B53 022 662
KT-144-823

Princeps

Tor Books by L. E. Modesitt, Jr.

The Imager Portfolio

Imager
Imager's Challenge
Imager's Intrigue
Scholar
Princeps

The Corean Chronicles

Legacies
Darknesses
Scepters
Alector's Choice
Cadmian's Choice
Soarer's Choice
The Lord-Protector's Daughter
Lady-Protector

The Saga of Recluce

The Magic of Recluce
The Towers of the Sunset
The Magic Engineer
The Order War
The Death of Chaos
Fall of Angels
The Chaos Balance
The White Order
Colors of Chaos
Magi'i of Cyador
Scion of Cyador
Wellspring of Chaos
Ordermaster
Natural Ordermage
Mage-Guard of Hamor
Arms-Commander

The Spellsong Cycle

The Soprano Sorceress
The Spellsong War
Darksong Rising
The Shadow Sorceress
Shadowsinger

The Ecolitan Matter

Empire & Ecolitan
(comprising *The Ecolitan Operation* and *The Ecologic Secession*)
Ecolitan Prime
(comprising *The Ecologic Envoy* and *The Ecolitan Enigma*)
The Forever Hero
(comprising *Dawn for a Distant Earth*, *The Silent Warrior*, and *In Endless Twilight*)

Timegod's World
(comprising *Timediver's Dawn* and *The Timegod*)

The Ghost Books

Of Tangible Ghosts
The Ghost of the Revelator
Ghost of the White Nights
Ghost of Columbia
(comprising *Of Tangible Ghosts* and *The Ghost of the Revelator*)

The Hammer of Darkness
The Green Progression
The Parafaith War
Adiamante
Gravity Dreams
Octagonal Raven
Archform: Beauty
The Ethos Effect
Flash
The Eternity Artifact
The Elysium Commission
Viewpoints Critical
Haze
Empress of Eternity

Princeps

A Novel in the
Imager Portfolio

L. E. Modesitt, Jr.

A Tom Doherty Associates Book
New York

This is a work of fiction. All of the characters, organizations, and events portrayed in this novel are either products of the author's imagination or are used fictitiously.

PRINCEPS: A NOVEL IN THE IMAGER PORTFOLIO

A Tor Book
Published by Tom Doherty Associates, LLC
175 Fifth Avenue
New York, NY 10010

www.tor-forge.com

ISBN 978-0-7653-3095-6 (hardcover)
ISBN 978-1-4299-9289-3 (e-book)

First Edition: May 2012

Printed in the United States of America

0 9 8 7 6 5 4 3 2 1

Once more, for Carol Ann . . .

CHARACTERS

Bhayar	Lord of Telaryn
Aelina	Wife of Bhayar
Kharst	Rex of Bovaria
Aliaro	Autarch of Antiago
Quaeryt	Princeps of Tilbor and friend of Bhayar
Vaelora	Wife of Quaeryt and youngest sister of Bhayar
Straesyr	Governor of the Province of Tilbor
Deucalon	Marshal of Telaryn
Myskyl	Commander, First Tilboran Regiment
Pulaskyr	Commander, Second Tilboran Regiment
Skarpa	Commander, Third Tilboran Regiment
Meinyt	Major, Third Battalion, Third Tilboran Regiment
Fhaen	Major, Fourth Battalion, Third Tilboran Regiment
Zhrensyl	Post Commander, Extela
Phargos	Chorister of the Nameless
Gauswn	Chorister apprentice, former undercaptain
Voltyr	Imager

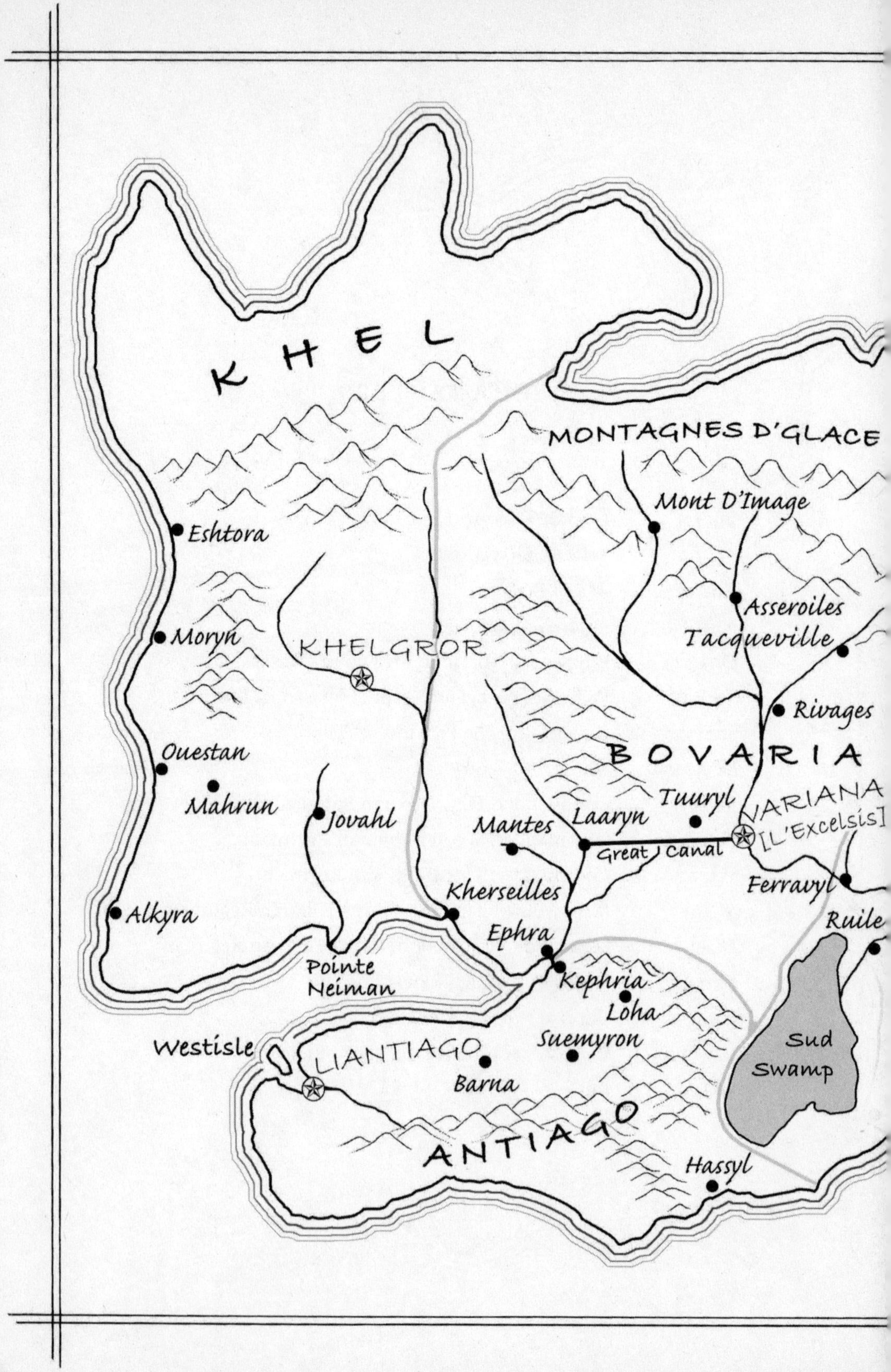

KHEL
MONTAGNES D'GLACE
Mont D'Image
Eshtora
Asseroiles
Tacqueville
Moryn
KHELGROR
Rivages
BOVARIA
Ouestan
Mahrun
Tuuryl
VARIANA
[L'Excelsis]
Jovahl
Mantes
Laaryn
Great Canal
Ferravyl
Kherseilles
Alkyra
Ruile
Ephra
Pointe
Neiman
Kephria
Loha
Westisle
Suemyron
LIANTIAGO
Sud
Swamp
Barna
ANTIAGO
Hassyl

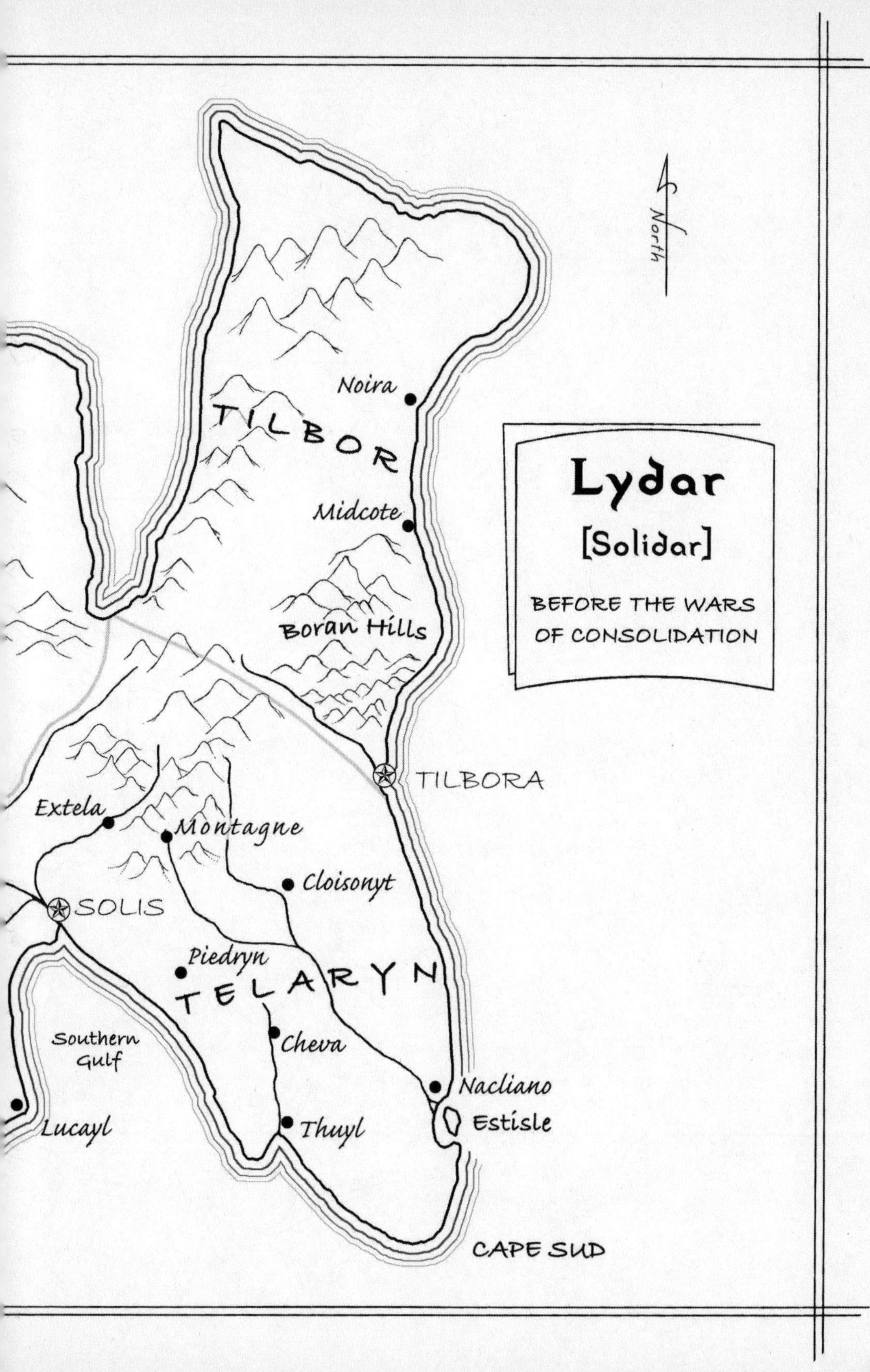
North
Noira
TILBOR
Midcote
Lydar
[Solidar]
BEFORE THE WARS
OF CONSOLIDATION
Boran Hills
TILBORA
Extela
Montagne
Cloisonyt
SOLIS
Piedryn
TELARYN
Southern
Gulf
Cheva
Nacliano
Estisle
Lucayl
Thuyl
CAPE SUD

Princeps

Quaeryt peered out from underneath the thick—and warm—comforter toward the nearest bedchamber window, its inner shutters fastened tightly. Even so, he could see frost on parts of the polished goldenwood. Supposedly, winter was waning, with spring some three weeks away, except that winter lasted into spring in Tilbor, even in Tilbora, the southernmost city in the province. The harbor in far-north Noira would not ice-out until the end of Maris, most likely.

A lithe figure wrapped her arms around him. "You don't have to get up yet."

"I do. It's Lundi, and I am princeps, you might recall . . ."

"Dearest . . . do you have to?" The excessively pleading tone told Quaeryt that Vaelora knew he needed to rise, but that . . .

He turned over and embraced her wholeheartedly, finding her lips on his.

All too soon, he released her, wishing that he did not have to leave their bed. But then, it had been her desire to remind him of that.

Bhayar had been right. Quaeryt and Vaelora were enjoying being married, even if he'd never seen it coming. Vaelora had protested that she hadn't either, that her brother had insisted she join him on his ride to Tilbora to keep her from the trouble she might have gotten into in his absence. Quaeryt had his doubts about her purported ignorance, but if that was the way she wished to portray matters, he'd certainly respect it. Then . . . it could have been that way. She hadn't brought anything with her but riding clothes, and women who planned on being married usually thought about what they'd wear . . . unless she'd wanted to be able to insist she hadn't known. And that was also very possible. He'd gone over all those possibilities for weeks, and probably always would . . . and he suspected she had planned that, as well.

He smiled.

"What is that smile for?" she asked, again in Bovarian, the language in which they conversed when alone—or in dealing with Bhayar.

"I was just thinking about the depths behind those seemingly guileless brown eyes."

"I cannot believe you are interested solely in *those* depths." Her slightly husky voice was both warm and slightly sardonic.

Quaeryt found himself blushing.

"You see?"

"Enough, lovely woman," he declared with mock gruffness. "Your brother did say that we were to keep each other warm."

"How, dearest, can I do that if you insist on getting out of this warm coverlet in this chilly bedchamber?"

Eventually, Quaeryt did leave the bed, as did Vaelora, and they washed and dressed quickly. Quaeryt was more than grateful for the warm water waiting in the bath chamber. Just the thought of the cold water in the officers' quarters made him shiver.

Although Governor Straesyr, when he had been princeps, had lived with his wife and family in one of the row houses along the north wall of the Telaryn Palace, Bhayar had declared that such quarters were not suited to his sister. Quaeryt had suggested that the apartments on the upper east end of the palace proper—those that had been occupied by Tyrena, the daughter of the last Khanar of Tilbor before its conquest by Bhayar's father—were most suitable for a princeps and that it would be most incongruous—not to mention grossly unfair—for the newly wed princeps to occupy the larger apartments of the former Khanar when his superior was the governor. That arrangement had been accepted by Bhayar and Vaelora and had certainly obviated possible tensions between Governor Straesyr and Quaeryt.

As Quaeryt began to pull on the fine browns of a scholar that Vaelora had insisted that he have tailored—because a princeps needed to look the position, as well as carry it out—he glanced at his left arm. It was still thinner than his right, while the skin was paler, not that his skin, ever so slightly darker than the pale honeyed shade of his wife's complexion, would ever approximate the near bluish white of the Bovarian High Holders and royal family. Given the beating his body had taken in the battles against the rebel hill holders, he was glad that none of the injuries had been permanent, unlike his left leg, shorter than his right, presumably since birth, since he didn't recall it ever being other than that.

Quaeryt waited until Vaelora was dressed—in light brown trousers, a cream blouse, and a woolen jacket that matched her trousers—before walking with her down the short corridor to the small cherry-paneled private dining room that had once been graced by Tyrena, who had been Khanara in fact, if not in name. There the ceramic stove radiated a comforting warmth.

Quaeryt seated Vaelora on one side of the table, then took his place to her left, at the end of the table, where Vaelora had insisted he belonged from the very first day of their marriage. In moments, a ranker in a winter-green uniform appeared with a teapot, a basket of warm dark bread, and a platter on which were cheese omelets and fried potatoes—exactly the same fare as in the officers' mess, if served on porcelain, and if not quite so warm.

Quaeryt poured her tea, then his. "I do enjoy breakfast with you."

"As opposed to dinner?" She raised her eyebrows.

"No. As well as dinner." He grinned, enjoying the game, holding the platter so that she could serve herself.

"What will you do today?"

"What I do every day. I have a meeting at eighth glass with Cohausyt—"

"He's the one with the sawmills who wants to pay to harvest timber on the lands Bhayar got from the rebel hill holders?"

"That's the one. I put him off because I needed to find out what finished timber and planking goes for in Tilbora."

"Did you?"

Quaeryt snorted. "In a way. I ended up finding out what the carpenters and cabinetmakers pay for wood. I had to work backward from that. Later, I have to meet with Raurem—he's a produce and grain factor—to see if he can supply grain cakes for the regiments." After eating several mouthfuls, and taking a swallow of the tea, he asked, "How are your plans coming for the spring reception?"

"Madame Straesyr has been somewhat helpful . . . as has Eluisa D'Taelmyn."

Eluisa D'Taelmyn? Then Quaeryt realized she was talking about Rescalyn's mistress, the Bovarian High Holder's daughter the former governor had introduced as Mistress Eluisa. "She's still here? I thought she had never married."

"That's her father's name. He's one of the lesser Bovarian High Holders. She has nowhere else to go, and Emra begged her husband to let her stay and teach their children singing and how to play the clavecin."

"I heard her play once."

"You told me. So did she. You upset her, you know?"

"I had that feeling. I was trying to see if Kharst was as terrible as they say."

"He's worse, according to Eluisa."

Quaeryt wasn't about to pursue that subject. "From your tone, I take it that neither one has been that helpful."

"They're really only interested in the wives of High Holders, not the wives of factors."

Quaeryt wanted to shake his head. "How are your writings coming?"

"I write some every day." She smiled. "The palace library has so many wonderful books."

"I know. I even read parts of some of them."

"You did mention that." Vaelora took a sip of tea. "I wish this were hotter."

"They have to carry it up from the kitchen."

"I know. What do you think she was like?"

"Who?" Quaeryt had no idea to whom his wife was referring.

"Tyrena. The Khanara who wasn't. You told me about those few scraps of paper you found with her writing."

"She was too strong in a situation where there were no intelligent men to marry and manipulate."

"Are you suggesting . . . ?"

"Me?" Quaeryt laughed. "All men react to women. All women react to men. Intelligent men and women react intelligently." *Usually, but not always, unfortunately.* "From all the documents I've read, none of the men in power after her father fell too ill to understand were intelligent enough to listen to her. Probably the only man in Telaryn who might have been was your brother, and he's much better off with Aelina."

"Why do you say that?"

"Because you said that, and you know them both far better than I do." He swallowed the last of his omelet, and the remainder of his tea. "I need to go." He stood, then moved beside her chair, bent and kissed her neck. After a long moment, he straightened.

"Remember," she said, "make the factors explain. In detail."

Quaeryt smiled. "Yes, dearest."

"You're close to disrespecting me." Her tone was bantering.

"Close doesn't count." *Except in bed.*

"I know what you're thinking."

He managed not to blush. "I'll see you later."

After leaving the third-level apartments, he made his way down the circular staircase to the second level, and then to the princeps's anteroom and the study beyond. After almost a month and a half as Princeps of Tilbor, he was still slightly amazed when he walked into the study, although the view to the northern walls and the hills beyond was largely blocked in winter by the mostly closed shutters and hangings.

Princeps or not, he still met with Straesyr at the seventh glass of the morning every Lundi, and once he had checked with Vhorym, the squad leader who was his assistant, he walked back across the second level to the governor's chambers.

"He's waiting for you, sir," offered Undercaptain Caermyt from his table desk in the anteroom.

"Thank you."

Quaeryt closed the study door behind himself and took one of the seats in front of Straesyr's wide table desk. "Good morning." He spoke in Tellan, because that was the language used normally by the military—although officers were strongly encouraged to learn Bovarian, and failure to do so was usually a bar to promotion above captain.

"I have to say that you're much more cheerful these days," offered the governor, squaring his broad shoulders and running a large hand through still-thick silvered blond hair, as he straightened in his chair and pushed a map to one side.

"No one's fighting or attacking, and the winter storms haven't been that bad." Quaeryt laughed ironically. "That's according to the locals. I've never seen so much snow and ice in my life, and they're saying it's not so bad as it often has been."

"You read Lord Bhayar's last dispatch, I take it."

That was a rhetorical nicety. Straesyr routed all dispatches to Quaeryt. Quaeryt, in turn, made sure that the few letters and dispatches, other than those of a personal nature, that came to him also went to Straesyr. "I did."

"Once the roads to the south are clear, he's ordered First Regiment to depart and take the route from Bhorael to Cloisonyt and from there to Solis."

"And from there," said Quaeryt dryly, "Bhayar will post them either to Lucayl or Ferravyl."

"Ferravyl's the greater danger," said the governor mildly.

"But, if Bhayar can determine how to conquer Antiago, that offers an opportunity to obtain greater resources and to deny them to Kharst. Not to mention the fact that Bhayar has never felt that Autarch Aliaro treated Chaerila with the respect she deserved." *Which is why you worry about his notes mentioning "respect."*

"Chaerila?" Straesyr's silver-blond eyebrows lifted.

"His oldest sister. She died in childbirth. According to Aliaro, her daughter died also. The daughter's death was mentioned as an afterthought."

"Did the Autarch express profound sympathy? Do you know?"

"I gained the impression that the sympathy was slightly more than perfunctory."

Straesyr shook his head. "Has Lord Bhayar conveyed anything . . . personally . . . to you?"

"Outside of brotherly missives to Vaelora and two rather short and polite notes reminding me to respect her at all times, I have heard nothing since the wedding." He paused, then asked, "How do Myskyl and Skarpa feel about the progress of Second and Third Regiments?"

"They feel that Second Regiment is largely ready and that Third Regiment will be ready for whatever duties it may be assigned by the end of spring. Commander Skarpa feels that if necessary, he could accomplish the last of the training while traveling."

Quaeryt missed eating in the mess with the officers, but as princeps, he was not in the military chain of command, except in the event that Straesyr was killed or incapacitated. Twice, he had taken the governor's place at mess night, once when the governor had the flux and once when a snowstorm had stranded him at High Holder Thurl's estate, even though the estate gates were less than five milles from the Telaryn Palace.

"I'll be meeting with Cohausyt at eighth glass," Quaeryt offered. "You saw the revisions to the calculations based on your recommendations."

"I did. Cohausyt will still do well, but Lord Bhayar can use the golds, especially if Kharst attacks."

Or if Bhayar attacks Antiago. "I'll be meeting with Raurem this afternoon as well. That's about whether he can supply those grain cakes for travel fodder for the regiments."

"He's a produce factor, isn't he, not a grain factor?"

"He is both, and Major Meinyt mentioned that he includes some rougher grains in his cakes, and they travel better, and the horses seem to do better. After you pointed out that there won't be much forage when they're leaving, I thought I should look into it."

Straesyr nodded. "I'm already getting to the point where I'll miss you when you go."

"Go? I'm not going anywhere, not that I know."

The governor smiled, and his icy blue eyes seemed to soften for a moment. "You manage to get things done. You're old enough to understand, mostly, and young enough to try the almost impossible. You also know the difference between impossible and not quite impossible. You're trustworthy, and Bhayar trusts you. There will be fewer and fewer advisors and officers whom he can trust totally. Sooner or later, he'll need you again. For your sake, I hope it's later."

So did Quaeryt.

"Is there anything else?"

"No, sir."

"Good. I'll talk to you later."

Quaeryt rose and made his way back across the second level of the palace. Cohausyt was already in the anteroom waiting when Quaeryt returned to his chambers.

"Princeps, sir."

"Do come in." Quaeryt smiled and kept walking.

The timber factor followed, and Vhorym closed the study door behind them.

Quaeryt gestured to the chairs, then settled behind his desk. "Lord Bhayar has agreed that the mature goldenwoods and oaks can be cut, but there are a number of conditions involved."

"There are always conditions in everything," said Cohausyt.

"There are indeed." Quaeryt picked up the sheet of paper from the desk and handed it over. "Here are the terms."

Quaeryt could see the tic in the factor's left eye begin to twitch as the older man read the sheet of paper.

"I don't know about leaving the softwoods untouched . . ." said the factor slowly.

"We know that the goldenwoods and oaks are heavier. There will be times when they bring down the evergreens. The terms state that you can only log those brought down incidentally . . . and not incidentally on purpose. Is that unreasonable?"

"Well . . . no, sir, but at times the best goldenwoods are surrounded by stands of pines, and there's no way to get to them . . ."

Quaeryt listened until Cohausyt finished, then said, "You'd best make those points of access very narrow."

"I suppose we can handle that . . . but no goldenwoods less than two-thirds of a yard across or two yards around at a yard above the ground?"

"That's what the best foresters recommend . . ."

"Begging your pardon, Princeps, but foresters aren't the ones who have to cut and mill the timber."

"That's true. They're the ones who have to make sure that there are trees there for your sons to cut and mill."

Cohausyt sighed and went back to reading, but only for a few moments. ". . . smoothing and tamping the logging roads?"

"Lord Bhayar doesn't want large gullies in the middle of his woods."

"But, sir, tamping takes men and time, and . . ."

Again, Quaeryt listened, before finally saying, quietly, "You are getting access to prime goldenwoods and oaks. There's not a stand like them anywhere else in Tilbor."

"But these terms . . ."

"I suppose I could post the terms and have others bid on them . . ." mused Quaeryt. Not that he wanted to, because Cohausyt was by far the most honest of the timber factors, and that meant that Bhayar would likely not be shorted on the golds from the sale of the timber. Quaeryt would have liked to have sold the rights for a flat fee, but there wasn't a timber factor in Tilbor who possessed that amount of golds to pay up front.

"No . . . I'll do what's right, Princeps." Cohausyt looked to Quaeryt. "I've heard you're fair. Hard mayhap, but fair. It'll take a bit longer, though."

"I understand." And Quaeryt did. *Everything has to do with golds . . . and time.* He understood that necessity, but even with the more honest factors, and Cohausyt was one of those, every term had to be spelled out in ink . . . and then explained.

He couldn't say that he was looking forward to the meeting with Raurem. With all the nit-picking and endless details required in everything, it seemed, he understood more than ever why Straesyr had been more than happy to relinquish his duties as princeps to Quaeryt.

Jeudi morning dawned clear and bright, but there was still frost on the windows, and Quaeryt was most happy that the dressing chamber had a large carpet, because he could see frost in places on the polished marble floor. Even the lukewarm wash water pitchers showed warm vapor rising into the air.

"The pitchers—they look like the hot springs below Mount Extel," said Vaelora. "Well . . . they don't really, but they remind me of them. I wish we had hot springs here. A truly hot bath would be so wonderful."

"If the springs were so wonderful, why did he move the capital from there?" bantered Quaeryt. He knew about the mountains of fire, but not about the hot springs. "Bhayar said his father did it because Solis was better located for trade and transport. He never mentioned hot springs in winter. But then, maybe he wasn't one for baths."

"Quaeryt . . ."

"Well . . . why haven't I ever heard about these wonderful warm baths?"

"It's not something we talk about."

Quaeryt frowned. "I don't understand."

"It's a family secret." Vaelora smiled.

"Am I not part of the family now?"

"You are, and I'll tell you because I don't want any secrets between us. Promise me that you won't keep secrets from me."

"I promise."

"I mean it."

"I understand," Quaeryt replied, and he did. He already knew that when she set her mind to something, nothing changed her course.

"He did it because of a vision."

"A vision? Lord Chayar was a most practical man. I can't believe he saw visions."

"He didn't, dearest."

Quaeryt sighed. Loudly.

"Father moved the capital to Solis because Grandmere had a vision. She didn't call it that. She said it was foresight. She was mostly Pharsi. Everyone knows that, but no one talks about it. She had more than a few visions, and

Father said he'd not listened to her only once, and he wished he had. So when she said she'd seen Extela in ruins and parts of it covered with ash and lava, he didn't argue."

"Well . . . so far as I know, Extela's still doing quite nicely."

"It is. Sometimes the mountain rumbles and at times it spews out ash, but the ash and hot springs are why the uplands are so fertile."

"And he uprooted everyone and rebuilt Solis because of a vision?" Quaeryt tried not to sound appalled. "One that never happened?"

"You didn't know Grandmere."

Quaeryt considered. *If her grandmother was anything like Vaelora, I can see . . .* "You take after her, don't you?"

Vaelora offered a rueful smile, one of the few that Quaeryt had seen on her face. "That was what Mother claimed. Bhayar said I have her spirit and that I was born to plague him."

Quaeryt grinned broadly. "So . . . that was why—"

He didn't get any farther because a good portion of the *cold* water pitcher splashed across his chest and face.

Later . . . when laughter subsided, with domestic order restored, and Quaeryt stopped shivering and got dressed, they did manage to reach the private dining chamber, where, thankfully, the stove had warmed the air to an almost pleasant state, pleasant for winter in Tilbora, reflected Quaeryt as he took a welcome swallow of tea.

"Dearest . . . are you still going to ride to the scholarium this morning?"

"Yes, even after a cold dowsing." Quaeryt managed not to frown, then saw the anxious expression on Vaelora's face, an expression he knew he was meant to see, since she was excellent at avoiding what she did not wish to reveal. "Would you like to accompany me?"

"If you wouldn't mind too terribly. Emra . . . I had thought to spend some time with her, but both her son and daughter are quite ill with the croup. So is Eluisa. That means I won't see her, either, and I was looking forward so to learning some of the pieces by Covaelyt and Veblynt."

"Isn't there sheet music? You play well enough . . ."

"She only has one copy of each, and she is most guarded in holding them. You can understand why that might be, and I'd rather not have to copy it line by line."

Left unsaid was that there were no copyists at the Telaryn Palace except those attached to the regiments, and neither Quaeryt nor Vaelora felt it proper to request personal copying from them.

Quaeryt looked at his wife. "You miss Aelina, don't you?"

"Terribly. I cannot tell you how much . . . She was the only one . . ."

"Except Aunt Nerya, of course," teased Quaeryt.

Vaelora looked at her husband with wide guileless eyes. "I should have mentioned her."

"Was she that bad?"

"You know what I feel."

Quaeryt did, and did not press. "I'll be leaving at half past seventh glass, and I'll have a mount for you. Please dress warmly. There's a bit of a wind."

"Yes, dearest," replied Vaelora in a voice that Quaeryt knew as her sweet and falsely submissive one—and that she knew he recognized as such.

He laughed.

The last quint of breakfast passed too quickly, and before that long, or so it seemed to Quaeryt, he had sent word down to have his mount and Vaelora's ready, finished reading the various dispatches, and was donning his heavy riding jacket, the fur-lined leather gloves, and the fur-lined cap he'd taken to wearing whenever he was outside for long.

"Vhorym . . . I'll be riding over to the scholarium. I likely won't be back until close to second glass."

Vaelora was actually mounted and waiting for him in the palace courtyard, as was the squad from Sixth Battalion who would accompany them. Quaeryt glanced at the sky, with the high gray clouds that were all too common in winter, then mounted quickly. As he and Vaelora followed the outriders through the eastern gates of the palace—the only gates—and down the stone-paved lane across the dry moat, now half filled with drifting snow, he could barely see over the snow piled on each side of the lane, even on horseback. The wind was raw and bitter, as it usually was when it blew out of the east.

Snow crunched under the hoofs of their mounts as they rode through the lower gates and onto the main road to the south.

"We're only a few weeks from spring," he said cheerfully.

"That's spring in Solis," returned Vaelora.

"True enough. We'll be fortunate to have frozen mud by then."

The wind was bitter enough that neither said that much on the glass-long ride to the scholarium. In fact, Quaeryt said almost nothing at all until they rode up the snow-packed lane and past the main building of the scholarium before reining up opposite the middle of the rear porch.

"Squad Leader, put all the mounts in the stable. You and the men wait in the tack room in the stable. If the stove isn't fired up, you have my authority to do so. I will need two rankers to escort my wife."

"Yes, sir." Rheusyd glanced at the stable to the rear of the main building. "Might already be fired up, sir. There's smoke rising."

"I hope so. It's been a cold ride, at least for us."

"Been on colder ones, sir, but a warm stove would be good for the men."

Vaelora and Quaeryt dismounted, climbed the steps, and crossed the wide and empty covered porch.

As he held the door for her, he said, "There's a stove in the main hall outside the master scholar's study. You can warm yourself there. I imagine you'll have company before long. Besides your escorts."

Vaelora raised her eyebrows, then brushed the combination of water and melting frost from them. "Oh?"

"There aren't any women here, except for the cooks and a few others, and none are as beautiful as you."

"Who could tell under all these garments?"

"They could tell." Quaeryt turned as the gray-haired and round-faced master scholar hurried toward them. "Nalakyn, I'd like to present you to my wife, the Lady Vaelora."

The master scholar bowed deeply, his eyes avoiding those of Vaelora, as was proper. "We are most honored to have the sister of Lord Bhayar here, and especially in weather such as this." He straightened. "I would offer you my study or that of the scholar princeps, but neither has a stove or a hearth. With your permission, I will have a comfortable chair brought for you so that you can warm yourself by the main stove here."

"You're most kind, master scholar."

Nalakyn flushed. "It is not often we are so honored."

Once Vaelora was seated before the stove, the two rankers discreetly standing against the wall several yards away, Quaeryt and the other two scholars were about to retire to the much cooler study of the master scholar when another figure hurried through the rear door, a young man wearing the robes of a chorister. Snow sprayed from his boots.

"Princeps! Sir?"

Quaeryt stopped and waited. "Gauswn! It's good to see you. How are you doing? How is Cyrethyn?"

"He is in good spirits, sir, but he is frail, and he begs your pardon for not joining me, but he is not so steady on his feet as once he was."

"Has he let you deliver any homilies?"

"Let, sir? He insists I do two a month." The young chorister looked embarrassed. "One of them was taken from what you said."

"I'm sure I probably gleaned it from someone else."

"I don't think so, sir. There's nothing like it in any of the chorister books." Gauswn paused. "I mustn't keep you, and Cyrethyn needs my help. I did want to come and thank you again. This is where I should be."

"Before you go," said Quaeryt, "you should meet my wife, Vaelora."

Gauswn bowed deeply. "Lady . . ."

Quaeryt smiled at Vaelora and eased away.

After he entered the master scholar's study, he took one of the chairs in front of the desk. "Let's see the ledger, Yullyd."

"Here, sir." The scholar princeps handed the master ledger he had carried to Quaeryt, then took the other seat. "The marker is where the entries for Ianus are summarized. I finished them on Lundi."

Nalakyn slipped into the chair behind the desk, but sat forward, apprehensively.

"Is there someone you can train to do the day-to-day entries?"

"Young Syndar has been helping me." Yullyd's voice was level.

Quaeryt wasn't surprised. From the time he'd delivered a letter from Syndar's father Rhodyn, he'd known that the student scholar would likely try anything not to leave the scholarium. "His father wants him to go back to Ayerne? Is that it?"

"He says he won't go, and that his younger brother is far better suited to being a holder."

"That's likely true, but it's not our decision." Quaeryt frowned. "How good a scholar is Syndar? Would he make a good bursar in time?"

"He's very accurate with the figures, and very neat," replied Yullyd. "He truly wants to be a scholar."

"He also assists in teaching the younger students. He's been most helpful there," added Nalakyn.

"Draft a missive to Holder Rhodyn for my signature. Make it very polite and most courteous. Tell him that I know of his desires and wishes for his sons, but I had thought he would like to know that I have learned that Scholar Syndar has proven to be exceedingly gifted as a scholar and is being considered for training as the bursar of the scholarium and that he has a future as a scholar. Because of this, tell him that I had thought he would like to know of this before making any final decision on what might be best for his sons." Quaeryt paused. "Write that up as soon as we finish. I'll wait for it."

The two exchanged glances.

"I can send it tomorrow. Otherwise, it will be another week. I want him to get it before his mind is even more set and before it's even close to spring planting."

During the winter, now that Bhayar had destroyed the last of the ship reavers, couriers from Tilbora could take the coastal roads directly south, well past Ayerne, and then turn west through Piedryn on a more direct southern route to Solis. There was no reason Quaeryt couldn't pay the courier out of his own funds to stop and deliver the missive to Rhodyn—the holding house was less than fifty yards off the road.

Yullyd nodded. "Yes, sir."

"Is there anything else?"

"Sir . . . we have . . . some difficulty," said Nalakyn.

"What kind of difficulty?"

"Ah . . ." Nalakyn drew out the single syllable, as if he were at a loss for words.

"Chartyn," said Yullyd. "He's not the problem. The fact that we accepted him is."

"There's another factor with an imager son?" asked Quaeryt.

"Actually . . . well . . . ah . . ."

"Yes," said Yullyd. "He's not a factor. He's a freeholder to the north. One of those with not enough lands to be a High Holder and too well off to be a mere grower or crofter. He heard about Chartyn. He's well able to pay for his son."

"I fail to see the problem. Has Chartyn created any difficulties?"

"No, sir . . . but . . . imagers in a scholarium?" asked Nalakyn almost plaintively.

"There are imagers in the Scholarium Solum in Solis. Why shouldn't there be imagers here?"

"We don't have any rules for imagers, sir," said the master scholar.

"Would it help if I wrote out a draft of some rules? I knew the imagers at the scholarium fairly well, and they did tell me some things." *Not that you don't know far more than Voltyr did, or even poor Uhlyn, but the scholars don't have to know that.* "You could start with those and refine them as necessary."

"But . . . this is a scholarium . . ."

Quaeryt looked hard at Nalakyn, feeling almost like imaging his disgust and anger.

The master scholar paled . . . then swallowed. His voice was barely audible as he replied. "Whatever you say, sir."

"Nalakyn," Quaeryt said gently, "I went out of my way to save the scholarium when most of Tilbora was ready to burn it and all of you because of what Zarxes, Phaeryn, and Chardyn—oh, and Alkiabys—were doing. Lord Bhayar and Telaryn need safe places for both scholars and imagers. Not just scholars. Not just imagers. Both."

Yullyd glanced at Nalakyn.

"I understand, sir, It's just that . . ."

"We all have to change with the times. I wouldn't be surprised if, in a few years"—*if not even sooner*—"Lord Bhayar will need imagers."

"You mean if Rex Kharst conquers Antiago and captures the Autarch's imagers?" asked Yullyd.

"That's certainly a possibility," agreed Quaeryt. "It would be useful to have some imagers who could create Antiagon Fire or combat it." Not that Quaeryt had any idea of how to do that himself.

"How . . . would they combat it?"

"Image sand over it, I suspect. That usually damps most fires, even bitumen fires." That was a guess on Quaeryt's part, but he thought it would work, since stone and earthworks were impervious to Antiagon Fire. "I'll have those draft rules to you within a week, sooner if I can. Tell the holder—what's his name . . . his son's name, too?"

"His name is Kryedt. The boy's name is Dettredt."

"Tell Holder Kryedt that the boy is accepted, under the usual provisions requiring good conduct and obedience to scholars."

"Yes, sir," replied both scholars. While Nalakyn's tone was not quite resigned, Yullyd's was more enthusiastic.

"Now . . . I'll wait outside in the main hall while you draft that letter to Holder Rhodyn."

Quaeryt stepped out to rejoin Vaelora, noting several students hurrying away as he neared. One he knew—Lankyt.

"What did young Lankyt have to say to you, dearest?" asked Quaeryt quietly, not wishing his voice to carry beyond Vaelora.

"Which one was he? The slim brown-haired one with the shy smile?"

"How did you know that?"

"I didn't, but you wouldn't have known who he was unless he stood out in some way. He was the most respectful and well-spoken."

"His father is the holder in Ayerne."

"Rhodyn, is it?"

"Yes. He was most kind when I escaped the ship reavers and was recovering."

"He spoke highly of you when we spent the night there."

"He's a good man. I just hope . . ." Quaeryt went on to explain.

Vaelora listened, then nodded. "You're offering a strong suggestion, but not demanding." She smiled mischievously. "You are suggesting, between the lines, that he'd be a fool not to agree."

"What else could I do?"

"You could let him do as he pleases without saying a word . . . but that's not who you are. You've proved that in dealing with my brother."

Quaeryt shrugged.

"The chorister? Gauswn . . . he was most complimentary. Is he the one who was an undercaptain?"

"He was."

"He said that it was almost a shame you hadn't been a chorister, but that he'd seen you were destined for greater deeds."

Quaeryt winced. "I fear he thinks I'm another Rholan."

"Would that be so bad, dearest?"

"For a man who doesn't know whether there even is a Nameless, it would be." Quaeryt shook his head.

"You're too hard on yourself."

"Not in that."

Vaelora shook her head.

Shortly, Yullyd reappeared with the letter. "Sir?"

"Thank you." Quaeryt read it, then nodded, took the pen from the scholar princeps, and signed the missive. "Very good, Yullyd."

"Thank you, sir."

After the ink dried, helped by Quaeryt's holding the paper near the stove, he folded the sheet and slipped it into the inside pocket of his jacket.

In less than a quint, they were on the road back to the Telaryn Palace, riding directly into the wind, which seemed to be slightly stronger than on the way to the scholarium.

"Are you still glad to be accompanying me?" asked Quaeryt dryly.

"Yes. It was good to get out."

"What did you think of the scholarium?"

"Everyone was most polite," observed Vaelora.

"You might have noticed all the deference was to you, my dear lady. Quite manifestly obvious, I would say."

"That might have been, but the respect was for you. Master Scholar Nalakyn looked somewhat chastened when he bid us good day."

"He was reluctant to take on another paying student because the boy is an imager." Quaeryt snorted. "As if the boy will not have enough problems. An education will help."

"It helps some, dearest. Others it is wasted on."

"True. But if he's one of those, he goes back to his father. He deserves the chance. What he makes of it is up to him. Did Chaerila ever write or say anything about the Autarch's imagers?"

"Not to me." Vaelora frowned in concentration. After a moment, she said, "I remember, though, something that Aelina said. Chaerila complained in a letter to her that she was almost a prisoner in the palace, but at least she wasn't walled up in a compound with metal behind the walls, the way the Autarch's imagers were." She paused. "What are you going to do?"

"Write up a set of rules. Then you'll read them and tell me what to change and improve?"

"You aren't asking me." A mischievous smile appeared. "Isn't that a form of disrespect?"

"I respect your judgment and intelligence so much that I know you'd want these rules to be as good as we can make them."

Vaelora laughed.

Quaeryt smiled happily—until the next gust of bitter wind whipped around and through him, and he shivered almost uncontrollably.

And this is a warm day for winter.

Another storm had buffeted Tilbora beginning on Samedi, and Quaeryt and Vaelora had remained within the palace walls. While the snowfall stopped by early on Solayi, the rankers of the regiment were still clearing snow in midafternoon, and Quaeryt was in his official study struggling with the draft rules he had promised Nalakyn and Yullyd.

He glanced up as the study door opened wide.

"What are you working on, dearest?" Vaelora asked as she stepped from the anteroom into the study.

"Rules for young imagers at the scholarium."

"Why didn't you have Nalakyn or Yullyd write them up and then just review them?"

Quaeryt had told her why earlier, but he didn't comment on that. Vaelora never asked a question, he'd discovered, without a purpose. "He'd write them, and they'd sound wonderful and mean nothing. Then Yullyd would rewrite them, and the poor youths would feel that they were in prison, and that would make their schooling worthless." His breath did not quite steam in the cold air of the study. "I thought you were practicing with Eluisa. That's why I came here. I'd already started work on this on Vendrei."

Vaelora walked around the desk to stand at his shoulder and read down the document. Then she smiled. "From those rules, one might think you had lived among imagers for your entire life . . ." She did not quite finish the sentence, but left the words hanging.

"I did spend several years at the scholarium, with Voltyr and, for a time, with Uhlyn, you might recall."

She looked down at the document and began to read, picking out a phrase from the middle of the sheet. "Imager scholars must not, under any circumstances, attempt to image metals. While there is always the temptation to image coins, the effort to image silvers and golds has often proved to cause great illness or death, even to older imagers. . . ."

Quaeryt nodded. "That's true."

"I don't doubt it's true, dearest." She smiled again, warmly. "What I have some doubts about is how you might happen to know that."

"I told you . . ."

"Dearest . . . I know that you would never tell me something that is not true or based in truth. I also know that, upon occasion, you have"—she paused—"been less than forthcoming about the details of certain events."

Quaeryt repressed a sigh. He'd known that, sooner or later, Vaelora would learn enough to suspect his imaging abilities. Perhaps she had all along and had waited for what seemed the proper time to discuss the matter. Still . . . he wanted to know what she knew, because it was likely Bhayar also knew at least some of what she had learned . . . and might have even learned it from him. "Such as?"

"One of the reaver captives—before he was executed—kept talking about the man who walked out of the storm and survived enough poison to kill two men, and then left three corpses and a dog—and none bore a single mark."

"I almost died from that poison. If it hadn't have been for Rhodyn and his wife—"

"Then there was the fact of how often you ate at various tavernas in Solis. Not expensive tavernas, but even the least expensive meals totaled far more than the stipend that Bhayar gave you. You are most honest, and no one ever slipped you coin, but you never seemed to run out. You usually paid in coppers. Very dirty coppers, not shiny ones."

Quaeryt could see that someone, most likely Bhayar, had been very thorough . . . and where she was headed, but he merely nodded. "Scholars seldom have more than coppers."

"Then there was the report about how you removed a crossbow quarrel from your own chest. Alone. A man who weighed fifteen stone couldn't do that. The captain surgeon couldn't believe you did it from the depth of the wound, especially without ripping your flesh to shreds. You're strong, dearest, but you're not that strong."

"Maybe I didn't report it right."

She shook her head. "One thing I do know is that what you say is close to the truth. Always."

"I try."

"Then there are all the reports about how you managed to save men and officers and how so many rebels seemed to strike at you and miss."

"They didn't miss enough," Quaeryt pointed out. "You saw that."

She moved behind the chair, reached down and massaged his shoulders, gently. "I didn't tell my brother all of that."

"But . . . how?"

"Nerya was always more than a duenna. She isn't an aunt, either. She's a distant cousin. She wanted to make sure that you weren't playing with woman after woman. When she told Bhayar all the places you'd been, I was the one who did the figures."

"Is there anything you don't know?" he asked with a laugh.

"She was also very impressed by your taste. You always chose reasonable places with good food, and you never drank too much. None of the servers had anything ill to say of you. That meant you gave them extra, all of them."

"What can I say? I was extravagant to the limit of my means."

She shook her head. "You also have black eyes and white-blond hair."

"And that means?"

"You know very well what it means." She bent down and brushed his neck with her lips. "My imager dearest." Then she straightened.

"You agreed to marry me, knowing that?" he said, easing the chair back and standing.

"Grandmere said I would wed a man with white-blond hair who was more than he seemed. That was one of her last visions. I was barely ten. It scared me."

Did she seek you out for that reason? He didn't ask that question. "Does it scare you now?"

She shook her head. "I didn't tell Bhayar that, either. Aelina knows, though. She might have told him. When I first saw you at the palace, I didn't even think about it."

"You were what then? Twelve?"

"Thirteen."

"What changed your mind?"

"You were respectful to Bhayar, but you never groveled or pled. You might have been the only one without position of whom that could be said." She smiled. "I couldn't imagine why. I know now."

"Imagers aren't invulnerable or invincible." He lifted his left arm. "I've scars and barely healed bones to prove that."

"What can you image?" she asked.

"It depends on what it's made of. Generally, the more common the material, the easier it is. That's not true of metals, though. They're harder. I tried to image a gold coin once. I almost died. Ice is easy, more so in summer, for some reason. I tried copper jewelry once. The copper wasn't too bad, but the shape was terrible. You really have to concentrate on the substance and the shape. It's hard work."

"You'll have to tell me more . . . when no one else is near." She glanced toward the open door to the anteroom, although no one else was there, not on Solayi. "I almost wish we didn't have to go to services tonight."

"As princeps, I should set an example. Besides, I like to hear what Phargos has to say. He usually does make me think."

"It seems . . ." She paused. "I don't know. Is there a Nameless? I know you don't think so."

Quaeryt shook his head. "I never said that."

"Oh, I know. You say that you don't know if there is or there isn't. But what is the difference between not knowing and not believing? Either way, you don't worship the Nameless."

"Do you?"

"We were talking about you, dearest."

Quaeryt waited.

"I feel that there's something beyond us. Is that the Nameless? Or is it something else?"

Quaeryt forbore saying that the belief in something greater than human beings and not knowing what it might be was exactly why that power was called the Nameless. "I don't know if such exists. I doubt that even if it does, it plays games with people, rewarding or punishing them for their belief or non-belief, or for whether they attend services or believe exactly what the choristers say that they should—although I have to say that most choristers I've heard confine their homilies to what I'd call reasonable guidelines for living."

"You're very reasonable, dearest, even when you're doing the most unreasonable things."

Quaeryt wasn't about to respond to *that*. "I can't help but wonder if Rholan really happened to be a charlatan," he mused.

"Why do you say that?" asked Vaelora.

"Because of the contradiction in terms he embodied. He talked endlessly about the sin of naming, and yet are not so many words spoken over so many years in themselves a form of naming?"

She laughed. "Greatness always includes great contradictions. It's not possible otherwise."

Quaeryt was afraid she was right about that. "We should get ready for dinner and services."

"So we should."

He slipped the sheet of draft imager rules into the desk drawer.

Yet another snowstorm blew in on Mardi afternoon and evening, but by midday on Meredi, bright sun and southern breezes were so much in evidence that wherever the stone pavement had been largely cleared, the remaining snow and ice had melted, leaving the stone dry. Even so, with the dray-horse plows and more than a company shoveling away the snow, it was close to late afternoon before the laboring rankers cleared the long paved lane down the hill on which the Telaryn Palace was situated.

As he stood before the window in the princeps's study, looking beyond the walls to the snow-covered hills to the north, Quaeryt reflected on the events of the first month and a half of the new year—beginning with Bhayar's arrival in Tilbora and the greater surprise of Vaelora's appearance . . . and their wedding. At the same time, being princeps was . . . well . . . close to demandingly tedious, and it certainly would have been depressing to some extent without Vaelora's presence. The position was one of keeping track of detail after detail, listening to unhappy and sometimes greedy factors, and managing supplies and expenses for the three regiments. Still . . . tedious or not, he had learned a great deal about finances, logistics, and what was required. He'd also learned that keeping everyone even close to happy took an inordinate amount of time. Then there were the odd duties, such as overseeing the reformation of the scholarium. He was just happy that he'd dispatched the draft imager rules to the scholarium early on Lundi, somewhat revised by suggestions from Vaelora.

He had to admit that he was relieved, not so much by her admitting she knew he was an imager, but by her almost matter-of-fact acceptance of his talent. He'd almost blurted out asking her if she had visions, as her grandmere had, but he'd decided to wait before posing that question. He suspected that she did and that was one reason why his imaging talent didn't seem to bother her.

He turned at the rap on his study door, opened immediately by Vhorym to admit Straesyr.

"Sir?" Quaeryt rose from his chair.

The governor closed the door behind him. He carried several sheets of paper, which he extended to Quaeryt. "I think you should read these."

Quaeryt took them and immediately began to read. The sheets were a dispatch from Bhayar, ordering the departure of First Regiment as soon as possible and practical, using the more southern route, if necessary because "events require the presence of additional forces in the west of Telaryn immediately." The next paragraph "requested" that Third Regiment be readied for departure as soon as practicable, but no later than the third week of Maris, while Second Regiment be split into two regiments, the bulk remaining with Second Regiment, and a new Fourth Regiment be created and reinforced with recruits and standing complement from Telaryn Palace.

Quaeryt looked up. "It would be good to know what those events might be. The way he wrote that could mean anything."

"He's concerned that someone besides us might read it," the governor pointed out.

"That suggests trouble with Kharst." Quaeryt paused. "Or that Lord Bhayar is planning some action to forestall even greater trouble with Bovaria."

"Either way . . ." mused Straesyr, "it points toward war before too long."

"Unless he thinks bringing two more regiments to the west might give Kharst second thoughts."

"From what I've heard, Rex Kharst is impulsive enough that he sometimes doesn't even have first thoughts."

"Impulsive, but effective. Or his marshals are good enough to make his impulses effective."

"That doesn't lessen the effectiveness," pointed out Straesyr.

Quaeryt noted that the governor didn't point out that those less charitable to Bhayar could have said the same thing about the Lord of Telaryn.

"Myskyl could have First Regiment on the road in less than a week," said Straesyr. "What about supplies?"

"Raurem is supposed to deliver a wagonload of those grain cakes on Jeudi, if we don't get another storm. The rest of the stores are ready to go."

Straesyr nodded. "The grain cakes will help, especially for the ride beyond Ayerne. There won't be any forage at all."

"I'll see about getting more of them for Third Regiment. We have the golds for them, and even if it's tight, we won't have the expenses for victuals and fodder later in the year with two regiments gone earlier than planned."

"Except that these orders to recruit and train another regiment will increase expenses." The governor's voice was dry.

"Creating a Fourth Regiment might not be bad. Some of the younger men who followed the hill holders might not mind food, clothing, and coppers, and sending them west would keep things quieter here. We might do a little planning along those lines. . . ."

"I already have," replied the governor. "Rather, I've adapted the plans Rescalyn had already made."

"Did he plan to split the old regiment into three regiments?"

"He planned for four, the way Bhayar just ordered." Straesyr smiled sadly. "He was a brilliant man. He just didn't anticipate that Bhayar would send an equally brilliant scholar to observe—and one who proved to be rather . . . durable."

"Fortunate," corrected Quaeryt.

"I've noted that fortune often tends to follow the most observant and best prepared in ways that reward them far more than mere chance, my dear princeps." Straesyr offered a smile both warm and ironic. "In any instance, we'd best prepare for recruiting and staffing another regiment. Who would you suggest as commander?"

"Would Commander Zirkyl prefer to leave Rescalyt for a more active command? If you gave him a choice . . . a real choice . . . so that he doesn't feel that he's being pushed . . . Or would Myskyl prefer to leave First Regiment? They're both good at training and discipline without overdoing it."

"Since Myskyl's senior, I'll ask him. I'd wager he'd prefer to head south with First Regiment, but he'd like the chance to have a choice, and I'd like to give that option to him."

Neither mentioned that the older commander had not been all that enthusiastic about the events surrounding Rescalyn's death in the last moments of the battle against Zorlyn . . . or that he might prefer greater distance between himself and Quaeryt.

Quaeryt nodded, wondering, again, what exactly might be happening to the west . . . and if Straesyr would happen to be right in suggesting that Quaeryt might find himself leaving Tilbor before that long.

After Quaeryt left the princeps's study on Vendrei and walked up to the private apartments, he looked first into the salon, then into the study where he thought Vaelora might still be writing. Both were empty. He found her in the dressing chamber, studying herself in the full-length mirror.

"What do you think of this?"

Quaeryt looked at what she wore, wide-legged purple trousers that, if she stood straight, looked like a skirt, above which were a yellow blouse and a tight-fitting jacket that matched the trousers.

"You don't like it. I can tell," she said when he did not immediately speak.

"I didn't say anything."

"You didn't have to."

"The trousers and jacket are good. The yellow doesn't go with your skin."

"You could have said that first."

"I . . . should have."

She took off the jacket, looking at the blouse in the mirror. "I knew it."

Quaeryt opened his mouth to ask why, if she knew it, she'd even asked him. Instead, he closed his mouth.

"The gray goes better . . . but it's dull."

"Do you have a pink or rose blouse?"

"If I had one, why would I be wearing the yellow? I didn't bring a trousseau, dearest."

The word "dearest" was not quite edged in acid, and Quaeryt kept still.

"And that's not something my dear brother has bothered with sending."

"And the seamstresses here are limited," he offered. They'd been married with him in his browns with the one formal jacket—retailored temporarily to accommodate the splint—and she'd worn the best of the riding outfits she had brought.

"Are there any? With any great talent?"

Quaeryt stood, thinking. He knew he'd run across one. Then he winced. *Why didn't you think of that earlier?*

"You have that look. What is it?"

"I just remembered. There is a seamstress in the harbor area. She used to create . . . tailor dresses for Tyrena."

"And you didn't tell me?"

"I didn't think of her until now."

"Oh?"

That word spoke volumes, but Quaeryt wasn't about to address the implications. "She was . . . is one of the Sisters. She was the one who first told me about Chardyn's link to the Khanar's Guard and the pretender. I went into her shop by accident. . . ."

Vaelora sighed. After a moment, she smiled. "I'm sorry. I know it's just a small dinner with Emra and Straesyr. But I did want to wear something different, and Eluisa offered me the yellow blouse. It doesn't suit her either, and she never wore it."

Quaeryt smiled ruefully. "At least, I remembered in time for something else." He handed her the oblong envelope with the card inside.

She extracted it quickly and gracefully, her eyes scanning the elegant script. "A ball? A real ball? Who is High Holder Thurl?"

"One of the High Holders whose estate is nearby . . . comparatively. We may have to ride." Quaeryt had never seen the carriages that remained at the Telaryn Palace in use, and he didn't even know if there happened to be a sleigh. *Probably somewhere, but why would anyone have used one in the last ten years?*

"Ride? In a gown?"

That did sound ridiculous, Quaeryt had to admit. "I hadn't thought about that."

"I doubt Emra would even attend if she had to ride . . ."

"I will see." Quaeryt held up a hand. "I doubt that we would be invited, except that as the sister of Lord Bhayar, you could not be overlooked, and so . . . I, as a mere lowly princeps, must also be included."

"Quaeryt . . ." She grinned. "That is almost disrespect."

"But . . . I did remember the seamstress."

"This is only two weeks away."

Two weeks and a day. He didn't voice that thought either.

"Can we see this seamstress tomorrow?"

"If it doesn't snow." He fervently hoped it would not be snowing on Samedi.

In the end, Vaelora wore the pale gray blouse with a rose scarf, conceding that it was "acceptable."

Quaeryt thought she looked far more than acceptable as they left their quarters.

The governor's apartments—those formerly belonging to the Khanar—were also on the third level of the palace, but to get there, Quaeryt and Vaelora had to descend to the second level, using the staircase on the east side of the second-level gallery, then walk to the west end of the palace, where a separate staircase, which could be closed off by two sets of iron doors, if decorated and gilded, afforded the only entry.

A single ranker stood by the staircase doors. "Good evening, sir, madame. The governor is expecting you." He gave two quick jerks to a bell-pull.

By the time Vaelora and Quaeryt reached the top of the pale gray marble steps, covered largely by a green carpet runner, Straesyr was waiting.

"Greetings! We'll join Emra in the private sitting room." The governor smiled cheerfully. "The salon would be overly spacious for the four of us. Also, it would take a great deal of wood or coal to heat it to be comfortable."

If the private sitting room happened to be the smaller chamber, Quaeryt definitely understood what Straesyr meant, because the sitting room was larger than his official study as princeps.

"Do join me," offered Emra, rising from where she had been sitting.

Quaeryt was still struck by the fact that Emra's hair was a striking silver-gray, in contrast to her husband's largely blond thatch.

The four of them settled into leather upholstered armchairs set in a semicircle around a low table, placed in turn before a ceramic stove that radiated a comfortable heat.

"Hot mulled wine . . . or red or white?" asked the governor.

"The mulled, please," rejoined Vaelora immediately.

Straesyr left the sitting room briefly, then returned and reseated himself. Shortly, a ranker in uniform appeared with a tray on which were four mugs from each of which rose thin wisps of steam. Vaelora took her mug and immediately clasped her hands around it. Quaeryt took a small sip and almost burned his mouth. He set the mug on the table.

"I spend much of my time here," said Emra. "It's the most comfortable chamber. Would you believe that the master bedchamber doesn't have a stove—just a fireplace that you have to keep fired up all the time if you want to keep the chill out?"

"It's not quite that bad," murmured Straesyr.

Emra raised a single eyebrow, but said nothing.

"The most comfortable room we have," offered Quaeryt, "is the private dining chamber. The fireplace in the bedchamber smokes so much that we ended up sealing it up. Temporarily, with some timbers and rags, behind a most ornate—and useless—fire screen."

"That works for you two. You're young and newly wed," replied Emra.

"How long before we stop getting snow?" asked Quaeryt, looking to Straesyr.

"Never," said Emra quickly.

"It should start tapering off in the next week or so, but we've had snow as late as in Avryl, and once even in Mayas."

"Like I said," added Emra, "never." Abruptly, she smiled. "I do tend to give Straesyr a great deal of grief about the chill, but I do prefer it to the heat of someplace like Thuyl. That's where I grew up, you know. Solis is dry and cool compared to Thuyl."

Quaeryt let himself wince.

"It's worse than that," Emra continued as she took in his expression. "I never worried about where we were posted because I knew it would be better than where I grew up."

"What is your family like?" asked Vaelora quickly, still cupping her hands around the warm mug of wine.

"I suppose they're still there, but they aren't the kind to write. They could certainly afford the silvers for it."

"They're into cotton factoring," added Straesyr. "They used to own all the warehouses in the delta. Emra married me against their wishes." He looked to Vaelora.

"It wasn't quite against my brother's wishes," she replied. "I just refused to marry anyone else."

"She didn't bother to inform me, either," Quaeryt said dryly, before his voice warmed. "It was, shall we say, the greatest Year-Turn gift I've ever received . . . or ever expect to."

"You're very fortunate he understands that, dear," said Emra.

"I am indeed . . . and for other graces that he possesses."

"Were we ever like that?" Emra looked to Straesyr.

"In our own way, yes."

"I suppose we were. Time does pass . . ." Emra paused. "I did persuade the kitchen to provide us with specially roasted game fowl. I do hope you like game fowl. . . ."

"Indeed," said Quaeryt, almost simultaneously with Vaelora's "Of course."

Their eyes met, momentarily, and they smiled.

Quaeryt understood both the warmth and the sadness in his wife's brown eyes, and resolved to make the evening as cheerful as possible.

Quaeryt felt as though he might be exceeding the bounds of his office in using a squad to escort him and Vaelora to Tilbora early on Samedi morning . . . but the half-staff he had obtained as a replacement for the one lost in the last battle against the hill holders was scarcely adequate by itself against brigands, and explaining imaging would have also created problems and questions better left unraised. Besides, she was Bhayar's sister, and had she not been married, or had she been married to someone else, and had she come to Tilbor, Straesyr certainly would have provided an escort.

Quaeryt was glad that the sun was out, and that there was no wind, so that the morning was almost pleasant, at least for winter in Tilbor. It was well before eighth glass, and both Artiema and Erion were still in the sky, although neither moon was close to being full, when they rode down the cold stone lane from the palace, with two rankers before them and the rest of the squad following, all of them riding far enough away from the couple so that they could talk privately—if they kept their voices low.

He turned in the saddle. "You were wonderful at dinner last night."

"So were you." She paused, then added, "It's so sad. They love each other, but . . ."

"Even when they talk about the very same things, they're not talking about the same things."

"They know it, and he still loves her, and she still loves him." Vaelora paused, and then looked straight at Quaeryt. "If I don't understand . . . talk to me until I do."

"I will."

"Promise me."

Quaeryt almost recoiled at the intensity behind those quietly spoken words. "I promise. I will. But you must do the same."

"I already do." She flashed a warm smile.

"I have a question. One I should have asked earlier."

"Oh?"

"You take after your grandmere—"

"Yes, dearest."

"I meant . . . about whether you see things as she did . . . visions?"

"I knew what you meant. I do . . . not often. She didn't, either."

"Did you see me?"

"Not exactly. But you looked familiar the very first time I saw you, in a strange way, and it wasn't because of what Grandmere had told me. There was one . . . farsight . . . that later proved to be about us. I didn't know that at the time. Years ago, I saw an image, as if I were there, and Bhayar and I were riding up a stone lane to a wall with gates. I didn't know what it meant—until I saw it again."

"The gates to the Telaryn Palace."

She nodded. "There have been a few others, but none that have not already come to pass."

"You'll tell me if there are others?"

"I will. Now you tell me more about this seamstress."

"I don't know much more about her skill, except that she'd mentioned doing clothes for Tyrena. I only recall her first name. Syen. I was trying to talk to people in Tilbora about what happened just before and after your grandfather defeated the pretender. Most people wouldn't talk to me, because I wore scholar browns. She was the one who told me why they wouldn't. That was likely because her husband—I think it was her husband—tried to kill me . . ." He went on to explain about the link between Chardyn and the scholars who had run the scholarium and how they'd been tied to the rebels, including how Chardyn had tried to kill him.

"You used imaging to kill this Chardyn?"

"I had to. He would have killed me otherwise. That was what got me to thinking about doing other things with imaging, like the shields I told you about."

"Do other imagers know how to do that?"

"Voltyr and Uhlyn didn't. I don't know any other imagers."

"Few can do that, or all would know."

Quaeryt had no doubts that Vaelora was right about that. "I wouldn't, either, except I feared that if I didn't try it, I wouldn't survive what Rescalyn had in mind for me."

"That is also farsight."

"A different kind," he replied with a laugh.

She smiled, but he had the feeling that she didn't totally agree.

When they neared the harbor, Quaeryt was careful to direct the squad to approach the shop from the south to avoid the brothel on the street to the north. While the brothel doubtless had its windows closed and shuttered against the cold, there was no point in going that way, especially since they would not be using the stable situated beside the pleasure establishment.

Once outside the shop, in the row of buildings fronting the harbor, Quaeryt dismounted and handed the mare's reins to the nearest ranker, then turned to offer help to Vaelora, but she already stood on the dirty snow beside her mount. He looked back to the squad leader. "Hernyn . . . we'll try not to be long."

"That's not a problem, sir. It's warm as winter days go."

Unlike the last time he had been in the harbor area, all the doors were unshuttered, although most shop windows were at least partly shuttered against the cold, and the air held the acridness of burning wood . . . and perhaps coal. As when he had come the first time to Syen's tiny shop, the single narrow window beside the door was shuttered, but the door was not, and it opened to his touch. He stepped through, holding his shields, recalling his last visit, when the seamstress's husband had tried to kill him because he'd mistaken Quaeryt for a colleague of Chardyn. Vaelora followed him and closed the door.

Syen looked toward them from where she stood beside the frame shaped like a woman's figure.

"This time, I definitely don't have the wrong shop," Quaeryt said.

"Greetings, Lady," said Syen, looking to Vaelora, before turning to Quaeryt. "I thought I might see you again, scholar . . . or is it Princeps these days?"

"Both, I suppose. Syen, this is my wife, Vaelora. I don't remember your surname."

"Syen . . . Syen Yendradyr." A faint smile crossed the lips of the trimly muscular woman who likely was not that much older than Quaeryt, despite the lines from the corners of her eyes and the streaks of gray in her short-cut hair.

"I'm pleased to meet you." Vaelora's husky voice was warm.

"And I, you." Syen inclined her head, as she had not done with Quaeryt.

"Quaeryt has told me how helpful you were to him," Vaelora added.

"As he was . . . later."

"She needs a ball gown rather quickly," said Quaeryt, not wishing to dwell on where that might lead.

Both women looked at Quaeryt.

He took a half step back, almost inadvertently.

"By two weeks from yesterday, if it is possible," added Vaelora. "If not, I do understand."

"Times are slow now." A smile and what seemed a twinkle in her eyes followed. "And we do owe your husband for several matters."

"I did what I thought was right," Quaeryt said.

"So you did. Would that more did." Syen turned her eyes back to Vaelora.

"The sewing and the fitting can be done in the time you wish, even sooner, but the gown will have to be made from the fabrics that I can find here in Tilbora."

"I understand."

"I would think . . . perhaps silver gray and black? Or red and black?" Syen frowned. "Then again . . ."

Quaeryt took a step farther back, content to let events take their course, but very glad that he was paid a great deal more as princeps than he had been as a scholar assistant. He might not know that much about being wedded to the sister of the Lord of Telaryn, but he did know that gowns did not come cheaply.

In the end, after Syen and Vaelora agreed on the design, and colors, and all the measurements were taken, Quaeryt handed over a gold for a deposit and to cover fabric. "Thank you."

"Thanks are not necessary, but your coin is welcome, Princeps, as are you and your wife. It is too bad you will not be here long."

Quaeryt raised his eyebrows.

"You—and your lady, by her very presence—have already done much of what was necessary, and Lord Bhayar will soon find other uses for your talents."

"I won no battles, performed no heroic acts. I only helped others."

Syen smiled. "The Sisters understand that more is often achieved by those who *only* help." She emphasized the word "only" just a trace. "We know who vanishes and who flees when no one else has been able to remove such pestilence." Syen turned to Vaelora. "Is that not so, Lady?"

"I would not argue with you on that, or anything else affecting Tilbor," replied Vaelora. "Until next week. Meredi . . . unless it snows."

"Until then."

Once they had left the shop and remounted, neither Quaeryt nor Vaelora said much until they were well away from the harbor.

"What do you know about these Sisters?" she finally asked.

"As I told you . . . I overheard a conversation between two women, another between two officers, and what I gleaned when I talked to Syen."

"You are truly Pharsi. To have determined what you did from so little . . ."

"You may be right You're not the first to say that. When I first rode up from Ayerne . . ." He went on to tell the story of how he had delivered the letter from Rhodyn to the holder's eldest son Jorem and how Hailae had spoken to him in Pharsi.

"White-blond Pharsi with black eyes . . ." mused Vaelora. "I have not heard of them, except as imagers, but that would explain much."

As she finished, a gust of wind whipped around them. Quaeryt shivered, hoping that there would not be yet another storm coming. "You'll wish we had hot springs like you did in Extela by the time we get back to the palace."

"You'll do quite nicely, dearest."

Quaeryt certainly hoped so.

The next few days were far warmer, enough to melt the snow near dark stone and uncovered ground—except at night—and that meant that in the morning ice covered much of the stone pavement of the lane down to the lower gates.

On Mardi morning, Quaeryt walked to the private dining chamber, thinking that Vaelora would be along in moments. She wasn't. After half a quint, he turned and headed back to the dressing chamber.

When he appeared, she stepped forward, shuddering, and put her arms around him.

"What is it?"

"Those shields . . . the ones you created for battle . . . can you still do that?"

"Yes . . . I haven't seen much need, not here in the palace . . ."

"Please . . . whenever you leave the palace . . . or even here when there are people you don't know . . . please use them . . ."

"Why . . . What did you see?"

"It was a hall . . . a long one, and you were standing by a doorway, and a man in dark clothes had a crossbow, and I saw the quarrel go toward you . . ."

Quaeryt stiffened. "Did you see any faces . . . anything else?"

Vaelora looked at him, and he saw the streaks of tears running down her cheeks. "It was so real . . . so very real." Her voice strengthened. "You must use those shields."

"But . . ." He knew better than to protest, but it seemed so unreal. So far as he knew, anyone who had a personal grudge against him was dead.

"Dearest . . . you are seen as a man of influence and power, and you have already changed much. You have done so quietly. Most people see the governor and the commanders as the ones who made the changes, but there are still those who know you were behind those changes."

"I'm just a scholar who . . ."

"Just? If the Sisters all know what you did, who else does as well?"

Quaeryt smiled ruefully. "You're right. I will."

"Promise me. Starting today."

"I promise."

She blotted her cheeks and eyes, delicately. "I'm sorry. It was so real that I wanted to scream and warn you. Then it was gone."

"Are these foresights always like that?"

"Farsight," she corrected him. "I told you. I don't have many. This is the first one in more than a year, but they all have felt so real when I see them."

"I'll go back to using shields," Quaeryt said, trying to reassure her once more.

"I know it sounds silly . . . in a fashion, anyway . . ."

"If you're right, then it will save my life or health, and if not . . . there's certainly no harm done." He shook his head and added quickly, "You're right in any case. It's just hard for me to believe that anyone would want to kill me. In a battle, yes, but as a regional princeps?"

"Who's married to Lord Bhayar's sister and who has come to power over so many younger sons of holders and High Holders," added Vaelora.

"I wouldn't even have been considered in a region like Ryntar or Montagne, or even Ruilan, would I?"

"I'd have considered you anyway," she replied with a smile.

"That might have been, but I have my doubts your brother would have been so accommodating."

"I'd have found a way."

The matter-of-fact certainty in her voice reminded Quaeryt of one thing—Bhayar hadn't needed to tell Quaeryt to respect Vaelora. *Not at all.*

"We should eat breakfast," he said gently.

"Oh . . . I almost forgot."

The inadvertent innocence in her voice reminded him of something else—and that was what a mixture of experience and inexperience lay beneath her determination. He embraced her once more. "I do love you."

"I know." Her arms went around him for a moment before releasing him. "We do need to eat."

He didn't mention that he'd just said almost the same thing.

They walked to the private dining chamber hand in hand.

After breakfast, Quaeryt made his way down the private staircase and to his study. He was early enough that he arrived before Vhorym. He didn't settle behind the desk, but walked to the center window and pulled back the hangings and opened the shutters, ignoring the chill off the glass as he stood there looking out to the north. The first snows had begun to fall near the end of Feuillyt, and by mid-Finitas snowstorms were regularly bombarding Tilbor, and that had been weeks before winter began. Spring was less than two weeks away, and everything was still covered in snow, so much that when he rode out the east gates he could barely see over what was piled on each side of the access lane to the palace.

His thoughts went back to what Vaelora had said—and seen. Who would want him dead, and what would he be doing in a long dark hallway?

He laughed, quietly.

How would you ever have believed you—a mere scholar—would become princeps of Tilbor and be married to Bhayar's daughter?

Then he turned to face the remainder of the day.

On Meredi, Quaeryt accompanied Vaelora back to Tilbora for a fitting of the ball gown—except that she insisted he wait outside. After the ride and while he stood and waited with the escort squad, he realized that he was somewhat tired, and he wondered why.

Shields . . . of course. Even though he was holding the lighter shields that stiffened only when something touched them, doing so was still an effort—one that he had not made in more than a month, except occasionally. He'd forgotten how long it had taken to build up his strength and endurance to be able to hold them much of the day.

He still couldn't help but wonder who might be seeking his death. Those who were mostly likely to hold a grudge as a result of the destruction of the rebellious hill holds would be sons or heirs of those holders—and he doubted that many of them knew of his small role or even cared about him, particularly since Rescalyn—who had planned and executed the campaign—had died at the end of the last battle. Chardyn was dead, and from what he had determined it appeared that Zarxes had died in the battle for his father's hold. The seareavers didn't even know who he was . . . if any of them had even survived.

He shook his head.

"Dearest?"

Quaeryt turned to see Vaelora leaving Syen's shop, carrying out what Quaeryt presumed was the gown, if rolled and covered in oilcloth.

When she reached him, standing beside the mare, she handed the gown to her husband. "Please don't drop it."

"I won't. Is it finished?"

"Of course. She had to make a few changes. That was why it took a bit."

"What do I own Syen?" he asked as he took the gown from her.

"Nothing. I paid her the rest of what was due."

"You . . . ?"

"I am not penniless, dearest. Bhayar did leave some golds for me. He told me to be careful of them. I have been. This is the first time I've spent anything. Major Daendyr has kept most of them in the regimental strong room." With a smile, Vaelora swung up into the saddle, far more gracefully than he ever did.

Quaeryt should have known. He just shook his head.

"Please hand me the gown, if you would, dearest?"

He did, and then mounted, wordlessly, wondering exactly how many golds his wife had stored away. *Certainly far more than you have.* At least, he could say to himself, if not to anyone else, that he hadn't married Vaelora for golds. He hadn't even thought of it, not that anyone was likely to believe him.

"Why are you smiling?" she asked as they rode away from the harbor area of Tilbora.

"Because I never married you for your golds and because no one would ever believe me if I said so."

"I do."

"No one but you."

"The young chorister at the scholarium—the one who used to be an undercaptain—he would."

Quaeryt laughed, ruefully. "That might be the one thing on which we'd agree. Otherwise, he thinks too highly of me."

"You want people to think you do well, but not too well. Is that because you're afraid that if they think too highly of you, you'll disappoint them?"

"Partly." *And partly because I don't want them looking at me too closely.*

"And partly for other reasons?" She glanced knowingly in his direction.

"You know me too well."

"A wife should," she replied playfully.

He wasn't about to argue with that, either.

"Dearest . . . I have not pressed . . . but I cannot wear that gown and ride . . ."

"Oh . . . I'm sorry. I meant to tell you. We will ride in a carriage down to the lower gates, and High Holder Thurl will have a sleigh waiting for us—the four of us."

"When did you learn this?"

"Yesterday," he admitted.

Her glance was not quite withering.

"I did find out," he said quietly.

After several moments of stone-faced silence, abruptly, Vaelora grinned. "Dearest . . . next time . . . I do hope there is not a next time."

So did Quaeryt, even if it had been his fault. *Especially since it had been.*

By the time they neared the lower gates to the palace, Quaeryt could feel the sunlight for the first time in more than a season. He was riding with his winter jacket open, and he noticed that small piles of slush had been thrown to the side of the road by the small sleighs used by many Tilborans in winter.

In a few places, he saw mud. He glanced toward Vaelora, noting she had loosened her coat as well.

"It's gotten warmer," he said.

"It has, but for how long?"

There was that, but it was a reminder that spring would come.

He kept thinking about that even after he escorted Vaelora back to their quarters and then made his way back toward his study. When he reached the gallery, he turned and made his way to the governor's anteroom.

Undercaptain Caermyt glanced up. "He's not busy, sir."

Quaeryt knocked on the half-open door and then peered in.

"Come in, Quaeryt. What's on your mind?"

"Sir . . . I just returned from Tilbora. I think that First Regiment should leave as soon as possible. If the roads turn to mud . . ."

"I agree. So does Commander Myskyl—and he does prefer to remain with First Regiment. They've almost made ready, another day at most, and they will leave on Vendrei." Straesyr smiled. "We'll still see freezing nights, but it's likely to get warmer and warmer during the day."

"Have you received any more dispatches?"

The governor shook his head. "I doubt we will for a time, unless we fail to send off the regiments in a fashion Lord Bhayar deems untimely, and neither of us would wish that, I think." His voice turned wry and sardonic with the last words.

"No, sir." Quaeryt paused. "Oh . . . I got a note from Raurem late yesterday. He can deliver another wagonload of grain cakes by the third of Maris."

"That should be acceptable. Muddy roads or not, Commander Skarpa won't have Third Regiment ready to leave before the end of that week."

"I'll let Raurem know, but I'll insist on that date, just in case."

Straesyr nodded.

After leaving the governor, Quaeryt walked back toward his own chambers, wondering what might be happening in the west . . . and whether . . . and if so, when events might involve him.

Thinking of Vaelora, he wasn't so sure he wanted to be involved, for all of his plans.

But you made those plans before she came into your life. Times change.

So they did, more than he had ever anticipated.

Quaeryt had only been in his study for a quint on Jeudi morning when Vhorym knocked on the door.

"Sir . . . There's a young scholar here to see you. His name is Lankyt, he says." Vhorym did not quite frown. "He says it's important."

"I'll see him. He's a good youth. His father saved my life." Quaeryt rose.

Vhorym left the door open, stepped back, and gestured.

Lankyt hurried in, bowing deeply, and straightening. "Sir . . . Chorister Gauswn . . . he sent me. Chorister Cyrethyn is dying. He would like to see you. Chorister Gauswn . . . he said you should know."

"I can leave now." Quaeryt stood. "You rode alone?"

"Yes, sir."

"We'll ride back together." Quaeryt gestured for Lankyt to follow him. "Vhorym . . . I'm needed at the scholarium. I don't know when I'll be back, but it will be later today."

"Yes, sir."

Quaeryt hurried down to the main level, stopping by the duty desk to request a squad to accompany him, and then out to the stable, where he saddled the mare, then walked her out of the stable and mounted. He rode across the courtyard to where Lankyt was waiting on a gray gelding. "Your mount?"

"Syndar and I share him."

Quaeryt glanced around the courtyard, looking for the duty squad that was to accompany him. "He's the one you used to visit the local growers? To find better ways to grow things?"

"Yes, sir."

"Have you discovered anything new since last harvest?"

"Well . . . not much . . . except that marigolds keep away many bugs. I was thinking that if we planted them around the orchards, that might help . . ."

Quaeryt listened for not quite another half quint, until the duty squad arrived, and then they set out through the eastern gates and down the stone lane to the lower gates. Once they left the upper gates, he raised his shields, the lighter ones that would stiffen into hard shields if anything neared them.

He noticed that the snow heaped on each side of the lane seemed a touch lower and stone gutters flanking the lane were carrying meltwater down to the moat. They weren't full, but it was more than a trickle.

After almost a quint of riding, Lankyt spoke again. "Sir . . . I meant to thank you, but I was worried about the chorister."

"Thank me for what?"

"Yesterday . . . my da—my father—I got a letter from him. He agreed that since Syndar seemed so much better suited to being a scholar, I should come home, but only when the roads were clear and when I could join someone trustworthy. You did that, didn't you?"

"Not exactly. Syndar wanted to stay. He's been a great help to Scholar Princeps Yullyd. I wrote that to your father. Nothing more."

"Thank you, sir. I liked what I learned at the scholarium, but I do so miss Ayerne, and I know I'm better suited to the land."

"I'm sure you are." Quaeryt paused. "Would you be willing to leave tomorrow?"

"Sir? Do you mean it?"

"First Regiment is heading that way, and they leave tomorrow. I think I can persuade Commander Myskyl to let you ride with them. They'll likely overnight at Ayerne anyway. But you'll have to gather your things and ride back with me when I leave the scholarium after I see Cyrethyn."

"I can do that, sir. I can."

Quaeryt nodded, his eyes on the road. So far the packed snow and ice, and presumably the ground beneath both in places where the roads were not stone-paved, seemed frozen solid. Of course, there would be mud farther south, but because the snow melted more in between storms, there wouldn't be as much mud as in Tilbor and the area just south of the river when everything did melt.

After they had ridden a while longer, Lankyt again turned in the saddle. "You said First Regiment was riding south. Will there be a war, sir?"

"There's always likely to be a war sometime. When and where the next one will be, I don't know, but I fear it won't be that long."

"Will you have to go or will you stay in Tilbor?"

"I serve here at the pleasure of Lord Bhayar. That's up to him."

The youth nodded thoughtfully.

It was close to a glass later when Quaeryt dismounted outside the stable of the scholarium. He was almost breathing heavily when he dismounted, and wondered why, until he realized, belatedly, that he'd been carrying shields for the entire ride.

Can you lower them? He frowned. *Surely, here . . .* He decided against it. He'd promised Vaelora, and if anything at all happened . . . he certainly didn't want to hear what she might say. Besides, the more he worked at it, the sooner before the effort required would diminish.

At that moment, he saw Gauswn hurrying toward him at almost a run.

"Sir!" panted the chorister.

"Where is Cyrethyn?" asked Quaeryt.

"He's in his quarters in the anomen, sir. He does want to talk to you, but he's so weak. I was afraid to leave him."

"We came as quickly as we could." Quaeryt turned to Lankyt. "You need to get your things ready. If any of the scholars need an explanation, I'll talk to them after I see to Cyrethyn."

"Yes, sir."

Quaeryt handed the mare's reins to the ranker nearest to him and looked to the squad leader. "I'll probably be here about a glass, Heisyn. There should be room in the stable for the mounts, and the tack room is usually warm."

"Yes, sir."

With that, Quaeryt nodded to Gauswn, and the two walked along the packed snow that covered the brick lane and then along the foot-packed path from the scholarium to the anomen.

Gauswn led the way to the main door of the building and stepped into the vestibule. "The private hallway is this way." He opened a narrow ancient ironbound door that Quaeryt had only vaguely noticed in passing on the few occasions he had visited the scholarium's anomen.

The long hallway, barely illumined by a single oil lamp, led to a narrow staircase whose stone steps bore the hollows worn by years of choristers' footsteps. At the bottom of the staircase, there was another passage to the right, again dimly lit by a single oil lamp in a wall sconce. Quaeryt found the near darkness oppressive, but less than five yards from the bottom of the steps was a door, beside which stood two older students.

"He's in his bed." Gauswn pointed to the door. "He said he needed to talk to you alone. I'll wait out here."

"I'll try not to tire him."

Gauswn nodded, but then said, "Please . . . sir . . . do let him say what he must, whatever that may be."

Quaeryt smiled sadly. "I will." He opened the door, stepped into the chamber, and shut the door behind him. The sole light came from a pair of high and narrow windows, only one of which was unshuttered, and just on one side. The furnishings were few, just the bed, a night table beside it, an armoire, a writing desk, and a chair—which had been pulled up close to the bed.

The old chorister, whose still wavy brown hair, without a trace of white, was so in contrast to the drawn and lined features of his face, smiled faintly as Quaeryt walked over to the narrow bed and sat on the chair.

"I came as soon as I could."

"I . . . thought . . . you would."

Quaeryt waited.

"Thank you . . . for Gauswn. He will be . . . a good chorister." Cyrethyn took a wheezing breath. "A better chorister than an officer . . ."

"He was a good officer," said Quaeryt.

"He will be . . . he already is . . . a better chorister . . . and you . . . you have not disappointed him. He will always look up to you."

That was something Quaeryt had worried about more than once. "I wish he did not."

"No . . . you must understand that he does . . . Never forget it . . . you . . . there is more about you . . . and . . . you must . . . must never . . . disappoint those who believe . . . in you. . . ." Cyrethyn was gasping as he finished those words.

Quaeryt wanted to ask if there was any way he could make Cyrethyn more comfortable, but knowing there was not, he remained silent until Cyrethyn's breathing eased somewhat. "Is there anything else . . . I should know?"

The slightest smile crossed the old man's lips. "You would make . . . a fine chorister . . . but . . . the world would be . . . poorer for it."

Quaeryt did not wish to dispute either, much as he doubted both of Cyrethyn's assertions, so he just sat on the stool and smiled warmly. "Is there anything I can do?"

"You . . . have done all I hoped . . . so far . . . just . . . do . . . not . . . disappoint them. . . ."

Even those words exhausted the old man, and Quaeryt nodded, rather than speak. For perhaps a quint he sat there, long after the chorister's eyelids closed and he drifted into sleep. Finally, Quaeryt rose and walked to the door, opening it quietly and stepping outside, trying to close it equally silently.

"Is he . . . ?" asked Gauswn.

"He told me what he wanted me to know. He's sleeping or dozing now."

"Thank you for coming," said Gauswn.

"I could do no less for him." Quaeryt shook his head. "But there is also little else I can do."

"You saved the scholarium and the anomen, sir, and he cared greatly for both."

"He was devoted to both." *Unlike some.*

After several moments of silence, Gauswn cleared his throat. "I'll see you out, sir."

"There's no need. Cyrethyn needs you more than I do."

"He'd be very disappointed, sir, if I didn't at least see you to the door."

Quaeryt smiled. He couldn't argue with that. "Just to the anomen door."

From the chorister's chamber they walked side by side, just far enough apart that Quaeryt's closely held shields were not triggered into full protection. Because the staircase was too narrow to be comfortable for two, Quaeryt led the way, with Gauswn close behind. Just before Quaeryt reached the top of the staircase, he frowned. Was there someone waiting by the door?

Something slammed into his shields, driving him back so hard that he staggered to one side and almost fell. Because of his shorter left leg, he barely managed to catch his balance after going down one step.

As he did, Gauswn sprinted past him, a long knife drawn from somewhere in his hand.

Quaeryt's eyes followed the chorister, and after a moment, so did his feet as he ran after Gauswn. He was close enough to see Gauswn's arm move in what looked to be an underhanded thrust to the chest of a man in black—whose face mirrored shock, even as the crossbow clattered to the stone floor.

"You . . . always . . ." The would-be assassin's knees crumpled.

Gauswn thrust the dying man backward, and his body hit the stone with a muffled thud.

Quaeryt reached the chorister and looked down at the sharp-faced and dark-haired figure, attired totally in black, who tried to gasp, then shuddered and was still. "Alkiabys . . . I thought he'd died in the last battle, along with Zarxes."

"He should have." The chorister turned to Quaeryt. "Again . . . the Nameless has protected you. . . ."

"Alkiabys just missed."

Gauswn looked straight at Quaeryt. "I saw you be thrown back by that quarrel. It was aimed straight at your heart. Yet it was as if it hit a wall and dropped to the stones."

"I didn't see that," replied Quaeryt. That much was true. He hadn't *seen* it; he'd only felt the impact.

Gauswn inclined his head. "You are blessed by the Nameless."

What can you say to that? After a moment, Quaeryt said, "I don't know that. I do know that I'm glad that quarrel didn't reach its target . . . and that you took care of Alkiabys. All I can ask is that I'd very much appreciate it if exactly what happened remains between us. I'm not asking you to lie . . ." Quaeryt paused. "You can say that Alkiabys fired his crossbow at me. That is true. You can also say that, for some reason, the quarrel didn't hit me. I will say, which is also true, that you leapt to my defense and killed him."

"But . . . why . . . ?"

"Gauswn . . . if . . . IF I'm somehow protected, and you tell anyone, how long before someone else tries . . . and if I survive, someone else after that? If, as you think, the Nameless is protecting me—and I have grave doubts about that—but if it is true, the Nameless might not wish to keep protecting me if the fact of that protection is flaunted . . . or even known to a single other person."

The chorister nodded slowly. "Sir . . . it will be between us."

"Thank you. I cannot tell you how much I appreciate that." *And I can't . . . at least not for a very, very long time.* Because, while two people could occasionally keep a secret, especially if one happened to be as honorable as Gauswn, three people never could.

Gauswn looked down at the body, then at Quaeryt.

"Give him an honorable pyre, but no memorial."

The young chorister nodded. "That would seem fitting."

"You attend to Cyrethyn. I'll have Yullyd or Nalakyn come and take care of the body."

"Thank you, sir."

When Quaeryt reached the rear of the scholarium, he saw Lankyt standing on the porch, with Nalakyn beside him. Several bundles were set at Lankyt's feet.

"Princeps, sir," began Nalakyn, "I understand that you have offered—"

"To have Lankyt escorted back to his father's holding? That's correct, but I'm going to have to task you with a less pleasant duty. You might recall Alkiabys?"

"Yes . . . sir." The round-faced master scholar sounded puzzled.

"He was hiding in the anomen and tried to attack me when I left after seeing Cyrethyn. Gauswn leapt to my defense and killed him. Because he once was a scholar, he deserves a pyre, but not a memorial." Quaeryt fumbled in his wallet until he came up with a pair of silvers. "I would not wish the expense to fall entirely on the scholarium. Use these to replace whatever wood is necessary. And because Gauswn must attend to Cyrethyn . . . could you have some of the scholars remove the body?"

"Yes, sir." After a moment, Nalakyn said, "About young Lankyt . . . ?"

"He'll be riding back to the palace with me. He'll be riding out with Commander Myskyl early tomorrow morning."

"Yes, sir."

Quaeryt looked hard at the master scholar. "We'll be leaving as soon as the horses are ready."

"I'll have the students on discipline duty and Scholar Weisyn remove the body."

"Thank you."

Nalakyn almost scuttled across the covered porch and inside the building.

"It really was Alkiabys?" asked Lankyt.

"Yes."

"I never liked him," blurted Lankyt. "He liked to hurt students in Sansang practice. He'd say that they needed to learn what would happen when they didn't defend themselves right. But he liked it. Scholar Chardyn was hard, but he was fair." There was a pause. "Do you know what happened to him?"

"Let's just say that he and Phaeryn would make certain that on the day that the visiting scholars or others said they would depart . . . they departed early . . . and left their coin for the Ecoliae. I suspect that one of those visitors took exception . . . perhaps many did, but one was finally able to prevail."

Lankyt nodded slowly. "That . . . I can see that."

Quaeryt bent and picked up one of the bundles. "Is this all you're bringing?"

"I left whatever Syndar could use, sir. I'll have more than enough at home."

That was certainly true, reflected Quaeryt as they walked toward the stable, but Lankyt's leaving anything that his older brother could use was still thoughtful.

"Father did tell me to ride the gelding home," Lankyt added. "He said that, as a scholar, Syndar would have less need for him."

A quint later, when Quaeryt, Lankyt, and the squad were a half mille away from the scholarium, Lankyt turned in the saddle, looked across the space between mounts, and said, "Master Scholar Nalakyn says that we should always tell the truth. I don't see everything, sir, but it seems to me there are times when the truth hurts more than not saying anything."

Quaeryt laughed ruefully. "That's true enough. The problem is that when you start thinking like that, it becomes easy, first to say nothing, and then to lie, and then lie more, and finally to justify all the lies you've told. Yet . . . there are times, when part of the truth, so long as that part is not a lie in and of itself, is better than the whole truth . . . For example, if a man loses his courage in a battle and turns and flees, but is cut down from behind, there is no harm, and a grace, in telling his family that he died in battle without saying that he tried to flee. If a man has done evil while doing some otherwise good deeds and is killed in trying to do evil, it is sometimes better to say that he had good qualities and qualities that were not so good. But . . . if you do not tell the entire truth, you must always remember that you did not tell the entire truth, and each time you are tempted not to, you should ask whether you do so to make your path easier, or to aid others . . . or whether you do so for your own interests. If you find you are too often 'helping' others in that fashion, then you are deceiving yourself." He shook his head. "As in everything, nothing in life is as simple as the maxims we teach. It is so easy to slip from the honorable . . . and yet, I have seen what many would call honorable used as a reason for cruelty and despicable behavior." After another pause, he concluded, "And I don't know that I've answered your question."

"I think you have, sir."

Quaeryt wasn't so certain. *It's so easy to self-justify, and so hard to be truly honest about why you do what you do. Rescalyn certainly believed that overthrowing Bhayar would result in better rule of Telaryn . . . and you believed that a slightly better ruler would not justify all the upheaval and bloodshed. Who was right?*

For all that he believed he had acted wisely, who was truly to say?

On the remainder of the ride back to the Telaryn Palace, Quaeryt managed not to reveal much more than he'd asked Gauswn to say, despite Lankyt's curiosity. Once they reached the palace, he found Myskyl, who was surprisingly amenable to letting Lankyt ride with the regiment, then made arrangements for Lankyt to take a room in the west wing, and to eat as a guest in the mess. Finally, Quaeryt hurried to the main section of the palace and up to his and Vaelora's quarters, where he found her in the study that had become hers.

She looked up from the table desk where she was writing. "Dearest . . . why are you here . . . now?"

"The scholarium sent a messenger to ask me to come see Cyrethyn—the old chorister. He's dying and wanted to talk to me. A few things happened. You were right . . . sooner than you thought . . ." He went on to explain what happened, ending with . . . "and I believe Gauswn will keep the details to himself. Asking that of him . . . it bothers me . . . yet . . ."

"You were right to do so. The longer before anyone knows what you can do, the better." After a moment, she added, "Grandmere said something like that."

"Oh?" Quaeryt truly did wonder what Vaelora's grandmother might have said.

"It's better that others guess than know, because guessing breeds uncertainty, and uncertainty clouds action. That's what she said."

"There's also another matter I had to deal with. The messenger from the scholarium was young Lankyt. You met him . . ."

"The young man who wants to be a holder?"

"That's Lankyt. His father has finally agreed . . ." Quaeryt went on to explain, then said, "I had to persuade Myskyl to allow Lankyt to accompany First Regiment." He smiled crookedly. "I shouldn't have had a problem with that, not when they'd planned to overnight near Ayerne, but I do need to make certain that Straesyr understands." He paused. "I did want to tell you what happened." He grinned, if raggedly. "And that I did keep my promise."

"Sometimes . . . a woman does know . . ."

"More than sometimes," he admitted. "Especially you."

"You'd better tend to Straesyr. You might also tell him that Lord Bhayar was most favorably disposed toward Holder Rhodyn."

"I will." He glanced at the papers on the desk. "More of your writing on governing and people?"

"Yes . . . I was thinking . . ." She smiled. "Let me finish. You can read it when I've thought it out. You should do what you must as princeps."

"You sound like Straesyr . . . as though we won't be here that much longer."

"I fear he may be right. I cannot say why." Her eyes flicked in the direction of the center of the palace.

"You cannot . . . or you'd rather not?"

"I cannot . . . it is just a feeling."

"Farsight?"

She shook her head. "Just a feeling. Go see Straesyr."

Quaeryt doubted that what she sensed was just a feeling, but he only said, "I will see you later." Then he stepped forward, bent down, and kissed her cheek, before straightening and leaving.

On Vendrei morning, Quaeryt was up earlier than usual to see Lankyt and First Regiment off, as was Straesyr, if more than thirty yards from where Quaeryt stood, barely after dawn under high clouds and with a northwest wind that suggested the spring thaw was not quite so imminent. Quaeryt also gave a letter of Vaelora's—addressed to Aelina—to the regular courier, along with the extra silver for carrying a private message. After returning for a hurried breakfast with Vaelora, he made his way to his study.

Once there, he settled behind his desk to sort through the various messages and missives that Vhorym had placed there.

He'd only been at that for less than a quint when the governor walked in.

"Good morning, Quaeryt. I saw that you were up early to see the regiment and your charge off this morning."

Quaeryt stood. Although Straesyr wouldn't have made a point of it, Quaeryt would have felt uncomfortable sitting while his superior was standing. "I was, sir."

"Let us just hope they can get to Ayerne before the weather changes one way or another."

"Today looks promising."

"It does, so far. I wanted you to know that I changed the weekly report. In addition to informing Lord Bhayar that First Regiment is on its way, I also told him that we were working to dispatch Third Regiment as soon as we could. I didn't tell him when that would be."

"You're worried about supplies—or the weather?"

"More about the weather. We could get a sudden thaw that turns the roads immediately south of Bhorael into impassable swamps. We could also get a storm so severe that sending men and mounts into it would be a death sentence."

"I'd bet more on the swamps," said Quaeryt.

"So would I, but you never can tell. Let me know if there's any change in when Raurem will deliver the grain cakes." Straesyr paused. "Is there anything else I should know?"

"I haven't heard any more about Chorister Cyrethyn, but he won't last much longer, and it's a good thing you and Commander Myskyl let Gauswn leave service early. He's already another presence to keep the scholars in line, not that Nalakyn wants to do anything but be a scholar and teach others."

"That's always good." The governor nodded. "We'll talk later."

Quaeryt nodded. Straesyr often used that phrase to indicate he had nothing more to discuss, rather than signifying something else to deal with later.

After Straesyr left, Vhorym brought in another missive, this one from a wool factor in Midcote. From the date, the petition to reduce the factor's tariffs had taken more than a month to reach Tilbora, not surprisingly. Quaeryt set that aside for the moment, although he knew he'd deal with it before the morning was over.

Addressing all the items awaiting him occupied him into the early afternoon, and he was far from finished when Vhorym announced, "Chorister Phargos."

"Have him come in."

The regimental chorister walked into the study. Quaeryt gestured to the chairs, and Phargos seated himself before speaking, this time in Bovarian, a tongue in which he was fluent, but usually only employed for conducting services. "I thought that you should know. Cyrethyn died late last night. Gauswn sent me a message this morning. He wrote that you visited him yesterday."

"I did. Gauswn thought I should. I'm sorry to hear of his death. He tried to do his best, and that could not have been easy under the shadows of Zarxes and Phaeryn."

"Gauswn also wrote that he is more convinced than ever that the Nameless has chosen you for great deeds."

Quaeryt winced.

"You know," said the regimental chorister with a laugh, "that's as good an indication as any."

"What is?"

"Your reaction. But . . . do you want to tell me why he feels that way?"

"He feels that I've escaped too many situations that should have killed me for them all to be a result of mere good fortune. I've tried to persuade him otherwise. I obviously haven't been successful." With the last sentence, Quaeryt's tone turned wry.

"Commander Skarpa doesn't think so either. He also told me something interesting. He said that you told him he would be a regimental commander—long before the fight against the hill holders."

"I did. It seemed obvious to me that it would happen sooner or later."

thousand golds worth last year, but it could do more. They didn't want to flood the east with silver. That would only drive its worth down."

"But . . . if Rescalyn had been successful . . ."

"He could have produced more and sold it or coined it and used it all over Telaryn. Zorlyn was minting coins, though. There were molds and stamps—close to identical copies of Telaryn silvers."

"That's counterfeiting . . . or is it?"

"I don't know that it is." Quaeryt shrugged. "He was using real silver, and now it doesn't matter. The mines all belong to your brother."

"I doubt he even knows it."

With all that Bhayar held, that was likely true, but it was yet another reminder of the vast difference between the life Quaeryt had led and the one Bhayar had.

Quaeryt was still thinking about Rescalyn's omission of the silver from the dispatches when he reached his study . . . and all the ledgers and records he needed to peruse . . . and all the time he would spend trying to persuade factors and others to do what was in their own best interests.

"I've observed that more than a few things that seem obvious to you, master princeps, do not seem obvious to others, and yet they occur."

Quaeryt shrugged as if helplessly. "I cannot change what is."

"I suspect you have already changed what might have been."

"In some few things, such as re-forming the scholarium, improving its acceptance and gaining it more students, or getting Gauswn released from duty early to become a chorister, I have been of some help."

"In a few other tasks as well. Major Meinyt owes his life to you, as do a score or more rankers. Your presence here also brought Lord Bhayar to Tilbor, and that quieted many who wondered about his dedication to its people, as did your marriage."

"Vaelora did that, not me," protested Quaeryt.

"Your lady would not have wed anyone without outstanding qualities, master princeps. Nor would her brother have let her. That, we both know." When Quaeryt offered a dubious expression, Phargos added, "Tell me that is not so . . . if you dare to do so honestly."

Quaeryt laughed. "She does know her own mind."

"As do you, my friend. Now . . . about that homily . . ."

"What homily?"

"The only one I'll ever insist on your giving here. I want a promise that before you leave, whenever that may be, you will deliver the homily at services in the anomen. Everyone has heard you deliver a homily . . . except me."

"Just one . . . one time?" asked Quaeryt warily.

"One . . . once."

"For you . . . I will. But just once. I'm not a chorister."

"But you could have been . . . and an excellent one."

Not when I don't even know if there is a Nameless, I couldn't. But Quaeryt only shook his head.

Phargos laughed. "We will see." He stood. "I did want you to know about Cyrethyn."

"Thank you." Quaeryt rose as well. "He was a good man in a difficult position, who feared he had not done as well as he should have. That is something all of us should keep in mind."

"I might point out that any chorister would be happy to have uttered the words you just did."

"Go back to your anomen . . ." But Quaeryt couldn't help grinning.

"For now, most honored master princeps. For now." Phargos was smiling broadly as he left the study.

Samedi and Solayi passed without incident. The weather remained unchanging—cold under high clouds. Lundi brought snow flurries that briefly changed to rain, and then to ice that coated the snow and pavements that night, all of which melted by Mardi afternoon, just in time for another light snow. When Quaeryt and Vaelora rose on Meredi, the day was cold, but clear.

As he walked with Vaelora to the dining chamber for breakfast, he hoped that all was well with Lankyt and First Regiment, although it was likely they wouldn't reach Ayerne until that evening.

After they seated themselves, and he poured tea into their mugs, Vaelora took a slow swallow and then set her mug down. "Quaeryt dearest . . . we are attending this ball held by High Holder Thurl. Can you tell me anything about those who will be there? Besides Straesyr and Emra, of course."

"Except in terms of their names and positions, I know little. I have met only two of them, and only one of their wives. I had a midday meal with Governor Rescalyn at the estate of High Holder Freunyt, and a visit by myself with High Holder Fhaedyrk and his wife. Freunyt has a large holding outside of Tilbora, not so near as that of Thurl. He is intelligent and most well off . . ." After describing Freunyt, he recounted what he could remember of the holding, which wasn't that much. "As for High Holder Fhaedyrk . . . he is younger, and his holding is a ride of some four glasses to the north. In this weather . . ." He shrugged.

"Tell me anyway . . . and what you recall of his wife."

"I asked to visit Fhaedyrk because he was the target of several assassination attempts by Zarxes . . ." He went on to explain the background and the events of the visit, and the fact that Fhaedyrk's holding brewed excellent lager.

"I don't believe you mentioned his wife, dearest."

"Oh . . . she struck me as very intelligent, but much like you in that she reveals little to those she does not know—except when it suits her husband's purposes and her wishes."

"What does she look like?" There was the slightest edge to Vaelora's words.

"She is blond, like many people here, somewhat stocky, and a bit shorter than you, I think. She is very much in love with her husband, it seemed, and

he with her. They were most charming and hospitable . . . and they did reveal, if indirectly, their concerns about the scholars . . . once I broached the matter. I was possibly more direct than another High Holder might have been."

"She did not flirt with you, then?"

Quaeryt detected a hint of amusement in her voice, for which he was grateful. "No, not in the slightest. She did serve a most tasty berry custard, though."

"You do have a weakness for sweets, dearest."

There wasn't anything he dared to say directly in reply to that. So he didn't. "Do you think your brother will attack Antiago this spring?"

"I doubt it. He is more likely to respond to what others do . . . and then turn their weaknesses against them. In that, you and he are much alike."

"Then he anticipates an attack by Kharst. Autarch Aliaro would not be so foolish as to attack either Telaryn or Bovaria."

"What one anticipates is not always what happens."

"Especially since matters sometimes do not go as planned."

"Were you thinking about Rescalyn when you said that?" she asked.

"No. I was thinking about Zorlyn and the hill holders. They assumed that matters would continue as they always had. Rescalyn let them believe that would be the way it was, even while he was planning to destroy them."

"Why was that necessary? If he really wanted to become Lord of Telaryn, why did he bother with the hill holders?"

"I can think of several reasons." Quaeryt served her the cheesed eggs and mutton strips, and then himself before continuing. "First, keeping the hill holders as a threat allowed him to build up the regiment to three times what it had been. Second, it allowed him to give all of the officers and rankers ex perience in fighting. Third, by taking over the holdings of Zorlyn and t others with silver mines, he would have obtained that silver to pay for war against your brother. And fourth, he couldn't afford to have a dang enemy behind him while setting out to fight another war. He planned ing the winter and the spring to rebuild his forces, and he would verted all the tariffs from Tilbor—" Quaeryt stopped abruptly.

"What is it?"

He laughed. "I just realized something. Well . . . I knew it . . put the pieces together. I read all those dispatches . . . years' never did Rescalyn ever mention the silver mines of the hill h

"How many golds worth of silver would they produce?"

"I've looked at the records for last year . . . well, for four They don't mine in the winter. Zorlyn's mine produced

Warmer weather on Jeudi and Vendrei was followed by a blustery wind on Samedi, and a return to freezing temperatures just before sunset when the sleigh sent by High Holder Thurl arrived at the lower gates of the Telaryn Palace where Quaeryt, Vaelora, Straesyr, and Emra waited in the gatehouse. Quaeryt had barely seen the gown Vaelora was wearing because she'd shooed him away from the dressing area until she was dressed, and then had immediately donned a long fur coat he had not seen before that afternoon. He was wearing his finest browns with his formal brown coat, over which he wore a heavy winter jacket.

"Look how gloriously red the sky is to the west!" exclaimed Emra as the four left the gatehouse to walk to the sleigh.

"There was a bit of that last night," observed Straesyr. "Just a touch."

Quaeryt looked, turning to face into the light wind, coming out of the west. Indeed the entire western sky was red, a glorious golden red, if with an undertone of a darker red, like that of drying blood . . . of which he'd seen far too much in the campaign against the hill holders. The brilliance of the color almost totally obscured the crescent of Erion, whose slightly sullen reddish white seemed pale by comparison. He glanced at Vaelora, walking beside him, her coat wrapped tightly around her. Her face expressed more puzzlement than wonder, and he asked, "What is it?"

"That looks familiar. I couldn't say why."

"The sunset?"

"The colors."

"Then you must have seen them somewhere . . ."

Vaelora nodded. "But I don't remember." She turned, and Quaeryt helped her into the sleigh.

As the driver eased the sleigh away from the gates and onto the packed snow and ice of the road, two squads of troopers followed them.

Quaeryt continued to study the western sky, and it seemed to him that the golden red and the darker red took longer to fade than was usual for sunsets, but colors or not, the air was chill. Although heavy fur wraps had been spread across trousers and gowns, after only a quint in the horse-drawn sleigh, Quaeryt's legs were colder than if he'd been riding. *But then, you haven't been riding at night . . . or even late in the afternoon.*

"Earlier this week, I wondered if we'd be using the carriage," said Emra. "The snow was melting so fast."

"That's the way it is at the end of winter and the beginning of spring," said Straesyr. "Warm, then cold, then warm. Each time the cold is usually a little less chill, the warm a trace more springlike."

After another three quints, the sleigh swung through a pair of gilded iron gates flanked by polished marble gateposts set against graystone walls. Torches lit both the entry gates and the way up the snow-packed lane to the estate house, a structure more like a Bovarian chateau, thought Quaeryt. The sleigh stopped just short of the covered entry portico, where the four disembarked and then walked across the stone pavement that had been swept clean of snow and the ice removed, before climbing the three wide marble steps to the entry.

The outer double doors were open, although Quaeryt could see that the decorative ironwork was gilded on both sides, and a doorman opened the inner goldenwood door for them as they approached. "Governor . . . Lady Straesyr . . . most honored Lady Vaelora . . . Princeps."

Quaeryt noted the difference in address between Emra, whose position was determined by that of her husband, and that offered Vaelora, who clearly outranked him.

Once inside the chateau, they stood in a hexagonal vestibule with a high vaulted ceiling. The walls above the goldenwood wainscoting were smooth plaster tinted to resemble golden-streaked marble, with deep blue velvet hangings.

"The robing room for the ladies . . ." murmured another functionary, gesturing to the left. "And for . . . you . . ." That gesture was to the right.

Two valets stood waiting in the narrow chamber to take Quaeryt's and Straesyr's outer coats. From there, Quaeryt followed Straesyr back into the main entry hall, where they waited for a good half quint for their ladies.

Vaelora's hair was swept back with black and silver combs, and her gown was of black velvet in a cut that accentuated her waist, and with a neckline that was a diamond cut just large enough to allow the silver pendant that held a modest emerald. The sleeves tapered to almost skintight at her wrists. Completing the ensemble was a silvered green sleeveless vest, held in place in front by a silver chain.

Quaeryt found himself staring in admiration.

"I see you like it, dearest."

"I like you in it." He dared not think what else he thought.

"You picked a very good seamstress," Vaelora added.

If by accident. "Thank you."

"The ballroom is at the end of the main hallway . . ." murmured yet another functionary, in what was clearly a reminder to move along.

Quaeryt and Vaelora walked quickly until they caught up with the governor and his wife. Then they waited, but for moments, to enter the ballroom.

"Governor, Lady Straesyr . . . welcome to Thurlhold." High Holder Thurl was an angular older man with thinning blond hair, who spoke in Tellan, which would not have been the case with a High Holder nearer Solis.

"We're pleased to be here, and I deeply appreciate the use of your sleigh," replied Straesyr. "Even more so does my wife."

"I thought it might be so." Thurl smiled, before turning to Quaeryt and Vaelora. "Lady Vaelora, Princeps . . . I bid you welcome. It is not often we entertain a couple who are both of position." Thurl turned his eyes back to Quaeryt. "The muted finery of a scholar suits you, Princeps, although it does not do justice to your reputation in the field, I understand."

"That was by necessity," replied Quaeryt. "We do appreciate your grace and hospitality." Glancing beyond Thurl, where but a handful of couples stood, generally near the sideboards offering wine, Quaeryt could see that his browns represented the most severe attire of anyone present.

"We can do no less." With a smile, Thurl turned to those following Quaeryt and Vaelora.

Quaeryt understood that Thurl had meant those words literally, no matter how graciously uttered.

"You would not be here . . . except . . ." murmured Vaelora.

"Except for you," he agreed. "They look down on the princeps as a functionary who deals with factors and low holders and others of less stature."

"They do not know you."

"As you suggested, my lady, in your correspondence, even before you knew all you now know about me, you recommended that it was better that people not see one as a threat if one wished to accomplish one's ends."

Vaelora laughed softly. "It is a compliment that you not only read my words, but recall them so well."

"I read them often."

"I can tell. For that I am grateful."

"As am I, because your advice and counsel are wise beyond your years."

"In some matters. Not in others." Looking over his shoulder, she murmured, "There's a couple approaching."

As he turned, he murmured, "Fhaedyrk and Laekyna."

"Princeps . . . and this must be the lady Vaelora." Fhaedyrk bowed.

"High Holder Fhaedyrk . . . Laekyna," Quaeryt acknowledged, deliberately bending social niceties by acknowledging Fhaedyrk's wife in her own right.

Laekyna's eyes widened just slightly, but she curtseyed, a courtesy Quaeryt had not seen in Tilbor before, but then, until the ball, he'd been at no functions where more than a single woman of position had been present.

"Lady Vaelora," offered Laekyna after the slightest hesitation, "I'm so pleased to meet you."

"And I you," replied Vaelora. "My husband has told me of your hospitality and grace when he visited you."

Laekyna smiled, shyly. Even so, the act transformed her face, and once more Quaeryt was struck by the similarity in expression between her and Vaelora, although the two were not at all alike in appearance. "He is most kind to notice."

Kind? Hardly. Fair . . . perhaps. "You were most hospitable."

"One could hardly be less to the princeps," said Fhaedyrk smoothly.

"That is true, especially if he happens to be the husband of the sister of Lord Bhayar," replied Vaelora with a smile. "But, as I recall, Quaeryt was only a scholar assistant at the time, and that speaks to hospitality."

"What can I say?" replied Fhaedyrk disarmingly.

"That you understand not all wisdom or power resides in those who are High Holders, perchance," said Vaelora. "Or that offering hospitality is not conditional upon position, but it is better to act than to speak such. Of course, as a woman, that is merely my youthful opinion."

Quaeryt noted that Laekyna was having difficulty concealing a smile.

"It is an opinion well worth considering." Fhaedyrk paused for but an instant. "Do you have news on what may be happening in the west?"

"Only through my husband. It appears as though Rex Kharst may be considering actions hostile to Telaryn. What those actions might be is not clear." Vaelora glanced to Quaeryt. "Is that not so, dearest?"

"That is indeed all that we know at the moment. We have been requested to prepare another regiment for deployment to the west, but not for what purpose."

"What do you think of Thurlhold?" asked Laekyna of Vaelora.

"It appears tastefully impressive," replied Vaelora.

After several more exchanges of polite comments, Fhaedyrk and Laekyna excused themselves.

Behind Quaeryt and Vaelora, the group of musicians began to play.

"We should dance," said Vaelora quietly.

"Perhaps we should," replied Quaeryt, "but I don't know how."

"That part of your education was neglected, dearest, but it's not hard. I'll show you how. You take my right hand in your left, and place your right on the middle of my back just above my waist . . ."

Quaeryt did his best to follow her instructions and her lead, but the best he felt he could have said when the musicians stopped for a moment was that he'd managed not to step on her feet or trip her and that he'd managed to look generally like he knew what he was doing.

Vaelora looked up at him. "You see? It's not that hard."

"No. Except that, without your instruction, I wouldn't have the faintest idea of what to do." *And I'm not certain that I still wouldn't.* "Would you like some wine?"

"Just a little."

As Quaeryt and Vaelora walked toward the nearest sideboard, the musicians struck up another tune, one livelier than the one played before. Quaeryt glanced at the dancers, still no more than a score, and wondered if he'd ever learn the intricate steps that he observed. *With Vaelora's insistence and instruction . . . most likely.*

When Quaeryt turned from the sideboard holding two goblets of white wine, he found himself facing a High Holder he did not recognize.

"Princeps . . . High Holder Heskhaeld." The trim but muscular holder who addressed Quaeryt smiled politely. "We have not met, but the governor suggested that I talk to you."

"I'm pleased to meet you." Now that he had the man's name, Quaeryt knew exactly what Heskhaeld wanted, and he doubted that the High Holder would be satisfied with what would likely happen.

"While a ball is perhaps not the optimal location for discussing matters of property, it is winter, and I so seldom can get to Tilbora . . ."

Quaeryt nodded and waited.

". . . more than a month ago, I inquired about the purchase of a section of land adjoining mine—certain lands belonging to the rebel holder Saentaryn . . ."

Quaeryt nodded. "And you have not had a response and wondered when you might?"

"Precisely."

"Those lands now belong to Lord Bhayar, and as princeps, I sent your request to him in Solis. As princeps, I have authority over supplies and other matters here in Tilbor, but not over Lord Bhayar's lands. Any decision on those he must make, and he will likely consult with his finance minister before doing so. As this is winter, to get a message to Solis takes some time, even with military couriers . . . and a return message also takes time . . ." As

Quaeryt explained, he understood, once more, how easily procedures could be employed to offer a negative response without ever directly saying "no," although he had recommended that the lands not be sold for the present, given their proximity to High Holder Eshalyn's coal mine. ". . . and when I receive an answer, you will be assured that we will inform you as soon as we can."

"I can ask no more." Heskhaeld bowed, clearly mollified, but less than satisfied.

Quaeryt slipped toward Vaelora and handed her the goblet of wine.

"What was that about?" she asked.

"He wants to purchase lands from your brother . . ." Quaeryt explained quickly.

"At a ball?"

"I'm only a princeps," Quaeryt said wryly. "He obviously felt the courtesies don't apply to me." *Unlike Fhaedyrk.*

"Lady Vaelora?"

They both turned to see another couple, neither of whom Quaeryt recognized, approaching.

The rest of the evening will be like this. Nonetheless, Quaeryt smiled.

Quaeryt had barely finished dressing on Solayi morning when the bells in their quarters rang so insistently that someone had to be yanking the bell-pull with either excessive enthusiasm or great urgency.

"Who can that be?" asked Vaelora.

"It's not good. Not on Solayi morning." Quaeryt turned and hurried down the private staircase to the access doors. He peered through the peephole and saw a squad leader he did not recognize standing there, most likely one on duty. Still, he raised his shields before opening the door. "Yes, Squad Leader?"

"Princeps, sir, the governor requests that you join him in his study at your earliest convenience."

"Tell him I'll be right there. You wouldn't know what this is about?"

"No, sir."

Quaeryt smiled politely and tried to use his imaging ability to project friendly and open curiosity.

"He did receive an urgent dispatch, but he didn't say what was in it, sir."

"Thank you."

Quaeryt took the steps back up to their quarters two at a time and strode to their dressing room.

"What is it?"

"As I said, it's not good. Straesyr just got a dispatch, and he wants to meet in his study immediately. The regular couriers never arrive on Solayi."

"You'll tell me?"

"As soon as I can. Save me some breakfast."

"I can do that."

Quaeryt bent over and kissed her neck, then made his way back down to the second level. When he reached the governor's chambers, Quaeryt hurried in past the empty table desk where Undercaptain Caermyt usually sat. The governor did not rise from behind his desk, but motioned to the chairs. Straesyr was wearing an old set of winter greens, suitable for the chill of the study where the stove had not been fired up.

Quaeryt sat. "What's the problem, sir?"

"There are several." Straesyr's mouth curled into a smile both sardonic and rueful. "Mount Extel . . . it erupted last week. A quarter of Extela is covered in lava . . ."

Vaelora's grandmere's foresight flash . . . Quaeryt repressed a shiver.

". . . Kharst is rushing troops to Ferravyl, obviously wanting to attack if Lord Bhayar removes any forces there at present. Lord Bhayar wants you and his sister to leave immediately with Third Regiment for Extela. You're to go to Extela and take over as temporary governor. Governor Scythn was killed by the flow of hot ash that preceded the lava. So were the princeps and most of their staff. I'm to send Second Regiment—somehow—to Ferravyl within two weeks of your departure." He handed a single sheet of paper, sealed, to Quaeryt. "This was included for you."

Quaeryt broke the seal and read quickly.

Quaeryt—

Extela was in chaos. I have a regiment there, but they need to return to Ferravyl before your arrival. Send a courier to Commander Zhrensyl when you're two days away. You will be governor of Montagne province, and you and Vaelora will be my personal representatives there. Don't neglect the safety of the people, but release as many companies from your regiment as soon as you can . . .

There was more, but the remainder of the missive expanded on the basic responsibilities laid on Quaeryt—and Vaelora.

"He's sent a regiment there to keep order, but we're to replace them, and Vaelora and I are supposed to use our presence to keep order so that most of Third Regiment can leave as soon as possible." Quaeryt paused. "You probably knew that already."

"In general terms."

"How soon are we leaving?"

"Mardi—if it doesn't snow."

"I'll send a messenger to Raurem and tell him to deliver whatever he can tomorrow. The rest can go for Second Regiment . . ."

For almost a glass, the two discussed what arrangements had to be made and which of them would do what.

Then Quaeryt headed back up to Vaelora to inform her before he went to deal with everything else.

Vaelora jumped up from where she sat at the table. "What did he want?"

"To tell me that your grandmere was right. He didn't put it—"

"She was right about what?"

"You'll need to pack up everything that will fit on a mount and in one trunk. Mount Extel erupted . . ." Quaeryt went on to explain.

When he paused, Vaelora asked, "What about the people? How many people were hurt?"

"A quarter of Extela was destroyed. Hundreds, perhaps thousands, are missing. They're likely dead, especially with the flooding."

"Flooding? In winter? Oh . . . the heat melted—"

"All the snow and ice at once," he finished.

"Those poor people . . ." mused Vaelora. "That was what Grandmere said would happen."

"Was she always right?"

"That was the only vision I know of that had not come to pass when she died. I don't know what Bhayar expects of us . . ."

"I don't know what we can do, either . . . but your brother expects us to make things better."

"You'll think of something."

"We'll think of something. Remember . . . your brother insisted you come, too." He shook his head. "On top of it all, I need to give a homily at services tonight."

"What?" Vaelora's voice rose just slightly.

"I promised Phargos I would give one homily—just one—before I left Tilbora."

"Oh . . . dearest . . ." Vaelora shook her head. "Do you know what you'll say?"

"No . . . but I'll think of something."

"I'm sure you will." She smiled. "I'd like to hear it as well." The smile vanished. "One trunk?"

Quaeryt shrugged. "Do you want your brother's soldiers commenting on how you carried everything you had in a supply wagon?"

"How much are you taking?"

"I think I can fit almost everything I own in an officer's kit bag." *Tightly.*

Vaelora made a face. "I can do the same with one trunk. If I can find one."

"If you can't, I'll get two kit bags for you."

"Go!" The single word was delivered with mock gruffness. "Do what you must."

"I need to eat something, first."

"Oh . . . I forgot. There's plenty left."

Quaeryt ate the cold omelet and the bread, if smeared liberally with a quince jelly that was so tart it was just short of bitter. Then he headed for his study to compose messages and try to begin to do what Straesyr had delegated to him.

Amid his efforts to make the arrangements for their departure, Quaeryt did locate Phargos, several glasses later, actually in the anomen.

"The word is that you and Third Regiment will be leaving in the next day or so."

"Mardi morning, if it's not storming." Quaeryt paused. "I made you a promise . . ."

"I hope you intend to keep it." Phargos grinned. "I was worried about the homily for this evening anyway."

"I will." *But you may well worry about the homily after it's delivered.*

After he left the anomen, Quaeryt returned to his various tasks, eventually getting back to his and Vaelora's quarters in time to eat and then for the two of them to make their way to the anomen for services.

They stood near the front, but to one side through the first part of the service.

When it came time for the homily, Phargos did not step up to the pulpit, but stood in the middle of the sacristy and began to speak. "As all of you know, Princeps Quaeryt will be leaving with Third Regiment. So I thought it would be fitting for him to deliver the homily this evening." Phargos offered a benevolent smile.

As Quaeryt turned to move to the pulpit, the first time he'd actually delivered a homily from there, he did catch the glimpse of an almost impish expression on the regimental chorister's face. Without being excessively slow, he moved to the pulpit deliberately, then stood there for several moments before speaking, in Bovarian, as was the custom at the anomen in the Telaryn Palace.

"Under the Nameless, all evenings are reckoned as good, but, unhappily, at times, we all have our doubts about that reckoning." After delivering that phrase as wryly as he could, he paused slightly. He could see several nods and heard a rueful chuckle before he went on. "The reason Third Regiment is leaving Tilbora early is that there is great destruction in Extela. Mount Extel erupted and destroyed much of the city. I doubt most seriously that many in Extela feel that this is a good evening. Nor would many of thoughtful mind have said that the Solayi following the fall of the last hill hold was especially good, not with all the deaths and the agonizing injuries. Yet all evenings under the Nameless are good . . . so it is said.

"Well . . . certainly being able to be alive and well enough to see the evening is better than the alternative, but is that what is meant by a good evening? Is mere survival enough to make the evening good? There's certainly nothing I've read or heard that makes such a claim. Nor has the Nameless whispered in my ear and said, 'All evenings are good because I said so.' And, while it may be personal vanity on my part, somehow I don't think that the Nameless would say that. I'm going to go out on a limb—or stand at the edge of a cliff, if you will, in this storm that we call life and say that what is meant by those words is something quite different from the simple meaning we hear in them." Quaeryt paused again.

"What if . . . what if those words really mean that all evenings are good because we have the ability to discern between what is good and what is not? That we have the capability to choose between a course of good or a course of evil or a course somewhere in between. Now . . . some will say that the Nameless has the power to do anything, and question why evil things happen to good people, especially evil things not made by people. In one way or another, we choose whether to fight, as do those against whom we fight, but no one chooses to have a mountain explode and kill them or their family. Yet . . . let me put the question in another way. What value, what integrity, would lie in life if the Nameless mandated and ordered life in such a fashion that there were no evils . . . of any sort? Or even a world where evildoers were struck down by lightning or plague sent by the Nameless? Could it be that all evenings are good, because each one offers us the possibility of affirming what we are and what we can be at our best?

"If there were no evil . . . could there be good? And what would that good be worth? Could it be that the good of every evening is that we are granted the power to choose what course we will follow, to make of ourselves what we can . . ."

When he finished, he surrendered the pulpit to Phargos for the concluding hymn and benediction.

Vaelora slipped up to Quaeryt after the service, but said nothing as Phargos approached.

"I can see that you don't mind touching the most fundamental questions," observed the chorister. "Yet I did notice that you did not actually affirm that there is a Nameless."

"I tried not to. I honestly don't know if the Nameless exists. I can't proclaim what I don't know."

"That's the beauty of faith."

"No . . . that is faith. Whether faith is beauty depends on whether the Nameless exists."

Phargos shook his head. "If you were young and had not seen what you have seen, Princeps, I would say that you did not understand the need for faith. But you have seen and endured much, and you have clearly felt the agony of others. So I will say nothing except that you will either break the world or it will break you."

"I doubt I will break the world, and it does not have to break me."

Phargos smiled softly, sadly. "We will see, Princeps." He turned to Vaelora. "You have graced us, Lady, and may you grace others as well."

Vaelora inclined her head. "Thank you."

Neither Quaeryt nor Vaelora spoke until they left the anomen and were walking across the courtyard in a blustery wind.

"You worry him," said Vaelora.

"I doubt that I worry him. He likes me, and he's concerned that my lack of faith in the Nameless will leave me bereft when times and life turn against me, as they likely will." *And have in the past.*

"Will it?"

Quaeryt laughed briefly, almost sardonically. "To me, it is obvious that if there is a Nameless, that deity does not interfere one way or the other in the lives of men and women. Life may indeed break me. Who can say what will happen? But if broken I become, life and the deeds of men and women will break me, not a lack of faith in a deity that leaves us to our own devices. . . ."

Vaelora reached out and squeezed his hand, and they continued walking through the cold wind.

The easiest part of leaving Tilbora on Mardi morning was departing the Telaryn Palace. The days before had been hectic for Quaeryt, to say the least. He'd taken the precaution of packing up blank spare ledgers, copies of the Tilboran and standard Telaryn tariff schedules, and all other manner of administrivia that might be helpful, especially given that apparently neither the governor nor the princeps had survived.

The lane down from the eastern gates was dry, and the snow heaped on each side frozen and coated with ice. The road to the west was passable, even for the last supply wagons. Quaeryt had wondered why Skarpa was headed west—until they reached the river, still iced over, and he understood as the regiment navigated over the uneven surface. Even without having to rely on ferries, the crossing of less than two hundred yards of ice took until almost midday, but it would have taken far, far longer had they had to rely on the ferries at the mouth of the river. Then the regiment turned back southeast and followed the west river road back down to Bhorael.

By the next day, some twenty milles south of Bhorael, the snow alongside the road was less than knee deep. By late afternoon, some ten milles farther south, the top mud on the roads had unfrozen, and the column slowed. All in all, reaching Ayerne took six days, and Quaeryt felt fortunate indeed that he was a princeps headed to be a governor, because at those stops where quarters were nonexistent, at least he and Vaelora could sleep in a wagon. Even so, by the time they reached Ayerne, both of them were tired of mud, frozen mud, and more mud. Both also had mud spattered over boots and trousers and occasionally higher.

Even the rations seemed to taste of mud.

Late on Solayi, just before sunset, Quaeryt and Vaelora rode up the narrow brick-paved lane that led to Rhodyn's main hold house and that was thankfully free of mud

Lankyt stood on the front steps, peering out into the low western sun. "Princeps? Is that you? And your lady?"

"Both of us." Quaeryt did not dismount. Although he was hoping for a warm reception, he knew Bhayar's forces had already imposed greatly on

Rhodyn, although Bhayar himself, according to Vaelora, had reimbursed the holder for his entourage.

"Let me tell Father. He'll want to see you."

"I'd like to see him."

As Lankyt reentered the dwelling, Vaelora turned in the saddle. "He is a sweet young man."

"He also loves the land, and his father."

"That speaks well of Rhodyn."

"It does." Yet Quaeryt wondered if such love of parents resulted just from the parents' acts. Jorem loved his father—that was also clear, even if the eldest son had not wished to leave Bhorael and the family of his Pharsi wife. Yet Syndar, who would likely make a solid scholar, did not seem to manifest the same devotion toward his sire, while Lankyt did. Was there something about being a middle son? Quaeryt didn't know, or have any way of knowing.

In moments, Rhodyn was standing on the front steps.

"Holder Rhodyn," announced Quaeryt, "I fear I'm here to take advantage of your hospitality once again."

"Nonsense, your presence is welcome, and that of your lady." The gray-haired holder inclined his head. "Lady Vaelora, it is a pleasure to see you again. You did not tell me that one of the purposes of your journey to Tilbora was to wed the princeps."

Vaelora laughed, huskily, but warmly. "I did not know that was what my brother had in mind. I had hoped for such, but he gave neither of us any choice."

"A wise man." Rhodyn looked to Quaeryt. "I can offer dry quarters to all, as I have before, such as they are, but my table is limited. Perhaps you might ask the commander and any majors or other officers he might wish to include?"

"I will certainly ask . . . but I do not know what his duties may entail. I do not know that you have heard, but Mount Extel has exploded, and much of Extela is in ruins. That is where we are bound."

"That does not bode well."

"No . . . and there are fears Rex Kharst may attempt to take advantage of the situation."

"That would be . . ." Rhodyn stopped and shook his head. "I should not keep you cold and mounted. You two, at least, must have a warmer room for the evening, and if you would convey my invitation?"

"I will accept that room, for my lady, especially, although I fear it is more accurate to say that I am her princeps."

"That verges on disrespect . . . again," murmured Vaelora, but Quaeryt could hear the unvoiced laughter beneath the words.

"Let me take your mount, Lady," insisted Lankyt, hurrying up.

"That would be most kind of you," replied Vaelora, her voice conveying relief, appreciation, and warmth without the slightest trace of condescension. She dismounted with a grace that Quaeryt could only envy.

"I will convey your invitation to Commander Skarpa and return as I am able," he said. "And I do thank you for the invitation and hospitality."

It took Quaeryt close to a quint to locate Skarpa, out near the largest outbuilding, and to offer Rhodyn's invitation.

"We'll take the invitation," said Skarpa with a laugh. "That way, we can save a few rations. It's better food, but we do pay holders what we can, anyway."

"I saw the golds on the manifest for the regiment, but what would you pay for what he's offering?"

"Ten golds."

"Can you do fifteen if I add a few personally?"

Skarpa laughed again. "The governor already told me to give him twenty, for all he's done, and not to take your coins. Not here, anyway."

"The men won't mind if we eat . . . there?"

"Most of them won't care so long as they're dry and fed. The company officers understand that holders like to feed officers and that means their men get quarters, even if they're just dry barns." He smiled. "They hope they get promoted so that they get fed that way someday."

In the end, after Skarpa and Quaeryt had seen that all the men and company officers were fed, Rhodyn provided a late supper for Quaeryt and Vaelora, the commander, and the battalion majors. Rhodyn sat at the head of the long table, with his wife Darlinka at his left and Quaeryt to his right, with Vaelora beside her husband. Lankyt sat at the end of the table.

As the serving women set the platters on the table, after all the glasses had been filled with ale or lager, Rhodyn lifted his glass. "To your health and safety on your journey to come."

The second toast was Quaeryt's, and he offered, "Our deepest thanks and appreciation for your kindness and hospitality."

"We cannot thank you enough," added Skarpa after the toast.

"Commander," replied Rhodyn, "most times holders bear the brunt of quartering armsmen, wincing and saying nothing. I've been more fortunate. The princeps favored me by going out of his way to do tasks that benefited me and my family. He offered counsel in an indirect way that let me keep my family and my pride, and his wife has graced my hold so that we will be able to tell our children and grandchildren how we've been favored. On top of that, Lord Bhayar removed the last of the ship reavers and made the Shallows Coast safe to ride and travel again . . . and that will allow us to graze lands closed for generations. All that would not have happened, I suspect, without the princeps's presence in Tilbor." The holder's eyes twinkled and he inclined his head to Vaelora. "And yours, Lady. Now . . . enjoy the fare before it cools."

The heaping platters held slices of mutton covered in dark gravy, fried potato/onion cakes, and large pickles cut into halves lengthwise. Another bowl held applesauce, and the bread in the baskets consisted of small warm golden loaves.

For a time, no one spoke.

Finally, with a grin upon his face, Skarpa did. "The princeps has never said much about his meeting with you, Holder Rhodyn, only that he praised your kindness and courtesy. Might you tell us more?"

"I only did what any good person would do," demurred Rhodyn.

"Since the good holder is too modest," said Quaeryt dryly, "I will offer a bit more. I was shipwrecked in a storm off the Shallows Coast. An elderly lady there offered me water, which I foolishly accepted, thinking water would be safe, although I worried about her very mien. After that I was chased by brigands through the fog following the storm. While I was able to escape them, when I reached Ayerne, here, I spoke but a few words to Holder Rhodyn before I collapsed. He and his wife nursed me through the poison and the injuries I had suffered until I was well. Then he even persuaded the local ostler to sell me the very mare I still ride for far less than she is worth. Mind you, he did not do this for the princeps, but for the mere scholar assistant to the princeps, and he did so without a thought of himself."

Rhodyn shifted his weight in his chair, and Quaeryt thought the older man had blushed slightly.

"As I said, I only did what any good man would do."

"And what very few men in fact do," added Vaelora softly.

"I was not quite so selfless as the princeps says," protested Rhodyn. "I did read the letters he carried. One appointed him as a scholar assistant. The second was from a lady, and it was written in a fine hand. It asked the kind of questions any ruler should ask. More than anything, it was her letter that told me about the man who lay close to dying in my house. Darlinka read it and told me that it would be a great loss to the lady and the world if I let him die."

"I'm so glad you did not," murmured Vaelora.

"As am I," stated Darlinka.

"Now that you have your answers, Commander," said Quaeryt, "might I turn the tables and ask how you came to serve Lord Bhayar?"

"You have me there, Princeps," replied Skarpa. "Simple enough, it was. My father was a cooper, and after I'd destroyed enough staves in trying to make barrels, he said that the only trade there was where a man got paid for hacking everything to pieces was being a soldier . . . and since he had other sons who weren't so destructive . . ." The commander shrugged.

From that point on, everyone talked.

More than a glass later, once the door had closed behind the departing officers, Rhodyn turned to Quaeryt. "Might I ask a question?"

"Of course."

"Why did you write me about Syndar?"

"Originally, I wanted to find some way to tell you that Syndar was not suited to be a holder, but that did not seem . . . right. When Yullyd told me how well Syndar did in helping with the ledgers, I realized that while my feelings had been correct, I hadn't fully understood why. Your son Jorem has made the produce factorage more successful because he loves his wife and what they do together. Lankyt will make a good holder because he loves the land so much that he has gone out of his way to discover ways to improve what can be grown and how. Those were obvious to me, but when I saw, through others, that Syndar truly loved the life of study and numbers, I wrote . . . because men and women, I believe, find the most in life when they love what they do, either because they always love that or come to find that they do."

"And you, Princeps," asked Darlinka softly, "what do you love?"

"Besides Vaelora?" replied Quaeryt with a smile.

"You still answer some questions with questions," said the holder's wife.

What do I love doing in life? After several moments of silence, Quaeryt replied, "That's because I question that myself. I don't know that I have an answer for you, not one that would be completely honest. I like making things . . . better. But 'better' is something that is different for each man, each woman." He offered a crooked smile.

Darlinka looked to Vaelora, questioningly.

"I would not dispute my husband's answer, nor would mine be much different."

Rhodyn laughed. "Then it appears you are well matched."

"I only hope that you are strong enough together to survive what you love," said Darlinka, her voice still soft, with a hint of sadness beneath the words.

So do I. Quaeryt did not voice the thought, but just reached out and squeezed Vaelora's hand.

South of Ayerne, the ice-covered snow of Tilbor and the north gave way to softer snow that was little more than calf-deep and soft and slushy. Even so, only by concentrating could Quaeryt make out the snow-covered remnants of the towns that Rhodyn and the other holders north of the Ayerne River had leveled years earlier. Progress for the regiment was slow until they reached the small town of Sullys, three days south of Ayerne, where they turned west on the solid stone-paved post road built generations earlier in the time of Hengyst.

Roughly at midmorning on Samedi, under high gray clouds, Quaeryt and Vaelora were riding beside Skarpa near the front of the column when a scout headed toward them from around a wide curve in the road. The scout reined in his mount, then drew alongside the commander.

"Sirs! The bridge is covered with water. It's deep, more than head-high. The water's running too fast to cross, even if we could see where the bridge is. There are chunks of ice everywhere."

"We might as well see how bad it is before we decide," said Skarpa, looking to Quaeryt.

Quaeryt nodded.

"I'd like to come, too," said Vaelora.

Quaeryt wasn't about to deny her, not when she was a far better rider than he was.

Skarpa turned in the saddle and raised an arm. "Regiment! Halt!"

As the command rippled back along the column, Skarpa, Quaeryt, and Vaelora rode forward with the scout. The road between two tree-covered ridges was level all the way around the curve, then descended gently to an expanse of murky gray water, dotted with chunks of grayish ice, that covered the bridge. The four reined up beside another scout, some ten yards back from the edge of the water, and surveyed what lay between them and the road on the far side.

The river ran between two long ridges, neither more than fifty yards above the road, and less than a hundred yards apart at the level of the road, before plunging over a barrier of frozen vegetation, branches, and tree trunks, at the top of what was likely the top of a moderate cataract most of the year, but the barrier formed a dam that had lifted the water level well above the road leading to the submerged bridge, and whatever eroding effect the frigid water might be having was more than outweighed by the vegetation and chunks of ice piling up behind the existing tangle.

"It could be days . . ." said Vaelora quietly.

"Is there any way around this?" asked Quaeryt.

"From the maps we have, and from what I recall from when I was here before, we'd have to go back more than ten milles to take a more southern road, and it's not paved." Skarpa looked at Quaeryt. "You know what that means, sir."

Quaeryt did. The southern road would be even less passable in spots, besides taking much, much longer.

After a time, he said, "Let me take a closer look." Before either Vaelora or Skarpa could say anything, Quaeryt eased his mount off the road, southward along the lower part of the hill on the east side of the slowly rising water, trying to let her pick her way over the soggy ground between dampened and flattened bushes and leafless trees.

As he neared a point opposite the tangle that comprised the barrier, he could see that part of the hillside had collapsed, perhaps because of rain or melting snow, if not both. The combination of the rocks and soil and trees that had slid into the river and the debris carried downstream and snagging on who knew what else below the surface of the water, not to mention the ice, had created a temporary but effective dam.

But temporary could mean it lasts for days or weeks.

He tied the mare to the exposed root of a tree partly ripped out of the hillside by the landslide, then took his half-staff from its leathers and slowly made his way downhill to the end of the debris, a mass of ice, soil, and twisted branches and roots. He put one foot on the end. The debris did not budge. He took three more careful steps, using the staff to probe for solid footing, but when he tried to extend his boot for the fourth, he could feel the makeshift dam shift, if ever so slightly. Less than three yards from where he stood, water poured over the middle part of the barrier, almost as if it were a spillway, and then cascaded down over and around icy rocks and huge boulders, dropping a good thirty yards over a distance of less than a hundred.

He glanced back upstream. The torrent of murky gray water and ice chunks seemed endless. He looked at the face of the "dam," trying to pick out places where the water was seeping through in more than mere tricklets. Finally, he located a streamlet of water almost as big around as his wrist, shooting out from the front, some two yards down and possibly four toward the center of the twisted mass from where he stood.

He bent and began to wiggle a root, not that his efforts did so much as even cause a stir in the debris, but none of those around Skarpa could have determined that from where they watched. Then he concentrated on trying to image away some of the debris above the streamlet.

He could sense that he'd moved something, but the flow of water remained the same. The second time, he concentrated on an area to the far side. He could feel himself begin to sweat, despite the cold and clammy air around him.

He waited and watched. The streamlet seemed larger, but not much.

The third time, he visualized removing debris and soil behind the last place from which he had removed matter, and the size of the streamlet again grew . . . but not that much.

Quaeryt made another effort. The streamlet tripled in size, and the entire dam shuddered, if slightly.

Quaeryt retreated several steps and waited. While the streamlet continued to expand, he could see that the increased flow still was far from enough to lower the water level. He bent and grabbed another branch, but that was for effect only as he attempted to image away more, visualizing the removal of a large cube of material.

Everything around him seemed to flash, and sweat poured from his forehead. For a moment, he could see nothing because of the flashes, while the makeshift dam shuddered more. At that moment, he lost control of even his lightest shields. Then a cascade of water poured through the area Quaeryt had enlarged, and the barrier began to shake.

Carefully, but quickly, he eased himself back off the end of the debris and took several unsteady steps back uphill toward the mare.

A dull rumble seemed to shake the air around him, and he tottered where he stood, trying to keep his balance on the slippery ground where the staff was of little use. He glanced back at the makeshift dam, where a small section began to sag into the dark waters. Then, after several moments more, another part of the debris broke away, and spray cascaded upward before the ice-filled waters began to pour through the gap. The debris at each end of the opening continued to break away.

He took one step, then another, until he was close enough to the mare so that he could untie her. Mounting took almost all the strength he had left, and by the time he was in the saddle, with the staff back in its leathers, he just sat there for several moments. When he looked down at the torrent, the gap in the debris dam was almost ten yards across and deepening.

Quaeryt rode slowly back northward to the road where Skarpa waited with Vaelora and the scouts.

"What did you do?" asked Skarpa, his forehead furrowed.

"It wasn't that solid. I just tried to wiggle things and hoped I could loosen holes in it." The last part was true enough. "Just have everyone rest for a bit. It's beginning to give way. The water is breaking it apart now."

"That didn't look like just ice, sir."

"It isn't. It wasn't, but the ice was what was plugging some of the gaps. I levered some of it away, and the water is beginning to work."

Sparkling lights flashed before Quaeryt's eyes, once more, and he felt so weak and dizzy that he had to lower his head, almost to the mare's mane.

"Dearest . . ." Vaelora edged her gelding over beside Quaeryt. "You worked harder than you let us believe." She extended a flask. "Take a swallow of this."

The cordial in the silver flask burned its way down his throat, but after several moments, the worst of the flashes before his eyes began to subside. Then she handed him a hard biscuit.

Quaeryt ate it slowly with another swallow from the flask, before he took several swallows from his own water bottle—that held watered lager.

"Are you all right, Princeps?" asked Skarpa. "What did you do?"

"I just worked at opening a hole in that mess."

"It looks like the water's getting lower," admitted the commander.

Almost two quints later, the water had dropped below the solid stone surface of the bridge except at one end. While the torrent had ripped away parts of the walls and railing, the bridge itself, built of massive slabs of stone, remained untouched, and Skarpa had the engineers working on clearing the debris away from the upstream side of the bridge.

Vaelora turned in the saddle to look at her husband. "Dearest . . . look at that boulder, the one near the middle of the stream where everything was piled up." Her voice was low.

Quaeryt looked. In the middle of the smooth and massive boulder was a channel in the shape of the bottom half of a square running through the stone, and through that channel ran murky water. *No wonder I feel so rotten.*

"I doubt that the water cut that channel," Vaelora added. "You do need to eat more after doing something like that."

Quaeryt didn't protest either her assumption or the biscuits that she handed him.

Skarpa rode back from where he had been surveying what the engineers had been doing, and his eyes drifted to the fragments remaining of the debris. After a moment he shook his head.

"What is it, Commander?" asked Vaelora.

"I don't recall that water channel in the middle of those boulders. It's so odd that I'd think I would."

"You probably didn't notice it before because the water level was much lower," replied Vaelora.

"That might be . . . but . . . why would they have cut that there?"

"Maybe the river used to run higher," suggested Quaeryt.

After a moment the commander shrugged. "I'm just glad you could loosen all that. I wasn't looking forward to retracing our path or waiting for days."

"Neither was I," admitted Quaeryt. He just hoped he could regain enough strength to carry his shields before they ran into more trouble.

Even by traveling the post road, it took Third Regiment until the following Jeudi to reach the outskirts of Cloisonyt. Quaeryt worried for two days, until he could finally feel his ability to hold shields begin to return on Lundi evening. Yet by Mardi morning, holding them was no problem, and by Meredi, he realized he was barely aware of them, leaving him to wonder if stretching his imaging ability almost to the point of his own collapse was required in order to become a stronger imager. That was frightening, because he worried that going too far would lead to his death . . . and yet, he had the feeling that if he did not become a stronger imager, the failure to do so might also lead to his demise.

Consequently, he'd decided to say nothing about that to Vaelora, not until he was certain that the last episode had truly increased his capabilities.

In late midafternoon, under a clear sky with a cool wind at their back, he rode beside her, with Skarpa on her right, as they passed the as-yet-untilled fields and woodlots on the outskirts of Cloisonyt. Ahead, Quaeryt could barely make out where the fields and small cots gave way to the conglomeration of houses.

They rode on for another half glass, and the extent of the fields surrounding each cot dwindled as they neared the ancient city located on the north side of the River Acliano. Since the post road entered the city of hills from the northeast, their first view was that of stone dwellings scattered closely, but seemingly haphazardly, up a gentle slope to a low ridge topped by a line of far larger dwellings, also of stone. Unlike in the north, the roofs were of many different types—slate, shakes, and brown and red tile, creating the impression of different colored plaques thrown carelessly from a gambler's deck.

"Is there somewhere for the men to stay?" Vaelora asked Skarpa. "Besides in barns and warehouses and stables and worse?"

"Yes, Lady. There is a post there. It is old, but well built, and can hold a garrison the size of a regiment. Most times, there is but a company stationed there."

"One of Hengyst's old posts built after his conquest?" asked Quaeryt.

"So it's said."

"Is it still the home of great artisans?" pressed Quaeryt, thinking of the graceful ancient vase of the innkeeper destroyed by the boorish patroller in Nacliano and wondering if such artistry still remained in Cloisonyt.

"There are many artisans. Their shops are everywhere." Skarpa offered a sound between a laugh and a snort. "Many of their works are pleasant to look upon. Whether they are great, I could not say."

"Where is the post from here?"

"On the other side of the ridge and to the north a mille or so. It guards the road to Montagne."

"That's a good road?"

"As good as the one we travel now," replied Skarpa with a smile. "The road from Extela to Montagne is *very* good." He paused. "Or it was before . . ."

"Mount Extel exploded?"

The commander nodded. "It's likely to be good until we near Extela. Then . . ." He shrugged. "Who can say? The engineers may have much to do."

Ahead of them was a pair of stone pillars flanking the road, signifying, Quaeryt suspected, the edge of the city proper, since immediately beyond it were houses with walled courtyards. The houses were not centered on the courtyards, as was the case in Solis. Instead, the stone walls enclosed a space behind the houses and appeared to encircle gardens and tiny orchards. Between the ground before each dwelling and the road were stone sidewalks, the first Quaeryt had seen since leaving Nacliano the summer before. Had it been less than a year?

There were few people on the streets or sidewalks, and while some hurried out of the riders' way, most gave them little more than a passing glance. The farther Quaeryt and Vaelora rode up the hill, the more winding the road became, and the smaller the houses they passed were. Before long, the houses gave way to small shops, scores of them, squatting side by side, their stoops and porches beginning almost at the edge of the sidewalk, with lanes so narrow that they resembled alleys more than anything. Many, as Skarpa had said, showed artistic wares in their display windows. In one potter's window, there was a beautiful white cat, and for a moment Quaeryt marveled at the artistry, until the feline moved, and revealed that the "artistry" was from nature and not from the potter.

Less than a half mille ahead, Quaeryt could make out a line of ancient trees, towering against the sky, if still leafless, and behind them, the beginning of the larger dwellings, some almost chateau-like, that he had seen from afar.

"Death to the Yarans! Death to the Yarans!"

Quaeryt jerked his head in the direction of the words offered in old Tellan just in time to see a man wearing a uniform he did not recognize. The man had apparently dashed out of an alleyway even narrower than a lane until he was less than a handful of yards from Quaeryt, if two or three yards forward of him. Even before the words were finished, the man released a long spear.

Knowing he'd never free his staff in time, Quaeryt tried to extend his shields . . . and did so barely quickly enough to block the weapon from hitting Vaelora. As the spear bounced off Quaeryt's expanded shields, he concentrated on imaging it back into the chest of the burly man who had thrown it.

A flash of light flared for an instant, and the assailant's mouth worked silently as his hands tried to grasp the shaft of the weapon whose barbed point had gone through his body and which protruded from his back.

Quaeryt managed to keep his mouth shut as he reined up. *How did you do that?* He'd imaged a crossbow bolt into Rescalyn, but a long spear? That did tend to answer his question about stretching his abilities, because he didn't even feel the slightest bit strained or tired.

"After him!" snapped Skarpa.

Quaeryt forbore to mention that the man wasn't going anywhere. In fact, by the time the troopers from the squad following them had ridden over and dismounted, the attacker was dead.

Several bystanders gawked, but edged back from the armed soldiers.

"Stay with him until the wagons reach you. Then tie him onto one," ordered Skarpa. "Make sure that spear comes with him."

"Yes, sir."

Vaelora looked to Quaeryt. He thought she was trembling, but as she saw him looking, she stiffened and offered a smile, if a very faint one.

"I'll be fine, dearest."

"You're certain?"

"I'm very certain. You're beside me."

Quaeryt eased his mount slightly closer to hers, letting his shields retreat to the lighter trigger shields, but keeping them extended enough to cover her. "You will be fine."

She forced a grin. "I think I said that."

"There doesn't seem to be anyone else," said Skarpa, "but we ought to pick up the pace a bit."

Quaeryt nodded.

"Send out two more outriders, fifty yards ahead. Forward!"

They resumed riding, and after several moments Skarpa leaned forward in the saddle to look across past Vaelora to Quaeryt. "What . . . what did you do back there?" The commander's voice was low.

"I caught it and threw it back," replied Quaeryt. "I was furious! No one . . . no one . . . attacks my wife." *Not and lives, not if I can do anything about it.*

"I can see that." Skarpa's voice turned dry. "I still don't know how you did that."

"Neither do I," admitted Quaeryt. "I just did."

The commander shook his head. "Might I ask . . . Princeps . . . what he yelled? What it meant?"

"Lord Chayar's forebears were called Yaran warlords. They defeated Hengyst's descendants and took over Telaryn. Apparently, some people in Cloisonyt have never forgotten, most likely because it was first a Tellan and then a Ryntarian stronghold." Quaeryt paused. "What I'd like to know is how he knew that Lady Vaelora would be coming."

"He must have found out from someone at the post . . . or from someone who knew someone at the post."

For all Quaeryt's caution and the extra outriders, or because of them, they encountered nothing else untoward for the remainder of the ride through Cloisonyt, up the hill, then down a quarter of the way on the west side before turning northwest for another mille. A half glass passed before they rode through the ancient stone-pillared iron gates of the post into the main courtyard.

They had barely reined up when a major hurried across the courtyard almost at a run. He came to a halt several yards short of Quaeryt and Vaelora. "Welcome to Cloisonyt Post, Lady, Princeps." He bowed, then straightened. "Major Duffryt, at your service."

A gesture of respect and caution to Vaelora, reflected Quaeryt.

"Thank you," she replied. "Have you received any news from Extela?"

"Very little, Lady. Only that part of the city was destroyed. The lava still flows, and ash still falls."

Quaeryt hadn't expected much more news than that, not when they had a good week's travel, if not more, to reach Montagne, with Extela three to four days beyond.

"How long will you be staying?" asked the major.

"That depends on the needs of the regiment." Quaeryt looked to Skarpa. "The horses need rest and grain and fodder." *Especially since we didn't get all of the grain cakes we'd expected because we left Tilbora early.*

"Two days would be good," offered Skarpa.

"Two or three days," said Quaeryt. Arriving in Extela with excessively tired men and mounts wouldn't help people much and would just tax even more whatever food and provisions remained in the battered city.

"The post commander's quarters are ready for you, Lady . . . Princeps," offered the major. "And we will have a fine dinner for you and all the officers."

"You're most gracious," replied Vaelora.

Quaeryt merely nodded.

Even so, it was almost a glass later before Quaeryt and Vaelora entered the quarters of the former post commander, a modest dwelling set against the north wall of the post, with a formal sitting room, a capacious dining room and kitchen, a small study—all on the first floor—and three bedrooms and a bathing chamber on the second.

"This furniture is beautiful," said Vaelora, looking around the master bedchamber, taking in the postered bed of dark goldenwood, the matching night tables, and even the twin armoires.

"It's not as old as the house," offered Duffryt. "Lord Chayar's father had it placed here for when he traveled to Cloisonyt."

That explains much. Quaeryt nodded.

"I will leave you to do what you must . . . and perhaps rest. The dinner will be in the officers' mess at half past fifth glass."

After the major departed and Quaeryt had closed the massive carved front door, the two studied the sitting room, then sat down in facing armchairs, waiting for the promised hot water for the bath chamber from the kitchen staff.

"What happened with that man . . . You couldn't do that before, could you?" asked Vaelora, keeping her voice low.

"Do what?" asked Quaeryt innocently.

"That kind of imaging."

"Not with something as big as that spear," he admitted. "I didn't think. I just did it. I didn't want you hurt."

"There was a flash of light around you . . ."

"I've never seen that happen before," he admitted.

At the footsteps in the hallway, Quaeryt stopped and looked to the archway.

"The water is ready and in the tub, Lady . . . Princeps." The sturdy graying woman bowed her head.

"Thank you." Both Vaelora and Quaeryt stood and made their way to the staircase.

Little more than a glass later, far cleaner and in fresh browns, Quaeryt escorted Vaelora, who wore one of the simple dresses she had packed in the kit bag that accompanied her trunk, across the stone-paved courtyard to the officers' mess. Everyone stood as they entered.

Quaeryt was seated at the head of the table, with Vaelora to his left and Skarpa to his right. Major Duffryt was beside Vaelora, and as the senior major in the regiment—which had taken Skarpa some considerable maneuvering to achieve—Meinyt was seated beside Skarpa.

"Perhaps . . . your wife might offer a blessing?"

Quaeryt looked to Vaelora.

"I would be pleased." She lowered her head slightly and spoke with the slight huskiness of voice that Quaeryt always enjoyed hearing. "For the grace we owe each other, in times both good and ill, for the bounty of which we are about to partake, for good faith and kindness among all peoples, and especially for mercies great and small. For these blessings, we offer thanks and gratitude, in the spirit of that which cannot be named or imaged. . . ."

"In peace and harmony," chorused the officers quietly.

After the blessing, Quaeryt immediately poured the red wine into Vaelora's goblet, then into his own. He waited until all the officers had wine, then raised his goblet. "A toast to the hospitality and grace of Cloisonyt Post."

"To the post," seconded Skarpa.

Then the servers appeared with platters of lamb and roasted potatoes.

Once everyone was served, Major Duffryt turned to Quaeryt. "Princeps . . . I heard that you picked a spear aimed at your wife out of midair and hurled it back at the man who threw it with enough force to send it through his chest. You broke most of his ribs and killed him on the spot."

"I don't know about the ribs," demurred Quaeryt.

"You have to be a strong man, but you're only a trace larger than average. I don't know how you could do that while mounted."

Quaeryt smiled, sheepishly. "Major . . . I wish I could answer that question. I just saw the man throwing the spear, and I reacted."

The major tried not to frown.

"The princeps is too modest," said Skarpa. "I have seen him in battle. With only a half-staff he unseated a rebel with enough force to break his neck. He took a crossbow bolt full in the chest, pulled it out, blocked the wound, recovered a stray mount, and rode back to the post. He was fighting again in a month. Another time, he broke a line of pikemen and cut down almost half a score from behind."

"Yet you wear brown . . ."

Quaeryt could see why the older officer was still only a major and in charge of a reserve post. That was where his nit-picking would be most valuable. "I'm still a scholar. I was riding with Sixth Battalion because the former governor felt I needed the experience to be able to report back to Lord Bhayar. Now . . . the man who attacked the lady Vaelora was wearing a uniform I've never seen." He looked at the major.

"Yes, sir."

"Tell me about the uniform. Commander Skarpa had you look at him."

"It's similar—I doubt it's identical—to the uniforms the Tellan troops wore when they lost the battle of Cloisonyt."

"How might you know that?" asked Vaelora sweetly.

"There was a parade or a march . . . last Feuillyt. A whole company of men wore them. They claimed they were celebrating the founding of Tela. They weren't carrying weapons . . . so there wasn't much the civic council could do.

"Might someone on the council know more about this?" Quaeryt smiled pleasantly.

"Chief Counselor Ghanyst knows everything that is going on."

"We'll have to pay him a visit tomorrow," said Quaeryt. "Now . . . if you would tell us about the post . . . ?"

From that point on, Quaeryt and Vaelora kept the conversation to the post and to the recent history of Cloisonyt, although the major and his officers could shed little additional light on the group wearing the replicas of ancient uniforms.

Much, much later, they retired to the master bedroom of their temporary quarters.

"Would you like to come along to visit the chief counselor tomorrow?" asked Quaeryt as he hung his jacket in the armoire.

"I would."

Quaeryt smiled. "Good."

"Dearest . . . was Skarpa telling the truth . . . about what you did?"

"That was the way it looked," Quaeryt admitted. "My shields weren't that strong when the quarrel hit, and it went into my chest. I knew the tip was barbed, and as you deduced, I managed to image it away before I pulled out the rest of the bolt . . ." He went on, reluctantly, to explain the other incidents.

"You were almost killed all those times . . . and you never even told my brother?"

"I wrote him about the quarrel."

"I read what you wrote. It sounded like a modest wound. It was more than that . . . wasn't it?"

"Probably."

"Why don't you admit to what you've done?"

"Because the imaging gives me an advantage. That means that I'm not in as much danger and that those deeds are not so great as others think. Yet I cannot admit that, or I cannot do what I must for you and for Bhayar. Nor will I be able to do what else I've planned."

She raised her eyebrows.

"I've told you about what happened to the scholars in Nacliano, and what almost happened in Tilbora. Scholars are cherished and revered compared to imagers. The first thing I want to do is to improve the conditions for scholars and get them to help and teach young imagers, the way the scholars in Solis did for me—even if they didn't know I was an imager . . ." He went on to explain what else he had in mind.

Just before eighth glass on Samedi morning, a squad of troopers from third company in Third Battalion—Meinyt's battalion—escorted Quaeryt, Vaelora, and Duffryt to the ancient graystone council building of Cloisonyt, an oblong two-story structure with windows almost as narrow as those common in Tilbora. The walls held no ornamentation, and except for the number of windows and the lack of a gold-colored dome, the severity of the structure could have identified it as an anomen of the Nameless.

The young clerk outside the chief councilor's study looked up as the major, Quaeryt, and Vaelora approached. "Sir . . . he requested—"

"Nonsense!" snapped Duffyt. "This is the new governor of Montagne, Choryn. Don't bother. I'll do the introductions."

Choryn swallowed. "Ah . . . yes, sirs, Lady . . ."

Major Duffryt was the first into the councilor's study, but he stepped aside quickly, waiting until Vaelora and Quaeryr entered before he spoke. "Councilor Ghanyst, I'd like to present you to Princeps Quaeryt. He's the regional princeps of Tilbor, and he's on his way to Extela to take over as governor of Montagne. His wife is Lady Vaelora, the sister of Lord Bhayar." Duffryt paused, then added, "Did I mention that he also brought an entire regiment with him?"

As Duffryt finished the introduction, and Choryn quietly closed the door, Ghanyst's expression changed from a polite impassiveness, concealing irritation at being interrupted, Quaeryt suspected, to a broad and equally false smile. "Lady . . . Princeps . . . how kind of you to call. Please . . ." He gestured to the chairs before his desk. "How might I be of service?"

After he seated Vaelora and then himself, Quaeryt smiled pleasantly. "I understand that you are the chief councilor of Cloisonyt, and that you have an expansive knowledge of the city, based on long and diligent experience."

"You are too kind, or perhaps the major has been far too charitable." Ghanyst offered a warm smile of the political kind—one whose warmth his eyes did not fully reflect. "I can lay claim to some knowledge and experience. It is far from expansive, for Cloisonyt is an old city with much history." He laughed gently and warmly. "That history is not dead. It lives in many inhabitants."

Quaeryt nodded. "Sometimes, what has happened long ago is not even past. When we rode into Cloisonyt, we saw a man in a strange uniform. When I asked Major Duffryt about it, he said that it was a reproduction of those worn by soldiers in the time of Hengyst . . . and that many wore such uniforms at times." He raised his eyebrows in inquiry.

"Oh . . . them. They're a bunch of small crafters and shopkeepers who believe that the old times were better. They want Tellan independence . . . or things as they were, maybe even before Hengyst. Some folks call them the Army of Tela and laugh about it when they're not around."

"When they're not around?" pressed Quaeryt.

"They're a mite touchy about it. Some people call them the Red Hands." Ghanyst shrugged. "They don't carry weapons. None of them have done anything to offend the patrollers."

"Until yesterday," said Quaeryt.

Ghanyst frowned. "Yesterday?"

"One of them wearing that uniform hurled a spear at my wife. He was yelling, 'Death to the Yarans!' I was too accurate in flinging the spear back. He didn't live long enough for us to learn what he meant."

"The patrollers didn't report that." There was a slight hint of accusation in the councilor's tone.

"That's why we're here," replied Quaeryt. "To let you know. They can pick up the body anytime—and the spear. At least an entire squad of troopers heard or saw the attack. Now . . . what else can you tell us about this Army of Tela?"

Ghanyst frowned again.

Quaeryt waited, smiling pleasantly.

After the silence dragged out, Ghanyst cleared his throat. "Well . . . I can't say I know all that much about them."

"If you know enough to say that they're small shopkeepers and crafters, you must know who some of them are," suggested Quaeryt politely. "You might even be able to introduce us personally."

"Ah . . . I would be more than pleased to provide the names and addresses of those whom I do know."

"That would be most helpful," said Vaelora sweetly.

"We'll wait while you write those down," added Quaeryt. "And you can send your assistant with us so that we can find the addresses."

"Of course . . . of course." Ghanyst's cheerfulness was less than enthusiastic.

A quint later, Choryn was riding Ghanyst's mount, awkwardly, and leading them down to Third Street where it intersected River Way. Two shops from the corner was the cobbler shop of one Chelgyst Antensyn. Most of the squad waited outside. Two rankers accompanied Quaeryt, Vaelora, and Duffryt into the shop.

The cobbler looked up from the bench where he appeared to be measuring or trimming leather. Even from the door, Quaeryt could see his eyes widen.

"Ah . . . sirs . . . Lady . . . what . . . are you interested in boots, perhaps?" the cobbler finally stammered, clear puzzlement in his eyes in seeing a major, a lady, and a scholar, followed by two armed men.

"You're Chelgyst?" asked Quaeryt.

"Yes, scholar."

"One of those who is a member of the Army of Tela?"

"No longer, sir. Not for more than a year." The cobbler's voice was tired. "Not since they started to carry spears. Spears are against the laws."

"Then perhaps you could tell us who was the one who decided that they should carry spears."

"There were several, but they were shouting from the back. I left right then. I wish I'd never gone to the first meetings. They were talking about marching in parades and reminding folks about the great deeds of the past. My great-grandfather had a knife that came from the fall of Noveault. We still have it."

Quaeryt asked a few more questions, but the cobbler avoided giving names, and Quaeryt didn't feel like pressing him, and they left the shop after less than a quint.

The second name on Ghanyst's listing was Aelphar, a cooper, but there was a tailor's shop at the address, and the tailor told Duffryt that Aelphar had died the fall before, and that he was renting half the space from the widow.

The third name was that of Shubatar, a fuller, five blocks to the west.

He was a stocky graying man, but voluble in his replies.

". . . went to some of the meetings. I really didn't care about all their parades. I figured that all those uniforms, the way they talked about them, they'd need fullering now and again . . . and some of them might come to me, rather than to Casseon."

"Who seemed to be the most outspoken?" asked Quaeryt.

"Chausyn was pretty loud. So was Dymeyt . . . and sometimes another fellow with him Shar-something or other . . ."

Once they left the fuller's shop, Quaeryt checked the names they'd obtained from Shubatar against those on Ghanyst's list. All three names were on the list, but near the bottom. Since Dymeyt was listed as a tinker, with a stall in the hill market, and that was the closest to where they were, according to Choryn, that was where Quaeryt directed the clerk to lead them.

Choryn swallowed.

Quaeryt noted his reaction and appeared to ignore it.

Another quint passed by the time they were riding up the rough cobblestones of the side lane that held the hill market.

"His stall . . . should be up there, past the poulterer . . ."

Quaeryt squinted. Did he see a man in grays easing away? He urged the mare forward at a faster walk. The man began to walk faster, then to run.

Quaeryt imaged goose grease—or what he thought of as goose grease—onto the bottom of the man's boots. The fugitive went down hard, then tried to scramble to his feet. By then Quaeryt was less than ten yards away, but the man staggered up and took two steps, before falling hard again—helped not only by the slipperiness of his boots, but by the momentary hardening of the air—similar to the composition of Quaeryt's shields—that the scholar had imaged in front of his shins.

"I wouldn't try to flee any farther, if I were you, Dymeyt!" snapped Quaeryt as he reined up.

Heads had turned from all around the market, but the onlookers backed away from all the riders.

"I didn't do nothing . . . I didn't." The man, still on his knees, looked up at the riders who surrounded him, including the rankers with unsheathed blades.

"Then why did you run? Might it have something to do with what happened yesterday?"

"I didn't think Sharmyt'd do something like that, sir . . . I didn't. I just thought he'd say something from the alleyway."

"How did he know we were coming?"

"He didn't, sir. Leastwise, he didn't say he did. He was headed over to Shubatar the fuller's place when we saw all the riders coming up the avenue. Then he saw the lady—begging your pardon, mistress—and he ran out. I saw his spear come back and go through him, and I ran back down the alley, fearing for my life."

"Why did he have a spear?"

"He said . . ." The man swallowed.

"Go on . . ."

"He said Shubatar wasn't no true Ryntaran . . . just a fat fuller wanting to make coppers off us all. He was going to talk to him. That was what he said . . . he really did, sir."

"Where did Sharmyt live . . . or work?"

"His brother's a tinsmith, down off the river road, Crafters' Way."

"What's Sharmyt's full name?"

"Sharmyt Frydersyn . . ."

"And his brother?"

"Sheam."

Quaeryt shook his head, then turned to the squad leader. "Bind his hands, and bring him along. The major's men can turn him over to the Civic Patrol when we're done."

"Yes, sir."

Getting to the tinsmith's shop required retracing their path back over the ridge and almost down to the River Acliano. Crafters' Way was all of a hundred yards long, and the tinsmith was at the end of the narrow street, distinguished by missing almost as many cobblestones as it had for what passed as paving.

Quaeryt had barely stepped inside the small shop when he faced a wiry man with a lined face—and two women, one a redhead nearly as young as Vaelora, and another who looked to be closer to Quaeryt's age.

"Sirs . . . Lady . . ." offered the man. "What can I do for you?"

"You're Sheam Frydersyn?"

"Yes, sir."

"You have a brother named Sharmyt, and he was seen yesterday wearing the uniform of the so-called Army of Tela?"

"He's my brother," admitted the tinsmith, warily. "What of him?"

"He tried to kill someone," replied Quaeryt, giving Duffryt a sharp glance.

"I told you!" hissed the younger red-haired woman. "I said he'd lead us all to no good with that foolishness."

For a time, Sheam said nothing. Then he shook his head slowly.

Quaeryt could see his eyes brighten, most likely with barely unshed tears.

"I told him . . ." The tinsmith shook his head again. "He didn't listen."

"He never did," added the redhead.

"Where is he?" asked the tinsmith. "In the patrol gaol?"

"He's dead," replied Quaeryt. "One of the people he tried to kill turned his spear on him."

The older woman sniffled. Tears rolled down her cheeks.

"I'm sorry, sirs . . . I'm sorry . . ." Sheam looked helplessly at Quaeryt. "His body . . . ?"

Quaeryt looked to Duffryt.

"It will be at the main patrol station," said the major.

After a few more questions that revealed nothing new, Quaeryt led the others out of the shop, and they remounted.

"We'll head back to the post now," he announced.

Duffryt looked puzzled, but said nothing.

"What are you going to do, Governor?" asked Choryn.

"I don't see the need to do anything more right now. If people want to wear old uniforms and praise the old times, they can do that. The one man who used a weapon is dead. Punishing others for doing that will just cause more of them to be unhappy." *And we don't need to waste men on something like that now.* "If there's more trouble, of course, we might send a company here to conscript the troublemakers and put them where they can wear new uniforms and fight for a live Lord of Telaryn, rather than for one long dead." Quaeryt smiled pleasantly.

Choryn shivered in the saddle.

Major Duffryt looked from Choryn to Quaeryt, but said nothing.

After dismissing Choryn to make his way back to the council building, Quaeryt eased the mare closer to Vaelora and her gelding. "I have the feeling that Ghanyst put the least likely names at the top of his list, including those no longer among the living. He obviously hoped that we would lose interest and would only make token inquiries."

"It would seem that way," she replied.

He nodded.

"You were serious about conscription," Vaelora observed.

"I was. People who have time to create replicas of old uniforms and weapons and who go to great lengths to stir up trouble have too much time on their hands and not enough useful work to do. Conscription would stop much of the trouble, put them to work, and pay them for it. Not that I think I'll have to resort to it." He laughed. "Besides, I don't even know that Cloisonyt is part of the Montagne regional governor's ambit. I've never seen a map."

"It isn't," replied Vaelora. "Your territory ends about halfway between Cloisonyt and Montagne."

"Then I'll have to send a dispatch to your brother telling him about Ghanyst's less than enthusiastic cooperation. I'll also tell him what I said about conscription and offer that as a solution if there is more trouble, perhaps giving Ghanyst a commission as an undercaptain."

"It is the sort of solution he likes."

"I know." Quaeryt grinned. "From whom do you think I got the idea?"

Just past midafternoon on Vendrei, Quaeryt turned in the saddle and looked to Vaelora. "How did you and Bhayar get to Tilbora so fast? We've been on the road for a little more than two weeks, and we aren't even to Montagne."

"The weather was drier, and we only traveled with a company of cavalry with a spare mount for every rider. Also, the roads are better, and it's quicker from Solis to Cloisonyt to Tilbora than from Tilbora to Cloisonyt to Extela."

Quaeryt nodded. "I see." *Even so, you must have ridden from sunrise to sunset and commandeered mounts along the way.* He was about to say something to that effect when, as they rode around the side of a hill, he saw a collection of houses and buildings less than two hundred yards ahead. The town was so small that there wasn't even a millestone with a name cut into it. At least, Quaeryt hadn't seen one.

"Do you know the name of the town?" Quaeryt asked Skarpa, riding on the far side of Vaelora.

"Ah . . . no, sir. It's on the map, but I don't recall."

"Gahenyara," said Vaelora brightly.

Quaeryt looked to his wife. "That must mean something."

"I was told it means the eastern end of Yara."

"The boundary of the Yaran warlord's lands? How did you know that?"

"Grandmere's mother came from here. Her father was a large holder to the north of town."

"A High Holder?" asked Quaeryt.

"What amounted to one. He only had daughters, and the lands went to Grandpere Lhayar."

"So they're Bhayar's now?"

"Unless he granted them to someone. I don't think he has, but he doesn't exactly tell me everything." Vaelora smiled mischievously. "He tells me very little, but he does tell Aelina."

"And you're very close to her."

"Without her . . ." Vaelora shook her head.

Quaeryt said nothing, although he had suspected Aelina's influence early on in his and Vaelora's correspondence.

Ahead of them was a narrow timbered bridge, wide enough for a wagon or three horses side by side, and little else, that extended a good twenty yards over a small river, supported by two sets of stone pylons, each one set equidistant from the end of the bridge and the other pylon. The river was running high enough that the water was less than a yard beneath the bridge deck.

As the scouts crossed the middle section of the bridge, Quaeryt noted that the planking and timbers flexed more than he thought they should, especially on the south side, but there was little give on the last third of the bridge, the one closest to Gahenyara.

"We can only do two at a time," suggested Skarpa as the three neared the bridge. "I'll drop back a bit."

Quaeryt could feel the bridge depress as the mare moved to the midsection, but there was no sense of recovery or rebound in the planking—only an ominous creaking that intensified. He immediately extended his shields to the planks and anchored the shield to the two pylons.

"Keep riding!" he hissed at Vaelora. He turned in the saddle. "Keep clear of the midsection of the bridge! It's going to give way!"

"Should I turn?"

"No. Keep moving." Quaeryt couldn't explain his words, but with each step the mare and Vaelora's gelding took, he felt more and more pressure on his shields—as if they were contracting around him. He concentrated on holding them, despite the pain and pressure, until both of them were on the far section, when he released all shields because he could barely hold on to them.

He glanced back over his shoulder, but kept riding until he and Vaelora were off the bridge, when he turned the mare and reined up. So did Vaelora.

The heavy planks on the south side of the middle section of the bridge—where he had been riding—slowly sagged into the water. For almost half a quint, nothing seemed to happen. Then the rushing water ripped away one plank . . . and then another . . . and a third, until even part of the bridge where Vaelora had crossed was gone. Before long, only the northern third of the midsection remained. The rest of the midsection had been carried away by the flood waters. The northern part *might* support a single horse and rider at a time, but what remained was far too narrow for any of the supply wagons.

Skarpa had retreated to the eastern end of the bridge, where the bulk of the regiment now waited.

Quaeryt's head ached, and his eyes burned so much that he could barely make out much beyond the bridge and the river.

"You're pale and shaking," Vaelora said. "You need to eat something." She reached back to the pack behind her saddle, then handed a hard biscuit to him.

He fumbled out his water bottle, filled with watered lager, took a mouthful, enough to make the biscuit chewable, and slowly ate it. "We're going to be here a while, until the engineers can repair the bridge."

"If you keep making a habit of this," murmured Vaelora, handing him another biscuit, "I won't have any extra food left."

You won't have a husband, either. Except . . . what else could he have done?

"You need to be more careful."

"I didn't think it was going to collapse when we started across, and I wasn't going to let you get swept away by the river."

"You were on the weaker part." A grin followed. "I do appreciate the thought, though."

Quaeryt refrained from pointing out that the planks where she'd been riding were also at least partly gone as well. "Thank you, dear one."

"Well . . . I was riding close to what collapsed."

"I worried." Quaeryt paused but slightly. "Is this under the administration of the governor of Montagne? Do you know?"

"On this side of the river. That's why—"

"The town is named Gahenyara," he finished.

Two men came running toward the riders from the town.

Quaeryt and Vaelora eased up beside the scouts and waited.

By nightfall on Vendrei, two battalions had walked their mounts across the remainder of the bridge one at a time. That portion of the regiment had taken over what empty barns there were in and around Gahenyara, and Quaeryt and Vaelora had occupied the best chamber in the ten-room local inn.

When Quaeryt woke on a very lumpy mattress beside Vaelora on Samedi morning, his headache was gone, and his eyes no longer burned. He could also hold light shields, but heavier ones only for a few moments before his head began to throb again.

After breakfast, the two stood on the narrow front porch of the inn, waiting for Skarpa.

"How long will the repairs take?" asked Vaelora.

"Several days, at least. I'd like to hear what Skarpa has to say."

"You didn't plan on stopping here . . ." Vaelora broke off what she might have said as the regimental commander rode up to the inn.

Neither she nor Quaeryt said anything until Skarpa joined them on the porch.

"The river's down half a yard from yesterday," said Skarpa. "The engineers have located some trees that look solid and tall enough, but getting them turned into planks will take another two days. Most of that will be felling the trees and getting the trunks across the river. The local mill can handle the logs. Barely." He shook his head. "Hate using green timber, but there's nothing long enough that's dried and seasoned around here. You'd think the locals would know better."

"If the former governor hasn't been here recently . . ." Quaeryt had the feeling that the previous governor, most likely a casualty of the eruption, hadn't been as far east as Gahenyara in a long time . . . if ever.

"You're as cynical as I am, Princeps."

"Can you get another battalion or two across what's left of the bridge while the engineers work on the trees?"

"I'd planned on that."

Quaeryt nodded. "I'd like to take a battalion and leave tomorrow."

"Thought you might have something like that in mind."

"We can't do anything to help you, and a battalion should be enough to deal with anything we encounter."

"I'd feel happier if you took two. We can unload two wagons and break them down and ferry the supplies across by hand. That should be enough to get you to Montagne, and it will keep everyone busy. We'll catch up as we can."

"That might be better in any case," Quaeryt said. "Gahenyara isn't provisioned to support a regiment. Not for long, in any case."

"I'll send Third and Fourth Battalion with you."

"Was that Meinyt's request?" asked Quaeryt.

Skarpa grinned. "He did say that he couldn't imagine you'd wait around when there was trouble in Extela. He volunteered Third Battalion in the event you did want to go on. Major Fhaen also volunteered."

Quaeryt knew little about Fhaen, because he'd been stationed at Northcote, except that Meinyt had high regard for the redheaded major. "Then we'll leave early tomorrow."

"I'll let them know."

After Skarpa had mounted and ridden back east toward the bridge, Vaelora cleared her throat.

"Yes, dear?"

"We can't do anything to help rebuild the bridge," she said. "Can we go look at the old chateau?"

"Is it still standing?"

"It is. It was still able to be occupied when we were children, Bhayar said. It's been empty for years, though."

"Why?"

"It costs too much to ship timber and crops from here to most places, and it's too far from anywhere, or other holders."

Meaning Solis.

". . . and it's also too big for the keeper to maintain anything but the building. He and his family live in the gatehouse."

"It might be a good thing to visit it," agreed Quaeryt.

"You're just not humoring me?"

"No."

"Why do you think so?"

"I couldn't say," replied Quaeryt. "I just feel that it would be."

"Good."

With one thing and another, including obtaining directions and arranging with Meinyt for a squad to accompany them, which became two squads led by the company commander at Meinyt's insistence, it was almost a glass later before they set out from the side courtyard of the unnamed inn. Undercaptain Jusaph rode ahead of Quaeryt and Vaelora as they made their way westward from town along the old stone-paved road.

Less than two milles farther on, they reached a stretch of stone wall extending a quarter mille on each side of a set of ironbound wooden gates. On the other side of the wall, west of the gates, was a stone dwelling, clearly inhabited, since a thin trail of white smoke issued from the chimney. Farther to the north, rising over the bare limbs of the trees, Quaeryt could see a long slate roof, from which sprouted a half score of natural stone-faced chimneys.

Even before Quaeryt and Vaelora reined up at the wooden gates, a man in a gray jacket and brown trousers had hurried from the iron-grated opening in the wall beside the gates. "These are the lands of Lord Bhayar."

"We know," said Vaelora. "He's my brother, and this is Governor Quaeryt. He's the new governor of Montagne. He's also my husband."

The black-bearded man glanced up at Vaelora, then to Quaeryt and then at Undercaptain Jusaph and the squad of uniformed riders behind him.

"A thousand pardons, Lady . . . a thousand pardons."

"We're here to inspect the chateau," Vaelora went on, "before we continue on to Montagne and then to Extela."

"The chateau . . . I do what I can, Lady . . ."

"We know. It has been years . . ."

"Since the time of my grandfather. That was when Lord Lhayar trained men on the lands to the north."

"If you would open the gates," suggested Vaelora.

"But . . ."

Quaeryt could see that trying to be patient with the man would only result in Vaelora losing respect. He tried to image the sense of authority toward the gatekeeper. "The Lady Vaelora has every right, indeed the duty, to inspect her family's lands."

The gatekeeper stepped back, his face suddenly pale. He swallowed. "Yes, sir . . . Governor, I mean. Just a moment." He hurried back through the archway, leaving the gratework open.

Shortly, the ironbound wooden gates began to creak open.

"What did you do?" murmured Vaelora. "All of a sudden, it was like you were Bhayar. You didn't look like him. You just had that presence. Except it was greater."

"Imaged authority," he replied in a low voice.

"You can do that?"

"I didn't know for certain. I thought it was worth a try."

"Don't let Bhayar know. He'll want you with him all the time." Vaelora smiled wryly. "He suspects, but he'd rather not know. Not at the moment."

"Deniability," suggested Quaeryt.

"Something like that," replied Vaelora.

Quaeryt nodded.

When the gates gaped wide, the keeper hurried forward and extended a heavy ring of keys to Vaelora. "If you'd return them when you leave, Lady . . ."

"I will indeed. Thank you."

The gatekeeper did not look in Quaeryt's direction as he backed away.

Vaelora raised the ring and keys, and Quaeryt eased the mare forward, through the gates and onto the rutted lane that might once have been heavily graveled—if the intermittently spaced heaps of gravel and dirt along the right side of the lane were any indication.

The lane curved to the left gently and gently uphill for only about fifty yards before splitting. The right branch led to a cluster of outbuildings some thirty yards from the east end of the chateau, while the left ended in a stone-paved square before the main entry—a wide but single ironbound door fronted by an oblong stoop of natural stone. There was neither a roof over the stoop nor any sign of a mounting block, although a good teamster might have been able to position a coach to use the stoop as such.

The stone-walled chateau itself had two levels aboveground, and extended no more than fifty yards from one end to the other, and less than thirty from front to rear. All the windows were shuttered, and most of the shutters sagged in some measure. While the shutters and casements had once likely been oiled or painted, any vestige of either had vanished, leaving the wood one shade of gray or another.

Vaelora reined up beside the stoop and immediately dismounted, handing the gelding's reins to a ranker. Quaeryt followed her example.

"If you wouldn't mind, Lady . . . Governor," offered Jusaph, "I'd feel remiss in my duties if my men didn't enter the chateau first."

"Of course." Vaelora smiled and waited.

The undercaptain gestured, and three rankers and a squad leader dismounted, hurrying forward. Vaelora handed the key ring to the squad leader, who inclined his head, then moved to the door. The door opened easily, but squeaked as it did, and the four troopers entered the chateau.

"It looks clear," called the squad leader after a time.

Quaeryt and Vaelora stepped inside, into a modest hall some four yards by four. Quaeryt almost tripped when the longer heel on his left boot caught the edge of the stone doorsill, but caught himself quickly enough that Vaelora didn't notice.

Off the foyer to the left through a square arch was a great hall, empty of furnishings. At one end was a hearth and a fireplace large enough to hold several grown men. To the right was a hallway that appeared to stretch to the eastern end of the chateau. Directly opposite the entry was a stone staircase some two yards wide, certainly the narrowest main staircase Quaeryt had ever seen in a holder's dwelling.

He looked to Vaelora. "Up or to the right."

"I'd like to see the main floor first." She turned and walked to the first doorway, where the open door had sagged enough that the end away from the hinges rested on the rough stone floor. Beyond the doorway was an empty square chamber with a hearth and modest fireplace.

"A parlor?" suggested Quaeryt.

"Most likely."

The doorway opposite the parlor revealed a larger room, also with a fireplace and without furnishings except for the east wall, where slightly drooping shelves of once-polished goldenwood had likely held books. The two proceeded through the main floor past a family dining room, and then into a large kitchen, still holding a massive trestle table and little else. Off the kitchen were several storerooms, one of which had rows and rows of shelves for dishes and platters and the like. There was also a narrow stone staircase down to the lower level and the storage cellars.

The upstairs held six modest bedrooms, two chambers for washing, and the holder's private apartments, consisting of a sitting room, a bathing chamber, a small jakes, and at the eastern end a large bedchamber.

Quaeryt followed Vaelora into the bedchamber, then stopped and frowned as he looked to the south side.

"There's a small room off here," said Vaelora. "It's barely large enough for a storeroom . . . but it has windows and shutters."

Or what's left of them. Quaeryt stepped forward and looked at the sagging narrow shutters in the wall and then at the archway, where a still polished, but heavy carved goldenwood door sagged on its heavy iron hinge pegs. "It's rather oddly placed, and that door is heavy enough to be used to guard a strong room. But there's no lock and no hardware for that, and the room has windows."

"Oh . . ."

Quaeryt turned to Vaelora. "Oh . . . what?"

"Grandmere said that her grandmother always slept alone. She never explained. She only said that it was safer for everyone that way."

"How did they have children?" asked Quaeryt wryly.

"She didn't say . . ." Vaelora shook her head. "Sleep alone, dearest, not make love. They are different. As you should know."

Quaeryt definitely understood the difference—especially after all the days on the road—but why had Vaelora's great-great-grandmere always slept alone . . . and why, in those days, had her husband acquiesced in that arrangement? "Did she have a temper?"

"Grandmere did. I don't know about her grandmere."

"Did they ever move to Extela?"

Vaelora shook her head. "They both lived here until they died, Grandmere said. Their son and his wife eventually moved to Extela after Grandmere married Grandpere. Grandmere's younger brother died in a hunting accident, and the lands became hers because he had no heirs."

Quaeryt nodded slowly. "It has to have something to do with your grandmere's visions. Did her mother and grandmother have that ability?"

"Grandmere never said. They were both Pharsi, though. From wealthy families."

Quaeryt would have wagered that one or both had had visions, but after all the years, who would know? "Have you seen enough?"

Vaelora nodded. "It's sad. This was once a place filled with people. They loved and cried and laughed. Now . . . there's no one." She stood in the chamber for a long time, saying nothing.

Quaeryt waited.

Finally, they left, walking slowly back along the rough stone floor toward the staircase. Neither spoke.

Quaeryt, Vaelora, and the two battalions reached Montagne by midafternoon on Mardi, through one rainstorm and more high waters, but did not have to cross any more flooded or damaged bridges. The post at Montagne was far older than the one at Cloisonyt, and the two battalions filled every available space in the barracks that could be called habitable. That did not include three barracks that resembled abandoned storehouses. After talking matters over with the two battalion majors and Vaelora, Quaeryt decided they would stay the one night in Montagne and leave the next morning for Extela.

Five days later, on Solayi afternoon, Quaeryt and Vaelora followed the outriders over the crest in the road leading out of the hills and down to the valley that held Extela—situated largely on the west side of the Telexan River. The sky was dusky orange, not with clouds, but with a heavy haze, and what looked to be a gray fog rose from a peak to the north of the city. As dry flakes fell intermittently around him, Quaeryt realized that the mountain had to be Mount Extel and that the gray plume rising from it had to be ash.

"The northwest quarter of the city . . ." gasped Vaelora, "it's all covered in black rock . . . only one tower left of the palace . . . and the north market . . ."

Quaeryt followed her gesture with his eyes. To the northwest, closer to the foot of Mount Extel, not all the rock was black. There were lines of orange—still-hot lava.

A light gust of wind swirled warm sulfurous air and ashes around them, some of which Quaeryt brushed off his browns before he looked at Vaelora. She looked back at him and shook her head. "I never imagined it would be this bad."

As the mare carried him down toward the river, Quaeryt studied the devastation. A reddish orange fountain of lava spurted intermittently from the side of the mountain and then oozed downhill, winding its way around and over earlier, but still recent, hardened and blackened flows. In some few places, such as the tower Vaelora had noted that jutted up from the black stone, a remnant of the old palace, the lava had seemingly flowed around a few structures while obliterating or covering most of the northwest section of the city. One flow had reached the river, well north of the city, and created a dam and a lake, over which poured steaming water, but the hills along the river south of the lava dam had diverted the molten rock back into a narrow area of streets and structures, leaving most of the destruction in the northwest quarter of the city.

Tents and huts and other crude structures dotted the east side of the river, but well south of the main part of Extela and only on the higher ground beyond the low hills that rose from the eastern shore.

"What about the posts?" Quaeryt asked Meinyt, who rode on the far side of Vaelora. "Can you tell how much they've been damaged?"

"The main post is well to the south of the city, and there does not seem to be that much damage to the south," said Meinyt. "There was a smaller post below . . ."

"Below where the palace used to be?" asked Quaeryt.

The major nodded. "We'll need to see if the main bridge is usable. Otherwise . . . it's another five milles to the south bridge."

The fields and meadows on each side of the road were covered in a thin layer of gray ash, along with piles of ash along the shoulder gathered by runoff from the lands. As they neared the river, Quaeryt noted the piles of debris from an earlier flood—or floods—and the ruins of houses and other structures within fifty to a hundred yards of the river.

What had once been a bridge was now more of a dam with gaps in it crossed by heavy planks over timbers and braced by oddly shaped chunks of stone, offering passage barely wide enough for a single supply wagon at a time.

"Looks almost as bad as the bridge in Gahenyara," observed Meinyt sourly.

Unstable as the bridge appeared, the heavy planks barely vibrated as the scouts, and then Quaeryt and Vaelora, crossed, followed immediately by troopers. Even before more than a squad of the first company of Meinyt's battalion had crossed the narrow makeshift bridge and formed up, figures appeared from what had appeared to be deserted streets and lanes. At first, there were but a handful, but the numbers began to swell, and all moved toward the riders, so that by the time all four squads of the first company had reached the ash-strewn plaza on the western shore of the Telexan River, close to fifty people in ash-smeared clothes were converging on the riders. Most were women, many with small children. Despite the damp chill, few if any of the women wore head scarves, although many had shawls across their shoulders.

"Do you have food?"

". . . food . . ."

". . . days since we ate . . ." A gaunt woman in gray and faded brown held up an infant. "Please . . . food . . ."

"First squad! Form up on the governor!"

Quaeryt didn't know the squad leader, but he appreciated the command. There was little enough in the way of provisions in the wagons that followed, and trying to distribute that small amount was more likely to cause a riot and more deaths. He could have used shields, if necessary, but armed men would provide a more visible and understandable deterrent.

"They're truly starving. Can't we do something?" asked Vaelora.

"We may be able to," he replied, "but not here and now. If we show food, hundreds more will appear, and they'll push those in front toward us. . . ."

Vaelora winced.

"Arms ready! Forward!" ordered the squad leader.

Slowly, the squad moved forward, farther into the plaza, to allow the companies behind to form up once they crossed the rubble-built bridge. The crowd swelled to close to a hundred, but some at the fringes began to fade back into buildings and lanes as it became clear that there was no food to be had. Meinyt's battalion was across the bridge, followed by the first supply wagon when a voice called out, "They have wagons coming!"

"They do have food! See the wagons!"

"Food!"

The movement away from the plaza halted, and then reversed. Even more people appeared out of the dust and ashes, heading toward the river end of the plaza and forming a human spearhead toward the bridge, giving the armed squad at the head of the column a clear berth.

"Protect the Lady!" snapped Quaeryt as he turned the mare and extended his shields, riding toward those leading the hunger-driven mob.

The force of the mare's weight and movement behind the shields cleared those at the edge of the mob's back, allowing Quaeryt to aim at the front of the near-raging crowd, forcing them away from the first wagon. As he reined up, Quaeryt forced himself to ignore the old woman who fell under the press of rioters forced back—and the child torn from her arms.

The crowd halted . . . as if those who had led it were uncertain.

"Ready arms!"

Quaeryt sensed, rather than saw, the flash of sabres.

The crowd stopped, but did not retreat.

Quaeryt stood in the stirrups, using imaging to project both his voice and the sense of authority and power. "Go back to your homes. Attacking soldiers for food will only get you hurt! Go back! Now!"

As he finished speaking, but kept trying to image authority across the crowd, he could feel a slight throbbing, but nothing more. He remained standing, watching, as slowly, and then more quickly, the hungry people began to disperse.

"Governor . . . ?"

Quaeryt dropped into the saddle and turned to see Meinyt rein up. "Yes?"

"How . . . ? It was . . . I even felt I needed to leave." The major frowned.

"I didn't want anyone hurt any more than they already had been." He glanced to his right, seeing Vaelora riding toward him, flanked by troopers. She eased her mount toward the old woman who had struggled into a sitting position and somehow found the small child she had lost in the crowd. Vaelora bent down from the saddle, with a flexibility and skill Quaeryt could never have come close to, and extended something, biscuits perhaps, to the old woman.

"The Nameless bless you, Lady . . ."

Vaelora straightened up in the saddle and rode slowly over toward Meinyt and Quaeryt. "Can she and the child come with us, at least to the post?"

The major looked to Quaeryt.

Quaeryt nodded. "She was hurt when I ordered everyone away from the wagons. That wasn't her fault." They'd only been in Extela a quint or so, and he'd had to image authority and threaten people with armed men. He feared that matters would only get worse . . . and that power might be the only way to keep order.

"Jusaph! Have your men get the woman and child in the wagons. We need to keep moving."

Before those in the crowd regain their courage and desperation. Quaeryt did not speak, only nodded.

"Yes, sir."

In less than half a quint, the two battalions, every man with his sabre ready, were riding down the ash-strewn boulevard that ran southwest parallel to the river. The doors of shops that had been secured with iron grates appeared largely untouched, as did those that appeared ironbound and sturdy.

But then, that just might mean intruders found easier access. Or that some crafters are still in their shops, waiting behind those doors.

There were some shops and dwellings where the ash had been swept away from doors and off shutters, and with the other signs he saw, such as footprints in the ash, unshuttered second-level windows, and the like, Quaeryt thought that not quite half the structures held inhabitants, probably those who had had fuller larders.

Another mille or so brought them to the main post, located on a low rise overlooking the river. The ironbound gates swung open as the column neared the stone walls of the post, but archers manned the ramparts, and two squads of cavalry were mounted up in the main courtyard. They remained so until the gates were closed.

Quaeryt immediately surveyed the structures inside the walls of the post. Directly to his right, beyond the mounted squads, was a modest anomen, with its dome of faded yellow-gold. Although it did not appear in poor repair, it had an air of disuse, and a length of chain with a lock on it secured the double doors, whose weathered oak had seen better days. Beside the anomen was the first of several structures that looked to be stables, and beyond them was a long barracks building. To Quaeryt's immediate left was an oblong black stone structure of one level that suggested a command building, perhaps with an officers' mess. Farther back was a two-story structure with a railed balcony and doors set at regular intervals opening on to the balcony, with matching doors below, most likely officers' quarters.

Quaeryt's survey was cut short as a graying commander hurried across the courtyard from the single-story black stone building, making his way directly to Vaelora, Quaeryt, and Meinyt. The commander's hair was not quite the color of the ash that still drifted down everywhere, if of a finer nature and in far smaller quantities south of the main party of Extela, and his face was drawn.

"Governor? Major? I'm Zhrensyl, the post commander."

Quaeryt studied the commander, whose eyes were red-rimmed, and who did not look to be in the best of health, but said nothing as Meinyt began to speak.

"This is Governor Quaeryt . . . and Lady Vaelora as well. I'm Meinyt, major in command of Third Battalion, Third Tilboran Regiment."

"Thank the Namer you're here, Governor, Major. You, too, Lady. We barely have enough men to keep the rabble from overrunning the gates. It's been that way for near-on two weeks, ever since the other regiment left."

"The rabble?" asked Vaelora coolly.

"Many of those who had the means began to leave weeks ago, Lady. Those that survived the eruption and the floods, that is. The rest . . ." Zhrensyl shook his head.

"What about the holders farther from the city?" asked Quaeryt.

"They just retreated behind their walls. They can hold off planting for a few weeks. They hoped that Lord Bhayar would send another force." The commander glanced toward the now-closed gates. "We had hoped . . ."

"There are two more battalions and the engineers following," Quaeryt replied to the unspoken inquiry. "We had to leave them to rebuild the bridge in Gahenyara in order to allow the rest of the supply and engineering wagons to pass. How are your provisions?"

"We have field rations for two regiments for another month. Little else."

"And water?"

"So far the springs remain clear and cool."

"What about fodder or grain?"

"Less than a month for a regiment."

"We'll need to plan how we can get more provisions here and more food to the city."

"There needs to be order. I have not had the men . . ."

"Commander . . . unless people see that there is food, the only order that will exist is that imposed by the edge of a sabre, and that order will only remain while the sabre is unsheathed and ready to wield."

Quaeryt's words were quiet, but the commander involuntarily took a step back.

"For the moment," added Quaeryt with a smile, "we need to get the men and their mounts settled and everyone fed."

"For you and Lady Vaelora . . . we only have the senior officers' quarters . . . since the palace and governor's house . . ."

"Those will be fine." *Especially after all the places we've slept along the way.*

"They will," added Vaelora with a smile.

"Ah . . . the officers' stables are the ones at the end . . ."

"Thank you." Quaeryt turned to Meinyt. "We'll need to talk with the commander after we eat." Then he looked at Vaelora, and the two eased their mounts forward toward the stables.

Almost two quints later, Quaeryt and Vaelora stood inside the senior officers' quarters, located at the west end on the top floor of an old black stone building holding quarters for squad leaders and officers. The quarters consisted of a sitting room, a bath chamber and jakes, and a bedchamber, much smaller than the apartments Quaeryt and Vaelora had occupied in Tilbora, and yet far more spacious than anything in which they had stayed since then.

As the door closed behind the ranker who had carried two of their bags, in addition to the kit bags each had lugged up from the stable, the pleasant smile dropped from Vaelora's face, replaced by an expression of concern. "How do you feel, dearest?"

"Just a touch of a headache, and it's going away."

"Are you sure?"

"I am."

"I saw what you did," Vaelora persisted. "Every time you do strong imaging, it takes effort on your part."

"Unfortunately, it does. But everything in the world takes strength of some sort."

"But there are different kinds of strength. Waterwheels work without horses or people pushing them."

"And sails on ships," he added. *Could there be any way to have the wind or water add force to imaging? Or something like that?* He shook his head. That seemed improbable. Most improbable.

After a moment he smiled. "The commander said that there was warm water in the bath chamber."

"You are so gallant."

Just hopeful. "I do try, dear."

Despite what Commander Zhrensyl had said about rations, the evening meal at the officers' mess consisted of a mutton stew with root vegetables and potatoes and fresh-baked bread, as did the fare for the other two battalions, served in the troops' mess at the west end of the compound. In a slight break with tradition, Vaelora also ate with the officers, at a long table that could have held fifty, instead of the sixteen who were seated there, most of whom were undercaptains and captains. The chamber itself was oblong and paneled in oak that had aged into a deep golden brown, as had the slightly battered if well-polished table and the straight-backed chairs.

After the meal, once the junior officers had been dismissed and departed, Zhrensyl, Meinyt, Fhaen, Quaeryt, and Vaelora reseated themselves around the end of the table, with Quaeryt seated at the head.

"The people need food, but commandeering it from the surrounding lands isn't advisable, except as a very last resort." Quaeryt turned to the commander. "Do you know what happened to the provincial treasury?"

"No, sir," replied Zhrensyl. "I imagine it's buried under all that ash and lava. Almost no one escaped from the first ash storm."

Fhaen raised his eyebrows, but did not speak.

"The ash came down like the worst rain anyone had ever seen. That's what the handful who escaped said." Zhrensyl went on. "It swept down the mountainside and buried almost everything in its path—the palace, the command base, the governor's building and quarters. The lava came later."

"Just ash?" asked Fhaen.

"It wasn't just ash, Major. There was a massive thunderclap, and the ground shook. Then a wall of ash roared down the mountain. It happened at night. The wind was so hot that it roasted people alive in their beds before they knew what happened." The commander shook his head. "We tried to help, but when we got there, we found people had either escaped, perhaps with a few burns, or they had died where they stood or slept. We found a few horses and oxen roasted in their traces or yokes . . . except there was little remaining of either traces or yokes. We had to leave after that, when the lava began to flow over everything."

"Did any clerks who worked for the governor or the princeps escape?"

Again . . . Zhrensyl frowned.

"We'll need clerks and others to rebuild the tariff system and the ledgers to account for spending. You also should have one or two." Quaeryt looked hard at the commander.

"Ah . . . there are two clerks. They've been staying in the barracks."

"Good. I'll see them in the morning. How hot is the area around the palace and the governor's buildings? Has it cooled off much?"

The commander shrugged. "Some places are still hot enough to be hearths or stoves. Other places are just unpleasantly warm. So they say."

"The palace is on higher ground, and the governor's square is on a lower hill below it," volunteered Vaelora.

"So there might be less lava around the governor's square?"

"It's possible." Vaelora frowned.

"Might I ask what you have in mind?" inquired Zhrensyl.

"I'm wondering if enough ash buried the building that held the strong room," Quaeryt said.

"Enough ash for what, Governor?"

"You know what a burned-out and banked fire is like in the morning? When there's ash covering everything, and the ash on top is barely warm, but there are still hot coals beneath? Well . . . if the ash came first, and then was covered with lava . . ." Quaeryt saw the comprehension in Vaelora's eyes immediately, but she did not speak.

Finally, Meinyt did. "You're saying that what's under the lava might be cooler?"

"It's worth looking to see," Quaeryt pointed out. "If we can get to the strong room, we'll have more golds for food and supplies. If not, I'll have to promise golds to the local High Holders . . . and getting them from Solis will take time and more golds." *Which Bhayar won't be happy to provide—assuming that he even can if Bovaria is building forces on the border or threatening an attack.*

"They won't sell. I've asked," replied the commander. "Said I couldn't pay enough."

"The High Holders did?" asked Quaeryt.

"That's what their stewards told the supply major."

"They wouldn't sell to you. If I have to ask, I'll have a regiment behind me and Lord Bhayar's sister at my shoulder," Quaeryt pointed out.

"That might be convincing enough. They won't be happy." Zhrensyl didn't look especially pleased as he spoke. "They stalled on doing anything until Commander Huosyt's regiment pulled out."

"No . . . they won't. They'll just be less unhappy than they would be with the consequences. Tell me . . . do you have shovels and picks here?"

"Some . . ."

"Tomorrow, we'll take some and look into the area around the palace and the governor's square. What about brooms?" After a moment of silence, Quaeryt went on. "One way or another, we're going to have to feed at least some people. We need to get the streets and sidewalks swept off. The more ash that accumulates, the more people will want to leave, and there's really nowhere for them to go, not at this time of year."

"Begging your pardon, Governor, but you don't know that the ash and lava won't keep coming or getting worse."

"You're right. I don't know. But . . ." Quaeryt waited for several moments before he continued. "If all that lava and ash covered everything that I've seen in the first days, and it looks like it did because almost all the lava I saw on the way here was dark and looked to be hardening, then it would seem that the lava and ashfall are lessening. What we can't afford to do is just wait and do nothing. That will also cause more people to leave." Quaeryt took a swallow of the bitter lager left in his mug, managing not to wince as he did so.

"Yes, sir." Zhrensyl's polite tone conveyed disagreement more pointedly than any words to the contrary could have.

Quaeryt laughed softly. "If you happen to be right, Commander, then you'll be able to say so to the end of your days, but we need to do something because Lord Bhayar happens to want the situation improved, and Extela is his ancestral home. We can't improve it by doing nothing. The only question is what will make matters better, and how we accomplish that. My task is to discover that and bring it about. We can't even begin to determine whether I'm right or you are unless we go and take a closer look at the damaged parts of the city."

"I haven't had the men . . ."

"I know that," replied Quaeryt as warmly as he could, although he suspected Zhrensyl had had more than enough men for what Quaeryt had in mind. "But I do, and we have more on the way. What do you have in the way of carts and dray-horses?"

"Three carts, and four wagons in good repair . . ."

For the next half glass, Quaeryt asked about what manner of resources remained at the post. He listened not only to what the commander said, but how Zhrensyl reacted to the questions. He also watched the two majors, Fhaen in particular because he hadn't spent much time at all with the younger major.

Then he rose. "It's been a long day for all of us. I'll see you all in the morning immediately after breakfast."

"Yes, sir." The others stood immediately.

Vaelora said nothing while she and Quaeryt walked back across the courtyard to the quarters building and up the outside stone steps. Quaeryt thought that the air seemed slightly clearer and that less ash was falling, but that might well have been wishful thinking.

Once he closed the quarters' door and slid the bolt, he turned to Vaelora, who had used the striker to light the lamp in the sitting room.

"You have some ideas, don't you?" she asked.

"Of course," replied Quaeryt with a grin, looking directly at her. "I always have ideas, especially . . ."

"I don't mean those ideas, dearest. I meant about the governor's mansion."

"I still have what you call *those* ideas, but they can wait . . . a bit. If I can find some paper, can you help me sketch out what you remember of the old governor's square?"

"The last time I was here was years ago."

"I've noted you have a *very* good memory." He grinned again. "But if you're not interested . . . there are those other ideas . . ."

"I can remember enough." While her words were tart, there was a hint of a smile at the corners of her lips.

Immediately after breakfast on Meredi morning, Quaeryt sat behind the desk in the small study that would have been that of the regimental commander. In the two chairs across from him were two men, clerks who had worked for the previous governor and who had sought refuge at the post. Quaeryt had been surprised that Zhrensyl had granted it until he'd learned that the older clerk was a distant cousin of the commander.

"Jhalyt . . . you were the assistant bookkeeper for the princeps?"

"Ah . . . no sir." The clerk had narrow-set green eyes below a high forehead and wispy receding brown hair. "I was the assistant to the bookkeeper."

"But you can keep a ledger?" At Jhalyt's nod, Quaeryt went on. "Can you set one up?"

"Yes, sir . . . but we don't have any records to start with."

"We won't for a day or so . . . if ever. We'll likely have to start new ledgers. What about a ledger for tariffs?"

"Ah . . . Caell did that. I only saw it once or twice."

"I can give you an example, and we'll work it out. That one we won't worry about immediately." Quaeryt turned to the other figure, scarcely more than a youth. "What did you do, Baharyt?"

"Just the supply ledger, sir. Mostly, I kept track of everything the governor and the princeps purchased."

"You can do that here. I'll be giving you more instructions as I know more." Quaeryt paused. "I need to know everything you can tell me about the governor's building. Everything. We're going to see if we can reclaim things from it." His eyes went to Jhalyt. "Tell me what was on each floor. Better yet . . . can you draw it out?"

"Yes, sir . . . I mean I can draw out where each chamber is . . . but aren't they under the lava?"

"That's what we'll find out. But it's worth the effort to see." Quaeryt pushed the pen and inkwell to the other side of the desk and handed the older clerk a sheet of paper.

Almost a glass later, after he finished meeting with the two clerks and taking their drawings, Quaeryt was out in the courtyard, inspecting the wagon and the cart that he'd decided would accompany the second company from Third Battalion, commanded by Captain Eleryt. The cart held an assortment of hand tools, mostly shovels and a few picks, but also a sledge and a mattock, as well as several buckets and two pry bars. The high-sided wagon contained chains and other gear that he hoped might prove useful. Quaeryt had tucked inside his brown scholar's working jacket four maps, one from the post, along with a set of directions as how to follow the streets, avenues, and byways so as to get as close to the governor's square as possible before encountering the hardened lava. The second map was the one Vaelora had drawn the night before. Then he had the two drawings from Jhalyt and Baharyt showing what chambers were where in the building.

When the company formed up in the courtyard, Vaelora was mounted beside Quaeryt because, as she had pointed out more than once, "Who else do you have who knows that part of Extela any better?"

Quaeryt knew better than to argue with her, and besides, she did know Extela. There was also little useful that she could do at the post, and Quaeryt had long since learned that his wife did not like to be left alone with nothing to do—and that she'd soon find more than enough to do, and possibly something he'd be less than pleased about. His eyes drifted to the locked anomen. While he'd seen abandoned and burned-out anomens, he'd never seen one simply locked.

Vaelora followed his gaze. "I wondered about that, too."

"I suppose I'd best ask the commander about that, too."

"There are a number of matters that still need explaining," murmured Vaelora, looking to him.

Quaeryt nodded.

"Ready, Governor?" called Captain Eleryt, as he rode up to join the two of them, easing his mount beside that of Vaelora, so that she was between the two men.

"Anytime."

"Company! Forward!"

As Quaeryt and Vaelora rode out through the post gates, he looked to the northwest, toward Mount Extel. The sky above the summit was hazy, unlike the clearer sky farther east or west, as if fine ash—or something—still issued from the volcano.

"The whole top of the mountain is gone," said Vaelora. "I couldn't see that yesterday with all the ash and clouds."

"How much taller was it?"

"It's hard to tell. It came to a peak. It was snow-covered, at least partly, all year round. How much higher? I don't know. A quint more?"

"Let's hope all that rock and lava isn't all on top of the governor's square," said Quaeryt wryly. His glance dropped from the mountain to the area of Extela that held the palace and the governor's square, if under ash and lava. "Is the main avenue the best way to go? I'd thought so, but . . ."

From the other side of Vaelora, Eleryt leaned inward in his saddle, as if to hear what Vaelora said more clearly.

"It will be fine until we're past the market square in the middle of the city. Then we'll have to see."

Quaeryt held his triggered shields so that they covered the two of them as they rode along the avenue toward the market square. Occasionally, shutters opened, usually those on second-level windows, but for the first mille from the post no one approached the riders.

Because of what happened yesterday afternoon? Or because everyone who is left is afraid?

Then a boy ran out from an alleyway, waving his hands. "Sirs! We need food! Please . . . please!"

"We're working on that," Quaeryt called back. "But we're not carrying food now. We'll be back later."

"My ma is sick. We need food."

Quaeryt could see the boy—barefoot and in a thin shirt—shiver. "Soon, but not now," he said.

Another youth appeared, begging for food, and then another, followed by an old woman, and then another scrawny boy with a crutch. Then came an older man, with a long gray beard, followed by a woman in a worn and ragged shawl thrown over little more than rags. By the time the company had ridden another long block, there were scores of people on the sidewalks begging . . . but none of them stepped into the street, most likely because the troopers all carried unsheathed sabres.

As they continued to ride toward the center market square, more scores of people appeared, pleading and begging. Most were ill-dressed or ragged, confirming Quaeryt's suspicions that those with food were either remaining behind barred doors or had already left Extela. "I don't see many who are decently clad."

"They're the poorest," replied Vaelora. "All they know is that they're hungry. They don't care that if you have to promise golds, rather than having them in hand, you'll pay more for the food, and there will be less."

"Or that I'll have to threaten the High Holders to keep the prices down."

"You'll have to do that anyway."

"You don't think they'll listen to reason?"

"The only reason they've ever listened to is the ledgers in their accounting rooms. That's what Bhayar is always saying."

She's right about that, too. "Do you think . . ." he began.

"No. You need to know what you have to work with. You also need to know more about conditions here in the city. You also can't spend too much on the poorest."

Because they aren't the ones who will rebuild and repair the city. Or produce and buy the goods to keep it alive. Still, he couldn't help feeling slightly guilty as he ignored the pleas that the poorest continued to call out.

Even before they reached the market square—appearing abandoned from a block away—Quaeryt could feel the warmer air . . . and see a rough expanse of blackened rock that had poured down the next street to the northwest, walling off the avenue. No one else begged from the sidewalks and alleyways as they neared the square, but he could see several shutters had opened, and one or two were ajar.

Once they entered the square, Quaeryt turned to Eleryt. "Have them halt here."

"Company! Halt!"

Quaeryt turned to Vaelora. "Is there a way east and downhill that will allow us to circle around that?" He pointed to the cooling mass of lava ahead of them.

"There are many ways, but any of them could be blocked."

"Then we'll just have to try them one at a time." He turned in the saddle. "Captain, I'd like you and two squads to stay where you are with the wagons for the moment. The lady and I will take the other two squads and see if we can find a better approach to the square."

"Yes, sir."

"Don't let anyone get too close, either."

"We won't, sir." Eleryt stood in his stirrups. "First and second squads! With the governor, under his direct command!"

Quaeryt turned to Vaelora. "Which way would you suggest?" He smiled, wondering if her foresight extended to picking routes.

"Downhill until we see a way back northwest," she replied so sweetly that Quaeryt winced.

"Squads one and two! On us!" Quaeryt did not immediately look at his wife as he urged the mare forward to the end of the square, then eastward down a narrower street that sloped gently toward the river in the distance.

At the next cross street, he looked northwest, but the lava still blocked the way, although the amount appeared noticeably less—and lower. After three more blocks, they could turn north once again, but an almost stifling heat permeated the streets, certainly one reason why those begging for food had gathered farther south.

"Not so chill now, dearest, is it? It's too bad we couldn't take the warmth back to those poor people on the south side of town. If only their problem were just keeping warm."

Quaeryt nodded, wondering if he could even do imaging in the heat. He frowned. There was something in the back of his mind, but he couldn't recall what it was.

Did you read something somewhere about using heat? Smiths and metal workers use heat all the time to form and shape metal. You're able to image things from one place to another? What about heat? Or would that just exhaust you? He didn't know, but he knew that he'd have to be very careful, whatever he tried.

At the next cross street, he looked uphill, but there was lava two blocks up. Another block farther on, and the street was clear. They rode uphill.

"The governor's square is only about four blocks that way." Vaelora pointed in the direction of Mount Extel, roughly west-northwest.

"The question is how close we can get to it and in a place where the lava isn't too high and is cool enough to approach."

"You don't want much, dearest, do you?"

"Not at all," he replied pleasantly. "Not at all."

Almost a glass later, after weaving back and forth, and up an alleyway to another cross street and then back south, Quaeryt and Vaelora rode along a street that, from what he could tell, had been covered with hard ash to a depth of more than a yard. While grayish ash or dust puffed up with each step of their mounts, the ash was hard-packed enough that the horses' hooves only sank into it a digit or so.

Finally, they reined up about ten yards back from an irregular mound of black rock that stretched roughly level across an open space, but the hardened lava directly before them was certainly not deep enough to have covered any buildings. While the hardened lava rose gradually from where it ended before them until it was high enough to engulf buildings, at the lowest point near them the black stone was a good yard above the packed ash.

"This is the east side of the square . . . I think." Vaelora looked around, then gestured. "It has to be. There's the old southeast tower of the palace. All the rest of it . . . well . . . not quite."

Following her outstretched arm, at first, all Quaeryt could see was black stone and more black stone, out of which rose the one tower. Then he looked more intently before he made out a section of wall joining the tower, but the wall looked blackened. He frowned. It wasn't blackened. The stones were black. He wanted to shake his head.

Exactly from what did you think all the black stone buildings were constructed?

"The tower stands out because the stone there is much older and something happened to it long ago. Grandmere told me that once when I was little, but I don't remember exactly why that was."

Quaeryt dropped his eyes to what remained of the square, and looking more intently, some fifty yards away, he could make out the black stone corner and slate roof of a building not entirely covered by lava—except that he was only a few yards below the top of the uncovered roof. Slowly, he eased the mare forward, but the heat didn't seem as intense as it had in other places in the city. Was that because the ash and lava had struck the palace and the square first and the later molten rock had flowed around them?

He turned in the saddle. "Squad Leader, if you'd have the scouts and a few others, as you see fit, ride back to the others and then guide them here."

"Yes, sir."

Quaeryt then dismounted and handed the mare's reins to Vaelora.

"Be careful."

"I will."

The first thing Quaeryt did was walk along the irregular edge of the lava, trying to gauge where it was the coolest and where it was the hottest. He did not quite touch the stone, but it didn't radiate much heat . . . anywhere. So he went back to the mare and took his water bottle, filled with watered lager, out of its holder and uncorked it. He walked along the stone again, flicking water at the rugged black surface, but the liquid remained. Only then did he touch the stone. While it was warm, it was not uncomfortably so, but he had no doubt that beneath the hard surface, there were places where the stone was far, far hotter.

He returned to where the hardened lava was the lowest and, taking the staff, pressed one iron-capped end against the top of the stone. The warm rock did not yield. So he jumped up, careful to concentrate on lifting his bad leg, so much so that he almost lost his balance before straightening on the rough surface, but the staff helped. He began to walk toward the lava-swathed building, one step at a time, testing the rock before him with the staff.

While he could sense greater warmth as the rock thickened as he climbed up the rock until he reached the uncovered stone corner of the building and the slate roof above it, the increase in heat was not that great. He bent over and lowered his hand to just above the solidified lava. It was warmer than he'd thought, almost warm enough to cook on. His boots were thick enough that they protected his feet.

He'd hoped that there would have been somewhere that they could have used picks to chip away the lava down to the ash, but especially given the heat of the lava under the crust, he could see that the easiest way to enter the building would be through the wall, and that might well be difficult with the limited tools they had brought.

He turned and walked back across the warm stone, very carefully. He could see that edges in places were sharp enough to slice through clothing and flesh.

Vaelora looked at him, raising her eyebrows.

"I think we can get in, but it won't be easy."

Before that long the rest of the company and the wagon and cart arrived, and Quaeryt accompanied several burly rankers with picks across the hardened lava to the exposed section of wall, choosing the lowest black building stone that was completely free of lava. If Jhalyt's hand-drawn map was accurate, and he was reading it correctly, behind the stone was a narrow chamber that had held file chests.

"We'll have to use the picks to chip out the mortar." He pointed to the first ranker and stepped back. "You start."

"Yes, sir."

The ranker took aim and swung, but the pick hit stone, rather than mortar, and rebounded. With a second swing, the ranker hit the mortar, but again the pick bounced away, leaving only the smallest scratch.

"Let me try," said Quaeryt. "If you'd stand back." He aimed the pick at the thin line of mortar and swung. Right as the pick struck he imaged away some of the mortar, leaving a deep line between the two stones.

"How . . . ?"

After another swing, and removing more mortar, he handed the pick back to the ranker from whom he had taken it. "You try it now."

Bit by bit, Quaeryt watched and quietly imaged away mortar, trying to draw strength from somewhere, as the rankers, with his unnoticed help, cut away the support for one stone and then another, until, after almost a glass, two sagged perceptibly. It took another half glass before they could pull the two free, only to reveal charred wooden lathe.

Quaeryt nodded. "Now the next two stones."

It was close to midday before enough stones had been removed for a man to climb through—assuming that the lathe didn't front more stonework.

"Bring up a sledge!" As Quaeryt waited for the sledge, he realized two things. He didn't have a headache, and that the lava around where the men worked seemed noticeably cooler. Had his efforts to draw strength from elsewhere worked? They must have, but why? Was that why the lava was cooler?

He frowned. When he'd done imaging in the cold rain during the battles with the hill holders, on at least one occasion he'd been pelted with ice when he'd seen rain all around himself. *They must be connected. But how?*

He'd have to think about that. He turned his attention to the ranker with the sledge. With the first crack in the lathing, a slight puff of warm air pushed the dust outward, but subsequent blows didn't bring more hot air, nor did the air seem sour.

That suggested to Quaeryt that the air inside wasn't too hot. *You hope.*

While they were enlarging the hole, Quaeryt walked back to where Vaelora waited under the hazy sky and took several long swallows of watered ale.

"Do you know where the strong room is?" she asked.

"The clerk said that it's in the middle of the lowest level—underground, I think. He said that only the princeps and the governor had the keys."

Another half glass passed before the sweating rankers had a hole big enough for men to enter. Quaeryt let one of them lead, bearing a small lantern, and then followed them over the charred remnants of file chests that had only partly filled the corner storage room. Quaeryt tried to open one of the chests, but the top gave way, and when he tried to extract a sheet, it crumbled under his fingers. The door to the corridor opened, if grudgingly against the ash in the corridor beyond that was ankle deep. The corridor walls that had likely once been white plaster above oak or goldenwood paneling were closer to a dark brown, and the wood was blackened and cracked. Still, the ash wasn't that deep.

Quaeryt's feeling of optimism died abruptly when he reached the stairs down to the street level. Halfway down, the ash covered everything.

"We'll need to shovel this up. You can put it in the hall that goes that way. We'll need to go back and get men and picks and shovels and buckets."

Quaeryt turned and retraced his steps and climbed back into the early afternoon that was probably almost chill at the post to the south of the city, but which felt almost muggy outside the governor's building.

Eleryt was waiting. "Sir?"

"The upper hall is clear, but the stairs are partly filled with ash. I'll need to have them cleared. They need to rotate. No more than two quints for each man at a time."

"Yes, sir."

Another glass passed before Eleryt reported to Quaeryt, who had spent the time drinking from his and Vaelora's water bottles and eating hard biscuits to regain his strength—and just waiting.

"Sir, there's a door blocking the steps below, and it's got a massive lock on it, sir."

"That might be good," said Quaeryt. "It might have kept the ash from filling the lowest level. I'll have to take a look. Oh . . . and bring one of the sledges."

"There's one inside, sir."

"Good."

Quaeryt made his way inside once more, down the corridor and down the ash-cleared steps to the solid, ironbound door and the massive lock.

"If I could have the sledge . . ."

One of the rankers handed it to him.

He'd already decided how to approach the situation. He took a solid swing at the lock, and as he expected, the sledge had no effect. He took another swing, moving so his body shielded the others' view of the lock, and after the heavy sledge rebounded, he imaged out two chunks of steel from the bottom of the lock hasp, but the lock remained frozen. He took a third swing, and the lock separated, the bottom dropping onto the stone and ash.

"I thought the heat might have made the lock more brittle. We were lucky in that."

". . . tried that . . ." murmured someone.

Quaeryt wasn't surprised that they'd tried without telling him, but he just stepped forward and slid the hasp out of the iron loop and lifted and slid the strap free. Even so, the door had warped, and it took two men with pry bars to wedge it free of the jamb. The stairs below were apparently clear, but totally dark.

"Who has the lantern?"

"Here, sir."

"Go ahead."

Quaeryt followed the ranker down the steps. The strong room was in the middle of the building, to the left of the bottom of the stairs, with an iron door and another iron lock.

Quaeryt shook his head. The sledge trick wouldn't work again.

"Sir?"

He turned to the nearest ranker behind him. "Would you inquire of the Lady Vaelora if she might happen to have a key or a straight piece of metal small enough to fit into a lock? Not too small a lock."

Although a puzzled expression crossed the man's face, he replied, "Yes, sir."

While he waited for the ranker to return Quaeryt studied the lock. The keyhole was smaller than that of the upper level doorlock, and the metalwork was finer, but the hasp was every bit as thick, as were the iron loop and strap that the lock secured.

Before that long, the ranker returned, breathing heavily, and extended a brass key.

"Thank you."

"My pleasure, sir."

Quaeryt turned to the lock. The key Vaelora had provided was far smaller than that required by the lock, but that mattered little, since he was counterfeiting picking the lock. While he manipulated the key, Quaeryt tried to image away the insides of the lock . . . and he found that far harder than imaging away the bits of iron from the lock on the upper door, so much so that when he finally managed to open the lock—gutted of all interior workings—his head throbbed and his eyes watered.

Why now? You didn't have that trouble before.

He removed the lock and stepped back, then swung the door open—only to find a narrow vestibule with a second locked door.

He couldn't help but sigh. Then he took a deep breath. "We'll have to see what we can do with this lock."

Before he tried any more imaging, he tried to think about what had been different about what he'd done with the second lock, as opposed to the first. Both had been made of iron, and he'd imaged away parts of each. *But why was the second so much harder . . . ? Because you're farther away from all the heat of the cooling lava?*

Belatedly, he realized that up the stairs he'd reached out for the heat. Down on the lower level, he hadn't.

Will that work down here?

He had to try.

As he manipulated the key, he concentrated on reaching out to the heat of the lava. While the imaging was easier than in the case of the previous lock, it was still far harder than it had been with the first lock, and light flashes blurred his vision when he stepped back to let others open the door.

. . . hope there's not another lock . . .

There wasn't . . . not exactly. But there were five locked chests in the strong room and a much smaller unlocked casket. Quaeryt lifted the lid of the casket and found it half filled with silvers. He closed it quickly, but held on to it.

"We'll need to carry these up to the wagon and cart." He offered a grin. "Be careful of them. Your pay's likely to come from there."

The squad leader swallowed, and Quaeryt judged that he'd never been in the presence of so much coin.

Eleryt was waiting outside the structure when Quaeryt emerged.

"We got the strong room open. They're bringing up the chests. They're all locked. There are five of them, and they're heavy. I took a quick look at the other rooms that weren't filled with ash, but there's nothing there but file chests and no sign of other valuables." *That doesn't mean there couldn't be some elsewhere in the building, but any looter will have to dig through a lot of ash on the main floor.*

The captain stiffened.

"Call it payroll and supply duty, Captain," Quaeryt said with an ironic smile. "We'll need every coin in it for supplies and pay."

"Yes, sir."

Quaeryt walked slowly toward Vaelora, who stood waiting in the limited shade offered by the single wagon. She held a water bottle.

"Are you all right?" asked Vaelora. "You look like something the Namer dragged in." She handed him the bottle.

Quaeryt put it under one arm and handed her the casket. "Be careful. It's filled with silvers. It didn't have a lock. The five big chests did." He took a long swallow of watered lager before replying. "It took some work to get into the strong room. I broke one lock with a sledge and picked the other two with the key you provided." He pulled it from his jacket pocket and extended it to her. "It was very useful."

"Especially since it was designed for my jewelry chest in Solis." The hint of a smile crossed her lips. "You're still pale. You need to drink more."

"Yes, dear." He wasn't about to argue. His head still throbbed, and he could barely hold the light trigger shields.

"You also need to eat." A biscuit followed her words.

"How many of those did you bring?" He took the offering and bit into it.

"As many as I could pry out of the cook. I had the feeling you'd need them. I was right."

"You were indeed," he mumbled through the biscuit crumbs. "Anyway, we did what we could. The chests might see us through for a while."

"For a while. It takes so much . . ." She shook her head. "You know as well as anyone."

"Unfortunately."

Two quints later, the chests had been secured in the wagon and cart, and the company prepared to head back to the post. After Vaelora and Quaeryt mounted, he glanced at the square opening in the wall of the governor's building. In all likelihood, in time, the upper floor would be stripped, but not for a while, but with what was likely contained in the chests, given their weight, he didn't want to leave any rankers behind.

His eyes flicked to where the sun hung just over the jagged peaks nearly to the horizon on the far side of the vast valley that stretched westward from Extela almost as far as the eye could see—and where the most fertile lands lay.

Even so, obtaining the governor's treasury, hard as it had seemed, was likely to be far less difficult than getting enough food for the city, the post, and the regiment would be.

"Dearest . . . what is it?" asked Vaelora as she eased the gelding forward and the column began the ride back southward to the post.

"I was thinking that this was the easiest part. It doesn't deal with people."

She nodded.

The company returned to the post just before sunset on Meredi . . . and without further incident—other than more of the poor begging for food. The chests were stored in the commander's strong room. Quaeryt had reluctantly "unlocked" one to assure himself that it actually contained golds, and it did, more than five thousand at a quick estimation, although he and Jhalyt would have to count out the coin to the last copper before he could have the clerk set up the ledgers. He left the other four locked, since he had no keys to them and did not wish to break the locks and thus subject others to unnecessary temptation. The strong room was certainly not as secure as the governor's had been, but far more accessible, reflected Quaeryt.

By Jeudi morning, the remnants of his headache had vanished, especially after breakfast, when he met with Commander Zhrensyl in his study. No sooner had Quaeryt seated himself across the table desk from the commander than the older man asked, "And how might I help you?"

"What happened to the Civic Patrol? There was one, wasn't there?"

"Yes, sir. Their headquarters was on the south side of the governor's square."

Now under ash and lava. "What about the patrollers . . . or the patrol chief?"

Zhrensyl shrugged. "The chief lived in the northwest. I imagine he's among those no longer with us. There are probably patrollers around, but . . ."

"You made no attempt to organize them?"

"That's not my responsibility, sir, and I didn't have the men. When Commander Huosyt came, he couldn't even find any patrollers "

Quaeryt managed not to snap at the older man. After several other questions that established that Zhrensyl felt he had no responsibility beyond the post itself, Quaeryt decided not to frustrate himself further and asked, "What can you tell me about the High Holders to the west?"

"Not so much as the governor could have, sir."

"Who purchases grain and food for the post?"

Zhrensyl frowned momentarily, as if the change in questions puzzled him.

Quaeryt waited.

"That'd be Major Heireg, sir. He's in charge of supply and the quartermasters."

"Then I'll be talking to him after we finish here. Now . . ." Quaeryt paused, trying to conceal the fact that he wasn't terribly impressed with the commander. "In your mind, who are the strongest and most powerful High Holders closest to Extela?"

"The nearest is High Holder Aramyn. His hold is five milles due west. Next is Wystgahl. He's about twelve milles south on a hill overlooking the river. The next nearest is Thysor, but his lands are more into timber, and he's to the east across the river."

"Who might be the strongest of the High Holders?" Quaeryt kept his voice pleasant, although he was less than pleased.

"That'd be hard to say, sir."

"What can you tell me about Aramyn?"

"I've never seen the High Holder, sir. Nor his place. I'd not wish to speculate on what I've not seen."

"What about Wystgahl and Thysor?"

"I've not met either, sir."

"Have you met any others?"

"No, sir. They'd be farther away."

Quaeryt was about to excuse himself when one other question, one he'd wondered about intermittently since he'd arrived in Extela, occurred to him. "I noticed that the anomen was locked . . ."

"Ah . . . yes, sir. That's because we've not a proper chorister. Well . . . not even an improper one, and there not being one, I felt it was best to secure the building. You wouldn't have a regimental chorister coming, would you?"

"No. There's no chorister with the regiment." Quaeryt wasn't about to get tangled up any more in providing homilies, especially given what he'd seen in Extela. For all that he'd said in the last homily he delivered—and he sincerely hoped it was indeed his last—he still had trouble reconciling a benevolent Nameless with the destruction wreaked on the city.

"That's a pity. The officers and men were hoping . . ."

"I can understand that." Quaeryt nodded as he stood. "Where might I find Major Heireg?"

"He has a study in the quartermaster's spaces—the end of the south stable."

"Thank you."

Quaeryt returned to the smaller study he'd claimed and immediately summoned Meinyt and Fhaen. As soon as they arrived, he waved them into the two chairs.

"Part of the problem here is that the Civic Patrol chief is apparently dead, the headquarters was destroyed, and no one bothered to reorganize the patrol, since the chief reported to the governor. Major Meinyt . . . I'd like you to have one of your captains or undercaptains scout around for a suitable building, preferably empty, that can be used as a temporary space for the Civic Patrol, one where cells or the like can be quickly built. Once we have a building, some of the engineers, and any stone or masonry workers we can find, will convert it, and chief clerk Jhalyt will write up some notices requesting patrollers who wish to retain their positions meet there. The sooner we can get patrollers back on the streets, the less patrolling you and your men will have to do."

"Yes, sir."

After going over a few more details with the two, Quaeryt hurried out into the courtyard, where Vaelora was waiting. As he walked toward her, he looked to the northwest. The sky appeared clearer, and there was only the faintest haze surrounding Mount Extel. At least, that was the way it seemed to him. *But are you seeing what you want to see?*

"How was your meeting?" she asked.

"Very polite. It would appear that Governor Scythn kept him very much in the dark."

"And his curiosity about High Holders is rather restrained?"

"Extremely. But that is the safest course for a military officer with limited talent. The other problem is that he's done nothing to keep order beyond the post walls. He didn't even try to gather what remained of the Civic Patrol." Quaeryt couldn't help but wonder how Zhrensyl had ever become a commander and why he'd been retained . . . unless Bhayar had judged that lack of curiosity was a requirement for the post in Extela.

"He must be close to the age for a stipend."

"Unless he had a long and glorious service when he was younger, I'm not sure that he deserves it."

Vaelora slowed and glanced to the outside wall of the rankers' mess hall, where the old woman they had rescued from the mob in Extela sat on the worn paving stones, her back against the wall, feeding bread from a loaf to the small child in her arms.

"You stay here," murmured Vaelora.

An amused smile on his face, one that vanished almost immediately, Quaeryt waited as his wife neared the woman.

"How are you doing?" asked Vaelora in Tellan.

The woman responded in what Quaeryt thought was Pharsi.

Vaelora said a few words back, apparently in the same tongue, then added in Tellan, "That's all I know."

"Then you are lost ones, you and the scholar."

Vaelora's eyes flashed to Quaeryt, as if questioning, before she replied, "He is the governor and my husband."

"Doubly lost are you both, then."

"We were fortunate enough to find each other."

"You will need to find more than that. Have you time to listen to an old woman's tale?" The woman handed another fragment of bread to the child.

Vaelora glanced to Quaeryt. He nodded.

The woman cleared her throat and began to speak.

In the time before the lost ones were lost, four young Pharsi, three men and a woman, were walking through the great woods of Khel. Two of the men were brothers, and strong-thewed they were. Afeared of nothing were they as well, even when they should have been. They led along a way too large to be a path and too narrow to be a road. Behind them walked their sister, with a young man like your companion, white-blond and black-eyed, and he was a distant cousin who had come to court her. Above them the trees were so thick that the day seemed like dusk. Before long, the four came to a scabbard lying beside the path, and a fine scabbard indeed it was, but bereft of its blade.

The older brother picked it up and thrust it under his belt, saying, "Where that came from there must be a blade to match."

The younger brother replied, "If the scabbard is yours, then the blade will be mine."

"Both will be mine, for I am the eldest," declared the older brother.

"Mine, for it is only fair that we share," insisted the younger brother.

"Mine—"

"Do not argue over what is not and may never be," said the sister, and her voice was soft, but firm.

"What say you, cousin?" asked the eldest.

And the white-blond and black-eyed Pharsi who had come courting said in return, "Your sister has the right of it."

The two brothers grumbled, but they were silent. Before long, they came to a fine velvet wallet lying in the path, and the younger brother grabbed it up, yet there was but a single tarnished copper within the wallet.

"So if there is a blade, it will be mine," asserted the eldest.

"Only if I do not find the golds that fell from this wallet."

And they began to argue once more. Again, their soft-voiced sister said, "Do not argue over what is not and may never be."

Once more, the brothers asked, "Cousin, what say you now?"

And once more, he replied, "Your sister has the right of it."

Grumbles followed grumbles, until they died away, and before long the four came to a clearing in the wood, where there were two men. They were well attired and well armed, and they fought with blades that glistened in the late afternoon sun that poured into the clearing. Then one struck the other a blow that clove through shoulder and near onto the heart of the other, but the dying man grasped a poignard and slipped it between the ribs of the other, and they both fell down dead.

The two brothers hurried into the clearing and immediately began to despoil the dead men of their belongings, seeing as neither would have need of such. Tied to one tree at the side of the clearing was young stallion, as handsome a stallion as anyone could want, and his coat was silver-white and as fine as silk, but he bore neither saddle nor bridle, but only a harness and a lead. But tethered to two other trees were even more splendid stallions, and they wore fine saddles and bridles as well.

The two brothers began to argue, each to claim what the other had, and the Pharsi woman turned to her cousin. "Dearest, let us take the stallion and lead him away."

Her cousin looked to the brothers. "There is much treasure there."

"Do not argue over what is not and may never be," she said. "Am I not more treasure than they will ever see?"

He smiled and said, "Truly, that is so."

And they untied the stallion and walked away from the clearing, leading the stallion between them, until the arguing voices of the brothers were lost in the soft sounds of the woods. They walked, and they walked, and the sun dropped lower and lower in the sky, until it, too, vanished behind the western peaks, and they came to the end of the woods and continued through the fields and meadows.

They had scarce come around a corner in the way that was too wide for a path and too narrow for a road when a man with hair as white as snow and as silver as moonlight and the face of a young warrior rode toward them across the meadow to the south. The silver-white-haired man looked from the young woman to her cousin and then to the mare. "Where did you come by that stallion?" he asked.

"Why, sir," answered the Pharsi woman, "his lead was tangled in a branch in the woods, and we untangled it. That was how we came by him."

"You did not try to ride him?"

"No, sir," replied the cousin most politely. "He looked not to be broken, and escaped from his owner."

"He is indeed not broken, nor will that ever happen, and he was stolen by two brigands, and they had two other rough fellows to help them, but they fell to fighting and they were still fighting when we came upon them and slew the last two. And I would ask that you not argue and return my stallion to me."

The woman was grieved so that she thought her heart would break, but she held her tears and said, "I would not argue over what is not and may never be."

"Wise you are, woman, and you as well, fellow." The white-haired man bent in the saddle and took the lead from her. "Wise you were, also, to lead the stallion between you, for to try to ride one so wild would only have left you dead and trampled in the dirt." He took a small pouch from his belt and tossed it to her. "Some coppers for your troubles."

Then he turned his mount, and he and his mount, like as to a twin to the stallion that trotted beside them, they rode off.

The woman opened the pouch and a score of coppers fell into her palm. She and her cousin looked up and saw the silver-white-haired man, a mighty bow across his back, riding up a shimmering road of reddish silver that stretched skyward . . . and vanished. And where the road had led, shining full in the night that had come on so suddenly, was Erion, the moon of the great hunter.

A single beam from that, the lesser moon, flashed across her hands, and she gasped, for the coppers had turned to gold.

And yet, the greatest treasure they had was not the wealth of the golds, but the wisdom of the hunter, and so that should be for you as well.

The wisdom of the hunter? Quaeryt did not voice his question.

The old woman looked from Vaelora to Quaeryt and back again before she smiled. "Remember the tale, lost ones, and you will be lost no more when you come to the road." Then she bowed her head to Vaelora. "I thank you, Lady, for your grace and kindness."

"And I thank you for your story and your insight," replied Vaelora. After a pause, she asked, "Is that an old, old tale?"

"I heard it from my grandmere, and she from hers."

"Why did you offer it to us?" asked Quaeryt pleasantly, feeling far more charitable to her than he had toward Zhrensyl.

"Because you need to know from where you come, lost one, governor that you may be." She smiled sadly. "That is all I can say. The rest you must find yourselves."

"Thank you," Vaelora said again.

As they walked away, Quaeryt thought about the woman's addressing them as the "lost ones." He'd heard . . . somewhere . . . about the lost ones. He just couldn't remember where.

The two walked slowly away from the rankers' mess hall.

"Who are the lost ones? What does that mean?" asked Vaelora.

"I'm trying . . ." Abruptly, he remembered who had first called him a "lost one"—Hailae, in Bhorael. *How could you forget that?* He shook his head ruefully. "I don't know all of it, but I've told you about Rhodyn's son Jorem . . ."

"The one who married the Pharsi woman he saved, you mean?"

"His wife is Hailae, and when she saw me the first time, she called me a 'lost one.' I'd never heard that. The lost ones are Pharsi who are marked by black eyes and white blond hair, but she couldn't, or wouldn't, explain more."

"You told me how she insisted you are Pharsi, but not about being a lost one."

"I thought I did."

Vaelora shook her head.

Rather than pursue that, Quaeryt said, "The way she told it, it has to be an old tale, but I've never heard it or read about it."

"She was certain it applied to us." Vaelora smiled. "Even if most Pharsi would have been beaten or killed if they'd been found with a horse and no way to have bought it."

"None of the old tales make any sense that way." He paused. "Do you really think that we're the lost ones?"

"You're from a Pharsi background, and so am I, but neither of us can speak more than a few words of Pharsi. We know nothing of their customs."

"So . . . from her point of view, we're the lost ones."

"I think 'lost ones' means more than that," mused Vaelora. "I wish I knew more. I should have listened more closely to Grandmere."

"She never talked about the lost ones?"

"If she did, I don't remember, and I think I would have." After a moment she asked, "What will you do now?"

"Meet with Major Heireg. The post quartermaster has to know something about the High Holders and who has what goods. Then . . . we'll begin visiting the High Holders."

"We? You didn't ask me." Vaelora's face was composed, severe in expression.

Quaeryt wasn't quite sure whether she was irritated or amused behind a facade. "Would my lady prefer to accompany me on a long ride to visit politely unpleasant High Holders or to remain here at the post in idle leisure?"

"That is most disrespectful . . ." Vaelora grinned abruptly, but the grin didn't last long.

"I am sorry. I'd thought we'd talked about this last night."

"We did . . . but you didn't ask. You just assumed."

Quaeryt didn't hide the wince.

"I would like to accompany you. I also think I can be useful, don't you?"

Her last words were delivered so sweetly that he winced again. "I do indeed, and I apologize for my assumptions."

"You don't have to apologize for all of them, dearest. Just that one. Your apology is accepted."

"Thank you."

Vaelora laughed softly.

"It might be better if I met with the major alone," said Quaeryt as they neared the stables.

"I would agree. I'll be outside here nearby."

"It's not likely to be long."

"Take as long as you need, dearest."

Quaeryt inclined his head to her, then turned and made his way to the narrow door at the end of the stable. Inside was a small space, barely large enough for the single narrow desk, the chair in front of it, and the records chests stacked head high against the outer wall.

"Governor!" The major rose from the desk and bowed. "What might I do for you, sir?"

"I'd like to hear what you have to say about procurement. Especially recent procurement." Quaeryt gestured for the major to reseat himself, then settled into the single armless chair in front of the desk.

"We haven't procured much in the past weeks. Nothing at all."

"Commander Zhrensyl indicated that you have a fair supply of rations and some fodder, but not that much more. Are supplies that hard to purchase?"

"It depends on what you mean, Governor," replied the round-faced man, whose cherubic visage was contraindicated by a lean muscular frame. "I could purchase more supplies, but we don't need them right now. The local holders, especially the High Holders, are holding their grain and flour dear. They're holding everything dear." Heireg smiled sardonically. "I've held off buying. I figured Lord Bhayar would send someone to replace Governor Scythn before long. Whoever it was would have more clout than I would in getting a fair price from those bastards. Pardon my language, sir, but they are. Some of 'em would run down a starving mother for sport. Especially Wystgahl."

That didn't surprise Quaeryt in the slightest. "I need to know what the range of past prices for simple goods has been—flour, a side of mutton, or a whole sheep, maize, potatoes . . ."

"Until the mountain blew, sir, flour was running eight silvers a barrel, sometimes nine. Potatoes were less than three coppers a bushel. Good ones, that is. In the fall, I could get a bushel for two coppers. Price of the other provisions bounced around from week to week. I can show you the ledgers with all the prices . . ."

"I'd appreciate that."

Heireg eased a ledger off the shelf on the wall, then stood, opening the ledger to the last page with entries. "You see here, almost a month ago, the last time I bought anything . . ."

Quaeryt listened as the major went over the costs of each procurement, then asked, "From whom do you obtain these massive amounts of goods?"

"Anyone who will sell at a decent price. Most times, the small holders offer better prices, but they can't supply all that we need. Right now, they've little to offer. The High Holders don't want to sell because they don't have to—not yet—and they think prices will rise."

"Who are the High Holders most likely to have flour and potatoes?"

"Wystgahl has wheat corn and a mill, and Aramyn has potatoes and some flour, I've heard. Chaffetz has both."

"Is Chaffetz the most powerful?"

"Don't know as he's the most powerful. Namer knows, he's the most stubborn. Don't go to him unless there's nowhere else to turn."

"Where is his holding?"

"He's got lands everywhere. His chateau is some three milles due south, off the stone post road to Solis that follows the river until it crosses at the bridge some twenty milles south."

"Can you think of any reason why I shouldn't visit those three and see whether they'd be amenable to selling some more provisions—at a decent price, that is?"

Heireg laughed gruffly. "You'd be the first governor to try, sir. Least in my time here. You get even close to a decent price from any of them, and I'd write a letter to Lord Bhayar spouting your praises."

Quaeryt laughed. "I think you've made your point, Major."

"Any other questions, sir?"

"Just a few. Do you know how many loaves of bread can be baked out of the flour in a single barrel?"

Heireg smiled broadly and shook his head. "The cooks and I go round over that. Should be around four hundred and a quint, according to their measurements. The best they ever do, from my figuring, is a shade over four hundred."

"How much flour do you have now here at the post?"

"Three hundred barrels. With your full regiment, we'll use close to two barrels a day."

When Quaeryt finished asking questions, he thanked Heireg and left.

As he walked across the courtyard to join Vaelora, he knew one thing for certain. He was going to need a lot more flour . . . and that was just the beginning.

Nearly a glass and two quints later, Quaeryt, Vaelora, and Undercaptain Jusaph rode behind the scouts and ahead of the body of Third Battalion's first company as they made their way up the gravel drive to the chateau of High Holder Chaffetz. A handful of men scrambled from out of a side gate toward the main entry, then came to a halt as they beheld the Telaryn uniforms and the company ensign.

Besides checking his shields and easing the mare closer to Vaelora's gelding, Quaeryt ignored the handful of men-at-arms and reined up opposite the main center entrance to the old-style three-story chateau, with its thick stone walls and narrow windows on the two lower levels, and wide windows on the third level.

Then, after Jusaph drew up the company in formation facing the chateau, Quaeryt dismounted, handed the mare's reins to the ranker who rode forward to take them, and walked up toward the entrance.

One of the iron doors opened, and a muscular figure in blue and white livery stepped out to meet Quaeryt. "High Holder Chaffetz is not presently available, sir." The functionary glanced at Undercaptain Jusaph and the company drawn up along the gravel drive. "Would you be interested in talking with the steward?"

Quaeryt smiled politely. "I might send Major Heireg to see him, but my business is with the High Holder."

"Sir . . ."

"I don't believe that you offered me the chance to make myself clear. As the new governor of Montagne, I am here to see High Holder Chaffetz. If I find it difficult to see him, in turn, he will find it difficult to see me."

The man froze for a moment.

"It might be best if you looked more closely inside the holding to see if he might be found to be available." Quaeryt's voice was pleasant. "Oh . . . and since my wife accompanied me, perhaps the lady of the chateau might wish to meet her while I discuss various matters with the High Holder."

"I will inquire within, Governor, to see if I might have been mistaken. In the meantime, if you would care to enter . . ."

"I will wait. There is little point to entering if Lord Chaffetz cannot be found."

When the door closed behind the functionary, Quaeryt turned and walked back to where Vaelora remained mounted.

"If he does not find the High Holder, and quickly, he is more of an idiot than he first appeared," murmured Vaelora.

"It is clear that the post of governor here has not been what it should be. That is something we must remedy. Now . . . under the guise of chatter . . ."

"I'm to let slip who I am and that you are a longtime boyhood acquaintance of my brother," finished Vaelora.

"Exactly . . . and anything else that will quietly terrify his wife or daughter or whoever entertains you."

Vaelora just smiled.

Less than half a quint passed before the iron doors—both of them—opened, and a man and a woman appeared.

"Governor . . . Lady . . . welcome to Chaffhyem," declared the man, his voice a resonant tenor. "We had not expected you, or we certainly would have prepared a more appropriate welcome."

Quaeryt held out a hand for Vaelora to dismount. She did so gracefully, and delicately, rather than in the athletic and more powerful manner with which Quaeryt was most familiar. Then the two of them advanced.

"High Holder Chaffetz, I am Quaeryt, and this is my wife, the Lady Vaelora." Quaeryt could sense the puzzlement behind Chaffetz's polite smile as the High Holder took in Quaeryt's brown scholar's garb. "We arrived in Extela late on Mardi, and this is the first moment we have had to call on you. I do apologize for the suddenness, but I fear that you and I have matters of a less than routine matter to discuss. My wife prevailed on me to let her accompany me, and since it has been many years since she was last here, I had hoped that she and your lady might have a chance to become acquainted while we discuss more serious matters."

"Of course . . . of course. Do come in."

Quaeryt ignored Chaffetz's forced heartiness, and he and Vaelora followed the couple inside the chateau. He did keep light shields around them both, just in case, although he doubted that Chaffetz was likely to be hasty in any action.

Once inside, they stood in an entry hall some five yards wide and less than ten deep, with a polished floor of black stones set in white mortar. Beyond the entry hall was a grand staircase and, just before it, a corridor that ran the length of the chateau, one branch to the left, the other to the right.

"If you would accompany us . . ." Chaffetz gestured to the staircase.

"Thank you."

At the top of the wide staircase, also of black stone, if with balustrades of well-polished and ancient goldenwood, the High Holder's wife escorted Vaelora to the left.

Chaffetz led Quaeryt to the right, past two closed doors and to a third that was open to a long and narrow study. Only the side walls held floor-to-ceiling bookcases, and the wood was of old oak. There were three wooden armchairs, if with leather padded seats, around a small table at one end of the chamber, and a desk with a similar chair behind it at the other end. Chaffetz gestured to the table and took one of the chairs, seating himself easily and immediately. Quaeryt took the one that left the third chair between them.

"For a call of courtesy, Governor . . . ah . . ."

"Quaeryt." Quaeryt ignored the fact that Chaffetz had not offered any form of refreshment.

"Governor Quaeryt," Chaffetz continued smoothly, "I am surprised that you found it necessary to bring such . . . an entourage, and even your wife."

"As you may have heard, the lava rendered the old palace and the governor's quarters uninhabitable, and I thought my wife might appreciate seeing a place of more refinement than the senior officers' quarters at the south compound."

"Ah . . . yes." After the briefest hesitation, Chaffetz went on. "I don't believe I've ever known a governor who had your apparent . . . training."

"As a scholar? No. There have been few." None, in fact, of whom Quaeryt knew. "But Lord Bhayar felt my background would be useful here in dealing with the problems."

"Where were you before, if I might inquire?"

"I was princeps of Tilbor."

"Ah . . . that explains it. You have both knowledge and experience in dealing with supplies and disorder. Tell me. Have you known Lord Bhayar long? In a close personal sense, I mean? I can recall when he summered here as a youth." Chaffetz smiled warmly, but condescendingly.

"Not that long compared to some," replied Quaeryt thoughtfully, letting the silence draw out for several moments. "Fifteen or sixteen years. We had the same tutor in Solis. He was trained in warfare and politics. I was trained at sea and in scholarship." Every word he spoke was true, if not quite in the way he implied.

Chaffetz continued to smile, but Quaeryt sensed that the High Holder was far warier than he had been moments before.

"Might I ask . . . if you would not mind, what forces you brought—you did bring forces, did you not?—to restore and maintain order in Extela?"

"At present, we have two battalions. Within a few days we will have a full regiment." Quaeryt smiled. "We came ahead while the engineers were repairing the main bridge in Gahenyara."

"And what is this matter of less than routine that brings you to Chaffhyem?"

"Grain and supplies, both for the garrison and for the city."

"I am always most willing to supply both. Of course, in a time when both are difficult to find . . ." Chaffetz shrugged. "We all do what we must."

"I am most certain, and in complying with Lord Bhayar's commands, I will also do what I must. I am seeking several hundred barrels of flour and an equivalent amount of potatoes . . ."

"They can be had . . . of course . . . but I must insist on payment in hard coin."

"You will receive payment in such . . . but I do doubt that Lord Bhayar would be pleased with the term you used . . . that you must . . . insist."

"A figure of speech, surely."

"I understand that the winter price of flour was eight silvers a barrel."

"That was before the difficulties in Extela, Governor."

"So it was. So it was. And for that reason, I will buy four hundred barrels of flour from you at nine silvers a barrel . . . and the flour will be the best you have. As for the potatoes, I will buy five hundred bushels at five coppers for every two bushels."

Chaffetz's mouth dropped open. "Those terms are preposterous . . . Governor. When grain is so dear . . ."

"There are costs, and there are costs," Quaeryt said gently. "If people get so desperate that those remaining leave the city and seek food where they can find it . . . that will ravish the small holders who have no walls and armsmen. In turn, that will reduce the tariffs I will have to collect for years to come. I will, of course, have to explain to Lord Bhayar that the desire to extort exorbitant profits on the part of the High Holders was the cause of this disaster, and I am rather loath to do this. Nor do I wish to use soldiers against poor starving people. If that were to occur I would lose some soldiers and blacken Lord Bhayar's name."

"I feel for your position, Governor, but I must look to my future as well." Chaffetz smiled with false sympathy.

"I fear you do not understand. Your wife has been talking with mine, I believe. I suggest . . . in fact, I *insist* that you talk with your wife before you make any decisions you will regret."

"Governor . . . I must protest . . ."

"Talk to your wife." Quaeryt smiled coldly. "I will wait."

Once Chaffetz left the study, Quaeryt walked to the narrow second-level window nearest one of the ancient oak bookcases and glanced out. Behind the chateau was a walled and slightly sunken garden with paths edged with cut black stone and surfaced with glittering white gravel. A boxwood hedge maze was centered on a fountain depicting a partly draped woman above an empty fountain pool. While there were trimmed juniper and pfitzer topiary sculptures in places, most of the trees were deciduous and leafless.

At the sound of bootsteps on the marble of the corridor Quaeryt turned and waited for Chaffetz.

The High Holder closed the door and walked to the edge of the table. His face was flushed, and he was trembling ever so slightly, largely with suppressed rage, Quaeryt suspected.

Quaeryt waited.

"You . . . you have placed me . . . in a situation . . ."

"No . . ." replied Quaeryt. "Circumstances and Lord Bhayar have placed us both in difficult situations. I am offering you an eighth part more than you would have received for the flour had there been no disaster, and one part in four for the potatoes. I am not commandeering your goods—and that I could have done."

"I doubt—"

"Do not doubt. The regiment that I command fought and destroyed the hill holders of Tilbor, and the least of them had many times the armsmen you could muster. This is Lord Bhayar's ancestral homeland. He would not see it prostrate. Nor would I. Nor would he think you were being unduly harmed by taking an extra profit of one part in eight. The other High Holders will take the same terms."

"You leave me no choice." Chaffetz's voice was hard. "But Lord Bhayar will hear of this . . . high-handed effort."

"Times leave me no choice," Quaeryt replied. "Nor do I have time to bicker and bargain, not while people are starving."

"You will regret this . . . in time."

Quaeryt smiled and said warmly, "I do hope, for your sake, that it does not come to that." He smiled. "Now that we have settled that, we should join the ladies, don't you think?"

"You think, Governor . . ."

"No . . . High Holder, I know, and I know Lord Bhayar far better than do you. The last thing he wants is to be petitioned by a High Holder who is *only* making a significant profit, rather than an exorbitant one." Quaeryt gestured toward the study door. "We should talk with the ladies, and you can tell us all about your holding and about that magnificent walled garden I observed through the window."

"You don't . . ."

Quaeryt image-projected total self-assurance.

Chaffetz seemed to shrink where he stood. Then he took a slow breath. "I suppose that would be for the best."

Quaeryt had no doubts that Chaffetz would never forget or forgive, but then, the man would never have offered reasonable terms for his goods except in the face of greater power. That, he'd come to learn, was true of most High Holders.

Quaeryt and all but one squad of his entourage, as High Holder Chaffetz had termed it, left Chaffhyem at slightly after ninth glass and arrived before the more modest chateau of Aramyn by two quints past noon. The squad that had been detached, at Vaelora's suggestion, was stationed on the post road to intercept any messenger that Chaffetz might be sending to Solis. Quaeryt did not intend to stop any such message, merely to delay it, add a message of his own, and send it on its way, but with the regular post rider to Solis. If Chaffetz dispatched no messenger, Quaeryt would simply report on his acts and the responses of the High Holders. What he didn't want was an inaccurate and inflammatory letter going directly to Bhayar, not without the full story.

Aramyn's chateau was not of stone but of a yellowish red brick, and appeared to be far older than Chaffetz's hold. It sat on a low rise in the middle of a park, set in turn in the middle of a vast expanse of fields and a few meadows. Aramyn was better informed, inclined to be more hospitable, or had better trained functionaries, because Quaeryt and Vaelora were immediately invited inside and promptly joined by the High Holder and his wife.

Almost as quickly, Quaeryt found himself in a goldenwood-paneled study, whose shelves were crammed with books, standing talking with Aramyn, who showed little sign of offering a chair or wishing to seat himself. The High Holder had thinning black hair and a narrow face, with deep-set brown eyes separated by a straight thin nose. His forehead was furrowed, although his skin elsewhere was largely unwrinkled. Quaeryt judged him to be some fifteen or twenty years older than Quaeryt himself.

"Governor, I take it that this is not exactly a visit of courtesy, even with your wife accompanying you." Aramyn paused. "Her name—Vaelora. It is not exactly common. I can recall only one other woman by that name, although she was but a child of four or so the last time I cast eyes on her. Also, while you are certainly no stripling, you are on the young side to be appointed a regional governor."

"I'm arriving from the position of princeps of Tilbor."

"Most interesting, I must say. I take it that you were involved in the last battles against the hill holders."

"I was involved in the entire campaign and wounded in the final battle," Quaeryt admitted.

"I wondered. I notice you have a slight limp."

Quaeryt did not disabuse Aramyn's conclusion, but waited to hear what else the other had to say.

The older man smiled. "Even more interesting. A scholar who has seen battle and who has served as a princeps married to a woman named Vaelora. You are both fortunate and unfortunate, Governor."

"Might I inquire as to why you think so?"

"Much will be expected of you, in terms of accomplishment and loyalty. Perceived loyalty can often conflict with accomplishment. That has proved to be especially true, given the temperament of the descendants of Lhayar."

Quaeryt certainly couldn't disagree with Aramyn's assessment.

"What are you here to ask?"

"For you to sell me supplies—at the price of nine silvers a barrel for flour and five coppers for two bushels of potatoes."

Aramyn nodded. "You offer a modest profit. Might I ask why you are not commandeering those supplies?"

"I have no interest in forcing High Holders to pay to help others, since much of what I buy will help feed those left in Extela. I'd prefer that they not feel obligated to complain to Lord Bhayar." Quaeryt grinned. "And that, if they do, he can see that they have no cause for such."

"I will meet your terms, Governor. I have two requests, however. First, that you inform Lord Bhayar that I have done so without complaint." Aramyn paused. "It is no secret that my sire and Lord Bhayar's sire did not see eye to eye. I would wish that be laid to rest."

"And second?"

"The answer to a question. How did you ever persuade her to marry you?"

Quaeryt couldn't help but laugh. When he regained his composure, he replied, "I didn't. Bhayar commanded us both. He said that I needed to be tied more closely to him, and that she needed to be married to someone suited to her—and quickly, so that he could actually spend time ruling."

A broad smile crossed the lips of the High Holder. "Only someone trained as a scholar would be bright enough for her, from what I have heard. He must have known you well, then."

"We had the same tutor years ago, and I have served him, on and off, since then."

"How did you end up in Tilbor?"

"I made the mistake of saying I wasn't about to advise him on how to handle matters in Tilbor without having been there. He sent me." Quaeryt shrugged.

"So you are not afraid to tell him what he may not wish to hear?"

"I have my concerns, but I've been able to do so and survive."

"May you always do so." After the slightest hesitation, Aramyn said, "Let us determine how much flour and potatoes you require and when. Then we will join the ladies for refreshments . . . if you have time. I will also offer some to your soldiers."

"We do, and I believe Vaelora would enjoy that very much. I know I would."

In the end, Quaeryt and Vaelora did not return to the post until after third glass.

The squad dispatched to watch the south road returned to the post less than a quint before sunset, reporting that no one at all had been riding south.

Once they returned to the post, Quaeryt, Vaelora, and Jhalyt went to the strong room and counted out all the coins in the unlocked chest. It turned out that there were some coppers, and silvers, and the total came to 2,891 golds, 43 silvers, and 11 coppers. Quaeryt had the clerk enter that as the starting balance on the master ledger. The other chests could be counted later, and their balances added in, but given that Quaeryt would soon be paying out golds, he needed to keep track from the start.

Then he met with Meinyt about a possible Civic Patrol building. Meinyt reported that Captain Taenyd had found a vacant factorage not too far from the east bridge.

"Good. We can get started on fixing it and gathering the patrollers."

"It's not in the best part of town, sir," Meinyt pointed out.

"That's most likely where we'll need patrollers. Can you work out with Major Dhaeryn how to get some men to make it usable? We can post notices asking for workers."

"He'll have more than he'll want," replied the major dryly.

"That might well be, but we don't want troopers acting as civic patrollers any longer than necessary."

"No, sir."

After Meinyt left, Quaeryt found Jhalyt and Baharyt and gave them instructions, with Baharyt getting the task of finding out exactly where the patrol building-to-be was and coming up with a simple map so that Jhalyt could include it on the notices that would be posted.

After they left, Quaeryt just sat for several moments.

Should you have started with trying to reconstitute the Civic Patrol? He shook his head.

That would have been foolish until he knew how he would have to pay for it . . . or anything else. But . . . it still bothered him.

Later on Jeudi night, well after dinner, and after he'd filled Vaelora in on what else had happened, the two of them stood on the stone balcony of the officers' quarters, looking eastward where the two moons had lined up, one above the other, a symmetry that occurred so seldom that he could not recall the last time that had happened—and this time, the red-tinged half moon of Erion was above the half disc of the pearly-golden Artiema.

"What are you thinking now?" asked Vaelora.

"The moon of vengeance above the moon of love."

"Isn't that the way it's been throughout time?"

"I suppose it has been." He took a deep breath. "It's been a long day."

"You handle officers and troopers, patrollers, and repairs well enough. It's dealing with High Holders that you're not fond of, isn't it?"

"I'm not fond of dealing with some of them. Chaffetz will be a problem. Aramyn went out of his way to be helpful."

"So did his wife. I wish I knew why Grandpere and his sire did not get along."

"Lord Chayar, from what I've heard in many places, was a just and fair ruler, but not always the most subtle of men, and his reaction to slights was said to be . . . disproportionate."

"He did have a terrible temper, but he was good to me."

That's because you were still young and cute when he died.

"You're thinking that's because I was still a little girl, aren't you?"

"Yes." He shrugged helplessly.

"That's not disrespectful." After the briefest hesitation, she added, with a smile, "Not quite."

"Truth isn't disrespect, dear."

Vaelora glanced back at the moons. "No, it's not, but some see it as such. I've talked to Bhayar about that. After you and I were married, he said that one of the reasons he did it was because you and I both conveyed unpleasant truths to him, and we both deserved to be married to each other."

"He said that?"

"Close to word for word."

Quaeryt could imagine Bhayar almost gloating over his plan to marry Quaeryt and Vaelora.

"You were going to say something more about High Holders, weren't you?"

"Not that much. There were several in Tilbor who were not only intelligent, but honest and honorable. Most were intelligent, but so self-centered as to be a threat as a group to your brother."

"A group of self-centered High Holders couldn't act together enough to be a threat, could they? Or are you saying that because they only see things through their own eyes that their acts result in threats to Telaryn?"

"You say that so much more diplomatically than do I."

"In what way?"

"The same fashion as here. Chaffetz was not satisfied with profits with which he would have been more than pleased a year ago, even three months ago. I suspect some of the others will not be, either. They wish even greater profits. Were they granted such, that would mean fewer golds will be available to your brother at a time when Rex Kharst is threatening. Yet if he or I force them to sell for less or commandeer their crops, then they become even more of a problem. Their desire to enhance themselves regardless of the consequences increases the threat to all Telaryn . . . and if that greed weakens the land to the point where Kharst defeats your brother, then they also will suffer."

"Do you think that likely?"

"No. But it is possible, and they know it is possible—or they should—but each thinks only of himself, and feels that the other High Holders should be the ones to be reasonable." He took another deep breath. "Tomorrow, when we visit Wystgahl, matters will be no different, and that saddens me."

"It's too bad that you have to deal with them all at once."

"I have little choice. Dealing with them in a way that will not offend most of them would take weeks, if not months . . . and time is what we have little of. Even if I spent that time, some would still refuse to offer fair terms for supplies . . . unless threatened. That is the way it was in Tilbor, and I doubt it will be different here—except there the threats could be so much more indirect and there was time for them to be considered. Here . . . I fear that most of those High Holders I visit here will complain that I've not been fair . . . or suggest even worse."

"I know. Why do you think I suggested you post that squad as a patrol?"

"I had that feeling."

Vaelora turned to face him directly. "You need some rest."

"Rest?"

Even in the dim light, he could see her blush, but she did reach out and take his hand as they moved toward the door of their quarters.

While both Chaffetz and Aramyn had agreed that they would begin to send barrels of flour on Vendrei, nothing had arrived when Quaeryt and Vaelora departed the post at just before eighth glass to pay a call on High Holder Wystgahl. Quaeryt hadn't expected that the provisions would arrive that soon, but he had informed both Zhrensyl and Heireg to expect them, and made sure that both Jhalyt and Heireg would be present to remove any golds from the strong room to make payment.

Because Meinyt had suggested rotating companies, third company under Captain Taenyd escorted Quaeryt and Vaelora for the twelve-mille ride south.

The entire front of Wystgahl's hold appeared to have been recently rebuilt with a portico supported by white marble columns above polished black stone steps up from a marble paved area under the roofed portico for coaches and riders. The tall thin man who stood waiting on the black stone step just below the marble columns had wavy red hair with a few white streaks.

His slightly nasal voice carried easily to the riders as he said, "You must be the new governor. I'm Gahlen, High Holder Wystgahl's son."

"Quaeryt, and this is my wife Vaelora."

"Do come in. Father would like to meet you both." Gahlen's voice was pleasantly cool. "Captain, if you'd care to ride to the courtyard, there is water for you and your men there . . . and for your mounts."

Taenyd inclined his head politely. "Thank you."

Quaeryt dismounted, handed the reins to a ranker, then offered a hand to Vaelora, who left the saddle so lightly and gracefully that her boots barely touched the mounting block before she and Quaeryt walked up the black steps toward Gahlen, who led them through shimmering bronze double doors into a circular entry hall some fifteen yards across.

"This is new, is it not?" asked Vaelora.

"It was finished last year," replied Gahlen. "This way, if you will." He walked directly back from the entry, through another high-ceilinged chamber graced by a double staircase, and then down a wide hallway past several closed doors to the last doorway on the right, gesturing for them to enter the chamber, a salon with wide windows overlooking a walled garden.

High Holder Wystgahl rose from an armchair, placed so that all the other chairs and the pair of settees faced to where he had been seated. He was even thinner than his son, with sparse white hair above a wrinkled and ruddy, but unbearded face. His watery green eyes were bloodshot. "So . . . you are here to insist I sell you flour. Is that it? Even accompanied by your beautiful wife."

"Should I be evasive and diplomatic?" replied Quaeryt.

"You don't look the type. Besides, you won't last long enough to be diplomatic."

"Then I'll be as polite as I can. How did you find out I was looking for flour? Your holding is not that close to any others."

"I have heard of your visit to Chaffetz. Gahlen had taken a mare there early yesterday afternoon to be bred to one of his stallions. He passed your patrol as well."

That might have explained why Chaffetz hadn't dispatched a messenger, reflected Quaeryt. Then too, Chaffetz just might have thought the better of it.

"Chaffetz was less than pleased. Then, he seldom is. He was less displeased when he discovered you were clearly on your way to visit Aramyn. He took great pleasure in telling Gahlen that you would soon be visiting me. He's like that." Wystgahl offered a hoarse chuckle. "Aren't we all?" He turned his eyes on Vaelora. "You're much more beautiful than your mother or your sisters. Did you know that?"

"That may be now," replied Vaelora, "but I'm certain they were more beautiful when they were my age."

"That may be. That may be." Wystgahl turned to Quaeryt. "So you were princeps in Tilbor. You look young for that position, Governor."

Quaeryt smiled politely, and image-projected assurance. "That was Lord Bhayar's decision, based on what I accomplished."

"You fight in those battles?"

"Yes."

"How many men did you kill?"

"I lost count after the first few skirmishes."

"You're a scholar, and you fought? I find . . ." Wystgahl broke off his words. "Well . . . whatever is . . . is. It won't change anything. I'll sell at my price or not at all." He snorted. "Governors come and go. Sooner if they cross High Holders."

Quaeryt could sense that Wystgahl wasn't about to respect a man he felt was younger and inexperienced. This time he image-projected death . . . the way he'd seen and sensed it.

Gahlen stepped back . . . and Wystgahl, who had started to open his mouth, closed it.

After a moment Wystgahl nodded. "You studied with the scholars. They even pronounced you one. You're not. You're one of those southern sons who knows power and death. The less I see of you, Governor, the better. What do you want?"

"Three hundred barrels of flour at nine silvers a barrel, and four hundred bushels of potatoes at five coppers for every two bushels."

"You'll get what you asked for, Governor. I expect my man to be paid on each delivery. In coin."

Quaeryt sensed a sliminess behind the words, but that certainly wasn't anything he could address. "He will be."

"The first barrels will arrive at the post on Lundi. If there's nothing else . . . I wish you well on your ride back to Extela . . . or what's left of it."

"I appreciate your understanding of the situation, High Holder," replied Quaeryt politely. "We look forward to receipt of the flour and potatoes in good condition."

Wystgahl barely nodded, then turned to face the windows.

"If you would, Governor . . . Lady . . ." offered Gahlen, who did not say another word until they stood outside on the portico, waiting for Taenyd and third company.

"You must understand, Governor . . . at times . . . my sire is not quite what he might be." Gahlen spoke in a low tone.

"That can happen," said Quaeryt, his voice equally low. "I am but Lord Bhayar's instrument. Lord Bhayar would not wish Extela to suffer more than necessary because a High Holder does not like the idea of a young governor."

"I will do what I can, sir."

"As will I," replied Quaeryt evenly.

Gahlen stiffened. "He is old . . . sir."

"Then you must guide him."

"That is . . . not easy."

Quaeryt nodded. "I wish you well."

Gahlen watched as they mounted.

Vaelora said nothing until they had ridden out through the ornate stone and iron gates of the holding. Then she turned in the saddle. "He was insulting . . . and rude. Even his son was shocked."

"He's the kind that believes that any younger man in authority knows less than he does. Anything I said would have been disregarded. He won't even listen to his own son. He's probably threatened to disown Gahlen if he crosses him in any way."

"What will you do?"

"Nothing . . . if he keeps his word. I don't have to like him. He doesn't have to like me. He just has to be cooperative."

"He won't be."

"We'll have to see." Privately, Quaeryt had no doubt that Vaelora was right, but he wasn't about to act against a High Holder unless and until Wystgahl broke his word.

Quaeryt and Vaelora had no more than dismounted in the post courtyard when Major Heireg came hurrying toward him, followed by Jhalyt.

"Governor, we've got a hundred barrels of flour from High Holder Aramyn and fifty from High Holder Chaffetz. I paid them for what was delivered, as you instructed."

"Start baking bread," replied Quaeryt. "I'd like to have a thousand loaves by midmorning tomorrow."

"Sir . . . we'll run out of coal for the ovens before long at that rate."

"Coal shouldn't be that expensive now, should it?"

"No, sir," Heireg admitted.

"We'll also need a wagon set up to take the bread into Extela tomorrow."

"Yes, sir. We can do that . . . but . . . they'll overrun the teamsters. . . ."

"I'm not sending it without a large force. I'm well aware of how desperate some of the people are. Have you seen Major Meinyt or Major Fhaen?"

"They were in the officers' mess, sir."

"Good. Thank you. I appreciate what both you and Jhalyt are doing."

As the two men turned and left, Vaelora looked to her husband. "You're going to be busy. I'll be in our expansive quarters trying to wash up."

"I know. It's scarcely what you're—"

"Not another word, dearest. The quarters are far better than those inns . . . or sleeping on a hard wagon bed."

That might well be true, but Quaeryt still felt slightly guilty, which was probably what Vaelora had in mind, as he walked into the officers' mess.

Meinyt and Fhaen were sitting at the end of the long table talking.

Quaeryt quickly motioned for the two majors to keep their seats and took the chair next to Meinyt and across from Fhaen. "Do we know when to expect Commander Skarpa?"

"We received word that the rest of the regiment should arrive sometime late tomorrow. They had more trouble with the bridge in Gahenyara than they anticipated. The river had washed out most of the base of one of the stone piers, and they had to reinforce it before they could put the planks in place."

"Tomorrow, we're going to begin restoring order to Extela. We can't afford to wait until we have the Civic Patrol back on the streets." He paused. "Have the engineers started on repairs on the factorage?"

"Major Dhaeryn says they'll begin tomorrow. They found a mason and some helpers. He thinks they can keep the materials to less than ten golds."

"That's good."

"Yes, sir. Rather not have the men spending too much time riding the streets."

"That's why I didn't want to have you sending out more than a few patrols until we could provide some food as well."

"They'll still fight over the food," predicted Meinyt.

"No . . . they won't. We'll take enough men to protect the wagon, and we'll make everyone line up if they want the bread. We'll have men every ten yards in each area, and they'll have orders to stop anyone who tries to steal from those given bread. If they have to kill a thief, so be it."

"People won't like that."

"If we don't do it, then whoever gets food will likely be robbed or end up killing those who try to rob them. Oh . . . I'll be with you, and I'll make an announcement first about how things will work."

"That will help . . . for about a quint," replied Meinyt.

"Then I'll make it again after we make an example of someone, as many times as we have to. I just hope it doesn't happen too often."

"You do have a way of persuading people, sir, " offered Meinyt, "but still . . ."

"I know. It won't be easy, but it won't get easier, either, especially if we wait any longer. But if we establish order that way, the Civic Patrol, once it's back on the streets, shouldn't have quite so much trouble."

"I hear we've already gotten more supplies," said Fhaen. "How did you manage that?"

"I just told them that Lord Bhayar wouldn't be very happy if they tried to profit excessively when his ancestral home had been prostrated . . . and that I'd make sure he knew it, if it came to that."

"That won't make you popular with the High Holders, sir."

"No. But I'd rather have them unhappy than have Bhayar being the unhappy one." *Especially now and in his ancestral home.*

Meinyt gave a sardonic laugh. "That's being caught between lava and a flood."

Quaeryt didn't dispute that.

In the end, on Samedi morning, Quaeryt decided to take twenty bushels of potatoes along with all the bread that the bakers had turned out and, just in case someone wanted it, two barrels of flour. The column left the post later than Quaeryt had planned, partly because he had to draw out golds for Major Dhaeryn for the Civic Patrol building repairs and go over the notices to the former patrollers with Jhalyt. Even so, it was just before eighth glass before they reached the point on the avenue a mille north of the post gates, where the dwellings began to cluster together—what most would have called the southern edge of the city proper. The two majors and Quaeryt had determined that he and Meinyt and the troops would ride to the south market square first, where they would surround the wagon and then let small numbers of people walk inside the perimeter of mounted troopers to the wagon to get bread . . . and potatoes, if they wanted them.

As he rode beside Meinyt, with a company directly behind them, followed by the heavily laden wagon, flanked by men with bare sabres, and then by another company, Quaeryt could see that the sky over Mount Extel was clearer than it had been since he had arrived, and the air was cool, but not chill. The patrols that he had sent out on the previous days appeared to have had some impact, because the sidewalks were largely swept clear of ash, although the occasional puffs of cool wind blew ashes off the slate roofs. There were a few people—invariably men—moving about, if with deliberate caution. Some second-story windows were unshuttered, but most ground-floor shutters remained fastened.

"How many do you think will come out?" asked Meinyt.

"Very few to begin with. Then we're likely to be swamped, and that's when the trouble will begin." As a boy in Solis, Quaeryt had seen how mobs behaved . . . and later as an apprentice quartermaster when his ship had docked in Liantiago during the rice riots there.

"That's the way I see it. The men will be ready for anything. Told 'em that things would start slow."

A gray-faced woman with stringy hair scuttled along the stone sidewalk, trying to keep pace with Quaeryt, who wondered from where she'd appeared so suddenly. "Food! Food . . . please, sir!"

"We'll be providing bread at the south market square," Quaeryt called out. "The south market square. If you want food, meet us there!"

On the other side of the avenue, beyond Meinyt, an old man cackled. "Food . . . they got food."

People began to appear, staying well clear of the armed troopers, but following the column and the wagon toward the square.

"Word spreads fast," observed Meinyt.

"Especially if they think they don't have to pay for it. That's why we're only doing this once. On Lundi, we'll be selling bread, flour, and potatoes in both the main market square and the south market square at the same prices as before the trouble."

"Some folks will be unhappy that it won't be free," said Meinyt.

"Some are always unhappy, and that includes High Holders as well as the poor," replied Quaeryt dryly. "We'll give out some bread to women with children, maybe outside the post gates, and from a wagon when we're selling." He paused. "Do you think your squad leaders will have trouble keeping it to ten at a time?"

"There don't look to be as many as there could be. I told them not to hesitate to use their blades, flat side if they can, edge if they can't. Can't let a mob get out of control."

More than several hundred people were already waiting when the wagon, surrounded by two companies of armed troopers, pulled into the center of the square.

As Meinyt supervised the deployment of troopers in a perimeter around the wagon square, Quaeryt rode over to the squad leader in charge of distributing the food. "You set, Squad Leader?"

"Yes, sir."

"I'd like you to pass the word to everyone who gets food. They can buy bread, flour, and potatoes . . ." Quaeryt repeated what he'd told Meinyt. "We won't be passing out much free food after today, and they need to know that."

"Sir?"

"We'll still give some to women with infants, but we can't feed the whole city, even part of the city. Not for long. We will keep the prices as they were."

"Yes, sir. We'll tell 'em."

"Thank you."

Making sure his shields were firm, Quaeryt rode out through the troopers on the west side of the square and reined up. Using his imaging, he did his best to project the words he'd already discussed with Meinyt. "We'll let a few of you at a time past the troopers, and we'll start with women and children. We'll start with you." He pointed toward a woman with two children, one in her arms, and one who clung to her free hand. "No more than ten. No one else gets past here until someone leaves. Every time a person leaves, someone else gets in."

Then he rode to the north side, the east, and then the south, delivering the same message, before returning to a position near the wagon, but from where he could observe both those approaching the wagon and those in the square beyond the troopers.

After watching for more than a quint, Quaeryt was surprised that while groups of men gathered beyond the square, some of them gathering and then separating, there were no efforts to break the perimeter. Nor did any of the men attempt to attack others—not within sight of the troopers. Most people who received food made a show of eating it inside the perimeter, although Quaeryt noted that more than a few women surreptitiously hid bread in their garments. He could also see that almost all the women also accepted the potatoes, and several had bags that they used to take flour.

The first woman he'd pointed to took her time feeding her children. Quaeryt didn't see her take a bite herself. He called out. "Squad Leader!"

"Sir?"

"Give another loaf to her." He pointed to the tired-faced woman.

The woman looked up as one of the rankers vaulted down and extended another loaf to her. Then she looked to Quaeryt. Her face showed nothing, but he thought there might be a brightness to her eyes before she took a bite out of the second loaf. *Then, it just might be your imagination.*

Almost a glass and a half passed before Quaeryt noted that people were trying to get back inside the perimeter for seconds. He signaled Meinyt that they needed to move on.

When the two companies re-formed around the wagon, and the column headed north along the avenue to the main market square, Quaeryt watched several of the men begin to follow. "That crew over there is following us."

Meinyt turned and looked. "They know they can't break the perimeter without taking casualties."

"You think they'll try a diversion."

"It's possible."

"Maybe I'll drop back to ride alongside the wagon."

"I've already got it flanked, sir."

"I know. But it can't hurt."

Quaeryt did slip the half-staff from its leathers, although he couldn't have said why, as he eased to the west side of the avenue and let the teamster catch up with him before matching his pace to that of the high-sided wagon.

Immediately north of the south market square, there were only a few people on the streets, and all those appeared to be hurrying away . . . except for the small group of men on the east side of the avenue who kept pace with the wagon.

After riding several blocks more toward the center of Extela, Quaeryt saw a group, almost a small crowd, ahead on the west side of the avenue. When they saw the column and the wagon, they began to cry out.

"Food! We need food!"

"All the food is gone . . ."

"Food . . ."

As he rode closer, he saw that the group looked to be composed entirely of women, many with scarves covering their hair and faces, especially those at the sides and rear of the crowd. Quaeryt frowned. He hadn't seen women crowded together so closely in Extela. Still . . . he'd only ridden the streets less than a handful of times.

"Please . . . food . . ."

"We're starving . . ."

He looked at the thronging women again. Only the ones in front had their heads uncovered, and most of them were young . . . and relatively attractive. They didn't look to be starving, unlike the gaunt older women who had trudged into the south market square, or even the tired-looking women with babes in arms who had taken bread and seated themselves on the stones and fed their children right in the square.

"Please . . . kind sir," begged a young woman, barely more than a girl, for all of the cleavage she let show as she turned to face the approaching governor.

Quaeryt glanced away from her toward the women with covered faces and hair, then immediately called out, "Arms ready!" He knew that the troopers already had their sabres out, but he didn't know the short command to alert them to an imminent attack.

Abruptly, the younger women dropped back, and the hooded "women" rushed toward the wagon and the troopers. There were also shouts on the other side of the avenue, but Quaeryt barely had time to bring down his staff on the sword arm of a burly man whose hood had fallen back as he rushed toward the ranker in front of Quaeryt. The ranker was already dealing with another attacker and didn't see or sense the second man.

Then an impact triggered his shields, and he turned in his saddle to strike at another assailant. No more than had he slammed the half-staff across the man's forearm, dislodging the blade, than both the women and the attackers fled down an alleyway less than three yards away. Quaeryt thought that the second attacker he'd struck was cradling an injured arm.

Abruptly, the avenue was empty except for the troopers and their equipment . . . and two women lying half on the sidewalk and half on the west side of the avenue and two men facedown on the street, one in a pool of blood.

Quaeryt rode around the rear of the wagon, slowed to almost a halt, to see another body on the stone pavement, and two troopers tying up a man with slashes on his arms and blood running from his scalp.

The dead man on the pavement wore a stylish and tight-fitting silk jacket. Quaeryt couldn't help but stare for a moment, then looked up as Meinyt rode up.

Quaeryt pointed to the dead man. "Quite a coat."

"Pimp's jacket," said Meinyt. "Haven't seen one of those in years."

"That can't be why they put the women up to it. I can't believe that they were starving."

"Most likely they weren't. I wager they thought there was coin in the wagon."

"Why?"

"Sometimes, when times were hard, the governors in some provinces would toss coppers and silvers along with the bread. You looked like you might be doing the same thing. The whole city probably knows you recovered the treasury."

"Do you think they'll try again?"

"You never know. I doubt it. They got close enough to the wagon to see that the barrel was a flour barrel, not one filled with coppers."

Quaeryt had never thought about the fact that someone would think he was going to toss coins to the crowds. He shook his head. "Toss the wounded one in the wagon for now." Glancing back, he could see that one of the fallen women had either gotten away or been dragged off. The other one's head was twisted at an odd angle that indicated she was dead. "Put the dead woman in the wagon. Leave the dead men."

"You heard the governor," said Meinyt, adding in a lower voice, "Good idea. The men's bodies will remind them."

Neither mentioned the fact that they didn't want to leave a dead woman, especially a young one, lying on the street.

While a few people watched from windows, no one approached the column or the wagon closely for the rest of the way to the main market square . . . or even immediately after Meinyt stationed the troopers into a tight perimeter around the wagon.

Given the momentary quiet, Quaeryt rode to the wagon to see what he could discover from the wounded captive, who, he noted, wore a tight-fitting jacket similar to that of one of the dead men.

"Who ordered the attack?" asked Quaeryt.

"Frig you," muttered the captive.

The ranker holding the man's left arm twisted it. The captive winced, but didn't speak.

"He won't say anything," said Meinyt, who had just reined up. "If he does, the others will kill him, and it won't be pleasant."

Quaeryt smiled coldly. "Then I think we should carry him outside the perimeter, cut him free, and thank him very publicly."

The wounded man swallowed.

"Of course, if he has something to say, we could take him back to the post, lock him up for a time, and then let him go some night."

". . . tell you . . . not here."

"We'll have to take him back, then," Quaeryt said.

"FRIG YOU!" screamed the captive, winking as he did.

Quaeryt didn't like it, but he understood. He also hadn't said where he'd release the captive. He nodded to the ranker holding the captive, then turned the mare and rode out near the perimeter, where, now that a few older women had gathered, he made the same statement he had at the southern market square.

After a slow beginning, the process of handing out bread and potatoes in the main market square went almost in the same fashion as it had at the south square, with the exception that not nearly so many men stood around looking on. Of the few handfuls who did, Quaeryt wondered how many, if any, had been in disguise in the group that had been part of the diversion in the attempted attack on the wagon. Were they looking for another opportunity . . . or waiting to see what happened to the captive?

In the end, though, the men drifted away, except for one, who kept looking at the wagon where the captive sat, trussed up.

After another glass and two quints, Quaeryt ordered Meinyt to re-form the column and head back to the post. While several handfuls of people watched them ride back southward, no one approached, and no one begged.

The first thing that Quaeryt noticed when he entered the courtyard of the post was that the anomen was unlocked, the ancient oak doors had been oiled, and the brasswork polished . . . and that Vaelora stood by the door, smiling, along with three rankers. Her riding clothes were smudged and stained in places.

Quaeryt rode across the courtyard and dismounted, then tied the mare to one of the ancient hitching rings.

The rankers eased away.

"I see you've been busy."

"They did most of the work, but I knew what had to be done and how to do it."

Quaeryt raised his eyebrows.

"Did you think that Father would train his son and not train his daughters?"

"But why?" Quaeryt's voice held far more exasperation than curiosity.

"I can explain . . . I can . . ."

At that point both Heireg and Commander Zhrensyl strode quickly across the courtyard toward the two of them.

"Governor!" called Zhrensyl. "The rest of your regiment will be here by fourth glass."

"I've got the cooks ready to feed them. Do you know how many?" asked Heireg.

"The entire regiment is four battalions of four companies each, with an extra company of engineers. All the battalions are mounted."

"No archers?" Zhrensyl's eyebrows lifted. "No foot?"

"Governor Straesyr's predecessor in Tilbor only had a company of archers. They were dispatched to Lord Bhayar with the first regiment to leave Tilbor. Another two companies are being trained, but they weren't ready. They'll come with the next regiment. The northern regiments don't have foot."

"The next regiment? I thought there was only one regiment in Tilbor, two at the most. How many were there in Tilbor?"

Abruptly, Quaeryt realized that Zhrensyl wouldn't have known, because Commander Myskyl had taken the southern route to Ferravyl, and there was no reason for Bhayar to have circulated what had actually happened in Tilbor. "Governor Rescalyn had been expanding the regiment there in order to train more recruits. That was because of the possibility of trouble with Bovaria."

All of that was true, if not quite in that context. "Governor Straesyr has been continuing that effort."

"You'd think they'd let us know."

"It could be that Lord Bhayar didn't want Rex Kharst to know until the men were trained and battle-ready. He certainly never explained his reasons to me."

Zhrensyl shook his head. "Don't know what this world's coming to, Governor." He smiled. "But we'll do our best."

"I'm sure you will, and I appreciate it. So does Lord Bhayar."

"Thank you, sir." Zhrensyl looked to Vaelora. "And thank you, Lady. The anomen hasn't looked that good in years." He offered her a broad smile, then looked back to Quaeryt. "Quite a lady you have, Governor."

"She is quite a lady, but I'm not so sure that she's not the one who has me."

"Either way, you're both fortunate, sir."

After the two officers had left, Quaeryt turned back to Vaelora. "I believe you were going to explain."

"Dearest . . . I really am a mess." She gestured to her soiled garb. "I'll explain, but I don't want to look like this for you and for the other officers. Besides, you need to take care of that poor mare."

Quaeryt sighed. Loudly.

"Dearest . . . you don't want to be disrespectful . . ." She offered a warm smile.

He shook his head.

"I'll be ready for dinner." With another smile, she hurried across the courtyard.

Quaeryt watched her for a moment, then untied the mare and walked her to the stable. While he turned her over to one of the ostlers to be unsaddled and groomed, he didn't get more than a few yards from the stable before Major Heireg requested more of his time, both to update him on the supplies they had received from Aramyn and Chaffetz, and to talk about coal, the supplies requested by the engineers, and provisions for the rest of the regiment. Then Quaeryt quickly checked the ledger entries posted by Jhalyt.

By the time Quaeryt finished with Jhalyt, Skarpa was leading Third Regiment through the post gates. Settling the additional battalions in took the remainder of the time before the evening meal, and Quaeryt barely had time to wash up himself and then escort Vaelora to the officers' mess.

After everyone finished eating, Vaelora excused herself quickly, leaving Skarpa and Quaeryt alone so that the commander could brief Quaeryt on what had occurred on the remainder of the ride to Extela. Quaeryt did wonder why she was being so accommodating, but suspected that she knew he was upset about the anomen and didn't want to cause any more friction, especially in public.

He couldn't help but wonder, then realized he'd missed what Skarpa had been saying. "Excuse me. Would you say that again?"

"Governor . . ." Skarpa said gently, "I asked if you wanted to wait until tomorrow."

"Oh, no . . . you might as well go over it now."

"You got the dispatch about the problems with the bridge at Gahenyara?"

"I did. I didn't mean to leave you with that much."

"You couldn't have done anything more there, sir. From what we saw coming in here, you've had plenty to deal with."

"We have indeed. Do you think the engineers can improve the east bridge?"

"They were already talking about that," said Skarpa with a laugh. "They'll manage. Anyway, we had more trouble with the wagons coming into Montagne. The rain we got flooded everything. Between the rain and the wagons, we lost two days. . . ."

Quaeryt nodded and kept listening as the commander briefed him on all that had happened to the bulk of the regiment.

When Skarpa finished, he looked directly at Quaeryt. "Like I said earlier, sir, looks like you've got your hands full."

More than that. "About a quarter of the city's buried in ash and lava. We distributed bread and potatoes today . . . and some flour." In less than half a quint, Quaeryt explained what had happened, including the missing Civic Patrol and the possible problems with the various High Holders and the fact that he hadn't even dealt with all of them.

"They're like that everywhere, most of them, it seems."

"Oh . . . do you have any other problems I need to deal with? Ones that I can do something about?" Quaeryt kept his voice light, trying to be humorous.

"Well . . . there is one," mused Skarpa. "And it's something you could do easily, sir, seeing as tomorrow is Solayi . . . and there's an anomen in good repair right here on the post."

No! Not again . . . But Quaeryt said nothing, knowing that any words that slipped out he would regret.

"Some of the officers, and a lot of the men . . . well . . . they saw all the destruction . . . They'd like a little reassurance."

"Comfort from the Nameless," Quaeryt managed to say.

"Yes, sir. I know it's not something you like to make a practice of, sir . . ."

"I don't know the service that well, but if they'll all bear with me . . ." Quaeryt shrugged helplessly. "I'm not a chorister."

"Everyone would appreciate it, sir."

"So long as they understand . . ."

"Sir . . . they understand."

Quaeryt took a long, last swallow of the bitter lager from his mug. "I suppose I'd better let you get to your officers and get some sleep in a decent bed." He stood.

So did Skarpa. "That'd be good. Really good."

Quaeryt walked slowly across the darkness of the courtyard to the officers' quarters and then up the staircase and along the balcony. The door bolt on their quarters was not thrown, and he opened the door, stepped inside, and slid the bolt. Vaelora rose from where she'd been sitting at the writing desk. Although her portable inkwell and a pen were on the desk, the single sheet of paper was blank.

"You're upset, dearest. What happened? Did Commander Skarpa lose men in another flood? Did another bridge go out?"

"You had to clean up the anomen, didn't you?" he asked quietly.

"It needed to be done," she replied.

"Why? Was it another vision?"

Vaelora stiffened ever so slightly. "Yes. If you must know. I saw you standing at the pulpit. Why do you ask?"

"Because Skarpa asked if I'd conduct services tomorrow." He shook his head.

Vaelora was silent.

"If the anomen were still locked . . ."

She nodded gently.

"But it's not . . . You *know* how I feel!"

"Then don't do it."

"I can't not do it. They need the services. There's no one else who can do it. Some of them, maybe a lot of them, are likely to die for Bhayar if it comes to war with Bovaria. And I'm going to complain about having to talk and inspire them?" *When you feel like a fraud doing it in an anomen?*

"I'm sorry, dearest."

"I don't want to talk about it right now." *Not when I'm so angry I might say something hurtful or that I might later regret.* Recalling what she'd said about not having secrets, he added, "I will later, but not now."

"Try not to be too angry . . ."

Her voice was so woeful that he stopped short, then realized that she was exaggerating the tone to excess, and he found himself grinning, even as he recognized the blatantness of her words and expressions. He shook his head. "No wonder . . ."

"Not another word, dearest."

He decided that was probably for the best—for the moment.

27

Quaeryt didn't sleep well on Samedi evening, between being upset over being maneuvered into acting as a chorister once more and worrying about how he was ever going to restore order and function to Extela, not to mention his unease about whether he had been unfairly angry at Vaelora, although he'd tried not to show it. Then too, he'd always been uncomfortable acting as a chorister for the Nameless when he had no idea whether there even was a Nameless.

On Solayi morning, his first thought upon wakening was, *If there is a Nameless out there, that Nameless has got quite a sense of humor.* The thought helped, but not much, as he and Vaelora readied themselves for the day. He was just glad she didn't press him to talk about why he'd been so angry; yet relieved as he was, he also wondered at her forbearance, because in the short time they'd been married, she'd always pressed to talk out matters when they disagreed.

Even so, she was pleasant at breakfast and later, as they readied to ride out.

Fhaen's second company escorted Quaeryt and Vaelora back across the rickety and makeshift bridge to the east side of the river and then south and east to the lands of High Holder Thysor. While Quaeryt had hoped Thysor would be available, given that it was a Solayi, the High Holder was out inspecting his timberlands to the south, and Quaeryt merely left a note saying that he hoped that they might be able to meet at some time during the coming week.

When they returned to the post, Quaeryt met with Major Dhaeryn of the engineers. Work had begun on modifying the old factorage, and the plans were complete for rebuilding the bridge, although Dhaeryn asked for permission to use stones from buildings in the northwest that had been badly damaged by the earthquakes and eruption. Quaeryt agreed, but only for buildings that were complete ruins.

Then he met again with Heireg to work out the arrangements for selling goods in the marketplaces on Lundi . . . and asked him to work with Jhalyt to set up payroll and supply ledgers for the Civic Patrol.

What with one thing and another, before he knew it, they were eating dinner, and then he was walking across the courtyard to the anomen, escorting Vaelora in and settling her at one side before he repaired to the rear chamber to wait until the bells rang the hour.

At that moment, he stepped out, walked to the middle of the dais that held the pulpit, then turned and faced the worshippers. The small anomen was filled, possibly with three hundred officers and men.

Quaeryt didn't even attempt the wordless invocation used by all true choristers to open a service. He just started with the greeting. "We gather together in the spirit of the Nameless and to affirm the quest for goodness and mercy in all that we do."

Following came the opening hymn, and the only one that Quaeryt knew by heart—that he could trust himself to sing—was "Glory to the Nameless." Thankfully, Vaelora knew it as well, and after the first phrase, he let her voice lead those in the anomen.

After that came the confession, which was one of the hardest parts of the service for Quaeryt, given that he was leading a confession of error to a deity he wasn't certain existed. Although he had no trouble confessing to error, only to the idea that he and those who followed his words would be forgiven by the Nameless, he'd observed precious little forgiveness in life, and wondered of what use it would be elsewhere, if there indeed happened to be an "elsewhere."

"We name not You, for naming presumes, and we presume not upon the Creator of all that was, is, and will be. We pray not to You for ourselves, nor ask from You favor or recognition, for such asks You to favor us over others who are also Yours. We confess that we risk in all times the sins of presumptuous pride. We acknowledge that the very names we bear symbolize those sins, for we strive too often to raise our names and ourselves above others, to insist that our small achievements have meaning. Let us never forget that we are less than nothing against Your Nameless magnificence and that we must respect all others, in celebration and deference to You who cannot be named or known, only respected and worshipped."

Quaeryt did lead the chorus of "In Peace and Harmony."

Before the offertory began, he announced, "The coins gathered in the offertory will be used to help poor mothers with children in Extela." *And Vaelora will decide who deserves such coins.*

Finally the time came for him to ascend to the pulpit for the homily, but he decided against that and merely stood on the middle of the platform holding the pulpit. Absently, he wondered if that meant he'd end up doing it all again, given Vaelora's vision of him at the pulpit. He cleared his throat and began. "Good evening."

"Good evening," came the murmured reply.

"Under the Nameless all evenings are good, even those that seem less than marvelous . . . and after seeing the devastation that lies to the north of us, we can all agree that there are some evenings that definitely seem less than wonderful . . ." Quaeryt paused just slightly before continuing. "Often we face daunting tasks, such as the ones that lie before us, and someone will say that all we need is faith and that we will prevail in whatever endeavor we must undertake. But what is faith? All throughout my life, I've heard choristers and others speak of faith, without ever explaining what faith might be except a belief in the Nameless, as if that were all I needed to know. Since the Nameless has not chosen to appear before us in any manifestation that one could call absolute proof, that faith is a belief in the Nameless without obvious proof. Another definition of faith is simply allegiance or fidelity, and yet another is confidence in another as being worthy of trust. From all these definitions, two things stand out as necessary elements of faith. We must have something in which to believe and what we believe must be worthy of our trust. If you will, faith is composed of belief and trust in the worth of that belief.

"There have been many deities worshipped throughout Terahnar over the past thousands of years, and I have no doubt that you have heard of at least a few of them in the course of your lives. Since it appears that the majority of men and women believe in something beyond themselves, what is most important is whether we can trust the guidance of our belief. Belief in itself is not enough. That belief must go beyond mere acknowledgment of the belief and its teachings.

"All of you are soldiers, and how well you fight the next battle or undertake the next duty depends in large measure on those who guide you and lead you, or if you're an officer, whether you make good decisions and whether your men have the faith necessary to follow you. Good officers and squad leaders inspire faith in their men, and good rankers inspire faith in their comrades.

"The Nameless is no different in that respect. What inspires faith is not just the fact of the Nameless, but the equally important fact that the guidance of the Nameless represents good counsel that can be trusted . . . if . . . IF . . . that counsel is followed without Naming, and without self-serving desires and motivations.

"What follows from this is the need to know what one believes, not just that it is, but what it means, and what it requires of us. We must understand fully what Naming is, and that is not just acting on or against mere names of things, but seeing how names hide the true nature of the world and those who inhabit it . . ."

After a few more sentences on Naming, Quaeryt concluded the short homily. ". . . in the end, faith requires knowledge, for without knowledge, blind belief is little more than Naming under the guise of worshipping the Nameless."

For a moment after he finished, he just stood there, before remembering that he had to lead the closing hymn and give the benediction. He chose one of the few closing hymns he knew almost by heart—"For the Glory"

For the glory, through all strife,
for the beauty of all life,
for all that is and will ever be,
all together, through forever,
in eternal Nameless glory . . .

He couldn't do the standard benediction, well as he knew it, because that would have, for him, presumed too much. He simply said, "As we have come together to seek meaning and renewal, let us go forth this evening renewed in hope and in harmony with that which was, is, and ever shall be."

After the benediction, he stepped down from the platform and walked to where Vaelora stood against the side wall, with Skarpa beside her.

"I still say you'd make a chorister, Governor," said the commander.

"You're kind. Let's leave it at that."

Skarpa snorted. "I'm not kind, and you know it. If you'd talked nonsense up there, I'd have told you." He glanced sideways at Vaelora and grinned. "So would your wife, I'd wager."

"She has been known to speak her mind." Quaeryt couldn't help smiling.

Vaelora smiled back.

"I'll be leaving you two, sir and Lady, and wishing you a pleasant evening." With that Skarpa nodded and departed.

"It is true," said Vaelora. "I have been known to speak my mind, but . . . did you have to tell him that?"

"I didn't. I just agreed with him."

"That just—"

"Might *not* be disrespect," Quaeryt concluded quickly.

"Sometimes . . ." But she smiled.

Once they returned to their quarters and Quaeryt had thrown the bolt, Vaelora turned to him and said quietly, "You were wonderful, dearest."

"Thank you." Quaeryt took a deep breath. "You know I don't like doing it."

"You like doing it. You like inspiring people and challenging them to think. What you don't like is feeling like a fraud because you're not sure that there even is a Nameless. You worry that you're doing good things under what are false pretenses." Vaelora stepped up to him and put her arms around his neck, then kissed him gently on the cheek. "I understand, dearest. I do."

There's something in her tone . . . "You do?"

"Women have to do it all the time."

"Even you?"

"Especially me . . . or Aelina. She has to do it even more."

Quaeryt couldn't argue with that. The impositions that scholars had to deal with were nothing compared to what women put up with in Telaryn, and from what he'd heard and read, women were treated far worse in Bovaria and Antiago. And he was all too aware that women had often had to do what they disliked for love of others . . . or even survival.

Vaelora moistened her lips. "I have to confess . . . Please don't be angry with me."

"Confess what?" he asked warily.

"I didn't have any visions about the anomen. It just looked . . . forlorn . . . and lonely, and then when I saw the faces of some of the men . . . when we cleaned it up . . ."

"Vaelora . . ." Quaeryt's voice held exasperation . . . and a touch of anger, he had to admit.

"Did you see the faces of the officers and the men when they left the anomen tonight?"

"I was looking at you," he admitted.

"They felt better. I could see it and sense it."

"Your Pharsi background?"

"You'd have seen it, too, if you'd looked." She dropped her eyes for a moment before lifting them to him again. "I am sorry . . . but . . . you need to do this. Not for me, not for you . . ."

"But for them?" He shook his head. "Why do you think it upsets me? They need that reminder of their faith, and there doesn't seem to be anyone else . . ."

"Do you think all the soldiers like killing?"

"Some do. I'd say most don't."

"But they do it because it's their duty."

"You're telling me that . . ."

"Yes, dearest. I am."

He couldn't argue with that. Unlike others, Vaelora had seen that kind of duty, or possibly the lack of it. After a moment he put his arms around her and just held her.

Her arms went around him, comfortingly.

On Lundi morning, under a clear sky, if with the slightest trace of haze, Vaelora departed with the companies that would be selling bread, flour, and potatoes, first at the south market square and then at the main square. Skarpa insisted on three companies, given that Vaelora was accompanying them, and put Meinyt in command.

Immediately after that, Quaeryt joined Major Dhaeryn, and they rode with some of the engineering rankers to the factorage that would soon be a Civic Patrol station.

One way or the other.

The southeast section of Extela was definitely the rougher part of the city, with older houses, some of brick, some of weathered wood, but most of the black stone that had to be ancient lava, with small areas of shops, and a tired feel to every street. Still, he did see a few people about, and many the dwellings were unshuttered, and even a few of the shops.

But then, where do these people have to go?

The empty factorage, like many structures in Extela, was of a single level, built of rough-trimmed black stone, with a slate roof. Quaeryt judged that it was thirty yards across the front, and perhaps twenty deep, with a wagon courtyard on the south side, where there was a single loading dock. Two men, not rankers, were replacing cracked and broken roof slates as Quaeryt and Dhaeryn reined up in front.

"The doors are heavy enough," offered the major, dismounting.

Quaeryt dismounted and tied the mare to the hitching rail, a worn pole suspended between two black stone posts.

"I got the masons to start yesterday, after we cleaned out all the junk and stacked it in the side courtyard. Walls are solid, but the place was filthy." The major shook his head. "I've got a couple of rankers who are good with wood, and they're setting up the front the way we drew it. It's like the patrol stations in Estisle, because that's what I remember."

Quaeryt looked to the major.

"My uncle was a patroller."

Once inside, Quaeryt glanced around. Two rankers had already framed what looked to be a counter with a built-in desk.

"That'll be a receiving desk. It also keeps a wall between the duty patroller and trouble. We'll need to put heavy doors in this archway . . ."

Quaeryt listened as he followed the engineering major, and as Dhaeryn explained.

". . . and this is the storage area I told you about. I've got the masons building twenty cells here. For now, we'll have to use double-thick doors with peepholes."

"We can only do what we can."

"Sirs?"

Quaeryt and Dhaeryn turned.

"There's a patroller in uniform outside, sir," said the approaching ranker engineer. "He wants to talk to the new chief patroller."

"Tell him I'll be out in a moment," said Quaeryt.

"Yes, sir." The ranker turned and hurried back through the archway.

"I was wondering if there were any patrollers left," said Quaeryt.

"Probably they lost everyone at the top. You lose too many officers or the like, and some outfits just fall apart."

That might have been, but Quaeryt had to wonder. "I'd better go talk to him." He walked back outside, checking his shields before he left the building.

The patroller who waited wore a gray uniform with black belt and boots, and a visor cap with a black leather bill. He was burly and a few digits taller than Quaeryt.

"You were looking for the patrol chief?" asked Quaeryt, stopping a yard from the man.

"Sir . . . begging your pardon . . ." The patroller looked curiously at Quaeryt's browns. "Are you the new patrol chief?"

"No. I'm the new governor. I don't know what happened to the old chief, but I assume he's dead or fled. The patrol building's buried in ash and lava. So I'm having the engineers convert this building for patrol use. We don't have the time or golds to build a new one. And you are?"

"Jaramyr, patroller first, sir. There's maybe thirty-five of us left. The others put me up to finding out what was going to happen." Jaramyr glanced to the roof, and then to the open doors.

"You're the most senior?"

"One of the most senior, sir. There are eight of us who are patroller firsts. None of us saw the chief or the two captains after the firestorm. The others are seconds and thirds, mostly. We've got three patroller recruits. They'd just started the first of the year."

"Can you gather them all together? Those who want to continue with the patrol. Here on Meredi morning at eighth glass?"

"We've not been paid . . . sir."

Quaeryt looked hard at the patroller. "I've ridden here straight from Tilbor, and I haven't been paid, either. Not in almost two months. . . ." That was a slight exaggeration, but Quaeryt didn't like starting on the note Jaramyr was voicing. "There aren't any records left anywhere—unless you have some."

"Chelsyr has a duty book, sir."

"Does that have a roster in it?"

"No, sir. Almost as good, though. It has every duty assignment from the first of the year to the time the mountain blew."

"Why didn't you keep patrolling?"

"We did . . . for the first three weeks, sir. But lots of us have families . . . The regimental commander left, and the post commander wouldn't see us. He said we'd have to wait for the new governor . . ."

Quaeryt could believe that. He managed not to sigh. "Have everyone here on Meredi morning. If you and the other firsts want to work on everyone getting paid sooner, meet me at the post at eighth glass tomorrow morning . . . with the duty book and any other records you've managed to save. We'll start straightening matters out then." Quaeryt image-projected both assurance and authority, although he didn't like relying on that as much as he was fearing he would have to.

The burly patroller seemed to shrink back, although he did not physically move. "Yes, sir. We'll be there."

"In uniform."

"Yes, sir."

"Good." Quaeryt smiled pleasantly.

Jaramyr inclined his head politely. "Tomorrow morning, sir." He stepped back, turned, and strode off.

"What did you say to him, sir?" asked Dhaeryn. "You looked at him, and he wilted. My men said he was belligerent, wanted to know why we were putting the patrol station here . . . talking about the worst part of the city . . ."

"It probably was," admitted Quaeryt. "But if they start carrying out their duties, it won't be."

"You think they will?"

"If they don't, they won't be patrollers very long."

Dhaeryn barked a sort laugh. "That's the way it should be."

After leaving the patrol building, Quaeryt, Dhaeryn, several engineers, and a company from Second Battalion rode through the largely undamaged southern section of Extela, as well as the areas farther north that had suffered from some damage from ash and lava, to determine what other repairs needed to be made to streets and drainage sewers . . . and what could be accomplished quickly. One matter they did discover was that of the two aqueducts supplying the city's water, only the east aqueduct, the one called the River Aqueduct, was functioning, but it needed cleaning and repairs, with heavy leaks in several places. A section of the northwest aqueduct almost a mille in length had been destroyed by the lava and ash, but that aqueduct had largely served the destroyed part of the city, and repairs, rebuilding, or a new aqueduct would have to wait.

Then, that afternoon, while Dhaeryn and his engineers developed a work plan, first for the River Aqueduct, and then for the order of other repairs and the materials required, Quaeryt joined one of the squads from Third Battalion's second company. In complying with Meinyt's instructions, both Eleryt and Taenyd had set up their patrol assignments on a squad by squad basis to patrol the city.

For the first glass that Quaeryt accompanied the squad assigned to the area southwest of the governor's square, he and the troopers saw little out of the ordinary, except that there were a few more people out and about than in previous days, at least from what he recalled.

Then, roughly two quints past the second glass of the afternoon, there was a dull roar, followed by a muted rumble and a slight trembling of the ground. Quaeryt glanced to the northwest as a thin plume of ash drifted upward into the hazy spring sky.

"Sir?" asked Squad Leader Shaupyr. "Are we going to get more ash and lava here in the city?"

Quaeryt studied the volcano for a moment. The ash plume did not appear to be thickening, and there were no more rumblings. "I don't know. We'll just have to be careful and be ready to ride south at any moment."

As he finished speaking, a violent gust of hot wind swept out of the northwest, and the bits of ash it carried were enough to trigger Quaeryt's shields, so that while the wind itself was like the heat of a desert on his exposed skin, the ashes seemed to circle around him.

". . . look at that!" hissed one of the rankers.

Before Quaeryt could decide whether to drop the shields, a scream echoed from the side street ahead.

"Help! Brigands! Thieves! Help!"

Quaeryt left his shields in place and urged the mare forward and then into the side street.

"After the governor!" ordered Shaupyr.

A heavyset man running down the side street glanced back over his shoulder, then turned in time to see Quaeryt's mount. He jumped to one side in order to avoid the mare, but the impact of the shields on him threw him to the pavement, and his body slid to the curbstone of the sidewalk. The bag he'd held flew from his fingers, and coppers scattered across the stones.

The second man was running the other way.

Quaeryt imaged oil under his boots, and the second thief went down hard on the stone pavement. For several moments he did not move, and by the time he staggered up and was starting to run again, Quaeryt was on him. A single blow of the half-staff to the back of the man's head was enough to bring him down again.

Before the man could rise again, the rest of the squad had filled the side street. Four rankers dismounted and trussed up the two thieves.

A graying woman dressed in a faded brown shirt and even more washed-out brown trousers stood in a narrow doorway, her head moving from side to side, and Quaeryt rode over and reined up short of her. "Are you all right?"

"They took my wallet. They took it . . . I heard the roar and the rumble, sir. Someone yelled that more ash was coming, and I peered out the door. It was like those two were waiting . . ."

"They probably were," said Quaeryt.

The woman looked at Quaeryt. Her eyes went to Shaupyr, who rode up and extended the pouch.

"Here's your wallet. I don't know if we found all the coins . . ."

"I had almost a silver's worth of coppers . . ." wailed the woman.

Quaeryt slipped a silver from his wallet and leaned down from the saddle to extend it. "This should make up the difference."

The woman started to grab for the coin, then restrained herself. "You're not a trooper. Not dressed like a scholar."

"No, I'm not, but the silver is yours."

"That's Governor Quaeryt," said the squad leader.

"But . . . he was the one . . . he stopped . . . both of them . . ."

"The governor is good with the staff," added Shaupyr. "He was riding patrol with us."

The woman turned back to face Quaeryt, and her eyes widened. "The Nameless bless you, sir."

"Just be careful."

"I will, sir." The woman darted back inside the narrow door.

Quaeryt heard the sound of a door bar dropping into place.

"What do you want us to do with this pair, sir?" asked the squad leader. "Take them to the south square?"

Quaeryt frowned. "No . . . take them to the patrol station. They can work off their crime rebuilding it, or the bridge, or whatever else the engineers need strong backs for."

One of the brigands stiffened, but said nothing.

Quaeryt belatedly realized that he'd never questioned the man who'd tried to attack the wagon on the day they had provided free bread and potatoes. *How could you forget? Because you're short of time . . . like everything else.*

He reminded himself to take care of that.

Within a glass, the ash plume from Mount Extel had dwindled away to nothing, and the rest of the afternoon patrol was without event.

After he rode back through the post gates late that afternoon and finished stabling the mare, little more than a glass before the evening meal, he immediately headed for the quartermaster's study. Heireg was there.

"Did we get any supplies today?"

"Yes, sir. High Holder Chaffetz sent another hundred barrels of flour. His man asked that he not be required to send any more until we return the barrels from the first hundred."

"That's reasonable, isn't it?"

"Yes, sir. High Holder Aramyn sent fifty barrels more, and a hundred bushels of potatoes. Lady Vaelora was pleased with that because they sold all fifty bushels of potatoes they took to the market squares. And High Holder Wystgahl sent fifty barrels." The major frowned.

"What is it?"

"Can't say as I like the looks of the barrels Wystgahl sent. His man wouldn't say much."

"You think we should look into those barrels?"

"I told the cooks to use one of them tomorrow night, just so we could see."

"Good. How much flour did they sell at the market squares? Do you know?"

"They took five barrels and came back empty. Jhalyt and I put the coppers in our strong room here. We took in 379 coppers for the flour and 120 for the potatoes. I got a chit from the chief clerk, and he entered the amounts in the ledger."

Quaeryt smiled. Vaelora or the rankers had been generous in what they'd doled out, but for the time being that was fine. "You seem to be working well with Jhalyt."

"I knew him slightly before. He was the one the princeps sent to check our accounts. Seemed to be a good man."

Quaeryt nodded. Jhalyt hadn't mentioned that to him.

When he left Heireg, he went to find the cell where the wounded captive was incarcerated, but had to return to have the duty squad leader provide a key and a pair of rankers. He also learned that the man's name—the one he gave, in any case—was Dhousyt Sleksyn.

Quaeryt didn't bother to take the fellow elsewhere, but just stepped into the small cell, if with his shields up.

"Took your time, Governor."

"That likely didn't hurt you. Your friends just might have forgotten as well. Who set up the attack on the wagon?"

"What's it to you?"

"That's not the question. The question is whether you want to end up in the river or being released quietly one of these nights." Quaeryt projected both authority and contempt, followed by indifference. Using image-projection on a man like Dhousyt didn't bother him, and it was far easier on both him and Dhousyt than any other technique available.

Dhousyt swallowed. "Bennar did. Bennar Fhandsyn."

"Was it his idea?"

"Bennar never had no ideas in his life."

"Then who did?"

"The swell who owns the pleasure house. Don't know his name. Bennar just calls him the spicer. You don't want to cross him. Just as soon carve his initials on you or your mother or sister. Did that once to Nordon's little sister . . . before Nordon disappeared. Heard it happened to others. Anyway, Bennar gave us each a silver. Told us we'd end up sow food ifn we didn't."

Quaeryt spend another quint with Dhousyt, but it was clear the man knew little more. It was also clear that the spicer, whoever he was, was truly despicable. When Quaeryt returned to the duty desk, he made arrangements for Dhousyt to be released after dark. He supposed he could have had him branded or the equivalent, but he'd held the tough longer than he should have.

He was ready to leave the duty chamber when a thought struck him. "Have there been any messages for me, Squad Leader?"

"No, sir. We haven't received any dispatches or messages today, sir. We usually don't get the report from Solis until Mardi afternoon, sir."

"Thank you." Quaeryt offered a pleasant smile and left the chamber, making his way across the courtyard to the officers' quarters, where he climbed the steps to the second level. Vaelora was waiting by the balcony railing outside their quarters.

"How did your day go?" she asked.

"I discovered large problems, and solved one small one . . ." He went on to explain about his forgetting about Dhousyt and the overall patroller problem. "They'll need someone to whip them into shape. It's not something that I'll have time to do. That was one reason why I forgot about Dhousyt."

"Major Meinyt would be good at shaping up those patrollers," Vaelora offered. "So would some of the other older captains."

"The ones who came up through the ranks." Quaeryt paused. "I'll have to talk to Skarpa about that." From there he recounted the remainder of his day before asking, "And you?"

"Fewer earth-shaking problems than yours," she said with a smile. "It was sad to see how many women had so few coppers."

"I talked to Heireg. I got the feeling you were generous in measuring the flour." He paused. "How many did you pay for?"

"I paid half the cost for more than twenty women. It could have been thirty."

"More likely, it was closer to forty."

"Some of them have so little." Vaelora looked at him. "I remembered what Father told me about helping people. You don't give them all of anything. They have to make an effort."

"Otherwise . . . they come to expect charity too much."

She nodded. "But it's still sad."

"Were there many who looked not to be too deprived?"

"Most of those who came had the coin for what they needed, and some said that they felt safer with all the troopers around."

"That was part of the reason for sending so many. Do you think Extela looks better than when we first arrived?"

"Yes. Paying coppers to some of the women to sweep up the ash has helped, too." Vaelora offered a faint smile. "We should wash up for dinner."

Quaeryt leaned toward her and brushed her cheek with his lips. "We should indeed."

"For dinner, dearest. Just for dinner."

He couldn't help grinning.

"You're being—"

"Impossible, but not disrespectful."

Vaelora laughed softly and took his hand.

For Vaelora, Mardi began in the same fashion as Lundi had. Quaeryt saw her off beside Fhaen, riding near the head of three companies from Fourth Battalion. As she had been readying the gelding to leave, he'd suggested that she didn't need to go to watch over the sales of goods every day, but she had been adamant.

"It makes a difference if the governor's wife is there. Besides, what would you have me do here at the post?"

Given the results of her last "free" day at the post, Quaeryt had offered no objections. He only said, "Please keep your eyes open for anything that seems unusual or out of place."

"Don't I always?" had been her response just before she had mounted the gelding and ridden across the courtyard to rein up beside Major Fhaen.

Quaeryt stifled the wince he felt and smiled. "Yes, you do."

Once Vaelora had ridden out through the post gates, Quaeryt went to the study he had made his own to meet with Major Dhaeryn to discuss the priorities for repairs to the city, especially those that could be done in addition to those on the River Aqueduct and the east bridge, both of which were absolutely necessary.

The first thing Dhaeryn said when he walked into the study and sat down stopped Quaeryt cold.

"We've had our first death, Governor . . . on the bridge."

"What happened? Did some of the stones shift or something?" The last thing Quaeryt wanted was another complication, like the makeshift bridge collapsing before Dhaeryn was ready to start rebuilding it.

The major shook his head. "A foolish thing. I had one of the newer rankers checking the east shore piers. He was careless, slipped and went into the river."

"He drowned?"

"In a manner of speaking." Dhaeryn shook his head. "He must have swallowed some water wrong, because he was lying on the stones when the others found him. They thought he'd had a dizzy spell or something. But he was cold. Dead."

"Then how did he drown, if he wasn't in the water?"

"He got too much water in his lungs. I'd guess he couldn't cough it all up somehow. You know, that's how some old people die. My great uncle did. He got consumption, and there was so much water in his lungs he just drowned." The major paused. "You don't think it would happen to a young man, but it did."

"I'm sorry."

"It's not your fault. I should have sent someone with him, but the rocks down there looked dry and solid. You never know."

Drowning . . . after getting out of the water? Quaeryt could see how it might happen . . . but that seemed so improbable . . . except it had. "Otherwise . . . how are things going?"

"The patrol station . . . the factorage has been neglected, but it was well built. It won't be fancy, but we'll have something the patrollers can use in a week, maybe sooner. The bridge and the aqueduct . . . they're going to take longer, and we don't have enough men or equipment to handle anything else."

"Then just work on those until you've done what you can. . . ."

After Quaeryt finished with the head engineer, while he waited for the group of patrollers first to arrive, he began to review the master ledger Jhalyt had created, albeit with his own improvements, based on the clerk's experience and some of the samples he'd brought from Tilbora.

All too soon, there was a knock on the door.

"Sir . . . the patrollers are here." The ranker looked around the small study.

"If you'd direct them to the officers' mess, we'll meet there."

Quaeryt gathered Jhalyt, gave him instructions, and the two walked to the officers' mess.

With Jaramyr stood five other patrollers first. All were in uniform, and all viewed Quaeryt warily.

Projecting both friendliness and authority, Quaeryt gestured to the table. "Please sit down, patrollers. This is my chief clerk, Jhalyt. We'll need him to recreate things like pay ledgers." Quaeryt sat down at the end of the table. "For those of you who don't know, I'm Governor Quaeryt. I was the princeps of Tilbor, and when he heard of the troubles here, Lord Bhayar sent me here to be governor. For the past few days, I've been having regimental troops patrol the streets. As Jaramyr may have told you, I have the regimental engineers converting a factorage in the southeast into a patrol station. We needed a building you could use quickly, and it's also removed from the area where the lava and ash might strike again." He paused. "I'd like each of you to introduce yourself and tell me what duties you handled as a civic patroller. Jaramyr . . . you can start."

The burly patroller swallowed, then spoke. "Jaramyr Delonsyn. Mostly, I was the senior patroller on the beats along the river from about a mille north of the piers down to the east bridge . . ."

"Chelsyr Catholsyn . . . senior patroller on beats north of the governor's square . . ."

"Waollyt Aolsyn . . . senior patroller . . . west end south of the old palace . . ."

When he had heard from everyone there, he asked, "Do all of you intend to continue with the Civic Patrol?"

Nods went around the table.

Quaeryt looked to Jhalyt. "Did you get everyone's name?"

"Yes, sir, except I'd like to check the spelling, sir."

"After we finish, please verify your name with Jhalyt. Now . . . it appears as though no one was patrolling when we arrived. That tells me that, at present, I'll have to appoint an acting chief from the regiment. Who that will be hasn't been decided. For the moment I'm acting chief." Quaeryt looked to the youngest man at the end of one side of the table. "Reyol, what is the pay of a patroller first when he initially becomes a first?" Quaeryt projected a touch of authority and the sense that lying would be unwise.

"Ah . . . a silver and two a week, sir."

"Chelsyr . . . a senior patroller first?"

"Tops out at two silvers a week after fifteen years, sir."

With several more questions, Quaeryt effectively had given Jhalyt enough information for a pay chart. "Now . . . when you verify your name, let Jhalyt know your years of service. If I find out that anyone lies, I'll put you up before a justicer for theft. Is that clear? Now . . . Chelsyr . . . you have a duty roster?"

"Yes, sir."

"I'd like you to go over that with Jhalyt afterward, with the names of patrollers likely to return and their ranks. You all will be paid. While you're giving your information to Jhalyt, I'll be getting your pay for the time from the Vendrei before the eruption to last Vendrei . . ."

All in all, the remaining details took close to a glass.

Then, after everyone left, considerably more cheerful, with coins in their wallets, and after more discussion with Jhalyt about revising the structure of the temporary pay roster for the Civic Patrol that Jhalyt and Heireg had created, Quaeryt had Jhalyt draft a set of tariff schedules and rules for Montagne, again based on the documents and records he'd had the foresight to have copied before he'd left Tilbora. That led to one other problem. Because

Tilbor had been governed as a conquered province, all the administration had been handled by the regiment. In Montagne, as in all other provinces, the governor's clerks were all hired by the governor . . . or the princeps . . . or the chief clerk, and that meant setting up another structure and set of ledgers.

When he returned to his own study, Quaeryt was still considering the possibility that such records might have survived, although his experience in entering the governor's building had suggested that probability was close to nonexistent. Even if some had survived under the ash in the lower level, he doubted that more than a few would be readable, and he certainly didn't have the time to go looking for them.

There was a knock on the door.

"Yes?"

The two clerks eased the door open and stepped inside.

"Sir . . . there are several other things," began Jhalyt.

"I'm sure there are." Quaeryt grinned wryly. "What have I overlooked? Or what am I about to overlook?"

"Vendrei will be the last day of Maris, sir."

For just a moment, Quaeryt wondered why the chief clerk was offering a calendar. Then he realized the reason. "We haven't finished setting up the master pay accounts, have we?"

"I have the accounts set up, sir. The regiment keeps their own ledger, and so does the post. I know how much we'll need. It's a month's worth for the regiment, and just a week's worth for the post personnel. After Vendrei, we'd planned to disburse weekly for the regiment while they're quartered here. That's the way . . ."

"I know that. Have you drafted approval forms for me to authorize?"

"Mostly, sir, but I thought you'd like to see the figures. Also, you directed me as how to set up your accounts as governor, but you didn't mention what your stipend and monthly expense draw would be . . . or what level . . ."

"Or what level you'd be paid at?" Quaeryt smiled faintly. "Caell was chief clerk, didn't you say?"

"Yes, sir."

"Do you happen to know what his pay was? When he became chief clerk?"

"I know he was paid a half gold a week as chief clerk the past two years. Before that . . . I don't know."

"Did he have an expense draw?"

"No, sir. He got an additional silver a week for food and lodging."

"But you didn't as his assistant?"

"No, sir."

"What were you making as his assistant?"

"Three silvers a week."

"Then put yourself down for half gold a week in pay." Quaeryt paused. "Do you or did you have a home . . ."

"No, sir. Couldn't afford one. Not in Extela. I rented a room on the west side. The place is gone."

"For now, then, since you're being fed by the post and have a bunk here, you don't need to pay for lodging and food. Once you both find other places, we'll talk over adjustments."

"Thank you, sir." The chief clerk inclined his head deeply.

"Baharyt . . . we'll pay you two silvers a week for now. After a month, the chief clerk and I will review how you're doing." Quaeryt was being more than fair, because he'd gathered the young man had barely been working as an apprentice bookkeeper and inventory clerk for three months.

"Thank you, sir!"

"You can go. I need to go over a few more things with Jhalyt."

Once Baharyt had closed the door, Quaeryt looked to the chief clerk.

"He was paid a silver and three. He'll get better." Jhalyt offered a half smile.

"About the regiment and post, first," suggested Quaeryt.

"Yes, sir." Jhalyt slid a sheet across the desk.

Quaeryt looked at the figures in neat columns, and then at the totals. Once again, he managed not to swallow. *Two thousand and eleven golds in pay, and three hundred golds in projected supply costs.* At least he'd recovered the chests from the treasury strong room. "The next tariffs aren't due until the end of Mayas, either," he mused. *What are you missing?*

"The second week of Juyn, actually, sir."

A month and a half . . . with no revenue. And likely the tariffs would be low, although not that low, since the collections in Montagne and areas away from Extela shouldn't suffer that much. "Do you know what the midyear tariffs bring?"

"Not exactly, sir. Caell said they were only about a third of all the year's tariffs. Many were paid late, also."

Quaeryt waited.

"I don't know for certain, sir, because Caell and the governor kept those ledgers to themselves, but I heard figures now and again. I'd guess . . . I'm only guessing . . . that the governor collected some fifteen to twenty thousand golds a year."

At close to two thousand golds a month, just for regimental pay, Quaeryt realized he couldn't keep the regiment in Extela for more than a few months—not without requesting payments from Bhayar. He also understood why the post had so few troopers for its size. Then he realized what he'd forgotten. "The regiment should be paying their own men out of what they brought with them. Through the end of Maris, anyway."

"Yes, sir. I checked with Captain Dimeark. They'll pay nineteen hundred and seventeen golds . . ."

Quaeryt almost sighed in relief.

". . . but you still have to authorize it. You'll have to pay them from the treasury here from Avryl on, until they're transferred to Solis or wherever they'll be stationed."

Still, that meant the immediate loss to what he'd saved of the treasury was still almost four hundred golds.

"There's the matter of your stipend, sir."

Quaeryt had wondered about that himself. As princeps of Tilbor, Quaeryt had gotten luxurious quarters and been paid five golds a week, ten times what he'd made as a scholar assistant, and half what Straesyr made as both marshal and governor—and as princeps, he hadn't even had to pay an officer's mess bill. He'd been stunned by the pay, but Straesyr had told him that most princeps made far more, because the other governors were free to set up their own budgets, so long as they met the guidelines established by Lord Bhayar and his minister of finance. Unfortunately, Quaeryt didn't have those guidelines, because those in the governor's square were either ashes or buried under the ash, and there hadn't been any in Tilbora because they hadn't applied to Tilbor.

"I have to confess, Jhalyt, I hadn't thought about that. Tilbor is run on a military basis. Do you happen to recall the basis for pay guidelines?"

"No, sir." A small smile appeared. "I do know that the princeps drew ten golds a week, and he once said that he earned less than a tenth part of what the governor did."

A hundred golds a week? Or more? Quaeryt managed to keep from showing astonishment. No wonder so many wanted to be governors! He managed to smile. "I don't think Montagne, and Extela especially, can afford to pay a governor that much. Not at present or in the very near future. For the moment, put me down for twenty-five golds a week." That was a calculated amount.

"Just . . . twenty-five, sir?"

"For now. I reserve the right to increase it if matters improve." He smiled again, ironically. "How can I take a larger amount when I'm asking everyone else to hold down their prices and what they receive?"

"Begging your pardon, Governor, sir, there's many that wouldn't even think that, sir. Most, in fact."

"Then we'll just have to change a few minds, won't we?"

There was silence in the small study for several long moments.

"Sir . . . word is that you grew up with Lord Bhayar . . ."

"You want to know if it's true? We've known each other for over fifteen years, and we had the same tutor. I wouldn't say that we grew up together. I was trained as a scholar, and then went to sea, and then came back to being a scholar, and then a scholar assistant to Bhayar before he dispatched me to Tilbor."

"And you fought in the wars there?"

"Just the last one."

"And your lady?"

"She's Bhayar's youngest sister." Quaeryt smiled wryly. "The marriage was his doing. Fortunately, we're well suited to each other."

Jhalyt swallowed. "Sir . . . there might be some things you need to know . . . about the old governor, I mean."

"I'm sure there are, and I'd like to hear what you have to say. The more I know, the more I can avoid unnecessary difficulties." Quaeryt waited.

"Yes, sir." Several moments passed before Jhalyt spoke again. "Governor Scythn . . . there were two sets of ledgers . . ."

After hearing what Scythn had drawn as his pay, Quaeryt was scarcely surprised as Jhalyt revealed the means by which the former governor had drawn almost double what he'd reported to Bhayar, and how the former princeps had drawn triple his stated pay. When the chief clerk finished, Quaeryt nodded. "Thank you. In a way, that's very good."

The slightest frown creased the clerk's brow.

"It means that in time we'll have more golds to work with. We just have to get through the next few months." He rose. "If you'd go find Major Heireg, I'll meet you outside the strong room. We need to count the rest of what's in those chests."

"Yes, sir."

In the end, between them, the other four chests contained 12,041 golds, 643 silvers, and 561 coppers. Quaeryt had just over fifteen thousand golds in the provincial treasury, a sum that made him more than a little nervous, but he also understood why provincial governors didn't like to maintain many soldiers . . . and, belatedly, why Rescalyn had thought he could have gotten away with what he'd planned.

A little after the third glass of the afternoon, Quaeryt was once more seated in the study that had been a regimental commander's, studying an old map of Extela, and adding to his notes of what areas were totally covered in ash or lava and where major repairs were needed.

There was a knock on the door, and a ranker stood there, holding an envelope. "Sir?"

"Yes?"

"There's a messenger here from High Holder Thysor. He sent this. The messenger will be waiting for your reply, he said."

Quaeryt rose, crossed the small room, and took the envelope. "Thank you. I'll have a response as soon as possible. If you'd see that he gets something to eat and drink and that his mount is watered?"

"Yes, sir."

Quaeryt opened the envelope and began to read.

Governor Quaeryt,

I would very much have liked to have met you when you called on me, but as my steward doubtless told you, I was in the south inspecting timber stands to see which areas would best be logged over the summer and did not return until late yesterday . . .

I would be pleased to meet with you anytime on Jeudi, Vendrei, or Samedi. I would suggest meeting at Thyhyem, given the infeasibility of meeting at governor's square . . .

"Infeasibility indeed," murmured Quaeryt as he picked up a pen to reply, thinking that Jeudi would be best for another trip across the river to Thyhyem.

He'd barely finished the reply to Thysor and had it given to the messenger when the duty squad leader appeared with a dispatch from Solis. Quaeryt opened it and began to read even before the squad leader was out the door.

Dear Governor Quaeryt—

I received a report from Commander Zhrensyl. He had just received a dispatch from you, saying you would arrive in two days. I trust I will receive a report from you shortly, once you have determined conditions in Extela. Commander Huosyt could not report damages because the heat of the lava precluded close reconnaissance, and a later report from Commander Zhrensyl stated that he could not determine the extent of damage because he had insufficient forces. Please send as accurate a report of the damage as possible immediately, if you have not already done so.

At present, Rex Kharst has moved three regiments into position west of Ferravyl. We have reports that a full foot regiment has been sent by barge from Variana and will arrive near Ferravyl shortly. Needless to say, the sooner you can reestablish order in Extela and release the Third Tilboran Regiment, the better. I do not expect Third Regiment to remain in Extela past the fifteenth of Mayas in any event, and would strongly prefer the regiment be dispatched sooner. Unless you receive orders to the contrary, Commander Skarpa is to proceed to Tresrives at the juncture of the Telexan River and the Aluse. From there he is to take the river post road directly to Ferravyl. . . .

When Quaeryt finished the dispatch, he just sat at the desk for several moments. He could understand Bhayar's concerns fully. Rebuilding Extela had to be secondary to defending Ferravyl—and all Telaryn—from a Bovarian attack. At the same time . . .

He shook his head. There was little point in arguing. What he needed to do at the moment was to compose a reply for immediate dispatch the next morning.

He had great difficulty in wording one paragraph of his reply, and wrote and rewrote that part several times, finally coming up with words that were accurate, but not too accusatory.

. . . Part of the difficulty in reestablishing order lies in the small size of the garrison remaining in Extela. Because the ash and lava covered the governor's square and almost all of the old palace, the heat destroyed all records, although we were able to recover some of the treasury—enough, with care—to cover modest expenses of rebuilding those facilities most necessary for daily life in Extela. It would appear, however, that Governor Scythn left little margin for unforeseen expenses in his handling of finances, particularly in view of a level of expenses that, in light of projected tariff receipts, appears rather higher than ever reported to you. This situation is likely to slow some rebuilding . . . since, before Third Regiment is released, we will need to expand the garrison forces remaining here by at least a company, and possibly two, to help maintain order until the Civic Patrol can be expanded from the core of surviving patrollers . . .

Quaeryt went on to describe the extent of destruction in detail, the areas of the city still intact, and the beginning of repairs to sewers and aqueducts, noting that with the complete destruction of the north aqueduct, the repairs and expansion of the River Aqueduct had become more vital, as had those to the east bridge. He also mentioned his acts to freeze prices of foodstuffs temporarily, if with a slight profit to the High Holders and growers. All in all, he ended up writing a five-page dispatch, and felt that he'd probably overlooked matters that he should not have.

He decided to have Vaelora read it over before he dispatched it.

Later that evening, after dinner, in the privacy of the quarters, he watched closely as she read through his carefully chosen words.

When she finished, she smiled. "It's better than most he receives, and longer."

"You're suggesting I should shorten it."

"No. A first report should be long, especially to protect you. If you don't tell him how bad things are, then he'll expect too much."

After they discussed possible changes to the dispatch, he then recounted the other events of the day, saving what Jhalyt had conveyed about Scythn and double ledgers.

Vaelora nodded calmly, clearly not surprised. "Most governors do something like that, in various ways. That's why Father made them pay for any soldier garrisoned in their provinces. It's why Bhayar continues the practice, and it's one reason why you're governor now. My brother knows you're honest, and Extela can't afford another governor lining his wallet at the moment."

Quaeryt shook his head. "It's not the pocketing of the golds that gets me so much as the amounts involved. A captain makes a half gold a week, a major a gold, a commander two, and a marshal five—along with quarters. Even as governor and marshal Rescalyn only made ten golds a week. Scythn was officially paying himself twenty times what a marshal makes . . ."

"Why do you think so many High Holders press Bhayar for governor's positions for their younger sons?"

"I knew that," replied Quaeryt dryly. "I just didn't realize how lucrative the position was for someone with few principles. But I couldn't justify that much. That's why I only set my own pay at twenty-five golds a week for now."

"Dearest, I think you're being too frugal. You could have taken fifty golds a week and still paid yourself a quarter or less of what Scythn was taking. And it would be nice to have a real dwelling . . ."

"I know. But we don't have the time to build one. We'd have to find one, if there even is one suitable . . . and we'd need to have a cook and a maid . . . and some guards, not to mention a stable . . . and there are furnishings . . ." The entire idea overwhelmed Quaeryt, who'd never had to worry about anything of a personal nature except having a room, a few garments, and feeding himself. Not only that, but he felt he had little enough time to do what needed to be done to return Extela to a semblance of its former prosperity.

"You've been governor, officially, since Scythn died. That was the middle of Fevier. That means you are owed two hundred golds. I know you've saved a few from when you were princeps, and I have quite a few remaining. Also, we could rent a place for a time, perhaps from a once well-off factor who would prefer the golds until his business improves."

"And who would not mind being owed a favor from the sister of Lord Bhayar?" Quaeryt smiled.

"My brother can afford that."

"I wouldn't even know where to start," Quaeryt protested.

"You don't have to. Those are matters I do know something about, dearest. All you have to do is tell me how many golds you have, and I tell you what I have, and we decide what we can spend, both to begin with, and each month. Then you leave the rest to me. Running a household is something that wives are supposed to do."

"And husbands are just supposed to pay for it?"

"Of course." Vaelora smiled gently, then added, "Within reason. But you already know I'm very reasonable."

Except about cleaning up abandoned anomens. "That's true." Quaeryt repressed a shrug. "Right now, I have forty-five golds, and a few silvers. That's before I'm paid."

Vaelora nodded. "I have almost a hundred, and Bhayar will give me at least two hundred after our first year anniversary. He said it would be a delayed dowry."

"We can't count on promises . . . even your brother's."

"I won't." She frowned. "I will need an escort when I look for something suitable. Don't object. It's reasonable that I have one, since the lava destroyed a very suitable dwelling . . . and I promise not to commit more than a hundred golds for the dwelling . . . or more than twenty golds a month to run it."

"And you can't obtain it by promising or even hinting at favors—or difficulties—from me," Quaeryt added.

"No, dearest. Even I understand that."

Quaeryt winced at the arch tones in her voice. "I'm sorry. After the way Wystgahl treated me, I just worry." What Vaelora proposed seemed reasonable enough under the circumstances, but he still worried, even as he said, "I'll let Skarpa know about the escort tomorrow morning."

"You'll be pleased," she promised.

And so will you. But then, he could certainly understand, given that she'd been raised in a palace and especially given all the places she'd had to sleep over the past month. "I'm sure I will be."

Meredi morning Quaeryt was up early, very early, so that he could rewrite sections of his report to Bhayar, and dispatch it with a special courier immediately after breakfast. As soon as he'd seen Vaelora off on her quest for a governor's house with two squads of troopers, he cornered Skarpa again outside the stables.

"Yes, Governor? You have that look . . . sir."

Quaeryt grinned. "I'm certain I do. You may have heard that I'm trying to re-form the Civic Patrol . . ."

"The guards told me that you left orders to admit up to eight patrollers yesterday, and Dhaeryn told me you're converting an old factorage. You seem to have that well in hand." Skarpa raised his eyebrows.

"The chief and his captains didn't appear to survive . . . or if they did, they're nowhere to be found."

"Some of both, I'd wager."

"I was wondering if you might have a very senior, hard-as-nails captain close to being stipended, who could finish his service as a chief patroller here. The locals need someone to keep them in line." *And then some.*

The commander shook his head. "Too bad they won't keep you as governor."

"Oh?"

"Sir . . . begging your pardon, you're here for the same reason I got promoted to commander. Lord Bhayar needs someone he can trust, someone who's honest, and someone who will do what's necessary . . . even if it means tromping all over the polished boots of every High Holder and wealthy factor in Montagne."

One aspect of the qualities mentioned by Skarpa immediately struck Quaeryt—and that was the separation of trustworthiness and honesty, suggesting that trustworthiness was more akin to loyalty. What Skarpa said didn't conflict with what Quaeryt had observed, but in a way it saddened him. "I'm well on the way to scuffing at least a few boots."

"You'll likely have to do more than that, sir."

"About one of those captains you or your battalion commanders could recommend?"

"If you'd give me a day or so to think about it . . . and talk to the majors . . ."

"I'm assuming it's not something you or Meinyt would want."

"No, sir. Not me. Couldn't speak for Meinyt, but he'd be better off elsewhere."

Quaeryt nodded. That suggested Meinyt might be useful in another capacity . . . perhaps.

"I'll talk it over with all of them," Skarpa added.

"Thank you."

Quaeryt had only taken a few more steps back toward the headquarters building when he saw Heireg hurrying toward him. He stopped and waited for the major.

The slightly rotund officer stopped short of Quaeryt and announced, "Sir . . . I have to report that the flour we got from High Holder Wystgahl is filled with weevils. By the time we strain it and sift it, we'll lose almost half of it."

"Is that true of all the barrels?"

"We've checked five of them. They're all like that."

Quaeryt sighed. "He delivered what . . . some fifty barrels?"

"Yes, sir."

"Check them all, and then let me know when I get back to the post. I've got to meet with what's left of the Extelan Civic Patrol."

"Yes, sir."

Quaeryt made his way back to the headquarters building, where he gathered up the items he needed, and then briefed Baharyt on what he expected of the young clerk at the meeting. Then he went to the strong room where he and Jhalyt counted out sufficient silvers and coppers to pay forty patrollers from the time of their last payday . . . with some extra, just in case.

Then, accompanied by Taenyd and third company, Quaeryt and Baharyt rode out from the post. The young clerk was clearly uncomfortable on a horse, much the way Quaeryt had been a year earlier.

Less than a year, really. So much had happened since the previous summer, and all because of his ideas for changing the positions of scholars and imagers in Telaryn, plans about which he'd done little enough, except for restructuring and improving the scholarium in Tilbora. Still . . . that had been a start.

The ride was uneventful, and Quaeryt noted that there were more people on the streets, even some women and children, and to him that was a good sign.

When they reached the patrol station, Quaeryt studied the roof and the front of the building before dismounting. While the places where the old slates had been replaced were obvious, the roof looked far better, as did the front of the building, with freshly oiled shutters in place on the four windows. Two men worked on planing one of the heavy double doors to the main entry. One might have been one of the brigands Quaeryt had captured, but he wasn't certain.

He dismounted and turned to Baharyt. "Just follow me."

"Yes, sir."

Quaeryt didn't see Dhaeryn after he tied the mare to the old railing and stepped up onto the narrow stone porch, but one of the senior squad leaders of the engineers appeared and said, "All of the patrollers are inside, Governor."

"Thank you."

When Quaeryt stepped inside the entry area of the Civic Patrol station, two things struck him. First, the receiving desk or counter was largely finished, the wood already oiled, and there were around thirty patrollers, all in uniform, standing in groups.

The murmurs died away as he moved toward them. While a few looked at him with what resembled hope, there was certainly an air of something that was not quite indifference, and certainly skepticism.

Quaeryt stopped several yards in front of them and smiled politely, image-projecting authority and confidence. "Good morning. Your patrollers first may have told you. I'm Governor Quaeryt, and I'll be acting patrol chief for a bit. This will be Civic Patrol headquarters, and in the next few days, there will be twenty cells in the back. For now, while we reorganize the patrol, the troopers of the Third Tilboran Regiment will patrol the streets. By next week, you—or those of you who wish to remain patrollers—will begin taking over those patrols. The engineers will finish converting this building and making other repairs around the city. . . ."

Quaeryt went on to explain what he expected of them and that those expectations would be posted as a written code for the Civic Patrol, although he would consider changes based on their suggestions and experience.

". . . We will clearly need more patrollers, and any of you who recruits a new patroller will get a bonus—after that new recruit completes three months of paid service. The bonus will be two silvers." He paused. "Do you have any questions?"

"What about pay?" came a question from the back of the group.

"The pay grades will be the same as before." Quaeryt knew that wasn't what the patroller who asked the question had in mind.

"The pay we didn't get," said another voice.

"That's an interesting question. When I arrived here a little over a week ago, there was no one patrolling the streets, and people were afraid to go out. So I've had troopers patrolling the avenues and streets. I've asked around, and none of you have been doing the duties that you were supposed to be doing, not for the last month, in any case." Quaeryt projected withering contempt for a moment. "Some of that is understandable. You didn't have a patrol building or a gaol. Nor did you have any captains or a chief, it appears. For that reason, those of you who wish to continue as patrollers will receive back pay after you sign up and renew your commitment."

"Why did you put the station here?"

"Because we could and because we needed it quickly. It also appears that we couldn't put it in the northwest part of the city," he added dryly. That did get a smile or two.

"Scholars . . ." murmured someone.

Quaeryt smiled. Coldly. "I am a scholar. I've also been a quartermaster at sea, and I took part in all the battles in Tilbor in the last year before I became princeps there. I've taken a crossbow bolt to the chest and broken an arm in battle. I'm not much impressed with muttered comments by men who are supposed to be honorable and uphold the law. As I said a moment ago, I expect every one of you to be polite and cheerful to every person." He paused, then smiled sardonically. "You don't have to be cheerful to lawbreakers—just polite and forceful enough to keep them well under control."

He could sense a certain confusion, even antagonism.

Again, projecting total authority, he said, "If you behave like toughs and lawbreakers, then the people will all regard you as worse than the lawbreakers because you're abusing your authority. More to the point, so will I . . . and none of you want that."

The authority projection worked better than the words, he suspected, but he could see the effect. "We won't go to shifts yet. All of you who intend to continue as patrollers will be here at seventh glass tomorrow morning. In uniform. Right now, you can line up at the end of the receiving desk where Baharyt is. Give him your name. He'll check it against the duty roster and your rank, and you'll be given your back pay. Then you can leave until tomorrow morning. Several of you have already been paid, but you still need to check with Baharyt."

Quaeryt stepped back and then moved to where he stood behind Baharyt, so that he could look at each man as he came forward.

Most of those who stepped up avoided meeting his eyes. Jaramyr did, nodding respectfully, if grudgingly, Quaeryt thought. So did Chelsyr and several of the others Quaeryt had already met.

Once all the patrollers had given their information to Baharyt and been paid, Quaeryt and the clerk left the building to the engineers. As Quaeryt mounted and started back to the post with Taenyd and third company, he could hear the murmurs from a group of patrollers who had remained outside, gathered together and talking.

". . . there he goes . . . bastard . . ."

". . . tough bastard . . ."

". . . you want to cross him?"

"Jaramyr . . . talked to some of the troopers . . . related to Bhayar . . ."

". . . not kidding about . . . killed a score with a staff . . ."

Quaeryt managed not to wince at the last. But then, he probably had.

As he rode back to the post, he had to wonder. Had he used too much force in facing them? What choice did he have? From meeting the patrollers first and seeing that group, he had few doubts that they'd been only slightly better than organized toughs, probably taking bribes and then some. What else should he have expected after learning the way Scythn had acted?

He didn't get back to the post until two quints past ninth glass. He barely dismounted before Heireg appeared.

"Sir . . . ?"

"How many barrels were spoiled?"

"All of them in some amount. We might save half of it . . . if we use those barrels first."

"Do that. It appears I need to pay another call on High Holder Wystgahl." Quaeryt turned toward Taenyd, who had dismounted. "Captain! Can you be ready to ride out in a quint?"

"Yes, sir. We can water the horses some and be ready to go. Where to, sir?"

"High Holder Wystgahl's."

"Yes, sir."

A little more than two glasses later, third company rode up to the portico of the hold. As Quaeryt reined up, he caught sight of the graying red hair of Gahlen, the holder's son, standing on the black stone step below the white marble columns.

"I don't believe you are expected, Governor."

"I'm here to see your father."

"I don't think he'll want to see you."

"I'm quite certain he won't." Quaeryt smiled coldly. "That's not his choice."

"And if I deny you entry?"

"Gahlen . . . for your sake, I do hope you don't try."

The heir frowned, then gestured. "This way. He's in the salon. That's where he always is these days. He says he coughs less there."

Quaeryt caught up with the redhead and asked, "Consumption?"

"Who can tell whether it's that or just age?"

Quaeryt could sense the mixed feelings swirling within Gahlen, but said nothing, thinking about what he could or might do. He did raise his shields, close to his body, before he followed Gahlen into the salon.

"Why did you let him in?" snapped Wystgahl, rising from the same armchair in which Quaeryt had last seen him. "I should disinherit you and settle the holding on your brother."

"It's rather hard to deny a governor with a company of armed troopers," replied Gahlen, stepping back, but not leaving the salon. "Haylen would have the same problem."

"Bah . . . you're both worthless." Wystgahl turned to face Quaeryt. "I sent you your Namer-cursed flour. Now . . . get out of here."

"You sent weevil-ridden flour, and more than half of it is spoiled and useless."

"You insisted on a price for the flour, Governor." Wystgahl smiled crookedly, a glint in his eyes. "I gave you the kind of flour represented by that price."

"The price was for good flour, and I offered you a profit of an eighth more than what you could have gotten two months ago. That's likely a profit of one part in four."

"I could have gotten more. You set the price. I gave you the quality you paid for."

"You don't intend to make good on what was promised?"

"A promise extracted by force has no value, Governor. Lord Bhayar has already upheld that precedent. Besides, you accepted that flour."

"My men accepted it in good faith. Your faith was anything but good." Quaeryt was at a loss. He didn't want to drag an old man out of his holding. Nor did he really have the authority to do so, and Wystgahl certainly knew that. "You effectively defrauded Lord Bhayar out of thirty golds."

"He can certainly afford it. Or you can."

"It's all right to cheat anyone you can if you're a High Holder? What about the next two hundred and fifty barrels?" asked Quaeryt calmly, although he felt anything but calm.

"That's your problem as well. Face it. You can't do anything . . . Governor. You don't dare bring your troops in here and seize my holding. You wouldn't last a season after that. Do you think that the High Justicer in Solis is going to even hear an appeal over a mere thirty or a hundred golds?" Wystgahl laughed.

And such an appeal would take weeks to get to Solis, longer to decide, and make Bhayar most unhappy, thought Quaeryt. *You don't have the time for that. Yet . . . if he gets away with cheating and defying me . . . putting Extela back together will just get harder . . . because he's the kind to flaunt his "victory" and let everyone know, and that will require that you use more and more force, and that will mean everyone will think you're even more unfair than they already do.*

Wystgahl coughed, once twice. "Namer-cursed phlegm."

Phelgm . . . water . . . consumption . . . that's it.

"You can't make me change matters . . . Not even a governor can do that."

"I don't intend to do anything of the sort. I'll leave you here, dreaming of your past glories that never were. I'll deal with your son, who understands the responsibilities of being a holder far better than you do. You're not a High Holder. You're a greedy old man who'd cheat on the Nameless to get an extra copper." Quaeryt sneered and image-projected withering scorn and contempt.

"You're a worthless scholar . . . a nothing! A nothing, do you hear me? Nothing at—"

Quaeryt imaged water—just plain water—into Wystgahl's lower windpipe as the old man continued his tirade.

The holder tried to cough and sputtered up some water. Quaeryt imaged more water, into where he thought the man's lungs were.

Wystgahl staggered, then gasped, tried to speak, coughed up more water, then began to choke and convulse.

Gahlen rushed forward, unable to catch his father as the old man collapsed on the rich maroon and cream of the salon carpet. He turned his father over, half lifting him, then pounding him on the back.

Finally, he lowered the body and stood, facing Quaeryt. "You did it! You made him so upset!" He rushed toward Quaeryt, drawing a poignard and thrusting toward the governor.

The blade slipped aside off the shields, and while Gahlen gaped, Quaeryt imaged a section out of the tang of the blade, so that the weapon snapped with the second thrust.

"Armor . . ."

"Don't!" snapped Quaeryt, reinforcing the single word with as much authority as he could order-project.

Gahlen stopped as though he'd run into a stone wall.

"Don't be stupid," said Quaeryt tiredly. "I offered your father a decent profit, but he was greedy. He wanted more. In trying to cheat the governor of Montagne, he was cheating Lord Bhayar. He got so angry he died. I'm not interested in pursuing the matter further . . . unless you make me. Enough people have already died in Extela, and more will likely die across Telaryn with the war to come. You're now the High Holder. All I'm asking is for you to keep the bargain he didn't."

"But you killed him."

"Oh? Did I ever even touch him? I only told him that he was selfish, greedy, and unreasonable and that I'd deal with you."

Gahlen was silent.

"Your father sent fifty barrels of flour. Half of it was worthless. You owe another twenty-five barrels, and those had best be good barrels, and so should the remaining two hundred and fifty, as well as the potatoes. I also want a letter of apology from you for your sire's attempt to cheat Lord Bhayar."

Gahlen flushed. "After this . . . ?"

"High Holder Wystgahl, and you are now High Holder . . . as I told your father, had any workingman or factor cheated Lord Bhayar—or you or your father—out of thirty golds, he would lose everything, possibly even his life. I'm only asking for you to fulfill what your father agreed to provide . . . and an apology. I'm not a High Holder. I'm a former scholar who happens to think that High Holders shouldn't get away with crimes that would condemn men of lower position to death."

"He didn't get away with anything. Say what you will . . . you killed him."

Quaeryt wasn't about to dispute that. *Not that you had much choice, given the circumstances.* He glanced down at the body on the costly carpet. "No . . . in the end, he didn't get away with anything. Should he have, just because he was a High Holder?" After a brief pause, Quaeryt went on. "I'm sorry for your loss . . . because he was your father, and it is your loss. I can't say I'm sorry for his death. He'd rather have had people starve than settle for a modest profit, and he defrauded Lord Bhayar . . . and took pleasure in it. That's neither right nor honorable. Now . . . if you will excuse me." He turned and walked out of the holding.

No one said a word.

Once they had ridden out through the gates, Taenyd finally looked at Quaeryt. "What happened, Governor? They all looked at you as though you were the Namer in person."

"High Holder Wystgahl became incensed when I accused him of fraud and providing weevil-ridden flour. He said that was what I deserved for forcing a sale. I pointed out that he would be making a profit on good flour, but that he'd defrauded Lord Bhayar. He said Lord Bhayar could afford it. I told him he was a greedy old man. He got red in the face, then blue, and collapsed.

His son accused me of making him so angry that he died. That's possible. He wasn't in good health. But my responsibility is not to allow Lord Bhayar to be cheated." Quaeryt laughed bitterly. "If you or I had stolen thirty golds from Lord Bhayar . . . or High Holder Wystgahl, what do you think would have happened to us?"

Taenyd shook his head. "I'd not even want to think about that."

When Quaeryt returned to the post, it was less than three quints before the evening meal, and he barely had time to go to his study and complete the rough map of Extela he'd been working on—one that showed the undamaged sections of the city, those that would likely need civic patrollers—if and when there were enough patrollers.

After that, he hurried over to the officers' quarters, where he found Vaelora coming down the outside steps.

"Did you have any luck, dear?" asked Quaeryt.

"There are several places. None is quite right. We can talk about them after dinner."

From her tone of voice, Quaeryt was immediately convinced that not "quite right" was an understatement.

"How about you?"

"Angry patrollers and a visit to High Holder Wystgahl over his weevil-ridden flour. He got so mad when I told him his actions were unacceptable that he ended up turning red and then blue and coughing and dying on his expensive carpet."

"Rather unfortunate for him." Vaelora raised her eyebrows.

Quaeryt could see she understood. "You heard how unreasonable he was to begin with. He wanted to keep the good flour and sell it at an exorbitant profit and pawn off the worthless on us. I'll tell you more after dinner."

She nodded.

Both Quaeryt and Vaelora were unusually quiet during dinner, if for differing reasons, he suspected.

Afterward, when they returned to their quarters, after he shut the door, he turned to her. "What did you find?"

"Tell me about the High Holder first, if you would."

Quaeryt did, ending with, ". . . I didn't know what else I could have done. I'd have had to have brought it to Bhayar, because no justicer can try a High Holder, only the supreme justicer or a council of High Holders, except in Tilbor, and that may have changed already. They would laugh at the idea of trying a High Holder for defrauding a lowly governor for a mere twenty to thirty golds, even for more than a hundred if he'd delivered the rest of the flour in the same condition. Even if they didn't, it would take weeks, if not months, to get anything done—and I don't have the time to pursue that and do everything else. The High Holders in the rest of Telaryn certainly would have upheld Wystgahl because they wouldn't have wanted to set a precedent that suggested they had to meet the same standards as mere factors." He shook his head. "What bothers me most about all this is that if a factor or grower did what Wystgahl did, he'd be whipped within a digit of his life, and he'd lose everything, and possibly his life."

"Dearest, he deserved what happened. He was arrogant, proud, greedy . . . and especially, he was stupid." Vaelora's voice turned cool. "There's a reason Bhayar usually appoints the governors he does. It's because they have some source of power besides the position itself. Rescalyn and Straesyr had huge numbers of armsmen. Other governors are the sons of powerful High Holders with close friends who have influence. Both Chaffetz and Aramyn saw that you represented power immediately. Chaffetz didn't like it, but he understood. Aramyn knew before you walked into his hold. Wystgahl was too old and too stupid to realize that."

"I still didn't like doing it. He was a foolish old man, but his son wouldn't stand up to him, either . . . and if he'd succeeded . . ."

"No . . ." Her voice was softer. "I understand that."

"And I had to force an apology out of the son . . . but if I didn't . . . then there wouldn't be any acknowledgment of the wrongdoing, even though he was cheating everyone who pays tariffs, and he was cheating Bhayar." Quaeryt gave a bitter laugh. "I think the other thing that bothered me was his insistence that a mere hundred golds was nothing . . . when most men would die or be crippled for life for stealing that."

"You did what you had to. Bhayar wouldn't have wanted a complaint over something like that. Do you think that Wystgahl is the first High Holder to die in a strange accident? Bhayar, and especially Father, had to arrange for a few accidents when High Holders got out of line. The smart High Holders understand that. Wystgahl wasn't smart."

"No . . . he was old and not thinking straight, and he threatened to disinherit Gahlen if he went against his desires. He didn't want to listen to anyone else."

"You couldn't do much else, not if you want to be effective as governor."

Quaeryt knew that. What he didn't know was how to avoid such complaints and still accomplish the task of returning Extela to at least a semblance of a functioning city. "You were going to tell me how your search went."

"It didn't go terribly well. The quarter that held the best dwellings was partly destroyed, and the owners of the remaining dwellings there want even more for them."

"Even with the palace and the square destroyed?"

"It's where the people who are important have always lived, and now that there are fewer dwellings, those remaining are more coveted. There's no open land there. One factor has bought two dwellings just south of there and razed them so that he can build another mansion to replace the one he lost."

"Are there any close to here?"

"There's nothing close to suitable less than two milles from here, at the closest." She grimaced. "And those dwellings aren't that suitable for a governor."

"We might—"

"Have to settle for something less suitable?" Vaelora interrupted. "I've thought of that. There's another area I'll look at tomorrow." A faint smile crossed her lips. "It would be closer."

"I'll be interested in what you discover." *And especially in what it will cost.*

He still needed to write up the draft of the code for the Civic Patrol. He hoped Skarpa could come up with some names for a Civic Patrol chief—someone who could inspire respect and discipline. And he'd never checked with Dhaeryn on how the aqueduct and bridge repairs were coming along . . . and if they were.

Every day there's something else . . . and so little time. But he had no doubts that would continue. He just hoped he could keep ahead of the problems . . . or not get too far behind.

31

"You never answered my question last night," said Quaeryt to Vaelora as they left the officers' mess early on Jeudi morning.

"You asked a question?"

In hearing her tone of voice, Quaeryt knew she was playing him, but he went along with the game. "I asked if you wished to ride out once more to seek a house today or to accompany me to Thyhyem to meet High Holder Thysor this afternoon?"

"When this afternoon?"

"I thought we would leave around noon . . . after I talk to Major Skarpa about possible candidates for patrol chief and then meet with the patrollers."

"I could still ride to some . . . nearer places, and meet you at noon."

"To see if such are even remotely suitable?" Quaeryt grinned.

"That, dearest husband, is perilously close to disrespect." But she grinned back.

"Then . . . at noon."

While Vaelora went to make ready with the squad assigned to her, Quaeryt found Skarpa waiting outside the study.

"Good morning."

"Of a sort, sir."

"What now?"

"One of the rankers in Major Chaestyn's third company went out to one of the local inns last night . . ."

"They're open?"

"If there's a regiment around, they find a way to be open." Skarpa's voice was dry. "Especially when other coins are short."

"What sort of trouble is it? Or should I ask whether it was a woman or a fight?"

"Both. After he left the public room, the fellow decided a local girl—a girl, not a harlot—ought to accommodate him. She was Pharsi. Her mother was nearby."

"Is he alive?"

"No, sir. Neither are three of his mates."

"Three?"

"The mother objected. The ranker slugged the mother. The daughter stabbed the ranker in the gut. Three other rankers charged in. So did some Pharsi men. When it was all over, there were four dead rankers, and several injured Pharsi. No one knows who the girl or her mother are."

"Except she was attractive beyond her years," said Quaeryt dryly. "I take it the ranker wasn't from Tilbor or from Solis. Or here in Extela."

"Piedryn."

From what Quaeryt knew, that figured. There were almost no Pharsi in the flat croplands around Piedryn, not after Hengyst's purges of the area. But, of course, that explained in part the Yaran enmity against the Ryntarans, given how many Pharsi lived in Montagne and how many Pharsi relatives Bhayar's grandfather Lhayar had had, including his wife. "Do you need me to do anything?"

Skarpa shook his head. "I don't think so. I've had all the majors pass the word, reminding them that Lord Bhayar doesn't look favorably on mistreating women, especially Pharsi women, and that neither do you nor I. I also said that any ranker who slugged a woman because she wouldn't bed him—or whatever the reason—deserved what he got."

"I hope that's enough. The last thing I want is what happened in Tilbor." Quaeryt shook his head, even thinking about the idiocy of the first governor after the conquest. He'd razed part of the city because the Pharsi women used their knives on some of the invading Telaryn soldiers after the troopers had been warned not to molest the women. The carnage and the disruption had cost the governor his position . . . and possibly his life, later, if some rumors were true. "Especially in Bhayar's ancestral home."

"I told them that, too. They'll get the word across."

Given Skarpa's discipline, Quaeryt was certain of that. "Have you had a chance to think about candidates for the Civic Patrol chief?"

"There are two senior captains who might be suitable," said Skarpa. "One's in Second Battalion. Major Aluin says that Captain Hrehn comes from Ilyum—that's a town to the southwest of here. He's less than four months from being stipended. You've seen him—the big, gray-haired captain. I saw him lift the end of a wagon once so his company could change a wheel."

Quaeryt remembered the captain, and he could see that Hrehn would definitely have physical presence.

"The other is Pharyl. He's got almost six months before a stipend. He's from Montagne, and Major Aluin thinks he might work out."

"Would you mind if I took both of them with me tomorrow? Since they're both from around here, I could ask each for their opinions, and their recommendations."

The commander nodded. "That might be best. How are the patrollers coming?"

"I'll see shortly. I'm not that impressed so far."

"They won't be as good as the best rankers."

"I'll have to find a way to make them that good—or one of your captains will." After the briefest pause, Quaeryt asked, "Is there anything else I need to know?"

"No, and I hope there won't be."

So did Quaeryt.

After Skarpa left, Quaeryt grabbed the map he'd worked with on Meredi afternoon and hurried out to the courtyard, where a ranker had the mare saddled and waiting. He mounted and rode over to where Captain Eleryt waited.

"Ready, sir?"

Quaeryt nodded. They had less than two quints to get to the patroller station, and he worried about being late. Not that anyone would call him on it, but he needed to set the example . . . and he still needed to write up a code for the Civic Patrol.

"Company! Forward!"

Neither Quaeryt nor Eleryt spoke until they were well away from the post and the gates had closed behind the end of the company.

"Like the other days, sir? One squad to stay at the patrol station, and the others to patrol their sections of the city?"

"Exactly the same. I hope we can start the patrollers taking over some of that before long."

"The men don't mind, and they like it better than training all the time."

"I suppose they do. They can see something beside the post." *Such as women.* Quaeryt didn't voice that thought.

He rode for another half quint before he noticed several women—more than several—ahead on the sidewalk to his right . . . before some of the shops that had been open for the past week or so.

"Governor!"

Quaeryt looked to see who had called out, and realized it was the older woman standing slightly out from the others—close to half a score of other women, some older, and some younger. Almost all were dark-haired and honey-skinned, a shade slightly darker than that of Vaelora's complexion. He gestured to Eleryt and reined up.

"Yes?"

The woman who had stepped forward followed the salutation with a brief phrase in Pharsi, one Quaeryt recognized.

He answered with one of the few phrases he recalled from childhood, and then said in Tellan, "I was orphaned young, and that is all I recall."

"You are a lost one, then, in more ways than one."

"So it has been said."

"Why do you let your soldiers attack our girls?"

"What he did was forbidden. She and you defended her honor. No one will come after you, and I will make certain that the few soldiers who did not understand will know to leave you alone. Most do. The man who attacked the girl was from Piedryn."

One of the younger women spat into the gutter . . . demonstratively.

The older woman nodded. "It is said that you listen and that you are fair."

Quaeryt understood what she meant—that she expected him to keep his word. "I will do what I said. There are more than a thousand soldiers. Most will be gone in two months, and I have already ordered my officers to remind their men about Pharsi women. I cannot promise that every single one of them will be wise in the ways of Pharsi women."

The woman nodded once more, then spoke the single Pharsi word that meant acknowledgment, thanks, and an end to the conversation.

Quaeryt replied with a nod.

The women all turned and moved away.

Quaeryt gestured to Eleryt.

"Forward!" Then the captain eased his mount closer to the mare. "Sir . . . if I might ask . . ."

"Last night . . ." Quaeryt went on to explain what Skarpa had told him. ". . . and the commander and I decided that to pursue the Pharsi women would be a very bad idea, especially after what happened in Tilbora under the first governor."

"Sir . . . I understood that. But . . . she addressed you in Pharsi . . . and called you a lost one. But you're blond . . ."

Quaeryt laughed softly. "I was orphaned as a very young child, so young I was barely able to speak. I knew I was an orphan, but I didn't know I was Pharsi until less than a year ago." He recalled that moment in the produce factorage when Hailae had spoken to him in Pharsi and proclaimed him a lost one . . . and wondered how he could have forgotten it, even for a moment. "Until then, I had no idea. Like you, I thought all Pharsi were dark-haired or at least had brown hair. So did everyone else. Blond Pharsi are called the 'lost ones.' Why, I don't know. There's some sort of legend, but I've never heard it."

"Lord Bhayar has some Pharsi ancestors, it's said."

"He does, but he didn't know I was Pharsi until after I knew."

"Lost ones . . . I've never heard of that."

"Neither did I." Quaeryt kept his tone light. "And I thought I'd found myself."

Eleryt smiled.

As they continued to ride toward the patrol station, Quaeryt saw the streets were cleaner, and that the ash was largely gone. He glanced toward the truncated peak that was Mount Extel. While he saw a waviness in the sky above the mountain that suggested the air there was warmer, he couldn't make out any sign of more ash.

As the bells from the nearest anomen finished ringing out seventh glass, Quaeryt dismounted and hurried into the still-uncompleted patrol station. A quick look across the waiting patrollers, actually drawn up in five groups, each headed by one of the patrollers first, heartened him somewhat. More than somewhat, when he realized that four of the groups held twelve patrollers each, eleven plus a first. The fifth group held ten.

"Governor, sir," offered Jaramyr, stepping forward slightly from the smaller group. "We've been passing the word that the patrol's being reformed. Some of the other patrollers came back. They didn't know. I have their names for you, sir."

"Excellent," replied Quaeryt. "It appears as though you've grouped the men in terms of patrols under a patroller first."

"Yes, sir. I've also listed each patrol here. You can change them as you see fit. . . ."

Quaeryt nodded. "We'll see about that as matters progress. Did the old patrol operate with eight-man patrols under a first? Or was it twenty under a first?"

"Twenty, sir. There were eight patrols, and each had two squads, one for the day shift, and one for the night shift."

"But you weren't at full strength, were you?"

There was the slightest pause, as if Jaramyr were considering how to reply, before he said, "No, sir. There were supposed to be eight patrols, but we had six patrols and five extra men."

Quaeryt waited.

". . . and most of the patrols had fifteen or sixteen men," the patroller first finished.

"Were you ever told why?"

"The chief said that he only received enough golds for that many patrollers."

Quaeryt snorted.

The faintest look of puzzlement crossed Jaramyr's face.

"I can tell you without even any records that the chief received enough golds for eight patrols. I'd also wager that whatever patrols covered the governor's square were at full strength."

A faint smile was the response Quaeryt got, followed by, "I wouldn't take that wager, sir."

"I didn't think so."

"I'd also wager that the former chief and his captains likely survived the eruption and were not seen soon after."

"Captain Hrolar and most of the two patrols he summoned were killed trying to warn people. The others . . . we never saw them."

Sometimes the exception does prove the rule. "I'm very sorry to hear that about Captain Hrolar."

"Yes, sir. He was a good captain."

From Jaramyr's tone, Quaeryt could easy infer that the other captain or captains were not all that good.

"There are a number of things we need to take care of this morning. I'd like to start by meeting with the patrollers first about which patrols should be assigned to which parts of the city and rotation patterns. While we're discussing that, I'd like each of the patrols to meet and come up with a listing of what equipment or gear that they need—at a minimum."

For the next glass, after passing word to their patrols, the five patrollers first and Quaeryt went over the map he'd brought. Several made corrections to streets and alleyways, but in the end they'd worked out a tentative plan for patrolling. Then he asked for suggestions on inclusions in the code for patrollers, before having each patrol leader return to his patrol and gather equipment requests.

Once they returned and he'd finished noting those requests, he asked, "Are there any questions?"

"Not about what you said, sir," replied Yuell, who looked to be the youngest of the patrollers first. "We heard there was a problem between some Pharsi girls and some soldiers . . . what are we supposed to do about that?"

"The ranker who attacked the woman is dead. I doubt there will be many more problems like that. Rankers have to obey the laws just like everyone else." He thought about saying something about coming to him if there were too many rankers to press a point, but decided against it. Then he caught the sharp glances between Chelsyr and another patroller first—Uhlen, he recalled—and added, "I'm very well aware that some of Lord Bhayar's ancestors were Pharsi . . . and that he doesn't like women being forced—especially Pharsi women. I don't either, and neither will whoever becomes patrol chief." He smiled the cold smile. "Are there any other questions?"

"Do you know when we'll have a patrol chief, sir?" asked Waollyt.

"I'm still working on that. One way or another it won't be too long."

"Sir . . ." began Uhlen, "if other patrollers who were patrollers want to join the patrol . . . what should we say?"

"Tell them that you'll have to ask me—or the new chief. Before we make a decision, I'd like to hear what the patrollers first have to say about that man . . . and I'd like to know why he didn't show up the way everyone else did."

That brought nods from the group.

After almost another glass, he released the patrollers first to go over the possible patrols with their men. He also gave the patrollers first the discretion as to when to release their men, as well as noting that he expected everyone present at seventh glass on Vendrei. Then he departed with the single squad detailed to escort him.

Quaeryt rode back through the gates to the post at roughly two quints before the ten bells marking noon would ring out. Vaelora was waiting for him in a narrow wedge of shade on the north side of the stable.

After he dismounted, he led the mare over to where she stood. "How did your explorations go?"

"I'll tell you on the ride." Vaelora grimaced. "I wish we didn't have to visit a High Holder in riding garb."

"We don't have a coach, and even if we did, I don't think I'd want to take it over the east bridge at the moment."

"Another loss to the mountain," she said ruefully. "I'm sure Governor Scythn had a coach."

"Among many other things."

"You don't like him, and you never met him." After a moment she added slyly, "I cannot imagine why."

"Neither can I, except that it might have something to do with his handiwork. I just found out this morning that it appears that he allowed the patrol chief to pocket the pay of what amounted to two patrols." He paused. "We need to ride out as soon as I water the mare and the squads are ready."

"Squads?"

"The one that escorted you, and the one that escorted me. Skarpa doesn't want us going anywhere with less than half a company, especially outside of Extela."

Even so, it was a good quint past noon before they left the post and headed for the east river bridge. Because Dhaeryn had not been able to locate any large timbers, the repairs so far had been limited to rebuilding and reinforcing the stone piers. That was another reason why Quaeryt needed to talk to Thysor, because, from what Quaeryt had been able to determine, Thysor was the closest High Holder with extensive timberlands.

As they rode into the area of Extela that Quaeryt had come to realize held a number of Pharsi shops, factorages, and homes, he saw several women turn, inclining their heads to Vaelora in respect. He knew that because he saw the lips of several murmur words about the Nameless "blessing the lady."

He said nothing about that until they were crossing the square on the west side of the river, just before the bridge. "You have more than a few admirers."

"On this side of Extela."

"I can't imagine that anyone would indicate anything else, even on the west side."

"Let us just say that many on the west side are more reserved."

"After all these years?"

"Especially after all these years."

Quaeryt understood. That had always been the problem the Pharsi faced. Because they were intelligent and worked harder than anyone else, they were successful. Very few people really wanted to attribute success just to hard work, and so they blamed it on cliquishness and conspiracy. Then when the Yaran warlords had married Pharsi women, Quaeryt had no doubt the marriages had "proved" the nefarious motives of the Pharsi clans.

Quaeryt could see engineers working on the middle pier of the bridge, but not on the piers closest to the riverbanks. "It looks like Dhaeryn and the engineers have the end piers on each side largely repaired."

"The planks and timbers don't look that solid," observed Vaelora.

As before, they ended up crossing the bridge in single file, widely spaced, and it took more than two quints to get both squads across.

Once they were on the main road, on the way to the crossroads where they would turn south, Vaelora asked, "How is the rebuilding of the patrol station coming?"

"I'm hopeful it will be usable by sometime next week. It's likely to be ready before the patrollers are." After a moment, he asked, "What have you discovered?" He tried not to sound wary or skeptical.

"There's one dwelling that *might* serve. It's more like a villa than a proper Extelan house. The factor who owned it died, and his daughter wants to sell it." Vaelora shook her head. "It's large enough, but it's been empty for a year . . ."

"Furnishings?"

Vaelora shook her head. "A few pieces, but even they'd need work before you'd trust them."

"What does she want for it?"

"Five hundred golds. The repairs would cost at least fifty, and furnishings . . ." Vaelora shook her head.

"We can't . . ." Quaeryt paused.

"You were going to say, dearest?"

"I was going to say that we couldn't afford that, but I realized that the governor can, since the villa will serve as well for whoever else is governor, and five hundred golds is not that expensive for a permanent residence."

"Later governors will not be so modest."

"That will be their problem, but it could also serve as the residence of the princeps."

"I had thought that, actually. If we can work matters out." Vaelora smiled.

And the greatest working-out will be between us. He returned the smile.

Another glass passed before they reached the severe iron gates to Thyhyem, gates attached to modest reddish black brick pillars, and flanked by walls that extended less than two yards on each side of the gates. Beyond the walls on each side was a thick hedgerow. There was no gatehouse and no guard.

Even on a second visit, Thyhyem wasn't exactly what Quaeryt expected, not with the mille-long flat graveled entry drive flanked by ancient and massive oaks, although in places there were younger oaks, clearly replacement trees, but even those were scarcely saplings, or anything close. The hold house itself was of two levels, also of the reddish black brick and formed a V, with the entry portico at the point of the V.

Thysor stood on the wide brick expanse in front of the brick pillars that supported the portico roof that sheltered the entry to the long dwelling.

"Greetings!" offered the High Holder as Vaelora and Quaeryt dismounted. "Refreshments await your men and the mounts in the north courtyard." Thysor gestured to his left.

"Thank you," replied Quaeryt, after handing the mare's reins to a ranker and extending the hand to Vaelora that she didn't need to dismount.

They walked up the three steps to join the holder.

"Governor Quaeryt," offered Thysor, his eyes going to Vaelora, "and

Lady Vaelora. I always told your brother that you'd grow up to be both intelligent and beautiful."

"I'm glad you offered more than beauty as a compliment," returned Vaelora. "Yet how would you know, since you've not seen me in years?"

Thysor laughed. "Your husband is a scholar . . . and a governor. Your brother has followed his father's example. The more closely related someone is to him, the more he expects. The governor is your husband and, if I understand matters correctly, had to prove himself in a number of ways. You were known as extraordinarily bright as a child, and you had the habit of tactfully puncturing vanity even then. Therefore . . ." The silver-haired High Holder shrugged, but his eyes smiled.

Vaelora offered a warm smile. "And you, Thysor, would have liked to flirt with every pretty girl and woman, but contented yourself with charming young girls. I can see some things have not changed."

The interaction between the two was a quick reminder to Quaeryt that he'd become part of a very small circle, about which he knew next to nothing—except for Bhayar's family.

"My dear lady . . . I would not dare. Already, the word has spread that your husband has single-handedly restored basic order in Extela."

"That's rather easy to do with a full regiment at your back," suggested Quaeryt mildly.

"It only seems so," replied Thysor. "But do come in. We can talk of that and other matters over refreshments and light fare." He paused. "I do presume you are not here for a mere courtesy call, Governor."

"For courtesy, but not just for that."

"I do appreciate the courtesy," replied Thysor as he guided them between the brick pillars and to the open but plain goldenwood double doors, "and your interest in more than courtesy. Your predecessor emphasized courtesy to the exclusion of all else . . . or so it seemed from this side of the river."

"Especially courtesy to his own coffers, it appears more and more," replied Quaeryt, hoping for a response from Thysor.

"That is a common failing among governors, one reason, no doubt, you were appointed." His voice turned wry as he continued. "It's also a failing not unknown to High Holders, as I suspect you've discovered."

Quaeryt wasn't certain if Thysor already knew about Wystgahl, and he wasn't about to ask. He just said, "Greed is common enough among all, I fear."

"So it is."

The entry hall through which they walked was square, with off-white plastered walls above goldenwood wainscoting, and a pair of portraits, one a woman, on the north wall, and the other a man, on the south wall. Neither resembled Thysor.

The High Holder led them through the receiving hall to another circular chamber, from which two corridors branched, one at an angle to the left and the other at the same angle to the right. At the back of the circular hall was an archway, with open double doors, toward which Thysor continued. Beyond the archway was an expansive chamber.

"Chaelyna is awaiting us in the salon. It is a treat to have visitors. We see so few, as far as we are from Extela." Thysor halted at the archway, gestured for them to enter, and then followed, smoothly moving up beside Vaelora.

Quaeryt surveyed the salon quickly, noting the wall of windows to the west, overlooking a private garden, with each window having dark gauzy hangings, most likely to mitigate the light of the late-afternoon sunlight, especially in summer, and heavier ochre draperies as well, for cold winter evenings. Set directly before the center windows was a table, already set for four.

The slightly stocky dark-haired woman who rose from the settee on the immediate right, while perhaps a good ten years older than Quaeryt, was certainly at least that amount younger than the High Holder. She offered a cheerful smile.

"Dear . . . Governor Quaeryt and his wife Vaelora. You might remember her." Thysor's eyes twinkled.

"Chayar's youngest. My . . . how beautiful you are . . . and married, no less."

"Only since the first of the year," replied Vaelora.

Thysor gestured to the chairs and the settee facing the one before which Chaelyna stood. Vaelora settled onto the settee in such a fashion that both women seated themselves at the same instant. Quaeryt was not quite as deft as his wife, but not so far off that it was noticeable.

"Shall we dispense with the less courteous aspect of your visit first, so that we may enjoy your company?" asked the High Holder.

Quaeryt couldn't help smiling at the way in which Thysor had framed matters, with the implication that the "less courteous aspect" still needed to be handled courteously and tactfully. "I may have been misinformed, but I gathered that you have extensive timberlands . . ."

"Do not tell me that the governor is becoming a timber factor . . ." Thysor laughed. "Pardon my little jokes. I notice that you have men working on the east river bridge. You are looking for heavy timbers and planks?"

"I am. At present, what remains of the span can barely hold a single mount at a time."

"What terms are you asking?"

"Your cost for the timber, plus a profit of one part in ten."

"And you would trust my costs?" Thysor raised his eyebrows.

"I trust everyone . . . until they abuse that trust. For some, I have trusted them only once."

Thysor looked not at Quaeryt, but to Vaelora. "Is it wise to abuse the governor's trust?"

"No . . . because he holds it as an abuse of Lord Bhayar's trust."

"Pardon me, if I ask a personal question, Lady. Did the governor serve Lord Bhayar before you married him?"

Vaelora laughed. "He has known Bhayar since I was little more than a babe, and he served as an advisor and more, most lately as princeps of Tilbor. He did not seek my hand. Lord Bhayar insisted that I wed him."

Thysor's eyes returned to Quaeryt. "Then you are high in Bhayar's estimation, and your accomplishments must be many, or you would not be a governor, coming from a background as a scholar."

Quaeryt smiled wryly. "There is no way that I can reply to that without seeming either excessively overweening or falsely modest."

"I think you just did." Thysor chuckled.

Across the table, Chaelyna smiled as well, but did not speak.

The High Holder's eyes lighted on Vaelora. "Again . . . my pardon, but you do not act as many women do when a marriage is arranged without their consent. Nor do your glances at your husband suggest indifference."

"I do believe, High Holder," replied Vaelora with a light laugh, "that we should discuss such matters after those of lesser courtesy."

"So we should." Thysor's voice and expression were both warm. He turned back to Quaeryt. "Seeing as you are who you are, and seeing as you are neither attempting to buy my favor by acceding to an exorbitant price, nor that of the mob, by forcing a sale on which I would lose golds, I will accept your terms. Your men can meet with my timbermaster tomorrow if they so wish."

"I will send Major Heireg and Major Dhaeryn to see him."

"Excellent." Thysor smiled broadly. "Then we can talk over more pleasant matters, and we can learn more about both of you."

"I had hoped to learn more about you," replied Quaeryt. "and what you can tell me about Extela and Montagne."

"I could not tell you half so much as could your lovely wife."

"I have not been in Extela in years. You have so much more experience than do we," replied Vaelora. "And experience is what enables understanding . . ."

"Then we will trade anecdotes," suggested Chaelyna, "but I do think we should repair to the table. Talking can be such a thirsty business, and you must taste last year's ice wine. It is delectable, all because of Thysor's care and hard-won knowledge. He won't say that himself, but I can." As she rose from the settee, she glanced to Vaelora. "As I am certain you can say much about the governor that he is far too modest to disclose himself."

As he stood with the others, Quaeryt knew he would have to force himself to keep his thoughts on the social side of the afternoon, much as he wished he could have departed earlier, if only so that he could get to work writing up the code for the Civic Patrol.

Except this is work, and necessary. Especially after the mess with Wystgahl, you need more High Holders who will support you . . . or not oppose you.

He smiled again, even as he wished that Wystgahl had been half as courteous as Thysor or at least as practical as Chaffetz.

In the end, Quaeryt and Vaelora spent close to four glasses with Thysor and Chaelyna, among the most pleasant four glasses Quaeryt had ever spent with a High Holder. As a result, they didn't return to the post until well after the evening meal, and it was almost dark by the time they retired to their quarters. Both moons were already high in the sky, on a warmish evening that foreshadowed the heat of late spring and summer.

"I'm sorry we missed the evening meal," said Quaeryt as he closed the door.

"I'm not," replied Vaelora. "We had far better fare with afternoon refreshments . . . and delightful conversation."

"Do you think he'll attempt to cut corners on the timber?"

"No. He's charming, and he's been very successful. He'll earn every copper he can, to the last letter of any agreement. He won't cheat you, outright or indirectly."

"Why do you think that?"

"He's sharp. He knows you're powerful. He doesn't know why or how. You're also close to Bhayar. Upsetting a young, ambitious, powerful, and well-connected man is dangerous, especially when that young man has guaranteed a profit. By doing it that way, whether you intended it or not, you told him that you wouldn't cheat him, but that you'd destroy him if he cheated you."

Quaeryt laughed softly. "I didn't—"

"You did, dearest, and you know it." Vaelora grinned at her husband.

"I wasn't intimating destruction."

"Whether or not you would go that far doesn't matter. He knows you could, and it was deftly done, honestly and directly. He appreciated your tact."

"I'm glad you—and Thysor—found my approach tactful. Or was it merely honest and direct?"

"You were indirectly direct, which is best in situations such as these." Vaelora sat down on the end of the bed.

"I'm used to being indirect when I've been the one receiving the orders or instructions, but I don't have that much practice at getting my point across indirectly without seeming either arrogant or weak."

"No one would ever guess. Just don't worry too much about it."

"I don't when I'm dealing with officers or patrollers, but the number of times I've dealt from a basis of power with High Holders I could count on my fingers." He paused. "Look at what happened with Wystgahl."

"That would have happened to any governor in that situation. Most would have handled it with greater difficulty."

Quaeryt certainly hoped he'd done as well as he could, but didn't see much point in belaboring his concerns. "How does your brother view the High Holders? It's not a question I was in a position to ask, and I never observed him with any."

"He is wary of any of them."

"They can't do that much to him . . . unless they unite, and I've not seen any evidence that many are dissatisfied."

"Most of them trust no one. That's because only one son can inherit. More than a few older sons have met their end in strange accidents. They're always looking over their shoulders. They can't help but wonder if Bhayar might be conspiring with a younger brother, especially if they think they've displeased Bhayar . . . or their father. You saw that with Wystgahl. So few High Holders tell Bhayar any more than they must. Except for the handful who wish to use Bhayar to gain an advantage over other High Holders, most avoid him except at functions and other gatherings that are largely ceremonial."

"Do you think that's why Aramyn was so cordial to us?"

"I feel that he was doing exactly what his actions implied. He was viewed unfavorably by Father, and he wants to change that. Because you weren't unreasonable, it won't even cost him anything . . . only a chance of forgoing a bit more profit . . . and that wouldn't even be certain."

"So why was Wystgahl so belligerent? I offered him the same terms."

"I can't say." Vaelora shook her head. "Except that he was greedy and stupid."

"Could it be that all that rebuilding overextended him? And that he saw the chance to make a greater profit on his grain and other crops? He had to use his own people, but when lien-tenants are doing stonework, they're not planting or harvesting."

"That's possible, but I couldn't say."

He smiled and asked, "If you would tell me more about the dwelling that *might* be suitable . . ."

"It's more like a villa. I told you that. It has a large main level, and only master sleeping quarters and the like on the upper level. The entire rear is a walled garden, but the walls are brick. They need much work. The garden is hopelessly overgrown. The interior looks solid, but every wall needs paint or plaster. There aren't any paneled walls at all, except for the main study. There's very little wood, either, except for the built-in bookcases in the main study. It might rather be called a library. . . ." Vaelora looked at Quaeryt.

"It sounds like there's a fair amount of work to be done."

"A great number of small things and several large ones, such as oiling all the outside wood, repairing and straightening most of the shutters . . ."

As Vaelora went through the list, Quaeryt nodded occasionally, torn between admiring her for all that she had noted and trying not to show the sense of being totally appalled at what needed to be done—and what that would likely cost. Yet they couldn't stay in the officers' quarters forever.

Vendrei morning saw Vaelora off to take another look at the old villa that might possibly be suitable, while Quaeryt met again with Skarpa and then Dhaeryn before awaiting the arrival of the two captains suggested by the commander.

They both entered the small study together, Quaeryt gestured for them to sit down, then asked, "Did Commander Skarpa explain why I wanted to meet both of you?"

"Yes, sir," offered Pharyl politely.

The taller and more massive Hrehn nodded.

"What did he say?"

The two exchanged glances. Then Hrehn spoke. His voice was a light baritone. "He said you wanted two experienced captains to come with you and look over the remaining civic patrollers and give you our opinions."

"That's true. I'd like to see what you two think."

"Might I ask why you—or the commander—picked us?" asked Pharyl. His eyes centered on Quaeryt.

"I asked him for captains who had the most time dealing directly with rankers." That was certainly true enough, reflected Quaeryt. "I don't have that kind of day-to-day experience with patrollers . . . or rankers."

"What can you tell us, sir, if you don't mind, before we see these patrollers?" asked Pharyl, wiry and shorter, with jet-black hair.

Hrehn nodded once again.

"Right now there are about half the former patrollers remaining," Quaeryt began. "Neither the chief nor the captains can be found. According to the patrollers first still in Extela, the one good captain was killed in the ash storm, along with several patrollers. He was trying to help people escape the eruption. The other captain . . . no one wants to say anything about him. The chief diverted the equivalent of twenty men's pay into his own wallet, as well as a disproportionate amount of the funds provided for Civic Patrol expenses. No one knows whether he died in the ash storm or scuttled away. The engineers are converting an unused factorage into Civic Patrol headquarters because the old one is buried under the ash and lava. The patrollers first have organized the remaining patrollers into five half-strength patrols. I have my opinions, but I'd like you two to accompany me this morning. After we return, I'd like your thoughts before I make any more decisions."

The two exchanged glances once more.

"We can do that, sir," replied Hrehn.

Quaeryt had the sense that both suspected more than mere opinion was likely to be involved, but he wanted to see just how perceptive the two might be. "We might as well get started. We'll ride over to the patrol station, and if you have any more questions, you can ask them on the way."

Neither captain said a word more, but followed Quaeryt outside into the courtyard. They'd clearly expected to accompany him, because their mounts were waiting with his, as was a company from First Battalion, led by Undercaptain Sengh.

Only after they were riding up the avenue away from the post did the gray-haired Hrehn ask, "How many patrollers are there now, sir?"

"There were fifty-four yesterday. That includes five patroller firsts. From what they told me, there should have been close to a hundred and sixty patrollers for the entire city, but there were only a few more than a hundred."

"That doesn't seem like that many," observed Pharyl. "Did they just patrol during the day?"

"Two shifts, I've been told. Day and night."

"Fifty men to cover the city," mused Pharyl. "Were they working in pairs?"

Quaeryt almost said "yes," except that he realized he'd never asked. "I assumed so, but I didn't inquire."

"Most patrols do send out men in pairs, from what I've seen," added Hrehn, "but you never know."

"Twenty-five teams . . . What equipment did they have?"

"Truncheons and belt knives . . . and a small coil of rope. Uniforms, of course."

"Leather wrist shackles would be better," offered Pharyl. "Heavy leather's harder to cut."

"Why not iron?" asked Quaeryt.

"It's too heavy, and to equip an entire patrol would take time."

Quaeryt nodded. That made sense, and he hadn't even considered it. But then, that was one reason why he'd asked for experienced older officers.

The three reined up outside the patrol station less than a quint before seventh glass, and Quaeryt could see several patrollers walking quickly toward the building.

"They're the younger ones," said Pharyl.

The front four windows were now protected by iron grates. Quaeryt wondered where Dhaeryn had found those, since two looked to have come from one source, and two from another. The narrow porch was clean and swept, he noted, as he stepped into the front chamber of the station. The area inside the freshly oiled heavy double doors, now in place and each held open by a square-cut black stone as a doorstop, looked completed, with a long desk counter some five yards back from the doors. The wall behind the counter had a single solid door. Looking closely, Quaeryt could see that the engineers and those locals that they had hired had joined sections of wood of differing sizes and grains, but the workmanship and the dark oil stain minimized the contrasts.

The waiting patrollers stood in five loose formations—their patrols. None stiffened as Quaeryt walked in, followed by the captains, but all conversation stopped. The receiving room was so quiet that Quaeryt could hear the unevenness of his own bootsteps as he walked to a point just before the middle of the counter and turned to face the patrollers. Hrehn took a position to his left, Pharyl to his right.

After a moment, Jaramyr stepped forward. He glanced from Quaeryt to Hrehn and then to Pharyl, his eyes taking in the Telaryn uniforms before he looked back to the governor. "Sir, all men are present. We also have three former patrollers who would like to rejoin the patrol. They were staying with relatives in nearby towns. Word was slow to reach them."

"Thank you for the report. You and the other patrollers first talk to them and tell me what you think tomorrow morning. Have them report tomorrow, and we'll let them know then. Oh . . . and everyone will be paid next Vendrei, and every Vendrei after that." Quaeryt paused, then went on. "I've asked Captain Hrehn and Captain Pharyl to accompany me today. After we inspect the progress of the building, we'll be meeting with each patrol and its patroller first separately. After we meet with each patrol and go over the patrol routes, I'll be dispatching each one to cover those routes and familiarize each man with the entire route the patrol will be responsible for. Pass that word to the other patrollers first."

"Yes, sir."

As Jaramyr turned, Quaeryt could sense the quick exchange between the two captains, but only said, "Let's see how the engineers are doing on the back area."

The door behind the receiving counter opened easily onto a short hallway. As in the walls of the receiving chamber, various sizes and lengths of wood planks smoothly joined and strained comprised the hallway walls. On the right side were three doors, one into a modest study, and two into small studies.

Each had a table desk and a single chair. On the left was a single larger chamber, empty of all furnishings. The hallway ended at a cross corridor. There, Quaeryt stopped and looked in both directions at the doorways set at even intervals across the back of the building. The stone and brickwork looked complete on less than half the cells. From what he could tell there were eighteen, nine in the front and nine behind them.

Major Dhaeryn hurried along the cross corridor, coming to a stop before Quaeryt. "Sir . . . I'd hoped to see you here. Major Heireg and I will be leaving as soon as he arrives to go meet with High Holder Thysor's timbermaster."

"Good. Just make sure you get the basis for his costs. He should be fair. How are we coming here?"

"We could only work in eighteen cells. Each should fit two men."

"That will have to do, then," replied Quaeryt with a smile. The smile faded as he recalled that he didn't have a justicer or even a justice hall, because the old justice hall had been on the south side of the old governor's square. "We may have to use the larger room back there for a justicing hall for a while."

"I'd thought that might be necessary. The men are working on a small dais that can be put at one end."

"Thank you." Once again, Quaeryt felt as though he'd plunged into water over his head and had been rescued by the competence of others. "How are the cells coming?"

"By Lundi we should have maybe half of them solid and tight. Getting the mortar has been the hard part, but you don't want a cell with anything but brick and stone walls."

"Don't let me keep you, Major. You need to work out the timbers and heavy planks for the bridge."

"Yes, sir. By your leave . . ."

"Go . . ." Quaeryt smiled warmly and gestured.

Then he crossed the hall and looked into the nearest cell, one that appeared nearly finished. The cell was roughly three yards deep and two and a half wide. The walls were a mixture of stone and brick, and there were two small openings high in the wall, one in front and one in the rear, and two smaller ones also in front and back, level with the stone floor on which the cells had been constructed.

"Not too small," murmured Pharyl.

"Wouldn't want to spend much time there," added Hrehn.

"This won't serve the city for that long, sir," said Pharyl.

"I'd thought that some of the offenders could be used for work parties to clean the city."

"They could, but they'd still have to be confined at night," pointed out Pharyl. "You could flog some of them and let them go for a first offense."

"We'll need to talk about that." *Something else you hadn't thought about.* "Let's go meet with the patrollers first and their patrols." Quaeryt turned and walked back to the receiving room and to Jaramyr and his patrol.

"Sir?" said Jaramyl, stiffening slightly.

"Have you drawn out individual areas for each patrol?" asked Quaeryt.

"Ah . . . no, sir. I've shown them on the map you had me draw," answered Jaramyr.

Quaeryt didn't want to press that too hard. "Then after you walk them through the entire area, you and your men need to come back here and decide on who patrols which of the areas. I want each team of two men to patrol the same area for a week, and then switch to another area. With five patrols, each team will spend a week a month in the same area. That should allow familiarity, but not too much familiarity."

"Ah . . . yes, sir."

"That may change based on how things go, and how the new chief wants to organize patrols, but that's the way it will be for now. I'd like to see the map with all the patrol areas drawn in when I meet with you tomorrow morning. After we meet then, you'll take the patrollers through their areas once more." Quaeryt paused. "Is that clear?"

"Yes, sir."

"You're dismissed to familiarize your men with their patrol area."

"Yes, sir."

Explaining what he had in mind took slightly longer with the other patrollers first, and it was almost a glass later when Quaeryt and the two captains left the patrol station and headed back to the post, accompanied by a single squad.

After they had ridden for a time, Quaeryt asked, "What did you think of the patrol station?"

"Not a bad place for it," said Hrehn. "Could be larger, like Pharyl said."

"The engineers have done a good job for the time they've had," added Pharyl. "In the future, it might be a good idea to build another station on the west side."

"You could make that one bigger," added Hrehn.

"Do you think they need to patrol all the time . . . or that they really ever did?" asked Pharyl.

"What would you suggest?" replied Quaeryt.

"Two shifts. One from fifth glass of the morning until third glass of the afternoon, the second from second glass of the afternoon to midnight. The time between second and third glass would be used to change patrol shifts and learn what happened and what to look out for."

"No patrols at all between midnight and fifth glass?"

"The patrollers wouldn't catch many people at those times, and the tavernas and inns aren't supposed to be serving then anyway."

"I hadn't considered that." *There's a lot you haven't considered or had time to consider.*

The questions offered by the two after that dealt mainly with administration and supply details, some of which, again, Quaeryt hadn't fully considered.

When they returned to the post, Quaeryt dismounted and turned to the pair. "I'd like a word with each of you. Alone in my study. I'll start with Hrehn."

Once he and Hrehn had returned to the study and seated themselves, Quaeryt immediately asked, "What do you think of the patrollers you saw?"

The big captain offered a slow smile. "They're scared to death of you, sir. That'd be good because they're not used to discipline. They need some work there. Like Pharyl said, they really need leather cuffs. Rope takes too much time. The armorers here could make up some."

"What else?"

"You'll need more men, sir. You know that."

"How or where would you suggest we get them?"

Hrehn frowned. "I can't say as I have the best ideas for that. I'd not want the present patrollers first making those decisions, though. Not for new recruits. Maybe . . . put out the word and have them come here to meet with you?"

Quaeryt asked questions and listened for another half glass, then let the big captain go, saying that he'd like to talk to him again later.

Pharyl came into the study and seated himself almost cautiously.

"What do you think of the patrollers and the patrol, Captain?"

"Might I ask a question, sir?"

"Of course."

"You were watching us as much as the patrollers. I got the idea that you had more in mind than just our opinion. Am I wrong, sir?"

Quaeryt smiled. "No. You're not. Are there any other reasons why you thought that?"

"Hrehn and I are the closest to finishing our time for a stipend, and we're both from this part of the country. There's also no patrol chief, and there are no captains."

"You're right about that. But I do want your opinion."

"There's a lot of work to be done if you want a decent Civic Patrol. You've got them in line for now, but in another month, unless you get a good chief and senior captain, you'll have trouble . . ."

Quaeryt noted the way Pharyl linked the chief and captain, but nodded and kept listening.

". . . They'll just go back to their old ways, and they'll have their hands out for coins and favors."

"You seem certain of that."

"I grew up in Montagne. You know that. Even when I was a boy, people talked about how you had to pay the patrollers in Extela for everything to avoid trouble. More than a few friends left Extela and came to Montagne." Pharyl laughed softly. "You only had to pay the patrollers in Montagne if you might be in real trouble."

"So how would a new chief stop that?"

"You'll never stop it all. You might keep it way down. The best way would be to let it be known that you wouldn't look too hard if a patroller got a free meal now and again, but that anything more might end them up in a cell, if not worse. That'd work if the patrollers thought the chief wasn't taking coins from their payroll or accepting golds from every factor or High Holder around. If the new chief ends up on the take . . ." The wiry captain shook his head.

"What sort of new chief would you suggest?"

Pharyl smiled wryly. "If I were looking, I'd want an older officer who came up through the ranks and wasn't too senior."

"Why?"

"A commander or a marshal would be looking for more golds, and the only way to get them would be the way you wouldn't want. So they'd either leave or end up on the take. A captain or major could expect more pay and less danger than in service. They wouldn't have any expectations about the patrollers, either."

"Would you be interested?"

"Yes, sir. I would. But not unless Hrehn would agree to be the senior captain. It'd take two of us. And I'd want to be paid as much as a major."

A gold a week was certainly affordable, reflected Quaeryt. "Do you have any idea if Hrehn would be interested?"

"I don't know . . . not for certain. He'd talked about whether he could be a captain of patrollers in Montagne. He didn't think it was possible here."

"Let's see. If you'd wait here a moment while the duty messenger finds Captain Hrehn."

"Yes, sir."

Quaeryt stepped out into the corridor, but couldn't find a messenger. Less than a half a quint later, he did find Hrehn talking to the duty squad leader, and the two walked back to the study. As Quaeryt closed the door, the gray-haired captain looked quizzically at Pharyl.

"Captains . . . you might have some idea why I asked you to accompany me to see the patrollers. Both of you were recommended as possible candidates for positions in the Civic Patrol here." Quaeryt turned and looked at Hrehn. "Would you be interested in becoming the senior captain if Captain Pharyl is the new chief?"

"I might be, sir."

"The starting pay would be eight silvers a week for the senior captain and a gold and two silvers for the chief. Oh . . . and you'd be carried on the regimental rolls until you'd served your time for a stipend."

Hrehn looked to Pharyl. "Was this your doing?"

"In a way," answered Quaeryt. "Captain Pharyl was blunt with me. He said that the challenges of rebuilding the Civic Patrol would require a senior captain whom he could trust and rely upon. He indicated that he would not consider the position unless I committed to also hiring a solid senior captain."

Hrehn laughed, warmly. "A man'd be a fool not to accept your offer, Governor. That's if Pharyl accepts it."

"Do you both accept, then?"

"Yes, sir."

Quaeryt spent another glass with both officers, and then a quint with Skarpa informing him.

The commander laughed. "I can't say I'm surprised, sir. You can be very persuasive . . . one way or another."

"I prefer honey to vinegar."

"Vinegar's sweet compared to your disapproval, sir."

Quaeryt could only shrug, but he had to admit he hadn't thought he was that hard. *Are you?* Then he thought about Wystgahl—except he still didn't see that he'd had any real choice.

He had no sooner returned to the study when there was a knock on the door. "Yes?"

The door edged open to reveal the duty squad leader. "Lady Vaelora sent a ranker back to inquire if it would be possible for you to be able to join her, sir."

Quaeryt managed not to frown. Then he nodded. "Tell him I'll be there in a moment . . . if someone could see to my mount."

"Yes, sir."

By the time Quaeryt reached the courtyard, the squad that had accompanied him earlier in the day was waiting, along with the mare and the ranker who had carried the message from Vaelora. In less than a quint, he and the squad followed the ranker out to the avenue, and then westward along a boulevard with a center strip that held trees and bushes. He couldn't tell whether the ash had killed the vegetation or whether it was simply slow to leaf out after the winter.

After a ride of slightly more than a mille, the ranker turned north past a pair of large brick pillars. Quaeryt would not have called any of the dwellings along the tree-lined avenue either modest or small. All were of at least two levels, and none was less than thirty yards across the front. All were constructed of either black stone or reddish black brick, if not both, with slate roofs, and the grounds of roughly one in three were enclosed by walls over which not even a man on horseback could see.

Even from over a hundred yards away, Quaeryt could see where a mounted ranker waited in the street in front of a pair of open gates in yet another wall. When Quaeryt reined up beside the ranker, he saw the villa through the gates—a dwelling certainly not modest in any sense, not to Quaeryt. The two-story structure extended some seventy yards from end to end, and that did not count the stable situated at the end of the drive that ran from the gates to the covered side portico and then to the stable, also of two stories. Nor did it count another structure located against the rear wall of the property, although Quaeryt could only make out part of that, shielded as it was by the bulk of the villa and the slightly overgrown trees to the right of the open space beside the stable.

Only five hundred golds? Quaeryt took a slow deep breath and then rode through the gates and to the portico. Vaelora was waiting there with an older man in olive livery. Beyond them, in the area to the right of the stable, waited the rest of the squad, dismounted and watering their mounts from the long stone trough opposite the stable.

Quaeryt dismounted and tied the mare to one of the ornate iron hitching rings, then walked up the four wide black stone steps to the brick-paved and columned portico.

"Dearest . . ." Vaelora smiled. "I'm glad you could join me. This is Calachyl. He's the steward for Factoria Grelyana. He's been showing me through the villa."

The steward bowed. "Honored Governor."

"I'm pleased to meet you, Calachyl."

"It is my pleasure, sir. Would you like to see the villa?"

"Yes."

The steward smiled and gestured for them to follow him.

The double goldenwood doors from the portico could have used oiling and polish, and the iron grilles that protected them showed traces of rust in places. Immediately inside was a square entry hall, some four yards on a side. An archway to the right opened into a small waiting room with windows overlooking the front garden, not that anything green was yet in sight. Opposite the archway was a doorway.

"That is the cloakroom," gestured the steward, before opening the door, then closing it and moving out of the entry hall. "The receiving parlor is on the right, and the library and study on the left."

Both chambers were large, five yards wide and close to ten long. Built-in oak bookcases comprised one entire wall of the study—the one backing up to the cloakroom—and in the middle of the outside wall were double doors opening onto the covered rear porch. A similar set of doors in the receiving parlor opened onto the front porch, also covered. Neither chamber held furnishings.

Quaeryt tried to note everything as the steward led them through the villa, showing them the formal dining chamber, the grand salon, the private dining and breakfast room, the kitchens and pantries in the rear, the grand staircase to the upper level, the master suite and bathing and dressing chambers, and six other bedchambers, and two bath chambers, as well as the upper level study for the mistress of the house. By the time they returned to the entry hall, Quaeryt briefly wondered why anyone would sell what he had seen for a mere five hundred golds, but then realized that the dwelling didn't match what Vaelora had described earlier.

So how much is this? He decided not to ask at that moment. Instead, he concentrated on what Calachyl was saying.

"The servants' quarters are separate in the building beyond the garden, and there are different cellars below for wines and produce, as well as a strong room."

"The stable even has quarters above it suitable for your personal guard," said Vaelora, "and there's a separate hidden staircase down from the study to the strong room."

Personal guard? That was another matter he hadn't even thought about, but should have, since the regiment would be departing in less than a month. With each passing day, there seemed to be something else that being a governor married to Vaelora required of him. *How many others would there be that you haven't even considered?*

He wasn't about to even try to guess.

"I'm glad you thought about that," he said with a smile. "Tell me more."

"I will wait outside," said the steward, bowing and then slipping away.

Quaeryt waited until Calachyl was out of earshot. "I don't think this is the dwelling you mentioned before."

"Isn't it so much better?" asked Vaelora.

"I wouldn't know. I never saw the other one," replied Quaeryt dryly.

"Are you angry with me, dearest?"

"Should I be?"

"This is so much better," Vaelora repeated.

"It might be so much more expensive also."

"It's only twelve hundred golds."

Quaeryt managed not to swallow.

"That's less than half what it's worth."

"So why is it priced that way?"

"Factoria Grelyana moved into a larger dwelling last year and needs the golds. She wants to present the lower price as a favor, but that's not the reason."

"How do you know that?"

"I have a few acquaintances left here. I asked them."

Quaeryt sighed. "Twelve hundred golds is a great deal more than we talked about. More than twice as much. This comes at a time when the provincial treasury isn't exactly healthy. And we have no furniture and no furnishings."

"Dearest . . . I've slept in other people's homes, and in wagons, and inns, and in cramped officers' quarters. I haven't said a word. Sooner or later, you or someone will have to build a governor's residence. Building something like this would likely cost thousands of golds . . ."

"It likely would," he replied. "We don't have that, either."

"Yes . . . you do. You have over ten thousand golds in the treasury. You'll have to use something like three thousand to pay everyone until the end of Mayas, and another five hundred or so for supplies. You'll start getting tariffs in Juyn. That gives you at least five thousand. Twelve hundred for a governor's residence isn't that much."

"That's just the beginning," he pointed out, realizing as he did that she'd remembered everything he'd said about pay and expenses.

"Paying for repairs and cleaning isn't that expensive."

"Furnishings?"

"Some of that can wait, if you think it necessary."

Quaeryt wanted to shake his head. His wife was Bhayar's sister, and she was going to get her way, especially since Bhayar had already made the point—when he'd insisted on lavish quarters for them in the Telaryn Palace—that Vaelora required "suitable accommodations."

"The villa we can do," he conceded. "Beyond basic furnishings for the main bedchamber and the kitchen and the parlor—"

"And the studies," added Vaelora. "You can't work without a desk and a few things."

He nodded. "The golds will have to go to the factoria directly, and we'll need a document of sale and receipt."

"I told her that would be necessary if you approved."

"When I approved," he corrected her ruefully.

Vaelora raised her eyebrows.

"That is not disrespect, dear," he replied. "Merely an acknowledgment of what is." *And what will likely be for many years to come.*

He didn't want to dwell on that too deeply at the moment, much as he knew he'd never escape that reality.

When he'd reluctantly agreed to the purchase of the villa, Quaeryt realized there would be more than a few details to complete the purchase, and he and Vaelora followed Calachyl to another villa more than a mille away. Except the word "villa" didn't begin to describe the small three-level palace that lay behind the high black stone walls. Nor was "luxurious" adequate to describe the paneled study to which Calachyl conducted them, a study twice the size of the one in the villa they had just inspected, with goldenwood bookcases, and a deep-pile Chevan carpet covering much of the polished pale green marble floor. The desk and chairs were pale goldenwood, recently and carefully crafted, with deep green cushions.

The woman who greeted them was perhaps a digit or two shorter than Vaelora, but so slender she appeared taller and more angular in the dark green silk jacket and trousers.

"Governor Quaeryt . . . I am so pleased to meet you." Factoria Grelyana smiled warmly, although her pale blue eyes remained cool. "I had no idea that the governor would turn out to be the husband of a friend of a close friend of mine."

"Neither did I," replied Quaeryt, wondering who was friends with whom as he inclined his head politely to the dark-haired woman who looked to be about his age—ten years or so older than Vaelora.

"I would not, of course, have parted with the old villa so easily, except to such a distinguished personage. But then, it is easier to part with something holding pleasant memories when one knows it will go to someone who knows how to care for it and who will preserve it as it should be."

"That is certainly our intent, with its character and history," replied Quaeryt. "I would have liked to have seen it furnished, so that we could have followed the same patterns."

"I am certain that Lady Vaelora's taste will more than do it justice."

"I will do what I can," replied Vaelora. "Still . . . I would not be surprised if there are several pieces that belong so much to the villa that they do not fit elsewhere. It would be a pity if they did not remain there," she offered with a caring smile, "now that you know they will be cherished and cared for."

"I had not thought of that, but it might be possible."

"I'm certain that Lord Bhayar would appreciate the thoughtfulness of gifts such as those," added Quaeryt, "especially when he has lost his ancestral home and so much of uncounted value."

For just an instant, Grelyana's eyes hardened. "We have all lost much in the recent past, but it is likely that Lord Bhayar has lost the most of a material nature."

"Given your losses, most honorable factoria, your kindness is especially appreciated," replied Quaeryt. "I know my wife deeply welcomes your continuing courtesy and friendship. I also appreciate your forbearance, at a time when any increases in tariffs would fall heavily on those who have suffered enough as it is."

"I will do what I can, Governor. You were princeps of Tilbora, it is said, and most instrumental in returning that unruly place to order."

"I can claim but a small part in that," replied Quaeryt.

"I doubt that part was so minor, not for a scholar who has wed the lady who stands at your side . . . and who has been entrusted with restoring Extela."

Meaning that it's too bad you don't have a fortune of your own and have to haggle over a villa. "I can claim a role in assuring that Lord Bhayar obtained certain silver mines and other rebel property that will replenish the coffers of Telaryn over time."

"Quaeryt is so very good at discovering . . . shall we say . . . wayward golds," added Vaelora brightly. "My brother was most impressed."

Grelyana smiled faintly, looking into Quaeryt's eyes. "One might even say that Lord Bhayar has found in you something lost."

"Quite true," replied Quaeryt cheerfully, "although I did not know I'd been lost, because I was orphaned young."

The factoria shook her head, an expression of amusement on her lips and in her eyes. "There are a number of pieces that should grace the old villa once again, and I am young enough to enjoy observing what will come of what Lord Bhayar has found in uniting you two."

"We are but a young couple in love and recently married in an unsettled time," professed Vaelora.

"Your husband may be young in love, Lady Vaelora, but he is old in other ways, as are you, and neither of you would be here in Extela, or in my villa, were those things not so." Another smile followed. "Would you join me in afternoon refreshments? I am certain that Calachyl and the governor's chief clerk can work out the details and the documents for conveying the property and making sure no golds are . . . wayward."

"Both are most capable, and your steward is the image of devotion and discretion to which my chief clerk could aspire. But then, he has you as an example." Quaeryt smiled, offering a rueful expression, "an example that the most ardent and accomplished of scholars would find it difficult to capture in mere words . . . and I am certainly not that skilled in the ways of phrase and word."

"And yet, Lady Vaelora, your husband's very words belie what he professes." Grelyana turned and gestured toward the wide archway. "The east terrace is most pleasant in the early afternoon, and I have some early tomatoes from the hothouse. And the lemon tart is absolutely delicious. You've always liked that, Lady Vaelora, from what I recall."

Quaeryt and Vaelora exchanged glances after the factoria turned. Then Vaelora offered the slightest of shrugs and a grin.

Quaeryt managed not to laugh, but that was the last time he felt that way for several glasses.

Just long conversations and the light refreshments offered by the factoria after the indirect agreement on the purchase of the villa took the rest of the afternoon and gave Quaeryt a headache—which he tried to conceal from Vaelora.

But by the time they returned to the post and Quaeryt had instructed Jhalyt on the necessities regarding the purchase of a governor's residence—and the clerk seemed not in the slightest bit surprised—the throbbing in Quaeryt's head had subsided even before he located Skarpa outside the officers' mess.

"I'm sorry . . ." he began. "I was called away earlier before I could find you. That's not the best reason for not telling you immediately that—"

"Pharyl and Hrehn are going to clean up your Civic Patrol?" Skarpa smiled. "It's better that way. Some officers—and they're probably not like that, but too many are—start to get too cautious once they're close to getting a stipend."

"I did say they'd stay on the rolls."

"We can do that. They won't draw pay for that time, but it won't affect their stipend, and since it won't, I don't imagine they'll complain."

"I do apologize . . ."

"Governor, sir . . . you've got more on your platter than you should have." Skarpa grinned. "And being married to Lord Bhayar's sister . . . that has blessings, too, and I'd imagine some of them come from the Namer."

The reference to the Namer reminded Quaeryt of something else he'd forgotten, that he'd have to come up with a homily for services on Solayi. "She's beautiful and intelligent, and she cares for me and I for her. I'm most fortunate in that."

"She was raised in a palace, and you'll always have to look over your shoulder for her brother. Better you than me, sir."

Quaeryt shrugged, not quite theatrically, then said, "Now all I have to do is find a justicer."

"Can't you act as justicer? Governor Rescalyn did for a bit."

"If I have to, I will. I'd rather not. Have Dhaeryn and Heireg returned?"

"I haven't seen either."

Quaeryt hoped that all had gone well in setting up the procurement of planks and timbers, but if it hadn't, he'd find out all too soon.

After taking his leave of Skarpa, he rejoined Vaelora in their temporary quarters.

She was sitting on the end of the bed when he closed the door. "Are you feeling better?"

"Yes. Was it that obvious?"

"Not to Grelyana, I think. Her husband was said to be quiet in social situations."

"I'm still not used to weighing the indirection of every last word."

"You were never bad at that, and you're getting better."

Quaeryt certainly hoped so.

"Grelyana knows about the lost ones," observed Vaelora.

"She almost said directly that we were going to upset your brother's rule and life far beyond what he expects and that she was going to enjoy it. Did he ever do anything to her . . . or her late husband? I assume her husband's dead," Quaeryt added quickly.

"He died five years ago. He never had children by his first wife. Their son is eight . . ."

"So she'll be in control . . ." Quaeryt shook his head. "The factors don't give the title of factorius or factoria unless it's earned. That means she's truly in charge."

"You think that she created the rumor that she had to sell the older villa at a loss?"

"I don't think so. I think she wants the thousand golds now because she can do more with the golds than with the villa, and some goodwill from the governor and Lord Bhayar's sister won't hurt, either. What does she factor?"

Vaelora frowned. "Metals . . . copper, tin, and her husband had an iron-works."

"*She* had the metals factorage before she married?"

"Oh . . . you wouldn't know. She had far more than that. Her family had only daughters, and she married Raansyd the day before the family estate would have gone to her cousin. Raansyd was kind enough, but it was the only way to hold everything. Besides, he needed her and her family. He was close to losing everything. She saved it all. Well, her family helped some."

"She's part Pharsi, then?"

"I don't know. No one's ever said, but many of the factoring families here have Pharsi blood. Not quite so many as in Khel."

"Not quite so many as there once were in Khel," said Quaeryt dryly.

"Thanks to Rex Kharst . . . and the Red Death." She paused. "Is it true that he attacked in the depth of winter after he heard that a third of Khelgror died?"

"I hadn't heard that before. I wouldn't put it past him. The plagues tend to die out after cold winters."

"He must have lost more men to the winter."

"That didn't seem to bother him."

Vaelora shook her head. "Now he wants to use our weakness against us. Have you heard anything else from Bhayar?"

"No. I only got his dispatch on Mardi, and I sent back a report on Meredi. He won't even have mine until next Lundi night at the earliest, I'd judge. If we get a dispatch now . . ."

"We'll be at war—or worse."

Quaeryt nodded. After a moment, he asked, "Are you pleased with the villa?"

"Oh, yes. It's big enough for a governor, but not too big . . ."

He smiled and listened as she began to tell him of her plans.

Quaeryt didn't sleep all that well on Vendrei night, because he kept waking up and asking himself what he'd really gotten himself into. Except it hadn't been totally his choice, and accepting Bhayar's decision and marrying his attractive sister hadn't seemed that onerous. He just hadn't thought through all the ramifications. *You only thought you had.*

But when he looked over through the dimness at Vaelora's sleeping face, he could only smile . . . and he did finally drift back into slumber.

After a breakfast of overcooked eggs and near rancid and greasy sausages, the idea of eating where Vaelora had some control over the food had even greater appeal, although he suspected it would be weeks before anything like that occurred . . . and it would likely take more golds than either of them anticipated.

Immediately after breakfast, after seeing Vaelora off to meet once more with Grelyana, he met with Dhaeryn and Heireg in the small study that felt even smaller. He didn't bother with pleasantries, but just asked, "How did you work out things with Thysor's timbermaster?"

"He can supply everything we need," replied the engineer major. "He won't give us a price until he delivers. His best estimate is three hundred golds for both planks and support timbers. It'll be another week before he can deliver the heavy support timbers. He's got enough seasoned stock, but they'll have to be milled."

"While you're waiting on the timbers, can you work on the mortar and repairs to the River Aqueduct?"

"We've started on that. The hardest part will be getting to the red clay quarry. The road's blocked in two places by lava. We'll have to use horses to pack it out." Dhaeryn shrugged. "We can do it, but it won't be quick."

Quaeryt couldn't help looking puzzled.

"We need the old red clay from near Mount Extel. We have to add that to the mortar mix and gravel to make the concrete watertight. Otherwise the water will wear away the repairs in weeks. No more than months anyway."

"Only that kind of clay?"

"It's the only kind around here, sir. I understand there's something like it in Antiago, but it's more grayish there. They say you can only find it near volcanoes. I wouldn't know. I do know that when we use the red clay, except it's not quite like other clay, the concrete will harden solid even under water."

"I didn't know that," Quaeryt admitted. "When will your men be able to finish the cells in the patrol station?"

"It might be Meredi. No longer than the end of next week."

When he had finished talking with Dhaeryn, and the engineer left, Quaeryt turned to the supply major. "Are there any other surprises?"

"Besides what we've paid out for flour and potatoes? No, sir."

"Good. Because I have one. I ended up agreeing to purchase a residence for the governor . . . and for every governor who follows me. We're going to have to transfer some funds to a Factoria Grelyana."

"The metals factoria. They say she's wealthier than most of the High Holders in the province."

"We need to make arrangements to pay her for the dwelling. Her former villa. The total comes to twelve hundred golds."

"Jhalyt mentioned that he was working on the documents with the steward." Heireg frowned. "For just twelve hundred golds? That's a big villa . . ."

"Factoria Grelyana was charitable . . ."

The major raised his eyebrows.

"Call it self-interestedly charitable. She suggested the price was a favor. I suggested that Lord Bhayar had lost far more to Mount Extel than anyone in Extela and that increased tariffs to pay for things, such as to replace a governor's residence, were in no one's interest. She preferred golds to the villa, and no one else was likely to buy the villa anytime soon." That was a guess on Quaeryt's part, but he would have wagered that was so, particularly since the villa had been vacant for some time, from what he observed when they toured it, despite what Vaelora had said earlier about the lack of suitable and available dwellings. "It's likely to be far less expensive—and take less time—than building one." *Particularly of that size in that kind of location.*

"No doubt of that, sir. What about furnishings?"

"I don't know yet. The factoria has agreed to provide some that were originally in the villa. I'll have to have Jhalyt set up an account ledger for the residence and staff. In time, when the regiment leaves, I'll also have to hire some guards."

"Governor Scythn detailed some of the rankers from the post to the governor's square."

"I might have to do that for a few weeks, but I wouldn't want to make that the permanent way of handling it."

"I can see that, sir."

Quaeryt could sense the approval behind the major's quiet words. *Every day you find out another place where Scythn was diverting funds or resources. Are all governors like that?* What he'd discovered so far suggested that Bhayar needed a better system of governing the various provinces, and especially for keeping High Holders like Wystgahl in line, but even considering how that might be done would have to wait . . . for some time. And who knew if Bhayar would even consider changes?

No sooner had Heireg left than Commander Skarpa was at the door. Quaeryt motioned him inside.

Skarpa sat down and announced, "One of the patrols caught some young fellows last night."

"The way you're saying that, I have the feeling I'm not going to like this."

"You won't, sir. They'd tried to break into a house on the west side."

"Women?"

Skarpa shook his head. "A factor from Solis. Well, he came from Solis, but he's been here several years. His name is Hyleor. He and his brothers take delivery of spices from Otelyrn in Solis. Then they bring them upriver and sell them. On the return, they buy mountain herbs and send them downriver and ship them . . . wherever."

"What happened last night?"

"Some locals dragged Hyleor out of his house and were starting to beat him. The squad rode up and ran them down. One of the men tried to gut one of the ranker's mounts. The ranker hit him with the flat of his sabre. Knocked him cold. The problem is that he took a couple of steps before he passed out, and he fell on one of those pointed iron fences. The point went through his eye. He's dead."

"There's more, isn't there?" asked Quaeryt.

"The young fellow who attacked the ranker was Versoryn. He's the nephew of a High Holder around Ilyum. The High Holder's name is Cransyr."

"What were they doing attacking a factor?"

Skarpa shrugged. "No one seems to know."

"Did they catch any of the others?"

"Just one. Versoryn's brother. He claims that the rankers threw Versoryn onto the fence. He said his uncle knows Lord Bhayar well enough to have them all executed."

"I've never heard of High Holder Cransyr." Quaeryt laughed sharply. "Unhappily, that doesn't mean anything. There are far too many that I don't know. What did you do with the brother?"

"He's in the brig here, and he's not at all happy about it."

"Did anyone see what he did?"

Skarpa shook his head. "Even the factor couldn't say who attacked him—except for Versoryn. Hyleor recognized him because Versoryn had a scar across his cheek and jaw."

"He didn't recognize any of the others?"

"He says he doesn't."

"What did Versoryn do? Was he a factor . . . or what?"

"No one seems to know. He was well dressed. So is the brother."

Quaeryt was getting a very bad feeling about what had happened. A factor had been attacked, but could only recognize one conveniently dead attacker, and both the dead man and his brother were well dressed, without any known profession, and claimed a High Holder connected to Bhayar as their "uncle." "I should talk to the brother. Do you know his name?"

"Vhalsyr. That's what he says, anyway. I can have the brig guards bring him here, if you'd like."

"That would be best, I think." Quaeryt understood Skarpa's quiet suggestion that governors did not visit offenders, as well as a recognition that Quaeryt had once . . . and a hint that he should not have.

"Then, I'll have the guards take care of it. They'll wait outside." Skarpa rose.

A half a quint later, a thin brown-haired man, scarcely more than a youth, stood before Quaeryt, his face holding an expression close to but not quite a sneer.

"Sit down, Vhalsyr." Quaeryt projected total authority.

The young man seated himself, his eyes not quite meeting Quaeryt's. "So you're the new governor."

"And you're an offender caught as part of a group beating up an innocent factor," replied Quaeryt, his voice level, sitting down behind the narrow table desk.

"He wasn't innocent. He was using those Otelyrnan spices to drug girls so he could do anything he wanted to do with them. When he was finished with them, they went to his pleasure houses."

"And how did you know that?"

"I just know."

"Do you have any proof?"

"Everyone knows what he's been doing."

"And no one has said anything?"

"He paid off the senior patrol captain."

"Who was that?"

"Faastyl. When he heard a new governor was coming, he left. They say he went to Nacliano."

Based on his own relatively recent experiences in the port city, Quaeryt couldn't say he was surprised—except a journey of that distance seemed unlikely for a patroller, even a senior patrol captain. Still, he made a mental note to have Pharyl inquire about both Hyleor and Faastyl.

"I'm supposed to take your word for all this?" Quaeryt shook his head.

"It's true. If you keep me locked up, you'll pay for it. Lord Bhayar will have your head. My uncle will see to that. He will."

"He might, but he might not. He might not want to see his sister widowed."

At that, Vhalsyr swallowed. "It's true. Everything I say is true."

"It might be. But you and your brother didn't come to me. Hyleor didn't attack you, either. You dragged him out of his house." Quaeryt smiled politely. "For now, you'll remain locked up. We'll see what we can find out."

"You'll be sorry. You'll see."

"I could turn you over to the Civic Patrol. We're rebuilding it. Almost two-thirds of the patrollers have returned."

Vhalsyr stiffened for just a moment. "You'll do whatever you want."

"I'll keep that in mind. What else can you tell me about Hyleor?"

"He's scum. He cheats the mountain people on what he pays for their herbs. He lies to the girls, especially the ones who are barely women. Some probably aren't even that old. Those are the ones he likes to use the best."

"Everyone knew this, and no one did anything?"

"Who would do anything? Justicer Tharyn just handled cutpurses and slam-thefts, that sort of offense. Graefsyr was in Hyleor's wallet."

"And the governor?"

"He didn't care so long as Graefsyr paid a share of his take to him."

"I suppose you saw all this."

"Everybody knew it. It was no secret."

Quaeryt questioned Vhalsyr for almost another quint, but the young man could offer no proof and no other names. At that point, Quaeryt realized he needed to leave or he'd be late in getting to the Civic Patrcl and announcing the appointments of Pharyl and Hhren. He had the guards take the young man back to the brig and hurried out to the courtyard where the two officers were waiting with the escort squad.

"I'm sorry. Something came up, and it might involve the Civic Patrol." Quaeryt mounted quickly, but didn't say more until they were beyond the gates and riding up the avenue, Pharyl to his right, and Hrehn to his left.

"Did Commander Skarpa mention to either of you what one of the patrols ran into last evening?"

"They broke up a fight," replied Pharyl, "and one of the men who started it fell on a fence spike and got killed."

"It's a bit more interesting than that," said Quaeryt dryly, as he went on to relate what he'd discovered, finishing by saying, "I'd like you two to see what you can find out from the patrollers."

"If they know anything, they won't want to say it," suggested Hrehn.

"Unless we point out that Lord Bhayar doesn't like women being used that way, and that four rankers are dead with no retribution because that's the way he and the governor feel." Pharyl barked a laugh. "I could point out that if the governor will stand behind Pharsi women against his own rankers, it might not be the best idea to hide anything."

"I'll leave it to you as to how you handle it," replied Quaeryt. "Just let me know what you find out . . . or don't."

"Yes, sir."

First Wystgahl and now the nephews of a High Holder . . . Quaeryt was almost afraid of what else involving High Holders might happen.

The anomen bells had just finished ringing out seventh glass when they reached the patrol station. Quaeryt hurriedly dismounted, and the three walked quickly into the receiving hall where the patrollers waited. After taking a position in front of the receiving desk, flanked by the two officers, Quaeryt waited for a moment to allow the chamber to quiet. He didn't have to wait more than a few instants.

"Good morning, patrollers. I promised that it would not be long before you had a new chief and a new senior captain. Effective immediately, Chief Pharyl will be in command of the Civic Patrol." Quaeryt gestured to Pharyl. "His senior captain will be Captain Hrehn. Both have had distinguished service as officers, most lately with the Third Tilboran Regiment in subduing the rebels in Tilbor. Both also were born and raised in the province of Montagne and have a certain familiarity with this part of Telaryn." He paused, then added, "But not so much that they'll tolerate certain ways of doing things that seemed to be prevalent under the previous governor and chief. I won't say much more. I'll leave that to them. After they finish what they wish to say, the chief, the senior captain, and the patrollers first and I will have a brief meeting." Quaeryt stepped back and motioned to Pharyl.

The wiry chief stepped forward and surveyed the patrollers.

"I don't believe much in talk just to be talking. Most of life's problems can be handled by being where you're supposed to be and doing what you're supposed to be doing. Being a patroller or a soldier is no different. That's what I expect out of each and every one of you. Be where you're supposed to be, and do what you're supposed to do." Pharyl nodded to Hrehn.

The tall captain offered a slow smile. "Chief Pharyl's said most of what I might have said. There is one more thing. We're here to protect the people. All the people. If any of you turn out to be more interested in filling your own wallets, the only question is how long before you get found out . . . and how much you lose, and that might be your neck." Hrehn glanced back to Pharyl.

"All patrols remain here. Patroller firsts to the meeting room," announced the chief.

Quaeryt led the way to the room beyond the door behind the receiving desk and opposite the studies. Once everyone was present, he began. "I have a few questions, and then I'll be leaving so that Chief Pharyl and Captain Hrehn can brief you in more detail on what they expect." He paused, then asked casually, his eyes lighting on Waollyt, "Who were the justicers here in Extela before the eruption?"

"Ah . . . well, the governor served as high justicer. There were two justicers for Extela. The one for serious offenses, that was Graefsyr. The petty offenses . . . well . . . they came before Tharyn."

"Does anyone know who was a high justicer in the time before Governor Scythn?"

After a moment Chelsyr cleared his throat. "There'd be two. One was old Fadruk, but he died sudden-like. The other was Aextyl. He stepped down when Governor Scythn was appointed. I think he still lives here somewhere. Leastwise, he did before the mountain blew."

"Does anyone know where Justicer Aextyl resides?"

Quaeryt had to wait some time before Yuell finally spoke. "He used to live in the square brown brick place on the corner eight blocks west of the southwest market square. That's if you go west on the south market avenue."

"Thank you." Quaeryt nodded. "I'm going to leave you in the hands of Chief Pharyl and senior Captain Hrehn." He wanted to make some comment about obeying them, but decided that would be weaker than saying nothing at all. Instead, he turned to Pharyl and Hrehn. "Good day."

"Good day, Governor."

Quaeryt walked out of the patrol station and mounted, then nodded to the squad leader of the escort squad. As he rode away from the patrol station, he realized he still didn't have the faintest idea what he would say at services on Solayi evening.

After leaving the Civic Patrol station, Quaeryt detoured to find the dwelling described by Yuell, only to be told by Aextyl's granddaughter that the former justicer was visiting his other daughter in Tulagne and wasn't expected back until the following Mardi. Once Quaeryt returned to the post, he went to work on a dispatch to Bhayar. In the end, he spent almost two glasses drafting and redrafting the report, explaining everything, including the problems with Wystgahl and his unfortunate death—something that Quaeryt still regretted and still could see no other practical solution for—and the purchase of the "new" governor's villa . . . everything except for the problem with Versoryn and Hyleor, since he wanted to know more before he put anything about that situation in writing.

Then he went over the ledgers with Jhalyt and calculated what the likely expenditures for Avryl might be. His figures showed that there should be a fair reserve, even if he had to pay out the same amounts in Mayas and Juyn, before all the midyear tariffs were collected . . . but then, he was spending far less than he would be once he had the provincial government replaced and restaffed, even at a lower and less extravagant level than that enjoyed by his predecessor.

He noted when both Pharyl and Hrehn returned, and much as he wanted to ask how matters had gone, he did not. The day-to-day operations of the Civic Patrol were now their duty, and while he intended to meet with them on a weekly basis—or at their request—more frequent inquiries would merely undermine their authority and sense of responsibility.

Abruptly he realized he hadn't checked with Heireg about the feasibility of stopping or cutting back on the sales of flour and potatoes . . . and he hurried from his study to the quartermaster's, where he waited for a third of a quint or so for the major to return.

"Sir? What is it?"

"The flour and potato sales . . . how are they coming?"

"As you told us, we're only selling on Meredi and Samedi. They just got back. That's where I was, counting the totals with Jhalyt and adding the coins to the receipts' chest. The locals are starting to try to bargain . . ."

"Do you think that means they're not so desperate . . . or that they're out of coins?"

"The squad leader says they've got more coins."

"Why don't you have them announce on Meredi that after this week, we'll only be selling on Samedi?"

"The squad leader suggested that, sir."

"How are we coming on flour and potatoes?"

"Gone through a lot, sir, with all that the regiment takes and what we've sold . . ." Heireg opened the ledger he had carried into the study. "Oh . . . and we got twenty-five barrels of good flour from young holder Wystgahl . . . and he left this for you." The major handed over a sealed envelope.

Quaeryt broke the seal, extracted the single heavy sheet of paper, and read.

> *Governor Quaeryt,*
> *As we discussed, I have delivered the additional barrels of good flour, and will fulfill the contract my father failed to meet.*
> *I apologize for that difficulty.*

Below was a signature and a seal. Quaeryt didn't quite wince. He had as much of an apology as he would ever get. At least, there was a written acknowledgment of the former High Holder's failure.

Quaeryt handed the note to Heireg. "You should read this."

Heireg did, then handed it back. "Right kind of him. He didn't mention all the bad flour and all the extra time it took us to sift it clean."

"High Holders sometimes have a different view of things," Quaeryt said mildly.

Heireg nodded.

Quaeryt finally got back to his study at a quint past second glass.

Vaelora returned to the post, although he didn't realize it until she knocked on the study door several quints after third glass. At that point he put aside the ledgers and walked with her to their quarters.

"How did your day go?" he asked as he closed the door.

"Grelyana returned some of the furnishings to the villa . . . almost enough for us to live there."

"Almost?"

"The master suite now has a bedstead, bedside tables, and two matching armoires . . . and a dressing table. They're a little worn, but they'll be fine with oil and polish. The main study has a desk and several chairs, as well as a table and four chairs . . . and there are several old-style parlor pieces that could go in either the receiving parlor or the salon. They're in the salon at present. There's nothing for the upstairs study, but I wouldn't have expected that. Those pieces were likely hers. There are several worktables for the kitchen, and a small and very battered dining table and chairs for the private dining and breakfast room."

"That's a beginning," he said cautiously.

"The beginning of a beginning. There are no linens, and we need a mattress for the bedstead. There are no kitchen utensils, no cutlery, no plates, no platters, no cauldrons, no pots, no table linens, no towels. We have no staff . . ."

"Do we have anything else at all?"

"There are platform beds in the servants' quarters and in the stable quarters, but no mattresses."

Quaeryt couldn't even imagine what it was going to cost to set up even a minimal household in the villa. More to the point, at that moment, he didn't want to.

"Some of that will not cost all that much," added Vaelora. "It will take time, and I will need a steward or someone in that capacity."

"Do you know where to find one that we can trust?"

"Shenna has some ideas."

Quaeryt had no idea who Shenna was, and it must have shown on his face.

"She's the older sister of Rhyena. Rhyena was a friend when we were both little. She—Rhyena, that is—married a High Holder somewhere near Cloisonyt. He was an older widower. Shenna hasn't married, and she's a governess for Aramyn's youngest daughter. When she found out I'd come back . . ."

"You're thinking of Shenna as . . . a female steward?"

"That would never be accepted. But she could be my private secretary and be a great help."

"Then ask her."

"I already have . . . but I'm glad you approve."

"What else . . ." Quaeryt stopped. "How long will setting up the villa take?"

"Several weeks before anyone else should see it. A week before we can move in—if we can find basic staff."

"Skarpa will agree to detailing some troopers for temporary guards. They'll only be available for little more than a month."

"That will help." Vaelora smiled. "How was your day?"

"I think yours was better. What do you know about a High Holder named Cransyr?"

"Dear Cousin Cransyr? He was always a nettle to Father, but he's tried to play up to Bhayar. Why do you ask?"

"Because his nephews and their friends tried to beat up a local factor. The patrol caught them, and one of the nephews—Versoryn—fell on the point of an iron fence. It went through his eye and killed him. We have his brother, the other nephew, locked up in the brig here. He says Bhayar will make sure all the rankers are executed. He also threatened me, but backed off that somewhat. He still believes, I think, that he can get me dismissed as governor."

"That won't happen. Nephews who aren't the sons of High Holders can't claim privilege. Even 'nephews' like Versoryn can't claim it."

"Privilege? That's in the case of wrongful death. Being caught in committing a crime and dying in trying to escape isn't wrongful death." Quaeryt paused. "And what did you mean with that cynical comment about 'nephews' like that? That there was a much closer relationship?"

Vaelora nodded. "Their mother was Cransyr's mistress. She died several years ago. It was quite a quiet scandal because everyone thought Cransyr's wife had poisoned her. It happened on his lands, and he had the right to apply justice even to his wife . . ."

Quaeryt knew that High Holders had that right for offenses taking place on their lands.

". . . but Cransyr pronounced it an accidental poisoning. He built separate quarters for his wife and hasn't spoken to her since . . . or so it's said. The boys were sent to live with the sister of the mistress here in Extela."

"Why didn't he find his wife guilty?"

"She was always Bhayar's favorite cousin. I never cared for her much, but I was only ten or so when it happened." Vaelora shook her head. "Still . . . it would be best to handle the boy carefully. You'd be surprised at what the High Justicer of Telaryn has found to be wrongful death, dearest, especially when well-connected High Holders and their sons are involved."

"I don't know that I'd find it that surprising. Depressing, but not surprising. I need to find a justicer. I could act as justicer. Scythn was his own high justicer."

"He was?"

"That's what several of the patrollers first said."

"Bhayar forbid that practice except as a very temporary expedient. I know. I heard him tell Aelina that."

That was another item that Quaeryt would need to put in the dispatch he planned to send off on Lundi. He wondered what else he'd remember to add.

Quaeryt had thought he might sleep late on Solayi morning, but he woke up with the first light. Because Vaelora was still sleeping, he lay there and thought about what else he needed to add to his report to Bhayar. He couldn't help but wonder and worry about whether Kharst had attacked Ferravyl . . . and how soon Bhayar would need Third Regiment, especially since the Civic Patrol wasn't ready to take over full patrolling duties in all parts of Extela.

He was still thinking about all the additions to his report when she woke.

"It would be so nice to wake up in a real bedchamber," she said with a yawn.

"Before long . . ." he said quietly.

"Longer than I wish to think about, dearest. There is so much to do."

"There's been so much to do for both of us," he pointed out.

"I should have gone to the market squares yesterday. Until life is better, the people should see me."

"You can't do everything."

"No, but some of them have so little. At times, it bothers me that I'm concerned about furnishing and setting up a villa when even these quarters are so much better than what they have."

The sadness and wistfulness in her voice moved Quaeryt, and he said, "You can't stay here forever, and someone has to rebuild a place for us and for the governors to come." After a moment he added, "It's better to purchase an existing villa, because I'll still need to build a place to house a justicing hall and studies and chambers for those who serve Lord Bhayar and the governor." His eyes were drawn to her . . . again.

She sat up in the bed and yawned once more, before looking at him. "Stop staring," she added, not quite sharply.

"Can't I appreciate how my wife looks?"

"You appreciated enough last night."

Quaeryt offered a mock wince.

"That's almost disrespect."

They both laughed.

Later, they dressed and ate at the mess, another meal that had Quaeryt wishing for either their own kitchen or even the meals fixed by the officers' mess in Tilbora. He supposed he could have gotten involved with the kitchens at the post, but that was just another problem . . . and one that was far from urgent, especially when he felt he didn't have enough time to do everything that needed to be done. Then he escorted Vaelora back to their quarters before heading to his study to write out the final version of his report to Bhayar. Close to two glasses later he scurried across the courtyard through the drizzling rain to their quarters.

While Vaelora continued to go through her lists of what the villa needed, Quaeryt tried to think of something that he could offer as a homily. Finally, he eased away from the small writing desk and went out onto the balcony, where he stood looking out into the chill rain and the mist sweeping eastward into the post from the river, trying to think of something that would inspire and not sound worn with time and repetition.

How long he stood there, he wasn't certain, but Vaelora seemed to appear beside him from nowhere.

"What are you doing out here? You're just staring into the rain."

"I don't know what to say for the homily for services this evening," he admitted. "I've been so busy trying to resolve this and that problem that when I finally have time to think . . . I can't."

"Talk about what you told me this morning," she suggested.

"What was that?"

"You said I couldn't do everything. Neither can you. Neither can most people. Life's not about what we can't do, but what we actually do."

"I might be able to do something with that."

She smiled. "I'm sure you can."

Quaeryt finally did manage to find a way to tie what Vaelora had suggested into a passable homily, enough so that when he finally stood on the dais in the anomen facing the officers and men of the Third Tilboran Regiment, he could begin the homily without feeling that he was repeating something they had heard from others too many times.

"Under the Nameless all evenings are good, even those filled with rain and mist . . ." The slight pause he offered allowed for a few smiles before he continued. "All of us have been very busy the past weeks. We've been trying to make things work here in Extela, to keep order at a time of disorder. For all of our efforts, there are as many problems arising as we have resolved . . . so many tasks uncompleted, and even more that we have yet to begin . . .

"As I thought of all those undone tasks, it came to me that dwelling on what one has not done, or what one plans to do, but has not done . . .

well . . . that it's a form of Naming. Why might that be? Because we're spending words in worrying about something that has no value. A deed not done is not a deed. It's one thing to acknowledge what needs to be done. It's another to fret and worry and talk endlessly about what has to be done. Spending time and words on nothing . . . if that isn't Naming, then what is?

"We think of Naming in terms of vanity, of using words to lift ourselves above others or to gain an advantage over them by word-painting them as less than we are or ourselves as more than others. And those uses of words are indeed Naming. But what of those uses of words and thoughts that distract us from what we must do? We all know people who worry and fret and worry so much that the worries keep them from even trying to do what is necessary. In such instances, the words erect a barrier between a man and productive accomplishment . . . and they make that man less than he could be. Naming is not just an offense against others. It can also be an offense against ourselves and how much better we could be . . ."

It wasn't one of Quaeryt's better homilies, but what he'd said was indeed true enough.

He just hoped that his next homily was more inspiring, for both himself and the men of the post and the regiment.

With the Civic Patrol under the control of Pharyl and Hrehn, Quaeryt concentrated on various other problems on Lundi and Mardi, the most pressing of which, Jhalyt reminded him politely, was to locate the tariff collectors and either continue them in their past employ or dismiss them, but not before obtaining their ledgers—since all records of who had paid and how much had presumably been charred in the lava.

Given how many records he was realizing were missing and would need to be replaced, Quaeryt requested a company from Skarpa and returned to the governor's square. After two days of digging through chambers and checking file chests, they were actually able to locate the tariff records for those paid two years previously. There was no sign—no uncharred and unburned indication—of any records more recent. Nor did they find any more golds or silvers, although there were signs that other looters had been there, but it appeared they had found nothing of great value either.

In his riding back and forth from the post to the entombed governor's square, Quaeryt also traveled different routes through Extela to see how repairs were coming and how many shops and crafters were back at work . . . and it did appear that the majority were actually open. How well they were doing was another question, but he could hope that their being open was a good sign.

In the end, until Baharyt's efforts were more urgently needed, Quaeryt assigned the junior clerk and a half squad of troopers to continue looking through the shambles that had been the governor's building in an effort to find and salvage any records of any possible usefulness. He wondered if he should have tried such reclamation sooner, but it still seemed to him that he'd been right to place restoring order and providing food ahead of finding tariff ledgers and other records. He then had Skarpa assign several rankers to accompany Jhaylt while the chief clerk tried to locate and contact past tariff collectors.

At eighth glass on Meredi morning, Quaeryt rode to Aextyl's dwelling to see if the old justicer had returned from Tulagne. Only half a squad accompanied him, since Extela had returned to an appearance of order, and since the troopers were better used in patrolling areas where the Civic Patrol did not have enough men to cover—and helping Baharyt and the engineers.

A sad-faced hound, chained to the side of the house, bayed once as Quaeryt dismounted, then watched him as he walked up the steps.

A narrow-faced woman whose blond hair was streaked with gray opened the door. "Yes?"

"I'm Governor Quaeryt, and I'm here to see High Justicer Aextyl."

The woman's eyes hardened, then looked past to the ten uniformed troopers, still mounted and waiting, one of whom was holding the reins to Quaeryt's mare. After a moment she looked reluctantly back to Quaeryt. "He's no longer a justicer, Governor."

"I know that, but I would still like to see him."

Another long moment passed. Then she sighed. "Very well. If you'd come in. He's in his study."

Quaeryt followed the woman through an entry hall that was more the size of a small vestibule and down a narrow hallway for only a few yards to an oak door aged to a deep golden brown shade. She stopped at the door, barely ajar. "Father . . . the new governor is here to see you."

"Send him in, daughter. Send him in," replied a hearty voice.

At the woman's gesture, Quaeryt stepped into the modest study, more like a small library, with bookcases on every wall. The door closed behind him. The man who sat in the worn brown leather-upholstered chair had a lined face with sunken cheeks, wispy white hair, and red-rimmed eyes. Even so, those pale green eyes were intent and imparted a cheerful expression.

"Good morning, Governor. Do sit down. You'll pardon me if I don't stand."

Quaeryt smiled as he seated himself in the straight-backed chair. "I appreciate your taking the time to see me."

"Time . . . time . . . these days I've got plenty of that." The alert green eyes continued to study Quaeryt. "Hmmm . . . a scholar. That's what they said, but you never know. How did Bhayar ever have the nerve to appoint a scholar? Or is your father a High Holder to whom he's beholden?"

"I was orphaned when I was barely more than an infant and raised by the scholars of Solis. I was scholar advisor to Lord Bhayar, and then a scholar to the governor of Tilbor, and then princeps there before Lord Bhayar sent me here. After I became princeps, he insisted I marry his sister."

Aextyl laughed. "Rather the other way round than the path taken by most ambitious young men. They usually wed the sister or daughter to obtain the position." He studied Quaeryt again. "You look more like a ship's officer than a scholar."

"I spent time at sea, six years before I returned to being a scholar."

"So . . . now you're the governor. I hear that you've already changed things. Any change is welcome, and if it took an eruption to get it . . . then things might have been for the best."

"With almost a quarter of the city destroyed?"

"Scythn was destroying it already."

"Was that why you stepped down?"

"I didn't have a choice."

"Did he threaten your family . . . or just suggest that their health might be better if you left the justiciary?"

"You don't have a high opinion of the late governor, do you?"

"I don't know that he's dead, but no . . . I don't."

"Might I ask why, Governor?"

"I think you know. He paid himself exorbitantly, let the patrol chief reduce the number of patrollers and pocket the wages not paid. So far as I can tell, it appears as though he received more than ten thousand golds a year, and I'm not certain I've tracked down all that he took."

"I'd wager he extorted even more, but what do I know? I'm just a has-been high justicer who tried to keep a certain amount of justice in the application of the law."

"That's why I'm here, sir."

"I appreciate your kindness, Governor. I can't do it. My mind and spirit are willing, but my body's not what it used to be. Come to think of it, it wasn't what it used to be when I stepped down, and that was close to six years ago."

"When Scythn became governor?"

Aextyl nodded.

"Are there any other justicers or advocates here in Extela who would make acceptable justicers?"

The old justicer barked a laugh. "You might as well ask if you could find an ox here that could wield a pen."

Quaeryt paused, then asked, "If I have to act as justicer, can I pay you to sit beside me and help with the law and the precedents . . . at least for a time?"

"I might consider it for a few cases. That's if you'd read Ekyrd's treatise on the law. That shouldn't be a problem for a scholar."

"Reading it wouldn't be a problem," Quaeryt said. "Finding a copy to read would be, since all of the governor's square is buried in ash and lava."

"I have a copy you can borrow. Over there, the second shelf down, on the end, the maroon binding."

Quaeryt rose, walked to the bookcase indicated by the justicer's bony finger, and extracted the comparatively slim volume. "This one?"

"That's the one. Read it. If you understand it, you'll know more law and procedures than most justicers ever do."

Quaeryt returned to the chair and sat down, still holding the book.

"Do you know why there's no scholars' house here? There was one, once, you know?"

"I can't say that I do."

Aextyl smiled. "That book you hold is one reason. The scholars had their apprentices copy it. Some of the local merchants and small factors read it. They disputed the findings and the handling of various trials and hearings, especially those dealing with some of the larger factors, particular factors, and one High Holder who, I hear, recently got so angry he suffered a seizure. No great loss there. Governor Scythn imposed a tariff on the scholars, claiming that the copying of books made them merchants. Other harassments followed, and then the scholarium burned in a fire. The surviving scholars dispersed."

Quaeryt winced.

"You think that is strange, Governor?"

"No. It has happened elsewhere recently. That was what bothered me."

"Knowledge held by those without power is always regarded as a danger by those with power."

"That is why we have laws," suggested Quaeryt.

"Everyone knows that power without law is tyranny, but they fail to recognize that law without power is useless. The laws here had no power. You are trying to change that. I applaud your efforts, but I fear you will fail, even with your ties to Lord Bhayar."

"We will see." Quaeryt smiled politely. "Will you consider advising me through a few hearings after I read this treatise?"

"I will consider it. I make no promises."

"On another subject . . . what do you know about a factor named Hyleor?"

"Ah . . . Hyleor Cylonsyn. He was a supporter of Governor Scythn. He also owned and still does, I believe, a share of at least one pleasure house, if not more. I have not had the dubious pleasure of meeting him and suspect I am the better for that."

"Are there any other factors whose acquaintance might be, as you put it, a dubious pleasure?"

"In recent years, there have been more than a few. Aerambyr, Thaltyn . . . and, of course, Lysienk and Pulam."

"Why should I look out for from them?"

"The usual . . . overcharges, delays in goods or substandard goods, and, occasionally, accidents to retainers or relatives. Your predecessor had a tendency to turn the other way, with his hand out, I suspect."

Quaeryt managed not to wince a second time. "I see. What do you know about a patroller first by the name of Jaramyr?"

Aextyl shook his head.

"What do you know about a Captain Faastyl?"

"Only that you would be best not to have him in the Civic Patrol, although I have heard he has left Extela."

"Are there any other factors or High Holders with whom I should be especially cautious?"

"High Holder Cransyr is known to be especially partisan, as is Suletar. For the factors, besides Hyleor, it might be wise to handle several others with care, Assoul and Dyetryn in particular. Factoria Grelyana can be vicious if she believes her interests are infringed, as can Lysienk."

"Any others?"

"All of them will be your friend to your face and whatever is necessary to advance their interests when your back is turned or your eyes are elsewhere."

Justicer Aextyl definitely had a skeptical, and probably realistic, view of people, reflected Quaeryt. "I suspect that is true of every governor."

"Indeed." Aextyl coughed, then lifted a large handkerchief to stifle the paroxysm that followed.

Quaeryt waited until the coughing spasms ceased before standing. "I will not take more of your time, but I do appreciate your advice and the loan of the law treatise."

"My pleasure, Governor. I trust it will do more good in your hands than on the bookshelf here."

Quaeryt inclined his head. "Thank you."

Then he turned and walked to the door, opening it, and started toward the entry hall.

The narrow-faced daughter met him there. "Governor . . . I hope you didn't press him. He's not well. Being a justicer took years off his life."

"I asked if he would sit beside me for the first few hearings and advise me. He said he would think about it—and only if I read this treatise."

Her eyes went from the thin book Quaeryt carried to the scholar's browns. "You're going to read it, aren't you?" Her tone was almost despairing.

"He made it rather clear that whether or not he decided to advise me, I needed to read it to have any chance of following the proper procedures. I'm taking his advice."

"Would that others had, sir." Gently as the words were spoken, bitterness suffused them.

"Sometimes, good men are treated ill by the times and their peers, but I do greatly appreciate his counsel and advice . . . and your courtesy in allowing me to see him." Quaeryt inclined his head, then left.

As he rode away, he considered what Aextyl had said about Grelyana . . . and that concerned him, especially given how they had pressed the factoria in dealings over the villa.

Upon his return to the post, Quaeryt checked to see if he had received any dispatches, but there were none, and he made his way to his study. There he wrote down the names of the factors mentioned as difficult by Aextyl. Once Pharyl was a bit more settled in as chief, Quaeryt wanted to have the chief make a few inquiries about each of them.

Almost a glass later, as he finished reviewing the master ledger showing expenditures, the duty ranker knocked on the door of the small study. "There's a fellow here to see you, sir. He claims he was a justicer, gave his name as Tharyn Ashsyn."

"I'll see him."

A few moments later the door opened, and a slender man stepped inside, wearing a tailored gray tunic and matching trousers. His polished boots were gray, and he wore a large gold ring on his right hand. He inclined his head. "Governor."

"What can I do for you?" asked Quaeryt, gesturing to the pair of chairs before the desk.

The man sat down and smiled, revealing slightly yellow teeth. "I heard that you're looking for justicers, Governor. I might be able to help you out."

"In what way?" asked Quaeryt politely.

"Being that I was low justicer for Extela under Governor Scythn, I bring some experience that might be helpful to you."

"I've heard your name, but not much more." Quaeryt smiled. "Why don't you tell me about yourself?"

"I grew up west of here in a little place called Wesron. My da was a smallholder, and I was the youngest. So when I was old enough I came to Extela and became a patroller. Worked my way up to patroller first." Tharyn shrugged. "That's just the way it happened."

"What have you been doing lately . . . since the eruption?"

"Waiting to see what happened. I was thinking about moving to Solis, but I heard you might need a justicer or two." Tharyn smiled broadly. "If you know what I mean."

"When did you become a justicer?"

"I was a patroller first for Chief Besant. That was under Governor Thailwyt. I told Governor Scythn that he needed someone who understood patrolling for the low justicer position. He thought about what I said, and then he appointed me."

Quaeryt doubted it had been anywhere that direct or simple. "From a justicer's point of view, how do you think the Civic Patrol was doing under the last chief?"

"The chief really kept 'em in line. Have to say that."

"I'd heard that the size of the patrol decreased some."

"No . . . it was always the same size, like around six patrols . . . leastwise while I was a patroller."

That was interesting, if true, thought Quaeryt, and it suggested that the previous chief hadn't changed matters so much as continued past practices. "Where did most offenses happen? In what part of Extela?"

"Oh . . . the southeast . . . all those Pharsis . . . always a problem . . ."

Quaeryt continued to ask questions for another quint before he finally said, "Thank you for coming in. I haven't made any decisions yet, and it was good to have the benefit of your experience."

"You're kind to see me, Governor. I would make a good head justicer. Knowing what I know, if you know what I mean."

"I do indeed." Quaeryt stood. "I do." *And I don't like at all what I know.*

Once the door closed, he sat down with a long deep breath.

Tharyn hadn't exactly impressed Quaeryt. *And he wants to be the head justicer?*

The encounter reminded Quaeryt that he still had to do something about the case involving Hyleor, and that meant he had to talk to the factor. Another thing to take care of on Jeudi.

After a moment he looked down at the thin maroon-bound volume on the desk. *Among other things, you have some reading to do.*

With Vaelora occupied in supervising repairs and cleaning of the governor's residence, as well as trying to locate kitchen equipment, pots, pans, and sundry other necessities for turning the villa into a functioning residence, Quaeryt left the post early on Jeudi to visit Hyleor. The only problem was that the spice factor had been traveling in the mountains to the north to purchase early spring herbs—or so his wife claimed—and was not expected to return until sometime late that afternoon or evening.

Quaeryt then rode to see how the repairs were coming on the east bridge and was gratified to see that the first timbers were being set in place. He was less gratified to learn from Major Dhaeryn that the cost of the timbers and planks would exceed 450 golds, and that more stonework would be necessary on the west end of the bridge before the last supporting timbers could be laid and braced.

On his return ride to the post, he swung by the patrol station, although he did not stop. From the outside, it looked complete, but he couldn't tell if the cells had been finished.

Two quints past the first glass of the afternoon, the duty squad leader hurried into Quaeryt's study to deliver a dispatch from Bhayar. As soon as the man left, Quaeryt opened the missive and began to read. After all the felicitations and appreciation of what Quaeryt had done so far there was just one other paragraph, stark in its simplicity.

> More Bovarian troops continue to move toward Ferravyl. Regardless of any difficulties you may have, Third Regiment is to depart Extela no later than Lundi, the sixteenth of Mayas, and to move with deliberate speed to Ferravyl. Because this may change at any time, Third Regiment should be prepared to depart any day after the fifteenth of Avryl.

The seal and signature were those of Bhayar.

When Quaeryt went to find Skarpa, who had effectively taken over the post commander's study, he waited until Skarpa had finished with Major Chaestyn before stepping into the study and closing the door.

"That dispatch that just came in? Bad news?"

Quaeryt handed the single sheet to the commander.

Skarpa read through the dispatch and handed it back before speaking. "It looks like we'll be fighting by midsummer, if not sooner."

"I'd wager on sooner. I just hope that the engineers will finish the bridge repairs in the next week or so. I am glad that the aqueduct is done."

"Is there anything else urgent you need from the regiment?"

"Besides replacements for fifty patrollers, trustworthy justicers, more clerks, tariff collectors . . ." Quaeryt shook his head. "So much was buried in lava and ash and burned that I don't really even know what else I need. I can't trust most of those who might know, and the ones I can trust are so busy that they can't do much more." *And your wife is trying to put together a governor's residence single-handedly as well.*

"You seem to be managing it so far, sir."

"Only with the help of the regiment. We need more patrollers, and soon."

"Pharyl and Hrehn can take care of that."

"If they have time."

"There are bound to be young men who need work. With Pharyl and Hrehn, all you need is some coin, and I imagine you have enough of that. Beginning patrollers can't cost you much more than trooper recruits."

After talking more with Skarpa, Quaeryt felt slightly less overwhelmed and returned to his study to try to think through what else he needed quickly from the regiment. Slightly before second glass, Pharyl appeared at his door, slipping into one of the chairs before the desk.

"How are things coming?" asked Quaeryt.

"The cells are finished, and three of them already are in use. We're feeding them bread and cheese and watered ale."

Quaeryt hadn't even thought about feeding arrangements, or dealing with prisoners, but there was no help for that, even if he still weren't certain what he would do about justicers. He feared that he'd have to act as one, and after having read little more than a third of Ekyrd Huelsyn's treatise *On Law and Justicing*, he was already painfully aware of too many things in law about which he knew nothing. "What are the offenses?"

"Two thefts and one assault. That's one reason why I wanted to talk to you. And there's another. An advocate for that young fellow you've got locked up here appeared. He wanted to know when Vhalsyr's hearing is scheduled. I said I'd have to check with you. He'll be back to see me tomorrow morning."

"We'll have to do that as soon as possible. His uncle is a well-connected High Holder. He's a cousin of Lord Bhayar. And since we have to deal with Vhalsyr . . . we might as well do them all. How long will it take you and the engineers to set up the large meeting room as a justicing hall?"

"We only need something that will serve as a justicer's desk. By Lundi, certainly."

"Set up the hearings starting at eighth glass on Lundi morning. I'll just have to act as justicer. I just met a while ago with the former low justicer."

"I gather he was as bad as the former chief?"

"How do you compare rotten apples?" asked Quaeryt dryly. "How is Hrehn handling the patrollers?"

"Very well. They need a big, strong, tough, and smart captain. No one's about to question him unless it's serious, and that's the way it should be."

"And you?"

"We need more patrollers."

"We need them soon. Lord Bhayar just sent a dispatch saying that Third Regiment will have to leave no later than mid-Mayas, and possibly in as little as ten days . . . if he sends orders. From the way he describes what the Bovarians are doing, it's going to be sooner than Mayas. Can you start looking for recruits?"

"I already have. Regular patrollers, patrollers second, that is, they start at a silver a week. I'd like to start recruits at five coppers until they complete a month's training, then pay them eight coppers a week for two months probation. That way, the existing patrollers don't see the new men as immediately being paid the same."

"You have my approval. Anything else?"

"No other problems. I did find out a few things you might find interesting. One reason why there were more offenses in the southeast quarter of the city was that the entire quarter was handled by one patrol. The northwest quarter—most of that's now under ash and lava—had two patrols assigned, and the northeast and southwest had three patrols between them."

That didn't surprise Quaeryt either. "So you'll just put two patrols in each of the remaining quarters?"

"That's my plan."

"It's a good one."

"There are a few other things . . . The pleasure houses . . ."

"The old high justicer told me that Hyleor owned part of them. What did you find out?"

"Faastyl did, like you thought. So did Scythn and Graefsyr, but they all sold out to Hyleor, even before the eruption, according to a couple of the older patrollers. They didn't put it quite that way, but it was clear enough." Pharyl paused. "Wasn't Graefsyr the one who was the head justicer?"

"He was. I didn't know that, but Vhalsyr—he's the nephew of High Holder Cransyr, the one the troop patrol picked up—he claims that Hyleor was feeding young girls Otelyrnan drugs and then sending them to the pleasure houses."

"Getting them to smoke elveweed, most likely."

"Are the pleasure houses still open?"

"They never closed. They never do. Except for the fancy one in the northwest quarter. It was just two blocks from the governor's square."

"Then there's likely to be a new one somewhere in the west part of the city before long . . . if it's not there already."

"We'll keep an eye out for it."

"What else?"

"Isn't that enough?" asked Pharyl sardonically.

Quaeryt laughed, briefly, then said, "There is one more thing." He handed a list to the chief, a copy of the one he'd jotted down after meeting with Aextyl. "These are factors here in Extela about whom the former high justicer, possibly the last honest one, had some concerns. As you can find out from the patrollers and others, anything you can learn might be helpful."

"Might take a while."

"That's why you're getting it now."

Pharyl nodded.

As soon as the chief left, Quaeryt hurried out to round up an escort to ride out to Hyleor's dwelling once more—since the trader apparently had no other place of business. He hoped the factor would be there, because he really didn't want to ride out on Samedi . . . although he would if he had to.

Two men were unloading a small high-wheeled wagon, carrying sacks into a shed at the rear of the dwelling, when Quaeryt approached the house, with a front garden surrounded by a waist-high brick wall topped with ironwork spikes on every post. The ends of the spikes would have been chest-high on Quaeryt. He frowned. For a tall man to fall on one was not impossible . . . but it was unlikely. Still, all the reports confirmed that Versoryn had attacked the trooper with a long knife and tried to gut the man's mount. After a moment, Quaeryt rode down the narrow rutted drive at the side, where he reined up and dismounted, handing the mare's reins to the ranker who had accompanied him.

The burly man, several digits taller than Quaeryt and broader as well, with heavy-lidded eyes, a fleshy face, and shiny black hair—presumably Hyleor himself—turned and waited.

"Trader Hyleor?"

"Who else?" His eyes flicked from Quaeryt to the ranker, and then to the squad of troopers drawn up in the street at the end of the drive. After a moment he studied Quaeryt. "A visit from the governor himself. What a surprise." The sardonic tone to his words was as heavy as the man himself.

"I came by earlier, but I understand you were traveling."

"You waited long enough. I had business."

"I'm sure you did. So did I."

Hyleor waited, as if challenging Quaeryt to speak.

Quaeryt didn't mind, but he did let the silence draw out for a bit. "My troopers reported that a gang of men tried to attack you."

"Tried? They dragged me away from the wagon and into the street. They laid whips on me. If that was just trying, I'd not want to know what succeeding might be."

"Did you know any of them?"

"I'd never seen any one of them before that."

"Then why do you suppose they attacked you?"

"Who knows?" Hyleor's snort was accompanied by an expression close to a sneer. "Rumors, I'd guess. Everyone thinks spice and herb traders trade in elveweed and curamyn . . . or worse. We're the last ones who do that."

"The last ones?"

"Everyone thinks we do. We get stopped and searched by the governors' men—or Lord Bhayar's—in every province. They never find anything. That's because we know we'll get searched, and it's not worth the danger."

"There's no law against it."

"Law? Who said anything about law? I suppose you've released that little snot your men caught. Too bad he didn't suffer the same sort of 'accident' his brother did."

"How did you know they were brothers?"

"It would have been hard to ignore. He was screaming that the troopers killed his brother. He kept yelling about it until they gagged him and carted him off. You didn't answer my question."

"You didn't ask one," replied Quaeryt pleasantly.

"Did you release him?"

"He's still locked up. I wanted to talk to you about testifying in the hearing on Lundi."

"Your men saw it all. You don't need me. I'm the one who got whipped. I didn't even know who they were until your men showed up and I saw the one lying on the fence spike. Besides, I'm headed to Solis tomorrow."

"I could require you to stay."

"You do that, and I'll have all the factors' councils protesting to Lord Bhayar."

Quaeryt shrugged. "The brother will have an advocate representing him, and without your presence . . ."

"That's your problem, Governor, not mine. Now . . . if you'll excuse me . . ." Hyleor turned away and walked toward the wagon.

After a moment Quaeryt turned and mounted, then rode back up the drive to rejoin the squad. As he rode back to the post, Quaeryt had to admit that he was amazed at Hyleor's arrogance and effrontery, but he hadn't really wanted to throw a factor—even one of dubious reputation—into one of the Civic Patrol gaol cells. *But why doesn't he want to testify? Because he doesn't want to get on the bad side of a High Holder and his bastard son?*

Either way, Hyleor's attitude was going to make life more difficult for Quaeryt.

It was half past four when Vaelora returned to the post, and Quaeryt was waiting in the courtyard as she dismounted. She wasn't smiling, and he decided not to ask anything. He just smiled warmly. "I'm glad you're back."

"It's not as if I'd been traveling to Solis and returned." Her voice was edgy. "It feels that way. It took me half the day to arrange for linens—bed linens, towels, table linens, napkins . . . even blankets. Half a day! I could have done it in a glass or two in Solis."

Quaeryt nodded, not wanting to point out the obvious—that they weren't in Solis, but in a much smaller city recently devastated by an eruption and earth tremors. "I know. It's much harder to get things accomplished here."

"Everything is an endless chore!"

"It does feel that way."

"Stop humoring me. You sound more condescending than Aunt Nerya at her worst."

"I do understand. I'm paying more for timbers, and they take longer to mill. I can't find an honest justicer . . . and I just got a dispatch from your brother."

Vaelora looked ready to snap back at Quaeryt until she heard his last news. "What's the matter?"

"Let's go up to our quarters, and I'll tell you. It's not terrible, but it's not as good as it could be."

"Tell me now."

"In the quarters."

"Fine."

Quaeryt didn't bother to hide his wince at the coldness of her tone. Unless he could calm Vaelora down, it was likely to be a long evening. He had to walk quickly to keep up with her as she marched across the courtyard and up the outside stairs. The heel of the boot on his bad left leg caught on one of the steps, and he barely caught himself.

Vaelora didn't even look in his direction.

Only when the quarters door was shut did she turn. "Well?"

"You don't have to shout at me," he said quietly.

"I hate it when you get that condescending tone in your voice. And then you refuse to tell me . . ."

"Did you ever think that I'd rather not say what he wrote in the courtyard with troopers all around?"

"You still didn't have to be so condescending."

"I shouldn't have been."

"No . . . you shouldn't, not with everything I've gone through today. And Grelyana showed up at the villa. She was so falsely sweet, and it was as though you and I had tortured her for those few pieces of furniture, and she wasn't using them. They would have dry-rotted away in the cellars of her palace. There was so much dust on them. That's where they had to have come from because they were so filthy. . . ."

Quaeryt listened for close to a quint before saying a word, deciding against mentioning what Aextyl had said about Grelyana as Vaelora moved on to detailing other problems. Then, when she paused, he said, "Bhayar requires Third Regiment leave Extela no later than the sixteenth of Mayas, but they have to be ready to ride out on notice from him any day after the fifteenth of Avryl."

"That's only ten days away! The bridge isn't finished. The residence won't be ready. You can't find trustworthy guards that soon . . ."

"The Bovarians are moving thousands of troops toward Ferravyl." From Bhayar's dispatch, Quaeryt didn't know the precise number, but it had to be thousands, if not more, given that there were already thousands of Telaryn troops already there.

"Oh . . ."

By the time they headed down to dinner, Vaelora was at least talking in a level, if slightly cool, tone of voice, and she was charming to the officers in the mess.

Quaeryt still knew it would be a long night, and he hadn't even mentioned his problems with Hyleor and justicing.

40

By late on Vendrei evening, Vaelora's coolness had warmed, and on Samedi, Quaeryt arranged for Vhalsyr to be transferred from the post brig to a cell at the Civic Patrol gaol. Then he and Vaelora both accompanied the contingent of troopers to the market squares and watched the sale of flour and potatoes. What struck Quaeryt was the range of people who came to purchase the goods, from those who appeared barely able to scrape together the coppers necessary to those who wore good linens and fine wool garments. That suggested to him that the prices he'd set were the lowest available, and that he might need to raise them before long.

Later on Samedi, both Vaelora and Quaeryt spent time at the villa, and on Solayi, Quaeryt read through another third of Ekyrd's treatise, concentrating on the procedures for handling a justicer's hearing . . . and the recommended sentences for various offenses. After that he managed, somehow, to come up with another homily—this one on vanity, how the excesses of attire, either being too elaborate or putting on a pretense of not caring, were both forms of Naming.

Vaelora left the post on Lundi morning to meet with Shenna and a group of women who provided goods to the poor, so that she could work with them to provide some of the coppers from the offerings at the anomen to the most deserving women, before going to the villa and looking into possible furnishings. After she departed, Quaeryt met with Jhalyt and Heireg to complete the final transfer of twelve hundred golds to Factoria Grelyana, then rode over to the patrol station, accompanied by a squad he likely didn't need, as well as the four troopers who'd been mostly involved in the incident between Versoryn and Hyleor. He doubted he needed that many troopers, since he'd continued to be most scrupulous in his use of and practice with his shields, but Skarpa felt the escort of a full squad was necessary.

While he didn't relish the idea of being a justicer, he also couldn't put off the hearings, not with Vhalsyr's "uncle" getting involved, if through an advocate, not to mention the limited number of cells available or the fact that Hyleor refused to testify. He wasn't looking forward to conducting any of the hearings, not at all, but he was especially dreading the one for Vhalsyr.

Pharyl came out to greet him at two quints before eighth glass, and the two walked back to the larger of the two studies in the building.

"The hearing room is ready, and I posted the notices where we could, and on the board outside. I put Vhalsyr first. His advocate has already been in to talk to him. He's still there." The chief looked quizzically at Quaeryt.

"You're still wondering why I'm going ahead with the hearings? Because I don't see any good justicers coming along anytime soon, and I don't want people saying that we're just locking people up and throwing away the key, especially High Holder Cransyr. Also, if some of them are innocent, unlikely as that may be, we don't want them locked away any longer than necessary. Also . . . since Hyleor isn't likely to show up, you may have trouble proving that Vhalsyr actually assaulted anyone."

"I've thought of that. If the patrollers had arrested him, that could be a problem. The older patrollers have the attitude that anyone they bring in is guilty. Since Vhalsyr was caught by troopers . . . if it turns out that way, it won't be quite that bad."

"The patrollers are likely right about that. Vhalsyr's guilty. I know that. So do you, but proving it with a High Holder's advocate defending him and ready to report any irregularity is another question."

"For the other three . . . what range of sentences are possible?" asked Pharyl. "Are they like in the regiment?"

Quaeryt realized, belatedly, that Pharyl was probably less aware of nonmilitary justicing than Quaeryt himself. *The half blind leading the blind.* "The possible sentences for conviction of lesser offenses—the first time—are various degrees of flogging and imprisonment, plus branding on the back of the hand for anything but misdemeanors such as public nuisances or drunken disorderliness. For a second conviction, much more of the same. A third offense merits death. Are any of the three branded?"

"No, sir."

"That's a relief. Can we get a branding iron made?"

"Ah . . . I took the liberty of asking around. I found an old one in an ironmonger's. It's Ryntaran, though, with the fancy 'C.' "

"If necessary, that will have to do . . . for now." *And something else needing to be done.* In recent years, most justicers had required differing brands—a "T" for theft, "A" for assault, and "F" for forgery or fraud—rather than general "C" for crime or criminal, regardless of the specific type of offense.

"The man who was assaulted wants to beg mercy for the fellow who attacked him."

Quaeryt almost asked why the man hadn't asked for the charges just to be dropped, but realized from his quick and intense study of the law treatise that charges could only be dismissed by a justicer after hearing the case—because all too often pleas to dismiss charges were offered by the victim in fear of retribution or because of threats to the victim or the victim's family.

After discussing the procedures for a time, Quaeryt just walked into the chamber and to the dais, where he seated himself behind the simple, almost crude, stained table desk. "The justicing hearing in the city of Extela, the province of Montagne, will commence. I am Governor Quaeryt, acting as justicer. The first hearing is the matter of Vahlsyr Brennasyn, charged with assaulting a factor and troopers of Telaryn in the course of their duties."

Immediately, a short stocky man attired in a black robe over his regular garb stepped forward. "Caesyt Klaesyn, representing the accused."

"Pharyl, Chief of the Civic Patrol, representing the city of Extela."

"Very well. Bring in the accused."

Two patrollers marched in Vhalsyr, his hands before him in leather restraints, and positioned him directly before Quaeryt. Caesyt stepped up beside Vhalsyr.

"You are charged with two counts of assault. The first count is that of dragging the factor Hyleor Cylonsyn from his dwelling and place of business and attacking him with various weapons, including knives and whips. The second count is that of attacking the troopers of the Third Tilboran Regiment in the course of their duties." Quaeryt paused. "How do you plead?"

"Not guilty, Honorable Justicer," said Caesyt smoothly.

The patrollers led Vhalsyr to the backless bench below and to the right of Quaeryt.

From there Quaeryt waited as Pharyl called in the first of the four troopers, Melnar. Melnar described the situation, and his description mirrored the one provided by Hyleor.

Pharyl asked a number of questions, then stepped back. "The patrol has no more questions."

"Do you have questions, Advocate Caesyt?"

"I do indeed, Honorable Justicer."

Quaeryt nodded.

"Trooper Melnar, at any time did you see the accused with a weapon or holding a weapon?"

"There were whips cracking all over the place when we rode up, sir, and the one who fell on the fence had a long knife."

"We know that Versoryn had weapons, but did the accused have one?"

"He must have. They all did . . . all of that gang."

"Did you see him with a weapon in his hand?"

After a long pause, Melnar answered, "No, sir."

"Did you see him strike Factor Hyleor or anyone else with his hands?"

"No, sir."

"Did you see him act in any way against anyone else?"

"He started trying to hit the other rankers—and me—when we caught him. He hit me, and he hit Estall."

"Did he inflict serious damage on any trooper?"

"Sir?"

"Did he hurt any of you?"

"I think Huryk got some bruises, sir."

"Thank you, trooper." Caesyt turned to Quaeryt. "I have no more questions for this witness."

Quaeryt looked to Pharyl. "Call your next witness."

Estall was the next trooper, and the patterns of testimony and questions—and Estall's answers—were almost exactly the same as Melnar's had been. So were the testimonies and answers from the last two troopers, although Huryk insisted that Vhalsyr had to have used a whip because the number of whips matched the number of people present.

"Vhalsyr Brennasyn, step forward," ordered Pharyl, who waited until Vhalsyr faced Quaeryt before continuing. "Would you please tell the honorable justicer what happened on the night of Vendrei, the thirty-fourth of Maris?"

"Honorable Justicer . . ." Vhalsyr swallowed, then went on. "My brother told me he wanted to go talk with Factor Hyleor. He said he'd had enough of Hyleor's shit with the girls, his getting them to smoke elveweed and snort curamyn. I told him that Hyleor was a mean sort. He said he'd take care of that. I wasn't sure I wanted to go, but I didn't want him to go alone. Except when we got to a block away, some more guys joined us. They carried whips, and some had knives. I didn't know any of them. When we got to this house, there was a fellow unloading a little wagon outside the place, and Versoryn, he said that was Hyleor, and they all ran down the drive and wrapped him up with their whips, and dragged him out into the street. I yelled at my brother not to hurt him because he'd get in trouble. He yelled back that Hyleor deserved what he was going to get. Before they could do much, all of a sudden, there were all these troopers riding up. There must have been twenty of them, and they had sabres out. Versoryn, he went crazy, yelling about how Hyleor even had the troopers on his side. He went after one of the rankers or maybe his horse with a knife, and the trooper hit him with his sabre a couple of times. I couldn't believe it. Everyone else ran, and I didn't see what happened next. I was still standing there, and the troopers came after me. I tried to run, but they caught me . . ."

After that, Pharyl spent another quint or so asking questions, but Vhalsyr said nothing at variance with his initial story. Pharyl finally said, "I have no more questions."

Then Caesyt asked, "Were you carrying a knife or a whip?"

"No, sir."

"Not even a belt knife?"

"Oh . . . I had a belt knife. It's barely as long as my little finger. I never took it out of its sheath."

"You didn't have a whip?"

"I never used a whip. I wouldn't know how."

"Did you ever strike any of the troopers?"

"Not until they jumped all over me, sir. I just kept trying to keep them from hurting me too bad."

Quaeryt had his doubts about that, but he listened while Caesyt continued his questioning, until the advocate finally said, "I have no more questions."

"Do you have a final statement?" Quaeryt asked Pharyl.

"Yes, sir. Whether the accused actually lifted a weapon does not matter. He willfully took part in a group activity that inflicted bodily harm on the factor and that assaulted troopers of Lord Bhayar. He admits to striking troopers, and to trying to escape, which is a sign that he knew what he was doing was an offense against the law . . ."

When Pharyl had finished, Quaeryt turned to Caesyt. "Your statement, advocate?"

Caesyt stepped forward and faced Quaeryt. "There is no doubt that the late Versoryn did in fact commit the offenses with which his younger brother is being charged, Honorable Justicer . . . but"—the advocate paused before continuing—"there is absolutely no evidence that Vhalsyr is guilty of anything but poor judgment in accompanying his brother. Not a single one of the troopers saw him with any weapon. The alleged victim of the assault has not appeared to testify—he was summoned, was he not?"

"He was," Quaeryt said.

"The most with which Vhalsyr can honestly be charged is being disorderly in public, and that only because he felt he was being attacked unfairly by the troopers. That is the only charge of which he can possibly be charged. For those reasons, I move that he be found guilty of that and only that, and that his sentence be limited to the time in which he has already been incarcerated." Caesyt smiled politely.

Quaeryt could see the situation quite clearly. *You'd be an idiot not to see it.*

"I will take your motion under advisement, advocate." Quaeryt looked to the patrollers flanking Vhalsyr. "Bring the accused forward."

Caesyt stepped back slightly and then moved beside Vhalsyr once he stood in front of Quaeryt.

Quaeryt waited several moments before speaking. "Vahlsyr Brennasyn, this hearing finds you not guilty of two counts of assault, but guilty of the lesser charge of disorderly conduct. Your sentence is limited to the time in incarceration that you have already served. You are free to go. This hearing is declared closed." After a moment Quaeryt nodded to the patrollers. "You can release him."

The advocate looked stunned. "You're . . . deciding . . . now?"

"You made your case, advocate. I don't have to like it; I just have to go by the evidence."

The three hearings that followed were anticlimactic. The accused had no advocates, and all three had been caught in the act with witnesses.

Quaeryt had no doubt that the entire matter surrounding Vhalsyr, Versoryn, Hyleor . . . and, of course, High Holder Cransyr was anything but over. He just hoped that he'd minimized the damage.

Surprisingly, at least to Quaeryt, the rest of Lundi, as well as Mardi and Meredi, turned out to be free of unforeseen difficulties, except for an afternoon rainstorm on Mardi, and some rumbling from Mount Extel on Meredi that died away within a glass—not that he wasn't busy almost every moment of every day, whether in meeting with the tariff collectors gathered by Jhalyt and trying to determine what factors and others liable for tariffs had perished, and who had not—or their heirs—in going over the comparatively few charred but barely readable records reclaimed by Baharyt, and in checking the master ledgers for receipts that were all too few, mainly coins from the produce sales, against the expenditures that were all too many.

He also had to detail one of the regimental wagons to help Vaelora move supplies and the additional furnishings she had purchased various shops around Extela to the governor's villa, just in order to make the villa "barely livable," as she had put it, rather starkly. That brought up the point that the governor needed a coach and team, a teamster, and a wagon for the residence. Every day that passed, he discovered something else that was required. Vaelora had engaged Shenna as her secretary and also hired a cook and maid. She had also persuaded Quaeryt that they would move to the villa on Jeudi, and that had required transporting some grain and fodder from the post to the villa's stable, among other things, along with working out a guard detail from the permanent cadre of troopers at the post . . . at least until he could make inquiries and get to work hiring governor's guards.

The more that had to be done, the more Quaeryt appreciated the two months they had spent at Telaryn Palace, in effect a honeymoon where they had had little worry over the everyday details of life—even compared to the comparatively privileged lives of a governor and his wife.

Jeudi morning, after he saw Vaelora off with the wagons, he sat down at his desk in the small study to read a petition that had arrived immediately after breakfast from a messenger from a Factor Ruent, someone whose name Quaeryt had never heard. From the very heading, Quaeryt sensed trouble.

Quaeryt Rytersyn
Governor, Province of Montagne
Extela

Most Honorable Governor Quaeryt:
It has come to the attention of the undersigned factors of grain and produce that you, as governor, have required large holders of grains and root crops to sell significant amounts of these crops at a price significantly lower than they would otherwise fetch in the marketplace. While we understand the immediate need for flour among the poor, we must protest the manner in which you have made the flour available . . .

As he continued reading, Quaeryt wanted to shake his head once more. From what was in the petition, the local produce factors wanted him to determine who was poor and only sell or give flour to them so that the factors could sell all their flour to everyone else. The fact that it would be at a higher price and provide greater profit to the local factors was not mentioned, except indirectly in the idea of a marketplace price. Quaeryt didn't have the manpower, the local records, almost all of which had been destroyed by the lava overrunning the governor's square, or the time to make that determination, and that meant he'd either have to risk the wrath of the factors or hurt the poor. All of that didn't even take into consideration the fact that Third Regiment might be ordered out of Extela and to Ferravyl in less than four days. Even if Bhayar did not issue an immediate withdrawal, the regiment would have to depart in little more than a month, and trying to keep Extela running without the regiment's manpower would take some doing.

He checked the signatures on the bottom against the list of "dubious factors," but none of the names matched, and that made the "flour problem" even more of a concern.

What if you increase the price somewhat?

Flour was still in short enough supply, with the destruction of the warehouses and several mills along the river to the north of Extela, that any price increase that the poorest could afford would be less than the factors would charge without Quaeryt's effective price limitations.

He laid the petition on one side of the small desk. He'd have to think about how to handle it, and if there were any way he could work something out with the factors. Sooner or later the price would rise, because he couldn't keep buying it comparatively cheaply from the larger High Holders, simply because they'd run out of grain and flour sooner or later. *Probably sooner.*

He had the feeling that he needed to get out of the flour business, but the situation irked him enormously. He stood, then walked from the study down the narrow corridor to the south door and then across the courtyard to Major Heireg's study.

"Sir?"

"I've been going over things. This Samedi will be the last one that we'll be selling flour and potatoes. We won't announce it at the squares, though. We'll post notices and pass the word on Lundi."

And Quaeryt wasn't about to write the factors back immediately, even if they did end up getting their way. He didn't want to admit publicly, or even semipublicly, that they'd forced his hand. *You should have stopped the sales earlier.* Except they'd been selling flour less than a month. How could he have stopped earlier in good conscience, when he hadn't even finished restoring order in Extela, and so many of the poor lacked coins?

Heireg nodded. "Better that way. We don't want people getting upset at the troopers handing it out." He frowned. "It's too bad for some folks, but you can't keep paying for it, and with the stocks we have . . . well, they might last to harvest . . . if Third Regiment leaves in Mayas."

"It's likely to be around that time," Quaeryt said.

"Word is that it could be sooner . . ."

"It could . . . if Rex Kharst decides that he wants to take over Ferravyl."

"Why would the Bovarians attack there?"

"It would give Rex Kharst total control of the river and the ability to use it to supply an attack downriver on Solis. That's why Lord Chayar invested so much in the bridge and the fortifications there."

As he walked back to his study, Quaeryt reflected on both his situation and Bhayar's. Everything in life involved trade-offs. Solis was better positioned for trade and for travel, but it was more vulnerable to attack than was Extela. On the other hand, Extela was out of the way, but close to a volcano. Being a governor offered more power to do things, but left him vulnerable to all sorts of problems for which imaging provided almost no solutions, and being married to Vaelora . . . That provided a set of trade-offs as well . . . as he'd come to discover over the past month in particular.

42

Vendrei morning Quaeryt woke up in the gloom of the master bedchamber of the villa—a semidarkness relieved by grayness seeping through cracks in and around the shutters that he had closed the night before because the window hangings ordered by Vaelora had not been finished. He bolted upright, swung his feet onto the cold ceramic tile floor before realizing that it was still early.

He glanced around, taking in the sparseness of the chamber that held only the bed, without hangings, two empty night tables and two armoires, in which their clothes had been hung or folded. There were no carpets on the old tile floor, and no chairs. The only items that were new were the horse-hair mattress, two pairs of down pillows, and the bed linens and blankets, as well as a plain green linen bedspread. In fact, from what Quaeryt had seen when he had arrived late on Vendrei afternoon, he wasn't sure that those weren't the only new items of furniture or furnishings in the entire villa, not surprisingly, since it would have been impossible to have had anything custom-sewn or fashioned in the time since they had purchased the villa.

While the bedchamber was neat . . . and sparse, as were the kitchen and the private dining/breakfast room, Quaeryt knew too well that the rest of the villa remained in a state of spare disarray—and that might have been describing the situation generously.

He turned to see Vaelora looking out from under the covers at him.

"It was so good to sleep on a good mattress and linens, wasn't it?"

Quaeryt had been so tired after moving and shifting everything that Vaelora had wanted moved—again—after he'd left the post on Jeudi night and ridden to the villa that he could probably have stretched out on a thin pallet on the floor and still slept soundly. "It's a far better mattress than the one in the officers' quarters."

"And not nearly so narrow. I could actually stretch out, and it didn't matter that you sprawled all over the bed. There's enough room for that."

"That's very true."

"Don't start the day by humoring me, dearest."

Now what are you supposed to say to that? "I'm not." Quaeryt grinned. "If you think I'm humoring you every time I agree with you, then you're asking for me to disagree."

"Quaeryt . . . dearest . . ." Vaelora's eyes almost flashed. "I can tell the difference."

Quaeryt shrugged helplessly. Anything he said was likely to make matters worse. *Dealing with Rescalyn and Bhayar was far easier . . .* But then, he hadn't loved them . . . or even had to like them.

She laughed. "You are a dear. A stubborn dear, though." Her arms went around him.

Shortly thereafter, not nearly so long as he would have liked, they washed up and dressed and made their way down to the private dining room.

Rebyah—the cook hired at Shenna's recommendation—had breakfast ready for them, as if she'd had Alsyra, the maid, listening . . . which she probably had. A pale blue linen cloth covered the worn and battered table in the private dining chamber, as opposed to the large formal dining chamber that could likely accommodate forty guests, if not more, assuming that they could find or commission a table of that size, along with the matching chairs.

"Good morning, Lady . . . sir," said Alsyra, as she set platters before Vaelora and then before Quaeryt. She offered a pleasant and warm smile, as if she were pleased to be serving them . . . and perhaps she was.

On each platter was an omelet, with strips of ham on the side and a biscuit for Vaelora, and two for Quaeryt. Quaeryt's omelet was also larger. Then came a pot of tea, with vapor seeping from the spout. Alsyra filled both cups, with saucers—not mugs—of plain bone china, part of a set that Vaelora had located . . . somewhere.

"Isn't this better?" asked Vaelora.

"It's much better." That Quaeryt had no trouble admitting, none at all, especially since he did like hot tea rather than the lukewarm brews he'd been drinking lately. He also liked their not having to eat with the regimental officers, although he had no doubts they would miss Vaelora. He doubted they'd miss him.

When they finished eating, Vaelora looked to him. "When will you be back?"

"Mid to late afternoon . . . if there aren't any problems. Do you need anything from the post?"

She frowned, thinking. "I don't think so. There's much to do here. We still need a wagon and a cart horse."

"And . . . when we can . . . we'll need a coach and a team," Quaeryt admitted.

"That can wait . . . for a little while."

Quaeryt wasn't about to ask how long that meant.

Since there was no practical way to house a squad of troopers in the space over the villa's stable, Quaeryt rode to the post with just two troopers as an escort. That seemed more in keeping with his sense of propriety, especially since Extela seemed less unsettled than it had when he had arrived close to a month before and likely as peaceful as it would be for the foreseeable future.

Once he stabled the mare at the post stable, he made his way across the courtyard to the building that held his "official" study. As he stepped through the door, he looked to the duty squad leader. "Any dispatches from Solis?"

"No, sir. No dispatches from anywhere."

That was good, given that almost any dispatch at the moment would have brought bad news. "Thank you."

Then he went to find Skarpa. The regimental commander was alone in the post commander's study.

"Any problems I should know about?" asked Quaeryt, closing the door behind himself.

The commander smiled sardonically. "There are always problems in a regiment. None of them are large enough to involve you. Some rowdy troopers last night, but not in the Pharsi part of the city, and our patrols caught them before the Civic Patrol did."

Quaeryt hadn't realized that Pharyl had begun night patrols, but the fact that he didn't even know was good.

"The other problem is that we've had more than a score of mounts dropping or breaking shoes in the last week."

"You think the farrier in Tilbora had a bad batch of shoes? Or could it be all the riding through the ash here?"

Skarpa shrugged. "Who can tell? The farrier here looks to be good, and we've gotten the ailing horses all re-shod. A couple will need a few days of rest."

"Have you picked up any recruits?"

"A handful. I gave them to Meinyt. He's good at training them. A few seemed better suited to the Civic Patrol, and I sent them to Hrehn."

"We can use some good ones."

"Can't we all?" Skarpa paused. "I heard you had to let that little idiot nephew of the High Holder up in Ilyum loose."

"No one could prove anything except that he followed his brother and that he resisted custody. The High Holder is married to Bhayar's favorite cousin, and he sent an advocate. Guilty as the nephew likely was, there was no way to prove it, and I didn't see much benefit in gaoling him longer and branding him. He and his 'uncle' will be angry enough as it is, especially since Hyleor's guilty of worse, even if half of it's not strictly against the laws, and the other half without evidence to prove it. Everyone seems to think he's not worth the firewood to send him to the Nameless."

"Don't envy you, sir. In some ways, fighting the Bovarians might be easier than putting Extela back together."

Quaeryt laughed. "You might be right . . . except more people get killed in battle." *A lot more.* As he'd discovered, even imagers with shields could get wounded . . . and if that one quarrel had been just a bit higher and hit his neck, even his shields wouldn't have saved him. Then again, his shields were better now, but he still couldn't hold them against constant attacks for a long time.

"That may be, sir, but you can win battles. There's no way you can win in putting a city back together. There's always more to do, and always someone unhappy."

Quaeryt nodded. He hadn't exactly thought of it in that way. He wasn't sure he wanted to, either.

When he finished with Skarpa, Quaeryt headed out to the courtyard to brief the captain who had the supply duty. He'd decided that the troopers should not make any statements about if or when they might be back to sell flour. They were only to say that any decision on selling more flour was up to the governor. And once the company and wagons had left the post, Quaeryt needed to check with Major Heireg about the situation with supplies and what needed to go with the regiment when it left for Ferravyl.

After that, amid everything else, he still had to come up with another homily before services on Solayi evening.

Quaeryt woke up tired on Lundi morning, but relieved that he'd managed to deliver another homily on Solayi evening . . . and one that stayed within the bounds of what he'd heard and studied about the Nameless and his own conscience. He needed to find a chorister for the post, but the problem there was simple. While there were enough believers to support the anomen when a full regiment was in residence, that certainly wasn't the case most of the time, and with the state of the province's finances, he didn't like the idea of committing golds, or even silvers, to maintaining an anomen that was poorly attended most of the year. That was no doubt why it had been locked and unused when he and the regiment had arrived.

Quaeryt left for the post right after breakfast, knowing that despite the light misty drizzle that enshrouded Extela, Vaelora would be shopping to see what other items she could find for the villa . . . those most needed, since it would take months, if not years, not to mention more golds than Quaeryt wanted to think about, in order to finish refurbishing the old dwelling.

When Quaeryt reached the post and made his way to his study, he found Pharyl waiting for him in the corridor. "Good morning, Governor."

"Good morning, Chief." Quaeryt gestured for the older officer to enter the study first. "Is your visit because of a problem or just to keep me informed?" He tried to keep his tone lightly ironic as he closed the door and took his seat.

"Just to keep you informed. I take it that Commander Skarpa told you that he referred several young men to me as possible recruits?"

"He did."

"They were quite suitable, all but one. When they discovered that the leadership of the patrol had changed, they suggested that others might well wish to become patrollers. We've had several more inquiries, and recruiting looks promising."

"Good."

"The work on the station is completed. It's rough in places, but I can have some of the recruits work on fixing up the small things as part of their training. I'd thought to schedule justicer hearings on Mardi and Jeudi mornings at eighth glass, as necessary. I wanted to check with you first, though."

"That sounds fine. Until I can find a true justicer, I'll handle them, but upon occasion, we may have to change the day or time."

"I thought that might be the case."

"Do you have any offenders that need a hearing?"

"Ah . . . not really, sir."

Quaeryt smiled. "A few disorderly types that you just wanted to lock up for a time and then quietly release?"

"Yes, sir. We've started some night patrols, and as we complete more training and retraining, we'll be putting more men on the streets at night. I don't think we'll be able to cover much in the time between midnight and fifth glass . . . I've also asked around, and so has Captain Hrehn, about those factors . . . the ones whose names were on the list you gave me."

"Have you found out anything?"

Pharyl laughed, half humorously, half ironically. "Sometimes what you don't find out tells you more than what you do. Paulam . . . he's really a renderer who calls himself a factor, but a few people who reneged on deals with him had difficulties or accidents. Assoul and Dyetryn take advantage of those who have no options. No one seems to know much about Thaltyn. Aerambyr . . . who knows? They say he's tough in dealings, but fair. The way they say it, I have my doubts. Then . . . there's Lysienk."

"What about him?"

"That's what I was talking about. He has a place out west, not that far from the new governor's residence. Not small, but not too big . . . but it has high brick walls all around it, and there are guards and dogs inside the walls all the time. Whatever he factors, he handles from there, in a separate building. The thing is, outside of finding out those few things . . . no one wants to say anything . . . nothing at all. They know more. They won't say anything."

"Nothing?"

"Not a thing."

Quaeryt nodded. "Just keep listening. Anything else?"

"Just small details . . . those Pharsi women . . . they watch every patrol. . . ."

Quaeryt listened quietly and intently, pleased that Pharyl had been able to accomplish so much so quickly. He had no doubt that Hrehn had been part of the reason as well.

Pharyl had not been gone from the study more than a quint or so when the duty messenger knocked on the door. "There's a chorister here to see you, Governor."

"Send him in." *Why would a chorister be here to see me?*

"Yes, sir."

Shortly, the study door opened, and Quaeryt immediately stood.

A trim white-haired man in a dark gray jacket, matching trousers, and polished boots stepped inside. He did wear a short version of the black and white chorister's scarf. "Governor Quaeryt, I'm Chorister Siemprit." His smile was wide and cheerful.

"It's good to see you, chorister. Please sit down." Out of respect, Quaeryt remained standing until the older man had seated himself, then settled himself behind the table desk. "What can I do for you?"

"Since my anomen is not too far from here, I thought I should introduce myself."

"Where is your anomen?" asked Quaeryt politely.

"To the west, off the western boulevard. It's only about three blocks farther west from where you've established the new governor's residence. That was one of my purposes in calling on you—to invite you to join us. When you can, of course. I understand that you and your wife have many demands upon your time."

"It has been rather busy since we arrived," Quaeryt temporized, doubting that a mere invitation to worship was the only reason for the chorister's appearance. "There was the need to reestablish order and provide food."

"Your immediate generosity to the poor was welcome and most necessary." Siemprit frowned slightly. "I did wonder why you required the poor to pay for flour and potatoes so soon . . ."

"We didn't for the first few times, as you may know. Then we set the price at what it had been before the eruption."

"Many could not pay that."

"We were not strict. We provided flour to many for far less."

"Still . . ."

"Chorister . . . unlike some governors, I am not a wealthy man. Nor was there much left in the provincial treasury. Nor, with Rex Kharst threatening from the west, does Lord Bhayar have golds to spare."

"I suppose that is true . . ." Siemprit sighed. "It is always a matter of coins, one way or the other. I see you were trained as a scholar, Governor. I did not realize you also were a chorister. Where did you study the ways and works of the Nameless?"

Quaeryt smiled ruefully. "Where I could, chorister."

"I'm told that you are very accomplished in explicating the ways of the Nameless."

"I do what I can."

"Being a governor and trying to restore order to Extela must take a great deal of your time. Yet you are acting as a chorister. Did you ever consider hiring a chorister from Extela?"

"In time, if it is necessary, I certainly will."

"I'm surprised that you haven't already. You seem to have accomplished a great deal in the time you have been here. Surely, hiring a chorister would not take that much effort . . ."

"Hiring a chorister probably wouldn't. Finding one suited to addressing a regiment might well take time."

"Your words suggest that you believe the Nameless regards soldiers differently from others."

"I doubt that the Nameless makes any such distinction, chorister," *assuming that there even is a Nameless.* "The distinction lies in the ways of making the Nameless and what is required by adhering to the doctrines of the Nameless relevant and directly applicable to soldiers."

"You're suggesting that soldiers are a breed apart."

"You don't think they are, chorister? How many men have you killed in your life? How many of them were likely guilty of only serving a different worldly master?"

"How many have you killed, Governor?" countered Siemprit.

"I didn't try to keep count, not after the first battles of the revolt in Tilbor."

Siemprit's forehead screwed up into a frown. "You're a scholar."

"That may be, but at the time I was a scholar advisor to the military governor, and I was ordered into combat." That wasn't technically true, because Quaeryt had only been ordered to accompany the regiment into battle, but he'd discovered that the only way to obey that order and survive had been to fight.

"Oh . . ." After the slightest pause, the chorister went on. "I hadn't realized you had also been an officer, as well as a scholar, and princeps of Tilbor. Most princepses come from a factoring background, those that aren't High Holders, that is."

Quaeryt had not been an officer, but because he'd been accorded that status and had men assigned to obey him, he didn't correct Siemprit. "Did you have a recommendation for a chorister here?" There wasn't any point in not asking, and it just might defuse some of the chorister's not-so-veiled polite hostility.

"My assistant, Neoryn, would make a most capable chorister."

"That is good to know, and I appreciate your bringing his name to my attention. Once we get matters here more settled, I'll have to meet him."

"I trust that will not be too long, Governor."

"No more than a few weeks, chorister." Quaeryt rose. "I do appreciate your coming to see me."

"And I appreciate your courtesy in hearing me out."

Once Siemprit had left, the door closed behind him, Quaeryt took a deep breath. *It seems as though no one likes what you're doing, and everyone wants something.* He knew he was overreacting, but that was the way he felt.

He was still wondering if—and when—he should see the junior chorister when there was another knock on the study door.

"Yes?"

"Some documents for you, sir, it looks like."

"Bring them in."

"Yes, sir." The door opened, and the duty squad leader stepped in and handed Quaeryt an overlarge envelope, one that clearly contained a number of pages within it, then quickly slipped out before Quaeryt could even say "Thank you."

He opened the envelope and immediately read the short missive on top of the more than ten sheets beneath.

> *Governor—*
>
> *The attached brief details a practice of the High Holders of Aramyn, dealing with unlawful water diversions, contrary to common law, established practices, and prior agreements, and seeks redress and damages commensurate with the injuries suffered by the plaintiffs. In keeping with the legal customs of Telaryn, I am lodging this brief with you, as acting high justicer of Montagne, for either your judgment or your referral, as you see fit, according to precedent and practice . . .*

The signature was that of Caesyt Klaesyn.

Quaeryt took a deep breath and began to read. After struggling through the nine long pages, far more abstruse than any scholarly treatise he had ever read, he set the brief back on the desk and massaged his forehead. *What did you do to deserve this?*

From what he could decipher, the local holders of the lands bordering those of Aramyn claimed that the High Holder and his father had both made the practice of diverting more of the water from the stream, identified as Minawa Creek, than was theirs by right to divert, and that they had left insufficient water in the creek for the downstream users to irrigate their lands and crops.

Quaeryt had no idea what to do—except pay a visit to former high justicer Aextyl and ask for his advice and counsel. He didn't even know how soon he had to act and whether he had to give notification to Aramyn and in what form, if he did—or if the so-called brief was a legal bluff of some sort.

He did have the idea that Advocate Caesyt, having seen Quaeryt make an immediate decision in the case involving Vhalsyr, believed the evidence was on his side and was trying to get an immediate judgment on this issue as well.

Less than a quint later, Quaeryt was riding the mare northwest to the dwelling of the former justicer, with the document he'd received and Ekyrd's treatise in one of his saddlebags. While the drizzle had stopped, the sky was still overcast, but at least it wasn't raining. He didn't see the sad-faced hound, either. After reaching Aextyl's house, he had not even tied the mare to the hitching ring when the front door opened, and the justicer's daughter stood there.

"He can't be a justicer, Governor. You'll kill him if you insist."

"I won't insist. I'm just here for his advice . . . and to return the book I borrowed." Quaeryt walked up the steps, carrying the book and the brief and leaving the pair of rankers mounted and waiting. "Might I see him?"

The woman nodded, sadly. "He's reading in the study." She turned and led him through the small entry hall and down the hallway. "The governor is here, Father."

"I thought he'd be back." There was a laugh.

Quaeryt eased his way into the study and closed the door.

"Good morning, Governor." Aextyl gestured to the straight-backed chair.

"I wanted to return this"—Quaeryt lifted the maroon-bound book—"and to ask you to read something and offer your opinion. I won't ask you to read it as a favor. I'll pay for your time."

"I just might take you up on that. Times aren't what they used to be. You can keep the book as long as you need it."

Quaeryt extended the sheets, then sat back and waited.

Almost a quint passed before Aextyl looked up. "Slimy ball of offal. You don't have any final jurisdiction on this, not as a governor or even as an acting provincial high justicer. Any petition or brief involving the rights of a High Holder has to be decided by the High Justicer of Telaryn, who must be a High Holder."

"Good—"

"But," the old justicer went on, "you have to write an opinion on the brief, and whatever Aramyn submits in rebuttal, and offer a recommendation."

"I could certainly write something, but it wouldn't be phrased correctly."

Aextyl smiled. "That's what Caesyt is counting on."

"What if I draft what I think, and you redraft it in the proper form? Would two golds be a fair payment?"

"More than fair, Governor, and I'd be happy to do that."

"There's one other thing. Don't I have to have a hearing and announce my decision or referral or whatever?"

"You do."

"Could I persuade you, for another gold, to sit beside me and advise me on anything that comes up? Caesyt knows I'm no advocate or justicer. I'll act as justicer, but I'd have someone come and get you, pay you, and return you here."

"Just advise you?" Aextyl's tone was somewhere between doubtful and weary.

"I've already used the treatise to get through four hearings, but I don't trust Caesyt."

"You shouldn't. He's slimier than an eel, and more disgusting than hog offal in midsummer . . . like I said before."

Quaeryt didn't want to press the old justicer. "I won't ask for your decision on advising me in the hearing now. I'd like you to think about it, but I do want your expertise in redrafting my opinion."

"I can do that."

"Is there any time period in which I have to respond?"

"No, but it's considered bad form and will discredit your opinion if you take longer than a month."

"Don't I have to inform High Holder Aramyn?"

"Caesyt's supposed to, but you should check with Aramyn. You'll have to wait for his reply."

Another problem that may drag on.

"Knowing Aramyn, you won't wait long—if Caesyt notified him. I wouldn't put it past him not to."

"Wouldn't that prejudice the case?"

"It should, but Caesyt just might want to discredit you as well."

Quaeryt had already thought about that. He nodded. "I think I'll be riding out to see High Holder Aramyn."

Aextyl smiled wearily. "I'll wait on your draft, Governor."

"Thank you." Quaeryt stood. "I do appreciate it."

"I appreciate your consideration in asking my opinion, Governor."

"I respect your knowledge, sir."

"You're one of the few who does, these days."

Quaeryt slipped a gold from his wallet and laid it on the desk. "That, I trust, is sufficient to cover your time and expertise today."

"You don't have to . . ."

"But I do. You've already kept me from making a terrible mistake." Quaeryt smiled, started to turn, then stopped. "Oh . . . you mentioned that I should be careful in dealing with a Factor Lysienk. What can you tell me about him?"

Aextyl frowned. "I can't say that I know that much. He arrived in Extela only about a year before I stepped down. He seemed to have golds, enough to buy the place he did, and then build a high wall around it. He supplied goods of various sorts to Scythn and others, claimed that he had the best produce, among other things. It seemed to me that people were always wary about saying anything about him. Oh . . . and he always rides with four bodyguards." The older justicer shrugged. "I never met him, but when an outsider gets that kind of wealth and influence that quickly . . . and when he feels he needs guards, it usually suggests the less than savory. I wish I could tell you more, but that's all I know."

"Thank you." Quaeryt nodded again, then made his way from the study, quietly closing the door behind him.

"You didn't ask him to be a justicer, did you?" asked the daughter, waiting in the narrow hall.

"No. I asked if I could pay him two golds to redraft an opinion correctly and if he would advise me on handling a hearing over water rights, I'd pay him more for the advice."

"Two golds?"

"I hope that's not unfair . . ."

The daughter laughed bitterly. "No. You're being more than fair, Governor. Unlike some."

"I don't want to take advantage of him, but I do need his knowledge and expertise."

"He'll be happy that you do."

Quaeryt hoped so. He nodded politely and made his way down to the hitching ring, untied the mare, and mounted. A quick glance to the northwest revealed no change around or in the air above Mount Extel.

The ride to Aramyn's holding took almost a glass, and when he stepped into the entry of the hold house, the High Holder met him with a puzzled expression on his face.

"Governor, I'm surprised to see you."

Quaeryt managed a laugh. "Unfortunately, that's not good. You shouldn't be. I thought you might be expecting me."

Aramyn frowned. "Oh?"

"I received a brief, a complaint this morning. It concerns you." Quaeryt handed the sheets to the High Holder. "Have you seen this?"

"A brief? Would you mind if I took a moment and read through this?"

"Not at all. That's why I'm here."

"Let us go to the study, then."

Quaeryt followed the High Holder down the corridor and then into the chamber he only vaguely remembered, and mainly for the expanse of goldenwood bookshelves. Aramyn gestured to the chairs before the desk, taking one himself.

Quaeryt took another.

Aramyn read the first page slowly, the second page less so, and then skimmed through the remaining pages. "Would you wait just a moment, Governor?"

"Certainly."

Aramyn stood, set the brief on the desk, and walked to a wall cabinet, which he opened. There he looked through several stacks of paper before extracting a sheaf of papers before closing the cabinet and moving to the desk. Standing there, he glanced at the first page of the papers Quaeryt had provided, then studied those he had taken from the cabinet. He repeated the process with each page before finishing and looking at Quaeryt.

"This complaint against me is almost identical to one filed by Caesyt two years ago, with one exception. There might be other little changes, but it looks to be the same. The only significant difference I see immediately is a clause alleging that the eruption has resulted in measurable and significant effects on water runoff and stream flows. He's using that as a basis for petitioning for a change in the decision handed down in Solis."

Quaeryt managed not to swallow. He hadn't caught that. He wondered if that were buried somewhere or so carefully disguised that he hadn't recognized it. "Could you point out that clause?"

Aramyn did—near the top of the second page.

Quaeryt read part of the wordage.

> Insomuch as recent geological events have impacted precipitation events and prevailing riverine flow patterns, the party of the second part asserts that any and all past judgments made on the distribution of such riverine allocations be reviewed in light of such recent impacts . . .

That was it. There was no direct mention of a previous hearing, or conflict or any sort of judgment.

"He wanted to sneak that by you, and he didn't send me a copy. He thought you might not inform me. That way he might get a favorable recommendation from you, and a reversal of the earlier decision. Even if he didn't, he could argue that your failure to follow procedures biased his claim." Aramyn snorted.

"I'll need your rebuttal."

"You'll have it in the next day or so. I have to travel to Montagne on a family matter, but I'll get it to you before I depart." He shook his head. "Thank you for letting me know. I do appreciate it."

"Do you need a copy . . ."

Aramyn shook his head. "But let me compare this to the original. Except for that one section, they look to be word for word. I will copy that one part."

In the end, Aramyn had to copy three paragraphs where matters changed, and it was close to fourth glass before Quaeryt left the holding, headed back to Extela and the villa. He was well away from Aramyn's before he realized that he'd meant to ask the High Holder about Lysienk, and it was late enough in the day that he wasn't about to ride back. Besides, he'd have other opportunities.

44

Quaeryt was quietly busy on Mardi, and he managed to deal with a number of minor problems, including straightening out the bookkeeping on payments to Gahlen, High Holder Wystgahl, the younger, and making sure that the offerings from the anomen were tracked in a separate ledger, as well as kept in a separate chest in the strong room so that they would be there when Vaelora had time to deal with the next distribution of them to the poor women of Extela. Major Dhaeryn offered a quick report on the ongoing repairs to the east river bridge—which was taking longer than the head engineer had planned, in part because of the difficulty in extracting the red volcanic clay needed for the underwater concrete used to repair the bridge pylons.

Without having to hold hearings at the Civic Patrol station, for which he was grateful, Quaeryt could also take time to reread the dense document from Caesyt several times, until he *thought* he had a better understanding of the issues.

Although it was two days past the fifteenth of Avryl, no message had arrived from Bhayar ordering Third Regiment to depart for Ferravyl, but Quaeryt was aware such an order could now arrive at any time. He hoped it would not come soon, given how much he was still relying on Skarpa and Third Regiment, especially the engineers.

The rest of the day was as quietly busy as the beginning, and Quaeryt was more than ready to retreat from the post to the villa, where Vaelora was pleased to inform him that she had located a matching settee and chair for the salon—which would, of course, require the use of a wagon to transport from the shop in Extela to the villa.

Still . . . it was pleasant to eat with just Vaelora and to linger over the evening meal that was neither bland nor overcooked . . . and the quiet of the villa was welcome as well. He also had to admit, if only to himself, that he was definitely enjoying the larger bed and the privacy of their own dwelling, governor's residence or not.

Shortly after eighth glass on Meredi morning a messenger arrived at the post and delivered Aramyn's rebuttal to Ceasyt's petition, and Quaeryt immediately read it. He ended up going through both the original petition and the rebuttal several times before he began to write his recommendation to the High Justicer in Solis, a recommendation he suspected Aextyl would have to rewrite considerably.

By just before the third glass of the afternoon, he had finished his final draft and was riding back out to Aextyl's dwelling. Several men and women on the avenue waved to him, and he inclined his head in return.

Even Aextyl's daughter greeted him with a cheerful, "Good afternoon," when she opened the door to let him into the justicer's dwelling.

The old justicer smiled warmly, as well, when Quaeryt entered the small study. "It's good to see you, Governor."

"It's even better to see you." Quaeryt set the stack of three papers on the study desk. "The short document on top is my draft recommendation. Beneath that is Aramyn's rebuttal, and beneath that is Caesyt's petition. Caesyt did not inform Aramyn. I did not put that in my draft, because I didn't know whether that was legally applicable, based on what you told me on Lundi."

"It's a common courtesy, but it's not required. It is required that you assure that Aramyn is notified, which his brief will substantiate that you have done. You will need copies of both the brief and the rebuttal to be sent to Solis with your recommendation."

"I hope asking you to redraft my recommendation isn't too much of an imposition."

"Nonsense. It's good to have something productive and useful to do."

Quaeryt eased the two golds onto the desk. "If you think your work is worth more . . ."

Aextyl laughed. "You're overpaying me, but I'm glad to take it. I would judge I'll be finished by midday tomorrow, but give me until third glass, just in case."

"I can do that. If I schedule a hearing for eighth glass next Mardi, would you be willing to come an advise me?"

"If I'm feeling well . . . and I should be."

"I would appreciate it. You know how I feel about Advocate Caesyt."

"I felt the same way when I was high justicer. I can't imagine his presence is any more pleasant these days."

Quaeryt stepped back and inclined his head. "Then . . . here, tomorrow afternoon?"

"I'm not likely to be anywhere else," replied Aextyl cheerily.

Quaeryt made his way to the entry hall, where the justicer's narrow-faced daughter stood, waiting.

"Thank you . . . Governor." Her voice was low.

"Thank me? He's the one helping me."

She smiled softly. "I haven't seen him this happy in a long time. He misses being a justicer."

Quaeryt thought he understood. Aextyl was too frail in body to remain a justicer, and too alert in mind not to suffer the loss of being one. "I'll be relying on his advice so long as he's willing to provide it."

"As long as he can, he'll appreciate being able to do so."

Left unspoken, Quaeryt thought, was the daughter's appreciation of the fees Aextyl received for that advice . . . but that was fine with him. After a parting smile, he stepped out into the gusty wind that had appeared from nowhere and untied the mare. He glanced northward toward Mount Extel, but while he could not see the truncated peak because of the trees, the sky appeared clear of ash or the waviness of hot air.

He mounted quickly and turned the mare back toward the post.

Quaeryt and Vaelora sat at the table in the private dining chamber, eating breakfast. Quaeryt was enjoying a puffy almond pastry and sipping truly hot tea when Vaelora, who had appeared pensive since before the two had seated themselves, set down her cup and looked at her husband.

"Dearest . . . I'm worried."

"So am I . . . about quite a number of things. So are you. This sounds like a specific worry. What is it?"

"We've been here a month, and we haven't received a single invitation to dine anywhere."

Quaeryt managed not to laugh or grin . . . barely. No invitations to dine when a quarter of the city had been buried in lava and ash? When he'd had to detail troopers to patrol the streets to restore a semblance of order. "We've only been here a month, and for the first few weeks, I doubt anyone was hosting dinners."

"Shenna tells me that there have been a number of dinners. We should have been invited. We weren't."

"It could be that you're being snubbed because you married a scholar," suggested Quaeryt.

"A scholar who is a governor and who has been a princeps . . . and who's wed to the sister of Lord Bhayar," Vaelora replied. "This is where I was born. It's not right."

"Grelyana, you think? Should we have pushed as we did on the furnishings?"

Vaelora tilted her head. "I wouldn't think so . . . but . . ."

"Why don't you see if Shenna can find out?"

Vaelora laughed softly. "She's been trying, but it's not something anyone's talking about, and there are only a few people she can ask directly."

Quaeryt nodded and took the last sips of his tea. Even after working in the Telaryn Palace as a scholar and then as princeps, he'd never realized just how complicated being a provincial governor would be, especially in a partly destroyed city.

Although it was Jeudi morning, there were no hearings scheduled, and

Quaeryt didn't rush in riding to the post. He did have the feeling that it wouldn't be long before his Mardi and Jeudi mornings, if not part of the afternoons on those days, would be taken by hearings . . . at least until he could find an honest justicer. And that was another task he needed to get on with. He did enjoy the ride, since the air was warm, if slightly damp, and the trees were beginning to leaf beyond mere buds, and even a few early flowers were peering out.

He glanced to Mount Extel, but the peak showed no signs of throwing out ash or even hot gases, and that was good.

After he arrived at the post, he went looking for Pharyl because he wanted to talk to the Civic Patrol chief about scheduling the hearing on Caesyt's petition, but Pharyl was already on his way to the Civic Patrol station. So he stopped to see Skarpa.

The commander looked up from what appeared to be a sheaf of papers containing rosters. "Haven't seen you around much lately, sir."

"I've been around . . . more places than I'd like at times and then spending more time than I'd ever thought likely on various things I never thought I'd have to deal with—from buying a governor's residence to acting as a justicer . . . and a supply quartermaster for the poor."

"That seafaring background still shows through."

"Oh . . ."

"For cavalry and foot, a quartermaster is supply. A supply quartermaster is redundant."

"Whereas for those of us who've trod the pearly deep, or some such, a quartermaster is a navigator. Old habits die hard." Quaeryt smiled, then asked, "How are the night patrols going?"

"We haven't had any more trouble, but the squad leaders are reporting that they're being watched, especially in the areas where the Civic Patrol isn't going yet."

"That will mean trouble for Pharyl once you leave for Ferravyl."

"Have you heard anything new?" asked Skarpa.

"Not yet." That was more a courtesy, reflected Quaeryt, because Skarpa would have known the moment a dispatch rider came through the post gates. So should the post commander.

Quaeryt frowned. "Have you seen Commander Zhrensyl lately?" Since he and Vaelora had left the officers' quarters for the villa and were no longer eating at the officers' mess, he couldn't recall seeing the older commander at all.

"He's around, but he avoids me."

"He's the one who offered his study to you, isn't he?"

Skarpa nodded. "He's only got five months before he can take a stipend. He doesn't want any sort of trouble . . . and you asked him a lot of hard questions."

"So far as I could tell, he did almost nothing."

"True . . . but in his defense, he had next to nothing to do it with. He doesn't even have a full company left here. Half his men were killed because they were stationed at the old palace or around the governor's square."

Maybe you were too hard on him. "I didn't say anything."

"Governor . . . you don't have to say much. The men follow you because they can tell you'll put yourself out on the line. They can also tell that you're not one to tolerate shiftlessness. Maybe it's because you're a scholar, but it's like it's written all over you."

Quaeryt shook his head. "Not always."

"No . . . you can be as inscrutable as a blank slate. You always were with Marshal Rescalyn. Sometimes you're like Artiema and sometimes like Erion. I think that bothered Rescalyn a lot."

After discussing how to organize the regiment's departure, either in mid-Mayas or when the order came, Quaeryt left Skarpa, still pondering about the commander's comparison of him to one moon and then the other—the open pearly warmth of Artiema and the reddish imperviousness of Erion, the great hunter.

He'd have to ask Vaelora about that.

Pushing that thought aside, he went to see how Jhalyt and Baharyt were coming with the restructuring of the tariff collections and the reassignments of the tariff collectors. Then he needed to check with Major Heireg on supply questions. What with one thing and another, the day slipped way, until it was close to third glass.

Quaeryt saddled the mare himself, then rode out to Aextyl's dwelling, arriving some two quints before fourth glass, dismounting so quickly that he almost tripped over his bad leg before going out of his way to pet the sad-faced hound, who rewarded him with a few wags of the tail. Then he made his way to the small entry porch, where the justicer's daughter opened the door with a smile.

"Good day, Lady," he responded.

"It is, indeed." She gestured.

Quaeryt hurried back to the study.

Aextyl waved Quaeryt to the chair. "You write well, Governor. Too well for a justicer or an advocate. Every word is chosen with little ambiguity, except, unhappily, over the years justicers and advocates have determined that all too many of the words that have no ambiguity or ambivalence in everyday usage do indeed have such when employed in legal documentation. So I have turned your apparently clear recommendation—one that justicers would find less than convincingly so—into one that seems far less lucid, but which should convey a single meaning to the high justicer."

Quaeryt couldn't help but smile. "Is there any time period I need to wait before holding the hearing?"

"No. You must provide two days' notice at a minimum, and a week is customary."

"I think we'll stick with two days and set it for next Mardi." Quaeryt frowned. "Do you know where Caesyt has a place of study or advocacy?"

"He used to have a small study on the east side of the south market square. I don't know that he still does."

"We'll have to see. Can I persuade you to join me and advise me on Mardi?"

"I don't see why not. I'd like to see Caesyt's face when he catches sight of me." Aextyl's smile was close to impish.

"There's one other matter. Is there anyone here in Extela that you could recommend for me to appoint as a justicer? I shouldn't be doing this, and I can't for long, not under the guidance put out by Lord Bhayar."

"That's true." Aextyl's brow furrowed, and he was silent for a time. "There's an advocate in Mynawal, a young fellow . . . well not so young as you. His name is Bieryn . . . Bieryn Blaksyn. You might talk to him. If I can think of any others . . . I'll let you know on Mardi."

"Thank you." With a nod, Quaeryt gathered up the papers Aextyl had waiting for him and made his way outside to the waiting mare and escort troopers.

He rode back to the post at a quick trot, because he wanted to catch the chief clerk before he left for the day. He almost didn't make it, because Jhalyt was leaving the small chamber that had likely once been a storeroom when Quaeryt hurried up.

"Sir? Is there a problem?"

Quaeryt extended the documents. "You don't have to stay tonight, but I'll need copies of these three documents as soon as you can manage. By tomorrow afternoon if possible. They have to be word-for-word copies, each line identical to the line in the original."

"Justicing documents?"

Quaeryt nodded.

"Baharyt's better at that, sir. Is there any reason he couldn't do it?"

"None at all, but I want you to proofread them after he's done, to make sure the copies are exact."

"I can do that."

"Also, I'll need several copies of a hearing notice, but I'll have to give that to you in the morning, since I haven't drafted it yet."

"Yes, sir." Jhalyt took the documents and carried them back into the chamber, then returned and locked the door with an overlarge and tarnished brass key. "Good night, sir."

"Good night."

Quaeryt was getting ready to leave for the villa when Pharyl hurried in.

"Sir . . . I'm glad I caught you. Would have preferred not to ride out to the villa tonight."

"That sounds like a problem . . . What sort?"

"Some toughs smashed the shutters on a cooper's place, then broke inside. He took a mallet and crushed one's skull. The other slashed his arm with a knife—blade more like a short sword."

"The kind that's too long to carry under the laws of Telaryn?"

Pharyl nodded. "Dead man had one, too. Cooper says that the third fellow had one also. He got away."

"Are you holding the cooper?"

"No, sir. I told him he'd have to appear when there's a hearing."

"Any others that will require a hearing?"

"One other. So far. Things are getting back toward the way they were, according to the patroller firsts."

"That's a mixed blessing."

"More like the Namer's blessing," snorted Pharyl. "The other is a killing. Girl knifed a man. Likely her pimp. At least, he was wearing one of those pimp's jackets, and she isn't saying anything."

Quaeryt winced. That was an offense he didn't want to hear, not in the slightest. "Will anyone else testify?"

"Not likely. No one else was around when the patrollers got there, and the people in the rooms around said they never heard anything. They're lying, but there's no way to prove it."

"We can certainly hear those on Mardi . . . but I have to handle a complicated civic hearing that day as well. It has to do with a complaint against a High Holder over water rights, and I have to refer that to the High Justicer of Telaryn. If you don't mind, I'd like to put that first. You'll need to post notices for it, but those won't be ready until tomorrow."

"A complaint against a High Holder." Pharyl shook his head. "Don't envy you, sir."

"The advocate is our friend Caesyt."

"He's the kind of friend no patrol chief needs."

"And the kind governors don't need, either."

"Better you than me, sir."

"That's one of the things governors are appointed for." *Or should be.*

After Pharyl left, Quaeryt walked out to the stable to saddle the mare. He had more than a few matters to consider on the ride back to the villa. He also couldn't help but recall Skarpa's comment about governing, that it wasn't something he could win like a battle.

That's becoming more and more obvious.

Once he reached the post on Vendrei, Quaeryt found himself immersed in a welter of details, some of which he'd anticipated, and some of which he hadn't, from not only making sure Baharyt finished the copies of the documents for the hearing on Mardi, but also that the hearing notices were copied and posted and that a trooper delivered a copy personally to Caesyt. That turned out to take several glasses because the advocate was no longer at the location recalled by Aextyl, but in what had been a narrow shop on the main avenue some three blocks south of where Caesyt had been situated formerly. Dhaeryn did report that the repairs on the east bridge had been completed, but that the south half of the bridge would remain blocked off for several days longer because some of the concrete and stone and brickwork required more time to cure.

Dhaeryn had barely left the study when the duty messenger appeared. "A Factor Lysienk here to see you, sir."

Lysienk? Quaeryt knew he had heard the name, but didn't recall it from the tariff lists he'd perused earlier. After a moment he remembered that Aextyl had called Lysienk a factor of dubious integrity and Pharyl had also expressed concerns as well. *You should have recalled his name immediately.* Why hadn't he? *Because your attention is split in too many directions?* "Did he say why he wished to see me?"

"No, sir."

"Have him come in." Quaeryt stood.

Lysienk was slender and blond, yet moved with a slinky grace that reminded Quaeryt of port rats, even though the factor displayed none of the furtiveness of such a rodent. He inclined his head politely. "Governor Quaeryt. It is most gracious of you to see me without an appointment, yet one wonders how one might make such an appointment. Indeed, discovering your whereabouts took a number of inquiries."

Quaeryt gestured to the chairs before the desk and seated himself. "You did not state your business to the duty troopers."

"Indeed, I did not . . ." Lysienk offered a smile that was likely meant to be apologetic, but held a hint of the furtive, again reminding Quaeryt of a rat. "I am here to discuss the continuation of my supplies of the best produce and meats to the governor's household. I would not trouble you personally with such a trivial matter, but alas, I have been unable to determine who your steward might be or how to reach him. If you would be so kind as to—"

"I am most certain that you do supply fine meats and produce, Factor Lysienk . . ." Quaeryt let the silence at the end of his words draw out for several moments before continuing. "But my wife, currently in the personage of her private secretary, will be handling such purchases for the governor's residence."

Lysienk presented an even more ratlike smile. "Then perhaps you could convey to that distinguished person that I have supplied the last two governors with the best of produce and meat . . . and my supplies are not only the best, but unlike those of others, there are never any difficulties with their quality . . . and especially not with their delivery. You, being the direct representative of Lord Bhayar here in Extela, understand above all others the importance of such reliability."

Quaeryt understood precisely what Lysienk was promising, especially after what he had learned from Aextyl and Pharyl. He was also irritated, for more than a few reasons, but he managed to smile politely. "You are most persuasive, Factor Lysienk, and most convincing. As you may know, however, the new governor's residence is not yet ready for such provisions as you supply, and it will likely be several weeks before it is. The villa is not yet even properly furnished. Perhaps . . . if you sent a note to the villa requesting an appointment with secretary Shenna for some time next week . . . ? I would suggest meeting after Mardi."

"Ah . . . I do understand, Governor." Lysienk bowed, gracefully. "You are most kind, and I look forward to making arrangements with your wife's private secretary."

After the sleazy produce factor departed, Quaeryt just stared at the closed door for a moment. Did everything in Extela work that way? He'd purchased some time, but he'd still have to deal with Lysienk . . . in a way that would preclude siphoning off extra golds as assurance that provisions and teamsters would not suffer unfortunate "accidents."

Once again, he had less than a quint before the duty ranker was announcing "Factor Andryt."

As the door opened, Quaeryt tried to recall where he'd seen or heard the name . . . then realized that Andryt was one of those who had signed the petition requesting that Quaeryt stop holding the price of flour down.

Andryt was short, stout, and bald. "Governor . . . I am here to throw myself at your knees . . ."

Please don't.

". . . I will grovel if I must, beg . . . whatever . . . but I implore you to do something before we are all destroyed, devastated, and desolated . . ."

Desolated? By the low prices of flour . . . that will go up before long? But the rotund factor was still talking, and seemingly doing so at an ever increasing speed.

". . . the eruption, it was bad enough, and the thefts and the violence that followed was worse, and the east bridge being impassable and the lack of water, and the low prices of flour . . . but now . . ." Andryt stopped abruptly and shrugged, as if whatever he might be asking could only be obvious.

"Factor Andryt . . . I am afraid I do not understand. You are suggesting something that is even worse than everything that has already happened, but you do not tell me what this disaster is."

"Is it not obvious? Did he not precede me into your presence?"

"Factor Lysienk? He's obviously less than honest, but it might help if you told me why he is a greater disaster than lava, ash, ground tremors, violence, and flooding."

"Those who do not sell their best to him . . . bad things happen to them . . . He has mentioned . . . my family . . . made suggestions about the daughters of others . . . he is an evil man . . ."

"You never did tell me what you factor . . ."

"The finest in fruits, the best apples, pears, and peaches, and all the berries that the hills support . . ."

"If your produce is so superior, why do you worry about Lysienk? Why is everyone so afraid of him, then?"

"Because everyone who crosses him suffers most terrible things. They are so terrible . . . he might be . . ." Andryt shook his head.

"He might be what?"

"I cannot say . . . only . . ."

"The spawn of the Namer?" suggested Quaeryt.

"He is worse . . ." Andryt shivered. "He might . . . might even . . . be an imager."

"Oh . . ." Quaeryt frowned. "Why do you think that?"

"Because of what has happened to those who cross him. They drop dead while at dinner. They are found lifeless in their beds. There are no wounds. There is no sign of poison. Leforyn's horse broke a leg while he was crossing the river, and Leforyn hit his head on the bridge and fell into the water and drowned. These things happen. They do not happen all the time. They happen often to those who cross Lysienk. They should not happen just to those who owe Lysienk golds and refuse to pay or to those who have crossed him.

Yet this is the way it has happened for the past years, ever since this . . . imager came to Extela."

"How much do you owe him?"

"Nothing."

"How did you cross him?"

"Why do you ask me such questions?"

"Because no one talks about Lysienk. I know. I've made inquiries. You're talking. You've come to me because you have nowhere else to turn."

"He wants me to sell my goods and warehouse to him. I do not wish that. Not now. He is most insistent."

"Why your goods and warehouse?"

"I have the best flour mill in Extela, and now that there are fewer mills, there are growers who will sell only to me . . ." Andryt shrugged. "I refused his request for my daughter's hand."

"She is beautiful?"

"Every father thinks his daughter is special, but Marah is indeed special and beautiful, and I would not see her in his hands. Yet . . . to who else can I turn? No one else will help . . . or even say anything."

Quaeryt nodded. "I can only say that I will see what I can do."

Andryt sagged where he stood, looking crestfallen.

"Factor Andryt . . . I cannot ride out of here with a patrol and throw this man into a cell in the gaol because accidents have happened. I can see that he is not a good man, and I will deal with him. That is all I can promise."

"I have your word?"

"You do."

"I asked . . . the soldiers. They said you were a man of your word. Will you keep that word, even if an accident befalls me?"

"I will . . . but please do not let us talk of accidents."

"There have been so many . . . so many around this evil man."

"I'll do what I can . . ." Quaeryt said again.

It took a bit more time before he succeeded in reassuring the nervous factor and saw him out. After Andryt left, Quaeryt just shook his head . . . but he had to admit that the factor might be right. Accidents such as those he had described were one way a hidden imager might well operate.

Quaeryt felt a tight smile on his face. He'd done things like that, most recently with High Holder Wystgahl. *But doesn't the reason count for something? You acted to stop fraud, theft, and starvation. If this . . . Lysienk . . . does what this factor thinks . . . he uses imaging in order to create a form of fraud and theft.* He shook his head. Some people would see no difference, would only condemn the act, and not the reason, even when the law, such as it was, was unable to stop such theft.

And all that meant . . . If Lysienk were truly an imager . . . and as evil as he appeared to be, Quaeryt would have to do something . . . both to implement his own plans to make Telaryn a better and safer place for scholars and imagers, and to stop the corruption in Extela that seemed to pervade everything. Still . . . he likely had few days, if not longer.

In addition to everything else, he also couldn't help but worry about the homily he needed to deliver on Solayi evening, and that led to worries about meeting with Siemprit's junior chorister, which was something he didn't really want to do, because the whole issue would be moot, one way or another, in less than a month, when Third Regiment left for Ferravyl. Part of his reluctance, he knew, was because he'd felt Siemprit was like too many he'd met in Extela. Even though the chorister had never spoken a word about it, Quaeryt sensed that Siemprit was far more interested in coin than in what chorister might be best for the officers and men of the regiment, something Quaeryt had never felt when he'd dealt with Phargos, the regimental chorister in Tilbor.

The business with Andryt and Lysienk concerned him the most . . . for more than one reason, including the fact that even if Lysienk weren't an imager, the slimy factor was giving imagers a bad name.

He decided that he needed to ride over to the Civic Patrol station, just on the off chance that Pharyl might be able to tell him more. He left the study and walked down the corridor to the duty desk.

"I'll need the mare," he said to the young ranker standing there—not the duty squad leader, who would have been there most times. "I'm going over to the Civic Patrol station."

"Governor, sir, you might want to wait just a few moments before leaving."

"Oh . . ."

"The factor who came to see you, the second one, he had an accident."

"What sort of accident?"

"He was going out through the gates. He got maybe thirty yards from the walls, and his horse bucked and threw him. He came down on his head. That's where Squad Leader Daerk is, sir."

Quaeryt froze for just a moment. "I think I'd better take a look."

"Ah . . . yes, sir."

Quaeryt did not quite run from the building, but he did walk as swiftly as his leg would let him, until he was approaching the squad leader and another ranker standing over a prone figure.

"Governor, sir."

"What happened?"

Daerk turned to the ranker. "You saw it. Tell him what you told me."

"Yes, sir. We didn't see it, sir, not exactly, because that other factor was yelling at his men. They were over there." The ranker pointed. "We heard the horse scream. When we turned, it was sort of . . . I couldn't say . . . but the factor was on the stones. We ran toward him, and he was half muttering, half yelling, and then he just sort of stiffened up, and he died."

"Did you hear him say anything?"

"There was something about an accident, but it didn't make any sense. That was the only word that I could make out. I wanted to ask the other factor, but he was gone by then."

"Do you have the horse?"

"Yes, sir. Over there."

"Would you check it for tenderness or soreness around the hindquarters and flanks?"

"Yes, sir."

Quaeryt could hear the puzzlement in the ranker's voice, but the man walked toward the two others who had a mount between them.

"You think something strange, sir?" asked Daerk.

"I just thought it might be a good idea to see if the horse was injured and that was why he threw the factor." He glanced down at Andryt, who lay on his back, his face still in a half grimace, as if he had suffered great pain, and then died so quickly that the muscles had remained partly distorted.

Less than a half quint later, the ranker walked back to Quaeryt with a quizzical expression on his face.

"Yes?" asked Quaeryt.

"Well . . . sir . . . there's no mark anywhere, but there's a place on the gelding's rump where, if you touch it, he shies away. Has to hurt a lot."

"Thank you. It might be an insect bite or something. Sometimes they don't show." Quaeryt knew it was likely nothing of the sort. "Thank you."

He looked back down at the contorted face of the dead factor. He had no doubts how Andryt had been murdered—something imaged into the mount's hindquarters, enough to make him buck, and then poison, most likely pitricin, imaged into Andryt's brain.

And that meant he had an even bigger problem on his hands.

The rest of the day was filled with details and more details, but the notices were posted, the document copies made . . . and Pharyl sent a message informing Quaeryt that there would be another theft hearing on Mardi. That reminded Quaeryt to send one in return, asking Pharyl to look into the family and business affairs of Factor Andryt, since the factor had died in a strange accident.

When Quaeryt finally reached the villa, it was a good two quints past fifth glass, and Vaelora had a worried expression on her face when he stepped into the entry hall, after having unsaddled and groomed the mare.

"You look worried, dearest."

"I am." He glanced toward the archway and the corridor beyond.

"Rebyah and Alsyra are in the kitchen. Shenna has gone to see her family. Why? What happened?"

"Another problem of a serious nature." He went on to tell her about his meetings with Lysienk and Andryt . . . and the results.

"That's terrible."

"Will Shenna be here tomorrow?"

"You're not thinking of still having her meet with someone like that?"

"I am. I think it's the only way to resolve the matter. It's very important that she meet with him, and that not either one of us is present."

"Quaeryt . . ."

"Dear . . . please."

"All right . . . I know you know what you're doing, but I still worry."

So do I. "Sometimes, the choices are between bad and worse."

"There are getting to be too many of those." Vaelora's voice was between dry and tart.

"I know. Can we enjoy dinner?" *Exactly what else can you do right now?*

Vaelora did smile, if faintly.

Samedi morning Quaeryt was groggy, but still managed to struggle out of bed, noting, as he had not the night before, that there was a more elaborate coverlet—which he had tossed back the night before. He also noted a pair of matching straight-backed chairs, one beside each armoire.

"It is looking better, don't you think?" asked Vaelora.

"I do indeed." He had to wonder about the costs, but Vaelora had not asked him for golds. *Not yet, anyway.*

He dressed quickly, as did Vaelora, but took his time over breakfast, so much so that Vaelora looked at him and asked, "Are you going to the post later this morning?"

"When will Shenna be here this morning? Remember?"

"She should be here anytime now. I still worry about her talking to Lysienk."

"Don't," said Quaeryt. "He can't get what he wants unless he talks to her. And I may need evidence from someone else . . ."

"But if he's that clever . . ."

Quaeryt just looked at Vaelora.

"Oh . . ."

"There may not be any other way. Not given the way he's done things."

Vaelora nodded sadly.

What are you supposed to do? Let him image person after person to death? When there's no proof that will stand up in a hearing? Quaeryt wanted to shake his head. He didn't.

Quaeryt was just finishing the last sips of a third cup of tea when Shenna arrived. He stood.

"Good morning, Governor."

Vaelora's private secretary was petite and pert, with wavy black hair. Quaeryt wouldn't have called her pretty. Cute, perhaps, if slightly chubby, but she had beautiful hazel eyes.

"We need to discuss a matter with you." Quaeryt glanced to Vaelora, and then back to Shenna.

"Yes, sir."

"You will be approached by a Factor Lysienk, either in person or through a note. He represents himself as a provisions factor. You are to agree to meet with him, but on a day after Mardi. If he does not wish to meet in the villa, you are to insist on meeting with him somewhere close to the villa, either right before or right after you are to begin work. If he defers, explain that your mistress keeps a close eye on you, that you are new to the position, that such positions are hard to come by. It is very important that Vaelora and I know where and when you will meet, but we will not be present." *Not visibly.* "He will suggest that you purchase various provisions for the villa through him. He may even offer you some inducement. You are to appear reluctant, but do not get angry or rebuff him. You do not wish to make him angry."

The young woman's brow furrowed into a frown. "He wants to bribe or force me into paying more for provisions?"

"That is most likely," said Quaeryt. "He has done this before. He may tell you that I have already agreed to the arrangement . . . or hint that. You tell him that I requested you meet with him and hear him out."

"He will want an answer," said Vaelora.

"Tell him that Vaelora has not completed making a listing of what the residence will need on a continuing basis, but that the list will be ready in a day or so, and that he or his man can call on you at the residence then."

Vaelora nodded.

"Will that not seem as though I am dishonest?"

"You will not have agreed to any price at the end of the meeting," Quaeryt pointed out. "Meeting with a produce factor does not make you dishonest. You will likely meet with a number to determine who will best serve for what."

"Then . . ." Shenna shook her head, then looked to Quaeryt. "You're trying to trap him, aren't you?"

"I need to see whether he is merely sleazy, or whether he is worse. What he tells you will tell me."

"I can do that."

"Good. But . . . we do need to know when and where you will meet."

"I will let you know if he contacts me."

"Thank you." Quaeryt smiled. "Now . . . if you ladies will excuse me." The form of address to both of them was doubtless improper, because Shenna, as an unmarried daughter of a factor, was not technically a lady, but within the confines of the residence, that scarcely mattered. He hurried out to the stable.

Even so, because of the meeting with Shenna, Quaeryt did not get to the post until close to two quints past seventh glass.

He immediately checked to see if any dispatches from Bhayar—or

Solis—had arrived. None had. Nor were there any other missives or messages for him, and he went to check with Skarpa to see how matters were coming with Third Regiment.

Both Skarpa and Zhrensyl were in the post commander's study.

"Good morning, Commanders."

"Good morning, sir," replied both officers, although Zhrensyl was a fraction later in responding.

Quaeryt looked harder at the older commander, who appeared both flushed and pale. "Are you all right, Commander?"

"I must confess that I have had better days and weeks."

"Commander Zhrensyl and I have been talking, sir."

"It's nothing," said Zhrensyl.

"He has but five months left on his last tour before he can take a full stipend, but he also has almost three months in unused leave."

Quaeryt understood immediately. If Skarpa had decided to bring up the matter, it meant that Zhrensyl was ill indeed, perhaps failing, and for him to remain in his position would not be best for either him or the post, especially after Skarpa left.

"You're suggesting a month or so of sick leave, followed by his unused leave?"

"Yes, sir."

"I can certainly recommend that to Lord Bhayar."

"You two are treating me like an invalid."

"No," replied Quaeryt. "Like an officer who has served long and faithfully, and who should not have to suffer over a month or so of forced duty. You could take the stipend in less than two months anyway."

"I can still . . ."

"You can, Commander," Quaeryt agreed, "but that wouldn't be right. You'll still be post commander until your stipend date, but we'll work out a partial delegation of duties as you see fit. That way, you can decide what you can devote full energy to, and what others should do."

Zhrensyl offered a wan smile. "You're most kind, Governor, Commander Skarpa. I have worried."

"You don't have to worry any longer."

"This has not been one of my better days." The older commander stood up slowly, and Quaeryt could see the effort, and that his hands were trembling. "If you two will excuse me . . ."

"Of course."

Neither Quaeryt nor Skarpa said anything until several moments after the study door closed.

"I worry about him, sir."

"So do I, but what else can we do?" Quaeryt wondered if Zhrensyl would even live to see his stipend date. "Who would you suggest to take over most of his duties?"

"Major Heireg. The position here is really for support of the governor, and he's diligent and hardworking."

"And he's already handling many of those duties, it would appear."

"From what I've seen." Skarpa nodded.

"Have you seen Dhaeryn this morning?" asked Quaeryt.

"He's in the post engineer's workshop. Or he was."

"I need to talk to him. Then I'll talk to Heireg. Is there anything you think I should tell him?"

"You might say that Zhrensyl has been ill, and since he will be leaving service, that you'd like Heireg to handle a few more things, as necessary."

"Thank you. I need to talk to Major Dhaeryn while he's still at the post." With that, Quaeryt turned and made his way from the room and then across the courtyard.

As Skarpa had indicated, Dhaeryn was in the small engineering workroom. Both Dhaeryn and Captain Ghaelt, the post engineer, were examining what looked to be two curved lengths of iron, connected at both ends.

". . . put weight here, and if the wheels jolt . . ." Ghaelt broke off and looked up. "Governor, sir."

"I'd like just a moment with Major Dhaeryn."

"Of course, sir." Ghaelt nodded and stepped out of the workroom.

Quaeryt wanted to say that the captain didn't have to leave, but the junior officer was gone before he could get the words out.

"What do you need, sir?" asked Dhaeryn.

"If you have time, Major, I'd like you to look through Extela and see if there is somewhere suitable for a governor's building, not a square, but a place where we can either modify an existing building or build one that will hold a justicing hall, and chambers for tariff collectors, clerks, and various functionaries."

"Sir . . ."

"I know. You won't be here long enough even to begin such a project, but I trust your judgment, and that will give me some place to start. If you could include Captain Ghaelt . . ."

"Yes, sir." The look on the major's face suggested that Ghaelt was better for the assignment.

"I want both of you," Quaeryt went on, "because you have no preconceptions and because he'll have to carry it out."

"I've noted that the captain has few preconceptions, sir." Dhaeryn pointed to the iron sections on the workbench. "He comes up with ideas that seem very original."

"Excellent." Quaeryt image-projected approval. "That's all I had."

From the engineering workroom, Quaeryt walked back into the courtyard and then across to the supply major's study, opening the door with a cheerful, "Good morning, Heireg."

"Good morning, sir."

"I met with Commander Zhrensyl earlier this morning . . ."

"Yes, sir. He stopped by to tell me that he'll be taking some sick leave . . . and that you might be asking me to take over some duties . . ."

"I suspect you've already been dealing with some of them."

A crooked smile appeared on Heireg's face. "As I could, sir, without . . . causing any disruptions."

Quaeryt nodded. "We'll make it more official. I'd like to hear your thoughts about how we should handle this . . ." As he spoke he could see what he thought was relief on the major's face. He forced himself to concentrate on Heireg, although he couldn't help but worry about needing to talk to Siemprit's junior chorister . . . and to work out a homily for Solayi evening.

Again, after he left Heireg, details and more details piled up through the day, from the handful of women in tattered clothes who appeared outside the post, begging for flour—to which he acquiesced, if with the statement that such disbursement would be the last free flour—to a handful of missives from various advocates touting their credentials to be appointed as high or low justicer. After the hearing over the water business, he'd go over the names with Aextyl.

In the end, he didn't get back to the villa until close to fourth glass of the afternoon. *And this was on a Samedi,* he reflected, as he dismounted outside the villa's stable.

Vaelora walked down to meet him.

"What is it?"

"Lysienk did not waste much time."

"Shenna heard from him?"

"Indirectly. Less than a glass after you left, one of his minions appeared. She is to meet with Lysienk himself on Meredi, most properly, here in the villa," said Vaelora, "after you leave that morning, around seventh glass."

Quaeryt nodded. "That will require a little arranging, but I can manage it."

Vaelora looked puzzled.

"I'll need to get back here without being seen, and without my escort wanting to come with me." He offered a crooked smile. "Some of the things that were the easiest when I was a simple scholar have become more difficult now that I'm a governor."

"You were never a simple scholar."

"One to whom few paid any attention, then."

"Some of us did." Vaelora smiled broadly.

"For which I am most grateful." And he was, even with all the complications entailed in wedding the sister of the Lord of Telaryn.

Thankfully, Samedi evening and Solayi were uneventful. They were not without effort, not once Vaelora decided to try several different arrangements of furniture in the master suite on Solayi, and then, after a brief respite, in the receiving parlor.

Quaeryt also listened, commenting appropriately, as Vaelora talked once more about the lack of social invitations. He had to admit, if only to himself, that she might well be right, although he couldn't understand why. He'd seen and read about the excesses perpetrated by other governors, and his attempts at rebuilding, reform, and reducing corruption seemed comparatively mild, almost harmless, by comparison . . . and he couldn't believe that factors and High Holders would snub the Lord of Telaryn's sister for marrying a mere scholar . . . would they?

Yet . . . if that were the reason, that suggested that he needed to find a way to implement his plans for improving the situation for scholars and imagers. All that would have to wait, of course, until he managed to get Extela back to a better semblance of order.

On Solayi evening, he managed a homily about vanity, and the fact that vanity was not merely about appearance and trappings, but about attitude . . . and some of the officers and rankers actually nodded in agreement.

He left the villa early on Lundi morning, and the first thing he did upon reaching the post and stabling the mare was to arrange with Heireg to have a wagon pick up Justicer Aextyl early on Mardi with a pair of rankers for an escort to the Civic Patrol station. The second thing he did was to check with the duty desk to see if any dispatches had arrived. None had. That bothered him almost as much as if Bhayar had sent orders for Third Regiment to move out immediately.

Why? he wondered, but he couldn't answer his own question.

After that, he went from one task to another. He read several letters from young men who wanted to be clerks for the governor, and kept them for future use, because, before long, he was going to need more clerks, except at the moment he had no place for them to work, although that would change when Third Regiment left. He read through the schedule of Mardi's hearings and the written report Pharyl had left for him. At the end of the report were a few lines about Factor Andryt noting that the factor had possessed a solid reputation for honesty and quality, if a certain stubbornness, and that Pharyl would pursue other inquiries as possible.

Especially in that light, Quaeryt couldn't help but worry about Shenna's meeting with Lysienk, but there was nothing he could do about that until Meredi. He also wondered when he'd hear from Dhaeryn on possible locations for a building that would house all the clerks and functions he needed to direct as governor. He pushed those thoughts away and began to reread the recommendation Aextyl had drafted in response to Caesyt's petition. After a time, he began to write what he would say at the hearing. All in all, he was busy until he reached the villa late that afternoon . . . when he ended up moving recently delivered furniture in the salon, since Vaelora wanted to try several arrangements.

Mardi morning he left for the post early because he wanted to make sure that the wagon got off to pick up Aextyl, but Heireg had just sent it and two troopers off when Quaeryt rode through the post gates.

With that in hand, Quaeryt went to meet with Skarpa, and then with Dhaeryn, before returning to the courtyard almost two quints later. He mounted and rode out and down the avenue, and then to the Civic Patrol station, where he waited for about a quint until the wagon carrying Aextyl arrived.

He dismounted, handed the mare's reins to the nearer ranker, and walked to the wagon as it pulled up. "Greetings, Justicer."

"Good morning, Governor."

Quaeryt extended a hand to help Aextyl down, then looked to the ranker teamster. "Shastyn, Justicer Aextyl should not be that long. I would judge it will be less than a glass, and I would appreciate your waiting nearby for him."

"Yes, sir."

Quaeryt and Aextyl walked from the wagon into the patrol station, past the receiving desk and the duty patroller and into the corridor behind the desk, where Pharyl hurried from his study to meet them.

"Chief Pharyl, this is former high justicer Aextyl. As I mentioned before, he will be assisting me in matters of the law this morning in the first hearing." While Quaeryt had earlier told Pharyl, he repeated the information so that anyone who might overhear understood, as well as reminding the chief.

"I'm pleased to meet you, Justicer."

"Thank you."

"Could we borrow your study until the hearing begins, Chief?" asked Quaeryt.

"Of course, sir."

Once inside the small study, Quaeryt had Aextyl sit down immediately, then handed him what he had drafted the day before. "Is this the proper way to introduce this?"

The old justicer took the sheet and read through it. "That's acceptable. I would strike the phrase 'who must be a High Holder.' The high justicer always is, for the reasons we discussed earlier, and that wording is unnecessary."

After that, Aextyl made several other small corrections.

"Is there anything else I should be worried about?"

"There are a number of motions he could make, but we don't have time to discuss them all. Besides, you'd likely get confused. At times, I got confused."

While Aextyl's remark was light and meant to be humorous, Quaeryt still worried. He wasn't a justicer, and he definitely needed to find one he could trust to be honest and impartial.

After another quint, Pharyl rapped on the door, and Quaeryt and Aextyl walked into the chamber and to the dais. As he and Aextyl seated themselves behind the simple table desk, Quaeryt glanced toward Caesyt, whose face had registered a momentary frown, followed by an impartial expression.

Quaeryt picked up the sheet he had drafted the day before, the one Aextyl had corrected, and began to read. "The justicing hearing in the city of Extela, the province of Montagne, will commence. I am Governor Quaeryt, acting as justicer. The first hearing is the petition of Holders Yepryl, Huslup, and Graustyrk versus High Holder Aramyn in the matter of the use of the waters of Minawa Creek." He looked up. "Who represents the petitioners?"

Immediately, the stocky Caesyt, again in the black robe of an advocate, stepped forward. "Caesyt Klaesyn, representing the petitioners."

"The petition you have lodged requests that the defendant, High Holder Aramyn, cease and desist in diverting a fourth part of the waters of Minawa Creek, reserving those waters for stakeholders downstream, to wit, Holders Yepryl, Huslup, and Graustyrk. Is that correct, Advocate Caesyt?"

"It is, Honorable Justicer."

Before Quaeryt could say another word, Caesyt immediately added, "In view of the gravity of the situation, with spring planting already under way, I would move, in view of the fact that the defendant has not responded to the petition, that you grant the terms of the petition in summary judgment." The advocate smiled politely.

"Your motion is noted," Quaeryt replied, then leaned toward Aextyl, murmuring, "denied, because the defendant has responded?"

Aextyl nodded.

"Advocate Caesyt, because the defendant has offered a rebuttal to your petition, your motion is denied."

"Honorable Justicer, I move that the petition be forwarded to the High Justicer of Telaryn, without recommendation, on the grounds that, as governor, your interest in the resolution of the petition cannot be impartial."

"Your motion is noted." Quaeryt didn't even try to suggest a response, but again leaned toward Aextyl.

Aextyl murmured a suggested response, and Quaeryt repeated it.

"Advocate Caesyt, your motion is denied, under the precedent of Gubernatorial Supersedense, which provides that a provincial governor may act as justicer for up to two months after his appointment." Quaeryt's eyes flicked momentarily to Aextyl, who watched Caesyt intently. "In accordance with the laws of Telaryn, which require any petition or case involving the person or the rights of a High Holder be referred to the High Justicer of Telaryn, I am hereby making such a referral, along with my recommendation for a finding. You will be provided a copy of that recommendation in due order, according to the laws of Telaryn." He paused briefly, then added, "The hearing on the petition is concluded. There will be a brief recess before the next hearing."

Caesyt looked hard at Quaeryt, then at Aextyl, before inclining his head briefly, then saying politely, "Good day, Honorable Justicer."

Quaeryt offered Aextyl a hand to help the old justicer off the dais. "Thank you."

"I did very little."

"Your presence kept Caesyt from offering motions that I wouldn't have known what to do with." He paused. "I think I may ride out to see that young advocate you mentioned. Tomorrow, in fact."

Aextyl laughed softly. "I wrote him that you might."

"Good."

Quaeryt walked slowly beside Aextyl, out through the Civic Patrol station, outside and then helped him onto the wagon. Once Aextyl was settled on the seat beside the teamster, Quaeryt handed a small cloth bag to the justicer. "Your fee, counselor."

Aextyl eased open the bag, then shook his head. "That's too much."

"Not with Caesyt waiting to pounce on any legal irregularity it isn't. I do appreciate your counsel and your presence. All I ask is that you ride home and get some rest."

"I can do that, Governor." Aextyl smiled widely.

"Good."

Quaeryt waited until the wagon and the two escort troopers were on their way before turning and walking back to the patrol station. He was relieved that he'd dispatched the petition, but worried about how tired Aextyl had been. Still . . . without the advice of the former justicer, things might well have gone differently, and not nearly so well.

He still needed to hear the three other offenses.

Late on Mardi, just before Quaeryt was ready to leave for the villa, Pharyl appeared to pass on a few more bits of information about Factor Andryt, all of which attested to the man's reputation, and also the fact that his widow had declared that, in respect for her husband, the family would be in seclusion for a month. While all that he had learned wasn't absolute proof, it was more than enough for Quaeryt.

Meredi morning, Quaeryt lingered over breakfast for a time, talking with Vaelora, but not about Lysienk or Andryt, since they might be overheard, but about the previous day's hearings, not only the one involving Caesyt, but the others. He had acquitted the cooper on grounds of self-defense, and after seeing the burn marks and whip scars on the back of the pleasure girl, found her guilty of assault, rather than murder, and sentenced her to time served, a hand-branding, and a recommendation to leave Extela. That sentence had bothered him, but it was the least he could plausibly do, and again he was wishing more and more that he could find a justicer who was honest and trustworthy.

A quint or so before seventh glass, he made his way out to the stable, where the rankers had already saddled the mare. Quaeryt didn't see any sign of Lysienk or the guards who reputedly rode with the factor as he and the two rankers who escorted him rode eastward along the avenue toward the post. He did note where there appeared to be peach trees, as he had previously on other streets around the villa. After five blocks, he reined up. "Wait here, if you would."

"Sir . . . ?"

"I need to take care of something, and I'd prefer that you remain here."

The two troopers looked at each other and then at Quaeryt.

He looked back at them and projected total assurance. Then he turned and rode back toward the villa, easing the mare toward the north side of the avenue. A block later he eased his mount close to a large fir and then behind it. Seeing no one near, he raised a concealment shield to cover both himself and the mare and continued riding until he neared the side street on which the villa was located.

Even from the avenue he could see four riders—guards in black, and another riderless mount. Holding the concealment shield, Quaeryt reined up and waited.

A quint passed, and still Lysienk did not appear. Finally, the slender blond figure stepped down from the portico and walked up the drive to the bay gelding, mounted and then gestured to the guards. The five rode in Quaeryt's direction. None of them spoke as they passed, clearly not seeing or sensing him.

Quaeryt waited until the factor and his guards were well past him, then eased the mare forward.

Lysienk looked back, a half-puzzled expression on his face, then shook his head and continued riding, turning westward on the avenue. Quaeryt followed them, some fifteen yards back, until they were a good two blocks from the villa. On the south side of the avenue, behind a low wall, were several peach trees. Quaeryt nodded and reined the mare to a halt. Then, mentally reaching out to the peach trees, he imaged pitricin into Lysienk's brain and waited, still holding the concealment.

Lysienk raised his hand, the one not holding the reins, toward his forehead, then tried to speak. He began to convulse, then collapsed forward in the saddle against the neck of the gelding, which stepped sideways. Two of the guards moved toward him. The other two turned their mounts, looking everywhere.

"Something's happened!"

"He's dying, I tell you."

"How can he be? There's no one around."

Quaeryt continued to wait silently, until the four were completely involved in dealing with the dead factor. Then he eased the mount around and rode back eastward. When he reached the side street on which the villa was located, he turned the mount north for several yards, then edged next to a fir, where, after looking around and seeing no one, he released the concealment shield, then rode back out to the avenue. From there, he rode eastward and rejoined the two rankers.

"I forgot something I had to do," was all he said.

He kept thinking about Lysienk.

Having killed Lysienk wouldn't bring back Andryt or all the others the imager-factor had harmed or killed, but it would stop those kinds of abuses, and it also would stop Lysienk from creating unsavory rumors about imagers and giving them a bad reputation.

Good points, but are they enough? No . . . but what are the alternatives? He's killed more than a few factors, never leaving any traces . . . and waiting will only result in more deaths. Still . . .

For the moment he pushed away those thoughts, not that they would remain absent, he knew.

The events of the petitioners' hearing had confirmed Quaeryt's desire to find a competent and honest justicer as soon as possible, and as soon as he arrived at the post, he had quick meetings with Skarpa, Heireg, and Jhalyt. Then, with an escort squad, he left the post immediately, riding westward toward Mynawal, in order to meet with Bieryn Blaksyn, the "young" advocate that Aextyl had recommended as a possible justicer. Although he passed close to where he had killed Lysienk, he saw no sign of the guards or that they had even been on the avenue.

Why was that so easy? Because Lysienk never thought he'd encounter another imager?

Quaeryt wanted to shake his head. He'd killed men before . . . too many, but it had been in battle or when he'd been attacked. *That's not true. What about the patrol chief and patrollers in Nacliano?* They had tried to kill him, and they had burned the scholarium and killed scholars . . . So why did his murder of Lysienk bother him? The man had used imaging to kill others. He'd been corrupt and abused power.

Was it because there were no checks on either him or Lysienk? *Most likely . . . and that suggests that imagers need a system to patrol themselves, both to protect others and themselves.* That was yet another problem, and he kept mulling it over, now and again, all throughout the ride.

As he neared his destination, he wondered why an advocate would be located in a small town some fifteen milles from Extela—until he reached the edge of Mynawal, some two glasses later, and discovered that while it was no city, it was not a small town, but a thriving place set on a slightly raised plateau above the groves and fields that surrounded it. From what he saw as he rode down the main street, careful to maintain his imaging shields, Mynawal must have contained several thousand people. While that answered one question, it also made locating the advocate somewhat more time-consuming, requiring a number of inquiries along the main street until he finally received a satisfactory one.

"Bieryn Blaksyn? Oh . . . the advocate fellow? The next block down, second door, past the silversmith's." The cooper, who had been lifting a barrel into a wagon, looked at Quaeryt. "You must be an important scholar, sir, to have such following you."

"There are those who think so. Thank you." Quaeryt smiled and urged the mare forward.

The directions appeared to be accurate. At least, there was a narrow building without a signpost past the almost equally small shop of the silversmith. Quaeryt dismounted, handed the mare's reins to a ranker, walked over to the door, opened it, and stepped inside.

A young man, barely out of schooling, stood from behind a table desk where he had been copying something in the small front room with single closed door at the rear. Several chairs were lined up against the front wall, on each side of the narrow window.

"Sir . . ." The young clerk looked past Quaeryt to the squad of uniformed troopers lined up in the street. "Sir?"

"I'm Governor Quaeryt, and I'm here to see Bieryn Blaksyn."

The young man looked at the troopers in the street, then swallowed. "I'll . . . I'll tell him you're here, sir."

The clerk hurried to the door behind him, opened it, stepped through, and closed it behind himself. Through the not-so-heavy walls, Quaeryt could make out some of the words that followed.

". . . says he's . . . governor . . . score of troopers outside . . ."

". . . tell you why . . . ?"

". . . just to see you . . ."

The door reopened, and the clerk stood there, holding it open for Quaeryt. "Sir . . ."

"Thank you."

When Quaeryt stepped into the small study beyond, he took a quick glance around, noting the plain desk, the file chests neatly stacked against one wall, and the two bookcases, only one of which held volumes, the other of which contained two miniatures and several stacks of papers. Two wooden and unupholstered armchairs faced the desk. Beside the desk stood a neatly dressed angular man who looked to be five years or so older than Quaeryt and a few digits shorter.

"Governor . . . I don't have comfortable chairs."

"These will be fine." Quaeryt could sense the door closing quietly behind him as he took one of the chairs and waited for Bieryn to seat himself before continuing. "You might know why I'm here, Advocate Bieryn."

"Justicer Aextyl wrote me. I can't say as I believed him."

"Why not?"

"Most justicers are either the sons of High Holders or their relations . . . or they have . . . ties . . . to the governor."

"That's exactly why I'm here. The only justicer I've heard of or met with a reputation for honesty is Justicer Aextyl. He declined to accept a position as justicer because his health is not good. I asked him who he would recommend. He named you."

"That was kind of him."

"Kind? I doubt it. From what I've seen, it's a mostly thankless job, especially for an honest justicer."

"For a governor who's looking for a justicer, you're not that encouraging," replied Bieryn dryly.

"I'd rather not be falsely encouraging."

"I don't know that I'd be that interested."

"The compensation isn't exorbitant." Quaeryt knew, having checked with Jhalyt. "Historically, it's been between a gold and two golds a week. At present, the amount of time devoted to hearings amounts to less than half a day twice a week. That will doubtless increase, but by how much I cannot say."

"Justicer Tharyn disposed of all his hearings in a half day once a week," noted Bieryn.

Quaeryt laughed. "You know more than I do about what it would take. That's why I'm here."

"I just don't know." Bieryn shook his head.

"I won't press you. I would like you to think about it for a week or so. Then we can talk again."

"What do you want from a justicer, Governor?"

"Justice under the law . . . where possible. Sometimes, it's not, as I've already discovered."

"I heard about the hearing you held on Vhalsyr."

"And?" asked Quaeryt.

"Under the law, you had no choice." Bieryn smiled faintly. "Some justicers tend to impose what they believe is justice regardless of the law."

"I've seen that elsewhere. In those instances, the law simply acts to facilitate the aims of the justicer or those who influence him, and before long, it offers no protection to the innocent and not even an attempt at justice for the guilty . . ."

Quaeryt and Bieryn talked for another two quints before Quaeryt left.

On his ride back to Extela, Quaeryt reflected on what they had discussed, deciding that as Aextyl had suggested Bieryn would make a good justicer. *If he decides to accept the position, and there's no telling if he will.*

Quaeryt finally reined up in the post courtyard at a quint past second glass. Even before he reached his study, in the corridor outside, the duty squad leader hurried up with an envelope.

"Sir, this was delivered in midmorning. The young fellow said it was urgent."

"Thank you." Quaeryt paused. "No dispatches from Solis?"

"No, sir. No dispatches at all." The squad leader turned and headed back to the duty desk.

Quaeryt entered his study, closed the door, and opened the envelope, wondering who could have sent it and what it contained.

Dear Governor,

In view of your kindnesses to my father, I thought you would like to know that he died in his sleep last night after a cheerful dinner. He spoke well of you . . .

The signature was that of Birgyt Aextyldyr.

Quaeryt realized, belatedly, that he'd never known Aextyl's daughter's given name, for all the times that he'd visited the house. He shook his head, then walked back out to the courtyard.

Given how far the mare had already carried him, he requested another mount and ended up on a gray gelding with two rankers he did not recognize as his escort.

When he reached Aextyl's dwelling, he left the gelding with the rankers. He started toward the door, then paused. The sad-faced hound lay on the ground, unmoving. He stepped toward, and saw the eyes move, but nothing else. He eased toward the dog, then stroked its head. The hound gave only the faintest whine and did not move.

"I'm sorry, too, friend." Quaeryt stroked the dog a last time, then rose and hurried to the door, where he knocked.

A man Quaeryt did not recognize opened the door. "I'm sorry, but we're not receiving . . ."

"That's the Governor, Caxtyl."

"Oh . . . I'm sorry, sir." Caxtyl stepped back.

Behind him, in the small entry hall, stood Aextyl's daughter.

Quaeryt stepped inside and inclined his head to Birgyt. "Thank you for your message. I am so sorry . . ."

"It wasn't your fault, Governor. He was so frail he could have died at any time. He went to sleep happy last night. He did appreciate what you did, because it redeemed him in his own mind."

"He was so helpful and knowledgeable. I wouldn't have asked him . . . had I known he was so weak, but he seemed strong enough when we began the hearing." Quaeryt shook his head. "It was a short hearing, and as soon as it was over, I saw he was tired, and I walked with him to the wagon . . ."

"Governor, he was a justicer. You let him be one again. He was happy."

Birgyt looked to Caxtyl, who bore a passing resemblance to both Aextyl and Birgyt.

Caxtyl nodded.

"I would have come sooner, but I was in Mynawal. I did not receive your message until I returned." He paused. "If there is anything I can do . . ."

"Governor, many people say that when it is too late. You did something he dearly appreciated before then. You should have heard him talk about the hearing last night." Birgyt offered a sad smile. "Thank you."

"I will not take more of your time, but I wanted to express my sympathy and concern." Quaeryt inclined his head again.

"It is appreciated, Governor. Thank you."

Quaeryt stepped back, then slipped back out the door. It closed slowly and quietly. He turned and walked to the gelding.

He just hoped Aextyl had died as peacefully as his daughter believed.

You've killed the just and the unjust in the same day. But he hadn't meant to kill the one, and the other should have died far sooner. *What does that all mean?*

At that moment, Quaeryt couldn't have said.

By late afternoon on Vendrei, Quaeryt had to admit that he was tired. He'd ridden through Extela on several occasions over the past two days with Ghaelt, the post engineer, looking at buildings and locations, before finally deciding on building a new structure on an empty lot a mille north of the post. Obtaining the land had cost another fifty golds from the treasury, but the plot was close to the existing sewers and aqueduct extensions, and Dhaeryn and Ghaelt had set to work on drawing up plans. Quaeryt had also spent glass after glass going over the tariff listings. When he had noted that some of the factors he'd come in contact with, such as Hyleor and Lysienk, weren't even listed, he sent Baharyt out with the task of walking the main streets of Extela and jotting down every shop and factorage. That would mean, when the clerk finished, that Quaeryt and Jhalyt would have to go back and check the tariff listings against Baharyt's list. It would also likely result in greater tariff collections.

Quaeryt hadn't heard from Bieryn, either, and didn't expect to until the following week, but he admitted to himself that he'd hoped he would. Pharyl had reported another ten recruits were undergoing training as potential civic patrollers, and the number of evening patrols had increased by two. Even so, it wasn't likely that full evening patrols would be possible until late summer or early harvest.

No one had contacted him about Lysienk or even mentioned the factor's name again, except Shenna. Quaeryt had told her to wait to hear from the factor for several days, and if she didn't, to pursue other suppliers and factors. On Vendrei morning, Shenna reported to Vaelora and Quaeryt, just before he had left for the post, that Lysienk had died on a morning ride, and that his wife was selling off everything that she could.

Quaeryt leaned back in the chair inside the small post study, reflecting that it would be good to have a place where he could actually feel as though he was the governor, but, he reminded himself, he'd essentially had to rebuild not only parts of the city, but most of the provincial governing structure, and he was still a long ways from completing that task.

"Governor?"

"Yes?"

"Justicer Tharyn here to see you."

Tharyn was one of the last people Quaeryt wanted to see, but he forced a cheerful tone into his voice. "Have him come in."

When Tharyn stepped into the small study, Quaeryt motioned him to a chair. "Good afternoon, Tharyn. What can I do for you?"

"Governor, I noticed that you are still acting as justicer."

"For the time being."

"I also heard that High Justicer Aextyl was helping you, and he died right after."

"High Justicer Aextyl had been in frail health for some time. That was why I did not consider him as a possible justicer. I did consult with him to make sure my decisions and recommendations were couched in the proper legal terms. I was very sad to learn of his death."

"Other folks, maybe some in places like Solis, might not see it that way."

"Oh?" Quaeryt kept his voice genial. "Justicer Aextyl was very helpful, and I was most careful not to tax his health. How would anyone think it otherwise?"

"There are always those who'd believe the worst, especially if those who didn't receive the most favorable decisions . . . recommendations . . . wanted to cause trouble."

"There are always those who want to cause trouble." Quaeryt smiled, trying not to seem false, but fearing that he did. "I do appreciate your concerns. You're being most thoughtful."

"Thank you, Governor. I always try to be thoughtful . . . and grateful to those who give me reason to be grateful."

"I'm certain you do."

"Seeing as you haven't yet decided on who you might be appointing as justicers here in Montagne, I just thought I'd stop by and see how you were coming on making those decisions. I mean, I know you're looking for experience, and you'd likely be wanting those who know how things are, and wouldn't be wanting to cause you difficulties."

"That's very true," replied Quaeryt. "I am considering those very things, and I appreciate your bringing them to my attention." He paused. "Who would you say the most effective advocates in Extela are?"

"Be depending on what you mean by effective, Governor. Advocate Warolyt, he's been good at representing the High Holders around Extela. Advocate Caesyt . . . he's kept many a poor man from being branded when he shouldn't have been . . ."

Quaeryt listened for close to half a quint before Tharyn came to an end.

". . . and that's why I really think I could do you some good as a justicer, knowing like I do which advocates do what."

"You make a very convincing case, Tharyn, and I'll keep your words in mind when I finally make a decision." And Quaeryt would . . . if not exactly in the way that Tharyn might have hoped.

When Quaeryt finally reached the villa that evening, Vaelora greeted him as he stepped onto the portico, out of the light drizzle that had oozed out of the northwest and over Extela that afternoon.

"You look more cheerful," observed Quaeryt.

"We finally got an invitation to a dinner."

"Where?"

"High Holder Aramyn's. It's a week from tomorrow." Vaelora paused. "We don't have a coach or even a wagon."

Quaeryt studied her face. "I take it that you have located a coach? Where?"

"Ah . . . there are two for sale, through the livery stable on the south avenue. The more . . . suitable one belonged to Factor Lysienk."

Quaeryt nodded slowly. "Shenna had said his widow was selling many items."

"She wishes to leave Extela. He had two coaches. She will keep but one."

"What about a team?"

"Two grays come with the coach."

"How much?"

"Thirty golds for coach and team."

"I suppose we should purchase them."

"Good. I already did. They will be here tomorrow."

"You didn't have to . . . A governor does deserve a coach."

Vaelora smiled. "I know. I thought you, the treasury, more properly, could reimburse me."

Quaeryt laughed ruefully. "What's for dinner?"

"Stuffed fowl and sundry other accompaniments."

"Sundry other?"

"Maize and mushroom stuffing, early asparagus, and lace-fried potatoes."

"That will be good." He extended his arm, and they walked across the portico and into the governor's villa.

On Samedi morning, Quaeryt had been late getting to the post, not arriving until two quints past seventh glass. By ninth glass, Pharyl had sent him reports that some of the poor had gathered in the southwest market square and were complaining that the governor was no longer selling flour and potatoes . . . or even giving either to the very poorest. Quaeryt and Skarpa met, decided, and immediately dispatched several companies from Third Battalion.

Quaeryt thought about accompanying the troopers, then decided against it. His presence was more likely to incite those who were complaining than to calm them because they'd all be yelling that he had somehow betrayed them, and to keep order, even more force would be required.

Still, as he waited, Quaeryt couldn't help but ponder about the situation in which he found himself. For far more than the first time, he wanted to shake his head. If he provided flour at a reasonable price for the poorer inhabitants of Extela, the factors and holders complained. If he didn't, the poor complained.

He'd gotten the aqueduct and the east river bridge repaired. He'd reformed the Civic Patrol and largely restored order. He'd recovered what was left of the treasury in order to pay the patrollers and to pay for the supplies needed to make the repairs. Except for the Pharsi women and a few others, it seemed as though, no matter what he did, someone was unhappy.

No wonder some governors find a way to pocket everything they can. Since they please no one, they might as well please themselves.

He pushed those thoughts aside because they wouldn't help and took out the master ledger just to see how actual expenditures compared to what he'd estimated and how much was left in the provincial treasury.

Less than a quint later, before he'd finished his calculations, Skarpa knocked on the door and stepped inside.

"Thought you'd like to hear what happened."

Quaeryt gestured to the chairs.

Skarpa smiled as he seated himself, a folder in his hand. "As soon as the companies appeared, the troublemakers slipped away. Pharyl's patrollers nabbed a couple who had weapons, and I ordered Jusaph to have his company patrol the square for the next glass, and the others to sweep through the city. All the reports are that the shops are open, and nothing seems much different from any other market Samedi."

"How long will it take not to have to use troopers?"

"Not too much longer, I'd guess. We barely had to show up. Pharyl's whipping the Civic Patrol into better shape."

"Still . . . we've been fortunate to have you here this long. Why do you think that is?" asked Quaeryt. "I'd have thought Bhayar would have ordered you to Ferravyl sooner."

The commander shifted his weight in the chair and offered a slight frown before speaking. "I'd guess that he wants to leave Third Regiment as long as he can. He knows things can't be settled in a month. But he'll need us before we can do all that needs to be done here. That's why you're governor."

"Go on," suggested Quaeryt.

Skarpa shrugged. "I don't claim to know much about governing, except it's not often done well. The men who govern aren't idiots, no matter what anyone says. That tells me that it's not near as easy as it looks. There aren't many who want good governors. Most want a governor who will help them. You're not like that. I think Lord Bhayar wants you to clean up the place, but he doesn't know how bad it got. No one would have dared to tell him. So he's thinking that if you've got a regiment for a month or maybe two, you can take care of things. After that, sir, you're on your own."

"I'm getting that feeling." Quaeryt paused. "Who's likely to be the best officer here at the post for training? Once you depart, we'll need more local troopers."

"I'd try Undercaptain Shanyt. Came up the long way."

"You already asked around, didn't you?"

"Now, sir . . . would I be a decent commander if I didn't learn the lay of the land?"

Quaeryt grinned, almost laughing at the mock innocence in Skarpa's voice. Then he shook his head. "Thank you. And have you suggested to him that he start recruiting?"

"I think he might have lined up a score or so . . ."

Quaeryt was going to miss Skarpa, far more than he'd realized. "I appreciate that. We'll need them."

"He's a good man. Make a good captain."

In short, promote him, you idiot. "If you'd have your clerks draw up the papers . . . if you haven't already."

Skarpa extracted several sheets from the folder. "As a matter of fact, sir . . ."

"And there are several others there as well, I take it?"

"If you wouldn't mind, sir."

Quaeryt laughed.

After Skarpa had left, Quaeryt took a deep breath. He'd been kept out of more trouble by a few others—Skarpa, Aextyl, Pharyl, for starters—more times than he wanted to count, and some of those he'd lost or would soon lose. He just hoped he'd learned enough.

After finishing the discouraging business with the master ledger, he decided to take a break and try to come up with at least a few thoughts for a homily. He pushed away the nagging feeling that he should already have paid a visit to meet with Siemprit's junior chorister.

What was the man's name? Quaeryt struggled to recall, then nodded. *Neoryn.*

Next week. He'd get to it next week.

Then he tried to think about the homily.

More than two quints later, he finally came up with something, and when he finished, he looked down at the few sentences he had written.

> A man I did not know long or well died this past week, but he was a man whom I respected, and who suffered because he was honest and he held to his principles. He was willing to help me up to the day of his death, and he saved me from making several mistakes . . .

His eyes strayed from the paper on the desk to the study window of the villa, still without hangings, out into the bedraggled remnants of what had once been a garden . . .

What else can you say?

After a time, he added a few more lines.

> He agreed to help me because he thought it was right, not for the fame or fortune that had bypassed him. He will not be lauded, except by me and a few others. Nor will his name be praised unto the generations, outside his family, yet I will remember and respect his dignity and honesty . . .

Quaeryt nodded. He needed more, but he had a good beginning for the homily.

52

The coach and team that Vaelora had purchased for the villa did arrive on Samedi afternoon, while Quaeryt was still at the post, but he had remembered and brought back the thirty golds to reimburse her. Outside of a scratch or two, the coach was in excellent condition, as were the matched grays . . . and on Solayi evening Quaeryt and Vaelora rode to the post in the carriage, where Quaeryt again conducted services.

Despite Quaeryt's worries, Lundi and Mardi came and went with no more than the usual kinds of problems, with three comparatively routine hearings at the Civic Patrol station on Mardi. He did review the preliminary plans for the governor's building and, based on discussions with Ghaelt and Dhaeryn, requested several changes.

Meredi morning, after checking for dispatches and meeting briefly with Pharyl, and then with Skarpa, he set out for the anomen west of the governor's residence to meet, of necessity, with Neoryn, the junior chorister, if only to be able to claim that he had done so. He halfway hoped that Neoryn wasn't even at the anomen.

That was not to be, Quaeryt could tell, almost as soon as he arrived at the anomen, a oblong and featureless domed structure, except for doors and windows, as were all anomens, built of the black stone that formed the walls of so many buildings in Extela. He'd barely tied the mare to one of the ornate iron hitching rings when two men, both wearing black and white choristers' scarves, appeared on the wide front steps of the building, clearly waiting for him.

"I have no idea how long this will take," Quaeryt told Venkyl, the senior of the two rankers who had been his escorts.

"We'll be here, Governor."

"Thank you." Quaeryt walked along the immaculate stone walkway to the anomen and then up the wide steps to meet the two. He smiled as warmly as he could. "Good morning, Chorister Siemprit. I told you I'd be here."

"So you did. I had wondered if we might be seeing you, Governor." Siemprit gestured to the younger man with him, who looked to be about Quaeryt's age. "This is Neoryn, my assistant chorister."

Neoryn was black-haired with brilliant blue eyes and an oval face that conveyed innocence. He inclined his head politely and said, "Governor," in a resonant and mellow voice that doubtless could fill an anomen with ease.

"I'm pleased to meet you, Neoryn."

"And I you, sir."

"You must come in and see the anomen," said Siemprit.

The smoothness of his tone made Quaeryt check his shields, although he couldn't imagine a chorister attempting anything. Yet . . . *You don't trust him.* "I'd be happy to."

Siemprit turned and walked back through the open double doors, doors of finely finished and well-polished goldenwood, Quaeryt noted in passing. The plain bronze handles shimmered in the warm spring sunlight.

Inside, the floor was of polished black marble, while the walls of the spacious vestibule were of plain white plaster, with simple goldenwood floor moldings. Twin black marble archways afforded access to the sanctuary from the vestibule. The sanctuary was a good thirty yards long and fifteen wide. The dais at the far end was of black marble as well, but the pulpit was of polished goldenwood.

"It's very simple in an impressive way," commented Quaeryt.

"As is the Nameless," replied Siemprit.

"Unfortunately, life isn't always that simple." Quaeryt wanted to hear what the chorister might say in return.

"We often make life too complicated, Governor. A good remedy for that complexity is acting in accord with the basic and simple precepts of the Nameless."

When one can . . . without creating even greater harm and complexity. Quaeryt did not voice that thought but only nodded as he stopped short of the dais and studied the workmanship of the marble and the pulpit—and the recently painted white plaster walls behind the dais. Two narrow and high windows provided light.

"I imagine you'd like a few moments with Neoryn, Governor."

"That would be helpful."

"I will leave you two." Siemprit smiled beatifically. "I will be in my study if you need me further."

"Thank you."

"We could go to my study," suggested Neoryn.

"Lead the way."

The assistant chorister's study was twice the size of Quaeryt's study at the post, but simple in the same fashion as the rest of the anomen, with the polished black marble floor, goldenwood moldings around the door and windows, and the white plaster walls. A desk, with a chair behind it, and three other chairs, a file chest, and a bookcase comprised the furnishings. All were plain and of polished goldenwood, and all showed the finest in crafting and workmanship.

Quaeryt took one of the chairs.

Neoryn took one of the others, but not the one behind the desk. "Chorister Siemprit said you might be looking for a chorister for . . . your anomen, Governor."

"He probably told you I've been acting as chorister. It's not my calling, but I've done the best I can. There have been so many pressing demands that, until now, I haven't had time to look into the possibilities for a chorister, or frankly to come up with the funding to refurbish the anomen and support a chorister."

"Would not the collections . . . help?"

"They might, but the collections were used to buy food and clothing for the poorest women in Extela. It seemed that they needed that help more than the troopers needed a refurbished anomen."

Neoryn nodded. "No one could find fault with helping the poor."

In spite of himself, Quaeryt had the feeling that Neoryn actually meant what he said, as opposed to Siemprit, whose every word he doubted. *But is that because Neoryn's voice conveys sincerity, whether he is or not?*

Quaeryt didn't have an answer to that question. "There will be times when there are very few congregants, and even upon those infrequent occasions when there are more, the collections will not be large."

"There is no anomen near the post. Could it not be opened to those who live nearby, and not just be limited to those stationed at the post?"

"That might be possible." Neoryn's suggestion made sense. Quaeryt just hadn't thought of that option, most likely because he hadn't wanted to think at all about dealing with the anomen and finding a chorister. "Why do you think you might be the right chorister for such an anomen?"

"I cannot say that I would be the right chorister, Governor. I am a chorister, and I would do my best. Whether a chorister is best for any anomen depends as much on the congregants as upon the chorister." Neoryn smiled crookedly. "Part of a good chorister's task is to persuade those who come to look beyond what they wish to see and hear without offending them so much that they do not return."

Quaeryt did not reply immediately, because while he certainly recognized the truth of what Neoryn said, he also realized that what the chorister said applied, in many ways, to what he was trying to do as governor. The problem was that, in governing, one had to do things for the common good that were often not popular or acceptable to those with one kind of power or another. And sometimes, the law worked against justice, as in the cases of Wystgahl and Lysienk, something that few wanted to acknowledge, even as they bemoaned injustices either created by the very laws they supported or ignored by those laws.

"You disagree, Governor?"

"No. I was thinking that your words applied to more than being a chorister." Quaeryt smiled. "Tell me about yourself."

"I don't know that there's anything special about me. I was born in Ilyum . . ."

Quaeryt listened, occasionally asking questions, while Neoryn explained how he'd come to be a chorister. In spite of how little Quaeryt trusted Siemprit, he couldn't help but think that Neoryn actually might make a good chorister . . . just about anywhere.

But why does Siemprit want so much for you to offer a position to Neoryn? Because he's what Siemprit isn't, and Siemprit doesn't want his congregation to find out? Or is there something about Neoryn that you're not seeing?

In the end, Quaeryt made no commitment, except that he would be in touch in the next few weeks.

He rode back to the post, still thinking about the questions his meeting had raised.

53

By Samedi morning Quaeryt had still received no dispatches from Bhayar. Because Samedi was the thirty-fifth of Avryl, the last day of the month, it was beginning to look more and more as if Third Regiment might actually remain in Extela until the fifteenth of Mayas. Since Quaeryt had heard nothing from Bieryn, he was getting the feeling that the advocate wanted no part of becoming a justicer. Quaeryt couldn't say that he blamed the man. Perhaps, at least, he could consult with Bieryn about the advocates who had put their names forward for the position . . . if he ever had time to spend a day riding out to see the advocate.

On the other hand, Pharyl was reporting success in both recruiting and initial training of patrollers, and Ghaelt was working on getting together the crafters necessary to construct the governor's building . . . and there were no more complaints on Samedi morning about the lack of cheap or free flour.

Quaeryt left the post earlier than he otherwise might have on a Samedi, although most military posts gave most of the men Samedi afternoons off, as well as all of Solayi—except, of course, those posts engaged in dealing with rebellions or war. It was slightly before third glass when he stepped onto the portico of the villa.

"Good afternoon, Governor," offered Shenna, clearly preparing to leave for the day. "Lady Vaelora is upstairs preparing."

"Thank you." Quaeryt inclined his head slightly. "Have you found other sources of provisions?"

"Yes, sir. They are much more reasonable, and so are those who purvey them."

"I'm glad to hear that."

"So was Lady Vaelora."

"She's quite pleased with all the help you've provided."

"I'm pleased to be of assistance." With a slight bow to Quaeryt, Shenna said, "Good day, sir," and headed down the steps to the drive and then up toward the street.

Quaeryt turned and made his way into the villa, glancing in at the now perfectly respectably furnished receiving parlor and then at his study. The doors to the formal dining room were closed, since that chamber remained empty—finding a suitable table and chairs for a reasonable price had proved impossible . . . so far.

The master dressing chamber was where Quaeryt found Vaelora, who had just donned the same gown she had worn to the last ball in Tilbora.

"You look wonderful."

"It's too dressy, but nothing else is right, either. If there's a ball here, I'll have to wear this again, and hope that Aramyn and his guests tonight won't say anything . . . unless I can find another good seamstress."

"Shenna might know one."

"She knows the same ones Grelyana knows."

Quaeryt wasn't about to address that issue. "I'll wash up and be ready before long."

"Your best browns are laid out, with the dress jacket."

"Thank you."

"Alsyra did that."

"But you told her, and I appreciate that."

"We'll need to leave in less than a glass."

Quaeryt understood.

He washed up and dressed, then went down to his study and wrote what he could for Solayi's homily, then waited for Vaelora to appear. When she did, he escorted her out to the end of the portico, where the coach was waiting, with a ranker teamster and two outriders.

Neither spoke much until the coach was headed westward on the avenue, partly because Quaeryt was half bemused by the fact that he was traveling in a well-appointed coach, with velvet upholstered and padded seats, and even with real glass windows that could be swung up and fastened in place to keep out rain or snow. More amazing was that the coach was effectively his, at least so long as he was governor. A former scholar in a villa with a coach and team and a beautiful and devoted wife?

"It almost feels strange to be traveling somewhere in a coach," said Vaelora. "Until this week, it's been so long since I've been in one."

Quaeryt glanced at the pair of ranker outriders, a precaution suggested by both Skarpa and by Heireg, who was now essentially the post commander, since Zhrensyl had taken a turn for the worse and was bedridden. He couldn't help but think about how quickly things could change. While Zhrensyl had looked worn when Quaeryt and Vaelora arrived in Extela, the commander's decline had been precipitous, as had that of Aextyl—at least, it had seemed that way to Quaeryt.

Health, life . . . everything could change so quickly. One moment, Extela had been a city where all had been going well, and a day later a quarter of it had been in ruins.

"What are you thinking about, dearest?"

"How things can change so swiftly."

"Is that for your homily tomorrow?"

"More likely for a later one. I'm got some ideas for tomorrow."

"Well . . . one day you were a scholar assistant and single, and the next . . ." She smiled.

"The next I was a princeps and betrothed to a lovely lady."

"And now you're a governor."

"And it's not exactly what I thought it would be," he replied with a laugh. "Very few people are happy with what I've done."

"But Extela is doing so much better."

"It will be harder when the regiment leaves, and that's in two weeks from tomorrow—unless I get a dispatch ordering them out even sooner."

"You don't really think that will happen, do you?"

"It seems unlikely, but even two weeks may not be enough to complete some of the work. It won't likely even be soon enough to begin work on the governor's building, and that will mean paying more to local workers."

"You'll make it work. You always do."

"So far . . . How are you and Shenna coming on finding a dining set?"

Vaelora shook her head.

For the rest of the ride out to Aramyn's chateau, Quaeryt listened as Vaelora explained how she was coming in refurbishing the villa . . . and the problems she faced.

The coach and team slowed as the teamster guided it along the curving drive through the High Holder's private park and up the gentle rise to stop before the main entry of the old yellowish red brick chateau. While a doorman immediately stepped forward to open the coach door, Aramyn, dressed in a deep red velvet jacket and gray trousers, stood at the top of the steps waiting.

"Greetings, Governor and Lady Vaelora," offered the High Holder. "That's a handsome team and coach."

"We picked them up for the governor's residence from a widow who needed only one coach," replied Quaeryt.

"Ah, yes, that fellow Lysienk. I heard he was riding and suffered a seizure. They say it couldn't have happened to a nicer fellow." The irony in Aramyn's voice was so light that it was barely discernible. "Well . . . that was good for you. Do come in. Everyone's wanting to hear about how you've managed to restore order in the city." There was a slight pause. "This is just a small dinner . . . the four of us and my nephew and his wife, who are visiting from Montagne."

While Quaeryt was more than happy for the smallness of the gathering, he could see the slightest hint of a frown on Vaelora's brow, gone so quickly he doubted anyone else had seen it.

"We appreciate the chance to see you again, in less urgent circumstances," replied Quaeryt.

"There are so many things that Lady Minya and I did not have a chance to discuss," added Vaelora.

"Good," replied Aramyn with a warm and broad smile, turning at leading the way to the same salon where Quaeryt and Vaelora had spent the better part of an afternoon once before.

The four others in the salon rose as Quaeryt and Vaelora entered.

"You've already met Minya. Might I present my nephew Jaekyt and his wife Buhlyn. Governor Quaeryt and Lady Vaelora."

"My pleasure," offered the trim Jaekyt with polite warmth.

"I so wanted to be you," offered Buhlyn, a tall and broad-shouldered woman with curves only slightly excessive for her frame, if accentuated by the clinging mauve velvet gown she wore. She smiled warmly at Vaelora. "I saw you and your sisters ride through Extela years ago, and you all carried yourselves so well."

"She still does," added Quaeryt.

"Would you like to try some of my white winter wine?" asked Aramyn. "I must say that it's better than the un-iced wine . . . this year, at least."

"Most years," added Jaekyt.

"Please," said Vaelora.

Quaeryt nodded.

While the group might have been small, it was obvious that he and Vaelora were more than welcome, and that the evening would be enjoyable . . .

. . . and it was, through the wine and apéritifs, the turtle soup, the braised and marinated beef with lace rice and other side courses, the lemon tarts, and the Montagne brandy that Jaekyt had brought with him. The conversation only touched the superficialities of the situation in Extela, and then moved on to other less substantive matters, such as the best wines from the hills around Extela, and the difficulty of finding good seamstresses.

Quaeryt was almost sad to go, except he was tired.

When they had left the chateau, in the darkness of the coach, he turned to Vaelora. "Did you enjoy the dinner?"

"I did indeed. The food and company were both excellent."

"Except what?"

"Did you notice that all the guests, except for us, were from his family?"

"I did. You think that signifies we're not in the greatest of favor among other local High Holders?"

"I do, dearest."

"That's doubtless because I've trod on the polished boots of all the others, except for Thysor."

"He wouldn't count. He's so far away that he's scarcely local. We'll just have to see how things turn out."

Indeed we will. Quaeryt reached out and squeezed her hand, as the coach rolled eastward, back to the villa. But he still worried.

Solayi was without event, and Quaeryt managed another homily, loosely based on what he and Vaelora had discussed in the carriage, rather than on what he worked on earlier, which he saved for the next time he had to give a homily. He rode to the post, cheerfully, on Lundi morning. There were no dispatches, which was likely for the best, but his cheer began to vanish when he saw Major Heireg waiting for him outside his study, a solemn expression on his face.

"What is it, Major?"

"Commander Zhrensyl . . . he died in his sleep last night."

"I'm sorry." Quaeryt nodded slowly. "I can't say I'm surprised. Does he have any other family we should notify?" Quaeryt knew Zhrensyl was a widower, but little more.

"His son lives in Ilyum, but Hrehn says that they weren't close."

"Arrange for services and a pyre tonight, then, and . . . if you'd draft a letter for me?"

"Yes, sir." Heireg paused. "He was a good man at heart."

"I know." *Perhaps not as strong as he should have been, but you might have only seen him when he was failing.*

Not moments after Heireg left, a fresh-faced patroller appeared, likely a recruit, since the young man wore the uniform without insignia.

"Governor, sir."

"Yes?"

"I have an urgent message for you from the chief." The recruit extended a sealed envelope.

"Thank you. Is he expecting a response?"

"He told me to wait to see if you had a response."

Quaeryt frowned. "How did you get here?"

"On the patrol wagon, sir. It's the only one left, Captain Hrehn said."

Quaeryt nodded. *Only one left?* There hadn't been any, but Pharyl was the kind who would work out how to get something his men needed. For that matter, so would Hrehn. "I'll let you know."

"Yes, sir."

Quaeryt entered the small study, closed the door, then opened the envelope.

Governor—

On Samedi evening, a patroller team consisting of two patrollers and a patroller recruit saw a fight occurring outside a café facing the south market square. Because passersby were endangered, they broke up the fight. Then a male companion of the man the patrollers took into custody knifed the recruit in the back and then slashed his neck. The recruit died right there.

I had planned to schedule the hearing for tomorrow, but Advocate Caesyt protested that Solayi does not count as a day of notice, and I have scheduled the hearing for Jeudi, along with several other less serious charges.

Quaeryt set down the missive. *Something like this had to happen sooner or later.* Then he frowned. Since when could a café brawler afford an advocate?

He sat down at the desk and immediately wrote his reply.

Chief Pharyl—

Thank you for the notice about the unfortunate occurrence involving a patroller recruit and the scheduling of hearings. Doubtless the advocate is well versed in the precedents, and we should use his expertise in that matter.

I would hope that the hearing would reveal all the details of the event so that justice may be done.

Quaeryt had no doubt that Pharyl would understand what he wanted. He sealed the missive, then rose and walked to the study door, opening it. The young patroller stood there waiting.

Quaeryt extended the missive. "My reply to the chief."

"Yes, sir. I'll get it right to him."

"Thank you."

Quaeryt didn't return to the study, but made his way to the small room where the two clerks were already at work.

"How are we coming on reconciling Baharyt's crafter and factor list with the old tariff listings?"

"There's good, and there's bad, Governor."

"Start with the bad."

"As many as one in ten of those on the old lists aren't in Extela anymore, not that we and the tariff collectors can find them, anyways."

Quaeryt nodded. "That's not unexpected after all that's happened. And the good?"

"We found almost a hundred shops and crafters and even fifteen factors that haven't been paying tariffs."

"But they likely won't make up what we've lost?"

"No, sir. Maybe a third part. Might be half, but that'd be pushing it."

"We'll just have to do what we can." In the future, he might have to ease up tariff levels, even with the lower level of spending he'd imposed, because the Civic Patrol needed to be larger, and there had to be more permanent troopers at the post. Both those were more than evident to Quaeryt.

When he finished with the clerks, a good glass later, he went to find Skarpa, to tell him about Zhrensyl, but discovered that the commander had the entire regiment out on "maneuvers." Given that Third Regiment was headed to Ferravyl before too long, Quaeryt didn't find that surprising. Certainly, Skarpa had been diligent in continuing training, although he'd said little enough to Quaeryt.

When he inquired after Dhaeryn and Ghaelt and discovered that they were already at the site for the governor's building, he decided to ride there and see how matters were progressing.

The two engineers had staked out where the corners of the building would be, and were using heavy cord and stakes to mark out where the foundation trenches would be dug. Two small boys peered at the two engineers from across the street and beside a cart where a woman was trying to sell what looked to be knitted goods in front of a boarded-up shop of some sort. Once the building was completed, Quaeryt had no doubt that someone would either buy or refurbish the old building, most likely for a café or the inland equivalent of a chandlery.

He rode closer to the engineers and reined up. "You look to have it well laid out."

"Not well. Not yet," replied Dhaeryn.

"That's a good way of putting it, Governor," replied Ghaelt. "Look to—that's if we don't run into problems with the foundation trenches. And if we don't hit an underground spring. Don't expect that here, but you never know."

"Do you have laborers ready?"

"Plenty of those around here, sir," said Ghaelt. "Even masons aren't that hard to come by. Finish carpenters, good ones, they're not so easy to find."

Quaeryt couldn't help frowning. "Carpenters?"

"The good ones leave for places like Solis or the shipyards in Estisle . . . or they work for the High Holders, or they become cabinetmakers. Make a lot more silvers doing those things."

Put that way, it made sense, although Quaeryt hadn't thought of it in that fashion. "Do you have any men at the post with those skills?"

"Torkyn's not bad, and we can hire his cousin, once we get that far along."

Seeing as he was only slowing matters down, Quaeryt said, "Thank you. I won't take any more of your time." Then he turned the mare and started back toward the post.

At least, if bit by bit, he was making progress. *Slow progress.*

On Lundi night Quaeryt did not get to the villa until late, because he had to stay at the post late and offer words of farewell, as chorister, before Zhrensyl's pyre was lit. He did the best he could for an officer he scarcely had known, as he tried to explain later to Vaelora.

Then on Mardi, Quaeryt spent the morning at the Civic Patrol station, conducting five hearings, four of them minor, requiring either confinement for a week or a few strokes of the lash, and a theft and assault requiring both a flogging and a branding. In that instance, the man convicted had grabbed the coin box in a public house while the two sons of the woman who owned it were within yards and then tried to beat the older woman with a chair he picked up.

Quaeryt almost felt guilty ordering the punishment of a man that foolish, yet someone that stupid was likely to do the same thing again . . . and again, and then find himself facing beheading, still wondering how it had all happened.

That evening, when he finally reached the villa, Vaelora informed him that she still hadn't located a proper table for the villa's formal dining chamber, let alone matching chairs, and she continued to fret over the lack of social interaction and the invitations they had not received.

"We were invited more places when you were just a princeps in Tilbor."

"Tilbora wasn't mangled by an eruption," Quaeryt pointed out, even while he silently shared her concerns. "And factors and High Holders expect us to entertain, and we can't. Not yet. You saw that in Tilbora."

"I didn't realize just how much you'd have to do for the city, dearest."

"Neither did I."

On Meredi, Ghaelt reported that the laborers had begun to dig the foundation trenches for the new governor's building, and that there appeared to be no problems, but that it would be several days before he could be certain of that. Jhalyt reported that the tariff collectors had taken in over a hundred golds in the first few days of Mayas, and that cheered Quaeryt somewhat, given how many shops and factors had vanished under the ash and lava.

Jeudi morning, he made certain he was at the Civic Patrol station by seventh glass.

Pharyl greeted Quaeryt even before he reached the long duty desk. "Good morning, Governor."

"You have that look, Chief. What is it?"

"We have another problem." Pharyl walked beside Quaeryt, back to his study.

"Besides a dead patrol recruit?" Quaeryt closed the door behind them.

"An interesting case of theft and assault also took place on Samedi evening. I've scheduled it after the murder hearing."

"Is there anything about the murder that won't come up in the hearing?"

"Besides the fact that Caesyt is the advocate? No. There's something else, but I shouldn't bring it up until the hearing. I'd like you to hear it without my opinions."

"What else can you tell me that won't come up in the hearing?" Quaeryt asked.

"This fellow Cauflyn in the second hearing . . . he's a hired tough. He keeps order in Hyleor's pleasure house. One of them. The one that's less than a block from the southern market square."

"What was he doing away from it on a Samedi night?"

"It wasn't night. It was a couple of quints before fifth glass, too early for much business, when he tried to grab the felter's wallet."

"That doesn't make sense. He's got a job."

"It does if you've pissed off your boss."

"But you said he has an advocate. That makes even less sense."

"I'm guessing. Cauflyn's been in a cell since Samedi. Where else in Extela would he be safe from Hyleor's other toughs? Already, people know the patrol isn't what it once was and that Hyleor can't buy someone out of gaol. If Cauflyn thought Hyleor was out for his neck . . ."

"Where else could he have a chance of being safe?" said Quaeryt. "That means whatever he did was enough to cause Hyleor to want his neck, and he had to hurry. Otherwise . . ."

"That was my thought. Because Caesyt is defending both of them, there has to be a connection."

"It could just be that Hyleor wants them both free . . . for very different reasons."

"That's possible, but I don't know."

Neither did Quaeryt, and he had the feeling that regardless of how the hearing turned out, he still might not ever know.

After finishing with Pharyl, and waiting until just before eighth glass, Quaeryt walked into the hearing room and to the dais, seating himself behind the table desk, and setting the two files before him. A good fifteen locals were in the chamber, including a younger woman whose red eyes suggested she had been crying, and several hard-faced men.

"The justicing hearing in the city of Extela, the province of Montagne, will commence. I am Governor Quaeryt, acting as justicer. This hearing is the matter of Jubyl Jonsyn, charged with the murder of Shannar Fhandsyn and assault." Quaeryt looked to the stocky advocate standing by the bench for the accused. "Are you representing the accused?"

"Yes, Honorable Justicer."

Pharyl stepped forward. "Chief of the Civic Patrol, representing the city of Extela."

"Very well. Bring in the accused."

Two patrollers marched in Jubyl, his hands in restraints, and positioned him directly before Quaeryt. The tough bore an expression close to a smirk, and his eyes kept flicking to Caesyt.

"You are charged with murder and assault upon a civic patroller. How do you plead?"

"Guilty to assault," replied Caesyt. "Not guilty to murder."

Quaeryt nodded and waited for the patrollers to escort Jubyl to the backless bench at the side of the hearing chamber.

"Do you have an opening statement, Chief?"

Pharyl stepped forward. "The offender willfully stabbed a young patroller recruit who had not even raised a truncheon. He continued to stab the victim viciously and in such a flurry that no one could get to the patroller before he was close to death. By the laws of the land, that is murder. In addition, because the man he attacked was a patroller, by definition that is assault against those who enforce the laws." The chief stepped to the side.

"Advocate?"

"I do have a statement, Honorable Justicer." Caesyt stepped forward. "Jubyl had drunk too much, but he is not a killer. As you will see, he was not in his right mind. Because he was not, I will prove that he did not commit murder under the laws of Telaryn and Extela." With that, the advocate nodded and stepped back.

"You may proceed, Patrol Chief." Quaeryt was concerned about the brevity of Caesyt's statement, wondering exactly what it foreshadowed and what sort of legal trickery might be forthcoming.

"Patroller Dienn, please come forward," said Pharyl, turning toward the benches at the back of the hearing room, on which several patrollers were seated.

A muscular, stocky man, Dienn rose and stepped forward with short quick steps.

"Please tell the justicer what happened outside Shyan's Café last Samedi evening."

"Justicer, sir, Haellen and I were patrolling the south side of the square, and young Shannar was with us. Seemed to be two men yelling at each other outside Shyan's, but neither one had any weapons out. No clubs, no knives. Just two fellows shouting. They were shouting loud enough to upset folks, and we walked toward 'em. I had my truncheon in hand 'cause you can never tell. So did Haellen. I told Shannar to get his at the ready, but I didn't look back. When we got near, one of the two fellows who was shouting turned and ran down the alley. Didn't see any sense in going after him. No one looked to be hurt. No one was complaining. Then Jubyl yelled something about the Tilborans coming after him, and he pulled out a pig-sticker and ran at me. I was ready to cold-cock him, when he turned to one side and gutted young Shannar. Then slashed his neck. Got him two or three times before Haellen and I could stop him. So much blood that we didn't even have time to call for a healer before Shannar was gone."

"What did Jubyl do after that?" asked Pharyl.

"Not a thing. We'd hit him hard enough on his thick skull that he was stretched out on his face. He didn't wake up until after he was celled at the station."

"I have no more questions," said Pharyl.

"Do you have any questions, Advocate Caesyt?" asked Quaeryt.

"I do." Caesyt stepped forward. "You said that Jubyl yelled that the Tilborans were coming after him. What else did he say?"

"That was all."

"Did he say it more than once?"

"He yelled something like that a couple of times. Might have been three."

"Did he seem to recognize you . . . as patrollers, that is?"

"He charged us. Usually that means an offender knows we're after him."

"He never said anything about patrollers?"

"I didn't hear anything like that," admitted Dienn.

"No more questions."

"Patroller Haellen, forward," announced Pharyl.

In effect, Pharyl asked nearly the same set of questions of the second patroller, and in turn so did Caesyt. Haellen's answers were similar to those of Dienn.

Once both had completed their questioning, Pharyl nodded toward Jubyl. "Have the offender step forward."

"You have heard the words of the patrollers," began Pharyl. "Is what they say true?"

"No. I didn't stab no one."

"Everyone saw you stab Shannar."

"I just waved my knife. He stepped into it. Nothing I could do. He was stupid. He shoulda known better."

"Jubyl, did you know the man you stabbed?"

"I didn't stab no one."

"You just said that you did."

"No, sir. I said I waved my knife. He stepped into it. That's not stabbing."

"Did you know the man who died?"

"No."

"You didn't know that he was the younger brother of one of the guards at the pleasure house where you sometimes work?" pressed Pharyl.

"I object to that question, Honorable Justicer," interjected Caesyt immediately, although his voice remained smooth and level.

The younger brother of one of Hyleor's guards? For a moment, Quaeryt was silent before saying, "Please rephrase the question, Chief Pharyl."

"Yes, sir." Pharyl turned back to Jubyl. "Is not Bennar Fhandsyn a guard at the place where you sometimes work?"

"I know Bennar."

Bennar Fhandsyn? Quaeryt knew he'd heard the name before. He just didn't remember where or when.

"Did you know his brother Shannar?"

"He never talked about a brother."

"Did you know Bennar's brother?"

"I might a' met him. I don't remember."

Quaeryt was convinced those statements were lies, even if there happened to be no way to prove that.

Pharyl asked more questions, but Jubyl's answers never varied, and finally the chief stepped away and inclined his head to the advocate.

"Jubyl, you have said you were waving your knife and that the patroller walked into it. Why did you have the knife out?"

"Because there were Tilborans coming for me. That's why. A fellow's got to defend himself. He's got that right."

The faintest look of disgust crossed Pharyl's face.

"Advocate," interjected Quaeryt, "if you would please clarify any past connection to Tilborans . . . or not . . . as the case may be."

"Why did you think the Tilborans were coming for you?"

"They're everywhere. They didn't stay in Tilbor."

"Why not?"

"I donna know. They just are. I saw 'em. I did."

"Have you ever seen any other Tilborans?"

"I told you. They were near the square. They were after me."

"Did you take out your knife to attack them?"

"No, sir. I was just showing what they'd get if they came after me. Then that fellow patroller walked into it."

After another half quint of questions, Caesyt said, "I have no more questions."

Quaeryt turned to Pharyl. "Do you have any more questions or any other witnesses?"

"I have a few questions, Honorable Justicer."

Quaeryt nodded.

"Jubyl, there are no records of your serving in any regiment posted to Tilbor. Why do you say that Tilborans were after you?"

"Because they were. They were." Jubyl's eyes went from side to side.

"What would you do if one of these Tilborans moved toward you?"

"A fellow can defend himself."

"Would you kill one?"

"If he tried to attack me."

"No further questions."

Both Caesyt and Pharyl looked to Quaeryt.

"Do you have a closing statement, Chief Pharyl?"

"I do." Pharyl paused for a moment. "Jubyl stabbed Patroller Shannar. That is without question. More than a score of people saw it. Jubyl claims he was waving his knife to keep away Tilborans. He has never been to Tilbor. The advocate for Jubyl will claim that the offender did not know what he was doing. Just a moment ago, Jubyl made a clear statement that he would attack only if attacked. That shows the ability to decide. He decided to kill Patroller Shannar. He did so. He is guilty and should be found so."

Quaeryt looked to Caesyt.

"Despite what the chief of the Civic Patrol has said, Honorable Justicer, Jubyl had no intent to kill, nor was he in his right mind. The fact that he is convinced he served as a ranker in Tilbor demonstrates this. Under the laws of Telaryn, a man not in his right mind cannot be convicted of deliberate murder if there was no intent to accomplish such. Therefore, while Jubyl may be guilty of involuntary assault, he cannot be guilty of murder."

Caesyt inclined his head politely and stepped back.

For just a moment, Quaeryt was more than puzzled by Caesyt's comparatively matter-of-fact defense. *He wants him executed. But why? So no one can find out who hired him to kill Shannar and why?* Even if the advocate did want that, Jubyl was still guilty of deliberate murder. "Bring the offender forward."

Caesyt stepped back slightly from Jubyl once Jubyl stood in front of the dais, effectively leaving the man standing alone.

In more ways than one.

Quaeryt had to clear his throat before he spoke. "Jubyl Jonsyn, this hearing finds you guilty of one count of murder, and one count of assault in resisting the Civic Patrol. You are hereby sentenced to death by beheading."

Jubyl twisted toward Caesyt. "You said you'd get me off! You said . . . you bastard!" His voice rose to a shout. "I did what you wanted . . ."

Three patrollers moved around Jubyl, one immediately applying a gag.

"This hearing is concluded," Quaeryt announced. "There will be a break of one quint before the hearings resume."

Slightly more than a quint later, Quaeryt was back on the dais, with almost the same onlookers—except for the young woman who had been crying. Shannar's sister, lover, wife? Or Jubyl's? No one had said, and unfortunately, it didn't matter. Either way, she had lost someone she loved.

"This hearing is the matter of Cauflyn Coersyn, charged with theft of six silvers and assaulting a factor and others following the commission of the theft." Quaeryt looked to the stocky advocate standing by the bench for the accused. "Are you representing the accused?"

"Yes, Honorable Justicer."

Pharyl stepped forward, inclining his head to Quaeryt, then stating, "Chief of the Civic Patrol, representing the city of Extela."

"Very well. Bring in the accused."

Two patrollers marched in Cauflyn, his hands in restraints, and positioned him directly before Quaeryt. Quaeryt could see purplish yellow bruises on the left side of Cauflyn's face and several scabbed-over cuts or scratches on the right side and on his neck. The muscular and brown-bearded man did not look up at Quaeryt.

Caesyt stepped up beside Cauflyn, who started to lean away from the advocate, then caught himself.

"You are charged with two counts, one of theft and one of assault. The first count is that of taking by force the wallet of the felter Heryd, and the second is of assaulting him. How do you plead?"

"Not guilty, Honorable Justicer." Caesyt's voice was as oily and smooth as Quaeryt remembered.

"A plea of not guilty is entered." Quaeryt nodded to the patrollers.

The patrollers led Cauflyn to the backless bench below and to the right of Quaeryt and sat him down.

The first witness was the felter himself, an older and almost frail-looking white-haired man, whose shaking hands suggested too many years close to too many liquids not best for the health. Heryd's words told a longer version of Pharyl's summary, and Pharyl asked questions, the answers to which filled in many of the details.

Then Caesyt began his questions.

"Felter Heryd . . . is it not true that Cauflyn only held the coin box for a few moments before throwing it to the floor?"

"He threw it to the floor . . . that's for sure. My boys were coming after him."

"They were in the back of the shop, weren't they?"

"That they were."

"And there was no one between Cauflyn and the door, was there?"

"I couldn't say."

"Was there anyone else in the front of the shop besides you and the offender?"

"No, sir." Heryd's voice trembled as much as his hands did.

"So he could have run out the door with the coin box?"

"I suppose so."

"But he didn't, did he?"

"No," replied the felter grudgingly.

"Did he hit you at any time?"

"He wrenched the box from me."

"But did he hit you?"

"No, sir."

Pharyl called the felter's two sons and began to question them. As questioning went on, Quaeryt couldn't help but note that both were very slight and slender, like their father. Quaeryt thought both of them together might not weigh as much as Cauflyn.

After Pharyl finished questioning the sons, Caesyt began his interrogation, offering variations on the same questions he had with Heryd.

After that, Pharyl called several patrollers, who recounted their stories. Under Caesyt's questions, they had to admit that Cauflyn hadn't actually attacked them, which suggested to Quaeryt that the felter's sons had been overenthusiastic in capturing and holding Cauflyn for the Civic Patrol, before the patrollers had taken him to the patrol station and confined him. That, again, raised the question as to why the strong, large, and heavily muscled Cauflyn hadn't simply broken free and fled.

"Cauflyn Coersyn, step forward," ordered Pharyl, who waited until Cauflyn faced Quaeryt before continuing. "Would you please tell the honorable justicer what happened on the night of Samedi, the thirty-fifth of Avryl?"

"I'd been to Sazyl's, and I'd had a tankard or two. I wasn't feeling that steady, and I went out for some air. I came back. I thought I was in Sazyl's. I wasn't. I picked up this box. Then I realized it was a coin box. For a moment, I thought about taking it. Then I dropped it. Those fellows tackled me and beat me, and the patrollers came and took me away."

Quaeryt listened carefully while Pharyl questioned Cauflyn again and again, but Cauflyn said little more than he had in his first statement.

He's trying to get a light punishment, but he doesn't want to be released soon. That was Quaeryt's feeling. The tough didn't want to give Quaeryt an excuse for losing a hand or worse, but he wasn't trying to slant his story in the way so many of those Quaeryt had heard over the last weeks had done.

Caesyt persisted in trying to show that what Cauflyn had done was little more than disorderly conduct.

When all the questions had been asked, Quaeryt turned to Pharyl. "Your closing statement."

"Cauflyn Coersyn entered the shop of the felter Heryd, seized the coin box, and attempted to take it. When he saw the felter's sons coming for it, he dropped it, and they caught him. Whether he dropped the coin box or not does not matter. He took it with the intent of theft."

"Your closing statement, Advocate Caesyt?" said Quaeryt.

"Cauflyn Coersyn was confused. He likely had stopped by a public taproom or café. He went into the felter's thinking it was someplace else. He took the coin box, then realized it was not his and dropped it. The most with which Cauflyn can honestly be charged is being disorderly in public. He made no attempt to escape, even when he was struck and could have. He struck no one, and there is no testimony here that even mentions assault, and that being the case, I move that the assault charge be dropped."

"Honorable Justicer . . ." interjected Pharyl.

"Yes."

"Cauflyn seized the coin box with force. Use of force in the case of theft or attempted theft is assault."

"Advocate Caesyt, your motion is denied."

Quaeryt looked to the patrollers flanking Cauflyn. "Bring the accused forward."

Caesyt stepped back slightly and then moved beside Cauflyn once he stood in front of Quaeryt. Cauflyn did not even glance in the direction of the advocate.

Quaeryt announced, "Cauflyn Coersyn, this hearing finds you guilty of one count of assault and guilty of one count of theft. You are hereby sentenced to five strokes of the lash and branding on your right hand, followed by incarceration for one to two weeks, at the discretion of the patrol chief. This hearing is declared closed."

"Honorable Justicer, I request an appeal."

"On what grounds, advocate?"

"On the grounds that merely holding a coin box and dropping it is not theft. On the grounds that the accused offender took the coin box from a shelf that was easily accessible and not from the felter. As such, no force was applied, and without force, there is no assault."

"This time, you failed to make your case, advocate. Your appeal is denied."

The advocate looked stunned. "You're . . . deciding . . . now?"

"I have, advocate."

"Appeals must go to higher authority, Honorable Justicer."

"They did. They went from the justicer to the governor."

"Such arbitrariness is not usually a feature of law in Telaryn, and those who act arbitrarily must answer to the High Justicer of Telaryn. I will be informing him of the particulars of this case."

"That is indeed your right, advocate," replied Quaeryt mildly.

"It might be best . . . for all involved . . . were I not required to file such a report. The events detailed in such a report might well be construed as illustrating the lack of judicial procedures in the province of Montagne."

"That is your decision," replied Quaeryt, before declaring in a louder voice. "This hearing is now concluded. Return the prisoner to custody." He stood. "Good day, Advocate Caesyt."

Quaeryt said nothing more until he left the hearing chamber and he and Pharyl were alone in the chief's study with the door closed.

"You didn't have to incarcerate him, you know?" Pharyl smiled.

"You know why I did."

The chief nodded. "So that we can hide him in the wagon and drive him to the river piers some night when no one's watching."

"Any man who will commit a crime for a flogging and branding to escape Hyleor deserves at least a chance to get away."

"He was one of Hyleor's guards. He's not exactly the spirit of righteousness or an advocate for the Nameless."

"No. That's one reason why it's not unjust to brand him. Do you think Jubyl knows something . . . and that's why Caesyt didn't try very hard to defend him?"

"That's possible," said Pharyl. "It's most likely that Hyleor was afraid Shannar knew something and would tell the Civic Patrol, and that it would get to you. With Jubyl and Shannar dead, no one else who knows is likely to say anything. If you'd released Cauflyn, he'd be dead before midnight, if not sooner. I'd say he knows too much as well."

Who else . . . Quaeryt shook his head as he remembered where he'd heard the name Bennar Fhandsyn before.

"Sir?"

"You remember when the pimps staged that attack on the flour wagon?"

"I heard of it. I wasn't there."

"The one who we captured and held for a while. He said that the attack had been set up by Bennar, who worked for the spicer . . . The spicer had to be Hyleor." *Why didn't you connect all that sooner? Because there's more than one spice factor? Or because you're trying to do too much?*

"So Hyleor was behind that as well."

"It's nothing we can prove in a hearing, but that's two more dead men and a dead pleasure girl."

Pharyl offered a sour look, then shook his head as well.

Quaeryt wondered if he'd ever know the entire story . . . and how long he'd have to worry about Hyleor and what the so-called spice factor was really doing.

Quaeryt finally returned to the post somewhat after noon and had barely entered the building when the duty squad leader hurried toward him, a dispatch in hand, a dispatch sealed with copious amounts of red wax—signifying urgency.

"Sir, this arrived at ninth glass."

Quaeryt took the sealed dispatch. "Thank you."

"There was also one for Commander Skarpa."

That suggested that Third Regiment would be leaving imminently, but Quaeryt merely nodded, then hurried to his study. He wanted to be alone when he opened the missive.

Once he closed the door he walked to the desk, but did not sit down. Instead, he took out his belt knife and slit the envelope, leaving most of the heavy wax in place as he extracted the two sheets of heavy paper. He began to read.

> *Governor Quaeryt:*
>
> *I had thought your position as governor of Montagne would resolve a number of matters. While you have done much of what was necessary . . .*

Much of what was necessary? Quaeryt didn't like that opening at all, but kept reading.

> *. . . the situation has now changed. Our informants report that the bulk of the Bovarian forces in eastern Bovarian are marching toward Ferravyl. The number of small and scattered attacks on our positions near Ferravyl are growing weekly. All available forces will be necessary to repulse the Bovarians.*
>
> *You are to be congratulated on your accomplishments in returning order to Extela, in repairing and restoring the basic facilities to use, such as the east bridge and the River Aqueduct, as well as building a new Civic Patrol station and securing a new permanent residence for future provincial governors. It has come to my attention, however, that the unrest provoked by your methods in achieving these worthy goals has created a situation where it is best that you leave Extela and assume a position as an advisor to me in Ferravyl. High Holder Cransyr has complained about your handling of*

the events that caused the death of one of his nephews, and the uncalled-for imprisonment of another. High Holder Wystgahl [the younger] charges that your unseemly interrogation of his father caused his death. The grain factors of Extela have complained that your sale of flour caused them great financial losses, while many in the city insist that after you gained control of the flour supply, you raised prices to enrich the governor's treasury. Spice Factor Hyleor, the spice factors of Solis, and High Holder Unseeld believe that your failure to pursue those who assaulted Factor Hyleor caused him and the spice and herb trade untoward damages.

The former justicer Tharyn has claimed that you refused his services and then acted as justicer yourself. In doing so, according to an advocate in Extela, you placed such strain on the former high justicer who was advising you that he died after a hearing. A respected chorister has protested that you were also acting as a chorister for the Nameless and using your position as chorister to influence the troops, in particular to grant special treatment to undeserving Pharsi women. It has also been reported that you requested sick leave for the post commander, but retained him on the rolls, and in doing so, created the circumstances that led to his untimely and early death. Lastly, but not insignificantly, Factoria Grelyana feels that you and your wife exerted pressure for her to lower the price on the villa you purchased for the governor's residence and to insist on retaining certain family heirloom furnishings.

While I have no doubt that there are mitigating factors in many of these cases, perhaps in all, and that it is likely some of these charges, if not the majority, are totally false, I feel it best that you be replaced as governor by Markyl Quintussyn, who has been princeps of Ryntar for the past several years and who is a younger son of High Holder Quintus of Cloisonyt. Because of the urgency of matters in Ferravyl, you are to proceed with Third Regiment immediately to Ferravyl, with the exception of one company, chosen by you, that will escort the Lady Vaelora safely to Solis. Obviously, you can travel together until the road splits at Tresrives . . .

The remainder of the dispatch continued with details of where and how Quaeryt should report once he reached Ferravyl with Third Regiment.

For several moments, Quaeryt just stood there, not really thinking, stunned as much as anything.

In not quite a month and a half, almost seven weeks exactly, he'd effectively restored Extela to a working city, an incredible achievement by any standard, given the conditions he'd encountered, especially with the loss of most tools of government and those who knew how to wield them both effectively and honestly. *Except there were few who were truly honest.*

And what was his reward—and Vaelora's? Removal and replacement, because in trying to put things back together, he'd stepped on too many pairs of boots. Yet it would have taken months, if not longer, any other way, and he still likely would not have accomplished all that had to be done. *Not that you have yet, either.*

He shook his head, then slipped the sheets back into the envelope. He needed to talk to Skarpa.

Finding the commander wasn't difficult because Skarpa was standing outside the door to the post commander's study, talking to Meinyt. Quaeryt was willing to wait, but when both officers saw him they stopped talking.

"We can finish this later," Skarpa said to the major.

Meinyt nodded and hurried toward the courtyard.

Quaeryt followed Skarpa into the small study, not that any of the studies were capacious, and closed the door behind himself. "So what did your dispatch say?"

A puzzled expression crossed Skarpa's face as he stood beside the desk. "The same as yours, I'd imagine. That we're to depart as soon as possible, but that one company will receive special instructions from you."

"That's all?"

Skarpa lifted a single sheet from the desk and handed it to Quaeryt.

Quaeryt read it, then nodded as he handed it back. "That's what it says. Now . . . you're wondering why I asked. I'll tell you, but only if it remains between the two of us."

"You know—"

"I know you don't talk, and some of this will be known in a day, but . . . you'll see why. You'll also understand why I want you to know." He handed the dispatch he'd received to the commander.

Skarpa began to read, first nodding, and then frowning. At the end, he looked up. "Since this is between us . . . it's all pigshit. He doesn't want to piss off anyone at the moment . . . and I'd wager he's got more trouble than he can handle in Ferravyl." A rueful smile followed as he returned the dispatch to Quaeryt. "I did tell you that we were just here because no one else dared stomp on enough boots to fix things."

"I remember some words to that effect."

"I'm also going to suggest that you pay yourself a travel allowance and expenses, and your pay as governor for all of Mayas. You deserve that, and more, and Lord Bhayar will expect it and the new governor won't miss it."

"I'll have to think about that."

"Don't think too hard. You've got your wife to think about . . . and it's likely to be a good while before any of us gets paid once we're in Ferravyl." Skarpa shook his head. "I still can't believe it. Well . . . I guess I can . . . I did tell you—"

"That governing wasn't like winning battles. You did, and it isn't. Any time you get anything done, someone else gets upset, and the faster you do it, the louder they complain." Quaeryt offered a grim smile. "Do you think I should pay the regiment in advance, or just send the coins in a pay chest?"

"Send the pay chest. Too many of the rankers will spend every copper they have as soon as they get it."

"I can do that." Quaeryt couldn't keep a true half smile from his face at the way Skarpa had conveyed the need to get his men paid. "How soon will you be ready to leave?"

"We've been mostly ready for weeks. Samedi morning, I'd thought."

Quaeryt managed not to wince at the thought of telling Vaelora she had only a day to pack and leave Extela behind. "Then we'll leave on Samedi." *Not that we have any real choice.* "Have you told Heireg and the others?"

"Only that we'd likely be leaving before long on short notice."

"Then I won't keep you."

Quaeryt spent the next two glasses with Heireg and Jhalyt, since the major would effectively be not only acting governor but paymaster for the Civic Patrol and the post until Markyl arrived. When he left them to carry out his instructions, he reclaimed the mare and rode out the post gates, heading for the villa, and what he knew would be another sort of eruption.

On the ride back, he couldn't help but wonder exactly what Bhayar had in mind for him in Ferravyl. Was it simply to give him something to do, a meaningless position? Or had Bhayar decided that because Quaeryt had done more than he had ever admitted in Tilbor that he might be actually useful in Ferravyl?

Either way, what awaited him in Ferravyl meant trouble. The only question was what kind.

Vaelora came out of the villa to meet him on the portico after he stabled, but did not unsaddle, the mare, and walked up from the villa stables. Her expression was quizzical as she asked, "What is it, dearest? You're never home this early. Is something wrong?"

Wordlessly, Quaeryt handed the dispatch to her.

Unlike Skarpa, Vaelora frowned from the moment she began to read the dispatch, and that frown deepened with each line. Finally, she looked up.

"They're all lies! That bitch Grelyana . . . all of them! What did he expect with a quarter of the city destroyed? He had to know that schemer Scythn was skimming off too much in tariffs."

"As are most governors," said Quaeryt dryly.

"Except you. We're both being punished for your honesty and effectiveness."

Quaeryt shook his head. "I had a choice. I could have acted the way Scythn did, and few would have said anything. Or I could have proceeded slowly and deliberately, flattering and toadying, and doing nothing until everyone agreed, and doing nothing where people disagreed. I would have accomplished almost nothing in the time we've been here. Instead, I did everything in the dispatch. I did keep the price of flour down—just for a few weeks and to help the poor. I did cause Wystgahl's death because he wanted to make golds off the suffering of others, while stealing from your brother. There was a reason for everything I did—a good reason, but people with influence felt they suffered because I was trying to do things I felt would help everyone . . . and in some cases, those who truly wanted or needed the help. Poor Zhrensyl was dying already. He couldn't really do his job. I set it up so that he wouldn't suffer, and he knew that. But he's dead, and the only people who know what really happened are a few officers. It's like that with everything in his dispatch." *Or most things, anyway.*

"Bhayar has to know better."

"I'm certain he does," replied Quaeryt. "There's the phrase about most of the charges being false."

"He won't stand up for you . . ."

"He's facing attacks by Kharst and the Bovarians. The last thing he wants is a bunch of unhappy factors and High Holders in his ancestral home. He replaces me, and it solves everything. This Markyl, if he's smart, and I'm certain he is, will placate everyone and blame me. Things are getting back to normal, and no one will complain if the Civic Patrol is better, and if Markyl can find a justicer who does a better and more honest job than Tharyn and the other one did, the new governor will get the credit for it. He won't have to take the blame for getting a governor's residence—"

"That I found and negotiated for, had cleaned and furnished, and had little enough time to enjoy after months of travel and poor accommodations," snapped Vaelora. "Bhayar didn't even think of me, except to order me back to Solis like a discarded plaque in a game he's playing with Kharst."

Quaeryt couldn't blame her for her anger as he added, "And replacing us will allow him to remove Third Regiment as well, which he needs immediately in Ferravyl."

"How immediately?" demanded Vaelora.

"We leave on Samedi morning."

"Samedi morning! One day to make arrangements and to pack! One day! And Shenna, poor Shenna . . . What will I do for her?"

"We could give her some golds . . ."

"Of course, but that's little enough . . . and for all we've done . . ."

Quaeryt realized that he was not going to have much of a chance to say more. So he listened for almost two quints before he finally slipped in another sentence. "I have an errand to take care of . . ."

"Now?!! For what reason when you're being rewarded like this?"

"If I don't take care of it, I will regret it, and Extela will suffer."

"What is all that important if we're leaving on Samedi morning?"

"I'll tell you when I return." Quaeryt offered the sentence quietly.

"Is it that important?"

"It is to me. It's something that needs to be done."

Strangely, at least to Quaeryt, the anger seemed to vanish from Vaelora's face, but she said nothing for several moments.

Quaeryt waited.

"You have to set something right, don't you?"

"It's the least I can do."

"Please be careful, dearest." After a moment, she added, "In every way."

"This time, I intend exactly that." Quaeryt took a deep breath. He wasn't looking forward to what he planned, for more than a few reasons. Still . . .

He used a concealment shield to walk back to the stable, and he held it over both the mare and himself when he rode out from the villa, rather than try to explain to the rankers assigned to the villa why he needed no escorts. Since he'd had to make several trips to Hyleor's dwelling before finally meeting the factor, Quaeryt had no difficulty finding his way there under his shield.

When he saw the house, and the brick wall topped with ironwork spikes that fronted the street and formed part of the enclosure around the garden between the house and street, he frowned again at the sheer ill chance that had befallen Versoryn.

Might have been better for all of us if they'd whipped Hyleor to death. Quaeryt shook his head. *Then you'd have had to execute him and the others . . . and that would have been worse, especially given High Holder Cransyr. Except Hyleor's caused at least five deaths you know of, and probably more that you don't.* Like so many things in life, there was no ideal resolution. *But that's why you're here this afternoon.*

As he rode closer, he could see that no one was outside in front, despite the open gates.

Holding a concealment shield over himself and the mare, Quaeryt rode slowly through the gates. He looked again at the drive. The last time he had seen Hyleor, the drive had been muddy and rutted. Now it was smooth and graveled. He slowed the mare, then almost a step at a time rode down the dirt on the side away from the graveled drive toward the dwelling and the small building behind it. He chose the dirt because the sound of hooves on the gravel would be noticed more than silent tracks appearing in the dirt . . . assuming anyone noticed at all.

He was halfway down the drive when two men stepped out of the small shedlike building behind the dwelling. One was the fleshy-faced and black-haired Hyleor, looking fatter and greasier than Quaeryt recalled. The other was wiry and dressed in faded gray, moving his head from side to side with a jerkiness that reminded Quaeryt of a wary rodent.

Quaeryt reined up and waited, listening.

". . . do about Cauflyn?"

". . . once he's out of the patrol gaol . . . the same as the others . . . except I'll carve my initials in his guts so big he doesn't have guts . . ."

"Patrol chief or governor might have something to say about that."

"Word is that the governor won't last long . . ." The spice factor looked up and turned his head from side to side. "You hear something?"

"Just the wind."

"Could have sworn I heard a horse whuffling."

"Do you see a horse, sir?" asked the man in gray, his head moving rodent-like from side to side.

"I heard one."

Quaeryt didn't bother to wait longer. He imaged water into Hyleor's lower throat and lungs.

The factor staggered, then tried to speak. No sound issued forth. An attempted cough spewed forth some liquid, but Quaeryt imaged more water into Hyleor's lower throat.

The man in gray pounded on Hyleor's back. Hyleor coughed out a small spurt of water, but his face was turning red.

"Elenda! Elenda!" yelled the man in gray.

Hyleor staggered, then bent forward, trying to clear his lungs and throat.

Quaeryt waited.

Abruptly, the factor pitched forward into the gravel of the drive. The other man pushed on his back and kept pressing intermittently. Water gushed from Hyleor's mouth, but Quaeryt imaged more into the factor's throat.

In time, Quaeryt could see that the factor's chest was moving slower and slower . . . until it wasn't rising and falling at all.

The man in gray rolled Hyleor over so that he faced skyward in the late afternoon. "Elenda!"

No one appeared.

The gray man ran for the rear of the house.

Once he was out of sight, Quaeryt turned the mare and rode slowly back up along the far side of the drive until he was outside the gates. He reined up and waited. Still . . . no one appeared.

After half a quint, he turned the mare.

He was just glad Hyleor had been there. He would have come back later that evening, or on Vendrei evening, had it been necessary. He just couldn't have left Hyleor to create more trouble for Pharyl and for the people of Extela.

But won't someone else just step into his boots? And what right did you have to act as justicer and executioner?

His laugh was silent and bitter. *No right at all, only the responsibility not to let a man who caused death after death keep doing it when no one else could or would stop it.*

Quaeryt didn't have any better answers to his own questions. He kept riding, back toward the villa that he and Vaelora had occupied for such a short time with such high hopes for a future that had not come to pass.

He'd been able to do nothing about improving matters in Extela or in any other part of Montagne for either scholars and imagers. He hadn't finished resolving many of the problems facing the city, and he'd already been dismissed and replaced.

57

Quaeryt's head was aching, and little flashes of light sparkled in front of his eyes by the time he returned to the villa, unseen beneath the concealment shield. Once in the stable, he released the shield, and took a deep breath. The imaging he'd done hadn't been that strenuous, but he was out of practice in holding both personal and concealment shields simultaneously . . . and for such a long period of time. After several moments he unsaddled and groomed the mare. Since none of the rankers were waiting or looking for him, his absence from the villa had apparently gone unnoticed.

He walked up from the stable to the villa, his thoughts on what might await him in Ferravyl. His boots had barely hit the floor inside the entry hall, echoing unevenly, when Vaelora hurried out of the main level study. She stopped a yard short of him.

"How did . . . your errand . . . go?" Her voice was soft.

"I took care of it," replied Quaeryt tiredly.

"Not Grelyana? She's a bitch, but . . ."

At the worried expression on his wife's face, Quaeryt shook his head. "Hyleor. He ordered one of his guards to kill another, deceived him, and got the man sentenced to be beheaded. The man who was killed was a patroller recruit. He was murdered because he knew too much about Hyleor, not that I'd ever be able to prove it. That's what I know directly. Then there are all the girls Hyleor drugged for his pleasure houses, not to mention all the elveweed and other drugs he's carted into Extela. Oh . . . and he was also the one who set up the attack on the flour wagon, where two men and a pleasure girl got killed." Quaeryt sighed. "Someone will replace him. There's always someone, but they won't know as much, and they'll have to go on the assumption that bad things happen if they get too far out of hand. That's the best I can do for Pharyl and the city . . . so far as that's concerned."

"They don't deserve your help," retorted Vaelora.

"Pharyl does. I'm the one who made him chief. So does Hrehn. Besides, the ones who caused all the trouble for me aren't really the productive part of the city. For the most part, they're parasites on the city."

"More of them deserve what Hyleor got."

"They probably do," Quaeryt admitted, "but I'm not sure I'd want to meet the sort of man I'd become if I took on that task for all those who deserve it." He paused. "I'm not even sure I'd want to meet the man I've become in trying to put Extela back together."

"What choice did you have?"

"We all have choices. I chose to go outside the law three times. I did it because the law failed . . . but the law fails so much . . ." He shook his head. "Bhayar's right. I'm better not being a governor."

Vaelora frowned. "No. You've been a good governor in a bad time. And those three . . . that's why they get away with it. If a governor or a patrol chief can't show publicly the evil someone has done . . . or if that evil isn't widely known to almost everyone, any punishment delivered is seen as unjustified and tyrannical."

"That's exactly what happened to me, in a way," Quaeryt pointed out. "It takes time to make people aware of things, especially if they don't want to know."

"Sometimes, they never want to know." Vaelora's words held a sour tone. "They'd rather ignore the problems."

"Especially if they're guilty of the same sorts of acts, even on a lesser scale."

"The ones like Grelyana."

Quaeryt nodded.

"Is there . . . anything else?"

"Besides the fact that I need to write a list of items for the new governor?"

"Why?"

"So that he'll do what needs to be done, knowing that Bhayar will have been informed as well."

"It might work." She shook her head. "What else for us?"

"Well . . . you still have to pack," he observed quietly, with a slight lilt in his voice.

"*We* still have to pack, you mean. You don't have that much, and it won't take me that long. I never had a chance to get any more dresses or gowns sewn, and half my clothes aren't worth packing."

Quaeryt nodded. "But you still look good in them."

"I couldn't wear some of them a day without the seams splitting and leaving me riding in undergarments." She gave him a mock glare. "And don't say a word about where that would be appropriate."

He offered a grin.

"I said not a word."

"I didn't say anything."

"You didn't have to."

But she smiled back, Quaeryt saw, if only for a moment.

He felt so tired . . .

58

Vaelora and Quaeryt rose early on Samedi morning and were at the post a good two quints before seventh glass, when Skarpa gave Third Regiment the orders to head out. The initial route was simple—southward on the road that led to—and past—the chateau of High Holder Wystgahl and continuing to the southern bridge over the Telexan River, a narrow stone span that had withstood the river floods, but was barely wide enough for a single wagon or two horses abreast. On the southern and eastern side of the river, the stone-paved road extended through various towns and hamlets, past two cataracts, and the portage stations used by the traders, hugging the banks of the Telexan for over 330 odd milles to Tresrives, where the Ruil River and the Telexan joined the mighty Aluse.

Just before sunset on the fifteenth of Mayas, Quaeryt and Vaelora rode past a millestone reading TRESRIVES—2M. To Vaelora's right rode Captain Taenyd, and to her left was Quaeryt.

They had just passed the stone bridge over the Telexan, its three arches aligned almost due west, a bridge that Quaeryt would be taking with Third Regiment before long on the way to Ferravyl to join up with the bulk of the Telaryn forces—and with Bhayar.

"We're almost there." Quaeryt again shifted his weight in the saddle and tried to ease the soreness in more muscles than he recalled having.

"We're not anywhere," replied Vaelora tartly, "except closer to being separated."

"You'll be better off in Solis than if you'd stayed—"

"Dearest . . ." she interjected, drawing out the endearment in a fashion that sounded anything but endearing, "you have said that every day for the entire journey. Even if I agreed with you, and I'm less inclined to be agreeable with each passing glass, I do not need to hear that piece of dubious wisdom again."

Quaeryt winced inside, trying to keep a smile on his face.

"And don't smile that condescending smile, either."

Quaeryt let himself wince.

"That's not much better."

Quaeryt laughed, if ruefully.

As Vaelora looked to Quaeryt, behind her Taenyd gave the smallest of head shakes, as if to say that nothing Quaeryt could do would placate Vaelora, before he quickly looked forward at the road that turned eastward toward Tresrives itself, just downstream from the junction of the Telexan and the River Aluse. Ahead of them rode the first company of Third Battalion, acting as vanguard and commanded by Jusaph, with Skarpa beside the captain. Behind them were the remaining companies of the battalion, and then the other three battalions, and the engineers, a column stretching more than a mille to the rear to the supply wagons and the rear guard.

"How much farther to the post?" asked Quaeryt.

"It's just upstream of the piers. It's really not a post, just staging barracks built in the old days when Lhayar wanted loyal armsmen closer to Solis."

"And it's still a staging barracks, except it's now for troopers headed west," said Quaeryt dryly. "Or a barracks to rest men and mounts before they move on."

"How long do you think Commander Skarpa will rest the mounts?" asked Taenyd.

"You'd know that better than I, Captain," replied Quaeryt. "I'd judge at least a day. What do you think?"

"He hasn't pushed us as much as he could have," mused Taenyd.

Quaeryt considered that. They'd moved at a good pace all the way, but then Skarpa hadn't pressed. He just hadn't allowed any dallying or wasted time, but he hadn't had the regiment start out until there was good light each day, and except for the present day, he'd called a halt a good glass before sunset.

"Two days, I'd judge," Taenyd finally said.

"That's at least another day before we have to leave for Solis," said Vaelora.

"You'll be safe there long before we get to Ferravyl," noted Quaeryt.

"In Solis, yes . . ." murmured Vaelora. "But back in confinement."

"Aelina will be there."

"That's about the only good thing about being back in the palace," she continued in a low voice.

"You can't very well accompany the regiment into battle," he pointed out.

Vaelora did not respond.

Rather than press her, Quaeryt looked past her to his right as they rode around the curve that followed the river. Absently, he wondered just how many of the "suggestions" he had left for the new governor would be implemented.

More than if you had left none. Not that the thought was much comfort.

Before long, they passed the point where the bluish gray waters of the Telexan flowed into the Aluse. Quaeryt could see plumes of blue extending into the larger river before being swirled away and mixed into the brownish gray of the Aluse, as if the smaller river had never been.

Is that how uniqueness gets swallowed, mixed into a swirling mass so much larger?

"I know . . ." said Vaelora quietly, easing her gelding closer to his mare.

"Know what?"

"You were looking at the river. I remember the first time I rode back from Extela and saw the Telexan's blue waters swallowed and vanish. Usually, the water is even bluer, but I think it's grayer now because of the eruption and the ash."

"I was thinking about that, and a bit more."

"You usually are, dearest. You can tell me later."

Quaeryt was glad for the softening in her voice, but still worried about her reactions to Bhayar's ordering her to Solis.

The raised stone road ran along what was effectively a levee from the west bridge over the Telexan River for almost a mille, so that on the north side of the road were marshes, and on the left was the River Aluse. Then the road passed through a cut in a low bluff and entered the town. Above the roofs of Tresrives hung a grayish haze, but Quaeryt couldn't determine what had caused it because the weather was warm and he knew that there were no metalworks near the town. Nor could he think of any other cause.

The other aspect of the town that struck him immediately, despite the fact that the day had been sunny and the sun had not yet quite touched the western horizon, was that Tresrives itself looked gray, even though the wooden dwellings and buildings were more like faded brown.

As they neared the river piers, Quaeryt could see that Taenyd had been right. In fact, the captain had been generous in his description of the "staging barracks." A low stone wall, barely chest-high, separated the west end of the dockyards that serviced the river piers from a rough brick-paved space between the wall and the stables. West of the stables were three long two-story buildings whose brick walls carried the soot of years. Farther west was a smaller building, the officers' quarters, Quaeryt presumed, and beyond that structure some twenty yards was a low building that might contain the troopers' mess.

A ranker rode toward Quaeryt and Vaelora, reining in his mount. "Governor, sir, Lady Vaelora, Commander Skarpa would like to invite you to join him, in order to make quarters assignments."

"Thank you," replied Quaeryt, before turning to Taenyd. "And thank you, Captain. If you will excuse us."

Taenyd nodded. "It has been my pleasure."

Skarpa had reined up opposite the building that Quaeryt thought contained the officers' quarters. He turned his mount slightly to face Quaeryt and Vaelora when they joined him so that he didn't have to turn in the saddle. "The officers' quarters aren't much, sir and Lady," said Skarpa. "There are two larger rooms for commanders, and I thought you should choose the one that suits you best. The officers' quarters are in the building between the last barracks and the mess building by the wall, and the commander's rooms are on the river end."

"You're most kind, Commander," said Vaelora. "I do appreciate that."

"And all the officers would appreciate your joining us for the evening meal."

"We would be pleased." Vaelora smiled pleasantly.

A ranker followed them as they rode toward the quarters building, in order to take their mounts back to the stables, so that they would not have to carry their gear past the three barracks buildings.

"We've slept in worse," murmured Vaelora. "Too many times."

"And just as you begin to get things the way you want them . . ." Quaeryt let his words hang.

"Exactly, dearest."

Quaeryt couldn't blame her, even if he didn't know what else he could have done in Extela. *Or what else you could have done and lived with yourself.*

One thing he did know. He wasn't the kind of man who was comfortable in using the law to justify doing nothing when people were being hurt or killed. *But . . . that might just mean you're the wrong kind of man to be governor for any length of time.*

On Lundi morning, Vaelora sat up in the bed barely big enough for the two of them and yawned, then looked at Quaeryt. "I am not staying in these quarters for two days. Or even close around them."

Given how lovely she looked, Quaeryt tore his eyes away from her before he said something that was inappropriate and looked toward the shuttered window. "What do you have in mind? Tresrives is not exactly Extela or Solis, and we can't use the horses."

"I wouldn't mind walking. Anything but sitting around here."

"We can do that, I'm certain." Quaeryt rose and strode to the window, adding, "If it's not raining." He eased open the inside shutter slightly and discovered that it sagged so much he feared it would rip out of the casement. Then he peered through the hazy glass. "It's not even cloudy." He gently lifted the shutter back in place.

"It wouldn't matter if it were."

Quaeryt nodded sympathetically.

"You're being condescending . . ."

"Yes, dear." He ducked and caught the pillow flung in his direction, hiding a smile.

"You can be most difficult, dearest."

"You knew that before you married me."

"I didn't marry you. Bhayar did, and I had no choice in the matter."

Quaeryt grinned and tossed the pillow back in her direction. "You weren't complaining last night. Not at all."

"You're not just difficult. You're impossible."

But she was smiling.

After he dressed, while Vaelora finished readying herself, Quaeryt sought out Skarpa. He found the commander in a small conference room adjoining the mess, by himself, looking over maps with a set of calipers in his hand.

Skarpa looked up. "Yes, sir?"

"Any word about anything?" asked Quaeryt.

"Only a dispatch from Submarshal Myskyl stating that our presence is needed and requesting that Third Regiment take no more than two days rest in Tresrives before setting out for Ferravyl."

"He's a submarshal now?"

"That's what the dispatch says, sir, and who am I to argue?"

"Neither one of us is in a position to argue at the moment," replied Quaeryt warmly. "And since I'm no longer governor, and since I never was comfortable with you calling me 'sir,' please don't argue with me when I tell you to stop it."

"I could say, 'Yes, sir,' " replied Skarpa, returning the smile, "but I won't." After a pause, he went on. "I know you haven't received any dispatches, but do you have any idea what Lord Bhayar has in mind for you? After you get to Ferravyl?"

"Besides report? No. The last time I saw him, he was talking about what I needed to learn as princeps of Tilbor. He wrote a letter or two to Vaelora while we were still in Tilbora, but none of that mentioned me, except in passing. I haven't heard anything since the dispatch I showed you." Quaeryt shrugged.

"I was just curious."

"As for today, I'd thought that we might ride around Tresrives, except I realized that wouldn't rest the horses. So we'll walk."

"You can see it easily—the parts that you and the lady would like to see. Take the main avenue behind the middle of the piers." Skarpa snorted. "There's little enough here these days, except a lot of empty dwellings and buildings. I'm not sure there's been that much for years, not since Bhayar's family unified Telaryn."

"That should make a comfortable walk."

"I'll send some rankers as an escort." Before Quaeryt could protest, Skarpa went on. "You may not be governor any longer, but your wife remains the Lady Vaelora, and she's Lord Bhayar's sister. I'm not about to risk my neck by not protecting her."

"I won't argue that."

"Good."

"How long will it take to reach Ferravyl?"

"With good weather, at least a week. If it rains . . . who knows?" Skarpa looked at the maps again. "Planning where to stop gets tricky because we're going in high water time and there are so many swamps and marshes along the river road—for the first hundred milles or so. After that, past the Great Bend, it's just flat."

"That should make traveling quicker, then."

"If . . ."

"It doesn't rain," finished Quaeryt, smiling.

"I'll have the rankers waiting outside the mess."

"Thank you." Quaeryt stepped out of the chamber and went to rejoin Vaelora.

After eating breakfast in the mess, Quaeryt and Vaelora set off, walking eastward toward the piers, followed by four rankers at a distance of several paces.

The piers were largely empty, with only a single barge and one flatboat tied up at the second pier. A single guard appeared to be watching both.

"It's almost sad," said Vaelora. "It's as if part of the town isn't here. Why aren't there more people here if Bhayar's mustering troops in Ferravyl?"

"There's no point in having them here. It's too far from where the regiments are to support them and too close to Solis that it offers much of an advantage."

The first shop opposite the foot of the westernmost pier was, unsurprisingly, a chandlery, if one whose weathered front siding suggested it had seen far better days. Quaeryt and Vaelora walked past it and past a second building, shuttered and seemingly deserted, then turned northward on what looked to be the main street Skarpa had mentioned.

The buildings nearest the piers largely held crafters, including a smithy, a coppersmith, a cooper, a rope factor, and a cabinetmaker. At the end of the first block, where there was a small square, was an inn with a brick and timber front, kept in better condition than many of the shops, and across the street from it, a tidy-looking café with a wide front window flanked by reddish shutters. Two pots of hyacinths were set on each side of the door.

"Given what you thought of breakfast and what you didn't eat, we might want to come back later and eat there," suggested Quaeryt.

Vaelora's eyes flicked behind them.

"They could use a meal besides barracks rations," replied Quaeryt. "It won't be that expensive." *Besides the rankers need to know they're appreciated with more than words.*

The main street continued northward past the square, and then angled slightly right, to the northeast. Quaeryt noted a narrow shop that looked to be that of a seamstress, but said nothing, although he noted his wife's eyes flicked in that direction.

"Even if she's good, I likely couldn't get anything finished before I have to leave."

"I imagine there are better seamstresses in Solis," replied Quaeryt.

"How would I know? I was never allowed to visit any. The only one I ever met was the one Aelina picked out, and she came to the palace."

Quaeryt decided not to comment on seamstresses again. Instead, he studied the more varied shops in the next block.

Close to three glasses later, Quaeryt, Vaelora, and the four troopers were walking back down the main street toward the square. As they neared the small café, Quaeryt turned. "We're going to eat there."

"Sir," said the trooper with the insignia of a junior squad leader, "we'll just wait outside."

"Absolutely not," declared Quaeryt. "You four need to eat as well." Seeing the dubious look on the squad leader's face, he swiftly added, "I'm paying for it, and besides, if you're worried about protecting Lady Vaelora, you won't be doing her any good if you're out here, and she's inside."

"Sir . . . we're not supposed to intrude . . ."

"You can sit at another table. That's the only concession I'll make," Quaeryt insisted.

"Yes, sir," the squad leader replied cheerfully.

The six of them walked into the café. The public spaces consisted of a large front chamber with eight tables, and a back room with a handful of smaller tables. From what Quaeryt could see, the only patron was a large man seated in the back room, facing away from the door and the front room.

A slender serving woman, barely more than a girl, appeared and bowed, gesturing toward the tables. Quaeryt and Vaelora took a smaller circular table on one side, near the wall, while the troopers took an oblong table against the other wall.

The serving girl moved to a position between and back from Quaeryt and Vaelora.

"What do you suggest?" asked Quaeryt.

"The hunter stew is good, very filling. So is the domchana. We use our own grain-fed game hens. The lady might like the lace rice fries as well."

"Do you have skelana?" asked Vaelora. "With dark rice?"

"Yes, Lady. That is my favorite."

"Then I'll have that with whatever your best white wine is."

Quaeryt didn't have the faintest idea what his wife had ordered. "I'll try the domchana, but with some dark rice as well. And a pale lager."

"We only have amber, sir."

"That will do."

"It's very good, and your meal will be, too."

"Oh . . . and I'm paying for the four over there."

As the server crossed the room to the troopers, Quaeryt looked at Vaelora. "What is skelana?"

"It's pulled lamb shredded and seasoned, then seared until barely brown, and warmed in a cucumber and heavy cream and lager sauce." She smiled. "You can try a bite of mine to see if you like it."

"Thank you." Quaeryt glanced up and toward the troopers.

The serving girl had barely stepped away from the other table and headed toward the kitchen when Quaeryt heard the sound of something falling and turned.

"He's one of them! They're both evil ones!" The burly gray-haired man charged from the back room, with something in his hand, lunging toward the table where Quaeryt and Vaelora sat. "Die! Pharsi scum!"

Triggering full shields and extending them, Quaeryt leapt between the man and Vaelora, then anchored the shields to the floor.

The attacker hit the shields with such force that the cudgel he wielded slammed into the shields and rebounded, tearing itself from the man's grasp.

"Evil protects him! Evil—" The man's words stopped cold as one of the rankers slammed the flat of his sabre against the side of his head.

Quaeryt contracted the shields so that they were almost against his body as two other rankers grabbed the attacker's arms and threw him to the floor. The squad leader whipped out a short length of rope and bound the man's hands behind his back. Then the two hoisted the groggy figure to his feet. The fourth stood with his sabre ready.

An older woman, who had appeared in the doorway to the kitchen, glanced from the man pinned to the floor to Quaeryt, then Vaelora, and back to Quaeryt. The serving girl, her mouth open, stood beside the older woman.

The silence was broken by the sound of the café door opening. A patroller stepped inside. At least, he appeared to be in some sort of uniform, despite splotches and spots on the khaki shirt and trousers, with black boots and a wide belt, from which dangled a truncheon on one side. "What seems to be the trouble here?"

"Governor Quaeryt and his wife stopped here to eat," answered the squad leader, turning toward the patroller. "His wife is the sister of Lord Bhayar. That man tried to attack them."

The patroller raked his eyes over Vaelora in a way that made Quaeryt think of imaging him dead. "Rush-high tale that is. Lord Bhayar can't be no stinking Pharsi." A snigger followed the words. "You boys just need to run along and take your *friends* back to the barracks with you, and there won't be no trouble."

"I don't think you understand," said the muscular squad leader. "She is Lady Vaelora. That's why we're here. Now . . . you can take this piece of offal back to your station and throw him in a cell for a few days . . . or you can do anything else . . . and your relatives can decide what to do with your ashes."

The suddenly dough-faced patroller looked at the four rankers and their drawn sabres and then at Quaeryt.

Quaeryt image-projected both authority and withering contempt.

The patroller swallowed. "Ah . . . begging your pardon, Lady . . . Maybe I'd best be going." He took a step back.

"You need to take your friend here. He'd better stay in his cell for the next few days. Until the regiment leaves. You might tell your chief that," added the squad leader. "He might not want a visit from the regimental commander."

One of the two rankers flanking the attacker sheathed his sabre and half led, half dragged the still dazed man toward the local patroller, then practically shoved him forward.

Neither local said another word as the patroller led the still-bound attacker back out through the front door, stepping to one side, once he was outside, to avoid the potted hyacinths.

"The lost one . . ."

At those words, Quaeryt turned, realizing that they had been murmured in the comparative silence by the older woman who still stood by the kitchen door. He thought about asking her why she'd made the comment, but didn't want to raise that question in such a public setting, especially with the troopers nearby. Instead, after a moment, he smiled at the older woman and the younger server beside her. "I think that good meal you promised would suit us all now."

"Ah . . . yes, sir." The server scurried toward the kitchen.

The older woman nodded at Quaeryt, then bowed to Vaelora, before following the server.

"The local people don't care for troopers much, do they?" asked Vaelora.

"That's true in most places," replied Quaeryt. "That's why Governor Rescalyn effectively built the cafés and . . ."

"Pleasure houses?" Vaelora raised her eyebrows.

"Well . . . after the problems caused by his predecessor . . ."

"It makes sense. I don't have to like it. Just like Bhayar's decision not to stand behind you. He's fortunate not to be in Solis. I'd . . ." Vaelora broke off as the server appeared with a goblet and a large mug.

The older woman followed with two platters, deftly sliding one before Vaelora and the second in front of Quaeryt. They returned to the kitchen and came back with mugs and platters of food for the troopers.

"It looks much better than breakfast," said Vaelora. "Even food on the road tasted better."

"The mess kitchens are old," suggested Quaeryt. "Or maybe the provisions were even older."

His words brought a faint smile to Vaelora's lips, before she took a bite of her meal. He picked up the batter-fried sandwich that held fowl strips, pepper slices, and cheese and took a bite, finding it hot and tasty, if not overwhelmingly so.

"You should try this," suggested Vaelora.

After taking a taste of her skelana, Quaeryt looked to her. "You made the better choice."

"It's nice to hear you admit that," she replied with a smile.

"But the domchana is still good. It's just not as good."

Vaelora took a sip of the white and set it down. "Your choice of beverage was better, I think."

"Do you want a lager?"

"No . . . this will do."

After they finished the meal, and as they walked southward toward the piers, Quaeryt strained to hear the low murmured words from the four troopers, but he could only catch snatches of words, because the troopers walked more than a few paces behind, obviously trying to give Quaeryt and Vaelora some space and privacy.

". . . like he knew . . ."

". . . say he knows more than . . ."

". . . said he was Pharsi, too . . ."

". . . blond?"

Even though Quaeryt did not look back, the troopers' words died away.

Quaeryt looked sideways at Vaelora. "Are you all right?"

"I'm fine." She shook her head ruefully. "You'd think, after all these years, that people would know that there's Pharsi blood in our family."

"How?" asked Quaeryt quietly. "Except for when you handed out flour and bread in Extela, this is probably the first time in your entire life when you've been surrounded by people who didn't know who you are." *Perhaps not the first, but there can't have been very many times.* He didn't voice that thought.

"But . . . the people who own the café . . . they're Pharsi. Why didn't he attack them?"

"They're subservient, in his mind. They serve. They're in their place. We weren't . . . and he didn't know who you were."

"People here seem to know who you are, even when they don't." Vaelora's voice held an edge.

"What do you mean?"

"The old woman in the café."

"She just recognized us as having Pharsi blood."

"Oh? She didn't say 'one of the lost ones.' She said '*the* lost one,'" said Vaelora, "as if it meant something. As if she knew you were that lost one."

"She bowed to you, not me. And how would she know?" Quaeryt shook his head even before he finished speaking, and quickly added, "A vision?"

"Farsight," suggested Vaelora.

"You haven't had any more visions lately, have you?"

"No . . . dearest. They're not that frequent. Not for me. Grandmere had them more often, I think."

"Why would she . . . ? Could it be a skill that improves with experience?"

Vaelora laughed, ironically. "How? It's not something you can exactly practice."

"I wonder . . ."

"Wonder all you want."

"Haven't all the visions you've told me about dealt with people close to you?"

"How was the eruption in Extela . . ." Vaelora stopped.

"Twice. Your family was there when she had it, and it influenced your life."

"But she didn't know that then."

"Do you know that? Or what else she saw? I told you about the young Pharsi woman in Bhorael, the wife of Rhodyn's son? She had a vision of me in her kitchen before she ever knew I existed."

Vaelora frowned, then smiled wryly. "It's best to think that what will be will be, and that at times we may get a glimpse of it."

Quaeryt nodded, thinking, *A glimpse of what lies before us might be helpful—except such visions don't appear to be that accommodating.*

He reached out and took Vaelora's hand as they continued toward the river.

Unlike Lundi, Mardi had been uneventful, and Quaeryt enjoyed spending time with Vaelora, if only talking or walking . . . not to mention other pleasures, but the day passed too quickly, as did the evening.

Despite the comparatively cramped room Quaeryt and Vaelora shared in the small post adjacent to the piers at Tresrives, officers' quarters that a year earlier Quaeryt would have found more than adequate, Quaeryt woke early and with dread on Meredi morning. In the gloom that was barely lighter than full darkness, he glanced over at the still-sleeping Vaelora and a smile appeared on his lips, one that vanished immediately as he thought about how soon they would be parted.

You never thought you'd feel this way . . . or even have the chance to.

So few scholars ever could afford a wife, and as for imagers, almost no families even wanted a child who might grow up to be one. Quaeryt had understood that as a very young orphan among the scholars. That was why he'd kept his imaging talent to himself for long, long years . . . until Vaelora had arrived, although he had to admit that she and Bhayar had suspected it earlier than that. *But Bhayar might not have without your letters to her.*

Vaelora opened her eyes and yawned, then rolled closer to him and kissed him gently.

As she leaned back slightly a while later, he asked, "What was that for?"

"You know very well, silly man."

"Tell me anyway."

"For loving me, and not the sister of the Lord of Telaryn."

"I only really knew you, as you. You are the one who saw to that." There had still been times when he'd seen a certain imperiousness, but although Quaeryt did not know, not for certain, he had the feeling that most women had moments of imperiousness. Certainly, most men did . . . often with women in particular. That, he'd seen from the outside, as it were.

"I did my best."

"You did it very well."

Vaelora looked to the riding clothes on the rack, then offered a sad smile. "We'd best dress."

All too soon, after a quick and cold breakfast in the officers' mess, and packing both their mounts, he was mounted on the mare, waiting beside Skarpa in the courtyard as Eleryt, Vaelora, and Third Battalion's second company rode out of the courtyard and swung eastward on the river road toward Solis.

How long before I see her again? He tried not to think about other, even less pleasant, possibilities as he finally turned the mare and followed the commander toward the front of the regiment about to ride out to the west and who knew what awaited them there.

For the next glass or so, Quaeryt and Skarpa rode westward, first from the barracks and over the bridge over the Telexan River, and then along the stone-paved river road. As the day grew hotter and damper, Quaeryt folded his jacket and laid it over the front of his saddle, then at the first rest and watering stop, tucked it into the left saddlebag.

Two glasses later, when they stopped again, Quaeryt dismounted and actually opened the tight saddlebag to reach for the hard biscuits he'd slipped inside before leaving Tresrives . . . and paused at the envelope tucked in beside the small sack of provisions.

How had she . . . ? He shook his head and extracted the envelope, slipping it inside his tunic for a moment while he took out two biscuits and closed the saddlebag. Then the biscuits went into a pocket, and he opened the letter, smoothed it out carefully, and began to read.

Dearest—

I know I have not been the most pleasant person at times over the last weeks. At such times, I have not been the best of wives, either. That has not been right, or fair to you. I can only hope you understand. For all of my life, until we were married, I have been confined and restricted, even more so in what I might say than what I might do. For all the difficulties, and the lack of proper quarters at times for the last months, I still appreciate, more now than ever, the freedom you bestowed upon me . . . and your grace in hearing me out.

Much as I love you, and would wish to be able to tell you that only your survival matters to me, I must tell you that you will not survive without Bhayar's support. Nor will my brother survive and prosper without yours. You have the burden of saving yourself and him. Nothing else matters, for I will not see either of you again unless I am able to see you both.

Another vision? Something she didn't want to tell you? Quaeryt frowned. Why hadn't she wanted to tell him?

He looked back down at the elegant script.

Do what you must, as much as necessary, but no more than that. Do so with the knowledge that I love you for the man you are, and not for the talents you have and will need to use in often terrible ways. For, as we both know, that is the nature of war.

Beneath those words were three others—"All my love"—and her signature.

He read the last lines a second time, and a third, before finally refolding the sheet and replacing it in the envelope.

61

Samedi looked to be another long day, thought Quaeryt, particularly after the regiment took almost a glass to ride around a line of supply wagons headed for Ferravyl, and that was only a glass after leaving the small unnamed town where they had spent Vendrei night in leaking barns and sheds. That rain had also softened the ground flanking the road so much that passing the wagons required the column splitting into single files and each file riding on the graveled shoulder of the road until the entire regiment was past and could re-form. The wagons mostly held barrels, either of dried and salted meat, pickled vegetables, and flour, at least from the lettering on the barrels Quaeryt could see. He rode beside Skarpa, at the head of Fourth Battalion for the day.

Once they were well past the wagons, Skarpa eased his mount closer to Quaeryt's mare. "I haven't mentioned it before . . . but I got a written complaint from the head of the town council at Tresrives. It was delivered the morning we left, but I figured it could wait until we were on the road . . . and then, somehow, I didn't get to it immediately."

"So you could claim you were too far away . . . or that you took care of it in the proper manner . . . and there'd be no way for them to know what you did."

"Something like that." Skarpa grinned. "You might know what it was all about."

"A very unhappy patroller, I'd wager," said Quaeryt. "He wanted to show a couple he thought were lowly Pharsis who was in charge, and he discovered that he was on the wrong end of a few blades and an angry husband."

"He claims that you assaulted a local merchant."

"The so-called local merchant came running at us with a cudgel. I took it away from him, but I never even hit him. He started yelling about how we were cursed Pharsis and the evil ones. One of the rankers quieted him with the flat of his sabre. They tied him up. The patroller came in and tried to order us out. Your squad leader was most persuasive in changing his mind."

"Did he actually threaten the patroller?"

"I don't recall anything like that. He did say something about the patrol chief not really wanting a visit from you because he'd offended Lord Bhayar's sister."

Skarpa nodded. "Your recollection matches the squad leader's. I wanted to make sure." After a moment he added, "Still say you'd make a good officer, scholar or not. We're likely to be at war with the Bovarians before long, if we're not already, and in war no one cares too much about officers who might step on the boots of merchants and High Holders. They do care whether you get the task accomplished without losing too many men. You've already proved that in Tilbor and as governor in Extela."

"I also proved that most people don't care whether a governor gets the job done, only how it affects them."

"You proved that High Holders and snotty factors think that. The men just saw that you wanted the best for everyone, not just in Extela but when lives were on the line in Tilbor."

"I just might have been fortunate in Tilbor."

"When an officer is fortunate time after time, especially when he's close enough to get wounded a few times and men and squad leaders risk their necks to save him, it's not luck."

"That's a different kind of fortune, riding with good men and squad leaders." Quaeryt gestured toward the road ahead, which curved northward in a barely perceptible arc. "This is the Great Bend?" He wanted to change the subject.

"For the next fifty milles, roughly." Skarpa smiled. "When we're through it, and heading due west, we'll be about a day away from Ferravyl."

"If it doesn't rain again."

"It always rains in the midlands here. Only questions are how long and how hard."

Quaeryt smiled.

"Squad Leader Demryn did mention one interesting thing," said Skarpa, after a long silence. "He said he offered to have the rankers wait outside the café, but you said they needed to eat. That was kind of you, but I wouldn't have expected otherwise. He also said you told them that they couldn't protect Lady Vaelora if they were outside."

"I just said that to make it easier for them to accept a good meal."

"From anyone else, I'd accept that unquestioningly. From you . . ." The commander shook his head. "Too many things you've said that seemed improbable when you said them have come to pass." One hand lifted, and he pointed to the gold insignia on his collars, a crescent moon. "Like these. And then I find out that you're actually Pharsi. I never would have thought it. Never saw a blond Pharsi, but you've got the eyes, when you look close."

"Fortunate guesses. That's all." *I really did want to make it easier for the troopers to eat.* Yet Quaeryt knew Skarpa wouldn't believe such a statement, and saying that it was so would only make it seem like he was protesting too much.

"Lord Bhayar sent you to Tilbor. He's got Pharsi blood, too. How did he know to send you?"

How are you supposed to answer that? "I don't know. I've told you what he said."

"I'm sure that is what he said. That doesn't mean it's what he meant or why he sent you. And then . . . why did he ride all the way across Telaryn—with his sister—just to marry her to you?"

"I don't think that's why he came. Not the only reason. I'd been sending him reports from the day I arrived at the Telaryn Palace."

"That's true." Skarpa fingered his chin. "Myskyl said something about you once. I'd wager it's true about Lord Bhayar as well. He said that everything you said was true, but that didn't mean it was true in the way he thought it was. I'd wager that's true of Bhayar as well."

"It's probably true of most effective rulers," Quaeryt admitted.

"You know . . . you did Bhayar a great favor in the way you cleaned up Extela."

Quaeryt had a good idea as to where Skarpa was headed, but he still asked, "Why do you say that?"

"Any halfway decent governor can finish what you started, and everyone will be more happy with him. No one will question why you were replaced, and everyone will think that wherever he puts you next is just as a favor to his sister. That's if the position looks easy. If it's hard, they'll say that he's looking for a way to get rid of a family embarrassment. Either way, no one's going to pay much attention to you, not for the right reasons, anyway. Just like Rescalyn didn't. He thought you were there so that Bhayar didn't have to travel to Tilbor and that if he watched you and intercepted your dispatches and had them copied so that he could read them, he'd be a step ahead." Skarpa turned and looked directly at Quaeryt. "You knew everything would be read, didn't you?"

"I thought it would be."

"So how did Bhayar know what was going on?"

"He didn't at first. I had to be careful in how I wrote things."

"When he got to Tilbor, he knew everything that had happened."

"He's very sharp."

"No. You're very sharp, scholar, and he's sharp enough to know it and to use you. Just like he uses his regiments."

"Good rulers know how to recognize and use the best tools."

"I think I said the same thing," replied Skarpa with a laugh.

"You did. I admit it."

"A lot of tools get broken in war, scholar. Even good ones."

"I know that." And he did. He also worried that Skarpa and the other commanders—and Myskyl—were building one imager scholar into something far greater and more important than he was. Even Vaelora might be doing that, if only because she loved him.

And all he'd been doing was trying to survive and to make things better for those who were scholars and imagers . . . and now, on top of that, to hold on to what he had with Vaelora.

After two days of following the river road along the Great Bend, Quaeryt was convinced that the only things great about it were that the land was greatly flat and that, even early in the year, the size and ferocity of both mosquitoes and red flies were even greater. His shields didn't help against the pesky insects, although attempting to use them against the pests definitely gave his shield-imaging skills a trial. That effort, he hoped, might strengthen his abilities, since he hadn't been as diligent in practicing as he might have been.

On Lundi morning, at sixth glass, Skarpa dispatched a message to Bhayar containing an estimated arrival on Meredi, late in the afternoon.

As the courier rode off, Skarpa turned in the saddle toward Quaeryt. "Now that I've given a date, sure as a full Erion in the night sky means trouble we'll run into something to delay us. Or more than one thing."

Quaeryt wasn't certain that a full Erion meant trouble, but he had already experienced too many times when committing to something inevitably invited difficulties. That had seemed particularly true in Extela, but then, that might just be because of the way things had turned out. So he just smiled and nodded.

At two quints past seventh glass, a scout rode past the outriders and pulled in alongside Skarpa. "Sir . . . there's a problem ahead."

"What's the matter?" Skarpa asked the scout who rode over and reined up.

"There's a bridge up ahead over a small river, and there's a wagon stuck somehow on the bridge. The teamster there has a pair of archers, and won't let anyone near. Says he'll fix his wheel and axle on his own. There must be fifteen wagons waiting."

Quaeryt wondered what a teamster would be carrying that required archers, but not an entire body of guards. *Spices? Silks?* Offhand, he couldn't think of much else. But why would they leave the wagon on the bridge? *So no one could flank them?*

"Probably headed to or from Amyal," said Skarpa, interrupting Quaeryt's thoughts. "That's the next town of any size. Could you tell what he was carrying?"

"No, sir. With those archers, I didn't see any point in getting too close. He was headed toward us, though."

"Shouldn't take that long if he's got spares. If he's that heavy, he ought to be carrying spares." Skarpa frowned. "That's the Myal River. It's the last river of any size entering the Aluse between here and Ferravyl."

Quaeryt cleared his throat. "Perhaps . . ."

"If you want to, be my guest." Skarpa turned in the saddle and gestured to Alusyk, commanding Third Battalion's fourth company. "Captain, take a few men and accompany Scholar Quaeryt to see if you can get these wagons moving."

"Yes, sir."

In moments, Quaeryt was riding beside the captain, with six troopers trailing them, half wondering why he had volunteered—except that there was something about the broken wagon that bothered him. His hand brushed the half-staff in the leathers, but he hoped he wouldn't need it.

The road angled more northward, away from the river, for almost half a mille before turning west again along what amounted to a levee on the north side of a series of marshes. The ground farther to the north of the road was low and swampy, and held what looked to be rice fields. After another quarter of a mille, they came to the end of the line of wagons.

"Captain, sir," called the first teamster they neared, the last one in line, with a fully loaded wagon, its contents covered with an oilcloth tarp, sacks of grain or something similar Quaeryt guessed. "Can you get them moving? I've been sitting here nigh on two quints, awaitin' for 'em to move."

"We'll see what we can do," answered Alusyk, guiding his mount to the north shoulder of the road in order to pass the waiting wagons and teams.

Quaeryt eased the mare behind the captain, and the other troopers followed him. A large farm wagon, piled high with hay from the previous fall's harvest, was the first in line, just short of the stone approach to the bridge.

The bridge over the Amyal wasn't quite what Quaeryt expected. It was a two-span structure, the spans joining in the middle, where it was supported by a stone pylon rising out of the murky river water. The spans were composed of heavy planks over timbers stretching from the stone approaches to the central pylon. Each span looked to be some ten yards long. As the scout had reported, a large high-sided and enclosed battered black wagon rested in the center of the bridge, almost directly over the center pylon.

Alusyk rode to the end of the bridge and reined up, then called out, "You need some help there?"

"I've sent two of my men back to Amyal for what we need." The man who spoke was broad-shouldered, almost massive, blond, and clean-shaven. "We're not moving until then."

"You're blocking the road in both directions," pointed out Alusyk politely.

"So?"

"So . . . these teamsters and the regiment need to get across the bridge."

"A little waiting won't hurt anyone."

Quaeryt was getting a very bad feeling about the placement of the wagon and the attitude of the man—who looked to be more of a mercenary type than a teamster. He eased the mare closer to Alusyk and murmured, "Stay here. Keep him talking. I'll start talking. If I yell 'charge,' send the others after me."

For a moment, a look of puzzlement crossed the captain's face. "Are you sure?" he asked in a low voice.

"Very sure. I'm just a scholar."

After another moment, Alusyk looked to the blond man. "Waiting is going to hurt these teamsters, and the commander won't be happy. That might end up hurting you, too. Why don't you just let us help you off the bridge?"

Quaeryt urged the mare forward as well, trying to use his knees and as little movement of the reins as possible while concentrating on strengthening his shields. "Let me help you. Surely, a poor scholar without weapons is no threat to you or your cargo."

"Now . . . don't you crowd me, scholar. Be better if you didn't."

"It might be better if you let us help you. If that regiment commander finds you're blocking his way . . ."

Quaeryt could see the two archers nocking their shafts, and he urged the mare forward. "Charge!"

The two archers fired shafts, and nocked and fired again. Quaeryt could feel one and then the other shaft impacting his shields, but he kept riding. The archers loosed more shafts, some of which hit Quaeryt's shields, and then they and the blond man scrambled off the wagon and dove off the side of the bridge. A moment later another man that Quaeryt hadn't seen dove off the bridge as well. All four began to swim downstream.

That worried Quaeryt, and he reined up short of the lead dray horse in the team, then turned to Alusyk as he neared. "We need to drag the wagon off the bridge and do it quickly. As quickly as possible."

"That will likely break the wheel and splinter the axle. That might damage the goods. I'd like to know what's in the wagon. He didn't want us any too close."

So would I. "That's the merchant's problem. We need the bridge clear. We can check the goods once the bridge is open."

One of the teamsters in the first waiting wagon volunteered to help, by taking the traces of the damaged wagon. Several others came forward, and with extra ropes and three other horses, they managed to drag the wagon with the working front wheels and two collapsed rear ones forward over the bridge whose timbers flexed more than Quaeryt would have liked and down onto the east side and then onto the shoulder.

"Unfasten the horses from the traces," Alusyk ordered the four troopers who had helped move the wagon. The other five held the mounts, including Quaeryt's mare.

Quaeryt looked from the wagon downstream toward where the Myal joined the Aluse, but he saw no sign of the swimmers. Then he looked back toward the wagon.

The captain walked around to the back of the wagon and opened the loading door. He looked inside. "They were carrying elveweed. I think it is anyway. Probably coming from the marshes around the Sud Swamp. The so-called spice factors in Ruile harvest it and sell it where they can."

Quaeryt wondered if some of the elveweed had been destined for Hyleor in Extela.

"Why would they try to stand up against us when they knew a regiment was coming?" asked Alusyk. "Just for elveweed."

"There are golds in elveweed," said Quaeryt dryly.

"Smells like something burned here." Alusyk bent over and lifted a bundle of the elveweed. He sneezed, once and then again. "Something under here . . . a steel plate."

"Get out of there. Run!" Quaeryt turned and sprinted toward the bridge.

WHUMPP!

Quaeryt felt himself being flung toward the river. Then he felt nothing.

Out of the darkness . . . there was dampness on his face. Quaeryt realized he was lying on his back looking up at scattered gray and white clouds. Between two of the clouds, he saw the partial disc of Artiema, barely visible in the bright sky. A trooper who had been kneeling beside him with a damp cloth in his hand rose and stepped back.

"Scholar . . . can you hear me?"

Quaeryt recognized Skarpa's voice, and he turned his head. Waves of dizziness washed over him, but receded. "I can hear you. See you, too." After a moment, he asked, "What about Alusyk? The others?"

"How are you?" asked Skarpa.

Quaeryt wiggled his fingers. They all seemed to move. So did his toes. He moved his arms, then his legs, then rolled onto his side. He felt dull throbbing in places all over his body, but everything seemed to work as he slowly worked himself to a sitting position. "I don't think anything's broken. I ache all over." He paused. "You didn't answer my question."

"Alusyk's dead. The wagon exploded. Something from the explosion crushed his skull. Two of the troopers are dead, and one has a broken leg. Another has gashes. Most of the blast went down. Dug a big crater in the shoulder of the road, and cracked the paving stones on that side."

"That's what it was supposed to do."

"Do what?"

"Blast through the center of the bridge and destroy or damage the center pylon so that it would take time to replace . . . or for us to find another way over the river."

"How did you know?" asked Skarpa. "Why didn't you warn the others sooner?"

"I didn't know. Not exactly. There were too many things that didn't feel right. I couldn't figure out why a wheel would break exactly in the middle of the bridge . . . or the archers . . . but when Alusyk said it smelled like something burned and there was a steel plate . . . Then I knew and I yelled for him to run. I'd wondered about all of the teamsters swimming away, too . . . How many teamsters swim?" Quaeryt slowly stood. "You said something about this being the last large river between here and Ferravyl, but that means it's the closest to Bovaria. The elveweed was for show, to explain the extra guards."

"That means Kharst is about to mount an attack . . . if he hasn't already."

Quaeryt thought about nodding, then, given the way he felt, decided against any such motion and said, "I'd wager on it."

"Are you able to ride, or should I have one of the wagons pick you up?"

"I'll ride." Quaeryt knew from experience that riding was easier than bouncing on a hard wooden wagon seat. "What about the teamsters?"

"I told the ones that were still here to cross the bridge and wait at the next turnout." Skarpa turned and strode toward his mount.

Quaeryt followed, his steps far less vigorous as he made his way to where a trooper held the mare.

Despite Skarpa's misgivings, Third Tilboran Regiment approached the east side of Ferravyl just before second glass on Meredi. By then, Quaeryt's dizziness had subsided, but his stiffness and soreness remained, so much so that he felt like a creaky old man whenever he mounted or dismounted, although he did his best not to show his discomfort. As they neared the city, and as small mean steads gave way to crowded huts and houses, Quaeryt found the air hazy and his eyes burning ever so slightly.

A major Quaeryt didn't recognize was waiting with a squad of troopers on the river side of a set of ancient stone posts flanking the point where the stone-paved highway narrowed into the brick pavement of the city.

"Commander Skarpa!"

Skarpa did not halt the column, but motioned for the major to ride up beside him.

"Major Lewyn, sir. I'm attached to Fourth Telaryn, detailed to Marshal Deucalon's staff. You and Subcommander Scholar Quaeryt are to join Lord Bhayar immediately at headquarters. Your regiment has been assigned to North Post . . ."

Quaeryt missed a few words as he considered what the major had said. *Subcommander Scholar Quaeryt . . . What does Bhayar have in mind for you?*

". . . and would like you to have your men proceed there immediately. You'll rejoin them within a glass or two. Lord Bhayar wanted me to convey that as well."

"The beginning of the north river road isn't that far from the main post," Skarpa said. "Why didn't you just wait there?"

"I was ordered out here so that you wouldn't have to be away from the regiment for long, sir. The Bovarians could attack at any time."

Skarpa turned in the saddle. "Major Meinyt to the fore! Pass it back!"

Quaeryt almost smiled. Meinyt was only riding a few yards behind them, at the head of Third Battalion, and within moments, the grizzled major pulled up beside Skarpa, easing between the commander and Major Lewyn, as if the headquarters major were insignificant.

"Yes, sir?"

"Major Meinyt, you're acting commander until my return."

"Yes, sir."

Lewyn glanced from Meinyt and back to Skarpa, but said nothing as Meinyt dropped back slightly, allowing Skarpa and Quaeryt to move out at a fast trot, leaving Major Lewyn and his troopers momentarily behind.

Lewyn had to urge his mount almost to a canter to catch up. "I didn't expect . . . You didn't give any instructions . . ."

"You said time was important, Major. You wonder why I said nothing more," said Skarpa. "Because I don't have to. Meinyt knows what to do. All my battalion leaders do."

"Yes, sir." Lewyn looked forward.

Skarpa turned toward Quaeryt and raised his eyebrows.

Quaeryt managed not to laugh, instead asking, "How many posts are there around Ferravyl?"

"The main post on the point, the South Post crossing the river and the bridge, and the North Post. There are smaller posts farther up the Vyl and the Ferrean."

From the maps he'd seen and from what he had read, Quaeryt knew that the two tributaries that joined the Aluse at Ferravyl were far smaller than either the Ruil or the Telexan, and he wondered why the border with Bovaria had developed that far west. Had it just been the way the rivers ran or that the previous rulers of Bovaria had been occupied more in dealing with Khel and Antiago . . . or the warlike nature of the Yaran rulers of Telaryn?

Quaeryt hadn't ridden more than another half mille before he found that the air smelled and even tasted metallic and the burning in his eyes was not an annoyance but uncomfortable enough that they were tearing. He knew that Ferravyl was a mill city, with the ironworks built by Chayar on the northeast side, along a canal constructed for just that purpose, and that both coal and ore came down the Ferrean on barges from the north. What he hadn't expected was that the air would be so foul, far worse than the rotten stenches off the harbor flats in Solis at low tide in midsummer. At least the rotten air in Solis hadn't burned his eyes and throat.

People in Ferravyl were used to riders in a hurry, because they scattered out of the way, unlike those in Extela, or to a lesser extent, in Solis or Nacliano. Even while riding through the center of the city, Quaeryt gained the impression that Ferravyl was a mean town, worn down for all of its prosperity, where even the brick walls of an inn under construction off the pier square looked soot-smudged for all that masons were working on the walls as Quaeryt passed.

The smoke and haze were almost gone in the area around the main post, perhaps because it was located on a low bluff jutting out from where the Ferrean joined the Aluse, a point of land that Quaeryt suspected was being whittled away year by year by the rivers, and because a solid breeze blew out of the northwest.

While Quaeryt had anticipated that the main post would be filled with troopers, especially given its four-yard-high stone walls, and even thicker siege walls on the three sides facing the two rivers, that was not obviously the case, because he initially saw only a few handfuls of rankers scattered around the stone-paved courtyard. Then he realized that the walls extended farther to the west, through a second gateway into a far larger courtyard, filled with troopers. Even so, the unrelieved grayness of paving, walls, and slate roofs created a mood of something close to grim isolated resolution.

The major reined up outside the large central structure dominating the front courtyard, three stories with a small tower extending another five yards above the west end. "Lord Bhayar is waiting within."

Quaeryt had his doubts about that. Bhayar had never waited on anyone, not in his experience.

After dismounting and handing the reins of their mounts to one of Lewyn's troopers, Skarpa and Quaeryt walked up two stone steps and through the weathered ironbound oak door and into a small rectangular hall with a large desk manned by two squad leaders.

One immediately jumped up. "Commander Skarpa? Subcommander Quaeryt? This way, sirs, if you would. Submarshal Myskyl was hoping you wouldn't be long, and I'll send a messenger to tell Lord Bhayar you've arrived."

That overwhelming deference and politeness chilled Quaeryt all the way through, and it must have bothered Skarpa as well, because when Quaeryt looked to Skarpa as they followed the graying squad leader down the narrow hallway, the commander nodded slowly.

The squad leader stopped at one door and rapped on it. "They're here, sir."

"Take them to the conference room. I'll be right there."

"This way, if you would, sirs."

The conference room was three doors down and on the other side of the hallway and contained a long table with six chairs on a side and one at the far end. Only the chair at the far end had arms.

The squad leader stood by the door, as if to say something, when Myskyl, wearing the single stars of a submarshal on his collars, hurried in, pausing just to nod to the squad leader, who stepped out without closing the door.

Myskyl looked the same as ever, gray-haired, with the faint scars across his left cheek and jaw that Quaeryt recalled. He also carried what appeared to be a rolled map. "Commander, Subcommander . . . welcome to Ferravyl." Myskyl did not look at Quaeryt, but kept his eyes on Skarpa. "Lord Bhayar will be here momentarily. How was your trip from Extela?"

"Uneventful until the Bovarian spies tried to destroy the bridge over the Myal," said Skarpa.

"Yes . . . yes. Good job in stopping them."

"That wasn't my doing. Subcommander Quaeryt and Captain Alusyk took care of that. As I noted in the report I sent along with our estimate of arrival." Skarpa's voice was cool, yet gruff.

"Yes. Subcommander Quaeryt is quite resourceful. He always has been." Myskyl glanced toward the door of the conference chamber. He quickly looked back to Skarpa.

"Unlike some officers, sir," Skarpa said, "he does not avoid danger if he deems it necessary to accomplish the task at hand."

"Many have reported that, Commander." Myskyl's voice was even, not quite flat, and he continued to avoid looking in Quaeryt's direction.

Quaeryt heard quick bootsteps on the stone floor of the corridor outside, and then a wiry man with slightly disheveled brownish black hair, wearing the green uniform of a Telaryn officer, if without insignia, stepped into the conference room and closed the door behind himself. Bhayar's dark blue eyes rested on Myskyl momentarily, then moved to Skarpa, and then to Quaeryt.

"Please sit down." Speaking in Tellan, Bhayar turned to Myskyl. "You have the maps?"

"Yes, sir." Myskyl moved to the end of the table that held the single chair and unrolled the maps, placing one on top of the other and placing a square metal weight on each corner. Then he straightened and stepped back.

Bhayar moved the chair away and stepped up before the map, waiting until the other three flanked him. "This shows Ferravyl and the surrounding area. With the fortifications on the bridge and our cabling here"—he pointed to the lines depicting the bridge across the Aluse from the middle of Ferravyl to the far side—"we can prevent the Bovarians from coming downstream, unless they wish to incur terrible losses." He smiled tightly. "They do not. So they will attempt to flank us to the north and south, with enough men so that we will be forced to move men from the city and weaken our defenses here to the point that they can destroy the bridge and use the Aluse to land forces behind us."

Quaeryt nodded slightly, waiting to see what else Bhayar had to say.

"Commander Skarpa, it is most likely that the first threat will be across the Ferrean somewhere between two and ten milles from the post here."

"Because the river is quieter there, sir?"

"That is part of the reason. The other part is that the farther north one goes, the more and more rugged the hills on the east side become. The terrain favors us, because, to take Ferravyl, which is Rex Kharst's objective, those troopers will have to march and ride back south. The longer that march, the more men they will lose before reaching the city."

"You want Third Regiment to hold the east side of the river for a distance of ten milles?" Skarpa raised his eyebrows.

"I'm optimistic, Commander. I'm not an idiot. I want you to keep small groups from crossing and to delay and cause great casualties if larger groups manage to cross. I believe they will try a north crossing first, but I do not want to commit forces there because they will see that and attack in the south. By leaving forces at the main post, ready to move, we have the best chance of repulsing their attacks with the least loss of men. While you are holding and delaying, we will be moving to reinforce you. Subcommander Quaeryt and his men may also be of some help in slowing or stopping their advance."

Quaeryt noticed that Myskyl did not even blink at that announcement.

"The subcommander will be in charge of a special group, which includes imagers and a company of troopers. While his command is independent of Third Regiment, he will report to you operationally. Is that clear?"

A wry smile flitted across Skarpa's face. "Yes, sir."

"Good." Bhayar gestured to the map again. "At present, from what we have learned and observed, Kharst's main force is located across the Ferrean and about two milles north in the town of Cleblois. There is no suitable ford or crossing there, but the piers were built to allow barges coming downstream to make their way across the main channel to the east side to dock at the old piers just north of the post here. He has four to five regiments in Cleblois, roughly half of foot and half cavalry. There are archers, but how many is uncertain He has a second, if smaller force, comprising three regiments, on the south side of the Aluse and west of the Vyl . . ." From there, Bhayar, with occasional additions by Myskyl, pointed out the possible routes of attack, and then went on to note the placement of the Telaryn troops, with three regiments south of Ferravyl, three more in Ferravyl, another deployed in companies to the south along the Vyl, and another to the north along the Ferrean, leaving Third Regiment to hold North Post, a position roughly across the river from Cleblois.

"That should give you a view of what we face." Bhayar rose. "I'll need a few moments with Subcommander Quaeryt. Commander, you can discuss any courier or dispatch schedules or other matters with Submarshal Myskyl in his study. Then you and Subcommander Quaeryt can rejoin Third Regiment."

Bhayar waited for Skarpa and Myskyl to leave the conference room before clearing his throat and continuing, switching to court-Bovarian, the language used in the palace and among intimates. "There are a few other matters we need to discuss."

Quaeryt couldn't help but be amused at the circumstances surrounding a war with Bovaria that had Bhayar speaking Bovarian to an imager with whom he had studied, and who'd been a loyal Telaryn governor, princeps, and scholar assistant. But then, that somehow fit in the chaos that seemed to surround and infuse all conflicts, at least all those with which Quaeryt had been familiar, either through study or experience.

"There are a pair of uniforms waiting for you at the front duty desk. They're tailored to fit you. They're a brownish green, rather than the lighter green of regular officers, but they're close enough that you shouldn't stand out too much. You're going to take command of a special company—five squads of troopers and as many imagers as I've been able to have rounded up."

"But . . ."

"They've been told that you're familiar with imagers and that I don't want a known imager in charge of imagers. I've also conscripted your friend Voltyr . . . as well as others from across Telaryn. None of them will be happy, but we're going to need imagers, and it's your job to make them understand that. You also need to make them effective."

"Does Kharst have imagers?" asked Quaeryt.

"It's likely, but we don't know how many. He can't have more than a few, because he's killed off most of them. Most came from Khel or the parts of Bovaria bordering Khel before he conquered it. They'd be little more than slaves."

Quaeryt wondered about that, but he wasn't about to question Bhayar. "What exactly am I supposed to do with this group?"

"Whatever you can to support Third Regiment and create disruption and chaos among the Bovarians."

"You seem to have close to equal forces, and at least half of yours are experienced in battle and well trained. Why do you need more?"

"I'll answer that in a moment. Why do you think I relieved you as governor?"

"Begging your pardon, Lord Bhayar, but that's what I'd like to know," said Quaeryt quietly.

"Oh . . . I'll tell you why. You'd have turned Montagne into a wonderfully well-governed province, and every governor and High Holder in Telaryn would have been demanding your head . . . or your replacement. Governing isn't just doing it well; it's doing it in a way where no one is truly satisfied, but no one with power is fiercely dissatisfied."

Quaeryt did not reply for several moments, thinking about the implications of what Bhayar had said. *. . . no one with power is fiercely dissatisfied . . . but that also means that those who are or will be greatly dissatisfied must not be allowed great power . . .*

"Quaeryt . . . ?" prompted Bhayar.

"I was thinking, deeply, about what you said." Quaeryt smiled tightly. "I take it that wasn't the only reason."

"No . . . Vaelora had to be checked in a way you could not. I hadn't anticipated how much you've come to love her . . ."

I was supposed to check Vaelora's desires for villas and a lifestyle you provided . . . when you insisted that I "respect" her? Quaeryt managed not to react as Bhayar continued.

". . . Besides, this way Markyl will be far more bounded than if he had succeeded Scythn directly. He was the one all the High Holders wanted to follow Scythn, you know."

"I might have guessed."

"My placing you as governor also served notice, in an indirect way, that any of them could be replaced immediately if they become too greedy. You proved you could be an effective governor, and you're far more valuable as a governor in waiting, so to speak, than an actual governor."

"Thank you," replied Quaeryt dryly. He extracted a folded sheet of paper and extended it.

"This is?" asked Bhayar as he took it.

"A copy of what I left behind for Governor Markyl, with a note that you had a copy."

Bhayar laughed. "Excellent! Excellent . . . you've just proved you make a wonderful governor in waiting." He paused. "That leads us to why you're really here. That's the problem of Bovaria itself."

"Bovaria itself?"

"Bear with me," said Bhayar. "The only port that can handle Bovarian sea trade that is even remotely close to Variana is Ephra, and it's on the north side of the River Laar, opposite Kephria, which belongs to Antiago. The Autarch has enough ships to shut down trade there anytime he'd like. In addition, all the trade that would come down the Aluse can't so long as we hold Ferravyl. That's because Kharst doesn't want his merchants to pay tariffs, and

I'm not about to let them use the Aluse to strengthen Bovaria without getting a healthy stream of golds to build up our defenses. So his traders have to use barges from the Aluse south of Variana along the Great Canal to the Laar and then go down the Laar to Ephra. That takes longer, and it costs more."

Quaeryt understood the higher costs of trading, but Bhayar had more than that in mind. "What you're saying is that Kharst wants Ferravyl so that he can eventually take Solis. Why doesn't he just take Antiago instead?"

"He'd take heavy losses, especially with all that Antiagon Fire, and he still wouldn't have direct access to a good port. The great canal is long and very narrow. It costs thousands of golds a year to maintain."

"But he can't possibly conquer Telaryn, even if he takes Ferravyl."

"Not this year or next. Perhaps not in ten years. He's thinking for the long term. If he can gain control of Ferravyl, he'll control the Aluse. Once he has that, it won't take him long to build up forces to take the grain lands from Solis to Piedryn. And then there's the iron."

"Iron?"

"Iron ore. Why do you think my predecessors fought to keep Ferravyl? The largest amounts of high grade iron ore in all Lydar lie to the northeast of Ferravyl. With control of that iron and the grain lands, it would only be a matter of time before . . ." Bhayar shrugged. "So . . . it's best we act . . ."

"You have something else in mind?"

"I have thoughts. Whether they become more than thoughts depends on how much damage we can inflict on Kharst's forces. According to Submarshal Myskyl, your very presence multiplied the losses suffered by the rebels and reduced regimental casualties comparatively. I expect you to do the same here once the Bovarians attack."

"How long do we have?"

"They could attack tomorrow . . . or next week. I wager it's sooner rather than later."

"Why did you pick me for this?"

"You're the only one that might be able to wield the imagers into a coherent force. That's always been a problem in using imagers."

Quaeryt wasn't satisfied with that answer, knowing that there had to be more. "What else?"

"There's a price for everything, Subcommander. If you don't pay it, what you get will eat you away until you're a shadow of yourself."

Quaeryt managed a smile and a nod. "There is indeed a price, one way or another." *And there's one you'll pay as well when this is all over.*

"Is there anything else you need to know from me, Quaeryt?"

"There doubtless is, but at the moment, I have no idea what it might be."

"Then I will let you and Commander Skarpa be on your way to North Post."

"Thank you, sir."

Bhayar walked to the door of the conference room and opened it, waiting for Quaeryt.

They walked out almost together.

While walking into and out of the headquarters building at the main post had loosened up some of Quaeryt's muscles, he still felt stiff and sore as he and Skarpa rode northward to try to return to Third Regiment as quickly as possible without straining their mounts.

For a time, Quaeryt said nothing at all, while he rode and mulled over what Bhayar had told him. He couldn't help but wonder if the causes of wars were as simple as the Lord of Telaryn thought. As he and Skarpa rode past a building that might have been either inn or tavern, a fragment of song drifted toward him on the acrid air, a song sung in a clear soprano to the accompaniment of a lutelin.

West of the lowlands, and near to the sea,
my true love did sing out his song to me . . .
He sang and he wept and his words sounded true,
that never the night did I think I would rue . . .

Quaeryt frowned. He'd heard that song before . . . although the words didn't seem quite the same. Then he nodded—at Jardyna in Tilbor, where the singer had also sung another song, the one clearly about the war in Tilbor . . . blaming it all on how a man and his daughter and a cousin fought, and how the singer ended up with a daughter with no father, all for naught.

He shook his head. *Is it ever that simple?* Certainly, being governor in Extela had been far more complicated than he'd thought, and he'd never thought it would be easy.

After they had ridden a bit farther, Skarpa cleared his throat. "Myskyl said your command has imagers in it." The commander's voice was neutral. "All those that Lord Bhayar could find."

"That's what Bhayar told me. I asked him why he was putting me in charge. He said they would more likely take orders from a scholar. He also hinted that I'd best find a way, if they weren't so inclined." Bhayar hadn't even hinted that, but it was true, all the same, Quaeryt felt.

"Aren't you the fortunate one."

"No more so than you," replied Quaeryt ironically.

Skarpa laughed. "I told you that you'd make a good officer."

"Apparently, someone told Bhayar, and it wasn't Myskyl."

"No. He's scared shitless of you. I don't blame him."

"Oh? What have I ever done?"

"Besides survive wounds that no one should? Besides lead troopers through ambushes and melees where most junior officers die? Besides killing close to a score with that half-staff? Besides somehow always being around when things happened that shouldn't? Besides having enough balls to face down angry High Holders and survive? And you never seem to raise your voice. You, my friend, are the kind of subcommander every marshal loves and dreads . . . and every ruler will use to his advantage. Without counting the cost to you."

Of that, Quaeryt was well aware. Bhayar would use any tool he could—Quaeryt, even his sisters—and he had. Quaeryt also suspected that Bhayar had a dual motive behind creating the imager force. He either wanted the imagers to be useful or to be expended so that he didn't have to deal with them later, and he wanted Quaeryt to use them to inflict horrendous casualties on the Bovarians. He hadn't said that, but it made perfect sense, given what Bhayar really had in mind. Not that Bhayar had ever said. He didn't have to. Quaeryt knew, and it made sense, except for the fact it was totally impossible.

Because he didn't want to address Skarpa's words, Quaeryt said, "I just hope we have some time before the Bovarians attack."

"We might. Myskyl thinks that won't happen as soon as Lord Bhayar believes."

"Why? Because they don't outnumber us sufficiently?"

Skarpa laughed. "Because there aren't that many barges available. He says there never were that many, and they haven't seen any for weeks because the factors are hiding them."

Or because Kharst gathered them together even earlier. "The rivers are too deep to ford anywhere near Ferravyl right now?"

Skarpa nodded.

"What about building a bridge to the north where it's narrow, across a gap or something in rough terrain? If we don't think it can be done there . . ."

"Once we get settled, I'll have some scouts head north and look. They can check with the regiment to the north as well. We'll need continuing patrols."

Quaeryt wondered what else they'd need that he or Skarpa hadn't even considered.

Third Regiment had just begun to stable mounts and offload wagons when Quaeryt and Skarpa rode through the gates in the stone walls of North Post.

Quaeryt had barely dismounted outside the stables when a hard-faced captain hurried toward him. From the lines in his face, and the few streaks of gray in his black hair, Quaeryt suspected he had worked his way up through the ranks . . . and not that quickly.

"Subcommander, Captain Zhelan, at your service, sir." The captain's eyes took in the scholar browns.

"My uniform was a casualty of the rebellion in Tilbor," said Quaeryt, exaggerating somewhat more than slightly, since his "uniform" had consisted of a single overlarge green Telaryn tunic. "I didn't think I needed new ones when I was made princeps and then governor of Montagne. Lord Bhayar was kind enough to provide some, but I haven't had a chance to change."

"It might be . . ."

"Yes, it might, Captain. Do we have quarters where I can change?"

"Yes, sir. If you would follow me . . ."

Quaeryt found that, on his own, he now rated senior officers' quarters, even not being a governor, although senior officers' quarters effectively meant a slightly larger room and bed, a full writing desk, and a leather armchair, and an attached washroom, which he used to wash up before stripping off his travel-worn scholar's browns and beginning to don one of the uniforms Bhayar had provided.

Quaeryt looked at the insignia, already fastened to the collars of the greenish brown undress uniform shirt—a silver crescent moon. Commanders wore a gold crescent. He shook his head and continued donning the well-tailored uniform.

Captain Zhelan was waiting, pacing almost, when Quaeryt left his quarters. "Sir?"

"Where are the imagers?"

"I had them gather in the officers' mess. They're all provisional undercaptains. They wear officers' greens, but without insignia. They're not command officers."

Quaeryt understood the unsaid "like you." He also understood the question behind the unspoken words, but did not address it. He'd see if Skarpa would quietly take Zhelan aside.

"Have they had any training in arms?"

"I've had one of my senior squad leaders work with them on using a sabre."

"And they're no longer totally hopeless?"

Zhelan offered a wry smile. "They know enough to protect themselves from the average attack and how to use it against foot without slashing their mount. Beyond that . . ."

Quaeryt understood. "Do you have a roster or a list of their names?"

"Yes, sir." Zhelan handed Quaeryt a single sheet of paper.

Quaeryt read it. There were six names.

Akoryt Korytsyn, Undercaptain
Baelthm Athemsyn, Undercaptain
Desyrk Fhortsyn, Undercaptain
Shaelyt Haelsyn, Undercaptain
Threkhyl Chylsyn, Undercaptain
Voltyr Rytersyn, Undercaptain

"The last one, sir . . . ?"

"No. I knew him in Solis, but he's no relation." Quaeryt kept his smile to himself. It didn't surprise him that Voltyr was most likely an orphan, although that was something the imager had never revealed at the Scholarium in Solis. "Do I rate a study here, or do I use my quarters?"

"You have a small study on the corridor leading from the mess to the front courtyard entrance. Your name is already in the placard there. Well . . . not your name. It says Subcommander, Third Regiment."

"Thank you. If you'd show me the way to the mess, then you can return to your men, and we'll meet again after dinner."

"Very good, sir."

Quaeryt walked down the steps from the upper level senior officers' quarters to the courtyard and then to the rear of the same building.

"Through that door, and the middle door beyond the vestibule leads directly into the mess."

"Thank you." Quaeryt nodded, then turned and entered the building.

A single imager was standing outside the mess, most likely the only one Quaeryt knew. The imager kept looking toward the side corridor that most likely led to the front courtyard entrance, the one that presumably held Quaeryt's study.

Quaeryt walked toward the man, strengthening his shields, then spoke quietly, but firmly. "Imager Voltyr."

The younger man turned, his eyes going to the insignia first. "Subcommander . . ." Voltyr's mouth opened, and he was silent for several moments before continuing. "Quaeryt. They never said . . . just that we were getting a subcommander who had combat experience and could understand the needs of imagers."

One of Bhayar's little jokes? Quaeryt almost shook his head. Bhayar's—or Myskyl's—approach had been correct, emphasizing experience and ability over the name. *A good application of the tenets of the Nameless.*

"Combat experience? You're a scholar. How . . . ?"

"I didn't have much choice. I ended up in most of the last battles, leading troops at times." *They even followed me.*

"So . . . since Bhayar found a scholar could lead troopers, he figured you could lead imagers?" Voltyr did not quite sneer.

Quaeryt image-protected authority, as he repeated the last of Voltyr's words, ". . . could lead imagers, *sir?*"

Voltyr stepped back, his gray eyes widening, and swallowed.

"Like it or not, Imager Undercaptain Voltyr, you are an officer, and I am your commander. Like it or not, Bhayar is the only ruler in all Lydar who is tolerant of those who are different, whether they be Pharsi, scholar, or imager. Like it or not, we will do what is necessary for him to prevail . . . because the alternatives are far worse. Is that clear?" Quaeryt kept his voice calm and level.

Voltyr swallowed. "Yes, sir, Subcommander."

Quaeryt smiled pleasantly. "Go on in. I'll be right behind you."

"Yes, sir." Voltyr swallowed again.

Quaeryt followed him, closing the door behind himself. There were five other men sitting around the smallest of the three mess tables. Quaeryt knew none of the undercaptains except Voltyr. One was nearly bald, with patches of gray hair above each ear, his face pallid. Another was a youth who was likely barely eighteen, if that. The other three looked to be in their late twenties or thirties. Only one of the five obviously looked to be Pharsi, at least have Pharsi blood, and that was the youth, with his honey-colored skin, black hair, and black eyes. He was the first one, besides Bhayar, to see Quaeryt, and he froze, if for just a moment, as he took in Quaeryt—and the uniform, and Quaeryt's eyes and hair, Quaeryt suspected.

"Undercaptains . . ." Quaeryt's voice was just loud enough to cut through the murmured conversation of the three men at the center of the group. He continued to project authority, absolute authority.

All five rose, swiftly, if not with military precision.

"You may be seated." Quaeryt walked to the end of the table, waiting until the six were back in their seats. Then he took the chair at the end. "I'm Subcommander Quaeryt. Among other things, I've been princeps of Tilbor and temporary governor of Montagne, sent there to restore order after the eruption destroyed part of Extela. I also served in the campaign to put down the Tilboran rebellion. Before we begin, I'd like you to introduce yourselves. While I have a roster with your names, the only one of you I have met before is Undercaptain Voltyr." He gestured to the oldest, seated immediately to his left. "We'll start with age and go around from there." Quaeryt forced himself to concentrate on each man, so that he could link names and faces.

"Baelthm, sir," replied the gray and partly bald undercaptain in a resonant deep baritone.

"Desyrk, sir." He was thirtyish, blond with limp hair and watery blue eyes.

"Akoryt, sir." The thin man's voice held a hint of supercilious condescension, and his flat brown eyes did not quite meet Quaeryt's.

"Shaelyt, sir." The youngest replied in a polite and respectful tone, even nodding his head.

"Threkhyl, sir." On closer inspection, Threkhyl might have been closer to forty, with a voice that was raspy, matching his ginger hair and beard, a beard that looked recently trimmed to military length.

"Voltyr, sir."

"Thank you." Quaeryt offered an ironic smile. "None of you volunteered for this duty, I am most certain. Neither did I. That we didn't makes no difference. I expect all of you to do your best in what will be required of you. As for why you should . . . I am going to ask you all a question. Are you not all serving as junior officers?"

"Did we have any choice . . . sir?" asked Akoryt.

"No, you didn't. Do you know how many imagers there are that are alive in Tilbor? Or Khel?"

Every face around the table looked blank, except that of Shaelyt, but who did not speak.

"Do you know how many imagers are officers among the Bovarians?"

Again, there was no answer.

"None. In fact, Kharst killed all the imagers he could find that lived in Khel while or after he conquered it, and there never were very many in Bovaria because the Bovarians don't like them."

"Sir . . . we're not exactly popular in Telaryn," volunteered Voltyr.

"No . . . imagers are not, but Lord Bhayar is the very pillar of support for imagers compared to Rex Kharst . . . and I can testify that Lord Bhayar is fair to those who support him and merciless to those who oppose him . . . and I will be the same.

"There will be a meeting of imager officers every morning. While we are here at North Post, it will be at seventh glass, until further notice. Now, unless you have any questions, I will be talking to each of you individually in my study down the hall, beginning with Baelthym . . ."

"There is one thing . . ." offered Threkhyl. "We don't have much choice, but we don't intend to put up with trooper bullshit . . . and I'll show you why."

Something jabbed against Quaeryt's shields, then dropped onto the table in pieces—several chunks of wood that had comprised a wooden arrowhead.

Threkhyl's mouth opened. "He's a frigging obdurate."

That was a term Quaeryt had never heard before, but the meaning was clear.

But before he could say anything, Akoryt demanded, "What's an obdurate?"

Desyrk nodded, as if he'd been about to ask.

"Someone that imaging doesn't affect," snorted Threkhyl.

To cut off further speculation, Quaeryt immediately interjected, "There was a reason why I was chosen, and that same reason is exactly why you will behave as officers and conduct yourselves accordingly." He stood and swept his eyes across the group. "There will also be no more of this sort of nonsense. Is that absolutely clear?"

"Yes, sir." The chorus of responses was not quite uniform, but several voices had a shaken timbre to them.

Quaeryt thought he caught the hint of a smile on the face of young Shaelyt. "Now, if you'd come with me, Baelthm?"

"Yes, sir."

The study to which Quaeryt led the older imager was small, with barely enough room for a narrow table desk with a chair behind it and two against the side wall before it. There was a single narrow window onto the courtyard. Quaeryt sat down. "Tell me about yourself."

The imager cleared his throat, then said, "I don't know as there's that much to be said, sir. I was born in Cheva and lived there all my life until Lord Bhayar's men came for me. I made my living imaging little things, spring pins, pieces to things that got broken, tiny stone flowers for the masons when they wanted something special for their building . . ."

"Have you tried imaging larger things?"

"Much larger than, say, a small dagger, sir, and my head feels like it's splitting apart. It's not as though I haven't tried . . ."

"Image me a small iron dagger. On the desk, here."

The dagger that appeared was indeed small, no longer than Quaeryt's middle finger, and with that, Baelthm was showing a sheen of perspiration on his forehead.

After a quint or so, Quaeryt sent Baelthm to fetch Desyrk, and after Quaeryt finished with him, he interviewed Akoryt, then the others, ending up with Voltyr sitting across from him in the small study.

"I've never asked before, but were you an orphan?"

"What difference . . ." Voltyr looked at Quaeryt, then stopped for a moment. "Not exactly. My grandmother raised me. She never talked about my parents. She wouldn't talk about my parents, and she insisted that my father's name was Ryter."

"When did you discover you were an imager?"

"I was around twelve, and I imaged a copper so that I could buy some fruit. It wasn't a very good copper." Voltyt smiled wryly.

When Quaeryt had no more questions, Voltyr said, "I never knew you were an obdurate."

"What point was there in revealing that?" countered Quaeryt. "You were the only imager I knew."

"But . . . can I ask . . . why you, rather than another . . . obdurate?"

"Most likely because I do understand. Scholars are facing the same problems as imagers. The locals have killed the scholars and burned the scholariums in Nacliano and Extela. They almost did the same in Tilbora . . . and likely would have if I hadn't straightened out the master scholar and scholar princeps there. Both scholars and imagers face similar problems. I'm a scholar, and Bhayar trusts me. Would you want an obdurate who understood nothing of the trials and fears imagers live with?"

"I'd guess not."

Quaeryt looked hard at Voltyr.

"No, sir."

"If you want to improve things for yourself and other imagers, we will have to work together and be as effective as possible. I'd like you to keep that in mind." Quaeryt paused. "Do you have any other questions?"

"You said that you had been princeps of Tilbor. I heard that Bhayar's youngest sister married the princeps of Tilbor." Voltyr looked at Quaeryt quizzically.

"It wasn't quite like that. He ordered us both to marry each other." Quaeryt smiled for a moment. "I'm glad he did, but I never expected it."

"She's here?"

Quaeryt shook his head. "She's in Solis. When I was dispatched here,

Bhayar had a company of troopers escort her there." He rose from behind the desk. "I'll see you at dinner."

"Yes, sir." Voltyt inclined his head and turned to leave.

Quaeryt stood there for a moment. After all the interviews, his head was filled with details, but he at least had a mental picture of all the imagers. The only one who promised trouble, day in and day out, was likely to be Threkhyl. While Akoryt had a tendency to be condescending, he was a realist at heart, as was Desyrk. Neither Voltyr nor Shaelyt would be difficult. The real problem was that Threkhyl was likely the strongest and most accomplished imager, although Shaelyt and Voltyr promised greater abilities, from what they had been able to image for him, because they hadn't appeared to be straining.

Then he stepped toward the door, waiting until Voltyr was out in the corridor before drawing a concealment around himself. Then he moved into the hallway, closing the door behind himself, so it would appear that it had been closed from inside the study. He followed Voltyr, making an effort to keep his steps quiet and not to limp, down the hall and in through the partly open mess door, taking a position beside it.

"What did he say to you?" demanded Threkhyl as Voltyr entered the mess.

"He asked about my background, how I became an imager, and asked me to image something. All the things he probably said to you. A few words about working together."

"Just like every other friggin' officer," muttered Threkhyl.

"He said he knew you before. What was he like?" asked the older Baelthm.

"He was always pleasant . . . fair . . . honest. He's changed. I mean, he's still honest and fair, I think. But he's harder . . . like he'd cut you down in an instant for disobeying . . ."

"He's an obdurate, not an imager . . ."

"He's a scholar, and he knows what it's like to worry. He told me about all the scholars that have been killed . . ."

"If something happens to him . . . just happens," offered Akoryt, "what can they do to us?"

"He's Bhayar's friend, and he's married to his sister," replied Voltyr. "How long would any of us last?"

"Frig . . ."

"You would do well not to cross him and to do as he asks," suggested Shaelyt, almost deferentially.

"Oh . . . and how would you know?" asked Threkhyl.

"He is a lost one. Lost ones make good leaders and terrible enemies. If you do not believe me, ask those who know him how many of those who have opposed him are still alive and well."

"Lost one . . . ?" murmured someone.

Surprisingly, Desyrk spoke. "Seems to me that most of you are against the subcommander just because he's in charge and you don't want to be here. Looks to me that he's been successful. Do we know that anyone else would be better?"

"Couldn't be worse," snapped Threkhyl.

"You, my friend," replied Desyrk, "have not seen enough of the world to know how much worse it could be. Until you do, don't say things like that. We've been made officers and given uniforms and food. There are much worse places to be."

"It won't last," declared Threkhyl.

"Nothing lasts," returned Desyrk, "except maybe the Nameless, and I'm not even sure of that."

"What is a 'lost one'?" asked Baelthm, looking to Shaelyt.

The young man flushed slightly, then replied, "The 'lost ones' are from the ancient times. They are like the subcommander. They have white-blond hair and black eyes. Sometimes, they are missing a hand, or they limp. Other times, they have strange powers."

"He is an obdurate," Baelthm said. "That might be a strange power."

"Do your legends say what those powers are?" asked Desyrk.

"No, save that they can sometimes call upon the powers of Erion."

"So he's a god, now?" sneered Threkhyl. "A limping god?"

"No," replied Baelthm. "He's no god. You're still alive."

"What do you—" Threkhyl pushed back his chair and jumped to his feet.

At that moment, a silver pin planted itself in the ginger-haired imager's forehead. Threkhyl grabbed it one-handed and started to frown, as if concentrating.

"Don't," snapped the older man. "I could have put that through your eye, dipped in pitricin."

"Stop being fools." Akoryt's voice dripped condescension. "I understand what Baelthm meant. You should too, Threkhyl. You don't attack gods and live. The subcommander's right about one thing. If we don't work together, we'll all end up dead. Afterward . . . that's another story."

Threkhyl tossed the pin on the table, then brushed away the tiny drop of blood on his forehead. "For now . . . for now."

"What does he want us to do?" asked Shaelyt.

"Things to win battles . . ."

". . . make life hard on the Bovarians . . ."

Quaeryt listened for a time longer before slipping away under his concealment shield. He definitely had his work cut out.

One of the imagers' comments stuck with Quaeryt, so much so that he brought it up before he and Skarpa entered the mess that evening. He did speak in a low enough voice that it was unlikely anyone else would hear. "Did Myskyl give you any idea what I'm supposed to accomplish with the imagers?"

Skarpa's words were simple, and not terribly helpful. "They don't know. They're counting on you to find a way to make the imagers more useful than they've been in the past. All imagers have done is assassination."

Quaeryt understood. Assassination was a waste of an imager's talent, at least in most cases, but Bhayar's—or Myskyl's—view left everything up to Quaeryt, which bothered him more than a little, since when everything had been left up to him in Extela, the results, so far as he and Vaelora were concerned, had been less than optimal. *But then, here you don't have to satisfy everyone immediately. You just have to get the job done and satisfy Bhayar . . . and Skarpa.*

Quaeryt moved quickly to the smaller table that held the imagers and a few other undercaptains, while Skarpa, as senior officer, took his position at the head of the main table.

Most of the conversation at the table dealt with speculation about the intent of the Bovarians and the possible venues for their likely attack. Quaeryt ventured almost nothing and listened intently.

When he left the mess that evening, more than a few questions swirled through his thoughts.

Can you even make these imagers into any sort of force? How? You don't even know what any of them can really do. In thinking about various imaging possibilities, another question came to mind, one so natural that he was amazed that he hadn't thought about it before. *If you can image things into being . . . why not out of being? Or from place to place?*

Why hadn't he considered it? Because all he'd ever seen or heard was about what imagers did in the way of creating things? Even when he'd killed people, it had been by creating something, whether water in someone's chest, bread in their windpipe, pitricin in their brains or guts . . . *Is it because we don't naturally think of the absence of something?*

He frowned. But he *had* done that. Once, anyway, and that was when he'd imaged a hole in a chunk of rock and imaged away ice to break the jam that had backed up the river. He'd just done it, but it hadn't thought about it in just that way. Nor had he considered the implications of doing that on a wider scale.

Could he train the imagers to do that? Imaging holes in barges might make it difficult for the Bovarians to cross the river.

That sounded simple enough, but Quaeryt knew that all too many things that sounded simple enough were anything but simple. He'd been practically standing on top of the place where he'd imaged a hole in the stone, and he'd barely been able to walk away without collapsing. While imaging a hole in wood should be easier than in stone, doing so from a distance was another question entirely. He also had the feeling that some of the imagers were not all that accomplished.

That's not surprising. Too many are killed before they become skilled. He also suspected that at least some of the more skilled imagers were more like him, in that they had largely managed to keep their abilities unnoticed . . . and were the least likely to have been discovered by Bhayar's men.

He decided to walk to the north end of the post, where he'd seen several trees beyond the wall, tall enough to be seen over the stone ramparts, although the walls at North Post were only about two and a half yards high, not designed to withstand a siege or even bombards, but then since the Ferrean River lay between where the Bovarians could place bombards and the walls they would be aimed at, it wasn't as though the Bovarians could batter holes in the walls and then easily charge through.

He had to walk between two stable buildings to get to the wall, but he could see the pair of trees, although he couldn't tell what kind they were, except they weren't oaks or poplars, possibly ash or elms. Both were leafed out, but with the brighter green of recent foliage. On his side of the wall, he was some ten yards from the nearest of the two. His eyes lighted on a small dead branch, hanging at an angle a yard or so higher than the top of the wall. He concentrated on a spot a yard from the end of the branch, trying to image away the wood there.

Abruptly the yard-long branch tip fluttered down and caught in the leafy branch below.

Quaeryt didn't even feel any strain. So he turned and walked back another ten yards and tried again, this time trying to lop off a section of perhaps half a yard. Again, he had no difficulty.

Rock is much harder than wood, remember?

Even at fifty yards, he didn't feel anything. At a hundred, where he could barely make out what was left of the dead branch, he did feel a momentary light-headedness. He decided against trying more for the moment, and turned and walked back southward.

When he finally entered his quarters and sat down on the end of the bed, he thought about writing Vaelora, but he decided that he needed to spend some time trying to work out how he would test the other imagers. That turned out to be harder than he'd thought, and by the time he had a plan with which he was satisfied, with notes on several sheets of paper, he was having trouble focusing his eyes on anything. That might also have been because the lamp over the desk didn't afford the best illumination, and it had been a very long day. *The letter will have to wait until tomorrow.*

He realized that, again, when he found his eyes closing as soon as he stretched out in the bed.

When he woke on Jeudi, the sky was barely turning gray, and he had a slight headache. Still, he wondered if he'd spent the night dreaming about everything he had yet to do. Could he image away wood in fine slivers?

After a moment, he looked at the corner of the table desk and concentrated.

A line of light flashed through his eyes, but the corner edge of the desk had vanished, and he could see the lighter wood that lay behind the severed section—no more than a finger's width of missing wood.

He massaged his forehead with his left hand and concentrated again. The corner was back in place.

Is it? He stepped forward to touch the wood, then noticed that a faint mist had appeared around the corner of the desk. Gingerly, he reached forward. The air around the corner was chill, but the piece he had imaged back into place was warm to the touch.

Why would that be?

He didn't have an answer, but he needed to get washed and dressed, because he had things to do before breakfast.

In less than a quint, Quaeryt was dressed and walking the post . . . until he found a narrow walled space, more than fifty yards long, that would serve his purposes. It might have once served as anything from an outside wagon storage area to who knew what. Then he located the carpentry shop, but no one was there. So he went to the kitchen and persuaded the head cook to lend him two empty flour barrels, a plank he found outside the kitchen, and a pair of rankers to carry them to one end of the courtyard, where he set the plank with each end resting on the butt of an upended barrel.

After breakfast, he gathered the imager undercaptains at one end of the mess, even while the servers were cleaning up.

"We are charged with finding ways to disrupt the Bovarian forces. Today, you—and I—are going to learn something about what your abilities truly are and how they might best be used."

"Why don't we just kill them?" asked Threkhyl.

"Sir," added Quaeryt quietly, fixing his eyes on the imager.

"Sir," added Threkhyl.

"How far away from you can you image, Undercaptain? Do you know? How large and how heavy an object can you create?"

Threkhyl looked puzzled, while, beside him, Baelthm nodded.

"If they bring archers against us, some shafts can be lofted two hundred yards, if not farther. We won't be doing much good if all we can do is slay a few hapless troopers trying to storm a wall we're standing behind. Lord Bhayar would prefer that the Bovarians never get that close. It would be even better if you could image across the river, but we might not have that choice. That's also why we have a full company of troopers assigned to us. Their task is to get us close enough to create damage. I don't know about you, but I'd prefer not to get any closer than we have to, and that means I have to know exactly what each of you can and cannot do . . . and what you may be able to do with practice. Now . . . we'll be heading out to the north end of the post." Quaeryt rose. "Follow me."

He did not look back, but he did listen intently to the words murmured behind him.

". . . don't see the purpose . . ."

". . . know what he's doing?"

Quaeryt certainly hoped so.

Once they reached the long courtyard, he walked up to where the barrels and plank were set, then took ten long paces back and half turned. "Line up even with me." He waited until they complied. "Each of you is to image a metal disk onto the plank between the barrels. You first, Shaelyt."

"Yes, sir." The Pharsi looked at the plank, and a copper disk appeared.

"Desyrk?"

The blond nodded, and a gray disk appeared beside the copper one.

"Akoryt."

A disk of a lighter gray appeared.

All six of the undercaptains managed the first trial, as well as the second—from roughly thirty yards—but Quaeryt could see a slight sheen on Baelthm's forehead as he told them to move to the end of the long and narrow courtyard.

Baelthm glanced to Quaeryt, a worried look on his face. Quaeryt stepped over closer to the older imager. "Image a very small piece of copper in the shape of a square on the left end of the plank."

"I don't know . . ."

"Try it. It can be small."

Something did indeed appear, but Baelthm looked drawn when he finished.

After all the imagers had created a piece of metal, Quaeryt walked back down to the plank, gathering up the small disks and squares of metal and setting them on one barrel butt. He turned the plank on its side, so that its widest side faced the imagers. Then he propped it in that position with small stones from the courtyard and stepped back roughly ten yards, to about where the undercaptains had begun the first exercise.

"Undercaptains, here!"

He waited until they were again lined up before speaking. "I want each of you to image a hole in the plank, one at a time. I'll tell each of you when to start."

"How are we supposed to do that?" demanded Threkhyl.

Quaeryt kept his smile to himself. He was glad he'd thought of the answer to just that question. "I could tell you many things, Undercaptain. I won't. For now. In the meantime, I would suggest you try imaging a hole full of air into the plank. Or, you could try imaging a circle out of the plank." He gestured to Baelthm. "You, first."

The older imager concentrated, but nothing happened. Finally, he said, "I can't do that."

"Shaelyt?"

A square hole two digits on a side immediately appeared.

"Good," said Quaeryt. "Desyrk?"

The blond imager managed a small circle, as did Akoryt and Voltyr. Threkhyl created a circle about the size of Shaelyt's square.

"Now we'll walk to the end of the courtyard. Those of you who managed it from the shorter distance will try again from there."

All five managed to create holes from the end of the courtyard, but when Quaeryt took them another fifty yards, only Voltyr, Threkhyl, and Shaelyt could.

"You can have a few moments to rest, and then we'll return to the courtyard, and we'll see how many disks you can create quickly, and then how many holes."

From a short distance, all six could create small disks fairly quickly, although Baelthm and Desyrk were sweating before they finished. Again, only Voltyr, Threkhyl, and Shaelyt could create more than a few holes without getting so tired they had to stop immediately.

During another short break, Quaeryt went to the carpentry shop, persuaded the chief carpenter to let him have two more planks, and carried them back to the courtyard, where he replaced the first plank with one of the two he had obtained. Then he lined up the undercaptains some twenty yards from the plank.

"This time, I want you to image a metal arrowhead into the plank, with as much force as you can muster."

"Why arrowheads?" asked Threkhyl. "Archers can do that better."

"The exercise isn't about arrowheads. It's about gauging your strength, and seeing what can be done to strengthen your abilities." Quaeryt turned to Baelthm. "You first."

As Quaeryt expected, Baelthm's near-miniature arrowhead barely stuck in the board.

"Threkhyl?" As he spoke, Quaeryt attempted to create a shield across the front of the board.

Threkhyl's heavy iron arrowhead bounced off the unseen shield, leaving the board unmarked.

"What the frig?" muttered Threkhyl.

"Try again," said Quaeryt, removing the shield.

The ginger-haired imager's second arrowhead went through the board, pulling the plank right off the top of the barrels. It dropped between the barrels and the stone wall.

"Much better!" Quaeryt's voice reflected appreciation for the effort, but also a certain pleasure in his knowing that there were ways he could continue to test his own skills without the others realizing that he was doing so. "Wait a moment. I need to reposition the plank."

After that exercise, he then had the imagers go on to other exercises and tests that he had devised.

By the time Quaeryt dismissed the six for a midday break, he was sweating himself. *Trying to train them is more work than doing it yourself.* He shook his head. The problem was that he couldn't be in seven places at once. *You just have to figure out how to use and improve what they can do, preferably before the Bovarians decide to attack.*

By the time he walked toward the mess for the evening meal on Jeudi, Quaeryt had a solid idea of which undercaptain could do what . . . and what each could not do. What he didn't know, and wouldn't for a time, was how much they would improve with training. Just from what he had observed from Shaelyt's actions, he had no doubt that he'd see more improvement from the young Pharsi. He also thought that Voltyr and Threkhyl would improve. Baelthm seemed limited in his abilities, as well as either reluctant or unable to try to learn more. As for Akoryt and Desyrk . . . he had no idea.

Is it easier for Voltyr and Shaelyt because they're younger? That might be, but he'd learned and developed skills as an adult, and he was older than both of them, considerably older than Shaelyt.

Skarpa was waiting outside the mess, well away from the door, and Quaeryt walked over to join him.

"Pain in the ass to be regimental commander, sometimes."

"Oh?" asked Quaeryt.

"I can't walk into the mess any more and talk to anyone before we eat. Not for the evening meal. I can't even be early, because . . ." He shook his head.

"Because that's the signal to serve?"

Skarpa nodded, then grinned. "Remember . . . if I'm gone . . . you're the next ranking officer. Then you get to worry about it."

Quaeryt hadn't even thought about that.

"How are those imagers coming along?"

"Not so well as I'd like. Right now . . . they'd be useless, or close to it. I'm working on training them on things that might be useful, like imaging holes in planks."

"Why . . ." Skarpa broke off. "Holes in barges holding troops?"

"That's one idea. Do you have any others where the placement or removal of small objects would make a difference?"

"Horseshoes in a cavalry charge." Skarpa shrugged. "Other than that . . . Small things don't matter as much once the fighting starts. They matter more before."

"Like supplies that don't get there because a wagon breaks an axle and holds up a whole line of wagons?"

The commander nodded.

So how can you make these imagers useful . . . as imagers? Outside of delaying or sinking troop barges, Quaeryt didn't have any ideas that would make a significant difference. "If you think of anything else, I'd appreciate it if you'd let me know."

"I will." Skarpa glanced at a captain and an undercaptain hurrying into the mess, then said, "I suppose it's time to make our appearance. Lead on, Subcommander."

Quaeryt couldn't help but grin momentarily as he walked toward the mess door.

Since the seating in the mess was not strictly by rank, except on declared "mess nights," usually Jeudi evenings, on the first, third, and fifth weeks of the month, perhaps because Skarpa wasn't one for excessive formality, rather than every Jeudi, as had been the case in Tilbora, Quaeryt ate with the imager undercaptains, most of whom doubtless would have preferred that he did not, but he felt he needed to learn what he could about them.

After a good half quint of silence mixed with pleasantries, Desyrk cleared his throat, then asked, "Sir, can you tell us why we're here? It doesn't seem like what we can do would help the other troopers much."

Quaeryt could sense the others looking to him and waiting for an answer. He offered a pleasant smile and replied, "It's not what you can do now. It's what you should be able to do. It's the same thing with new troopers. If you put them into a fight the day they became troopers, most of them would end up running or dying. They have to be trained, and so do you. The problem with being an imager anywhere today is that no one really wants you to do anything because they're afraid of what you can do. You're not encouraged to get better at imaging, and you're not pressed to improve. That's my task."

"But you're not an imager . . . sir," said Threkhyl.

"I'm a scholar, and I've studied what imagers have done. Have any of you?" Quaeryt looked at each undercaptain, one after the other. When there was no answer, he went on. "Just by watching you after less than a day, I can see that I've pressed some of you to do ways of imaging you hadn't tried or considered."

"But can we improve enough to make a difference before the Bovarians attack?" asked Akoryt.

"I don't know," admitted Quaeryt. "I hope so. Even if you don't, though, this war won't end with one battle or even a few battles. You'll learn more with each fight or battle." What he didn't say was that those who didn't might not survive to the next fight . . . and even some who did might be unfortunate anyway. "How much better you become as you train will be more important than what you can do now."

"Have you ever been wounded, Subcommander?" asked Shaelyt, his voice very respectful. "Seriously, I mean?"

"Not seriously enough to die, obviously," replied Quaeryt. "But . . . yes. Twice." Before anyone could follow up on that, he added quickly, "Commander Skarpa, I think it was, made the observation to the effect that most officers only learn by surviving their mistakes, and getting wounded is a serious mistake." He managed to deliver the words dryly enough that several of the undercaptains smiled.

He managed the rest of the meal with pleasantries, and in asking gentle questions.

While sitting there, he lifted his mug after drinking all the lager, then concentrated on refilling it with lager—by imaging. Immediately, there was lager in the mug, but the outside of the mug was chill. He took the smallest sip of the liquid. It was lager, but not terribly good lager, possibly because he knew nothing about being a brewmaster. Still, that ability would come in useful in the weeks and months ahead.

Later, after leaving the mess, Quaeryt walked out through the main gates of the post and then north for a hundred yards or so along the river road, past an area that had been largely cleared of brush and trees, except for the handful near the wall—which really should have been removed.

A task for your imagers—from a distance?

He'd have to suggest it to Skarpa. He could see that dropping branches on advancing troops might help in a fight in a woods, but he had the feeling that most cavalry commanders would try to avoid getting their troops caught in a heavily wooded area. Working on the tree would help strengthen the imagers' abilities, anyway.

Quaeryt walked down the uneven slope toward the river, avoiding boulders, and the remnants of what looked to be the foundations of a large building, perhaps a warehouse, or even a barracks. He stopped some fifteen yards from the water, where he stood on a grassy patch at the back of a small knoll a few yards above the level of the water in the marshy area beneath him. Between the marshes on the east side of the river and the sand spits beyond the reeds, the distance from where he stood to solid ground on the west bank was less than three hundred yards. Across the river, if another hundred yards upstream, he could see the wooden barge piers and behind them various structures of the town of Cleblois. The piers were empty.

How far can you image? To those piers? Quaeryt wondered if he could image out a chunk of wood from the piers.

He looked at the piers and picked out a pole fastened to and rising from a bollard at the south end of the piers. Then he concentrated.

A line of light and pain flashed through his eyes and straight to the back of his skull—or so he felt. The pain was so intense for several moments that his eyes filled with tears, and he could not even see for a time. When he could finally see again, his head was still splitting. He closed his eyes and massaged his forehead. When the pain had subsided to a dull ache, he looked across the river.

The top part of the pole was gone. Was it because he'd de-imaged it? He thought so, but the pain had blocked his vision for a time, enough so that he couldn't be absolutely certain. He'd have to try again . . . later. With that thought, he turned and walked back up the slope to the road, far more slowly than he had descended.

Once he returned to his quarters, he lay down on the bed, wider than a mere bunk, and dozed, waking abruptly in near darkness to the sound of the bells sounding the glass. He bolted into a sitting position.

How long did you sleep?

He counted four more bells, then walked to the window and looked out. There was still a haze of gray in the western sky, indicating that it wasn't that long after sunset.

Probably eighth glass. And that meant he'd slept a little over a glass.

At least his head no longer ached, and he could get on with writing the letter to Vaelora that he needed to dispatch on Vendrei, assuming he could find a courier headed to Solis.

He seated himself before the desk, with paper and the pen and inkwell he had brought from Extela, and began to write.

My dearest,

I have arrived safely in Ferravyl, although not without an adventure along the way, from which I escaped uninjured, if exhausted and momentarily strained and stiff. I do trust that your journey to Solis was less eventful, and that all is well with you . . . and Aelina.

You cannot imagine my surprise to discover, upon my arrival in Ferravyl, that Lord Bhayar had commissioned me as a subcommander. I am now in command of a special force of troopers and imagers. When I asked why, he told me that he thought that a scholar with combat experience was the best choice for the position, and he had already conveyed that to the imagers, who all rank as undercaptains. At present, their skills are not greatly suited to combat, but I am working to discover what they can do and to train them toward abilities that may be more useful against the Bovarians. I fear, given the positions in which Lord Bhayar and Rex Kharst find themselves, that the coming conflict will be anything but short and believe that any small advantage may make the difference in the eventual outcome. Whether I can develop that advantage remains to be seen. . . .

Ferravyl is perhaps the least attractive city through which I have ever passed, and the very air burns one's nostrils. That we are fighting over such a mean locale emphasizes the importance of its location.

Would that I were with you still in Extela, or even in Tilbora, but we do not yet choose where we would be. Yet I look for the days when that is so, and when we are again rejoined.

When he finished the last lines of the letter and signed it, he realized that his head was aching once more.

After letting the ink dry, he folded it, slipped it into an envelope, and sealed it, imaging the seal rather than melting wax. Even that minor bit of imaging sent a twinge through his skull.

Why? You've done more than that before. Because you've been doing it all the time while you've been carrying heavy shields?

He hoped so . . . and that his straining his imaging abilities all the time would result in more improvement.

Then he began to disrobe. Sleep would help . . . he hoped.

On Vendrei, Quaeryt added more drills to what he had begun, starting with having the imagers image small items, first while mounted and not moving, and then while riding. Following that, he required them to try to image holes in a swinging board as they rode past it, first at a distance of a few yards, next at twenty yards, fifty, and then a hundred yards. Only Threkhyl and Shaelyt could manage to create holes at the longer distance. Then he gave the undercaptain imagers a break from imaging and had one of Zhelan's squad leaders spend another glass drilling them with the sabre. After that, he worked the imagers with more imaging drills.

That evening, after eating, Quaeryt walked through a light drizzle that had begun to fall in late afternoon back down to the river, where he again attempted to image away another section of the pole affixed to a bollard at the barge piers that served Cleblois, while holding the strongest personal shields he could, slightly extended away from himself. While the effort gave him an almost-splitting headache, he could see well enough afterward to determine that he had in fact imaged away the pole.

You just have to keep stretching yourself, no matter how painful it is.

He did smile, briefly, as he made his way back to the post.

On Samedi, he repeated the drills he had conducted on Vendrei, noting that both Voltyr and Desyrk could at last create holes in the swinging board at a hundred yards, although Desyrk could only manage tiny holes, but Akoryt did create larger holes at fifty yards, and even Baelthm managed one hole at a few yards. Quaeryt said nothing as they rode past the board, just listening when they re-formed and waited for the next exercise.

". . . don't see the point . . ."

". . . just watches and makes us do what he can't . . ."

". . . waste of time . . ."

". . . no real use for any of this . . ."

Only Voltyr and Shaelyt said nothing negative, but the practice, no matter how much the undercaptains disliked it—and from their comments, most did—seemed to work at improving their imaging skills, and when Quaeryt walked back toward his quarters to wash up and for a brief respite before the evening meal, he was satisfied that they were making progress.

"Subcommander, sir!"

A ranker hurried toward him with something in his hand.

Quaeryt turned and stopped. "Yes?"

"There's a dispatch for you, sir."

On the envelope were written two names, one above the other. The upper line read, "Subcommander Quaeryt, North Post." The lower line read, "Governor Quaeryt Rytersyn." Quaeryt recognized the lower handwriting immediately.

Quaeryt smiled at the duty ranker. "Thank you very much."

"My pleasure, sir."

Quaeryt did not even inspect the missive until he was alone in his quarters. As he suspected, the seal appeared to have been heated and then replaced, suggesting that the letter had been read. But Vaelora would have known that before she ever penned what lay inside. He opened the envelope, extracted the single sheet, and began to read.

Dearest,

We have not yet even reached Solis, but I do miss you and felt that I should write to let you know that I do. I am sending this through Lord Bhayar as the most certain way to reach you, in an envelope within an envelope. Our journey from Tresrives has been swift so far, but I will be glad when it is over, although I know that you will still be traveling.

The sky has been mostly clear until this afternoon. I can see heavy clouds to the northeast. They remind me, more strongly than mere dreams, that the warmest rain can turn to ice and ice can imprison the unwary. For as you love me, please remember that in the days ahead . . .

". . . more strongly than mere dreams . . . the warmest rain . . ." he murmured. *What does she mean by that?* Then he nodded. It had to be one of her visions—that was the reference to being stronger than "mere dreams," and it was something important, because she would not have worded it the way she had. He only hoped he could recognize the situation she described.

"The warmest rain . . ." he murmured again.

After a time, he continued reading.

. . . I did so enjoy the last day at Tresrives, and your care and concern. I must also confess, I have worried too much about where we have lived rather than understood how much I need the joy of living with you . . .

Quaeryt swallowed as he read those words. *For Vaelora's sake . . . and yours . . . maybe being relieved as governor was for the best.*

Before leaving his quarters for the evening meal, he reread Vaelora's latest letter and the one she had left in his saddlebag. Then, outside the mess, as officers were hurrying to enter before the glass rang, he met Skarpa, as was getting to be their custom.

"Tomorrow is Solayi, you know," offered Skarpa, his voice even.

"That would follow," returned Quaeryt lightly, "since today is Samedi."

"We don't have a chorister . . ."

"You know that one of the reasons I was replaced as governor was that the local chorister complained that I was acting as a chorister and teaching false values in my homilies?"

"I didn't know, but I can see that some of them might complain. You always preached something of value, rather than empty sayings. The men, and some of the officers, need what you have to say." Skarpa grinned. "And since you are a subcommander, and I am a commander . . ."

Quaeryt groaned, semidramatically. "Yes, sir."

"I thought you'd see it that way." Skarpa's grin was even broader.

Quaeryt shook his head, then asked, "Have you thought any more about what the imagers might be able to do to help directly in a battle or skirmish?"

"Could they do anything against archers . . . keep the shafts from hitting troops?"

"Not now, but if you could lend me a few archers on Lundi, we could see what might be possible."

"If we're not under attack by then, you'll have some archers."

"One other thing . . ."

"Yes?"

"There are trees just beyond the north wall. I'd like to see if the imagers could remove them. They shouldn't be that close to the wall, anyway."

Skarpa smiled. "If they can do it, have them. It's one less thing to worry about."

"Thank you."

As the bells rang the glass, Skarpa turned toward the mess door. Quaeryt walked beside him, but once inside, Skarpa made his way to the head of the main table, while Quaeryt walked to the small table that had become that of the imagers.

What else can you offer as a homily? That was a question that kept intruding on his thoughts, even as he began to listen to the comments by the imager undercaptains throughout the meal.

". . . why don't the Bovarians attack?"

". . . even think they will?"

". . . no way that Lord Bhayar would spend all the golds to assemble an army here if there isn't a threat . . ."

"Or gather imagers," suggested Shaelyt.

Several of the undercaptains exchanged glances, but Voltyr was not one of them. Instead, he looked to the youngest undercaptain and gave the slightest of nods.

Are golds always the final reason why rulers act? Or are golds merely one of the ways to measure a ruler's power? As the conversation drifted to barges and flatboats and whether the Bovarians would use either to send troops against Telaryn, Quaeryt couldn't help but keep thinking about whether it was a mistake to equate golds with power, especially in the case of the ruler of a land.

Is that why the precepts of the Nameless urge one to pay a ruler what the ruler is due, but no more? Because the power of the Nameless, or any deity, does not rest in golds but in the strength of the deity's believers? Wouldn't that also be true of troopers? That the winner is the one with better arms, better training, better strategy, and greater will? Quaeryt smiled wryly. *If . . . and only if . . . that ruler has enough troops. The best of everything else doesn't matter if you're massively outnumbered, assuming, of course, that the enemy has weapons and equipment somewhere near your level.*

Still . . .

Quaeryt nodded. He could do something with the idea that resolving problems required looking at what one truly needed, not merely golds, or what "everyone said." He also needed to practice imaging better lager.

Quaeryt spent the first part of the day on Solayi thinking and writing, first about the homily he had to deliver that evening, and then about more exercises that would help develop the skills of his imagers.

Then he went to find Captain Zhelan, who was just finishing meeting with his squad leaders in a tack room in the second stable. Quaeryt stayed out of sight until the squad leaders dispersed, then stepped forward as Zhelan was about to close the door.

"A moment, if you will, Captain."

"Yes, sir." Zhelan stiffened, far more respectfully than the first time that Quaeryt had met him.

"I've been so busy trying to get the imager undercaptains into shape that I fear I've neglected meeting with you."

Zhelan smiled. "I thought that might be so."

"You were right."

"What will you be needing from us, Subcommander?"

"When the time comes, escort duty to keep the imagers from getting killed while they do what they're supposed to do. At times, it probably won't be anything except keeping watch. Other times, it's likely to be quite a bit more."

"Begging your pardon, sir . . . but what can they do? I know imagers can kill people when they're close. Some of them, anyway, but it seems to me that a blade or a quarrel or an arrow will do the same . . ."

"You're right, Captain. But there are other things that they can do. What would happen if the Bovarians launched boats and barges to bring troops across the river . . . and a number of them sank in the channel? Should it ever come to a siege, and it probably won't, what would happen if the Bovarian siege engines all failed? Those skills some of the undercaptains already have. I'm working to develop others."

Zhelan nodded slowly, then spoke again. "Sir . . . if I offended you in any way when we first met . . ."

"You were surprised that I was a scholar. That's understandable. I may be the first scholar ever to become a subcommander."

"Commander Skarpa explained . . ."

Quaeryt smiled politely, but not coolly. "The commander and I have been through quite a bit together."

"Yes, sir. He said he'd been trying to get you to take command of a unit for years."

That was a bit of an overstatement, Quaeryt knew, but he merely said, "It's probably better that I had the experience in Tilbor and Extela before it happened."

"He said you were wounded several times."

"That's right. The first time because I didn't duck quickly enough, and the second because I tried to hold the line against heavy armored cavalry just a shade longer than necessary." That also wasn't quite true, except in spirit, because he'd been holding his position to get to where he could keep Rescalyn from leading a revolt against Bhayar.

"He also said that those were just the times when you almost died."

"In battle, Captain, as you must know, almost anyone who is seriously wounded is very close to dying. I was fortunate enough to survive and to learn from it." *Of course, what you learned was the necessity of building shields strong enough so that you don't get put in such positions again.* "I hope I'm never in a position to learn that way again." Quaeryt punctuated his words with an ironic laugh.

"No, sir. None of us do."

"I don't know that I've totally answered your question, Captain, but it's the best I can do right now."

"Yes, sir. I appreciate it."

After leaving Zhelan, Quaeryt again made his way down to the river south of the post, an area slightly less uneven, and without any trees or bushes. Before long he stood on what resembled a ridge some five yards back of the point where the ground dropped to the river, a low bluff whose lip was perhaps five yards above the shallows below, where the water swirled in a slight backwater. Where he stood on the south side of the post was more than another hundred yards farther from the piers than from the grassy knoll where he had tried imaging across the river earlier. The sky had cleared, and the air was so clean that the piers of Cleblois appeared far closer than they really were.

This time, Quaeryt concentrated on trying to remove the top of a bollard, the part above the uppermost iron band. He looked at the bollard, half wondering if he dared to try to remove the iron bands as well, then focused on the bollard . . . only to find himself thrown back by a wave of blackness and freezing chill, casting him into a deeper darkness.

A deep throbbing in his skull was the first thing he noticed. The next were rocks and sharp objects gouging his back. His eyes opened, and through intermittent flashes of light he could see the sky overhead. He realized that he was sprawled on his back, looking upward. Slowly, he rolled onto his side and then rose, slightly unsteadily, to his feet.

He had to squint to make out the piers. He swallowed. The entire upper section of the bollard, including the iron band, had vanished.

Your concentration varied just a little . . . and look what happened. He winced at that thought, a reminder of what care he needed to take in imaging.

He did his best to brush the dirt and grass off his uniform before walking slowly back to the post and through the main gates. He'd no more than approached the officers' quarters when Major Meinyt hurried over.

"Sir . . . did you see what happened on the river a bit ago?"

"On the river?" Quaeryt frowned, trying to ignore the pounding in his skull.

"There was a line of ice across the entire river, and then it broke up in chunks. Never seen anything like it."

"I have to say that I didn't see it. A line of ice, you say?"

"Yes, sir. Right strange."

Quaeryt nodded. "That sounds very unusual." After a moment, he added, "Thank you for telling me."

"It couldn't be something one of your imagers was doing, could it?"

"I've never heard of something like that, but I'll certainly check on it."

"Well . . . I just thought you should know."

"Thank you." Quaeryt smiled, then turned and made his way up the stairs to his quarters, thinking.

A line of ice that broke up into chunks? Abruptly, he recalled that when he'd tried to create a shield out of fog that ice pellets had fallen around him . . . and he'd always been uncertain about one of the skirmishes in the Boran Hills, right after he'd expanded his shields to deal with pikes. Drizzle had been falling everywhere else, except there had been ice around him. And when he'd imaged lager, the mug had gotten noticeably colder in his hands.

Is there something about greater use of imaging that creates cold, even ice? Why would that be?

He considered. If one put ice in a pot over a fire or on a stove, the heat melted the ice, and if the pot got hot enough, the water turned into steam. Did imaging do the opposite? Did it actually require heat, so that when great imaging was done, things turned much colder where the imaging was accomplished? He'd wondered about that in Extela, but never followed up on it.

How could you test that? With his head still aching, he decided any testing would have to wait . . . for at least a while.

After resting a bit, Quaeryt spent more time thinking about how he might train imagers to deal with arrows in flight, as well as other drills. Before long, or so it seemed, it was time for dinner.

Later, after the meal, Quaeryt once again acted as a chorister in the small post anomen, pushing back his qualms about it, although he doubted that any local chorister would know or care about what happened inside the gates of a totally military establishment involving an officer. The problem in Extela had been as much that he'd been governor as that he'd acted as a chorister . . . and that he'd been trying to deal with too many problems at once. *Yet what were the alternatives?* He almost smiled wryly. *The problem was that you didn't want to accept alternatives that hurt the troopers or the people . . . and that resulted in High Holders and factors opposing you.*

He was almost relieved when he finally began the homily.

"Under the Nameless all evenings are good, even those with the Bovarians a few hundred yards away . . ."

Quaeryt waited for the smiles to subside, then went on. "In these times, there seems to be a preoccupation with golds, as if golds alone will resolve every problem, provide a solution to every difficulty. But golds themselves seldom solve any problem. Let us think of it in this way. If you are starving and in the middle of a desert or on a raft in the middle of the ocean, can you eat golds? Can you drink golds? If you are in a battle, can you stop a blow from a sabre with a handful of golds? Yes . . . I'd be the first to admit that, in most cases, golds will buy food or weapons, or many other things, but golds are only a tool. They are one way to obtain the necessities of life, and I'd also be among the first to admit that in most cases, having golds, or silvers, or coppers makes life far, far easier. But we should never forget that golds are a tool, a highly useful tool. How do we obtain golds? If we're honest, we work for them. Those golds represent our effort. But other things also represent effort, and those other things are sometimes more important than golds. Golds cannot buy courage . . . or discipline. Those come from within. Golds are bought by skill, courage, or determination, if not all three. For that reason all the things that golds purchase are paid for by someone's skill, courage, or determination. Gold is merely a way of making the exchange easier . . . but we tend to forget that, and concentrate on the golds . . . and not what lies behind them . . ."

When he finished, he saw Skarpa nod.

That was good . . . at least until he had to come up with another homily next Solayi.

Clang! Clang! Clang!

In the grayness after dawn and before sunrise, Quaeryt had just pulled his boots on when he heard the alarm. He immediately hurried down to the courtyard, looking for Skarpa. He found the commander with the battalion majors gathered around him . . . and listened as Skarpa issued orders.

"Barges are loaded up at Cleblois. They're likely heading toward the point. Maybe beyond. Form up your battalions on the road, spaced at quint-mille intervals. First Battalion, take position just south of the south wall. Second Battalion . . ."

Quaeryt listened as Skarpa gave his directions for spacing out the battalions, then looked to Quaeryt. "Subcommander, take action as you see fit, so long as you don't put your men directly between the enemy and a battalion about to engage the enemy."

"Yes, sir." Quaeryt turned and hurried to a less crowded section of the courtyard where he image-projected his voice. "Imagers! On the double! Mount up and form on me!"

Zhelan appeared even before Quaeryt's words died away.

"Sir?"

"The imagers will be moving to the bluff on the south side of the post. For now, form up just on the side of the road toward the river to let the other battalions move into place. Once I get the imagers mustered, we'll see what we can do with the enemy barges."

"Yes, sir."

"Imagers aren't used to discipline, and I haven't had enough time to make it clear." *Except you should have set up procedures for where to muster if an alarm were sounded and told them what to do.* Quaeryt realized that he'd taken for granted all the procedures he'd learned with the regiment, and that he hadn't instilled all of them in the imager undercaptains. *I just hope I survive learning yet another thing I should have thought out earlier.*

As he waited impatiently, about to head for the officers' quarters to roust out the imagers, if they did not appear momentarily, another thought came to him. He couldn't help but appreciate the irony that, after all the time and effort he'd spent trying to instill and improve skills, they might not even be able to use them because he'd forgotten the elementary point of telling them when to muster and where.

At that moment Shaelyt appeared, still pulling on his uniform shirt as he ran from the junior officers' quarters, followed by Voltyr and then Desyrk, then the others, although Threkhyl was bringing up the rear.

"Get your horses and mount up right here, as fast as you can! Any time an alarm sounds, this is where we assemble."

When Shaelyt returned almost immediately and mounted up, Quaeryt was relieved—the ostlers had obviously saddled the imagers' mounts, for which he was grateful. He made a mental note to thank them personally.

While it seemed as though a glass had passed, little more than a quint after the alarm had sounded, Quaeryt and the six imager undercaptains reined up on the flat just above where Quaeryt had prostrated himself on Solayi. Still in the saddle, Quaeryt peered through the grayness. The barges were still tied at the piers, except for a pilot boat with a guide rope back to the piers. Where had they come from? A stream entering the Ferrean River upstream . . . or from somewhere concealed even farther north?

From what Quaeryt could determine, the barges contained heavy foot, with spears, since he could see more than a few spear shafts and points protruding above the high sides of the nearer barges. The pilot boat moved slowly toward the middle of the river, propelled by a good twelve men at long oars that resembled sweeps more than oars. The boat then appeared to halt, holding position against the current, as if it had dropped anchor, and the men at the oars stopped stroking.

Why are they waiting? They've already lost time for surprise. At the thought of time, Quaeryt stiffened for a moment, then looked to the undercaptains. "Imagers!"

"Sir?"

"At my command, when I call out the word 'Image!' you all concentrate on putting holes in the hull of that boat in the middle of the river. Make sure you put the holes in the part of the hull below the water. They need it as a guide of some sort. If it sinks, then they'll be delayed. Stand by . . . Image!"

As he gave the command, Quaeryt concentrated on putting a pair of holes in the pilot boat, one fore and one aft. Possibly because the boat was closer, or because the hull was thinner than the bollard, or because he was feeling stronger, he did not get a headache or pains in his eyes, and not even a momentary feeling of light-headedness.

For several moments, nothing happened. The pilot boat remained stationary in the middle of the Ferrean River, the current rippling by it. Then, abruptly one of the rowers dropped his oar and began to bail with a small bucket. The others began to row, and slowly, almost imperceptibly, the pilot boat turned toward the southwest heading toward the western shore and the marshy land there. Even after moving less than a score of yards, the boat was noticeably lower in the water, and moved less with each sweep of the oars. Before long, the gunwales were awash, and several rowers jumped from the craft, trying to stay afloat and swim toward a marshy spit of land. The remaining rowers clung desperately to the largely submerged hulk that the current carried southward past the marshes and toward the point where the smaller Ferrean joined the mighty Aluse.

Quaeryt managed not to frown, for he hadn't seen any ice on the river. *Because it wasn't as far and the wood was softer?* Those kinds of questions would have to wait.

"Imagers!"

The undercaptains stiffened in the saddle.

"This time, I want holes in those barges at the piers. Again, at my command. Ready . . . image!" Quaeryt concentrated on the lead barge, imaging what he hoped was a line of holes across one side.

Light flashed across his eyes, but his head didn't throb, and there was none of the pain that had accompanied either of his efforts on recent days involving the Cleblois piers. He squinted at the piers once more, then looked to the undercaptains. Baelthm was swaying in his saddle, and Akoryt appeared pale. Threkhyl, Voltyr, and Shaelyt had sheens of perspiration on their foreheads. Desyrk was massaging his forehead with the hand that didn't hold the reins to his mount.

Quaeryt had no idea how much the others had contributed, or if any of them had been able to reach the piers at Cleblois and put holes in the barges there, but for the moment, that didn't matter. He could only hope that the effort improved their skills, and that they'd be able to offer more before long.

Again . . . there seemed to be no motion around the barges, save for one or two dockworkers walking back and forth and doing seemingly meaningless acts with the hawsers tying the barges to the piers. Despite his headache, Quaeryt frowned. There was something about the hawsers . . .

Then he noticed something even stranger. The lead barge was sinking, and not slowly. But no one leapt out. The barge just went under, and the bow hawser ripped away the entire forward cleat.

"Look at that!"

". . . didn't know we could do that . . ."

". . . did we . . . really . . . ?"

Quaeryt understood immediately—and wished he had even earlier. Certainly the signs were there. "Captain Zhelan! To me!"

Zhelan trotted over and reined up. "Sir?"

"Send a courier to Commander Skarpa. The barges and the pilot boat were decoys. The Bovarians may already have crossed the Ferrean to the north, or they may have something else in mind, but those barges were flimsy copies of real barges. That's why they didn't move, and we could sink the one at the piers so quickly and why no troops tried to swim away. There weren't any."

As Zhelan rode off to relay the message, Quaeryt turned his eyes back to the river. The waterlogged hulk that had been the pilot boat was out of sight, and the dockhands on the barge piers had moved another barge dummy forward, as if they hoped no one had noticed. Looking closely, Quaeryt could see that the dummy rode higher and that the "hull" was far from as battered as any real barge would be.

In less than a third of a quint, Zhelan and a courier rode toward Quaeryt.

"The commander requests your presence, Subcommander," announced the captain.

Quaeryt turned in the saddle. "Imagers! Hold your position here. Undercaptain Voltyr is in command until I return. Voltyr, you're to take orders from Captain Zhelan, as necessary."

"Yes, sir," replied Voltyr.

Quaeryt eased the mare around, then followed the courier back to the post and to the river side of the post, where he could see Skarpa standing just back of the ramparts, surveying the river.

Quaeryt reined up, handed the mare's reins to the courier, then dismounted. "I shouldn't be long." He hurried up the ancient stone steps to the upper level of the wall.

"Good work," said Skarpa as Quaeryt approached. "You've probably gained us a bit of time. I've sent a message to Lord Bhayar and to Marshal Deucalon. The question is whether the diversion was to keep us here while the Bovarians attack somewhere to the south, or whether they'll be attempting a crossing in force farther north. Or if they'll attempt both." Skarpa paused. "What do you think?"

"You have much more experience than I do, sir, but . . . I'd wager that there's a crossing to the north, of some sort. It might only be a company or a battalion, but they'll want to do something to keep you and some of the regiments away from Ferravyl itself. Preferably far away."

"That would be my thought. I'm sending you and the imagers north with Meinyt and Third Battalion. I don't know what you can do, but Meinyt will need any aid you can give. The Bovarian objective has to be Ferravyl and the destruction of the bridge and its fortifications and the capture of the city, and I can't hazard more than a battalion until I know where the bulk of the attack is likely to be."

That made sense to Quaeryt.

"There's one other thing. You outrank Meinyt," Skarpa said.

"I don't have his experience, and I don't intend to override him."

"That's for the best, but . . . if anything does happen to him, you will have to take over the battalion. I've already informed him of that."

"You're sending him, rather than another major, because of me." Quaeryt offered the words as a statement, not a question.

"You've ridden with him before. He understands what you can do better than do the other battalion commanders. You've worked well together before." Skarpa offered a barking laugh. "He's almost ready to go. Have your men prepared for a week."

"Yes, sir."

As Quaeryt hurried back down the stone steps of the old post, he couldn't help but worry about what awaited them to the north—and how he could best use his scarcely trained imagers. But because he also needed to thank the ostlers and their assistants, he headed for the stables first.

By midday on Lundi, riding with Meinyt some ten milles north of the post, Quaeryt was sweating heavily under a hot sun that reminded him too clearly that it was indeed full summer . . . and no longer spring.

"How far north do you think they are?" asked the major.

Quaeryt looked at the low hills beginning less than a mille ahead, hills that were especially rugged where the Ferrean had cut through them over the ages. "I'd guess another few milles at least."

Meinyt nodded, then looked at the long gentle slope from the road down to the river. "Good time and place to take a break, water the mounts, and let the scouts see what more they can find." He turned in the saddle. "Battalion! Halt!"

As the battalion came to a stop, Quaeryt rode back past Jusaph's first company, serving as vanguard, to the imagers' company, where he reined up before the undercaptains and Zhelan. "We're taking a break here to rest and water both men and mounts—and officers. Undercaptains, we'll wait until first company and Captain Zhelan have their squads watered." Quaeryt nodded to Zhelan.

"First squad! Lead off on watering!"

"Imagers, dismount. Form a circle holding your mounts." Quaeryt turned to Desyrk, who'd shown far more horsemanship than the others. "If you'd hold my mare as well, Undercaptain. That way you all can see and hear what I have to say."

"Yes, sir."

Quaeryt waited until the six had formed a rough circle, then said, "We're likely to run into Bovarian forces in the next glass or so. Major Meinyt has sent out additional scouts, and I'll let you all know once I do."

"What do you expect we can do?" demanded Threkhyl.

"Well . . ." said Quaeryt, drawing out the word, "you can certainly image holes in Bovarians if they get close enough. Soldiers aren't as tough as those boards you put holes in. I'd rather have you be able to do things like that from a greater distance, but in a war you don't always get what you want, and when you do, you're just as likely to discover that getting your wish is often worse than not getting it."

"Begging your pardon, sir . . ." offered Desyrk, "but why are we here, then?"

Quaeryt smiled. "There are a number of answers to your question, Undercaptain. The first and most important is very simple. Because Commander Skarpa is in charge, and he ordered us to be here. The second is because no one knows what we can do, and the commander wants to find out before we get into a massive battle. The third is to give you all some understanding of what happens in a fight, because for most of you, it's not like you thought it would be."

Desyrk nodded.

"Any other questions?" Quaeryt glanced around.

None of the undercaptains spoke.

"Then stand by." Quaeryt walked past Desyrk and the mare and to the river side of the road, where he surveyed the troopers walking their mounts to the water. Upstream from where the horses were being watered a detail was filling water bottles. Quaeryt wasn't about to fill his water bottle with river water. Instead, he'd imaged watered lager into it. Admittedly, what he had imaged was still poor lager, but it was better than his first attempts and far cleaner than river water.

The river itself was far narrower—less than fifty yards wide—and deeper than it was in the stretch between Cleblois and North Post, and the water ran more swiftly. That suggested to Quaeryt that the Bovarians had to have made a crossing, assuming that they had, even farther north, and perhaps even a day or two earlier.

Behind him, he could hear mutterings.

". . . didn't do anything this morning," murmured Threkhyl, "just sat on his horse and ordered us around."

"He saw what the decoys were before anyone else," countered Shaelyt.

"Looking and seeing isn't hard," replied the ginger-bearded imager. "Wager that nothing was ever that hard for the subcommander. Not since he married Bhayar's daughter, anyway."

"Would you want to have Lord Bhayar always looking at you, Threkhyl?" asked Desyrk.

"Wouldn't bother me none."

"Then you're stupider than you look," said Shaelyt quietly.

"Who are you—"

"Enough!" snapped Voltyr. "Do you want your arms broken with the subcommander's half-staff?"

"What by the Nameless do you mean?" asked Akoryt.

"I asked around," said Voltyr. "He's been in battles, a lot of them, with this battalion. He's killed so many men with that staff that no one could count them, and he's an obdurate. Just how long will you last if he decides you're not worth the trouble to keep around?"

"He is a lost one, too," added Shaelyt.

"You keep saying that. What does it matter?" asked Threkhyl.

"The lost ones are under the protection of Erion."

Quaeryt decided that the undercaptains' current conversation had continued quite long enough, and he turned and started back toward the circle of undercaptains and their mounts.

"You make him sound like some sort of god . . ." Threkhyl's voice died away.

"Time to water mounts," Quaeryt announced, moving into the circle and taking the mare's reins from Desyrk, then leading the way down toward the river, following Zhelan's last squad.

Once the undercaptains had their mounts watered and had returned to the road, Quaeryt left the mare with Desyrk again and walked forward until he saw Meinyt talking to a ranker, presumably a scout or outrider. He waited until the two were finished, then approached the major.

"Subcommander. I was about to come looking for you."

"I thought I'd save you the trouble."

"There are two battalions headed our way, according to the scouts. One of foot and one mounted. They're less than two milles ahead."

"What do you plan to do?" asked Quaeryt.

"Attack. What else? The ground south of us is so flat that we'd be at more of a disadvantage there. We can take a position on the heights just north of here." Meinyt gestured toward the low ridge ahead on the east side of the road. "That way, if they try to get by, we can attack from above. They'll be faced with a cavalry charge down on them, or they'll have to come to us . . . or to try to go around us."

Quaeryt glanced farther north, where the next ridge was even higher. "Why not the one farther north?"

"It's too exposed and the ground leading to the road is too rough. If they take it, they'll lose mounts trying to charge down on us, and they'll wear out men climbing it. With us on the lower heights, I'm wagering that they'll attack, especially if I only show their scouts two companies."

"How will you do that?" Quaeryt didn't see all that much cover.

"There's a woods below the lower heights on the back side. There's nothing like that on the northern ridge. That also gives us a way to withdraw if matters don't go as planned. I'd prefer not to retreat, but . . ." Meinyt shrugged. "If it comes to that, it would give us the ability to attack in quick thrusts to slow them down while sending word back to the commander."

"You'd rather try to inflict greater damage first, though?"

Meinyt nodded. "My men have fought recently. The Khellan War ended over two years ago, and I'd wager they have more men who've never seen battle."

"Then we should see what we can do." Quaeryt offered a smile.

Another two quints passed before the battalion finished watering mounts and re-formed on the ridge that Meinyt had selected. The two companies in plain view were first and third companies, while the forces concealed in the woods consisted of fourth company and the imager's company. Quaeryt left Zhelan in charge and remained with Meinyt, insisting on that because he needed to see how the fight developed, at least in the beginning, in order to determine how and where to use the imagers and Zhelan's men.

His initial plan was to have the imagers follow Zhelan's regular troopers, because he felt that Meinyt would need every company he could muster and because the imagers would be safer in the rear than in remaining behind and largely unprotected on the ridge.

From the position of the sun, Quaeryt judged that it was slightly before the second glass of the afternoon when the first Bovarian outriders came around the gentle curve in the road that followed the course of the river. They immediately reined up, and one turned and galloped back north. Quaeryt could just make out a haze of dust farther north, which likely indicated the position of the main Bovarian body.

For the next quint, the outriders remained where they were, but the dust haze continued to move southward until a host of riders appeared on the road. The Bovarians moved to a point just below the larger northern ridge and then halted.

Another quint passed, and then a Telaryn trooper galloped up the ridge and reined in short of Meinyt. "Sir, there's a troop of mounted circling around the east side of the large ridge there. It looks to be the size of a company."

"Thank you. Head back where you can see them and let me know whether they're going to attack on the flank or try to come up through the woods."

"Yes, sir."

Meinyt turned to Jusaph. "You may have to use two squads to keep them off us."

"We could just use one, sir."

"If the main body comes up the ridge at us, you'll need two. If we attack them, you can use one."

"Yes, sir."

Meinyt looked to Quaeryt.

"I'll send Zhelan wherever you need him. The imagers will follow."

"And you?"

"I'll be with them."

"In the van, no doubt."

"Close, but not in the first line."

Meinyt nodded, but Quaeryt knew what he was thinking, and he couldn't help thinking, *Somehow you always end up in more action than you planned. No matter what else you had in mind.*

More time passed, and then the Bovarians advanced once more, stopping less than three hundred yards from the Telaryn position.

"Let's see if they'll come to us," said Meinyt quietly.

Yet another quint passed before the scout returned.

"Sir, the Bovarian mounted company is preparing a flank attack. They're at the base of the ridge, just out of sight."

No sooner had the scout reported than the main body of the Bovarians began to move, with several mounted companies forming a wedge flanked on each side by the foot.

"Where do you think we'd be most effective?" asked Quaeryt, although he had his own ideas.

"If you can swing and hit them from the north . . ."

"We'll see what we can do." With that, Quaeryt turned the mare and rode to the north of the first two companies.

The two concealed companies were already moving out of the woods by the time Quaeryt reached Zhelan.

"Sir?" asked the captain as Quaeryt rode up beside him.

"Hold them back just a bit. Let the other company join up with the battalion. There's a Bovarian mounted company coming. We'll take their rear and then move downhill and north of their main body. The men aren't to stop when we hit the first company. We're to do what damage we can in passing. Then at the bottom of the slope, we'll re-form and try to smash the rear of the main body. Pass that to your squad leaders." Quaeryt slipped the half-staff from its leathers.

"Yes, sir."

While Zhelan barked commands, Quaeryt watched. Two squads peeled off from the north side of the battalion to meet the oncoming Bovarian mounted. Quaeryt waited until the Bovarian cavalry was well engaged, then nodded to Zhelan. "Now!"

"Charge!"

Urging the mare forward, Quaeryt strengthened his shields, but extended them only slightly from himself to cover his mount.

Less than a squad of the mounted Bovarians saw and reacted to Quaeryt's attack, and more than half of the riders in the rearmost squad went down as Zhelan and Quaeryt swept across the side of the hill.

Quaeryt edged the mare closer to the captain. He could see where the Bovarian foot was bunching up near the rear of the main body, too close to several mounted companies. He used a touch of image-projection to strengthen his voice. "Zhelan . . . the second standard—the gray and red one? Charge them right there. You take two squads after we hit there and swing more to the west before coming south. I'll take three squads and push them into the force that's fighting the rest of the battalion." Quaeryt slipped the half-staff from its leathers.

Zhelan turned in the saddle. "Squads three, four, and five, on the subcommander! One and two on me! Charge!"

Most of the Bovarian foot did not see or hear Quaeryt's force until the Telaryn mounts were within a score of yards. A handful turned, and then yelled. Others turned, but by then the three squads were almost upon them. With the momentum of the mare behind them, Quaeryt's shields flung several men sideways into others before he contracted them close to his body so that he could use the half-staff.

A footman threw up a shield, more like large buckler in size, against Quaeryt's staff, but Quaeryt just went over the top and slammed his staff into the man's skull below the back of the helmet. Then he reversed the staff and braced it against his own shields to use it as a lance on the next footman, who went down.

For the next quint or so, the battle was at close quarters, but the charge had packed the Bovarian foot against the rear of the mounted Bovarians, who were being pressed from the front by Meinyt's force.

Suddenly, the fight became a slaughter as the invaders found themselves with less and less space to move, surrounded on all sides, except the river, and being backed downhill and to the south toward the water.

Scores broke and ran for the river, flinging away shields and helmets. They were likely the fortunate ones, thought Quaeryt as he continued to wield the staff against any Bovarian within reach.

A good glass more passed before Quaeryt pulled the mare away from the continuing slaughter and rode back to the road where a squad had re-formed around the imager undercaptains.

Shaelyt's eyes were wide as he studied Quaeryt.

The subcommander could lip-read the murmured words—or most of them. ". . . lost one . . . covered in the blood of his enemies . . . son of Erion . . ." Quaeryt just didn't believe them, but it didn't suit his needs or purposes to dispute them.

"All right! Did any of you image against the Bovarians?"

"Yes, sir." Every undercaptain nodded.

Quaeryt couldn't see any overt deception. "Good. Hold here. Take out any stragglers who try to escape in this direction." He turned and rode in the direction of the Third Battalion standard, where he hoped Meinyt was—and that the major was uninjured.

As he passed the grouped imagers, he heard another comment.

". . . didn't even look back to us," muttered Threkhyl. "Could have died, for all he cared . . ."

Voltyr and Desyrk glared at the ginger-bearded imager. Shaelyt shook his head, almost sadly.

Threkhyl closed his mouth.

Still holding a staff he realized was streaked with blood, Quaeryt said nothing as he rode past them and toward the standard, guiding the mare around the Bovarian bodies that seemed to be everywhere.

Meinyt and a half squad held a position on the road overlooking the slope where the troopers were now largely disarming the Bovarian survivors—of whom there looked to be only a few hundred. Quaeryt glanced to the river, where he saw the heads of scores of swimmers either letting themselves be carried downstream or trying to reach the western shore.

Quaeryt had no more than reined up beside the major than Meinyt announced, "We need to return to North Post. The battalions we fought weren't that good. Some of the survivors say they'd only been conscripted and trained in the last few months. They were sent out to keep us occupied while the main attack goes on somewhere else."

"What were our casualties?"

"A score or two killed in the battalion. Don't know about your company. Less than a hundred wounded. We'll lose some of those. That's not bad for this kind of mess." Meinyt shook his head. "The scouts can't find any sign of any other Bovarian troops anywhere on this side of the river. Not within milles."

"So they'll be attacking Ferravyl from somewhere else now?"

"I'd guess that right after we left there was an attack on south Ferravyl, on the far side of the Aluse."

"Anything to keep us spread out."

"That's my guess."

"I'll have my company ready to go." Quaeryt paused. "Is there anything else I should know?"

"Only that this is going to be a bloody mess. But you already knew that."

Quaeryt did, as did every man and officer that had come out of the Tilboran revolt.

Third Battalion—and some three hundred Bovarian captives—reached the gates of North Post just before seventh glass on Lundi night. Zhelan had reported eleven deaths and twenty-two wounded, three seriously. In both the battalion and in Quaeryt's command men and mounts were exhausted, and none of the imager undercaptains looked particularly pleased. That might have been partly due to the fact that they'd missed the evening meal and had to rely on travel rations of dried meat, hard cheese, and harder biscuits.

The first officer to reach Meinyt and Quaeryt was Major Fhaen. "Commander Skarpa is at the main post. He departed as soon as he received your dispatch, Major. He left word that you were in command in his absence, Subcommander."

With the hope that you don't do anything stupid. "Thank you. Has there been anything happening across the river since he left?"

"No, sir."

"Do we have word of any attacks elsewhere?" Quaeryt pressed.

"Not yet, sir."

"Once we dismount and deal with mounts and gear, I'll be on the upper west wall, checking the river, if anyone needs to find me."

"Yes, sir."

In less than a quint Quaeryt and Meinyt were looking out from the old stone ramparts at the river, seemingly peaceful under the orangish light of the setting sun.

"What's the weakest point of the defenses of Ferravyl?" Quaeryt finally asked.

"Where we are here is the weakest point. If the Bovarians cross the river to the north, and get beyond where we stopped them, there are a score of ways to attack the city. Three regiments couldn't cover the ways they could come. Doesn't make sense that they sent two weak battalions."

Quaeryt frowned. "Maybe that's not the right question. What is the key to holding Ferravyl . . ." He stopped. "No. That's not right, either. What does Kharst want? Really want? He wants unfettered use of the Aluse all the way to the sea. If he gets it, in time he can dominate Telaryn. What keeps him from that?"

"The Narrows Bridge," replied Meinyt.

Quaeryt had never seen the bridge, only heard and read about it. "How narrow is the river there?"

"Can't be much more than fifty yards in the channel. Maybe another twenty or so on each side in the shallows, but the water there is barely head-high. Swift, though."

"How many spans?"

"Four, as I recall. But you can't take a boat under the end ones. Well . . . maybe a shallow draft flatboat or a small rowboat."

Quaeryt looked back toward the Ferrean River without really seeing it. "Skarpa and Deucalon have likely already thought of this, but why did the Bovarians use flimsy copies of barges, if they were just going to sit at the piers at Cleblois? Why weren't there plenty of real barges around? Especially if they weren't going to be damaged?"

Meinyt frowned, but did not answer.

"I'd guess," Quaeryt said slowly, "that's because they have another use for those barges, and one that's far more destructive."

"They're going to fill them with powder and iron and send them against the Narrows Bridge? To try to take out the bridge?"

"All they need is to take out enough that it would take months to rebuild the center part, and then they'll bring all their forces across the Vyl and take all the Telaryn lands on the south side of the span. Without the bridge, Lord Bhayar would have problems getting his men across the river, especially under fire, and it would be impossible to rebuild it if the Bovarians held the south side. Commander Skarpa and Marshal Deucalon likely know that, but I wonder if they've thought about the barges. It wouldn't hurt to send a dispatch off immediately."

"No, sir, it wouldn't." Meinyt looked to the stone steps down to the courtyard, as if suggesting that Quaeryt ought to draft the message immediately.

"Still . . . I can't help but ask why the Bovarians haven't already put that into action."

"I'm no strategist," offered Meinyt, "but I know one thing."

Quaeryt waited.

"Too many marshals either attack too soon or wait too long. When you attack matters most. They may be waiting to hear what happened with us in the north, instead of using those barges now."

"Let's hope so." Quaeryt turned and hurried down the steps to the courtyard and then across to the building holding the commander's study.

There, he immediately drafted a message and dispatched it. Then he returned to the west wall, alone, and studied the river again, thinking.

What could he and the imagers do against barges loaded with explosives?

The immediate answer to the question was to image something flaming into the explosives.

But can you even do that, especially when great imaging effort creates chill and ice? He paused. *There's only one way to find out.*

He turned to face the river, about to image a flaming wick in oil. He did not, as another thought occurred to him. If he tried to image a lit candle or a wick into a bag of powder or a cannon shell, wouldn't the powder just suffocate the flame? Even before it could touch off the powder?

He glanced at the bombard at the end of the wall, then walked down to the armory.

"Sir?" asked the duty squad leader.

"Do you have any cannon powder here?"

"Not any I'd want to use, sir. The bombards haven't been fired in years. The marshal said we have to keep some powder on hand." The squad leader shook his head.

"I need a bit for the imagers. A small bag to begin with."

"Sir . . . ?"

"If you please, Squad Leader. If something happens, it's my fault, not yours."

The squad leader looked to the young ranker standing in the archway. The young man swallowed. "I heard that, sir. Please be careful."

The squad leader did not quite sigh. "This way, then, sir, and watch your step."

Quaeryt followed the bearded and grizzled armorer back through the shop, past grindstones and workbenches to a narrow stone staircase with an ironbound door at the bottom. When he reached the bottom, the squad leader lifted a key ring from his belt and inserted a large key, then turned it. The door did open smoothly, revealing a largely empty magazine chamber lit entirely by green glass prisms set in the ceiling and funneling light from the floor above, providing but limited faint illumination, since there were but few lamps lit.

The squad leader picked up a cloth bag from a wall peg and walked to the back of the magazine where stood two kegs. He eased open the end of the nearer keg with a wooden wedge and a wooden mallet, then used a wooden scoop to ladle the power into the bag.

"That be enough, sir?"

"That will be just about what I need."

"It isn't clumping. Ought to be all right if you take care."

"Thank you."

After the armorer closed the keg and they retraced their steps to the upper level, with the bag of powder in hand, Quaeryt left the armory. He walked across the main courtyard and then to the north, heading for the narrow auxiliary courtyard where he'd conducted some of the earlier imager training.

He glanced to the wall, noting that the trees were still there barely visible against the stars. *Never had the time to get around to dealing with them.* That was like so much of his life recently.

When he reached the narrow courtyard, he set the bag of powder gently down on a dry paving stone, and then stepped several paces away. First, he concentrated on imaging a tiny piece of iron, a quarter the size of a gold piece, making it red-hot. The small chunk of iron appeared, and Quaeryt lowered his fingers almost to touching the metal. He could definitely feel the heat.

Leaving the iron on the stone pavement, he retrieved the bag of powder and walked down to the north end of the courtyard, where he carefully poured out a small pile of powder. Then, taking the bag with him, he walked back more than thirty yards. Since the powder wasn't confined, if the red-hot iron did ignite the power, it should burn, but not explode violently.

He concentrated on imaging another red-hot piece of iron, this time into the middle of the small pile of cannon powder.

Almost instantly, a flash appeared, higher than Quaeryt expected, followed by a haze of smoke, barely visible in the light of the stars and little else.

Good thing you were careful.

Quaeryt then picked up the powder bag and walked back to the north end of the courtyard. Avoiding the place where he'd placed the first pile of powder, he poured out a smaller pile of powder and then retreated with the powder bag, setting it down on the stone pavement again and stepping away from it before he began to image. The second time, he imaged a piece of red-hot iron the thickness of a knitting needle, but less than half the width of a fingernail.

Again, the powder flared, and the acrid smell of burned powder drifted toward Quaeryt.

The third time he tried with an even smaller piece, and while that also ignited the powder, he had the feeling that the smaller needle-like section was about as small as would work reliably. A fourth attempt with an even smaller needle-like piece failed, but a fifth attempt with just a slightly larger needle piece did not.

But was that because of the way you felt?

He shook his head. One way or the other, most, if not all, of the undercaptains should be able to image the amount of iron required.

But can they do it and have it red-hot?

He didn't have an answer to that question.

He imaged a larger piece of red-hot iron into the remaining powder, which he left in the bag. The powder burned, but the flash did not seem that much different from the earlier efforts.

In the darkness of a cloudless sky, lit but dimly by partial crescents of both Artiema and Erion, he collected several of the small pieces of iron he had used to flash the powder, then made his way back toward his quarters, worrying about whether the Bovarians would attempt to destroy the Narrows Bridge that night. Then he smiled wryly. It might happen in the early morning, but it wouldn't happen at night, not when there wasn't enough light to guide such barges against the bridge piers.

Still . . . he hoped Meinyt was right and that the Bovarians were being too cautious.

72

As on Lundi morning, the alarm chimes rang again on Mardi . . . except they didn't wake Quaeryt, because one of the duty rankers had rapped vigorously on his quarters door two quints earlier, informing him that all of Third Regiment and the imagers had been ordered to form up and ride to the north approach to the Narrows Bridge as soon as possible.

Quaeryt was waiting for the imager undercaptains in the courtyard. Before he had left his quarters, he'd made certain he had the small iron pieces in a bag tucked into his saddlebags. This time the undercaptains all appeared relatively quickly, then proceeded to saddle their mounts and return in a short enough time that they did not delay the regiment's departure. Quaeryt rode near the front of the column with Skarpa. The sky was covered with high featureless clouds, and although it was before sunrise, he had the feeling that the day would be hot and muggy, even if the sun didn't break through the overcast.

Again, on the ride through the city, Quaeryt's eyes began to burn from the smoke and stench of the ironworks, possibly because the light wind was out of the north.

When the regiment halted on the stone-paved approach to the bridge, an undercaptain quickly rode forward. "Commander, Subcommander, Marshal Deucalon and Lord Bhayar await you on the north parapet."

Parapet—on a bridge?

Quaeryt looked in the direction of the undercaptain's gesture. There was a walled structure ahead and to his right, attached to the west end of the bridge. The low stone wall that extended the entire length of the west side of the bridge roadway curved into the wall of the stone structure toward which the squad leader pointed. Although Quaeryt couldn't be certain, from what he could see, he gained the impression that the structure had been built almost to the edge of the cliff that formed the north bank of the Aluse just west of the bridge. Belatedly, he realized that the entire long and connected set of structures comprised South Post.

Quaeryt and Skarpa followed the undercaptain through an iron gate that was fastened open with chains and into a courtyard. A ranker was waiting to hold their mounts.

"The steps to your right, sirs," offered the undercaptain.

"Thank you," replied Quaeryt, almost in unison with Skarpa.

As soon as he reached the top of the stone steps, which opened onto a walled parapet, Quaeryt immediately looked westward. There were no signs of any barges or other river craft. So, as he turned toward the raised stone platform at the back of the walkway behind the parapet wall, where Bhayar and several senior officers waited, he took a moment to study the bridge's construction and its position. Over time, the river had cut through a ridge of grayish stone, leaving the sheer cliff over which the long and narrow fortress was perched. Each end of the bridge was anchored in that stone, although the cliff on the southern side was lower, and that had necessitated the building of a stone-walled structure to raise the southern approach to the same level as that of the north. The other aspect of the bridge's construction that struck Quaeryt immediately was that the central pylon was not centered. Then he realized that it had been built on what remained of stony isle in the middle of the narrows—and that the isle was possibly the only thing that had made the bridge feasible.

Heavy cables and nets were set in place so that they almost reached the surface of the river, leaving less than a yard between the base of the nets and the water, but Quaeryt could also see that cables attached to the bottom of the nets ran to winches on the bridge itself so that the nets could be raised and lowered as necessary.

"Quaeryt . . ." murmured Skarpa.

"I needed a quick look. I've never been here before," returned Quaeryt in a low voice, turning directly toward Bhayar, who, with an officer in the uniform of a marshal, presumably Deucalon, had stepped down from the platform. When Quaeryt was several yards from the Lord of Telaryn, he stopped and inclined his head. "Lord."

His single word was echoed by Skarpa.

"I don't see any barges, Subcommander," said Bhayar evenly.

"I believe my dispatch only mentioned the possibility and suggested that you might already have considered that," replied Quaeryt.

"I had. Marshal Deucalon"—and with the mention of the marshal, Bhayar inclined his head to the slender, if wiry, gray-haired officer standing beside him—"thought it a possibility also. But he believed that the Bovarians would first attack all points of weakness before attempting a direct assault on the bridge. We have positioned cannon on the solid stone at the end of each approach to the bridge. They will attempt to sink any vessels approaching the bridge. They likely will not succeed in sinking all of them." Bhayar looked directly at Quaeryt. "Should the Bovarians launch barges filled with explosives at the bridge, can your imagers do anything to stop the barges that the cannon cannot sink before they strike the bridge piers and supports?"

"We can likely stop some of them, sir."

"If you can stop some," asked Deucalon, in an edged voice that Quaeryt found grating, "why not all of them?"

"The greater the distance from the imager to the barge, the harder it will be. Imaging can take great effort. I have only six imagers. If the Bovarians have scores of barges loaded with explosives that are all coming at the same time . . ." Quaeryt shrugged. "I suppose it's like a very good battalion. That battalion will likely prevail against one or two or three less able battalions. It's unlikely to prevail against three regiments."

The marshal frowned.

"That makes sense to me," replied Bhayar. "I don't like the idea that some may still strike the bridge, but anything that reduces the chance of damage will be helpful. Where would you place your imagers?"

"Most likely up here, sir. But I don't know where the channel runs, sir. I'd not wish to commit definitely until I know."

"Barges don't have enough draft for it to matter," said Deucalon. "There aren't any shallows in the Narrows."

"That's true, but the current runs faster in the main channel." Quaeryt understood Deucalon's point, but from the marshal's first words, the senior officer had annoyed him. "That affects how much time an imager has, and the main target will be the center pylon."

"You think so, Subcommander?"

"If they can bring down the center pylon, that will make repair the most time-consuming and difficult. It will also allow them to sail past and make it most difficult for you to stop barges carrying troops or goods in the future."

Before Deucalon could speak, Bhayar did. "The subcommander spent considerable time at sea, Marshal. He knows vessels as well as imagers and other scholarly matters."

"Major Ghesal knows the channel. I'll have him brief you." Deucalon was not quite dismissive. He turned and gestured to an undercaptain. "Summon Major Ghesal."

Quaeryt said quickly, "What I don't know is how they will detonate the powder at the right time. Would the crew just light fuses, and dive overboard, with the tiller roped in place?"

"That's most likely," admitted Deucalon. "They've got small boats. We've seen some of them."

"I take it that you have some other indications that a barge attack is likely," Quaeryt offered politely.

"Our spies have reported that there are more than a score of heavy barges upstream. They are moderately laden, and their cargo is covered with oilcloth waterproofs. Also, brimstone has become extremely dear in recent months." Bhayar smiled. "Last night there was a fire, and then an explosion on the Vyl, just upstream of where it joins the Aluse."

"There are also reports of more than two regiments crossing the Vyl well to the south," added Deucalon sourly. "There are four regiments on the west side of the Vyl." He looked to Skarpa. "Once we determine what attack is most imminent, Third Regiment will be sent to block or delay the advance of the southernmost Bovarian forces. We'll be leaving other regiments closer to the city until we know the disposition of the Bovarian troops."

Skarpa merely acknowledged the situation. "Yes, sir. We'll stand by."

Deucalon half turned away, then turned back. "What do you plan, Subcommander?"

"I'll bring the imagers here, and we'll walk to the best position, depending on what the major tells me."

"You can stable your mounts below," Bhayar said quietly. "That way, they'll be close at hand if you need to move."

"Thank you, sir."

Quaeryt waited until Deucalon was farther away. "I take it you don't have much faith in the cannon."

"I have great faith in the cannon. I have little faith in the cannoneers. There was no time to send word to Solis to obtain a truly experienced officer or squad leader. The cannon have been fired often enough, but not against moving targets."

Quaeryt nodded. Bhayar had never built a navy, and there were only two Telaryn warships worthy of the name. "That's why the cannon aren't on the bridge itself?"

"Would you put powder and shell on the bridge?" asked Bhayar dryly.

Quaeryt didn't need to reply to that question.

"I need to meet with the other commanders now," Bhayar went on. "I'll check with you later." He turned and walked toward the steps down to the courtyard, accompanied by Deucalon, and followed by two undercaptains and a major, none of whom had said a word.

Quaeryt looked to Skarpa, then shrugged.

Skarpa grinned, and then the two headed for the steps.

At the bottom, the commander looked to Quaeryt. "Do you think what you plan will really work?"

"It will work," predicted Quaeryt. "The question is whether it will work well enough."

Skarpa laughed. "You've been with Meinyt too much. You sound more and more like a grizzled old major every day."

"Better that than a young scholar."

"You were never young. Inexperienced, maybe, but not young."

Quaeryt wasn't sure he agreed with Skarpa about that, especially after what he'd learned that he didn't know in Extela, but he didn't dispute the commander. Instead, he took the mare's reins from the waiting ranker, and the two of them rode back to the regiment.

Less than a quint later, Quaeryt and the undercaptains were back in the same courtyard, turning their mounts over to the duty ostlers. After he dismounted, Quaeryt removed the cloth bag from his saddlebags and took it with him as he led them back up to the north parapet.

As Deucalon had promised, an officer was waiting.

"Subcommander, I'm Major Ghesal. Marshal Deucalon left word that you had some questions about the channel."

"I do. If you'd tell me what you can and where it gets closest to either bank . . ."

"I'll do what I can, sir. The rivers change some every day . . ."

Quaeryt listened as Ghesal explained, especially when he began to describe the flow closer to the bridge.

". . . the Ferrean's bigger and got a stronger flow, and so the channel's more to the south after they meet, but all that water pushes off the stone there"—the major pointed—"and it swings back more toward the middle so that, just about opposite the west end of the parapet, it's almost straight west of the isle pylon. There used to be more of an upstream point to the isle, but two years ago . . . think it was two, we had a hard winter, and the river froze there. When it thawed, a whole lot of rock crumbled into the Aluse. The west part of the isle ends no more than five, six yards west of the base of the pylon. It's mostly underwater. It used to be ten, twelve . . ."

"So a barge could run up on the stone and hit the pylon?" asked Quaeryt.

"It's possible. But the isle's not much wider than the base of the pylon. Sharp enough to rip the bottom out of a boat. I saw that happen years back."

Ripping the bottom out of a barge wasn't going to do much to help the imagers, Quaeryt thought. That would just ground the barge right below the pylon.

Three rankers appeared with an array of poles and a roll of canvas. While the major continued with his explanations and answers to Quaeryt's questions, the men assembled a framework at the back of the parapet and then tied the cloth to the top of the framework, creating an awning of sorts, similar to the one over the raised platform from which Bhayar had earlier observed the river.

The squad leader in charge eased his way over to Quaeryt. "That's to give your officers shade, sir, while they wait."

"Thank you."

When the major finished, Quaeryt thanked him, waited until he departed, then turned to the imagers. "You may be wondering why I was asking about the river flows and the channels. It appears as though the Bovarians will mount at attack on the Narrows Bridge here. They're bringing up troops from the south, and they will likely send barges filled with powder and iron or metal fragments downriver against the bridge itself. There are cannon positioned on the approach ways to the bridge. They will attempt to sink those barges at greater range." As Quaeryt thought about it, he realized another reason why the imagers were necessary. Given the height of the approaches and the bridge itself, the cannon couldn't be trained on the river close to the bridge itself. "Our task will be to stop as many of the barges that get past the cannon as possible."

"Sir . . ." began Threkhyl.

Quaeryt looked hard at the undercaptain. "I'm not asking you to stop a barge. And putting holes in the barge likely won't help much, because by the time a barge is close enough for you to do that, it will reach the bridge before it sinks. But . . . there is an imaging way of dealing with the barges." He extracted one of the small pieces of iron from the bag he held, the larger needle-like fragment. "Most of you have seen a smith at work, have you not?"

"Yes, sir," came the reply. Only Baelthm did not answer.

"Your task will be to image small pieces of iron into the kegs and bags of powder on the barges. But . . . you are to image them as red-hot, the way they would be if a smith had forged them."

"Why not image a lit candle?" asked Akoryt.

"Because the powder would smother it before the flame could heat it. Haven't you ever put out a candle with your fingertips? You do it quickly, and your fingers don't even get warm. That's what would happen to your lit candle. The powder will smother it. Red-hot iron will set off powder."

"How do you know this?" asked Threkhyl.

"Because I tossed red-hot iron into powder," replied Quaeryt. "I don't advise standing close and doing that."

There were no other questions.

A glass passed, and another, and Quaeryt and all the undercaptains were sweating, despite standing under the canvas awning. Finally, a ranker appeared with rations and water. Nearly another glass passed before Quaeryt saw a dark blotch on the water to the west, and then another one, and then more.

Bhayar and Deucalon knew more than they bothered to tell me. But then, he knew more than he'd chosen to tell them.

In less than two quints, more than a score of barges filled the river, each towed roughly to midriver by boats powered by rowers. During that same time period, the crews manning the bridge winches had raised the nets so that they were a good six or seven yards above the water.

As the current carried the barges downriver, Quaeryt could see that in the stern of each barge was a raised platform with a man standing on it and a tiller to a long rudder. Both platforms and tillers had to have been added.

"Undercaptains! To the parapet!" Quaeryt ordered.

Once they had lined up, Quaeryt stood at the eastern end of the line they formed.

Bhayar appeared at Quaeryt's shoulder. "What do you think?"

"I wonder how reliable those steersmen will be."

Bhayar shrugged. "I imagine the men steering the barges have been paid extra golds, most likely at least partly in advance. I'd also judge that they will have to light a fuse and fasten the tiller in place and then jump overboard. I'd also wager that those who are successful, if they survive, will get more golds. Bovaria is a large land, and finding twenty men who will take great risks for golds is not impossible."

"And paying large amounts to a few men is far cheaper than losing hundreds or thousands of men in an assault on fortifications," added Quaeryt.

Bhayar nodded without speaking. After a moment he moved away, back to the raised stone platform in the middle of the parapet, where Deucalon remained, a sour expression on his face, with several undercaptains, captains, and majors flanking them.

Just as Major Ghesal had predicted, once the leading barge reached the point where the waters of the Ferrean joined the Aluse, the barge swung toward the southern side of the river, and after traveling more than a hundred yards, eased back toward the middle of the river.

Thwump!

The sound of the cannon jolted Quaeryt, but he looked to the river. The cannonball struck the water a good fifty yards aft of the first barge, and well short of the second one.

". . . what are they aiming at?" demanded Threkhyl.

". . . not as easy as you think," murmured someone.

Desyrk, Quaeryt thought. "Don't even try to image the iron into one of the barges until it's abreast of us. Don't all of you try to image into the same barge. Threkhyl . . . you take the first barge, but not until I give the order. Voltyr, you take the second, and Shaelyt, the third . . . If one of you is having trouble with a given barge, I'll direct another imager to help."

Two more cannon reports echoed between the stone walls of the Narrows, but neither shell was anywhere close to the first barge. Yet another shell splashed into the dark water short of the first barge, and another behind it. The next shell hit beside the barge, spraying a sheet of water over the front section, but apparently doing little damage.

Quaeryt studied the first barge as it neared a point even with the west end of the parapet. The steersman was lashing the tiller in position, and the barge looked to be positioned directly at the tiny stone isle from which the central pylon rose. Then he bent down for several moments, then dived off the rear of the barge. After a moment, he bobbed up and began to swim toward the south side of the river, awkwardly. Quaeryt noted two white ovals under each arm.

Bladders . . . filled with air. He returned his concentration to the first barge.

Right after it came abreast of the western end of the parapet where Quaeryt had stationed the imagers, Quaeryt ordered, "Threkhyl! The first barge! Image now."

He watched as Threkhyl concentrated . . . and kept concentrating. Then, the oilcloth tarps covering the cargo area shivered . . . and exploded. Fragments flew everywhere, and spray and smoke obscured the spot where the barge had been. For several moments Quaeryt couldn't determine how the barge had fared.

Then he saw that it had broken into two pieces, with the aft section clearly sinking, but the forward part remained floating, and a section appeared to be burning.

Bitumen-treated?

The cannoneers had shifted fire to the second and third barges, presumably the crew on one end of the bridge targeting one, and the crew on the other end aiming at the other.

While the next two barges weren't that close together, Quaeryt worried because the remainder of the barges were far more closely clustered.

"Voltyr, take the second barge!" Quaeryt ordered.

Voltyr concentrated, but nothing happened—except that the cannoneers finally successfully targeted the third barge, which exploded in a hail of fire and fragments. Yet the second barge was already past the middle of the parapet, and the tillerman had fastened the rudder lever and bent to light the fuse. The Bovarian straightened and then jumped off the barge, heading toward the southern pier that rose out of comparatively shallow water. Even so, if the pier went . . .

Quaeryt imaged two small chunks of red-hot iron, and then a third.

A flash of light-headedness followed. *Somehow imaging iron over water takes more effort.* Another aspect of imaging that he hadn't known or counted on.

He watched the second barge, then took a deep breath as it exploded—before he looked back upriver, only to see three more barges, almost abreast of each other, but separated enough that the explosion of one wouldn't trigger the explosion of another. Gouts of water sprouted across the river, but none struck the next group of barges. Another round of shells was equally ineffective, except one cannonball struck close enough to the middle barge to send spray over the Bovarian guiding it.

"Shaelyt! Try for the barge on the far side."

"Yes, sir."

"Desyrk . . . the middle one, and Akoryt, the nearest to us."

"Yes, sir."

Quaeryt turned to the oldest imager. Baelthm was actually shaking. "Don't worry, the explosions won't reach us here." *Not unless it's a misaimed shell from our own cannon crews.* "I want you to be ready to deal with any of the next barges that come close to this side of the river."

"Can I try hot silver? Silver's easier for me than iron."

"You can certainly try it first. All I care about is getting metal hot enough to fire the powder."

"Yes, sir."

Quaeryt turned his attention to the raft of barges. The one closest to the bridge was the one nearest the south side of the river. He glanced to Shaelyt, intently looking out at the river, hopefully concentrating on the barge aimed at the far bridge pier. The tillerman had fastened the rudder and had stooped to light the fuse when the barge flared into light, flinging the body of the hapless Bovarian skyward and then into the river.

Shaelyt shivered, but straightened.

The cannoneers bracketed one of the barges farther upriver, and after several misses hit the craft with two shells and enough force that the steersman jumped from the stern and the barge began to sink . . . without exploding.

Desyrk's face was drawn, but little shivers struck the oilcloth waterproof of the barge he'd been assigned. Nothing happened.

Quaeryt wondered if he should offer unseen assistance when two things happened. The barge exploded, and Desyrk grasped at the stone parapet before his knees buckled. Voltyr managed to partly catch Desyrk and ease him to the stone before returning his attention to the river.

The barge assigned to Akoryt exploded. Quaeryt didn't see it happen, just the fire and remnants, but he didn't think it had been a cannon shell that had accomplished the destruction. From somewhere, another barge pushed through that smoke, and Quaeryt called out, "Threkhyl! The lead barge!"

Then he saw another barge, one that had escaped his notice, hugging the north edge of the river, a course that kept it shielded from one of the cannon emplacements. He stepped forward, to Baelthm's shoulder and pointed. "Baelthm . . . you take the barge headed this way, but don't try to image until it's right below us." Quaeryt just hoped that the older imager could account for at least one barge.

"Got it!" announced Threkhyl, triumphantly.

"Voltyr! The next one!" Quaeryt watched as Voltyr straightened his shoulders, then waited.

Voltyr's target barge exploded.

Quaeryt smiled.

Baelthm was the next imager to collapse, right as the barge that passed almost directly below the rampart exploded.

One barge, and he's finished. But hot silver does work. Quaeryt scanned the river.

"Akoryt! That one!" Quaeryt gestured.

Akoryt concentrated on his second target . . . and crumpled. Quaeryt looked to the barge he'd assigned Akoryt, then imaged his own hot iron. After a long moment the barge went up in fragments.

A flash of pain seared through Quaeryt's eyes, followed by burning tears, such a flood that he could see nothing until he blotted them with his sleeve.

"Shaelyt! Get that lead barge."

While the barge went up in smoke, and little flame, the young imager leaned forward over the parapet and vomited, then remained slumped there.

Quaeryt scanned the river. Eight barges remained. *Seven,* he corrected himself as the cannon claimed another barge. But of the imager undercaptains, only Voltyr and Threkhyl remained standing.

"Voltyr . . . can you do another? The one with the black splotch on the oilcloth?"

"I'll . . . try." Voltyr's face was pale, but he turned back toward the river.

The splotched barge exploded, and Voltyr sat down on the stone, holding his head in his hands. "Can't see . . ."

"That's all right. Just rest." Quaeryt stepped up to Threkhyl. "Try for the one in the middle of the river."

"Two of them there."

"The one farthest downriver . . . closest to the bridge."

Sweat poured down the face of the ginger-bearded imager. Then his face went lax.

Quaeryt barely managed to catch him and lower him to the stone.

Quaeryt concentrated on the lead barge . . . and watched it explode and then sink through burning tears. He took a deep breath, then looked to the next barge, imaging just two small chunks of iron.

This time, the pain was so intense that it was several moments before he could see anything at all. *Iron over water . . . why so frigging hard. Think the Namer was blocking you.* Absently, he almost smiled, knowing that he hardly believed in the Namer, but the smile ended before it began as a second wave of pain knifed through his eyes.

He took as deep a breath as he could manage, then imaged again.

A quick wave of blackness hit him, and he had to reach out to the stone parapet to steady himself. When he could see again, there were still three barges on the river, two in the middle, and aiming for the isle that held the center pylon.

One was already close to a hundred yards from the isle, where the cannon could not be trained on it. Quaeryt forced himself to concentrate again.

This time the blackness was worse, and his guts twisted inside himself.

Two left . . . just two.

He managed to image two more small chunks of iron, then grasped the stone as blackness and nausea swept over him. The tears in his eyes were like red-hot pokers. When he finally straightened, he barely could keep himself from staggering, unable to focus his eyes on the last of the barges. By the time his eyes cleared, the craft was less than twenty yards from the isle.

If you image now . . .

He watched helplessly as the last barge grounded on the rock from which the central bridge pylon rose.

CRUMMPTT! A column of flame and metal shot upward.

Through the pain and tears that filled his eyes, Quaeryt winced. *One last friggin' barge . . . and you couldn't do anything in time.* He just stood there as stones rained down from the center span of the bridge, except there were not as many as he had expected.

He blotted his eyes, trying to see the damage.

Finally, he could make out that while there was a hole in the span, at least half, if not more, of the roadway appeared to remain. Repairs might be possible comparatively quickly . . . at least repairs allowing troops to use the bridge. *Maybe.*

He glanced around him. Voltyr was rubbing his eyes. Shaelyt had pushed himself away from the parapet, although he appeared pale. Threkhyl was groaning as he rolled over, pushed himself onto his knees, and then staggered erect.

Quaeryt swallowed back bile, then spoke. "Voltyr . . . you're in better shape than the rest. Help the others. I'll be back in a moment." He paused. "Everyone here did the best he could, and we managed to destroy most of the barges. You did well. Voltyr . . . for those who didn't hear that, tell them that if they come around before I return."

He turned slowly, trying not to show any unsteadiness, and walked toward the raised platform where Bhayar stood, still surveying the river.

Were there more barges coming? Quaeryt turned and scanned the river, much as his eyes and head throbbed, but the waters were empty, except for what looked to be one of the towboats, a good mille to the west. He turned back and continued toward the platform.

Bhayar stepped around two officers and then walked down to meet Quaeryt.

"Between us and the cannon, we got all but one, sir."

The Lord of Telaryn nodded.

"We ran out of imagers and time before they ran out of barges," Quaeryt added.

"The bridge looks to be passable," Bhayar said. "Or it will be when the engineers finish immediate repairs." He paused. "I didn't think you could do half what you did. Kharst sent twenty-one barges. Undercaptain Sehaak counted six barges taken out by cannon, and fourteen by your imagers."

"I wasn't counting," Quaeryt said. *Except that we took out fifteen or sixteen.* Bhayar's face kept blurring, in between the flashes of light.

"I had that feeling. All those lost barges are going to stop a lot of upriver trading in Bovaria." Bhayar laughed, although his voice contained a trace of bitterness. "We need to get your officers some rest and food. I didn't realize it was quite that much work."

"We had to image red-hot iron into the powder in the barges. Imaging iron across water seems to take much more effort than anyone thought."

"Who thought . . . ? You did, didn't you?"

"The powder would have smothered a lit candle or flame."

"You don't look much better than your men, Quaeryt. Go take care of them."

"Yes, sir." Quaeryt turned and forced himself to walk back toward the undercaptains, trying not to limp too much.

Obviously acting under Bhayar's orders, Deucalon ordered a major to find and assign a small chamber where the undercaptains could sleep on Mardi night. Quaeryt had a tiny chamber to himself with a pallet bed, almost directly under the parapets from which they had imaged. He collapsed onto that bed almost immediately after returning from the evening meal in an overcrowded mess.

On Meredi morning, he woke well before sunrise, fully alert. He glanced around the chamber he'd barely taken in the day before, noting that it was both bare and spare, with the only furnishings being the pallet bed, a chair, and a writing desk with a single drawer. He walked over to the desk and opened the drawer partway. It appeared empty, but when he pushed it closed, he felt something move. He opened it all the way, to discover a leather-bound volume at the back, so small that it was little more than the length of his hand from wrist to his middle fingertip. The volume was so covered in dust that when he lifted it from the drawer, gently as he did, dust flew upward and everywhere, and Quaeryt sneezed time after time.

When he finally controlled his sneezing, he carefully removed the remainder of the dust and then, more curious than ever, opened the volume, which bore no title on the cover or spine, to the title page. It read, *Rholan and the Nameless.* There was no author's name given, either there or on or behind the frontispiece. Finding that strange and intriguing, he moved to the small window, where there was more light, and began to read the opening page.

> All know of the words of Rholan and his thoughts and observations, as well as the precepts he formulated in support of the Nameless. Yet for all those precepts, and the wisdom behind them, few, if any, have dared voice or write one fact. There is no proof that there is a Nameless. There is also no proof that there is not a Nameless, but proving a negative is effectively impossible, particularly when one speaks of a deity whose invisible and unnameable presence and voice have never been seen or heard, except by those claiming to be its prophets.

For these reasons, over the years, I have made thoughts and observations about the Nameless, the Namer, Rholan, and others, and since the Nameless is without nomen, so will I remain as well. For the interested reader or the casual peruser, I hope you will find what follows thought-provoking, informative, or at the least entertaining.

Quaeryt stopped reading and examined the small volume more closely. There was no date anywhere, only the words "Cloisonyt, Tela," which indicated the volume had been written before Hengyst had conquered Tela and that the writer had likely lived in the time of Rholan or close to that time. The leather was relatively soft, but clearly older, but the binding had been painstakingly done, and the text had been carefully hand-scripted, suggesting that there were few copies of the volume. Indeed, he might be holding the only one.

He turned to the second chapter of the volume.

In practical terms, Rholan has become synonymous with the worship of the Nameless. Therefore, to understand the appeal and growth of the cult of the Nameless, one must begin with Rholan. Already, the word has begun to spread that the man was mysterious and unknowable. He was neither. He was a physically unprepossessing scholar, the bastard son of High Holder Niasaen of Tela, possessed of a deep, melodic, and mesmerizing voice and an intellect surpassed only by his own sense of destiny . . .

Quaeryt looked at the book again. He couldn't believe what he held in his hand. It might technically belong to the Lord of Telaryn, but Quaeryt was going to keep the volume with him, at least until he had read it all the way through. He slipped it into his gear bag and then began to dress for the day.

Immediately after an early breakfast with the other senior officers, Quaeryt was summoned to meet with Bhayar—this time in a spare study overlooking the narrow courtyard.

The Lord of Telaryn sat behind a table desk on which was spread a map. He did not rise as Quaeryt entered and closed the door behind him, but gestured to the chairs across the desk from him.

As he sat, Quaeryt noticed the dark circles under Bhayar's eyes immediately. "You didn't get much sleep last night, did you?"

"No. You wouldn't have, either, except you wouldn't have been any good at the staff meeting anyway. You did most of what happened yesterday, didn't you?"

Quaeryt didn't bother to deny it, because Bhayar already knew he was an imager, but he did shake his head. "A third or a quarter. Threkhyl is capable, and so is Shaelyt. Voltyr had a little trouble at first, but he figured it out. Baelthm, Desyrk, and Akoryt could only do it once, and Baelthm only when the barge came toward the north side of the river and was practically right underneath him."

"That's done for now, thank the Nameless," said Bhayar.

"There have to be more barges . . ." began Quaeryt.

"Kharst can't afford wasting that much powder again. The powder he used would charge cannon thousands of times, and he needs that for the cannon that keep the Antiagon fleet at bay. By the time he could gather the barges and make them ready, it wouldn't matter." Bhayar smiled politely. "I have a question for you."

"Yes?"

"How did you know the Bovarians would try to use the exploding barges to destroy the Narrows Bridge?" asked Bhayar. "I never asked you how you knew."

"How did *you* know?" countered Quaeryt.

"Spies. They're more useful than guessing."

"How many did you lose?"

Bhayar's lips quirked into a tight smile. "More than I would have liked. How did you figure it out without spies?"

"It made sense after you'd explained how Kharst could take over Telaryn. He wouldn't have to do it all at once. First, he'd destroy the bridge. That would allow him to invade the south side of the river. He could spend years fortifying and building emplacements."

"I understand that, but what about the barges?"

"When they used mock barges for the false diversionary attack from Cleblois and then used unseasoned troops against Third Battalion, I had to ask why. Why would Kharst spend all that time and effort building mock barges? Why not just use real barges, especially if they weren't really going anywhere? And if he were going to use real barges for a direct assault on Ferravyl, why alert us with a false attack? That suggested that the barges were already being used. That meant either a direct attack or an attack on the bridge."

"Both, it appears. Kharst used some of those barges to carry at least two regiments to the east side of the Vyl some ten to fifteen milles south."

"Is that where you're sending Third Regiment?"

Bhayar nodded.

"Just Third Regiment?"

"It's more to slow them down. Deucalon doesn't want to send more, not with at least four Bovarian regiments still across the Vyl and enough barges remaining to ferry them across."

"Do you think they'll still attack?"

"We've already taken steps to encourage them. Third Regiment crossed the bridge well before dawn this morning. We had artists paint a canvas so that the bridge looks more damaged than it is, and we've strung a cable from bridge pier to bridge pier, and we're having boatmen use it as a guide across the river."

"To give the Bovarians the impression that the bridge isn't safe to use?"

"That's the idea. Now . . . Commander Skarpa has requested your presence. That brings up another question. What if the Bovarians try another attack here . . . at the same time that you're with Third Regiment?"

"I could split the imagers, and leave several under Voltyr's command for whatever use you can make of them." Quaeryt paused. "But how are you going to get Zhelan's company across the bridge without anyone seeing them?"

"They crossed with Third Regiment this morning. They had your mare as well. You can walk across after you choose who will accompany you."

"You knew I'd suggest splitting the imagers?"

"No. Commander Skarpa said you were more of an officer than you would admit, and that you'd end up with him."

Somehow . . . even as Skarpa's assessment amused Quaeryt, it also bothered him. *Are you that easy to read?* "He needs Zhelan more than he needs me."

"He said you'd say that, and his answer was that he needs Zhelan *under* your command." Bhayar laughed.

All Quaeryt could do was shrug helplessly.

Jeudi morning found Quaeryt riding southward on the river road on the east side of the Vyl, its channel barely more than thirty yards across, if deep enough to make crossing a chancy business. Still, during the previous day, they'd seen no sign of any Bovarian forces, although they had moved slowly through small village after small village, some barely even hamlets, resting men and mounts frequently. Quaeryt had ended up bringing Shaelyt and Desyrk with him, and leaving the others, because Threkhyl was still the strongest imager; Voltyr had a head on his shoulders; Akoryt was limited in what he could do, but helpful; and Baelthm wouldn't do well in a battle, anyway.

"I don't see why they didn't cross somewhere along here," observed Quaeryt. "You could run cable across between two trees, one on each side, and hand over hand the men and harness the mounts and pull them over. That's if you didn't want to cross at a known ford."

"But they didn't," Skarpa said.

"So the whole point of all of this is to split our forces again?"

"Yes. We don't have a choice. Not really. If we don't find them and slow them down—or stop them—then they could circle and catch our forces from the flank or behind."

"So they weaken Bhayar's forces one way or another."

"That's what they hope. But Third Regiment's better than they think, and you and that overlarge company are worth close to another regiment."

Quaeryt snorted. "You actually told Bhayar that I'd end up with you? You're going to get in trouble, my friend, wagering on me."

"That may be, but those who wagered on others fared far less well," replied Skarpa with a cynical grin.

"A mere matter of chance." And Quaeryt wasn't even certain Skarpa was right. Certainly, anyone who had wagered on Quaeryt's ability to remain as governor of Montagne would have lost . . . although Quaeryt was less and less certain he personally had lost, since governing was a thankless position and since he had learned more than he'd originally wanted to admit, especially about trying to avoid situations where the choice was between getting something done and making people with power happy.

"I think not."

At that moment a scout appeared, riding back north on the river road toward the outriders and the vanguard that Skarpa and Quaeryt led.

"The scouts have found the Bovarians," suggested Quaeryt.

Skarpa just nodded and raised an arm, gesturing for the scout to join him and ordering, "Column! Halt!" Then he rode out to the side.

Quaeryt followed.

The scout, a junior squad leader, reined up.

"What did you find?" asked Skarpa.

"The Bovarians are about two milles ahead," began the scout. "That's where those hills are. They've formed up in two positions. One regiment is on the south hill, in plain view. The other is on the back side of a hill north and east of there. The space between the northern hill and the river road is mostly fields. I think they're bean fields. There aren't any walls, but there are ditches on the west end of the fields . . . look to be mixed regiments, maybe half foot, half mounted . . ."

When the scout finished, Skarpa asked, "How far apart are the two regiments?"

"Close to half a mille. Could be a bit more, sir."

"Did they see you?"

"We tried to be careful, but they might have. Didn't see anyone moving, though."

Skarpa frowned. "I want you to go take another look, but stay off the road and out of sight. We need to know if they're holding those positions or getting ready to move."

"Yes, sir."

"We'll move up another bit, but take our time."

Once the scout had turned and headed his mount back southward, Skarpa turned in the saddle and looked at Quaeryt. "What do you think?"

"What if you form up on the flat in those bean fields?" asked Quaeryt. "They'd have to leave the heights to engage you."

"They won't. The longer they can keep us occupied . . ."

"Exactly," said Quaeryt. "But what would happen if they were attacked from the rear? From behind the hill they're on?"

"They'd see anyone coming. They'd pull back to the hilltop and use the heights," Skarpa said.

"I think there's a way to get close enough so that they're surprised. The attacking company could split off before you get in eyesight of the nearer regiment. What if you posted scouts, so that when the Bovarians are surprised, you know when to start up the west side of the hill. The regiment to the south would likely wait, wouldn't they? Even if they didn't, it would take them time to reach the hill, and you'd have the higher ground."

"I'd be caught between two regiments."

"No, you wouldn't, because you'd still have the north side of the hill open to withdraw, if you have to."

"And you're going to be the one to make that hidden attack?"

"Well . . . I'm not very good at following other people's orders . . ."

Skarpa shook his head. "You realize what will happen to me if you fail?"

"It won't be any worse than what happens to me," Quaeryt pointed out. "And you just said that the Bovarians would wait for days if we don't attack."

"You don't have enough men to make that work. You need a battalion, at the very least."

"See if Meinyt would support me."

"He'd support you to the Namer's door," snorted Skarpa. "I don't have to ask."

What Quaeryt realized was that what Skarpa was also telling him, if indirectly, was that commanders had to know what their officers could and would do, and they had to know it without ever asking. He nodded. "Thank you."

"You don't learn everything in one campaign."

At times, Quaeryt wondered if he'd ever learn near enough to survive the battles he kept getting caught in, let alone succeed in his long-term plans . . . plans that seemed further from realization than ever. And they'd seemed so simple back in Tilbor—just find a way to make life more secure for imagers and scholars.

"We'll move up and rest everyone. While they're resting, you and I and Meinyt can go over what you have in mind."

What with one thing and another, it was close to midmorning when Quaeryt addressed the two imagers who had accompanied him. "Shaelyt, Desyrk, I want you to ride or stay just behind Commander Skarpa. Your orders are simple. Kill anyone who gets close enough to injure him. Don't be fancy. Do whatever is easiest for you. If you know how, image pitricin into their brains . . ."

At that Shaelyt nodded, but Desyrk looked appalled.

". . . or image a thin blade through their eyes. This isn't honorable combat. It's war, and we didn't start it."

With a nod, Quaeryt turned the mare and rode toward the rear of the column, where Meinyt and Zhelan had gathered their troops.

"We're going to make a surprise attack on a Bovarian force that's waiting to ambush the main body of Third Regiment." Quaeryt looked to Zhelan, and then to the other company officers.

"Ambush the ambushers," added Meinyt.

"That's the idea. We'll be taking a back lane to get in position. Once we get near, we'll have to be silent. No noise at all, after I give the command for silence. No talking, clanking . . . swearing. We're going to try to get as close to the rear of the Bovarians as we can. Being quiet means more surprise and fewer casualties. When we finish here, I want you to pass that on to your squad leaders, and they need to make sure every man understands that." Quaeryt paused.

"Yes, sir."

"We're going to have to travel a lane for part of the way that's narrow, and when we get to the end of that lane, you'll need to shift your men into an attack formation. Can you do it without calling out orders? With hand signals or something like that."

"So long as we only have to do that once," said Meinyt.

"Can you do that twice, once for the formation, and then a charge right after they're in position?"

"Should be able to do that." Meinyt looked to Zhelan.

"Yes, sir."

"How fast can you shift your companies from a four abreast column to an attack formation?" Quaeryt asked.

"Be a lot quicker if I could use five abreast."

Quaeryt considered, then said, "Then set them up five abreast, but they'll be crowded on the lane."

"Better crowded than taking too much time."

Less than half a quint later, one of Skarpa's scouts was guiding Quaeryt's force through a meadow and past a woodlot, and then onto a rutted and slightly muddy lane that headed southward, if in a more winding way than the main river road. The lane followed a brook, in a general fashion, and moved in and out of woods. Farther ahead were several outriders, whom Quaeryt had cautioned to avoid being seen, if they could, and to return and report immediately if they saw signs of any Bovarian troopers.

Before that long, they came to a hamlet of less than a score of small houses, cots, dilapidated wooden outbuildings. Immediately, the handful of crofters and growers vanished into their dwellings . . . or into the woods to the east of the hamlet, as did their children. Seemingly, in moments, the entire hamlet was silent, and the only animal Quaeryt saw was a calico cat on a woodpile, regally surveying the troopers in the way only cats can, Quaeryt thought.

"Just keep riding," Quaeryt said quietly.

Beyond the hamlet the lane moved through an area that was lightly wooded with grass between the trees, and then toward a narrow stand of trees below the low hillside that held the Bovarians, a hillside low enough that the trees provided somewhat of a block to seeing the lane.

Even so, Quaeryt signaled for silence, then dropped his personal shields and took a deep breath. After a few moments, he concentrated. *How long can you hold a concealment shield this large?* He'd already abandoned his personal shields, and he wasn't even certain how long he could cover the front of the formation . . . but every yard that they could get closer to the Bovarians meant that much greater the surprise, even shock.

In another quint, the first part of the column neared the point on the lane where it wound around the base of the hillside. The Bovarian regiment was stationed on higher ground and facing westward, and away from the lane, except for a rear guard of perhaps a company, set a good hundred yards down the slope, arranged in four separated squads.

Quaeryt signaled to Meinyt, and the battalion moved out of the lane.

Quaeryt could see a number of the Bovarian rear guards looking around, clearly puzzled, but not yet seeing anything, but obviously hearing the muffled sounds of riders. He hoped they would think that the Telaryn force was simply much farther away.

Quaeryt himself could feel the strain of holding the concealment, but Third Battalion was still not in position.

Come on. Move! Get those mounts in place. Gritting his teeth, he eased his half-staff from its leathers.

He could see more than a few Telaryn troopers were as puzzled by the reaction—or the lack of it—by the Bovarians, but to their credit, none of Meinyt's and Zhelan's troopers said a word.

"Telaryns somewhere!" came the call—in Bovarian.

"Where?"

"Can't see them!"

"Send scouts down that lane."

"Scouts went up the path to the north!"

"Send more!"

Another half quint passed before Meinyt looked to Quaeryt.

Here goes! Quaeryt raised his staff . . . then dropped it.

Without a verbal command, not all the companies charged up the gentle slope exactly in an even line, but Quaeryt could see that they were all moving.

He decided against dropping the concealment, even when his company slammed into one of the rearguard squads, although the Bovarians could see within it, as could his own troopers, but it would appear to the Bovarian troops higher on the hillside that the rear guard had simply vanished—if many of them were even looking.

Without personal shields, Quaeryt found himself knocking aside one Bovarian's sabre and then slamming his half-staff into the skull of another Bovarian.

"At the main force!" Meinyt yelled as the battalion largely swept through the scattered, outmanned, and confused rear guard.

Quaeryt dropped the concealment when the troopers before him were some fifteen yards short of the Bovarians. Even as he managed to rebuild personal shields he doubted he could hold for much longer, he could see the shock and consternation as Third Battalion crashed into and through the rear of the Bovarian regiment.

Two large cavalrymen, wearing breastplates and skullcap helmets, spurred their mounts toward Quaeryt, one swinging a sabre and the other thrusting. Quaeryt's shields turned both blades, but not without him feeling like he'd been hammered across his upper body. Still, he managed a backcut with the staff that dropped one from the saddle before recovering the staff and bracing it against the saddle and using it as a lance of sorts against the next Bovarian.

For a time he couldn't even guess, all Quaeryt did was try to avoid blows while delivering them.

Then he heard an unfamiliar horn signal, and the fighting around him and around Zhelan's company seemed to fade, and Quaeryt could see that the foot and the cavalry of the first Bovarian force had scattered, although several companies on the south end of the hill managed to withdraw in a half orderly fashion toward the second Bovarian force.

"On the left flank . . . follow me!"

As Meinyt swung Third Battalion to the south, Quaeryt saw exactly what the major had in mind by pursuing the withdrawing companies into the other Bovarian force.

"Zhelan! Take the right of Third Battalion!" Quaeryt image-boosted his voice, despite the momentary light-headedness that caused, then swung the mare to parallel the captain's charge.

Skarpa's front moved slowly, almost hesitantly, and Quaeryt wondered why, until he saw the Bovarians charge downhill toward Third Regiment. Then the Third pulled back even more, redressing their lines. A good score of mounts of the heavy cavalry leading the Bovarian charge went down at the edge of the bean fields.

Must have been a bigger ditch there . . .

That was all Quaeryt had time to think about, because he and Zhelan's company were almost upon the flank of the Bovarians, all foot. While the foot had turned to face the riders, none of them had spears or pikes, and most of the first few ranks went down under sabres and hooves. Quaeryt used the half-staff as a thrusting weapon, braced against his saddle and shields.

Halfway into the foot formation, the charge slowed, and some of the riders went down, their mounts cut from under them, and more foot swarmed toward Third Battalion.

Quaeryt found himself near the edge between the armed foot and stalled cavalry. Widening his shields slightly, and hoping he could hold them long enough, he urged the mare forward, and then turned her upslope at a slight angle. The impact of the shields threw back the footmen enough, Quaeryt thought, that the rest of the company could press forward.

After riding some fifty yards, as the mare slowed, he turned her back downslope, again at an angle. By the time he pulled back from the front edge of the fighting, he could barely see, but he could sense that Zhelan and Third Battalion had broken through the foot and were attacking the rear of the main Bovarian body . . . and they had the higher ground.

Quaeryt just pulled up in an open space, holding on to his shields, hoping he didn't have to use them more, barely able to hang on to the half-staff.

After another quint or so, gradually and then in a rush, the remaining Bovarians broke, fleeing westward into and through the marshy ground to reach the river, struggling in various ways to cross. More than a few drowned, Quaeryt judged, although he could barely see at all by that time, between the throbbing pain in his head, and the flashes of fire in his eyes.

Shouldn't be making a habit of this.

In the end, Quaeryt remained reined up on the middle of the slope of the southern hill, hardly noting the squad of Zhelan's troopers that surrounded him. Every so often, he could see enough to determine that the Bovarian casualties had been enormous, with bodies everywhere, horses standing as if shocked in places and other horses sidling out of the way of Telaryn riders.

Sometime later, how much Quaeryt couldn't tell, Meinyt reined up beside

Quaeryt, who was bent over, his head practically against the mare's neck and mane.

"Sir?"

Quaeryt straightened slowly. "Yes, Meinyt?"

"The Bovarians never saw us, did they? The first ones, I mean."

"They didn't seem to. I hoped they wouldn't. I'd appreciate it if we could leave it like that."

Meinyt smiled. "I can do that, sir. So long as you ask for Third Battalion if you can."

"I can do that." *I certainly can.* Quaeryt forced a smile, not that he didn't appreciate Meinyt's words, but his head throbbed, and he could barely see. "Thank you."

"Our thanks to you, sir. I think the commander would like to see you, sir."

Quaeryt rode slowly downhill, through the dead and dying, the mare avoiding fallen men and mounts.

Skarpa was waiting on the road. He waved the two imager undercaptains away and rode over beside Quaeryt, then reined up almost stirrup to stirrup. "How did you manage that?"

"Manage . . . what?" Quaeryt replied, his mouth so dry he could hardly speak. Belatedly, he realized he should drink something, and he was about to reach for his water bottle when he realized he still held the bloody half-staff in his left hand. Slowly, he replaced it in the leathers and then extracted the water bottle, taking a long but slow swallow of the watered lager.

The flashes across his eyes lessened slightly, as did the pounding in his skull, and he finally looked at Skarpa.

"You broke the entire flank by yourself."

"No. I just gave them a little space so that they could attack."

"That's the same thing," snorted the commander.

"How many did we lose, do you think?"

"More than I'd like, but less than anyone would believe. Probably three hundred, at a guess, another couple hundred wounded. Some of those won't make it." After a pause he added, "The Bovarians had about as many survivors as we had casualties."

"That's a victory, isn't it?"

Skarpa nodded. "Meinyt said you managed to get them close enough that the first regiment was completely surprised."

"We were fortunate."

"No. The only fortune involved was that you were with us."

Quaeryt took another swallow of the watered lager. It tasted better than he recalled.

Skarpa smiled. "At least, I won't have to explain how you got yourself killed." Another pause followed. "Or why you didn't when anyone else would have."

Just don't ask.

Skarpa didn't. Instead, he turned in the saddle and looked to Shaelyt and Desyrk. "Undercaptains, you'd best escort the subcommander to his company."

"Thank you," murmured Quaeryt.

Skarpa just nodded.

75

By the seventh glass on Vendrei morning, Third Regiment was riding back northward on the river road. Skarpa had left the most seriously wounded in the only small town, barely more than a large hamlet, commandeering what passed for an inn to take care of those men for whom travel would be a death sentence. At the rear of the column marched 150 Bovarians, half of whom were wounded. Just behind the company acting as vanguard rode Quaeryt and Skarpa, with the imager undercaptains and Quaeryt's command immediately following.

Quaeryt had felt tired most of the previous afternoon, but after even the passage of a few glasses and more than a little watered lager, he'd been left with only a vague headache. When he had awakened on Vendrei, even after sleeping on straw in a barn, he'd felt remarkably fit. That in itself surprised him, but he wasn't about to question his good fortune.

Like Jeudi, Vendrei had dawned hot and sticky, but as he rode he could see clouds to the northwest, and usually clouds foretold cooler weather.

Cooler . . . and wetter . . . and then hotter and stickier in summertime.

After a time Skarpa turned in the saddle. "I've been meaning to ask you, again, Quaeryt, just how you managed to get an entire battalion so close to the Bovarians yesterday without them noticing. I asked Major Meinyt, and all he'd say was that he was too busy following orders to notice that." Skarpa looked hard at Quaeryt.

"We took the back lane, just as your scouts said. I asked Major Meinyt if he could move into a line of attack from a four abreast formation. He asked for five abreast. I agreed. When we reached the part of the lane close to the back of the hill, I ordered silent riding, and the men were very good. The Bovarians started yelling that they could hear us, but they didn't immediately form up. By the time they realized how close we were, most of them couldn't get prepared enough."

"That sounds like what some of Meinyt's captains said." Skarpa frowned. "Several of the captives kept saying that you and Third Battalion appeared from nowhere."

"It certainly didn't seem like nowhere to me. I was worried the whole time we were riding up toward them." *And that had certainly been true enough*, reflected Quaeryt.

"Then there was . . ." Skarpa shook his head. "There are some things a commander just shouldn't look into too closely, I suppose. It's just that, around you, that gets hard to do. I think Gauswn had the right idea. He thought you had a special relationship with the Nameless."

"You know that I'm not even certain that the Nameless exists. How can I have a special relationship with a being whose existence I doubt?"

"What you believe doesn't matter. Gauswn pointed that out to me before he left the regiment. You're the one who turned him from a good officer into a chorister, you know?"

"He always wanted to be one. He was a good officer, but he's already a better chorister."

"The same could be said about you. You're a good scholar, but you're a better officer."

Quaeryt was the one to shake his head.

"You do things that are impossible, and the men follow you."

"They only look impossible. No one else is stupid enough to try them, and sooner or later, I'm going to attempt something that is truly impossible . . . and men will be hurt and die." In retrospect, politically some of what he'd attempted in Extela had also been impossible . . . and he and Vaelora had paid the consequences.

"You worry about that, don't you?"

"Yes."

"That's also the mark of a good officer. Good officers always push their officers and men beyond what seems possible, but they never stop worrying about the costs to those they lead. Sometimes, they push too far. It happens. But I've seen, and heard, about how many more men are lost through excessive caution. If you lead a regiment through three hard-fought battles and push through to victory, and lose a third of your force, ministers in the capital will claim you're a terrible commander. Yet they'll praise a commander who only loses a hundred or so men in ten smaller battles, and never realize that he's lost half his force. Lord Chayar understood that. I can only hope his son does as well."

"We'll see, won't we?" *Do you really know? His replacing you in Extela doesn't fit what Skarpa would like, but political battles aren't the same as military ones.* That he'd discovered as governor. *But will there be other political constraints that will cause the same kinds of problems in the end?*

Quaeryt didn't have an answer to his own question. Only time and events would answer it. "Bhayar said that the Bovarians had at least six regiments around Ferravyl. Does anyone really know?"

"We fought half a regiment up north and two down here. Seems to me that Kharst wouldn't have sent two up the Vyl with only four left to try to take the city. I'd wager on eight."

Quaeryt nodded. "So would I."

"And I'd not be surprised if we don't see them right soon, late this afternoon, certainly by tomorrow. They'd want to attack before we got back and before Bhayar gets all the other troops from the east."

"How many more has he called in?"

"I don't know. Deucalon and Myksyl wouldn't say. If he stripped all the garrisons, I'd judge another eight regiments. Maybe ten. They say he started building regiments as soon as he left Tilbor at Year-Turn."

That was something Quaeryt hadn't heard.

"Right now . . . we need to worry about dealing with the Bovarians with what we've got."

Quaeryt couldn't argue with that, either.

At less than a quint past ninth glass Quaeryt caught sight of a Telaryn courier, flanked by two rankers, riding hard toward Third Regiment. The three were not riding down the road, but approaching through the plots of small growers from the northeast.

Skarpa looked to Quaeryt. "Thought something like this might happen."

"I said I wouldn't wager against you." Quaeryt blotted his forehead, then glanced northward. The heavy gray clouds had moved far enough south that they covered more than a third of the sky, but had not reached the sun, and the air felt damper and more muggy than ever. He looked at the approaching riders again. "That's an undercaptain."

"Frig!" muttered Skarpa. "More trouble. Sow's belly worth and more." He did not slow the regiment, but waved for the undercaptain to join them.

The junior officer eased his mount up beside Skarpa. "Commander, sir . . . Marshal Deucalon requests that you move forward with deliberate speed. There are six or seven Bovarian regiments about to attack." He handed Skarpa what looked to be a quickly sketched map. "You can see here, sir. Submarshal Myskyl is holding the approach to the bridge with two regiments. Marshal Deucalon holds this ridge with three regiments. The Bovarians have a regiment or more on the triangle, but their main body is to the south of Marshal Deucalon's force. Your attack on the rear of the main Bovarian force would trap them between you and Marshal Deucalon."

"Where is Commander Pulaskyr?" asked Skarpa, passing the map to Quaeryt.

"Commander Pulaskyr and Commander Claeph are engaged to the north against several other Bovarian regiments."

Skarpa almost uttered something, then clamped his mouth shut.

Quaeryt scanned the map. He could guess what had happened. Deucalon had learned of the approach of the Bovarian main body from the south, and had positioned his main force on the ridge a mille south of the bridge, so as to hold the higher ground. He'd left Myskyl and two regiments as a rear guard at the bridge, but once Deucalon had moved to the ridge, somehow the Bovarians had barged troops across the Vyl onto the triangle. If Deucalon moved against the Bovarian main body, that would allow the Bovarians on the triangle to use the river road to attack Myskyl and threaten the bridge and city. Myskyl couldn't move to reinforce Deucalon—or to attack the Bovarians on the triangle without abandoning the bridge approach, and it appeared that the Bovarians might have enough troops in the main body to split out and send a regiment or more east and then due north to take the bridge. Also the Bovarians on the triangle had the option of attacking Deucalon's rear.

Was the use of all the barges against the bridge also to give the impression that Kharst didn't have enough left to carry troops over the Vyl? After a moment Quaeryt answered himself. *More than likely.*

Quaeryt could see why Skarpa had wanted to swear . . . and then some.

"How far are we from the rear of the Bovarians?" asked the commander.

"Near-on a mille and a half. They're just beyond that low rise."

"So they likely can already see us?"

"Most likely, sir."

"Tell the marshal that we'll do what we can," Skarpa finally said.

"Yes, sir. I'll convey that."

Once the undercaptain headed back northeast, Skarpa turned in the saddle to Quaeryt. "I know what I think. What about you?"

"Deucalon has to be outnumbered," Quaeryt said. "If we just attack the rear of the Bovarians, we'll be swallowed."

"And?"

"If we attack from the road, and we're unsuccessful, we'll have very few places to go. If by some chance we are successful in moving them, they can just head east and around Deucalon toward the bridge."

Skarpa nodded. "So we'll have to trample lanes and maybe the fields of all these poor growers to avoid getting trampled ourselves. We'll have to leave a couple of squads with the riding wounded to guard the prisoners and their wounded, too. Hate doing that, but there's no help for it." He shook his head. "Might as well get on with it." He rode forward to the lead squad, Quaeryt following him, and shortly, the entire regiment was moving down a lane heading east-northeast, with scouts spreading out to the north and east.

"Can you and the imagers do anything to get us closer . . . the way . . ."

Quaeryt rode without speaking for several moments. *What could you get Shaelyt and Desyrk to do that would help so that the Bovarians wouldn't see . . . or wouldn't see clearly?* He considered, then nodded.

"They can probably see us right now," replied Quaeryt. "If we can pass by a woods or even a woodlot where they can't see us for a bit, they might lose sight of us."

"Might lose sight?" Skarpa raised his eyebrows.

"Might lose sight," Quaeryt repeated flatly. "There's also something else that might work, but I'll need to talk to Shaelyt and Desyrk."

The commander nodded.

Quaeryt eased the mare out to the side and then back to where the two undercaptains rode.

"Sir?"

"We're going to have to attack the rear flank"—*except it may not be the rear when we get there*—"of a large Bovarian force. I'd like you two to try something when we're not too far away from their lines." He paused. "I'd like you to image the most acrid bitter coal and wood smoke you can possible think of across their lines."

Desyrk looked puzzled for a moment, then nodded.

Shaelyt grinned. "Yes, sir."

"You've done something like that?" asked Quaeryt.

"Only in the cot, sir, when I was little and wanted to go outside. My da—"

"Good. Just stay close to me and listen for my command."

"Yes, sir."

"Follow me up front." Quaeryt moved out and then back up beside Skarpa.

"I've given the orders to the majors," Skarpa said. "We'll hit their flank at an angle, then move north to join up with Deucalon. I wasn't ordered to sacrifice the entire regiment, just to attack. Besides, sacrificing won't do any good. We can always move across Deucalon's rear and take on the Bovarians on the triangle. That would immobilize them and allow Deucalon to engage without being attacked from the rear."

Left unspoken was the fact that the marshal might not appreciate Skarpa's interpretation of his orders.

"The scouts have found a path—it's not even a lane—up ahead that goes north past a small woodlot. There aren't any Bovarians there, except there might be scouts."

"They won't matter," Quaeryt said. "They'd have to ride back and report, and by then we should be close enough." *You hope.*

"We'll have to re-form on the flat beyond the woodlot and then advance as a body."

"We'll do what we can," promised Quaeryt.

As the vanguard neared the end of the woodlot, Quaeryt dropped his personal shields and raised a concealment screen. He wasn't even about to try to hold a concealment shield across the entire regiment for all that long, especially since the distance from where the small woodlot ended to the

Bovarian flank was close to half a mille. *But if we can get within half of that, and Desyrk and Shaelyt can smoke them . . .*

That would help. Would it help enough?

Quaeryt kept scanning the main Bovarian force, which had formed up on the flatter ground a good half mille from the ridge where Deucalon's regiments were positioned. So far the Bovarians were not moving.

Why? Because they want Deucalon to attack? That seemed more than likely, since any movement by Deucalon would put him at a disadvantage. That explained why Third Regiment was being ordered to attack.

Quaeryt was beginning to feel the strain of holding the concealment, but continued to wait as Third Regiment re-formed. He looked to Skarpa. "How much longer?"

"Another half quint, at least."

Frig! Quaeryt managed a nod.

Skarpa added, "Don't lead. Let Zhelan do it. I need you to hold back with me. We'll move northeast and pick up the regiment as it withdraws after the first attack. They all have orders to hit hard and then turn north."

"Understood." Quaeryt turned in the saddle. "Shaelyt, Desyrk, you heard the commander. Stay with me."

"Yes, sir."

Quaeryt thought it was more likely to have been a full quint before Third Regiment began to move westward, but this time he'd taken the precaution of drinking more watered lager, and even eating several hard biscuits, the last of which he washed down hurriedly as the regiment trampled through half-grown maize, and then through a bean field. Finally, when the regiment reached what appeared to be meadow, Quaeryt ordered, "Image smoke! Now!"

Almost instantly, a thin brownish mist appeared—not across the entire front of the Bovarian flank, but for an expanse of perhaps a hundred yards—the center of where Third Regiment was headed. At that point, Quaeryt released the concealment and rebuilt his personal shields.

Third regiment covered almost another hundred yards before there was any noticeable reaction from the Bovarians, and only those to either side of where the smoke/mist had settled. Quaeryt could see more than a few of the foot on the flank that faced in the general direction of Third Regiment rubbing their eyes.

He also saw the pikes, not that the foot bearing them had all turned to face the Telaryn attack. Quaeryt turned in the saddle. "Desyrk . . . Shaelyt! Stay with the commander. Stay with him."

Whether Quaeryt liked it or not, if he didn't do something, the attack would end in disaster. He urged the mare forward, glad that he'd finally learned to ride well enough to match the troopers, until he was in close to the first line. Then he took the half-staff and balanced it across the front of the saddle and extended his personal shields.

As he rode closer to the flank he urged the mare into almost a full gallop and angled her to the south, then with less than fifty yards between him and the pikemen, he turned her back so he would graze across the front line of the pikemen.

As he struck the first pike, a spike of pain vibrated through him, but he kept riding as the intensity of the pain built until he could barely see. Finally, after a sweep of perhaps a hundred yards he turned into the ranks of the oncoming Third Regiment, slowing and contracting his shield to cover but himself and the mare, and hoping the rankers could avoid him.

Miraculously, most did, except for one rider who bounced off the shields at an angle.

Quaeryt just let the mare move at a quick trot toward the company to the north where he trusted Skarpa was slowly moving to join up with Deucalon's forces. Quaeryt glanced back over his shoulder.

The battalions of Third Regiment had most definitely torn a hole in the flank of the Bovarians and were already withdrawing. As the Telaryn cavalry troopers rode back north, most of them it appeared, Quaeryt could see that at least part of the Bovarian mounted was beginning to pursue.

He urged the mare into a faster trot. He felt damp spots on his face. Was he bleeding and not even aware of it? Then he realized that the sky had darkened, and a slight drizzle had begun. While the clouds directly overhead were light gray, those to the north appeared far darker and more ominous, but there wasn't too much he could do about that.

"You got them all riled up. Here they come!" called Skarpa as Quaeryt neared. "I was hoping they'd do that. We're headed east of Deucalon's force. If there aren't too many Bovarians on the triangle, we'll take them. If there are, we'll rein in and see if we can hold them in place."

As Quaeryt eased past the two imagers, Shaelyt, his eyes wide, looked at Quaeryt.

Quaeryt just nodded, slowing the mare to match Skarpa's pace, looking back. From what he could tell, most of Third Regiment had disengaged . . . except for what looked to be a company at the south end of the attack that was largely surrounded. Quaeryt managed to get out his water bottle and take several swallows and then recork it.

At least some of the beleaguered company, or companies, managed to break free, if by heading back due east, and after a time, the Bovarians pursuing them turned back more north and moved to join the growing attack on the main Telaryn force.

Skarpa slowed his mount as he and his escort company reached the lower part of the sloping grassy ridge.

An undercaptain rode toward Skarpa. "Commander, you're to hold the east flank. Those are Marshal Deucalon's orders."

"We'll hold!" Skarpa called back, adding in a much lower voice that could not have carried to the undercaptain. "Until we see if there are any attackers at this end."

The first companies of Third Regiment were halfway up the slope when Skarpa began to pass his commands. "Third Regiment, re-form uphill of the van! Attack formation! Uphill of the van."

When Skarpa took his final position, Quaeryt moved beside him, then looked down the slope at the Bovarians moving forward across the last yards of the flat of the meadow at a measured pace. For all that he'd seen Third Regiment inflicting numerous casualties on the attackers, the mass that moved forward seemed little diminished. He glanced to the west, realizing that Deucalon's force looked almost as large.

After studying Deucalon's defenses, with the ranks of pikemen across the front, Quaeryt could see why the Bovarian mounted units weren't moving at a faster pace. They'd wait until the foot engaged the pikemen . . . or until Deucalon sent mounted companies to stop the foot. Even as Quaeryt recognized the situation, a mounted battalion moved out from the west end of the Telaryn line and charged the Bovarian foot.

In turn, the foot companies split, half moving toward the pikes on the east and half toward those on the west, while a mass of Bovarian mounted charged forward to meet the Telaryn cavalry battalion. At that moment, flights of arrows arched from the rear of the Telaryn forces down into the Bovarian mounted, while the Bovarian archers targeted the pikemen on each end of the Telaryn forces.

Before long, Quaeryt suspected, the entire slope would be a confused mass.

"We may need to attack those foot," Skarpa said.

Both looked to their right as an undercaptain rode toward them.

"Commander! The Bovarian forces on the triangle have split. Half are moving to engage the bridge defenses. The other half are moving toward our rear. You're to take Third Regiment and stop those moving to our rear."

"Third Regiment! . . ." Skarpa began to issue orders.

In moments, or so it seemed to Quaeryt, the entire regiment had reversed itself and was riding northward. Quaeryt and his company rode slightly behind and between Second and Third Battalion, close enough so that Quaeryt, after a fashion, could see Skarpa's command group.

He glanced up. While the clouds had continued to thicken overhead, the raindrops falling remained scattered and intermittent. *For now.*

Before long, Quaeryt could see the dull gray-blue uniforms of the Bovarians—all mounted—as they charged up the back of the ridge. The riders of First Battalion ended up meeting the charge almost two-thirds of the way up the slope. Second Battalion attacked the middle of the Bovarian charge, and it appeared as though Major Aluin's men would leave the leading Bovarian units isolated.

At that moment another Bovarian unit rode uphill, directly toward Quaeryt's force.

"Sir!?" asked Zhelan.

"Charge them!" replied Quaeryt. One thing he had learned was that standing still in the middle of a battle was usually the prelude to a disaster.

Zhelan's company moved downhill, and although Quaeryt rode with them, he let others lead the charge, which in less than half a quint had stalled into a mass of hand-to-hand fighting.

Quaeryt used his staff as necessary, trying to save his shields and energy until imaging might produce some results, but there were so many men and mounts that he didn't see much point in trying anything except in using the shields for self-defense.

At some point, the Bovarians withdrew to the east, re-forming on the river road, but facing the ridge. Skarpa ordered, chivvied, and pushed Third Regiment back into formation on the east end of the ridge.

Quaeryt stood in the stirrups and tried to get a sense of what had happened as the rain began to fall more steadily, with large warm droplets splatting on his exposed skin. The Telaryn forces formed a unified front from the bridge approach across the ridge. The Bovarians began to form into a wide wedge.

Quaeryt looked farther south, where he could see yet another Bovarian foot regiment, possibly two, marching northward to join the massed Bovarian forces.

Where did that regiment come from? How many regiments do they have?

Quaeryt eased the mare forward, until he was positioned at the front edge of the defenders, then turned, "Shaelyt, Desyrk!"

Neither imager undercaptain looked particularly pleased, but both rode up beside him.

The rain began to fall even more strongly, still remaining warm.

Quaeryt looked to the road below, a narrow stone-paved strip in the middle of what was turning into a sea of mud. *The weather is going to turn this against us, and we're outnumbered. The frigging rain, hot warm rain.*

He stiffened in the saddle, as the words of Vaelora's letter came to him. . . . *the warmest rain can turn to ice, and ice can imprison the unwary* . . . Warm rain turning to ice? Was that what she had foreseen?

Could he and the other two imagers imprison the Bovarians in ice? But he couldn't very well just image ice. The ice came as a result of imaging something else, something massive.

"Desyrk, Shaelyt . . . you need to image a stone bridge, from the lower ground south of the point of the triangle over to the far side of the Vyl."

"What?"

"Don't argue with me. Not now. We need a stone bridge over the Vyl. Make it two spans with a single central pier. I want you to concentrate on that when I give you the command. Do you understand?"

Shaelyt nodded. After a moment, Desyrk nodded, although his eyes held confusion and puzzlement.

"Desyrk . . . when I tell you, just image the stone for the bridge, as much as you can."

He looked again at the massed Bovarians. *Do you dare to try? Should you?*

A horn call echoed through the rain, and as one, the Bovarians began to advance.

Quaeryt cleared his throat, extended his shields to encompass Desyrk and Shaelyt, then called, "Image the bridge! Now!"

He visualized the structure he imagined, with high slight arches to a central pier, and knowing he needed power, he didn't limit himself to just the rain. So he attempted to draw warmth from the Bovarian mounts, with thin tendrils of thought, and from the river itself—it had to have heat somewhere because when it didn't the water froze into ice. He even tried to link to the imagers who weren't near them . . . somehow.

From everywhere came lances of pain, strikes like cold lightning.

In instants, the clouds darkened from thick gray to black masses . . . and liquid ice poured down like sheets in an arc around him.

Quaeryt could feel that pervasive chill trying to suck heat from himself, yet being blocked by his shields, but that intense cold impacting his shields, even though they were not against his skin, made him feel as though ice were building all around him and the other two imagers.

Brilliant lines of white ice-lightning flared through his skull, and his tears seemed to freeze for an instant on his cheeks, and white fog billowed below him . . .

. . . and icy whiteness froze him into stillness.

Hot rain swirled around Quaeryt, and he shivered, even as lightnings of jagged ice cut him, and blood dripped into scarlet icicles hanging from his face and arms and legs . . . and when he turned and looked into the fog, a stone span receded and vanished . . . and ice flowed over him once more . . .

Quaeryt shivered . . . and slowly opened his eyes.

He was lying in a wide bed. Quilts covered him, but he could feel sweat beginning to form on his forehead. He tried to push back the quilts, but his arms did not seem to want to move. He tried again. Every muscle in his arms quivered, and lines of pain flared from shoulder to fingertip. Slowly . . . oh, so slowly, he pushed back the covers, barely enough that he did not feel as though he were being roasted alive.

Then he turned his head, although the movement sent lightning through his skull, to see a young man sitting on a chair lean forward, his mouth opening—Shaelyt.

"You're awake!"

"I . . . am," Quaeryt attempted to say, but the words were muddled. He wanted to sit up, but wondered if he even could.

"No one knew . . ."

"Knew what?" His lips were stiff and chapped, and each word was an effort.

"When they found you in the middle of the ice . . . you were warm . . . but no one could rouse you, sir."

"Help me . . . sit up." Quaeryt hated to ask, but his body was anything but cooperative.

"Yes, sir." Shaelyt stood and leaned forward, easing pillows behind Quaeryt and steadying him.

Quaeryt just leaned back against the pillows for several moments, not that he had any choice, weak as he was. "What . . . about . . . you . . . the others?" He found himself still unable to speak clearly because his mouth was dry.

"All of us . . . we made it. We were cold for a long time, but not like you." Shaelyt handed him a mug. "It's watered lager."

Quaeryt eased himself forward just enough to be able to drink, glad that Shaelyt was supporting the mug. His stomach muscles ached as well.

"You did something—"

"No . . . all of you worked together. You must have," Quaeryt added quickly, ignoring the furrowing in Shaelyt's brow. "I just gave you the ideas." He frowned. "You and Desyrk . . . how is he?"

"I told you. We all woke up. Even the others who weren't with us collapsed. The last was Baelthm. He woke yesterday. We're all fine. Well . . . maybe a little sore."

"Yesterday? What day is it?" Quaeryt took the mug from Shaelyt's hands and lowered it so that it rested on the quilt across his midsection.

"It's Mardi . . . morning."

"Mardi?"

"Yes, sir." The young imager stepped back. "I'm supposed to send word to Lord Bhayar."

"If I wake . . . or expire?"

"Yes, sir."

"Send away." Quaeryt's tone was dryly ironic.

When the door to the chamber closed behind Shaelyt, Quaeryt took another long swallow of the watered lager, before setting the mug on the bedside table. His hands were trembling, and he almost dropped the mug. He could do little more than lean back against the pillows Shaelyt had put behind his back to prop him up against the dark wooden headboard. As he rested there, he noted as he did that he was in a spacious bedchamber and that he'd been undressed and put in a long flannel nightshirt. The small effort he had made in setting aside the mug brought another sweat to his forehead.

You're weaker than you thought. Frig . . . you're fortunate to be alive with what you tried.

Had it worked? He frowned. It had to have worked to some extent, because Shaelyt had looked more relieved than worried and Bhayar was still around. That suggested that they'd managed at least a standoff.

After a time he reached for the mug, his hand and arm trembling, and took another swallow before he set the mug down, afraid he might drop it.

The chamber door opened, and Bhayar stepped inside, closing the door behind him, but not before Quaeryt caught sight of the armed guard outside. That worried him, for more reasons than one.

Bhayar stepped toward the bed, shook his head, then looked at Quaeryt before speaking quietly in Bovarian. "I've never seen anything like it. Either that bridge or the desolation on the east side of the Vyl."

"Did the bridge hold?"

"The engineers say it will last for centuries, if not longer." Bhayar frowned. "You don't know what you did?"

"I tried to have the imagers turn the rain that fell on the Bovarians into ice. I couldn't think of anything else to do against so many troops."

"You and your imagers slaughtered almost eight regiments of Bovarians. They were coated in ice and froze to death before they could move. Less than a battalion survived. You also killed some four hundred of ours. There was fog over the triangle and the river and the south of Ferravyl until yesterday." Bhayar paused. "It will be called a great victory for us, and a tragedy for Bovaria."

Eight regiments? Eight? More than twelve thousand men? Despite the sweaty dampness on his forehead, Quaeryt shivered. "A great victory," he repeated, hearing the words come out flat.

"The way matters were going it would have likely ended up with no winner, and just as many dead, except that half of them would have been ours."

Quaeryt hadn't thought of that, but it didn't make him feel any better.

"What did the bridge have to do with it?" prompted Bhayar.

"Imaging it was the only way to freeze the rain."

Bhayar frowned. "I can't say I understand."

"Neither do I," Quaeryt replied, for he didn't, not entirely, at least. "I just hoped that it might work."

"Might work? It worked indeed. With what Pulaskyr and Claeph did to the three Bovarian regiments that came down from the north, Kharst doesn't have enough men left in all of eastern Bovaria to stop a single regiment . . ." Bhayar paused. "Can you do that again? What you did here?"

Quaeryt laughed raggedly. "How often is there warm rain? How often are that many soldiers gathered in one place? How often could any group of imagers manage building a bridge like that?"

"That's not an answer," said Bhayar coolly.

"It's . . . the best answer . . . I can give." Quaeryt wanted to snap back, but that would have taken more strength than he had. "Do you think I like the idea of having imagers and scholars linked to the biggest massacre of troops in the history of Lydar? In fact, if you even mention imagers and scholars . . ."

Bhayar actually stepped back. "I beg your pardon." His words were sardonic.

Quaeryt ignored the tone. "Even if we could do something like that again, do you really want it known? Second, if you suggest it, what happens when it doesn't work? It might not ever work again. Imaging is never that certain. If you don't believe me, ask the imagers you put me in command of." He closed his eyes for a moment. Even those few sentences had been an effort.

"I did. They don't know how they did it."

"That's why you're better off claiming that the Nameless punished Rex Kharst with a mighty storm for trying to invade a neighboring land that never threatened him."

"I have suggested something like that."

"Keep suggesting it," Quaeryt said tiredly. "It can't hurt . . . if Kharst and Autarch Aliaro are worried . . . the Nameless is on your side."

"What would you like to do now?" asked Bhayar, his voice deferential, or almost so, for perhaps the first time in all the years Quaeryt had known him. "After you're stronger. You're not going anywhere for another few days or maybe longer."

"Visit my wife. I think I deserve that."

Bhayar nodded slowly. "I thought you might have that in mind. About a glass southeast of here is a small estate—Nordruil. My father seized it years ago for failure to pay tariffs. I think you will find it more to your liking than traveling to Solis. Besides, you're in no shape for a ride like that."

"Why there?" asked Quaeryt warily. "What about Vaelora?"

"Because . . . when it became clear that you—or the Nameless," added Bhayar archly, "had succeeded in annihilating the Bovarian forces attacking Ferravyl, I sent for Vaelora. I had no idea if you would live. I just said that you'd been wounded and requested her presence. I imagine she has been riding eight glasses out of every ten."

"Why else?" asked Quaeryt, although he had a very good idea why Bhayar wanted him to recover at Nordruil.

"Because the war with Bovaria has just begun . . . and because you couldn't even start to ride to Solis for a week at best, maybe not for several weeks. The time you would have taken traveling to and from Solis will not be wasted. It will take that long, if not slightly longer, to reorganize and refit the army for the campaign ahead—"

"And for the other regiments you called up to arrive," interjected Quaeryt.

"For the campaign ahead," continued Bhayar implacably, "in which you will play a vital role, I am certain. While you recover at Nordruil, you and Vaelora can discuss how both of you can help in such matters . . ."

Quaeryt could not have expected anything else, he supposed. "Not Vaelora. Don't bring her into it—"

"I won't, not so long as I can count on you."

You truly are a bastard. Quaeryt didn't speak those words. "What other choice do we have?" He kept his voice level.

"Not much. You more than anyone should know what Kharst—or any other ruler—would do . . . has done to imagers and scholars."

"Why do you think I've done what I've done—even before Vaelora?"

"As soon as you're able, I'll have escorts help you to Nordruil to wait for her. You should enjoy Nordruil," said Bhayar pleasantly. "So should Vaelora."

I'll enjoy making you pay double when the time comes . . . and Vaelora can help me figure out how. "I'm certain we will." He forced himself to remember that Vaelora would be at Nordruil. Soon, he hoped. Soon . . .

Then, at that, he smiled, ignoring the frown on Bhayar's face.

78

Quaeryt swayed slightly in the saddle of the mare as he neared the midsection of the old fortified bridge across the Aluse, guiding the mare to the left side of the span away from the damaged roadbed and wall ahead on the right.

"Are you all right, sir?" asked Undercaptain Jusaph, turning back to watch Quaeryt.

"I'm fine." Quaeryt forced heartiness he didn't feel in his voice. Even after resting and recuperating for another three days since waking up, his entire body ached, and he had bruises and strained muscles in improbable locations.

"Yes, sir." Jusaph's voice contained doubt, and he continued to look back every few yards as they rode past the stoneworkers and engineers already working to repair the damaged bridge.

Quaeryt straightened himself in the saddle, trying not to wince, and turned his eyes to the southwest once he was clear of the workers and riding down the bridge's unharmed southern span. Everywhere he looked there were wagons and carts moving, and hundreds of troopers toiling in the steamy air to bury the Bovarian dead before the sun of full summer corrupted the bodies. Two long and deep trenches stretched across the front of the low bluff of the triangle below which the rivers met, and in those trenches lay body after body. Another square pit had been dug, closer to the Narrows Bridge, then filled and heaped up with earth packed into a pyramid. That had to be the grave for the Telaryn fallen, Quaeryt knew, although no one had told him. In fact, few had spoken to him, except for Skarpa, Zhelan, and Shaelyt. And, of course, Bhayar.

Quaeryt looked back at Jusaph, noting the muffled murmurs of the two squads of first company escorting him to Nordruil. He could not hear the words and was just as glad he could not. Yet what else could he have done?

He looked ahead at where the road branched below the southern approach to the bridge, the one turning westward and then running south along the smaller river past the dark stone structure that he and the imagers had created to span the Vyl—and destroy thousands of Bovarians. That dark structure pointed like a crossbow quarrel toward Bovaria . . . and Variana, like the quarrel that once might have killed him, and had forced him to develop the imaging abilities that had seemed inevitably to require greater and greater destruction on his part.

Deliberately—and abruptly—he turned his eyes to the road leading southeast, first along the greenery of the river and then angling southwest toward Nordruil. Bhayar had said the holding was peaceful and quiet. He could use both.

He smiled faintly as he turned the mare southeast where the roads split, riding toward a respite, a time of rest . . . and a place where he could wait for Vaelora.

Vaelora . . .

He smiled once more.